VALKYRIE FREED

USA TODAY BESTSELLING AUTHOR
SHANNON PEMRICK

Valkyrie Freed
Valkyries Rising | Book Eight

Copyright © 2025 Shannon Pemrick
www.shannonpemrick.com

Cover Design by Covers by Combs
Editing by Sandra Nguyen
Chapter art by BRoseDesignz

First Edition © 2024

Print paperback ISBN 978-1-950128-55-8
Print hardcover ISBN 978-1-950128-54-1

This is a work of fiction. Names, characters, businesses, places, events, and incidents are either the products of the author's imagination or used in a fictitious manner. Any resemblance to actual persons, living or dead, or actual events is purely coincidental.

ALL RIGHTS RESERVED. In accordance with the U.S. Copyright Act of 1976, the scanning, uploading, and electronic sharing of any part of this book without the permission of the author constitute unlawful piracy and theft of the author's intellectual property.

BOOKS BY SHANNON PEMRICK

VALKYRIES RISING

Valkyrie Lost
Valkyrie Unknown
Valkyrie Destined
Valkyrie Renewed
Valkyrie Restored
Valkyrie Confused
Valkyrie Condemned
Valkyrie Freed
Valkyrie Shattered
Valkyrie Transformed

LOOKING FOR GROUP

Spellbinding His Ranger
Protecting His Priestess
Summoning Their Elementalist
Binding Their Elementalist

EXPERIMENTAL HEART

Destiny
Pieces
Secrets
Exposed
Surrendered
Reborn

ORACLE'S PATH

Prophecy of Convergence
Prophecy of Unbroken Oaths

See all books and learn more at
www.shannonpemrick.com

For everyone who know the lengths they'd go for those they love.

CONTENT WARNING

VALKRIE FREED contains mentions, discussions, and depictions of content some readers may find distressing. Reader discretion is advised. Please review the listed topics below and proceed with caution if needed. Your mental health is important.

Abduction & hostage situation

Child abuse/trauma (recovery from)

Death & the afterlife

Consensual non-monogamy

Familial, parental, & spousal death

Graphic (consensual) sexual content including: anal, degradation & praise, DP & DVP, impact play, light bondage, multiple partners, oral, rough sex, swallowing

Magical curses

Magical prosthetics/limb regrowth

Manipulation & abuse

Matricide

Nudity

Pregnancy

PTSD & mental illness

Profanity

Radicalization & extremism

Resurrection & reincarnation

Toxic familial relationships

Violence, gore & death

AUTHOR'S NOTE

VALKYRIE FREED is a Norse-inspired, polyamorous paranormal romance that concludes Astrid's story in the Valkyries Rising series. It relies heavily on events that have transpired throughout the series. I strongly recommend you first explore the other stories in Valkyries Rising before continuing with Astrid's conclusion for the best experience.

Power comes at a price. And Odin's just came due.

Pain ricocheted through my body. Blood dripped from healing gouges. My vision came in and out of focus, my body strained from fighting and overexerting my magic. I wheezed out a breath as my partially collapsed lung fixed itself through my accelerated Valkyrie healing.

Something hard touched my hand that lay in an unnatural position. Pain pierced my mind and I hissed, too tired to cry out. Broken, the wrist was definitely broken.

I flicked my gaze to my hand when the painful tapping persisted. A raven pushed on my hand frantically with its beak. *Muninn…*

"Up, Sister. Please get up." His telepathic voice penetrated my mind. His panic surged into me through the connection. *"Don't die again, please."*

Odin roared wordlessly. His fury and despair rolled over me, my Valkyrie soul twitching—demanding healing. My other hand clutched the empty syringe I'd injected into him before he knocked me away. Even after everything he'd done, my Valkyrie instinct to heal someone lost and broken wouldn't allow him to suffer.

Starkad—fully transformed into his wolf Berserker shape—circled Odin, as did Tyr, weapon poised for any more resistance. Fen prowled beyond them in a massive wolf form even larger than the truck-sized one he normally took.

I lay prone where Odin had flung me after my and Magnus' coordinated attack. Magnus had managed to teleport away safely, but Odin's powerful punch to my chest had put me in a bad place.

Kirby landed in front of Odin, angling her sword at his throat. "Give up, Odin. You lost."

Odin's good eye flicked around wildly. He clutched his spear with desperation, the last bit of power he still held. "What did you do? What did you ungrateful bitches do to me?"

I struggled to my feet, my body protesting. Three broken ribs and a wrist that had yet to heal screamed pain through me. Gasping for breath, my wings hung limply on my back and dragged on the ground more than they usually did. Muninn croaked and hopped around, happy I wasn't dead, though I sure felt like I was.

"We took your throne, god of a stolen crown," I rasped.

In a flash of iridescent feathered wings, Mia flew toward Odin, her syringe poised to deliver the final dose that would bind Odin forever.

Odin threw out power that knocked Mia back, his attention fixed on me. His lips pulled back into a sneer. "I am the Allfather. How dare you—"

He twitched his sword arm gripping his spear, and Fen lunged. Air rushed into my lungs as the sound of crunching bone echoed through the battlefield. Odin roared and staggered back. Blood gushed out of his now-severed arm.

Fen's jaw flexed and something snapped. Odin's spear clattered to the ground in several pieces. Fen's jaw continued to move and then he swallowed Odin's hand.

Mia appeared behind him, this time aided by Callie in her shimmering silver half-dragon form. Mia jammed the needle of her syringe into his neck and pressed the button.

Odin gasped and collapsed to one knee, the serum sapping him of his remaining strength in tandem with his new injury. "What did you… Bitch."

His breathing labored as his panic set in, eye flicking about those who had finally bested him.

I took a weak step toward Odin, my arm clutching my side.

"Valkyrie," Tyr murmured, an edge to his tone.

I flicked my gaze to him briefly. He had the face of a battle-hardened warrior, but I saw the creases of worry. I always saw past his jagged edges to the softer man inside. I knew what he feared right now. I knew he was remembering the battle he lost me to, and didn't want to experience that again.

But there were no wolves prowling in the shadows. There were no more wolves going for my throat today. The biggest bad wolf had just had his fangs ripped out.

Soft scuffles sounded around me. My Valkyrie sisters moved in closer with me until we surrounded Odin. Muninn landed on my shoulder and gazed down at the fallen god. His brother, Huginn, flew in and defiantly stood on Odin's shoulder. If a bird could glare, he would be at his brother. The sensations of betrayal that rolled off him were unmistakable to my Valkyrie soul.

Kirby sneered. "You are done, Odin. You have been stripped of all your power—the only thing you ever cared about."

Odin's eye flicked to each of us until he settled on me. Instead of the hate and disgust I knew I should feel, I only had pity for this man who had fallen so far by his own hand.

"Once, you had everything you ever needed." I winced when my broken wrist popped into place. "But you decided it wasn't enough. You couldn't be happy until you had more than what you were supposed to. You schemed and lied until you found your opportunity to take a throne that was never meant to be yours."

I ran my hand gently over Muninn's head. "And your paranoia over someone finding out became your undoing."

His eye burned into me, his unspoken questions of how the truth I spoke had come to light. Yet he didn't ask for those answers. Instead, he asked, "And now that you have me on my knees, battered and broken, what do you Valkyries intend to do? Kill me?"

Magnus snorted. "That would be dumb to try a third time."

"You've been reduced to nothing more than an immortal human," Azzie said. "Everything you've schemed for is gone."

"That's it? That's all you planned to do?" Odin asked.

"No." I shifted my gaze to Mia. She met my eyes with steely resolve and she nodded. We hadn't gotten to discuss this act beyond me telling her it was possible during her training, but the sisterly Valkyrie connection between us allowed her to understand my need. She knew what came next, and she was ready.

Mia swiped at her forehead, coating her hand in fresh blood from an open wound, then tangled her fingers with mine. Magic hummed through her, amplifying with her fae blood. My own magic built in my chest and surged through my hand, coiling with hers until it was difficult to know where one side started and the other ended.

We stepped forward and I placed my free palm on Odin's forehead. Golden magic sprang from my hand, brighter and more powerful with Mia's magic, surging through me in an intense buzz. The magic wrapped around him. My sisters shifted uncomfortably as I healed Odin's wounds. His arm was the last to heal, the injury becoming a sealed stump.

The golden light dissipated, leaving the odd single black tendril of magic that I had, now empowered by Mia's blood magic. It wrapped around Odin, and then seeped into his skin. My lower lip trembled as my unspeakable action left me.

"I, Astrid, völva and Valkyrie both, by the power of my magic and the blood of fae-Valkyrie, lay this curse upon you, Odin the raven god. You shall walk and wander alone, to learn and understand that which you have been so blind to for so long. Let eternity pass, unless Creation itself deems you worthy before. So it is spoken, so it shall be."

"So it is spoken, so it shall be." The ominous words echoed off my Valkyrie sisters' lips, chilling the air.

Something pulsed in my chest and through the connection I maintained with Mia. Her hand spasmed with her own reaction to the curse. Odin's eye went wide, and black magical runes appeared on his skin where the magic had touched him. Then they sunk into his skin, disappearing. I lifted my palm. A golden rune glowed on his forehead before it, too, was absorbed into his body.

Disbelief rippled through my Valkyrie sisters—except Kirby. Grim satisfaction was clear on her face. When I told them to trust me to have a solution to keep Odin from causing trouble, it was because I couldn't bear to admit what I'd planned to do.

It had been hard enough bringing Mia into the plan, but I knew I'd need her blood magic to help curse a god like Odin. Never in any of my lives had I cursed someone. I had seen my mother Randi do it, and she taught me how, but this was the first time I'd ever had to use what she taught me.

Odin glared up at me and I faked indifference, as difficult as it was. *Stupid bleeding-heart Valkyrie soul.* "Amend your curse to allow me my ravens."

"You have no familiars," I said. "Or did you not notice the bond break when your power left you?"

His eye widened and I thought I caught traces of fear. No, I knew I did. He'd always been afraid of losing his ravens. It was why he hated me so much when Muninn and I formed a special bond long ago.

Muninn and Huginn made displeased sounds and puffed up.

"I offer a new familiar bond to them," I continued. "If that is what they want."

Muninn perked up and Huginn snapped his beak. Odin's face twisted, his lips curling into a snarl. "You cannot take them from me! You cannot command—"

Kirby and Azzie leveled their swords on Odin when he tried to stand. I slashed him with an irritated look. "I will not command them. I offer them the chance to stay as they are, that is all. If they wish to remain with me, then I will care for them. If they wish to leave and make their own choices, they are welcome to."

I turned away, glancing at him from the corner of my eye. "I'm not you, Odin."

With tired, heavy steps, I walked away. Each step, the fight in me cooled. Sleep sounded so good right now. I winced when a rib popped into place. *And some pain killers.*

Familiar bond first. Given how long the ravens had been familiars, I suspected it'd take a few days at least for them to revert, but I didn't want to risk anything.

I found a safe place to sit, my legs thankful for the reprieve. Another rib shifted in my immortal self-healing.

Muninn hopped off my shoulder and gazed up at me. *"I am ready, Sister."*

I smiled. His quick answer didn't surprise me. It was Huginn I wasn't so sure of. A stolen glance showed he still sat on Odin's shoulder, watching me. Muninn called to him, and his brother flew over after a moment of hesitation.

I rested my hand gently on top of Muninn and he made a low purring sound. I touched Huginn and his only sound was a low warning and puffing of his chest. He wouldn't speak to me, he never did, but the meaning was clear. He was only doing this because he didn't want to revert to a regular raven or be without his brother. And I was fine with that.

Closing my eyes, I focused inward. My magic lingered under the surface, low in reserve but enough for this. I pulled it up and extended it to the two ravens under my touch. The magic swelled in my chest, and for a brief moment, two secondary palpitations pulsed out of sync with my heart. Then my magic died, and an awareness in the back of my mind that wasn't there before bubbled.

My eyes snapped open when Huginn croaked and his displeasure flashed through me. He flew back to Odin, who had sat alone. *That was strange.* Each familiar bond was unique. Bonding with these two ravens would bring me new experiences I didn't have with Angel, and show me potentials where mine and Angel's bond could grow.

Muninn pushed against my hand, his happy contentment rolling through me.

Weariness set in. I had nothing left in me now.

I glanced up when Tyr approached. He didn't say anything. What was there to say?

He stooped and collected me in his massive arms, cradling me in safety. Muninn hopped on my chest and nestled in close as I wrapped him into me.

It was over.

This nightmare that had plagued us for centuries was finally over.

TWO·

ASTRID
TWO MONTHS LATER

Magic comes at a price. Not all believe that, but as a witch-Valkyrie with centuries of experiences, I knew to be careful.

So as Frey reiterated to Diego and me how this dimensional magic worked—the best way anyone could explain magic, since much of it was intuitive—I hung on every word to make sure I didn't fuck this up.

I'd used this magic before. Many of our resident cabins had been slowly converted, between Dad's efforts and mine. It was one of the magic lessons Dad made sure stayed between us. But this was the first time I'd be combining my magic with someone else. Not only had Dad never done that before, but he was off with Tyr, infiltrating a cult of Malsumis location.

After months of dating and being cramped in my tiny room with two men as they slowly moved in, I was ready for something bigger. As it happened, I'd gotten that in the form of a gift, and now that it was done, I could have that and still be connected to this house. Sure, I could teleport, but why would I do that, when I could just walk through a door whenever I wanted without needing to expend magic?

Frey swept his long blond hair over his shoulder with a fair hand. "Are the two of you ready to try?"

I fidgeted with the tree-engraved pendant of my necklace, my most precious gift from Diego. I turned to Diego, gazing into his warm, silver-flecked brown eyes. I had to crane my neck up to do so with his six-foot tall wall of hotness compared to my five-two short—respectable height. My eyes roamed him, taking in his striking features. Lean, but still broad-shouldered and muscled in the right places, with tousled dark brown hair, a strong profile accentuated by a delicious amount of stubble, and dusky brown skin, I could stare at him all day if we didn't have this pressing task. "I am."

Diego took a strong breath and nodded. "Same."

I understood his nervousness. He'd been slowly learning the limits of his own magic as it manifested over these last few months. His cousins had gained theirs far quicker after coming into their dragon nature, but Diego wasn't bothered by the pacing difference. He liked making sure he had time to master the skills little by little, instead of being overwhelmed all at once. Besides, he'd taken to shifting into a dragon shape far easier than some of his cousins.

And this would be his first big magical task. I would use the most magic, since I was more experienced, but Diego still needed to add the right balance to ensure the connection we made would be seen as his as much as mine. When Tyr returned home, he'd weave his power in to claim our place as part of his domain, and then it'd be fully ours. *First things first.*

I took Diego's hands in mine, entwining our fingers and giving him a reassuring squeeze. He bent down and kissed me on the forehead. I may have swooned a little.

Frey hummed his appreciation. As a god of sex, all affection, even something innocent like this, in his presence would turn into payment for his assistance. Not that paying him for his help was a requirement. We were family, and he offered his assistance without me having to ask. But that didn't mean I wouldn't give him something in return for his help.

I pressed my hand against the closed door of what would be my former bedroom. Diego laid his hand over mine, his fingers elongating into claws, and patches of scales appeared on his arm. A thick appendage—his tail—wrapped around my leg and pulled me hard against him. My pulse skipped and I mentally chastised myself. Now wasn't the time to get horny.

You'd think after months of dating, and having every whim and need satisfied by two men—physically, financially, and emotionally—my libido would chill out finally, but no. It still decided I needed to act like a horny teenager just for being in the vicinity of such amazing men.

Diego inhaled deeply against my hair and chuckled. His lips brushed my ear. "After."

His smooth voice rolled over my skin like a warm caress. I sucked in a tight breath. That didn't help my distracted brain or, now, my pulsing lady bits. Neither did Frey's chuckling. *Focus.*

Pushing out all distractions, I closed my eyes and drew up my magic. Tingling spread through my body and out my hand, pressing against the grain of the door. The warmth of Diego's magic wrapped around mine until they mingled and fused.

I pictured my room as it was, barren of all furniture and personal belongings we removed earlier, creating the perfect empty host. I then imagined the layout of the home that had been built elsewhere. It wasn't entirely necessary, as just visualizing the door this one would connect to should work, but I wanted to be sure the connection was solid. Especially with the wards protecting this place.

Each aspect of the new home, from the living room to the kitchen and bathrooms, I visualized until the whole place existed in my mind. Then, it didn't.

My magic flared, taking the image with it.

I opened my eyes and stared at the door. "It's done."

Nothing about the door had changed, but I knew we'd been successful. It was this strange feeling in my chest that hadn't existed before. *Didn't expect that feeling.*

The small pieces of the fae domain Dad and I utilized to extend the cabins weren't tied to either of us like this. They existed. There was more freedom in their design, as we could change aspects of them on a whim, but it was also more dangerous. The fae didn't like it when others used pieces of their realm. They only wanted fae in there. So, there was a risk we'd have to remove them at a moment's notice, and I didn't want to deal with that.

Besides, designing my own home had been a lot of fun. My Valkyrie sister, Tatiana, had an architect friend, and a good one at that. She'd walked me through the whole process of laying out something for all our needs that also fit in the stunning new location.

Diego curled his fingers around my hand and dragged it toward the doorknob. "Shall we?"

I gripped the cool metal and opened the door to the home few had been able to see until now.

A small hallway with a laundry cubby to our right, and another door in a tiny recess to our left, opened to a spacious open-concept kitchen and living room. I walked in, gazing around at our handiwork.

Pictures hung on the walls, and other décor from plants and knick-knacks that embodied our interests made the place look lived-in.

The kitchen featured sleek granite countertops and modern appliances. A stunning island with a sink took up a decent amount of space, an ideal size for cooking and eating.

Beyond the island, a plush sectional sofa sat in front of Tyr's favorite flatscreen on the wall in the living room, all of Diego's surround-sound equipment perfectly hooked up, along with our gaming consoles. Diego's guitar sat in its stand by the TV.

On the far side of the room, a sliding glass door led to the patio.

The dining area flowed seamlessly from the living room, marked by a sturdy wooden table Tyr and Dad made. Several windows allowed a generous amount of light in, bathing everything in a soft, welcoming glow.

The house branched in two directions where the bedrooms and bathrooms were, along with some annexed rooms, like my part-office-part-potion-part enchanting room. I knew how to enchant items, and I had been bringing that back into my skill set, while also expanding it. The potion part was newer.

We did have some potion-making knowledge in our family history, and I had some basic experience in the past, but I never truly delved into it. Not all witches could make them, so it wasn't a guarantee I'd get far. But I liked the challenge, and some dabbling already showed promise.

Aya knew a verdant witch—a witch who specialized in potions and had magic that favored nature—from Las Vegas who was interested in teaching me once she had more time. So, until then, I'd turned potions into my hobby for now.

"Astrid, what is this?" Frey asked.

I turned around. He stood in front of the recessed second door. It stood higher than him, tall enough for Tyr or even someone as tall as Davyn to easily walk through without ducking, like all the arches and doorways in this place. The door had intricate carvings of a Norse and Celtic mix, and two cuts, one at about my height and then one about half my height, that looked a lot like smaller doors.

"That's the door to the Norway house," I said.

He pursed his lips. "Should I ask why it's three doors in one?"

I smirked. "One is Ùna-sized. One is Astrid-sized. And the last is why-do-I-date-fucking-giants-sized."

Frey snorted with amusement. It was a running joke even I had to lean into.

He opened the door to check the connection, only for a wall to greet him. Questioning blue eyes flicked back to me.

"Oh, uh, we haven't actually connected it yet. We wanted to do this first connection and then work on that one. I also want to incorporate Ùna's magic if we can, since her magic is laced into the Norway house."

He nodded. "Smart idea."

He then wandered off to check stability elsewhere, like Diego had done. Theoretically, we shouldn't have any issues, since it wasn't a pocket dimension, and connections from one place to another were fairly straightforward. But, magic sometimes didn't work as we expected.

I walked farther into the living room and pushed open the multi-slide door to the patio. Stepping out under the pergola, humid heat and a light salt-stained breeze greeted me. Soft white sand spread out from the patio where it met expansive blue-green water. The warm sun danced across the sparkling surface lapping at the shore. Above, the sky stretched out in an endless expanse of blue, dotted with puffy white clouds.

It worked. It really worked. I could hardly believe it.

This past Christmas, Tyr had surprised me with my own private island in the Caribbean. Yeah, a whole damned private island.

It wasn't that I was uncomfortable with the spoiling—okay, I was still getting used to that—but damn, he could have waited a year or two before going full nuclear on gifts, not six months into our renewed relationship. *He's trying to make up for all the lost time, I know.*

Of course, I was grateful. He'd put a lot of thought into which island to pick, and had been playing twenty questions with me for a while as a way to ensure I'd be happy. And he wanted to be sure I had my own active input, which was why I got to design the house he and Dad built in their spare time to keep them occupied… which was a lot when we weren't dealing with the Malsumis cult.

Someone knocked on the house door. I turned around to find Xavier, a man who looked like a bit shorter, middle-aged Diego, and Urd, a tall woman with pale hair that shimmered slightly, and even paler skin, poking their heads inside. "Open for visitors?"

I smiled and nodded. Urd had a habit of trying to take over any sort of magical training that involved Diego. And since I wasn't willing to bend on Frey's involvement after we'd come to an agreement, Xavier had whisked her away to keep her occupied.

Xavier looked up at the much taller woman with the same affection-ate gaze Diego shared with me. They entered, their hands entwined. The sight of them like this brought a bigger smile to my face. The two had gone through a lot to mend what had broken between them, even facing the very event Urd had feared. It was nice seeing them happy together again. *Now, if only I could work magic with Dad…*

Diego walked out of one of the bedrooms, and Frey did the same for one of the smaller bathrooms.

"Everything looks in order to me," Diego said.

Frey nodded. "I'm not detecting any broken connection points, either. I believe it's safe to say you two did a perfect job."

Urd swooped over to her son and framed his face affectionately with her hands. "Of course they did."

My attention shifted from them to Xavier. He walked around, taking the house in, but there was something… off about the way he did. He didn't pause on anything in particular, and completely glossed over the different landscape views out the windows—something Diego had thought up and worked with Urd to make happen to keep things interesting.

"Xavier, what are you doing?" I asked, cautiously.

He hummed. "Just looking, *mija*."

I pursed my lips. "What are you looking for specifically?"

He made a thoughtful sound as he scoped out the bedrooms, and then made a face. "There is no nursery."

Frey and Urd laughed. Diego groaned. And I shook my head, bemused. *Knew it.* This was his and my dad's thing. They wanted to be grandparents so badly. They weren't quite pushing—they did respect my, Diego's, and Tyr's mutual decision to take things slow—but that didn't stop our dads from poking a little. I didn't mind, and if it got to be too much, I'd asked them to stop and they would.

"I'm not hiding some secret pregnancy," I said.

Xavier's eyes flicked to Frey, who shook his head while grinning. "My sister would have already failed to keep her excitement at bay if Astrid was pregnant."

Sex and fertility deities were the world's quickest pregnancy test. And having three in my life, my best friend Aya—Freya—her twin brother Frey, and Min, Kirby's partner, I was in no shortage of early confirmation when that day finally came.

"And you can't use the *I'm not getting any younger* excuse anymore," I added.

Xavier huffed, knowing I was right.

I still wasn't quite clear what happened to make that the case. Something about ancient fae lineage and guardian vaults… or something like that. It happened during the fall and winter craziness, dealing with Odin and bringing Mia in as a Valkyrie sister, and more magical blocking nonsenses, so I hadn't really gotten the chance to listen when he and Urd explained what happened. *One of these days I'll ask them to repeat everything to me.* But today wasn't that day.

Urd swept over to Xavier and wrapped her arms around him. "Patience, my shield. Eternity is not to be rushed."

Diego slid his arms around my middle and pulled me into his hard body. My pulse jumped when the tip of his tail brushed my thigh, just under the skirt of my dress, before wrapping around my leg.

Frey chuckled, not missing the *zing* of sexual tension that spiked between Diego and me, and angled for the door. "I'll go check on my sister to see how the others are doing. You know how to thank me for my help, Astrid."

Of course I did. And from the way Diego slid his hands along my middle, he wouldn't be waiting long.

Urd and Xavier saw themselves out as well. No awkwardness, just acceptance. It was something I loved about my family. Affection was never to be hidden—as long as you adhered to privacy etiquette.

Unlike my immortal friends, who managed to get me to punch the *orgy* space on my sexual bingo card, not once, but twice. Two times more than past, non-immortal Astrid ever thought she'd punch that card.

Diego nuzzled my neck. "You did amazing."

His hot breath, mixed with his smooth voice dipping to that pleasant gravelly tone I so loved from him, sent a shiver of anticipation down my spine. "It was a simple connection. And I had your help."

He made a thoughtful sound that sounded more like a growl and had me clenching my thighs together. "You still did most of the work, *mi cielo*, and you should be rewarded for that."

Biting my lower lip, I turned in his arms to face him. I gazed up, taking in all his draconic features he hadn't tucked away after they appeared as he used his magic. Black and silver scale patches, tail and horns, but no wings. He tended to find those cumbersome. I understood that. My own Valkyrie wings were a pain sometimes.

My pulse intensified, need pooling in my belly. Call me a monster fucker, I didn't care. I loved looking at this man with these features, or without, if he wanted to walk around looking like a normal-ass human instead in his pseudo-dragon-human form. Whatever he wanted, because I just wanted him.

My hands slid up his chest, my finger playing with the button of his shirt. "And how do you plan to reward me, my dragon?"

Diego trailed a black clawed finger down my cheek, over the tip of the scar that cut diagonally across my face, to my lips. His other hand slid up my hip, his claws trailing along my skin, sparking tingles of anticipation through my body until it pooled between my thighs.

He was always gentle, a stark contrast to Tyr's roughness, and I liked it that way. But his claws, when he used them, added just enough of a thrilling edge to spice things up between us.

His soft curls curtained his eyes, but did little to hide the simmering desire in them. He tucked his fingers under my chin, tipping my face up. He dipped down, his lips brushing against mine. "The only way a good girl should be."

My stomach dissolved in a surge of molten heat and hot tingles shivered down my spine just as his lips captured mine. I groaned, falling into the wave of desire rippling through me. My fingers fisted his shirt and I yanked. The garment gave easily and buttons clattered on the floor.

Diego broke the kiss, chuckling and leaving my lips cold and wanting. "Impatient. Two can play at that game, Cielo."

His claws tucked under the fabric of my panties and he tugged lightly in warning. Eyes half-lidded, I murmured against his mouth. "Don't you dare."

He grinned wickedly and the fabric tore.

I blew out a breath, not mad like I should be. "You're picking up bad habit from Tyr."

Diego nudged away the ruined fabric and slid his claws along the apex of my thighs, sending a *zing* of anticipation and want through me. "Don't pretend you don't like it."

He was right, as long as it wasn't a favorite piece of clothing of mine, I loved it. And as Diego teasingly slid the back of his claws along my wet folds, he knew it, too.

My palms pressed against his hard abs. "Just make it worth it."

He grinned and wrapped his hand around the back of my neck. I surged up onto my toes and met his kiss with urgency. My veins simmered with my building desire. I needed him. Now.

Diego's claw disappeared, replaced by tender fingers. They teasingly slid between my folds, sending tantalizing pleasure through me, though never quite giving me enough. His mouth devoured mine. My mind swam. I reached up and tangled my fingers into his curls, desperate to have us closer. Too much separated us.

Diego seemed to agree because he released me and clutched the front of my dress, yanking down. I gasped as cool air slid across my sensitive skin. His deft fingers made impressively quick work of my strapless bra, and it clattered to the floor.

I moaned into his mouth, pressing against him. His hot skin seared mine. I wanted more.

Tugging at his shirt, I forced his teasing to cease just long enough to get his shirt the rest of the way off. Diego was determined to keep his mouth locked with mine, even as I attempted to slant my mouth south, down toward his neck.

All I wanted to do was claim every inch of his body. But he had other ideas.

His hands grabbed my thighs and he lifted me up with ease. I wrapped my legs around his waist, my core pressing hard against him. Heat seared my veins, and roared to an inferno when his tail slid up between our bodies.

I groaned into his mouth, forgetting how to breathe as I ground against the slightly opposable appendage enough to rub my clit. Diego growled something, and bent over until my back lay on a hard surface—the kitchen table.

Diego tore his mouth away and we gasped for air. He ran his mouth along the side of my neck and I tightened my grip in his hair. I rocked my hips against his tail, pleasure stroking my clit in a burning frenzy.

"That's it," he murmured against my skin, sending hot tingling waves through me. "Be a good girl for me. Show me how much you enjoy this."

The tip of his tail flicked side to side just right, and I moaned, rubbing against him harder. I needed more.

His tongue trailed along my collarbone, around the chain of my necklace, in time with his tail flicks. Desire crawled along my skin. I gasped and moaned when he licked my sensitive nipple. I arched into him, desperate for him to ease this overwhelming need inside me wanting to burst.

Diego licked again and again, each brief touch more teasing than the last. My pulse pounded in my ears, every bit of me alive with molten desire.

"Please, my dragon," I begged. Diego was a gentle and attentive lover, but he could also be a teasing or demanding one, too. I never knew which side of him I'd get. It was thrilling, and maddening.

A pleased rumble came from his throat and he murmured something in Spanish, too quiet for me to hear over the pounding of my pulse in my ears. He pulled my hard bud into his mouth, his other hand reaching between us. He tugged on his pants, the material dropping on the ground.

Diego's tail slid away. I whimpered. *Not now. Not—*

I gasped. His fingers slid inside me, another pressing perfectly against my needy clit. My mind fuzzed as sensations overwhelmed me, and I lost myself in the pleasure.

A deep moan tore through me when his hard cock surged into my needy pussy. My back arched as my body accepted his frantic thrusts.

Diego released my nipple with a pop, groaning out, "Fuck."

I panted, hot flames burning in my veins. "Yes. Please, fuck me."

My head rolled back, and a strained groan burst into a scream as an explosion of euphoria tore through me. Diego thrust into me harder, losing all control, and cresting over the edge of release, warmth filling me.

I lay languidly on the table, pleasure pulsing through me. Diego braced himself over me, our mingling breaths coming in heavy pants. Satisfaction and the need for more ebbed and flowed within me.

Diego chuckled when I pressed soft but wanting lips against his. "Give me another moment to bounce back, and I can give you everything you're after without magic."

I made a sound as if I were thinking, and then slid my hands along his chest. "How about, no."

Magic sparked from my fingers and followed the trail of runes I wrote down his taut abs. A low groan rumbled through Diego. My breath caught as he hardened inside me.

Diego slid his arms under my legs and gripped my ass. He tugged me hard into him, filling me deeply and making me gasp. "Hold on tight, Cielo."

I threw my arms around Diego's shoulders as he lifted me. He slid deeper into me. He groaned. "Fuck, you feel so good."

I bit my lip, my eyes hooding as he slowly slid his cock into my slick pussy. I gasped when he thrust hard into me, my fingers digging into his hot skin. Diego grinned and bounced me hard against his cock. I moaned, threading my fingers into his damp hair and falling into the intense pleasure bursting through my sensitive body.

"Eyes on me, Cielo," he growled out, his motions slowing.

My eyes blinked open and met his intense stare. Slowly, he slid his cock in and out of me. Painstakingly. Deliciously. I bit my lip, my grip in his hair tightening. I needed more.

"Good girl," he praised.

He thrust into me hard and I gasped, making him grin. Again he thrust hard, and then gentle. Another gentle slide in and out, followed up by a harder thrust.

My mouth gaped, pleasure fogging my mind, unable to focus on the erratic rhythm and increasing burning of desire in my veins. "Diego, please."

"Please what?"

I needed more. I needed all of him. I needed something I didn't have the words for.

Words failing me, I pulled his head down, meeting him halfway. Our lips met, melding together as passion took over. Every movement, every gasp and moan, it swirled in intoxicating pleasure until I lost track of anything but us.

Desire burned in my veins, building hotter and hotter, until I came undone. My head flew back, a scream tearing through me. I convulsed with the intense orgasm, clamping hard around Diego and milking his simultaneous release.

He grunted, his grip tightening, and his thrust jerking hard.

We came down, stilling. I breathed hard into his neck. Diego delicately extracted himself from me, and laid me back on the table. He fiddled with my pendant, laying it perfectly between my breasts. My languid body pulsed in euphoric bliss, and yet, it yearned for more.

It was always like this with Diego. I swear, if it were physically possible to go forever, we would, and I'd love every second of it. It was so strange to me.

I felt a strong bond with Tyr, but it was so different than the one I had with Diego. I knew it was a dragon thing. I talked with Azzie and Mia on a number of occasions about their connections to their dragon boyfriends, and compared it to what I had with Diego.

There were many similarities our bonds shared, but also differences. Sometimes those differences were the strength in which we needed to be near our partners, or knowing when our dragon partner was in trouble, and vice versa. Mia's bond with Caleb was a good example of the latter. Theirs was so intense, I was a little jealous I hadn't found that with Diego yet.

There was something special between a Valkyrie and dragon, we just weren't quite sure what caused it, or how deep it really went.

Diego made a sound in his throat and nuzzled the side of my face. "What are you thinking about, *mi amor?*"

My heart skipped a beat. He didn't call me that often, preferring to call me his cielo. Before we got together he'd use it in a teasing way, his way of hinting to me how he was feeling, and I was interpreting it as him telling me how deep he saw our friendship, since that's how I understood its use in his culture for close friends. But after we'd gotten together, he used it less.

It didn't bother me. It made the times he did use it feel special. Especially considering we'd yet to exchange "I love yous." Yeah, eight months into this relationship and that phrase hadn't come up by either of us.

It wasn't that I didn't feel love with him. It was... I don't know.

Something told me it wasn't yet time. Like we were missing one more piece between us that would tie us together better, making those words mean the most they ever could.

"You," I finally said after another moment.

He kissed my cheek and hovered over me again. "Not Tyr and how pissed he'll be that I got to break in the new kitchen table with you?"

I grunted. "He'll just take 'break in' to the literal level to one-up you."

A moment of silence and then we burst into laughter. It took us a bit to calm down, but when we did, he rubbed my cheek with the back of his finger while gazing affectionately at me. I smiled at him.

I was so grateful the three of us were working out. I'd been so worried. Especially early on when communication and balancing everyone's needs was so difficult. I thought we were going to have to call it quits and I'd lose them both.

But we worked through it, and Christmas had been evidence of that.

Seeing me get a private island from one of my partners would have been off-putting for most. Diego didn't have the kind of money Tyr had accumulated over the centuries. But he'd been able to keep up just fine, by surprising me with a getaway for two in Venice.

Like me, Diego could teleport us almost anywhere. No risky war-aura teleportation that might land you in the middle of a gun standoff. That was fun—not. Which meant, he could afford getaways without the need for expensive airplane tickets.

Could we go anywhere in Midgard whenever we wanted? Of course. But a planned romantic getaway felt special, even if it wasn't that much different from what we could already do.

I propped myself up on my elbows when a sensation bubbled in the back of my head. It was sporadic and familiar.

"What?" Diego asked. "Is it Angel?"

I shook my head slowly, trying to piece together if the tug was worrisome or good. "No, it's Muninn. I think… he's excited."

I'd had months to get familiar with the bond I had with Angel. The familiar bond I'd created with Huginn and Muninn after Odin's defeat was still new. There was so much more with them because of their advanced intelligence that I was having to adapt and learn.

Diego straightened and offered me his hand. "Then let's go see how they're doing."

THREE

After we cleaned up, and Diego decided to pull back all his dragon features, we left the beach house. We headed for Diego's old room, now converted into what we called the war room. The murmur of activity from residents downstairs drifted up to the loft, so calm and warm, and unaware of the activities we were conducting to keep them all safe.

Reaching the room, I knocked on the closed door once and then entered. Computer and monitoring equipment filled the room. I didn't know how even half of the stuff worked, but our three tech gurus did.

One of those said gurus, Aya, a tall woman with fair skin and a well-toned body, sat in the middle of the room, computers and monitors surrounding her. One of her huge fluffy cats, Buggy, lounged on the keyboard of an unmanned computer next to Aya where Dahlia would have worked, had she not had to handle something important last minute.

Aya's keyboard clacked as she worked at an inhuman speed. She had a captive audience standing around her, watching monitors with intense attention. Something was up.

I walked up behind Aya, gazing at all the monitors. "How are things?"

She grinned, brushing a few wayward blonde dreadlocks over her shoulder. "Jackpot."

My pulse skipped and my eyes darted around the available screens. Several were filled with lines of code. Others were surveillance videos. Many were still, angled on a singular location—most likely security cameras she'd hacked into, while others moved, as if attached to someone, which they were: Dad and the rest of the infiltration team.

"This is the facility, then?" I asked.

I hated how often we went into these infiltrations blind. There was always so little to go off of when we found traces of possible movement or got a tip about a potential location. And so many had come up as dead ends, it was hard to believe we'd actually caught a lucky break.

"It was definitely a main base of operation before we showed up," she said. "Though, we're pretty sure they knew we were coming."

I chewed my lip. "What happened?"

"They were clearly in the middle of relocating. There's a lot missing, from what's being reported." She tapped away. "But they hadn't gotten to deleting all their files. Magnus and I are finding quite a bit of useful data. I think. I'm no scientist, but it looks promising."

"Any issues getting it downloaded?"

She nodded. "They were smart enough to encrypt everything, even on their own server. Not surprising they were that paranoid."

I grunted. Bunch of cultists working for a goddess of chaos? Yeah, paranoia would be second nature to them. "Anything on the physical front?"

Having the chemical notes on the prize we sought was possibly the best thing to have tracked down, but having the physical prize would help us understand the whole picture of how the Malsumis cult was operating.

There'd been an influx of reports through the supernatural community of magic going awry. Many of them had been routed here for their safety and monitoring. Those who didn't come here were either sent to safe locations with the help of Mia's father, Ronan, welcomed into Runavík by Bjarke, or taken in by Nyx, one of the fates who wasn't as neutral as she portrayed herself to be.

So far, there was no clear connection between the victims, or an understanding of what they'd done to be subjected to such a terrible fate. And without a good antidote, we couldn't fix them yet.

We may have created our own version to deal with Odin, an act that still made my skin crawl, but that knowledge was still fairly limited. We weren't even sure if our version would last, given it was based on the experimental version Mia had been subjected to. We already knew the iteration used on her had been vastly different than the one my "mother" used on me. And with over two decades of more research on top of that, who knew how far the cult's serum had come?

That made this lucky break so crucial.

"Not yet, but the guys are searching," Aya said.

I nodded and flicked my gaze between the security cams. The footage wasn't great, most of the screens displaying muted colors and high grain. Some were in black and white. I suspected these locations didn't have any lighting.

Magnus, Kirby, and Azzie were together. Looked like my Valkyrie sisters were watching Magnus' back while she worked on her data collection. Fen prowled through a corridor. I couldn't tell if he was a man or a wolf from this angle.

Dad, Davyn, and Tyr also moved through the compound building. I caught sight of Tyr on a security camera. The enormous, muscled warrior of a god moved with practiced ease, his gun poised for use, and his attention alert for any danger. The stern expression he always had on his face had turned even more serious, if that were possible. I always enjoyed poking him about his unapproachable, resting-bitch-face problem.

Movement on another screen snagged my attention. My nerves wound tight. But as I peered at the stationary camera feed, I saw nothing. "Hey, Aya, might be seeing imaginary movement—"

"But best not to take chances," she finished. She used her equipment to move the hacked camera, but we couldn't get anything else on it.

"Tyr," she said into the microphone in her ear. "Astrid noticed some movement in a corridor you're heading for. I can't pick anything up, but be extra cautious."

She received a classic Tyr grunt response. Normally I'd crack a smile, but I couldn't. My nerves were wound too tight. Instinct screamed at me that something wasn't right.

It wanted me to be there, but I'd agreed to sit this out. I didn't have the needed training for an operation like this. I didn't have the right training for much that was useful beyond slinging some magic around and healing the injured. The fight with Odin had been a good example of that.

No matter how hard I trained, it didn't seem to be enough. I wasn't—I shook the thoughts from my head. I couldn't think that way. I had a specific set of skills, and they were useful. Just not in this situation.

Tyr walked through the camera I'd seen the movement from. I rubbed the vambrace on my forearm—Baldur's armor. It'd become a bit of a habit to do so when I grew nervous. The action calmed me, as if he were pushing a little bit of courage my way. *If only he actually could…*

Gunshots echoed in Aya's earpiece. I held my breath, and searched for Tyr's POV camera. He stood still, a body lying prone on the floor just feet in front of him. Tyr murmured something into his headset to Aya.

She grinned up at me, her bright blue eyes sparkling. "Nice eyes, Valkyrie."

I smiled. At least I'd helped. A gunshot couldn't kill a god, not unless it was those immortal killing bullets TOM had, which I doubted the Malsumis cult had gotten their grubby mitts on, but that didn't mean I wanted him to get hurt.

However, while Tyr was a little safer for now, the feeling of something being wrong hadn't gone away. *What am I missing?*

My eyes roamed the cameras, stopping on two labeled "familiar 1" and "familiar 2". Number one sat still, and gave a view from the outside of the compound—Muninn. Number two—Angel—also remained still, but because she had crouched under something inside the building.

I didn't like using Angel for these types of situations. She was supposed to be a therapy dog, and search-and-rescue on the side. But becoming a full-fledged familiar had changed her. Yes, she still did those things, but she'd gained enough intelligence over the past few months to push feelings through our link to indicate she wanted to do more. She wanted to protect me, as a shepherd did, and dealing with the cult encompassed that.

She did make a good ground lookout, too, which is why Dad wanted to bring her along. Our agreement was that she would stay with him, or at least near him. I could not lose her.

But as I stared at her feed, I didn't see him, and a swift look at Dad's feed showed he wasn't next to her. *Did he tell her to hide and stay put, or was this something she'd done on her own?*

My hand hit something on the desk. Looking down, I spied a small camera perfect for a bird to carry. Pain pricked my chest. This was our third familiar cam, meant for Huginn. But, he still wanted nothing to do with me. He'd taken my offer out of necessity, and he'd made that clear.

I didn't push for him to like me, but I wished he did. I wasn't preventing him from seeing Odin. I wasn't even using Huginn to spy on Odin, much to Kirby's annoyance. And it pained me to see Muninn so much, but not with his brother.

I shook the thoughts from my head. Now wasn't the time to be distracted. Especially not with that insistent feeling something still wasn't right. *But what is it?* It couldn't be my Valkyrie instincts, right?

My eyes flicked over all the video feeds and settled back on my familiars. Was it something to do with them? I still struggled to figure out when a feeling was mine or theirs.

I bit my lip and tapped the desk. *"Muninn?"*

His presence filled my mind. *"Hi, Sister. I'm helping."*

I smirked, and I was sure it bled into my communication with him. *"I felt your excitement earlier."*

"I found our enemies setting up an ambush and watched Fluffy eat them."

I choked on a laugh. Muninn had begun calling Fen that a few weeks ago for fun after hearing me call him that name a few times, and it stuck because Fen did not like it.

"Do you see any more enemies?"

"No."

I bit my lip. Then was my anxiety because of Angel?

"What's wrong, Sister?"

Something I had to get used to, being connected to Muninn and Huginn, was the telepathic link wasn't just limited to communication. We could hear each other's thoughts and they could relay what they'd seen to me like a movie in my head. Nothing was secret. That was how I knew when Huginn was with Odin. It was possible the connection with Angel was the same, but without her able to communicate with me in the same way yet, I couldn't be sure.

"Something doesn't feel right."

"Do you wish to see? I can fly so you can see more."

I pursed my lips. Actively seeing through his eyes instead of him replaying a memory was a new skill we were practicing. I couldn't hold it for long, but it could be helpful.

Closing my eyes, I concentrated on our connection. I lifted one hand to cover one of my eyes, to reduce the risk of visual distractions in the event I opened it by mistake—learned that lesson the hard way how much the brain didn't like seeing two places at once—and when the connection completed, I snapped my other eye open.

My world shifted. Instead of a room in my house, I now saw a clearing in the forest with an ugly concrete building. All the colors were so vibrant and alien to my human brain, which was also struggling to process the smells of the room I still stood in not matching my vision.

Muninn leapt off his perch and flew high into the sky, making all the appropriate ordinary raven motions, and presumably calls I couldn't hear but sensed, as he moved. I never worried anyone would suspect him of being anything but a common raven. It made him perfect for these types of situations.

He tipped his head in many directions to give me a good aerial view, but nothing seemed out of the ordinary. Everything was quiet.

I twisted my lips. *Then why—*

Movement.

Muninn's head twitched, noticing exactly what I had. He darted in the forest and landed on a tree branch. He didn't have the best angle, but, thanks to the intimate connection created by our familiar bond, I could feel his thought process as if it were my own.

Pretend to be a wild raven.

Dart somewhere else.

Fly closer.

And he did just that. He landed on top of the roof eave, croaked, and tipped his head so I could see the source of the movement I continued to catch glimpses of in his flight.

I stiffened. People moved next to the building. No, not just people. Equipment.

"Aya," I said.

She touched my elbow to indicate she was listening. Everyone knew how difficult it was for me to hold this connection. They always tried to keep the noise down.

"There are people outside. They're using a window to move equipment. I think… I think it's the stuff we're after."

She swore and quietly relayed our findings. I focused on my connection with Muninn, pushing against the strain in my mind. We were reaching the length of time that I could usually handle this visual sharing, but I needed to push it further. Their lips moved, and I needed to know what they were saying.

Muninn felt my need and projected an idea. He could try to share a memory—a memory of what he was hearing right now. While delayed from what was going on, it was the best he could offer until we got better at this active sharing.

"Can we do that with sound?" I asked him. Memory sharing wasn't new for the two of us, but it was only something we'd been practicing for a few months and we'd only gotten the hang of sharing visuals.

"Just sound, yes."

Then we'd have to try it.

I closed my eye and Muninn cut the connection. Emptiness met my mind, but only for a moment. His presence returned and this time, sensations around my ears tingled.

I clamped my hands over my ears to drown out the room, and listened, and repeated out loud what I heard but couldn't see.

"Move quicker. We can't let them spot us."

"Where are the rest?"

"They'll be the diversion."

"Will they make it?"

"Doubt it, but it doesn't matter. Between them and the decoy data we left for these fools, we'll be long gone before they realize what we pulled off."

"They think—"

"Hey, what's that?"

Muninn let go, and panic flooded in. Had he been seen? Was he—

"I'm fine," he said. *"They're stupid."*

I released the breath I'd been holding, and flicked my attention around the room, now that my senses had returned. Aya spoke furiously with the others, everyone else in the room now crowding in, making the *zing* of tension palpable. The ground team were all on the move. The only camera not moving was Angel.

I swallowed when I realized the sensation that something was wrong still pinged in my mind. Dread sunk in my gut. It hadn't been my instinct at all. It had been Angel trying to warn me.

My hands slammed down on the desk and I clamped my eyes shut, desperately seeking Angel's connection. It smashed into me like a raging Berserker, making my body physically shudder.

Warning. So much warning from her. Wherever she was, she was in trouble and it would harm everyone in that facility.

"Aya, they need to find Angel," I said as I simultaneously tried to send calm reassurance to Angel. "Wherever she is, there's danger, and she's hiding from it. It may be the force those cultists were discussing."

I didn't hear her response, too focused on my connection with my familiar. I couldn't do anything for her here, except apologize for not realizing sooner and reassure her help was on the way.

Angel pushed against the bond, but not to shut me out. She wanted more from our connection. Something like what I had with the ravens. But I didn't know how to make that. Aya told me familiar bonds were always different, and the age of the bond made a difference, too. I may have only been bonded with Huginn and Muninn for a few months, but they had centuries, if not millennia, with Odin, and they retained all of that when their bond transferred to me.

Still, I tried. I concentrated hard, thinking of ways I could help her. *What can I do from here? Should I just teleport to Angel's location?* Everyone told me to stay, but I could use my magic in person. I could protect Angel, and stop these cultists.

It wasn't just my witch magic that would be useful. My Valkyrie abilities were at my disposal. I could shield Angel while reserving my magic for something else.

Power churned in my chest. It crawled under my skin through my limbs. Garbled sensory input slammed into me. Thoughts, feelings, sound. It was all so fast, and mixed with my power, I was too overwhelmed to process anything.

I gasped and stumbled back, the power and overwhelming sensations disappearing and the room around me returning all at once. Strong arms caught me. I looked up to Diego gazing down at me, his face scrunched with worry. That was when I realized everyone in the room crowded me, and I was on the floor. Diego had caught me from hitting my head. My wings were also out and sprawling across the floor.

Wooziness rolled through me and I grimaced. "What happened?"

Diego's eyebrow arched. "I was going to ask you that. You went all Valkyrie and magic on us, then collapsed."

I squinted. "Did I pass out?"

"I don't think so." His eyes skittered across my face. "Are you okay?"

I sucked in a full breath and nodded. "I think so."

He helped me up, and Zeke, Diego's cousin and our mutual close friend, pulled out a chair for me. I put away my wings before accepting the offer.

"Thanks, Doomsday," I mumbled. The silly nickname I gave him long ago helped me ground my mind and push through the slosh of sensations buzzing in my head.

"What happened?" Zeke asked, repeating Diego's question.

I chewed my lip and described what I'd experienced the best I could recall. When I finished, everyone looked to Aya. She was the one here who had the most knowledge about familiars and magic. Well, second to Urd, but she wasn't forthcoming with information most of the time—a bad habit she was working on.

Aya's attention was on listening to the person on the other side of the headset. "In Magnus' exact words, 'Angel looked like a flaming tentacle land shark.'"

I laughed. That was quite the mental image.

Aya continued. "My best guess, is you somehow channeled your power through Angel. Not something I've personally witnessed before, but I'm sure other familiar bonds have been used that way."

I chewed my lips. "She's okay?"

Aya listened. "They all are. It was a good catch by you two. That would have been a nasty surprise."

"What about the cultists who were outside escaping?" Xavier asked.

A bubble of amusement pinged in my head. Then Muninn's voice came through. *"Fluffy ate them."*

I choked and relayed his words, as well as his apparent amusement over the action. Raucous laughter filled the room. Muninn was always a source of entertainment.

Aya calmed and focused on the infiltration again. One final sweep was made while Magnus, Kirby, and Azzie met up with Fen to go over the contents he secured.

"This is the real stuff," Aya confirmed, typing away on her keyboard. "Thank Creation you and Muninn noticed."

"Are you going to dump the decoy data?" I asked.

She shook her head. "We'll keep what we collected in case it has some legit info."

"Could it be useful to gain insight on how this cult works?" Frey asked. "We don't even know how this cult is structured."

Aya frowned. "I doubt it, but I won't rule it out. It's hard to even tell right now if these people have structure to analyze."

I scowled. "My egg donor can't be the only one with sanity, even if she's unhinged in her own way. There would have to be some sort of structure for them to be able to pull all of this off."

"They definitely have it," Zeke said. "Growing up around preppers and enthusiasts who were cultists in all but name, I can say with confidence it's more difficult to understand from the outside. While most of the cultists we've run into don't seem to have much sanity to them, if they're even alive rather than some freaky magic zombie, or annoying soul-stealing lizards, a cult like this wouldn't run smoothly and with the success it has without stable enough people to run it. They'll still be paranoid and unhinged, but there is a method to the chaos we're going to struggle to understand."

"I still don't get why they do this," Diego muttered. "What do they gain by helping the world go to shit?"

That was the million-dollar question. We all agreed Malsumis was a major player in Ragnarök. And, no matter how you interpreted what Ragnarök was about, and if us trying to prevent it again was just as futile as when the dragons tried in the past, it made sense a goddess of chaos would want chaos to reign. But why would anyone else want that?

Aya removed her headset and shut down the surveillance. "They're coming home."

I jumped to my feet, thankful my equilibrium was back to normal, and practically skipped out of the room and down the stairs.

Ùna met me at the bottom. "Are they on their way back? Should I make something for them?"

I smiled. "They should be here any moment. I'm sure a few of them will be a little hungry."

Her broken, gossamer wings vibrated and she limped into the kitchen. Ùna may have sworn herself to Tyr for saving her life, but she was no servant. Anything she did for us, was of her own choosing, and she chose to take care of us and the home to the best of her ability—something she reminded me of several times in the last few months when I tried to tell her she didn't need to go out of her way. That was how she felt she was most useful.

Leaving the house, I stepped out on the porch. A gentle breeze teased my hair, carrying the woody, evergreen scent of the mountain forest mingling with the sweetness of fresh blooming flowers. A raven called, and as I turned toward where the team had teleported in, Angel and Muninn rushed me.

Angel jumped up to slobber me with kisses and Muninn landed

on my shoulder, grabbing a lock of hair to lightly tug on it. I laughed and captured Angel in a restraining hug to keep her wriggly body from knocking me over.

"They act like you're the one who left," Diego teased. He slipped out of the house around me.

I laughed more. "Right? How dare I."

Muninn croaked and tugged my hair again. I released Angel, who had stopped wriggling, and gave her and Muninn affectionate pats on the head.

"*Reward?*" Muninn asked.

I snickered. "Yes, you both get a nice reward for your help."

Angel's ears perked and she sat up with her paws poised in the air. She cocked her head for good measure and my heart melted. Holding up my hands, a steak appeared in one, and a chocolate-chip muffin in the other.

Muninn croaked and made some other excited sounds, and Angel pushed her paws into the air more. I offered them their treats, and they snatched them faster than I could blink.

Angel hopped into a nearby chair and Muninn landed on the arm next to her. The two were adorable. They spent a lot of time together when Muninn wasn't off flying around or spending time with Huginn. Sometimes the two would antagonize each other for fun, and other times, they were like this, getting along like they'd been around each other for years. I'd even caught them a few times taking a nap together.

"And where is our treat?" Fen's deep and rough, almost growly voice said. I glanced up at the big, muscular man with dark-golden blond hair cropped tight above his ears. "It's not fair a dog gets a wagyu steak."

I snickered. "Didn't get enough meat action on the mission, Fluffy?"

His lips pulled back in a wolfish grin. "Never enough."

I stuck out my tongue. "Then ask your favorite belly rubber. You're getting nothing from me."

He swiped a large hand at me. I ducked and jumped off the porch to get away. He spun around and lunged for me, muttering something about being stingy, and I laughed as I danced around him.

If you'd told me a year ago I'd have a brotherly bond with the Norse wolf-god Fenrir, I'd have said you were off your rocker—in the most professional therapist way, of course. Now, with all my memories of my past and present fitting together like a completed puzzle I was missing pieces of for years, the bond Fen and I shared felt as natural as it had been centuries ago when we'd first known each other.

A quiet "oof" escaped me when I bumped into something solid. Strong, calloused tan hands wrapped around my upper arm, the right hand not gripping as tightly. I tipped my head up, gazing into Tyr's stunning blue eyes. His expression was softer than when I'd watched him in the video feed. It always was when he looked at me.

"Good, hold her there, Tyr," Fen said.

Tyr grunted out something that sounded like, "Mongrel," and scooped me into his arms.

I wrapped my arms around his neck and dramatically declared, "My hero!"

I then planted a kiss on his cheek. Tyr chuckled and Fen rolled his eyes. When Tyr set me back on the ground, I gave him a quick assessment.

His chestnut hair, which normally hung free down to his chin on one side of his head, was pulled back and braided to keep it out of the way, though a few strands had worked their way free, making him look a little disheveled. His scarred, tattooed skin didn't appear to have added any more marks, though there was dried blood on him. That was the only thing out of order I could see. "No injuries?"

He cupped my cheek. "Not a scratch, Valkyrie."

I touched his hand, the one he'd regrown after we killed Garmr. He didn't react to my touch, not that I'd expected him to. Even though he couldn't feel with the hand yet, Tyr didn't shy away from touching me with it. The lack of feeling didn't bother him, though he was always concerned the lack of sensation would result in him hurting me, so he was always extra careful when he touched me. He could be rough with me when we were intimate, but he never hurt me.

I peered around him to look at the others. "Everyone else in one piece?"

Kirby placed her hands on her slim, athletic hips. "Everyone is fine. Nothing our Valkyrie healing couldn't handle."

My healing ability wasn't unique to my brand of witch magic. Even if I hadn't been a witch first, I'd still be able to heal as a Valkyrie. Though, as we were learning as of late, Valkyrie healing seemed to have more restrictions compared to mine.

I nodded. "Okay. Just wanted—"

"Don't you say you want to be more useful as if you weren't," Azzie said as she crossed her arms. Her vibrant red hair, pulled back to keep it out of the way, swished behind her. "You nuked a group of twenty people with a magic dog torpedo after being the reason we found out about their little trap."

I tried not to grimace. They knew me too well.

"How did you do that?" Kirby asked.

I shrugged. "I don't know. I was focused on my bond with Angel. I didn't even realize I'd gone Valkyrie mode, let alone used magic, until I'd collapsed."

Tyr's grip on me tightened. "You collapsed?"

I smiled at him reassuringly. "I was back on my feet feeling fine in a few minutes. I'm fine, really."

The frown and worry lines on his face deepened.

"I'll look into all that another time." I didn't really feel like focusing on what happened to me. "I'd rather we focus on what we got from this."

Magnus held up a bulky briefcase. Another sat at her feet, and Dad carried two more. "Dahlia and I will start working on the digital data after I check in with Bragi and Nico. We'll loop in Aya as we do."

"I'll get all this set up in FU's labs so we can begin the chemical analysis," Dad said.

FU, the Followers of Urd, was the organization Urd oversaw. She didn't create it, however. That was her sister, who had taken on the male identity Lance, and made a mockery of Urd's name until they put themself at odds with Kirby, resulting in their death. Urd took over to better the organization and use it to actually help prevent Ragnarök.

Dad had infiltrated the organization in the past on Urd's behalf, which was where he'd met Ingrid. I felt bad involving him again with that past, but I also had to remind myself, he willingly inserted himself into everything. *Dad will do what he has to, to ensure we can all live in peace.*

A phone rang and then buzzed against my leg. I blinked and then slipped my hand into the pocket of my dress. I pulled it out and checked the ID on the screen. *Dahlia.* Or, goth dragon, as I'd labeled her in my phone.

I tapped the green call button. "You're on speaker."

"Excellent, I love a captivated audience," she said.

I snickered. "I hope you didn't put too much effort into your costume; no one can see you."

She huffed. "Way to spoil my fun."

Amusement rumbled through the group. Dahlia was a burlesque dancer at Frey's club. While we poked fun of her now and then, we were all supportive of her career, which she was amazing at.

"Sounds like everyone is back, which is good. I've got an update on my super-secret project. And it's a big one."

My brow lifted. "Oh?"

"I found Loki."

Silence.

Utter silence.

I wasn't sure anyone even breathed. That was, if I could hear beyond blood rushing to my ears. *That name.*

Much like Aya, Dahlia had the ability to find almost any immortal she wanted, though Dahlia had a computer program she'd created and somehow infused her magic into, that performed the task more reliably. How it worked, I didn't know, but it'd never failed her. Until Loki disappeared. She'd been trying to figure out how he was dodging her search with no success.

Until now.

She huffed. "Tough crowd. Not even a single clap."

My hand clutched my phone tighter, until my knuckles turned white and my fingers ached. "Where is he?"

"Someone is impatient."

He has to pay. "I just don't want us to miss our window."

Tyr's grip tightened in warning. I needed to get myself under control. Any mention of Loki, and fury threatened to take over me.

"Don't worry. I've been following his movements for the last few weeks. He's been popping in and out of existence. I don't know how, but that's not important. He's been visible for a while today."

Kirby scowled. "Sounds suspicious."

Zeke crossed his arms. "Anything Loki does is suspicious."

"I'm not saying it's a trap," Dahlia said. "Actually, I'm saying it's definitely a trap. Loki knows all about my program. And he knows Azzie and Davyn are after him. He'll expect me to notice him and rat him out. But he won't be expecting a feisty redhead witch-Valkyrie to be back from the grave."

"We can work out a plan of our own," Davyn said.

Dahlia snorted. "Let's hope you're not the one making it."

A rumble of laughter echoed through the group while Davyn scowled.

"Send the coordinates, and we'll take things from there," I said to Dahlia.

"Done. Good luck. If you need my help, just shout."

The call cut at the same moment my phone pinged. I opened the attachment she'd sent with coordinates and a map, as well as some photos of an old square building made of brick and concrete. A warehouse from what I guessed, and a clearly abandoned one with its broken windows, wild growing vines, and the thick forest surrounding the small overgrown concrete yard. *Yeah, does he really think no one would see this as a trap?*

I corrected that thought almost immediately. Single-minded, over-protective, lumbering bear Berserker Davyn would absolutely fall for something like that.

Showing the location to those around me, I allowed them to come up with a plan. I wasn't an expert at this, and in my current state, I couldn't trust myself to provide any helpful suggestions.

My mind whirled, and the conversations dulled to a buzz as my emotions swelled. A choking tightness clutched deep within my chest. Any time Loki was brought up these days, I felt it. But today, today it dug deeper than I ever had felt before, urging me to find him. Urging me to go now—to avenge Baldur.

I nodded and responded whenever anyone addressed me, but I

wasn't aware of any words. I knew my clothes had changed magically to something more practical for this attack on Loki, though I didn't recall using my magic to do so. I felt a concerned pulse from my familiar bonds, but I didn't acknowledge them.

I was aware enough to know the makeup of our attacking force: Dayvn, Tyr, Azzie, and me, with Zeke and Diego accompanying us for… some task. Kirby, Dad, Aya, and Magnus were on call for backup, but I had no idea what the plan was. I didn't know why I had suggested Angel and Muninn stay behind, but the others agreed with whatever reason I gave.

That should alarm me. I should be fighting against the tides of these emotions to ensure I got this right. But all I could see were the long-ago memories of a man taken from me, and with him, a piece of my heart.

Everyone gathered around me, and a moment later we were at the edge of a clearing with a windowless wall of the warehouse before us. Zeke and Diego broke off from our group while we hurried over to the wall, careful of the noise we made. Or, I thought we were careful. My breathing and pounding heart were all I could hear.

We slipped into the building through an open doorway, the door hanging on broken rusty hinges. Everyone scanned the small room filled with a broken desk, a few cabinets, roof debris, and plants.

"Be careful," Davyn whispered. "There might be—Astrid, what are you doing?"

Debris crunched under my shoes. I walked in a specific direction, the tightness in my chest yanking me.

"Valkyrie," Tyr hissed.

Their warnings bounced off me. My attention zeroed in on the double doors on the other side of the room. The pounding of my heart in my ears intensified. My shoulder blades itched. My fingers twitched, magic thrumming beneath my skin.

The doors flung open and I walked into the large, spacious chamber beyond, not questioning whether I'd thrown them open, or if someone else had. In the center of the room, a tall, lean, and smartly dressed man stood, his back to me.

Gravel crunched under my shoes, and he turned. He chuckled and rubbed his short beard as he did. "You're so predictable."

His hair was far shorter and a little darker from when I knew him in the past, now a dirty blond instead of golden, but I could recognize Loki just the same. The dark, twisting ache in my chest dug deeper, like an axe to the heart.

"So easy to—" He paused, his pale green eyes widening. "You…"

My breath quickened. I clenched my teeth so hard, my jaw ached. The itching of my shoulders increased. Boiling fury roiled through me in a consuming wave, until I saw red. My hand twitched, my axe manifesting. *He will pay!*

In a blink, I was in the air behind him, silver and gold wings spread, Valkyrie armor adorned, and axe poised. "Your soul is mine, Loki."

I swung my axe down on his neck.

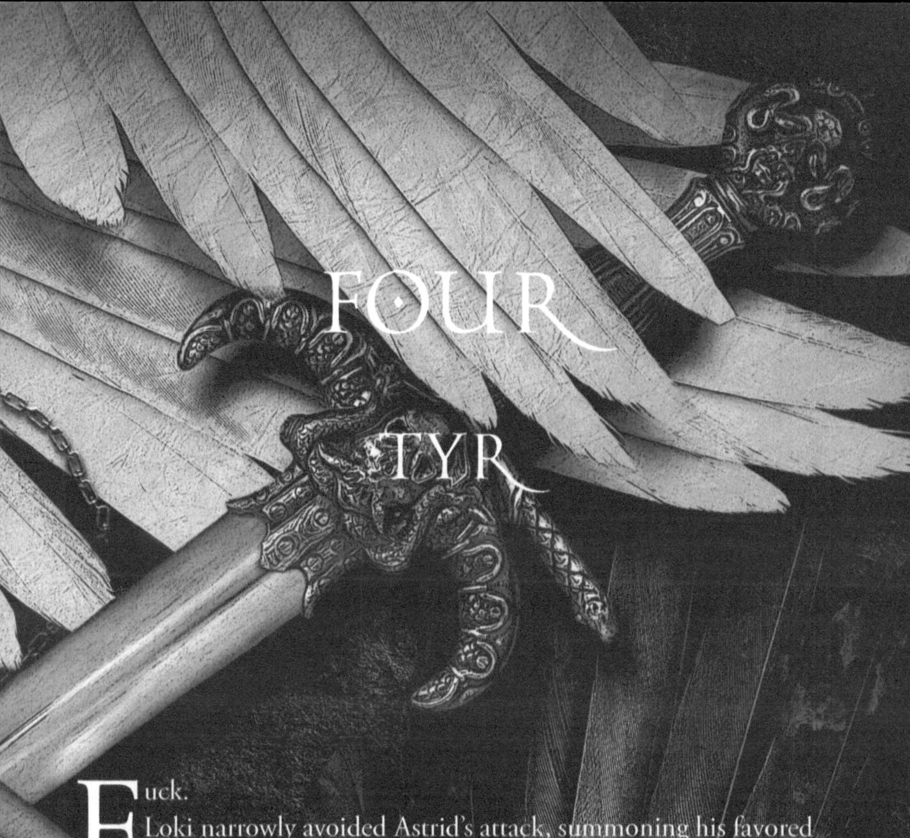

FOUR

TYR

F uck.

Loki narrowly avoided Astrid's attack, summoning his favored daggers to help deflect the blow. Dayvn snarled next to me, his body shifting and growing hair as he transformed into a bipedal bear. He grumbled something, though his transformation cut it off into unintelligible growls, and he didn't repeat himself. I suspected they were unkind words directed toward Astrid.

Normally I'd feel the urge to defend her from such vitriol, but I couldn't blame the Berserker this time. I knew Astrid was acting strange. All her responses and agreements during the planning lacked her usual lively delivery. She always acted out of sorts when Loki was brought up, but to blatantly disregard a plan and attack like this? I should have spoken up when I first noticed.

Her golden feathers shimmered violently. Gold feathers were associated with protection. But a failure to protect led to the path of vengeance. I remembered a number of golden-winged Valkyries being labeled vengeance Valkyries after they dedicated their purpose to avenging those who couldn't be protected.

I made the mistake of underestimating a vengeance Valkyrie before. The pure destruction that woman had caused for the sake of avenging a fallen warrior couldn't be erased from my mind. I should have been more careful with Astrid.

Her silver wings personified her need to heal souls—to take on their burdens. But her gold feathers couldn't be ignored either. I allowed myself to be blind to her soul's need to avenge the souls she couldn't protect.

Astrid was so sweet and gentle most of the time, I tried to put her into a box of peacefulness that she didn't belong in. And we were now paying that price.

Davyn charged in, and Loki threw a hand his way. "Not now. Astrid and I have business. You'll have to wait your turn, Davyn."

An invisible force slammed into the bear Berserker. He grunted and threw himself against what appeared to be some sort of invisible wall. Azzie shot me a concerned glance and raced over to Davyn. She probably hoped to find a gap in the barrier. I hung back, knowing that wouldn't be as easy as it seemed. Loki didn't have a lot of magic, but he knew how to use what was at his disposal. My eyes tracked him and Astrid.

Loki deftly moved out of the way of Astrid's next strike, an amused grin on his lips. "I'd heard rumors of a scarred, red-haired Valkyrie, but I hadn't guessed you were back. And with improvements from your last body. I'm quite curious how this all worked out."

Astrid bared her teeth, her fury ceasing any banter Loki was after, and a dozen swords materialized out of nowhere. They plunged for the trickster god.

He disappeared and then reappeared a few meters away, an irritated scowl breaking his usually cocky grin. "Seems those two you left outside are making themselves a nuisance."

A muscle in my neck twitched. *He knew about Diego and Zeke. But how?*

Loki shrugged. "I planned for that, of course. And it'll keep the rest of you occupied while I deal with this out-of-control Valkyrie. You really should do a better job leashing her, Tyr. Though, maybe you still can't. You're not the god you used to be."

My lip curled. Before I could spit out a retort, glass shattered. I whirled around. Human figures dressed in tattered garments with gray and decaying parchment-thin skin clinging tight to the contours of their body's bones climbed into the building in any gap or window they could find. Their eyes, lifeless and burning with an ominous ghostly light, peered into me so deep, I felt it in my soul.

Fuck. How the hel did Loki have control over draugar? We still didn't understand the exact cause for a draugr's reanimation or if souls powered them, or if it was some sort of magic. It wasn't the same type of possession Malsumis had over the dying.

Mortals had their stories, but that's all they were. Whatever it was, their existence wasn't a natural occurrence.

The how doesn't matter. I didn't have patience for Loki's idea of games. Astrid couldn't take Loki on her own, and neither Azzie nor Davyn were making any headway against that barrier.

Summoning my sword, I rushed the nearest draugr and sliced through it at the neck, severing its head from its body. The creature evaporated in a cloud of thick ash. Davyn slammed into a draugr, throwing it into a cluster, tripping the uncoordinated undead.

I used my momentum to take out three more draugar rushing me. These weren't the slow, shambling zombies from the movies Astrid enjoyed watching with the girls. They were real threats we couldn't ignore.

"Now, Astrid, let's talk," Loki said somewhere behind me. "I know Valkyries are protective of their own, but you and I haven't had issues in the past. Can we just come to—"

"Shut your mouth and just die," Astrid snarled. I jerked my attention back. That wasn't a response I was used to hearing from her, especially not in this life.

Fury twisted her face and magic flew from her fingertips at Loki. He used his own magic to defend, but he didn't attack. His expression gave away curiosity.

I turned away for a moment, to deal with three more pests, and when I turned back, Astrid had summoned her sword, dual wielding both weapons, and even more magic twisted around her. It grew in power, until I could taste it.

"You will pay, Loki, for what you did to him." Her voice cracked with the emotions playing across her face.

His eyes widened. "Shit, that's what this is about. Astrid, we can talk about this."

The muscles in my neck tightened, the warning of impending power coursing through the battle aura pulsing through the room. My breath caught for a moment and then I grabbed Azzie and summoned my shield before throwing us both to the ground.

The rim of my shield slammed into the age-broken concrete and the enchantment activated, throwing up a magical extension. Davyn ducked behind the magic, using his body as another shield against the draugar still advancing on us.

Astrid let out a spine-chilling scream, and power exploded. The ground beneath us quaked and shifted. Metal crashed down from the rafters and ceiling as it caved in. Brick smashed, sections of the building obliterating. Magic collided with my shield, pushing against all the strength I had.

Then it was quiet.

Davyn's weight lifted off me. I rose to my feet, my head snapping back and forth, surveying the destruction. The draugar were gone, as well as at least an eighth of the building.

Astrid rarely showed this lack of restraint. She always had her magic under control, unless she was under extreme duress. In the time I knew her, this life and previous, she'd only lost control like this a handful of times.

I shouldn't be surprised, however. This was Loki, the god who killed Baldur. She'd reacted poorly to the news the first time, and being in Loki's presence certainly didn't help her maintain any level of control.

"What the fuck?" Azzie said. "What's going on with her magic?"

I shifted my attention back to Astrid and Loki. My blood ran cold.

The concrete around them jutted up, and briar twisted out of the exposed earth, adding to the tormented landscape. I'd seen her do something similar, the day she lost her mother Randi. Grief was a dangerous emotion for a witch.

But that wasn't what Azzie meant. She was talking about the wild magic lashing out around Astrid. Most were gold, but black tendrils clashed with them.

We'd seen a black one now and then over the past months, mostly when she used her magic offensively. After learning Ingrid was also a witch, we assumed it may have been an inherited quirk. But now, it was as if half of Astrid's golden light had been replaced. And that wasn't all.

An inky blackness seeped into one of her eyes. The skin around her eye, pale as moonlight, was a stark contrast to the network of veins crawling beneath the surface down her face. The veins, dark as night, pulsed with ominous energy. *Randi.*

There was no mistaking that look. That was the same magic Randi had wielded. The only difference was when Randi wielded it, it took over both sides of her, where Astrid only exhibited half.

"Tyr, what is happening with her magic?" Davyn's words rolled through my mind, though my ears heard harsh growls and snarls.

My jaw clenched. I had no idea what the hel was going on.

Astrid breathed hard out of her mouth, her face twisted with her rage. Loki had managed to protect himself with his own magic, but it was clear her unhinged behavior unsettled him. It unsettled me.

My Valkyrie threw up her hands and the twisting magic around her shot out. Loki disappeared and reappeared a few meters away. It did him no good. Astrid was quick to use more, adding flying weapons to the mix.

"What do we do?" Azzie asked.

I didn't know. I didn't know how to help Astrid when she was in this state. I didn't know if she'd turn on us if we got too close.

"We wait for an opening," Davyn said. *"Then we strike."*

"Is that a good idea?" Azzie asked. "*Tyr,* an answer would be great about now. What. Is she. Doing?"

I wanted to say it was just her, enraged. But, that didn't seem right, either. Was this a result of the blood oath she swore? I knew all too well how those could twist your actions, even if it was subtle.

Loki teleported again, this time closer to Astrid, his dagger poised. Astrid grinned in a way that unsettled me. She threw up her hands, and gold ribbons sprang from her fingers. The trickster god scrambled back, but her magic was faster.

The ribbons wrapped around his arms and legs. Loki struggled against the binding, slashing at the ribbons as if they'd sever. They didn't. There was a reason Gleipnir had the mythical reputation it did. As long as Astrid's concentration held, so would those bindings. And in her current state, there was no way she'd falter.

Loki pulled against the tension, trying to fight Astrid with strength. Her wings flared wide, aiding her.

He huffed, as if inconvenienced rather than worried for his life. "Fine. Have it your way, little Valkyrie. You really want him back that badly, you can have him."

Something appeared in his hand and he tossed it at her. To my surprise, Astrid didn't dodge the projectile. The ribbons went slack and she caught whatever it was. I squinted. *Is that... armor?*

Astrid stared at the object. Loki slashed at his bindings again; this time, they dispersed into sparkles of magic.

He straightened his clothes, as if he'd only been mildly inconvenienced. "And you can figure out the rest on your own."

Loki's gaze slipped over to us. "Oh, and two baby dragons is hardly enough to keep me here."

He gave a mock salute and disappeared.

I ground my teeth together. This had all been a game. He could have left at any point. He'd only pretended he couldn't get away. *So what was his angle?*

Davyn shifted back to his non-bear form, though he still growled as he whirled toward Astrid. "What the hel—"

Azzie grabbed his arm and said his name in a low warning. And I understood why. Astrid still hadn't moved. She stood in the same place, staring at the object Loki had thrown at her.

"Valkyrie?" I said tentatively.

For a moment, she didn't respond, just stared. Every ounce of vengeful fury had disappeared. Even the strange magic about her had vanished.

Then, she lifted her gaze, her eyes glassy. "His soul is in here."

My fingers drummed on the island counter where I perched watching Astrid. She sat on the deck swing, unmoving and gazing down at her lap. The late evening sun cast orange hues into the kitchen and illuminated Astrid's red hair, making it look on fire.

Kirby and Aya stood in front of her, their lips moving, but I couldn't catch what they were saying to her. Astrid didn't react much to their presence. Only when Kirby reached down did she flinch back.

It'd been like this since we'd gotten back twenty minutes ago. Astrid's focus stayed on that vambrace Loki had given her. She barely acknowledged anyone. And if we got too close, she'd act like we were going to take it from her.

I understood the behavior. When Zeke and I joined them in the damaged warehouse after Loki's escape, Tyr filled us in on what happened. They'd had to deal with the same annoying creatures—draugar, he called them—and Astrid had gone berserk. She'd only been distracted by the vambrace because there apparently was a soul inside it. Baldur's, specifically. At least, that's what Astrid had said.

Being a Valkyrie as well, Azzie confirmed there was a soul trapped in the vambrace, but she wasn't familiar with Baldur, so she wasn't able to verify anything beyond that. That's why Kirby and Aya were trying to get Astrid to cooperate with them. Both could sense souls and had a past with Baldur.

And me? I could only watch and wait. None of my dragon abilities made me useful in this situation. Hell, Zeke and I had been useless keeping Loki from escaping. We'd thought we had a good grasp on the barrier, even when those draugar were inconveniencing us. Loki had bounced off the barrier a few times. But either our hold had weakened, or he had only been testing us, because he slipped through that final time with barely any resistance.

I shook the thoughts from my head. I needed to focus. Keeping an eye on Astrid was my self-appointed job now. I had the training to sort out whether her state was grief-related or something else. Signs pointed to grief, but I knew Astrid better than just about anyone. She was known to withdraw when trying to figure something out and didn't want help yet. This might be an extreme case, which was where I suspected the grief came into play. But I needed to monitor her longer, and without risking pushing her to talk before she was ready.

Everything inside me coiled and pushed to be near her—to gather her in my arms and protect her from everything, even herself if necessary.

Go to her. Protect. Claim my mate. The dragon part of me was incredibly protective of Astrid. Some days, stupidly so. And its mental urgings—the deeper primal thoughts of myself—didn't help.

Power prickled behind me where Papá and Ùna worked on dinner. It was nothing they were doing in particular that made me aware; they weren't using magic of any sort right now. No, it was the mate-bond mark Mamá left on Papá after they rekindled their relationship.

She told me once it was something dragons could do, as well as phoenix, and as such, we could sense one whenever it was around. Some other powerful beings could sense it as well, but I wasn't sure if anyone else here could.

Its presence brought me joy and comfort. Seeing them together again and us being a family, was like seeing all my childhood wants and dreams come to life before my eyes. Yet, the presence of the bond caused conflict with me, too.

My and Astrid's connection was stronger than anything else I'd ever experienced. The day Mamá and I had reunited, just after Astrid and I had one hell of a fun romp, Mamá had thought I'd bonded with Astrid. Ever since then, the thought stuck with me. She and I hadn't, but that pull to do so was there.

The dragon I was urged me to make her mine forever. But I wasn't ready yet. I would be at some point. But now wasn't the time. And that meant I had to fight any urge I had.

The deck door opened, drawing my attention. Kirby and Aya entered the house, an air of uncertainty about them. Tyr and I both stood.

"Well?" Tyr said when the silence stretched too long.

"It is Baldur's soul," Aya confirmed. "That's about as far as we got with her."

Kirby ran her hands through her blonde hair and let out a frustrated sigh. "Astrid is being too defensive and reactive. If we get too close, she acts like we're going to take it from her, or release his soul."

My jaw clenched. I was afraid of that. "You wouldn't do that to her, right? Release his soul?"

Kirby's brow furrowed. "Of course not."

Aya brushed a dreadlock over her shoulder and crossed her arms. "To be honest here, neither of us want to."

Tyr tipped his head. "What do you mean?"

"The thought of releasing Baldur's soul doesn't feel right," Kirby said. "That isn't based on personal attachment, either. Well, not for me, at least."

I was starting to understand. "Your Valkyrie instinct is directing you to do something else."

She nodded. "I don't know what we're supposed to do, but that may be why Astrid is acting the way she is. She's just a little too entrenched emotionally right now to do more than be defensive."

"So, what do we do?" Tyr asked.

She shrugged. "Give her time? She went in thinking she was avenging Baldur, and came out with his soul in hand. That's a lot to process."

Tyr nodded. "I don't think anyone could have predicted Loki's little trophy was more than just a vambrace."

The two women murmured their agreement. My attention had drifted to Astrid. Angel now sat next to her while Muninn hopped around on the back of the swing, his attention on her and the vambrace. At least she wasn't alone right now. *Go to her. Comfort and protect her.*

I refocused when a presence appeared in our group. Darius had returned.

Papá was the first to greet him. "Welcome back, *hermano*. What did you learn?"

While we had stayed to keep an eye on Astrid, Darius had gone to look into a development that seemed to have happened with her magic. From what Tyr and Davyn had described, the dark magic we'd seen every now and then had amplified and resembled the magic of her first-life mother, Randi.

Darius blew out a breath. "Not much, unfortunately. Randi isn't aware of anyone in the family having magic like the first Randi."

Randi, not to be confused with Astrid's past mother Randi, was a cousin of sorts who lived in Runavík. She was a descendant of Darius' non-immortal twin sister, who lived a few centuries ago. The family had a tradition of naming their first-born daughters Randi, unless it was Astrid who was reincarnated back into the family line.

"As far as she's also aware, no völva in the family has ever had their magic change like Astrid is experiencing," Darius continued. "She has similar speculations as me that it may be related to the reincarnation process she went through. We don't know much about the magic Aya used. It was an ancient spell, and spells that old always have some sort of heavy ramification. It's why most have been intentionally lost to time."

Which meant ancient immortal beings hid them away. Darius and Mom always talked about how magic has its price, even if it was a small one. It was why they always cautioned Astrid and me to be careful when trying something new.

Darius ran his fingers through his salt-and-pepper hair. "She also doesn't agree it's related to Ingrid. Even though Ingrid's magic looked similar, what Tyr described coming from Astrid was too close to Randi's magic for Astrid to have inherited it from Ingrid."

That was even if Ingrid's magic could be inherited. We knew nothing about her abilities, though we assumed much of it came from her worship of Malsumis.

I drummed my fingers on the counter. "It's a shame we can't talk to the dead. Randi may know something."

"Actually, we can," Aya said.

My brow lifted. "How?"

"Seeing as I took her soul to Fólkvangr, I can communicate with her whenever I need to." Her blue eyes brightened. "I don't know why I didn't think of that before. She may not know anything, but Randi was an exceptional witch, and she may know of something related to the family that she forgot to relay to Astrid before her death."

It was a long shot, but better than nothing. Whatever we learned, I just hoped it was nothing to worry about with Astrid. She deserved a peaceful, happy life. But until then, I'd do my best to keep her safe.

And that's what I did.

Hours turned into a day, and then two. Astrid didn't respond much to anyone. She performed basic life tasks, like eating and sleeping, but conversation couldn't be had with her. She focused only on the vambrace. It was like a trance she couldn't break. Or maybe she didn't want to break it, hoping that if she focused long enough, Baldur would magically appear.

My emotions ran the gamut. Frustration, jealousy, and anger were the most recurring of them: anger toward Baldur for dying and causing this pain in her; jealousy because her focus was so strong and I wanted that on me for once; and frustration because I couldn't do anything to help her, and because I was feeling those two other strong emotions and had those unkind thoughts.

It wasn't Baldur's fault he died. He didn't plan that any more than she had planned on dying. And the jealousy was mine to own up to. It wasn't like it was new. I'd had to work through it a number of times when I didn't feel as connected to Astrid as I wanted to be. And with her out of sorts, I definitely didn't feel connected to her.

It was all so exhausting to feel and not know how to change any-thing about it.

Today, late afternoon on day two, we sat out on the grass of the Norway home island. The environment wasn't much different from back home, but I thought the location might help her connect to whatever it was that locked her into this trance.

Plus, it gave Tyr something to do. He wasn't handling this well. His temper was off the charts, lashing out at every little thing. Any different movement or slightly new action from Astrid set him into a fussing panic that rolled into frustration when it wasn't her finally coming out of her trance.

He didn't want to talk it out, so keeping him busy with continuing to modernize the Norway house after centuries of stagnation was the best thing for the god at the moment. I'd sent Angel to be his helper, and keep an eye on him as well. It also kept her from being a pest, as Astrid's continual state was starting to agitate her familiars. I'd even convinced Muninn to go spend time with his hermano, away from Astrid, in hopes it'd help him.

I couldn't blame any of them. Seeing Astrid like this made me want to get up and pace or take off flying as a dragon and find Loki for doing this to her. The distance I felt made me desperate to want to find her, as if she weren't right here in front of me. But I managed to stay rational, for the sake of everyone.

My fingers slid along the frets of my guitar. Astrid loved it when I played, and I hoped it was helping her in some way. The gentle tune wrapped around us and floated out across the clear, calm waters of the lake mirroring the cloudy sky and towering evergreens on the far side.

I didn't know what I was playing. Maybe it was me making sense of random notes, or maybe I'd picked something up in the last few months, but the melody was almost haunting and evocative.

My eyes hooded, the sound drawing me in. I blinked slowly, and the lake and music disappeared. Lush, vibrant greenery surrounded me. A strong, earthy pine scent filled my nose. Evergreen trees, ancient and tall, grew as high as the sky, creating a dense canopy that filtered the sun, casting dappled light on the forest floor.

A familiar voice spoke. "Don't just stand there, come."

I turned and blinked at Astrid. Or, what looked like Astrid. She was younger, maybe fourteen or fifteen, and her clothes and hair were styled similarly to how I'd seen her at the reenactment.

Astrid's eyes sparkled and she laughed before skipping off. "I'll leave you behind."

My feet moved on their own, as if I were dreaming—or reliving a memory.

The soft carpet of moss along the ground cushioned my steps. Birds flitted in the canopy above and a raven cried angrily in the distance. A hare hiding in the underbrush startled and bolted deeper into the woods.

Astrid hummed a tune, one I swore I didn't know but I also did. I didn't know where we were going, but hel if I cared. I was with her. I always wanted to be with her.

Ask her.

Ask her what? What did I need to say?

Make sure you're not the only one who wants this.

I didn't understand these thoughts that were mine but weren't.

My pace picked up. "Astrid."

The voice that came from my lips wasn't mine, but it was.

She spun around and gazed up at me, those vibrant, soul-piercing green eyes of hers sending my heart racing. She waited, expectant but patient, like she always was.

My fingers curled, muscles in my neck tightening. My lungs rebelled and struggled to find air, and my throat threatened to close and cut off the words I needed to say.

I didn't care what others said. I didn't that care she wasn't a völva like the women before her. I didn't believe she was cursed. I didn't agree that her scar made her hideous. She was the most stunning creature I'd ever had the pleasure to meet, and I couldn't let her go.

"Ragnvald?" she said.

My mind paused. *Ragnvald? Who's that?*

"Ragnvald," she repeated. "Ragnvald. Ragnvald. Diego?"

I blinked and the lake view flashed back into my vision. I sucked in a deep breath of crisp air and sat up straight. A soft hand slid along my arm. I jerked my attention toward Astrid, my eyes being met with that familiar, soul-piercing gaze. No longer distant and unfocused, Astrid watched with me a liveliness that matched the dream.

"Astrid?" I murmured.

Her brow knitted together. "Are you okay?"

My guitar clattered on the ground, making an awful sound as it went. Astrid gasped when I grabbed her and pulled her into me. Her vanilla and lavender scent enveloped my senses. My pulse roared in my ears and it took all my control not to suddenly transform into a dragon and fly away with her. *Take her. Claim her, now.*

She mumbled something. I realized I'd smashed her face into my shoulder in my haste. I loosened my grip and she breathed deep in response.

"*Lo siento*," I mumbled.

"That's my line." She pulled out of my hold and scanned our surroundings. "I worried you, and for good reason it seems. How bad was it?"

I blew out a breath. "Two days. You functioned, but… Do you recall anything?"

She bit her lower lip. A spark of desire flared deep inside. "I was vaguely aware of things going on around me, or me performing basic tasks. Muninn and Angel also tried to connect with me through the bond, which was stronger, but still muted. All I could focus on was his soul."

I pulled her into my lap. "Do you want to talk about it?"

She leaned into me, but before she could respond, a shrill cry pierced the air. We looked up, finding Muninn speeding toward us. At the same time, the door of the house flew open and Angel bolted out.

She got to us before Muninn, whining her shepherd whine and shoving herself into Astrid's, and subsequently my lap, and rubbing herself all over us in her excitement. Muninn landed on the ground and hopped around, trying to avoid the wriggling mass that was Angel.

Astrid struggled to get her to calm down, and fell into laughter when she tumbled out of my lap. Muninn hopped onto Astrid, avoiding

Angel's squirming, and made a number of sounds I was still trying to learn the meanings to. I blinked bemusedly at the sight before me.

Heavy footsteps. I tipped my head, spotting Tyr running out of the house. He almost slid on his knees as he reached us and pulled Astrid into his arms. Muninn croaked unhappily and Angel still tried to push her way into Astrid's arms. I had to pull her back, which she was not pleased by. I gave her a comforting pat and did my best to get her to calm down.

"Don't you ever do that to me again," Tyr practically growled out into her hair.

Astrid rubbed his arm. "I'll do my best."

He eventually released her, allowing Astrid to love on her two familiars like they wanted. She still clutched Baldur's vambrace in her hand and Muninn took notice.

He balanced on her wrist and touched his beak to the old leather. He was surprisingly gentle, and the strangest cooing sound came from him. *"Baldur?"*

The raven's words flooded in my mind and not my ears, yet felt like I was hearing them physically. If I weren't used to it by now with Fen and the Berserkers when they were transformed into their animal shapes, I might find it difficult to process. Though, unlike them, Muninn and his brother could control who heard them on a whim.

Astrid's lips twitched. "Yes, his soul is in there."

My brow lifted. Muninn could sense the soul? Was that an effect of his bond with Astrid or something else?

Muninn looked up at her. *"What are you going to do with him?"*

"I don't know yet." She chewed on her lower lip again. My eyes flicked to those perfect lips of her, desire stirring again. *Fuck. Claim. Mate, now.* She really needed to stop doing that.

"I don't know what I'm doing," she confessed, her grip tightening on the vambrace. "I should break this spell trapping his soul and let him finally rest. But the very thought of doing that..."

Her jaw tightened and she shook her head, the words too difficult for her to say.

I wrapped my hand around her free one. "Then don't. Trust your instinct. Even if you don't know what you need to do right now, if all you know is that breaking the magic is the wrong decision, then so be it."

Her lip trembled. "But… what if this is just my grief talking?"

"It's not," Tyr said. He gently took her arm into his massive hands and removed the other vambrace of Baldur's she wore. He touched the soul-binding one, and this time Astrid didn't flinch away protectively. She let him take it, her eyes tight and trained on his movements, but there was no panic, showing her trust in him.

Tyr slid the armor onto her arm and tied it. "You're a Valkyrie. This is your job. Even in your grief, if you were meant to release his soul, you'd feel it. This means, you're meant to do something else with it, but we don't have enough information to know the best course of action yet. So, he'll have to wait a little longer until we do."

"But what other option is there?" Her words cracked. "If not death, then it's life, but the moment I think of the spell Aya used for me, I get this recoiling sensation, like that is an even worse idea than just releasing the soul. I don't know why I feel that, but that's clearly not the right path. So, what else is there? Reviving the dead is…"

She didn't need to answer that. Mamá told me how unique the spell Aya used was. It was ancient and powerful, one no one should have been able to find, for a reason she didn't explain. And as far as she knew, it was the only spell capable of catalyzing some sort of revival.

I squeezed Astrid's hand. "We'll figure it out."

She took a deep breath. "And if we could revive him some way, is it smart to do? Midgard has changed so much in the last six hundred years. It's one thing to live through all that, even if you don't experience every little change or event, but to just be teleported through time, with your last memories of a world that basically doesn't exist anymore…"

Tyr brushed her cheek with a gentle finger. "Don't worry, Valkyrie. Baldur is one of the most adaptable gods I know. Give him a little time and he'll be better at technology than me."

This got her to laugh—that beautiful, carefree sound that warmed the soul. I smiled, warmth rolling through me. I missed that sound.

Muninn croaked. *"I will search for information."*

Astrid pursed her lips. "I don't know what there is to find, but I won't stop you from trying."

Muninn may not be human, but he was an exceptionally intelligent raven, given the magic in him, and his age. I didn't doubt he'd be capable of finding some sort of clue to help us.

Her raven familiar unfurled his wings and took off, disappearing into nothing thanks to a magical artifact on his leg that allowed him to teleport anywhere he wanted.

Angel licked Astrid's cheek and trotted into the tranquil lake water. My brow furrowed and then deepened more when Astrid said, "Stay inside the wards."

"Where is she going?" Tyr asked before I could.

"She wanted to check out the forest. She wants to be helpful, too, so patrolling the borders became her logical choice."

It was still a little strange hearing Astrid and Angel interact like this. And I was also fascinated to witness how Angel would change the longer she was a familiar. Maybe one day Angel would be able to do what Muninn could.

Astrid looked up at us through her lashes, a demure smile on her lips. The simmering desire in me from before stoked even hotter. "You're both okay with this? If I find a way to revive Baldur…"

I cupped her cheek. "I am more than okay with it."

There wasn't a part of me that was concerned or even jealous of the idea of her having Baldur back. I wanted her to be happy. I knew a part of her still loved him, and if there was a way for her to get him back, I would support her.

"You know I don't have an issue with it, Valkyrie," Tyr rumbled.

I leaned in, pressing my forehead against hers. "Just, don't forget about us, okay?"

She snorted. "I'll never forget about you two."

Astrid let out a startled squeak and pulled away from me. Or, she was pulled away by Tyr. He dipped down and pressed his face into the crook of her neck. "We'll make sure you don't."

Desire pulsed deep inside me. My primal dragon thoughts beat in my head, demanding her. After two days of worrying, I was game to remind her what she'd forgotten about.

I blinked when something small and wet smacked me on the forehead. And then again, this time my arm. We all looked up when more rain fell from the gray sky.

"Living room it is," Tyr murmured before hauling Astrid over his shoulder. She squealed and complained, which only stopped when he gave her a quick swat on the ass in reprimand. "Careful, Valkyrie, or your punishment will be worse."

Her cheeks turned a deep pink. "Punishment for what?"

"Two days."

Astrid bit her bottom lip. I grinned. I wasn't one for punishment. I'd rather praise and worship. But Astrid enjoyed both, and me being a voyeur for punishments always increased her pleasure, which I was coming to enjoy more and more.

Tyr shoved the door open before the enchantment could do so on its own. It hit the wall with a *bang* which made Astrid bite her lip again, her lips curving up. Tyr was giving himself away too much. She was not going to cooperate, making this worse on him.

He marched into the small living room and set Astrid on the floor. He summoned his axe, making both my and Astrid's brows raise with surprise; however, all he did was remove a leather tie from it before banishing the weapon back into its pocket dimension.

"You've lost the privilege of using your hands," he said. "Offer me your wrist."

Astrid didn't respond right away, her eyes carefully watching him, but eventually she held up her wrist.

Tyr tied the leather to her wrist. "Now turn around."

Slowly, Astrid complied. As her back faced him, her lips pulled into a brief grin. I lowered myself on the plush chair to enjoy the show.

"Give me your other wrist."

She hesitated again like the first time, but responded to the order. Tyr restrained her hands behind her back. His hulking frame pressed into her back and he loomed over her.

With surprising gentleness, he reached around and tipped her chin up. His words were far rougher. "On your knees."

She gazed up at him and smirked. "No."

Tyr's jaw set and his fingers slid down her skin until they wrapped around her delicate neck. "What was that, Valkyrie?"

She paused for effect. "No, my god."

His grip on her neck tightened. She inhaled deeply, her back straightening. "You will do as I say."

"Or what?"

Without releasing her, Tyr grabbed the front of her shirt. The fabric bunched around the curves of her breasts.

Astrid's tongue slowly swiped along the backside of her lip. "Is that supposed to be a threat?"

I shifted in the chair, anticipation building in me. She hadn't put on a bra this morning. She knew exactly how hard she was pushing Tyr today.

Fabric ripped and Astrid only grinned as he tore her shirt open. A groan built in my throat, seeing her perky, large breasts break free, their bouncing movement hypnotic. Her tattered shirt framed them just right, and the pendant of her necklace disappeared between them, tempting someone to reach between and pull it out.

Somehow Tyr refrained from touching them—from touching her. I didn't know where he found the restraint. Even from here, all I wanted to do was take her in my hands and fondle and tease and worship her soft delicious curves until she was a begging, panting mess.

"Are you going to behave now, Valkyrie?" Tyr rumbled. "Kneel and beg for my forgiveness, and you'll only get twenty-four. Half of what you deserve."

She snapped her teeth and grinned. I bit the inside of my cheek. I'd never seen her this bratty before, but I liked it.

Tyr's grip around her throat tightened and her eyes hooded. "Forty-eight now."

Astrid wiggled her jean-clad hips. "Like I'll feel it."

I chuckled and slowly twirled my finger, magic springing from my hand. Her pants seemed to melt away into colorful wisps of smoke, an illusion that made it a little more fun to look at than just snapping them away.

Astrid's eyes popped wide, not having expected me to partake. She knew Tyr wouldn't have risked ripping a favorite pair of pants of hers. He knew better. But now her one protection was gone, especially as she apparently had gone commando today.

Tyr bent her forward and his hand smacked her bare ass. Astrid inhaled sharply and bit her lip. The tiniest of moans escaped her. Tyr waited a moment for any other response.

Astrid glanced up at him and grinned while still biting her lip and shook her ass as if to taunt him. "You call that a spank?"

The following *crack* to her backside echoed through the room, followed by her grunt. My back straightened. That was not the typical force he used with her. And that hadn't sounded like an enjoyable reaction from Astrid.

Tyr's stern expression softened in only a way it did for her. "Too much."

"You think?" Her voice was hard, no hint of playfulness to be found. There went the fun. "I understand you're upset, and I am sorry I worried you both, but that was uncalled for."

Tyr's grip on her neck loosened to something tender and he bent down. "I apologize for going too far. It wasn't my intent, but that doesn't matter, and I own that."

With my arm propped up on the armchair, I rested my cheek on my hand. Healthy communication wasn't easy, but necessary. These two had established where their boundaries were months ago, and it was good seeing them communicate through them here, even with emotions running high.

Tyr kissed her, devouring her mouth until she moaned and leaned into him. Astrid tugged her wrists against her restraints, but she didn't see what I could. I couldn't help but grin as Tyr slid his other hand down her arm and wrapped it around her smaller hands.

Astrid broke the kiss. "Tyr."

He chuckled low and deep. "You seem to think we're done here. We're not. We're not even close."

She rolled her eyes. "I'm done with the—"

Tyr's mouth covered hers again and he sank down onto the couch, pulling her with him. She let out a startled squeak. He grinned down at her and dragged his fingers down her neck. "I can punish you in other ways, Valkyrie. You're not getting out of that."

Instead of a snappy retort, she inhaled and arched her back as he trailed his touch between her breasts, along several lines of her mandala sternum tattoo he'd memorized, and down her belly. I watched, fascinated by this new behavior. I'd never seen Tyr this gentle with her during sex. That wasn't to say I didn't think he ever was, just that I'd never witnessed it.

Tyr slid his fingers all along her body, never going low enough for her, or me. He chuckled in her ear when he teasingly traced the underside of her breast and she groaned quietly. "Where's your bite, Valkyrie? Don't tell me I've doused your fire already."

Astrid's lips parted as he trailed his fingers up her outer breast then promptly shut them when he traced her arm. I grinned and repositioned myself in my chair. The brat in her was alive and well, just working in another way. She refused to give him what he wanted—her words.

Tyr continued to tease, and every time I thought Astrid might finally give in, she managed to resist. With each stifled gasp, each squirm and bite of her lip, my blood ran hotter. This was becoming torture for even me. I wanted to hear her beg just as much.

His fingers slid down her belly again, lower and lower until they nearly reached the apex of her thighs. Astrid gasped quietly, and her hips tipped up. Tyr withdrew his fingers immediately and chuckled when she failed to bite back a quiet whimper.

"Beg for it, Valkyrie," he murmured in her ear. "Beg your god, and I'll grant your prayer."

Astrid set her jaw, refusing to give in. Tyr smirked and repositioned his legs into a wider stance. He wrapped his thick fingers around her thighs and lifted them over his legs, suspending her and putting her on full display for me.

My tongue ran along my lower lip while my eyes drank in every curve, down to her glistening pussy and every shallow breath she took.

My fingers curled into fists and my cock strained too hard against my pants as the heat building in me burned in my veins.

Claim. Mate. Mate. The dragon in me shifted and nudged, desiring to touch her, to taste and claim her and mark her as mine forever. I did everything I could to control that urge, but hell was that getting harder and hard to do. Especially after what'd happened in the last two days.

Tyr curled his strong fingers around Astrid's neck again. "Look at what you're doing to him, Valkyrie. You're only going to make it worse the longer you disobey. I can't guarantee he'll be nice to you."

Oh, I'd be nice. I'd please her until she couldn't walk tomorrow. Maybe we'd sequester her away for an extra day, to make up for the same time lost.

"Be good and beg me," Tyr rumbled as the fingers of his free hand slid up her inner thigh.

Astrid bit her lip. "Make me."

Fuck.

Tyr chuckled and teasingly slid his fingers along her soft folds. Astrid sucked in a tight breath through her nose, as did I, and she tipped her hips, trying for more. But Tyr was too quick and pulled his fingers away, instead teasing her inner thigh. He released her neck to trace patterns around her breasts and along her tattoo.

Astrid squirmed and bit down on her lip harder. But as Tyr continued to tease her pussy again until she tried for too much, it was her eyes that gave away her weakening stubbornness.

When Tyr slid his finger along the slit of her pussy, Astrid moaned. "Please."

Tyr paused and grinned. "What was that, Valkyrie?"

She breathed in and out, as if that was all she could concentrate on.

He dragged his finger across her perky nipple and Astrid let out a strangled moan.

"Please," she finally repeated. "Please, Tyr."

He rolled her nipple between his fingers and she arched into his touch. He continued to tease her lips, making her squirm.

Astrid whimpered. "I'm sorry. Forgive me for forgetting about you."

Tyr's chest rumbled in a way even I felt over here. "Good girl. I'll make sure you never forget what your god gives you."

She leaned into his touch. "Remind me, please."

Tyr's fingers slid between her folds. Astrid's mouth fell open with her pleased sigh. He stroked and teased her clit and played with her breast. She writhed and moaned. She twisted against her wrist restraints, begging and pleading with him for more.

Just when I thought she'd hit her peak, Tyr pulled away.

Astrid whimpered and twisted, trying to catch his fingers. "Tyr, please don't. Please, I'll be good."

Tyr rumbled a thoughtful sound. "Will you?"

She gazed up at him, her chest heaving with her need. Something passed between them because he smirked and plunged his fingers inside her. Astrid arched and moaned something deep and primal that ignited the need burning in my veins. *Take mate. Claim her.* If Tyr didn't hurry up, I'd take her from him. Not even a god could stop me.

I pushed the intrusive thoughts from my mind. That level of possession wasn't safe, and I knew it was the dragon in me that needed to be tamed back.

Astrid arched and squirmed, Tyr increasing his attention on her until she finally crested over that edge. She screamed and her hips bucked. At the same time, magic suddenly sparked from her, and my and Tyr's clothes vanished.

Tyr and I stared at her as she came down. She panted for breath and weakly smiled. "Oops."

Tyr chuckled and grabbed a fistful of her hair, yanking and making her gasp. "That was no oops, Valkyrie. You're a greedy little, unsatisfied—"

He cut himself off with a stifled groan. Astrid had bitten her lower lip and grinned in the middle of his rant.

"Is that you saying you don't want my worship, Tyr?" she purred, her arms moving in long, gliding movements up and down.

I had to bite back a groan of my own. What I wouldn't give for her to be stroking me instead. I needed some relief.

Wrapping my hand around my strained cock, I pumped slowly, careful to only give myself a small amount of relief. Creation did I need it.

"Very well, Valkyrie," Tyr rumbled. "Have it your way."

He lifted her and then plunged his large cock inside her. The most primal groan came from Astrid, the sound caressing and taunting me. He thrust into her and she responded by meeting his motions with her own, pushing him fully and impossibly into her.

"That's it, Valkyrie. Take your god's cock like a good little whore."

"More, Tyr," she begged, her eyes practically rolling into the back of her head. "Fuck me more. I need all of you inside me."

Tyr grabbed her throat and made her look up at him. "Don't you dare close your eyes. Your eyes stay on me."

Her perfect breasts bounced with each of his thrusts, their motions luring and begging me to leave my spot to come play with them.

Tyr pushed his fingers between Astrid's thighs, stroking her sensitive clit as he fucked her. She bucked and begged, drawing him closer and closer to release. Or maybe that was me. I had to force myself to ease up. I needed her to finish with me.

Astrid's back arched more and Tyr's thrusts became more punctuated. He claimed her mouth with his, devouring her. Her body convulsed, and they both groaned into each other as they came.

Their mouths parted when they came down, breaths mingling, but Tyr didn't stop. Astrid squirmed and writhed as she gasped, her body sensitive but wanting.

Tyr grinned down at her. "That's it, Valkyrie, worship your god's cock and like it. A slut like you needs to be filled with my cum."

A flash of envy slashed me. The two of them had this special bond, where if she did something just right with him, something to do with prayer, he didn't have to stop immediately. Creation did I wish I could have something like that with her. Immortality gave me a quicker bounce back than before, but still. The most I could do was hope she used her magical blue pill.

Astrid came quickly again, her unrestrained cry of pleasure filling the house. Tyr wasn't far behind, filling her pussy with reckless abandon. They slowly stilled, Tyr pressing his face into her neck and Astrid laying languidly against him, her expression blissful.

He kissed her on the temple and then extracted himself with a low groan and set her feet on the floor. "Go give him attention now. He's been patient."

Tyr gave her a light slap on the ass, making her squeak adorably before he leaned back on the couch. I grinned at Astrid as she sashayed toward me. I drank in the sight of her hips' hypnotic sway and her breasts bouncing with each step. With her hands still tied behind her, her chest jutted out more, punctuating each bouncing movement.

I reached for her and pulled her into me by her luscious hips. She slid into my lap, fitting against me like the perfect piece, and pressed her forehead against mine.

I relished this closeness with her. "How are you feeling?"

Astrid hummed. "Good."

I tugged a bit on the leather restraining her, and it came undone, freeing her arms. She slid her fingers up my chest, igniting heat under my skin. I tangled my fingers into her hair. "Do you need a moment, Cielo?"

She smiled sweetly and leaned in, pressing her lips gently against mine. "I want whatever you're willing to give, my dragon."

Claim her. She is mine. I need to claim her. A dragon growl caught in my throat. I'd give her everything she asked for and more.

Mate. Mate. I couldn't get carried away. I still didn't understand how dragon mating worked—Mom was oddly vague about it every time I brought it up—and I didn't want to mate Astrid without her permission. I also wasn't sure I was ready for that step. I knew I wasn't. Soon. But not now.

I kissed her deeply, pouring everything I felt for her as if this were the last time I could. My tongue tangled with hers, taking in her taste and searing it deep in my memories.

Her fingers threaded into my hair, pulling me closer. Her slick pussy dripped all over me, practically begging for me to fill her as much as Tyr had. My cock twitched. Astrid giggled and rocked her hips. Not willing to deny her, I grabbed her hip with my free hand and slowly slid inside her.

Our kiss broke as Astrid's mouth fell open and she moaned. I pulled out as slowly as I'd entered her until just the tip remained inside, and then pushed back in. The pace was as delicious as it was agonizing.

"Diego," she whispered.

"You like this?" I said.

"Yes," she purred. "Yes. I want more of this."

I kept up my pace, slowly fucking her—loving her like she deserved.

My fingers trailed over her soft body, teasing and playing with every sensitive spot she had. I cupped her full breasts and ran my thumbs along her sensitive skin.

She moaned. "Do more of that. Play with me."

I slid my fingers over her rigid dusky-rose nipples. Teasing and circling, flicking and pinching, slowly fucking, I played while enjoying the range of pleasured expressions flashing across her face. She arched under my touch, begging.

I dipped my head, trailing my mouth and tongue over her collarbone, past the pendant bouncing against her skin, along her heavy breast. Astrid whimpered as I teasingly kissed around her sensitive peaks and rocked into me, increasing the potency of my thrusting.

"Give it to me," she said, her breathing heavy.

Sliding the taut bud into my mouth, I sucked hard once. She gasped, her grip on my hair tightening, sending a pleasant sensation down my spine. I licked and sucked, and nipped and sucked some more. Astrid arched and rocked faster and faster, aching for more.

"More," she begged, the sound intoxicating and sending my pulse pounding in my ears. "Give me more, my dragon."

I obliged, not interested in denying her anything. One hand released her and tangled in her gorgeous hair, while the other slipped between her thighs, finding her slick, needy clit. Astrid gasped, and then moaned rocking into me, driving me further inside her. My desire burned so hot under my skin I thought I was going to combust.

I thrust harder into her, losing myself in everything she was and everything I needed from her. Astrid moaned, her breaths laboring. Her fingers tightened in my hair and she tried to pull herself impossibly close, as if trying to fuse us together forever.

"That's it, mi amor," I growled out around the mouthful of her breast, my voice deepening as my dragon surfaced. "Tell me how much you like this."

She tried to. Her mouth gaped and tried so hard, but she was too lost in the pleasure.

I grinned. "Tell me, *hermosa*, I know you can. *¿Eso se siente bien?*"

Astrid nodded. "Sí. Yes. Yes, please more. I need you—"

Her moaned cut off her words as I rubbed a new pattern along her clit in time with the way I sucked her perfect nipple.

Hearing even the slightest Spanish off her lips drove me crazy. And now all I wanted was to hear her screaming in ultimate pleasure. "*Vengas para mí.*"

Her head rolled back and her hips bucked as an orgasm tore through her. Her walls clamped down around me, squeezing and milking my cock. Tension coiled and then it exploded in one euphoric release. I groaned, spilling inside her, abandoning myself to pleasure.

I thrust until I couldn't anymore, coming down from the high soon after Astrid. Breathing deep and hard, satisfaction coursed through me. I gripped her hips firmly, refusing to pull out so I could relish being inside her as long as I could, regardless how spent I was. I'd bounce back for another round soon.

My dragon's presence bled into my senses until the line between us was hard to differentiate. It wanted more from this connection with her, but it was also as pleased as me.

I gently kissed Astrid on her forehead and she hummed. She pressed her soft body into me, her fingers still tangled in my hair. My fingers glided over the sensitive skin of her back. She sucked in a sharp breath and arched. Our lips brushed, our breath mingling. Grinning, I dipped my head enough to kiss her.

Tenderly, slowly, I savored her like the most intoxicating memory.

My fingers slid up the smooth skin of her arm, bumping into the vambrace on her forearm. My breath caught, and my body seized. Images flooded my mind and sound assaulted my ears.

I jerked back, overwhelmed by everything flashing too quickly to make much sense of it. Some of it felt familiar, like I'd experienced the event and was remembering, while some were foreign, like watching a movie filmed in first-person. There wasn't much connection between the moments, except one thing: Astrid.

Air filled my lungs when the images abruptly disappeared. I gasped for breath, relishing the sensation as if I'd held it for hours.

Astrid's gentle hands framed my face and she turned me toward her. Her face was pinched all over with worry. "Diego, are you back with us?"

I blinked and vaguely noticed Tyr looming over us. "I… yeah, I am."

"What happened?" Tyr asked.

My eyes squinched as I tried to process. A headache built the longer I attempted, making my eye twitch. Golden light sprang from Astrid's hands and soothed the pain away. I leaned into her touch, relishing the feeling. "I think I saw memories."

Astrid cocked her head. "You saw Baldur's memories?"

I nodded and swallowed, struggling for words to explain, because I wasn't convinced it was just Baldur's memories I'd seen, given what I experienced earlier outside. But I also didn't know how to explain that side of the memories, because the only ones that made sense were triggered by me touching the vambrace.

"He touched the armor, so it makes sense," Tyr said.

"But it's never been an involuntary thing," Astrid said.

Dragons were known for their visions. The first dragons, our mothers, were the most famous of them all. However, not many understood us beyond that, or how unique our abilities were.

Each dragon had a uniqueness to them that made their visions and other abilities special. It was reflected in the way we hoarded, too. Dahlia's all revolved around information and her tech. Zeke saw several possibilities of a prophecy all at once and expressed them through art, which he hoarded. Caleb saw the truth of hidden pasts and broke barriers by holding all languages close to his chest, while his twin, Callie, saw deceit even in chaotic future visions. Me? Mine was memories.

My visions were almost always ones already seen, but came from a different perspective or played out a little differently. And more recently, I'd learned to tap into an object that had memories attached to it.

It wasn't easy for me to do right now, and not all items had memories. But through that, I was getting a better grasp of what were memories, visions, and basic dreams. Or I thought that until today.

These moments with this Ragnvald individual and whatever else I saw because of the vambrace were puzzling.

I sucked in a deep breath. "It was definitely memories. I think Loki's magic is just a little strong. I'll try not to touch it just in case."

Astrid frowned and touched the vambrace. "I could take—"

I pressed my thumb to her lips. "No."

She pulled away, a crease in her forehead. "Are you sure?"

Wrapping my hand around the back of her neck, I pulled her close and closed my lips around hers, devouring her. I would never ask that of her. I could accommodate. That would be easy. And I could tackle what happened, after I was done indulging in this amazing woman.

Darkness.
Emptiness.
Numb.
Where am I?
Unknown.
Floating.
Existing.
Who am I?
Baldur Odinson.
But what did that mean? What did anything mean?
What are these sensations?
Fear, palpable and luring.
Pain, twisting and deep.
Rage, burning with fury.
Calm, soothing and welcoming.
Desire, hotter than the sun.
Sun.
Sunshine.
Valkyrie.

SEVEN

ASTRID

Information scrawled up the laptop screen on the coffee table in front of me. Most of it was technical jargon I didn't understand in the least, but I did my best, hoping something might jump out at me. Sitting around me in the great room of the retreat house were much smarter people than me who were capable of dissecting the data. I just had to hope when they discussed it, it was in not-smart-person-speak.

My phone chimed and I took a peek. It was an email from the town council with image attachments. There were a few designs, ranging from basic to artistically detailed. They all had New Fensalir scrawled on their surfaces, and some also referenced Valkyries' Sanctuary.

Diego leaned to peer over my shoulder. "Whatcha got?"

"The council finally decided on an established date and got sign designs made up for approval. They want my input."

He shifted his gaze to me, the corner of his mouth twitching as if he were amused. "You sound so happy."

I rolled my eyes. "They don't need my approval for this. I told them that."

Kirby, who sat on my other side on the couch, nudged me with her elbow. "That's what you get for creating a sanctuary."

I blew out a breath. Back in the fall, when we took in a large number of refugees, it was decided the town would become an official sanctuary. The townsfolk decided to rename the town to reflect this, especially since we were now semi-hidden from the world. Two names had been proposed, the same two on the signs.

Ultimately New Fensalir was the winning name during a town vote, but Valkyrie's Sanctuary still held prominence with the locals for the entire surrounding area the sanctuary wards encompassed. And it was that second name that made the situation so strange for me.

Apparently, even though the wards were powered by a few of us, I was seen as the main guardian of sorts. Possibly on account of me running the retreat, and sticking my nose into saving people when I could, but I didn't exactly ask to be some sanctuary leader. *I also didn't reject it, either…*

Luckily the town still had Bernard, our original mayor, even though the council and mayor positions had been combined and restructured, and the town mostly ran itself without me having to be involved. They just liked involving me in what they thought were bigger matters. Like a damned sign most people would never see.

The town wasn't exactly invisible, and people could come and go as they pleased, but the magic protecting our sanctuary did lessen some of the tourist traffic, as it dissuaded anyone who might pose a threat to the residents. That mostly affected humans, as the supernatural community living here rarely lived behind glamour and magical masks.

Dahlia—who lounged in a beanbag chair in the most awkward way possible—sighed, drawing my attention back to the more important situation at hand. "There's so much here, where do we start?"

"Is there anything in the notes to reveal why the magic community is being targeted?" Diego asked. May not be the most pressing thing to talk about, but it was important. And it was something we average-intelligence people could help discuss. "They're going through so much effort to do this, when there are far easier ways to cause chaos."

"They pose a threat to whatever her insane plans are," Aya said. "Fae, demons, gods, and other creatures like them are powerful. Even humans pose a threat. While their ability to touch magic is significantly less than before the first Ragnarök magical sacrifice, it's still great, considering the sheer number of humans on the planet.

Urd crossed her legs. "Magic has been having a resurgence as well. Artura and I had noticed this century, and even in the last year especially, there was new magic cropping up, even amongst family lines that never had magic before. There have been a greater number of non-dragon seers as well, as seen with some of the new Valkyries. This is a new phenomenon. It's why I've been more active this century. I was afraid it was a sign Ragnarök would be upon us again."

There seemed to be more unstated information in her eyes, but she wasn't going to divulge that right now. I wasn't sure why the older dragons were like this. Either out of habit, stubbornness, or something else, it was frustrating regardless, to have to pry important information from them. *I wonder if what she's not saying has to do with those vault-thingies Xavier mentioned.*

The other day, I'd finally gotten around to asking him to re-explain what happened to him, and he did, but he was really vague about the vault, only mentioning it had something to do with magic. I was pretty sure I'd gotten even less info about them than the first time he explained. Like it was some big secret he had to keep for some reason, and he'd said too much the first time.

Ronan, a tall elf man with thick, dark hair, captivating eyes, and an air about him that commanded respect, but still had an easy elegance that made him approachable, cleared his throat. "I don't believe this is the most pressing thing to discuss. The motives don't matter if we can't reverse what they've already done and prevent further damage."

He had a good point. "So, what do we have here, for us average people trying to understand all this jargon?"

"Most of the magic-blocker data is compiled from the new data we stole and what Ronan remembered, since Ingrid ran off with the data when they had their falling out," Aya said. "We've tried to find similarities between the iterations, but it hasn't been easy, with the lack of resources from the original formula."

"The original formula was intended to be temporary," Ronan said. "At least, that's what I'd wanted when I started with the project, and what Ingrid had claimed she was after as well when she approached me for funding. I wanted the side effects to be minimal when anyone decided it was time to stop taking the pills. From this data, it's clear just how much she pushed the formula to make it permanent after I refused to continue taking part in her schemes."

"Luckily, the data we stole goes into detail of how Malsumis' energy is used in this new formula," Aya said. "It's complex, and done in ways not many would have guessed was possible."

We already knew Malsumis' essence was used in some way. When Thac found out Mia had been using the first iteration of the magic blockers in the form of pills, he'd sensed the corruption in the medication. Ronan, once he was freed from Odin's mind control and allied with us, also used the last of the batch in his possession to replicate the pills into the serum weaponized against Odin.

However, it couldn't be all that was used, not with the differences between the blocker administered to me compared to Mia.

Whereas her blocker was a constant daily renewal that broke down in a matter of a day or two if not renewed, mine had been a medical shot. Or, at least we presumed my egg-donor had given me one as a child, disguised as a vaccine. And it took over two decades for it to break down. Two decades of my magic hammering away at the blocker until it weakened enough for my Valkyrie abilities to destroy it.

With such wildly different results from formulas that we were guessing only had a few years max separating their iterations, there had to be more to it. There was also the fact that, to anyone's knowledge, there were only two individuals who could suppress magic the same way the magic blockers did.

One of Loki's brothers, Helblindi, now going by the name Blake, had once been able to do this with others. However, it came at such an insurmountable cost—he'd lost that power when he used it to restrain the goddess who was trying to kill Blake's love.

In a strange twist of fate, Marley, the partner of Byleist—now Eli—Loki and Blake's other brother, gained the same ability when she ascended as one of the newest gods. But it would come with the same heavy cost, so she, too, refrained from using the power.

Ronan insisted he knew nothing about either immortal's power during his time involved in the magic blockers, and the timeframe of Blake losing his power didn't lend itself to it being used by the Malsumis cult. He also wasn't a bad dude.

We'd paid Blake and Marley a visit to be sure, and to see if either of them could share some insight with us. They were more than happy to help where they could, but the information shared didn't shed enough light to understand how such an ability could be replicated in this current situation, especially without sacrificing something in return.

"But it is the main component of blocking," Aya said.

"How is that possible?" Tyr asked.

"Because of how it's used," Dad said. He had a folder open with paper files, which he handed Tyr a sheet from. "It's manipulated to wrap around the source of magic and bind it."

Kirby squinted at her computer screen. "It's not the only component, though. This here says it can't bind indefinitely on its own, and that there's an undocumented second binding agent."

Ronan let out a heavy breath. "The other component was fae blood."

My lips twisted, as did my stomach, discomfort settling in deep. Blood had a potent effect on magic, but fae blood had unusual magical properties. It was best known for its ability to bind magic into artifacts that anyone could use. Ronan's line in particular was one of the rare few fae lines to be able to extensively utilize the power in fae blood and not risk death.

However, I doubted anyone in his line helped with this stronger binding, which implied fae had died for this new serum.

Ronan continued. "The blood is used to bind the magic to the body, and then her essence is layered on top, where it traps the blood-sealing magic, preventing any magical leakage. This process used to be handled by me for the original formula. We haven't yet discovered, in the retrieved data, how they're managing something so complex without me."

"How is it different from how you used the magic for the nullifier serum we used on Odin?" I asked.

Ronan hadn't explained to us how the blood magic worked in the serum, just that we could trust it would work as long as he or Mia administered the last dose. It was an uncomfortable serum to trust with him, since it wasn't exactly different in my book from Ingrid's magic blocker.

The only major difference was that Ronan gave people a choice, if they weren't Odin at least. *And Ronan isn't mind-controlled.* Even still, I couldn't help but worry if it landed in the wrong hands, or someone regretted the choice later. I already hated that I'd used it on Odin out of desperation.

"My version had Malsumis' essence removed, and relies heavily on my blood magic. If they don't have a blood mage altering the fae blood, then that's the major difference," he said. "Fae blood on its own, while potent, doesn't have the same range of properties as manipulated blood. Blood manipulated through magic is much stronger and more difficult to break. This means we still have a chance to reverse what the cult has done with the magic blockers."

"There's also a note here talking about a weakening agent in order to do it," Kirby said. "What's that about?"

I leaned over to see what part she was referencing. My eyes stopped scanning when I noticed two words, with hastily scribbled notes saying there were inconsistencies with its inclusion. "*Phoradendron Leucarpum.* Isn't that… mistletoe?"

Had I not been studying herbs and plants for potion-making, I wouldn't have had a guess at what that scientific name was. Conveniently enough, I'd recently gotten into learning more about the Viscaceae family of toxic plants, which included several species of mistletoe.

Ronan nodded. "Yes, one of the North American variants. This is the weakening agent. Neither fae blood nor Malsumis' energy can latch onto magic contained inside a body without issue. Even if the magic user isn't powerful, the magic inside them is still too volatile to be contained easily."

I pursed my lips, my mind racing. Mistletoe. It kept coming up in my life. *There are no such things as coincidences.*

"Why would you use mistletoe instead of something else?" Dahlia asked. "It's a toxic plant."

"Astrid had Mia drink it in a tea," Diego said. "Can it really be that toxic if she turned out okay?"

"The tea didn't hurt Mia because she's fae," Ronan said. "We're immune to most natural poisons and toxins."

"But Astrid didn't know that at the time," Tyr said.

"I'm familiar with how it can be used." I played with my necklace pendant. "Mistletoe has a long history of being used in toxins on humans. It was something I was taught by my mother Randi. Those with magic, even if they're human, have higher resistances to the toxic nature of mistletoe, so witches would craft potions that attacked the magic of another witch or a fae."

That's what gave me the idea to make the tea for Mia. I could feel her magic trying to burst through, so I assumed at the time another magic was imprisoning it. I believed I could neutralize the magic without harming her if I gave her a highly diluted amount.

"So, the mistletoe is used to neutralize the magic enough for binding agents to seal it away," Dad mumbled.

Ronan nodded. "That's correct. The original formula was only approved to use a minute percentage, as I didn't intend for it to be a permanent situation. We don't have enough data here to tell if that amount has changed."

"It could be either way," Dad said. "Even if the dose of mistletoe compound was too high and killed their targets, it'd add to the chaos they're looking for."

I pressed my lips together. I couldn't shake something about the mistletoe inclusion.

"I know," Kirby said. "It's strange to me, too."

I shifted my gaze to her. Diego shot us a questioning glance and Kirby shrugged. "Obviously this has solid proof of working in this formula, but when you think about the other big event involving mistletoe, it doesn't quite make sense."

Magnus looked up from her laptop. "Are you talking about Baldur?"

Lucia, who sat next to Ronan, piped up. "Who is Baldur?"

Lucia was a young Latina woman barely in her twenties, with golden brown skin, who stood around my height and had a loud presence that matched her louder mouth.

Crystal jewelry and brightly colored clothes adorned her petite frame that hid the fact she could put down as much food as a Berserker. Her long black hair had a bright green streak, though with the use of magic, changed day to day based on her mood.

She was as new to us as Mia. She was Thac's "niece." They weren't actually blood related or anything. It was more akin to the relationship Dahlia and Magnus and Fen and I had with each other when we called each other siblings.

And despite her being a bruja, a Central American witch, with magic that manifested as enhanced physical strength that got her in trouble when she didn't control herself, she didn't have a lot of experience with the true inner workings of the world.

Despite her knowing her family had magic, she hadn't been brought further into the truth until the last few months. It was why she was here. She wanted to know more, and this was a safe way for her to do it.

"He was a European god who died many centuries ago." Thac said.

Thac, known to his followers as Tlaloc, was a large man just taller than Tyr and with similar bulk. Dark, thick wavy hair curled around the collar of his shirt, and Central American-style tattoos adorned his scarred light brown skin. His brown eyes spoke of centuries of experience.

Lucia blinked. "Gods can be killed?"

He nodded. "Through specific circumstances, yes."

"What does this have to do with him?"

Mia, a tall, curvy woman with long dark hair and dark eyes, rubbed her neck over a wine-colored birthmark in the shape of an apple that was accentuated by a snake tattoo trying to eat it. "Correct me if I'm wrong, as my knowledge of Norse myth, let alone actual reality beyond that myth, is a bit spotty, but wasn't he the perfect son of Odin who died to mistletoe?"

I nodded. "The myth says Loki used mistletoe because it was the only plant that couldn't promise not to hurt him. Reality, nothing actually swore that of course, and Baldur was only immune to physical pain. But, if myth is based on truth, why was mistletoe mentioned?"

"Because he had it in his hand," Tyr said. "Remember, I caught him hovering over Baldur's dead body. I saw the mistletoe."

My brow squinched. "And he confirmed that's what he used to kill him?"

Tyr shrugged. "I attacked him without asking questions."

Of course he did.

Aya leaned back in her chair. "To be fair, Loki never denied the use of mistletoe. And he was quite proud of TOM's name."

"Confirmed he did kill Baldur that way, or only never denied it?" I asked. Something was pinging in the back of my mind, making it difficult for me to let this go.

"Does it matter?" Lucia asked. "Every time this Loki is ever mentioned, it's never good. He sounds like a *mamaverga* who needs a good face beating."

She pounded her fists together in emphasis. Thac shot her a stern look while Diego and a few of us laughed. Thac didn't particularly like her foul mouth, and unfortunately for him, we didn't discourage it.

"It does matter," I said. "Because doing something versus not denying it are two completely different things."

And if Loki sealed Baldur's soul, he did it for a reason. And that reason had something to do with the mistletoe, and it wasn't what everyone thought.

I rubbed Baldur's vambrace. His soul pulsed beneath my touch, a sense of calm rolling over me. *What was he doing?*

"We're off track," Magnus said. "We can research the mistletoe part of this to be sure, since the weakening agent of the blocker is important, but what we really need to worry about is the Malsumis essence."

She tapped her dragon claw ring on the top of the laptop screen. "We have Ronan and Mia to help us combat the fae blood use. What we don't have is a way to dissolve the goddess's essence. If we remove it, the weakening agent is less likely to hold on its own. The problem is, we've only managed to break the essence twice, and both times it had been weakened beforehand. We don't have that luxury when it's a freshly administered dose. If we want to develop a true antidote, we need to first get past that part."

I sat back in my seat. This was where I drew a blank. "How do you combat a god essence?"

"Usually with an opposite god essence," Aya said matter-of-fact.

Diego's brow furrowed. "What do you mean?"

Aya tapped her lips as she thought how to word herself. "All gods have their domains, but those domains have classifications, like life, earth, fire, and even chaos."

"So, with Malsumis clearly being a chaos goddess, we need to have her opposite. Which is… order?"

Aya shook her head. "Light. Order falls under light, which is why it's good Tyr is on our side."

Mia squinted. "You're a war god. That conflicts with light—and order, while we're at it."

Tyr shook his head. "War isn't inherently an agent of chaos. It's turmoil, yes, but not all turmoil is chaos. My domain oversees the order and justice of that turmoil, both externally and internally."

Mia turned to Aya. "What about you?"

"I'm a life deity, like my brother," she said. "My war domain oversees passion—passion to live, love, and protect."

"Does life deity essence help us?" I asked.

Aya's lips twisted. "Possibly. Life and light don't conflict, so I may be able to boost light essence, but I'm not sure. We'll be better off finding other light gods to help us. Theoretically it shouldn't be difficult, as our cause is something they could get behind, but we all know how well gods, especially of different regions, get along."

I grunted. That was an understatement. The fact that so many different gods and immortals worked together in our group was a rarity.

"Hopefully, Astrid can figure out this thing with Baldur's soul," Tyr said. "He'd be more than happy to help."

Thac's brow furrowed. "You'll have to explain that one. He was known for being chaotic on the battlefield. Plenty of us non-European gods knew of his reputation."

Tyr shook his head. "To most he seemed that way, but if you knew him, it was all a carefully laid tactic."

Aya stretched. "Baldur was a cunning man. He understood his domain of courage well, and what helped bolster it in men and women who saw him fight. He led them to believe, if they prayed for courage, he'd take their fear away and into himself and convert it into a primal and vicious energy to use on the battlefield. His supposed recklessness made others more courageous, even if he couldn't answer their prayer."

"He was also well known for his kindness and wisdom outside battle." Memories flitted through my mind as I stroked his vambrace. "People saw this side of him as the result of tossing aside fear, and strove to do the same. It brought hope to a darker time in our history."

Silence filled the room. Everyone appeared to be thinking about something, but who knew if they were all the same topics. I knew my mind had shifted to all thoughts of Baldur. Having another light god working with us was crucial to winning against Malsumis and stopping Ragnarök for good this time. *But, what if when he comes back, he isn't a god anymore?*

Of course, I needed to be competent enough to actually bring him back. Between taking care of the sanctuary, training, and allowing myself to enjoy life despite everything going on, I had spent the remainder of my time trying to figure out this whole bring-Baldur-back conundrum. And I wasn't doing all that well.

Urd rose to her feet, her eyes unfocused. "There's a situation I must see to."

Then she was gone. Xavier popped in from the kitchen to clarify that she just up and left without another word and then disappeared, using the magic around the house as a pseudo-fae doorway. I was still getting used to the fact that he'd unlocked some magic within him.

With that brief distraction over, we were left to brainstorm some more. But the longer this continued, the more restless I became. I found myself pacing and alternating between rubbing my vambrace and fiddling with my necklace.

Diego grabbed my hand, pulling me to a stop. "You're going to burn a hole in the floor if you keep that up. What's wrong?

Was there anything wrong? I wanted to say no, but I rarely knew anymore these days. I shook my head and continued my pacing.

A raven's call filled the room and then Muninn appeared.

"Sister. Sister!" he cried. *"I found it. I found it."*

He flew around the room like crazy before banking toward me. He landed on my shoulder and tugged on a lock of hair, shouting the same phrase over and over in my head.

I laughed and scooped him up by cradling his body in my hands. "Calm down, Muninn."

The raven's wings went limp over my hands. He let out a half-croon, half-irritated sound. Muninn both liked and hated this manner of being held. I'd discovered it by mistake when he got a little too excited once.

"Now, calmly tell me what you found," I said.

"Loki's magic."

All eyes shifted to the raven.

My brow furrowed. "Where did you find his magic?"

"Baldur's home in Breidablik."

My brow furrowed. *Why would—*

"Breblek?" Lucia said, mispronouncing the name.

"Breidablik," Tyr gently corrected. "It's a small coastal town in Norway Baldur used to protect. Hlín oversees it in his absence now. It's a sanctuary town."

I pressed my lips together, a strange thought coming to me. "Which burial ritual was performed for him?"

Tyr and Aya exchanged a perplexed glance. Aya spoke. "I… don't know if we did."

Lucia cocked her head. "How do you not know if you performed a burial?"

Tyr smoothed his beard. "It's not often a god needs burial rites. We never thought we'd have to do it for him of all gods, either. And the problem was, our most common form of burial is a funeral pyre."

"How is that a problem?" Magnus asked.

"Everyone thought Baldur was fearless, but that's far from the truth," Aya said. "He was afraid of a few things, but nothing as much as he was fire."

My brow creased. That wasn't even something I knew. *I wonder why…* I took a deep breath. "What happened, then, if you didn't give him a funeral pyre?"

Tyr worked his jaw. "I remember bringing him home until we could figure out where it would be ideal to bury him. But… I don't recall going back to finish the rite."

Aya shook her head. "I don't, either. And I don't know why we wouldn't."

All week I couldn't shake how to bring Baldur back to us. I had his soul. I assumed I needed to figure out how to get him a new body. *A body…*

I straightened. "I'm going."

Tyr's brow furrowed. "Going where?"

Kirby rose to her feet. "Not without me."

I smiled, grateful for her support. It was the one thing I needed most right now.

Dahlia sat up. "You two can't be serious. This screams a Loki trap."

Kirby and I shared a glance, understanding zinging between us. "It's not."

Even if by some chance trouble was waiting for us, I trusted Kirby to have my back. The start of her life may not have been the bright, happy one she deserved, but much of her training came in handy. It was something I greatly valued.

Magnus' brow furrowed. "You're joking."

I set Muninn on my shoulder and he pressed against me, cooing in an almost cat-purr way. "Look, I know you two have only known Loki as an evil dickhead, and I'm not saying he isn't an evil dickhead, because the fucker has done a lot of terrible shit."

Lucia snorted on a laugh and Thac shook his head.

I continued, not missing a beat. "But several of us here have known him far longer than a few decades. Before he went down this rabbit hole of shittery, Loki was just an annoying dickhead-trickster god. His pranks usually went too far, but they were never intended to maim or kill anyone. That's what makes this whole 'Loki killed Baldur' thing so fucked up."

I ran my fingers through my hair. "Loki gave me this vambrace with Baldur's soul trapped inside on purpose. There's a reason he also has his magic all over Baldur's house. And that reason predates him becoming an evil dickhead."

Dahlia's intense eyes flashed. "Are you hearing yourself right now? This is the same Loki who's actively trying to kill Azzie, even though she wants nothing to do with him, and he's the same asshole who sent you into a murderous, trickster-god-chopping rage upon seeing him a week ago."

I held up my arms. "And look at me now."

Silence fell over the room, everyone watching me. It was Ronan who broke it first. "Whenever Loki has been mentioned, you have acted peculiarly. You are not acting that way."

I nodded. "My heightened irritation and rage are out of character for me. I've got a temper, yes, but it's normally nothing like what I've been experiencing."

"It's the blood oath," Aya said, realization dawning on her.

I nodded again. "Yes. But I'm not acting that way right now when talking about Loki. I'm calm. What isn't calm about me is this incessant need to go, right now, to Breidablik. I can't ignore that shift in me."

Tyr rose from his seat. "Then let's go."

Diego and Aya nodded. Mia raised her hand. "I'm going with you, too."

I tipped my head, curious about her insertion. She involved herself with the magic blocker stuff when she could because, like me, she didn't want anyone else to suffer the way we had. But she had no stakes in Baldur and Loki.

"I just feel like I need to go with you," she said. The reason why escaped her, but the need to act pulled her regardless. I understood.

I held out my hand. Those coming with me clustered around and made contact. Dad wished us luck and promised the rest of them would keep working hard on the Malsumis problem.

Dahlia mumbled out for us to be extra careful about traps and not to die because she wasn't going out of her way to find forbidden resurrection spells.

Diego chuckled. "Love you too, *prima*."
Her dark lips quirked up, and then the room disappeared.

The briny tang of salt water and the sweet fragrance of flowers, mixed with the faint aroma of pine, assaulted my nose before my eyes registered the change in scenery.

The afternoon sun hung low in the sky over Breidablik, casting a warm golden hue over the seaport town. The surrounding fjord's cliffs towered the landscape, covered in lush green forests. Plaintive cries of seagulls created a haunting sound through the harbor that mixed with the clink of ropes against masts and the creaking of the wooden docks. Water gently lapped against the sides of brightly colored anchored boats.

The dock we stood on creaked as I turned, taking in a town so different from my memories.

Quaint wooden buildings painted in pastel hues lined the waterfront, their reflections shimmering in the harbor's mirrored surface. Window boxes overflowed with blooming flowers, adding an extra touch of color.

Activity on the docks had come to an abrupt halt at our appearance, eyes of all types turning to us. I didn't have time to take in their reaction, or the changes of the town any more than they had. Munin took off and something deep in my chest tugged me to follow.

My wings growing and spreading wide, I took to the skies and followed Muninn's path down the coast. Kirby and Mia followed close behind. A beating of large, leathery wings sounded, and I turned to see Diego's black and silver dragon form keeping pace with us.

He had no riders on his back, leaving Aya and Tyr to follow on foot, no doubt their choice. Given Hlín now protected this place, they'd make her aware of the reason for our sudden appearance, as it wouldn't have gone unnoticed.

I didn't know the goddess; I only knew she'd once sworn herself to Frigg before the queen goddess died, long before even my first life existed, and her domain was associated with protection. Hopefully she was a welcoming and forgiving goddess, especially if she had any love for the son of the goddess she once served.

Just outside the town, up on a high cliff, a lone house stood overlooking the water. Muninn frantically flew around the sod roof. Even from this distance, Loki's magic hit me like an invisible beacon.

We landed several feet away from the building. My wings tucked close to my back, but I didn't fold them away. I took in the wooden structure; it looked untouched by time. Loki's magic crawled over everything, including the ground. But the god himself was not here.

Kirby turned to me. "What do you want to do?"

Her question caught me off guard. Kirby was a leader by nature, it was why following her was so easy. I had expected her to take one scan of the area and start figuring out the best plan of action for us to follow, and I wouldn't have questioned it.

Yet as we shared a look with each other, I saw the other side of her—the side that recognized this was the most important thing to me right now and that calling the shots would be overstepping. It didn't bother her. She easily accepted she wasn't the leader in this "mission," even if I made shots that she wouldn't normally agree with for a chosen approach. It was something I could admire in her.

"Probably best if we split up and check for any traps." I shrugged. "Even if this isn't a death trap by present evil-dickhead Loki, past annoying-trickster Loki may have left something unpleasant for us to deal with."

She chuckled and nodded, stepping away from our formation toward one side of the house, her eyes scanning everything. Diego shifted out of his dragon shape, keeping several of his draconic features, and walked in the opposite direction. Mia stuck with me as I walked right up to the front door. Muninn watched us from his perch on the roof over the door.

"Hey, look." Mia pointed to a plant growing in a small bush on the side of the house.

I squinted at the yellowish-green plant with strap-shaped leaves and similarly colored flowers. "That's European mistletoe, but it doesn't make sense to be growing there. They're parasitic, so they need a living host to germinate."

"Meaning it's been placed there on purpose?"

I glanced up at her. "I don't believe in coincidences. Especially when Loki is involved."

Placing my hand on the door, I pushed. To my surprise, the metal hinges creaked, and the door opened. I hesitated in the doorway, unsure all of a sudden. *Shouldn't that have been locked?*

"Go on, Astrid," Mia whispered. "I'm right here with you."

Swallowing back my nerves, I nodded and stepped over the threshold into a time from long ago. Everything was as my memories recalled, from the long common room with center hearth, kitchen table, tapestries, and candle light fixtures, to the storage room on the left, and his room on the right.

A door clacked open and a moment later Kirby and Diego strolled in from the storage room.

"Nothing out of the ordinary outside," Kirby confirmed.

"Besides what looks like food that should be beyond moldy but isn't, that pantry is good too," Diego said.

That left the only remaining room. My feet carried me toward it. Loki's magic grew stronger until I tasted it on my tongue. My pulse pounded in my ears in time with my steps.

I halted in the threshold, staring into the small room filled with artifacts, weapons, books, and discarded clothes. On a large bed was the one thing to stop me in my tracks. Seven feet tall, with long golden blond hair framing his painfully still, lean yet sturdy and muscled frame, was Baldur.

I couldn't move. I couldn't breathe. He was here. After all this time.

"Go on," Kirby murmured as she touched my lower back. "You can do this."

Swallowing, I forced myself to take a deep breath and stepped forward. Then another step. In several small steps, I found myself looming over him.

He had a symmetrical face with high cheekbones and straight nose complemented by a neatly groomed beard I was tempted to run my fingers through and along his square jawline. Runic tattoos wrapped and covered him all over, including his face, stomach, and fingers. His pants were the only clothes he wore, reminding me how much of a toss-up it was if he was half naked or fully clothed and respectable. *He's exactly as I remember.*

He looked so peaceful, but far too still.

I lifted a shaking hand and reached out. Barely a hair's length away I paused, fear skittering around in my veins.

Then I touched him.

I inhaled sharply. "He's warm."

Kirby and Mia crowded in, both cautiously touching his tattooed arm. The three of us shared wide-eyed glances that reflected the same question. *How the hell did Loki do this?*

My hand slid up his pale chest accentuated with runic tattoos and a light smattering of pale hair, clinical and professional, feeling out the extent of this preservation magic. My heart skittered when I felt the faint pulse of his heart in his chest.

"Now what?" Mia whispered, as if afraid talking might break the spell prematurely.

The vambrace around my arm bumped his body, and his pulse jumped. A pulsing sensation came from the armor as well. I took steadying breaths, trying to think. "The mistletoe out front."

Diego murmured something and left to retrieve it. That was one element that felt right. Problem was, I didn't know how to move Baldur's soul. *Fuck.*

"Um…" I bit my lip. "Could we use our Valkyrie shields to trap his soul to his body long enough for me to do something? There are three of us, so we might be able to layer it in a way that would work?"

Kirby's brow knitted. "I think you're on the right track, but we'd need a little more than just that."

"My blood magic might work to bolster the shields," Mia said. "I think I can weave it into at least my shield, if not both of yours, too."

Kirby tapped her chin. "That might work. We just need to ensure the soul doesn't disappear in the moment between being released and us creating the shields."

"Couldn't we make them before Astrid releases Loki's magic?" Mia asked.

I shook my head. "They'll be destroyed if they're active while I'm using the mistletoe."

"How do you plan to use that?"

I puffed out a deep breath. "I don't know if I can explain it more than… instinct."

She nodded. "What else do we have that will help?"

"We're Valkyries," Kirby said. "And we're dealing with a soul."

Very few beings could touch souls. It was one of the most important abilities that made a Valkyrie what she was.

We normally took in a soul, mostly warrior souls, and brought it to their final resting place, either Valhalla or Fólkvangr. But this time, we would do the opposite, something Kirby had done once before with Starkad. "I'll take on the burden."

Kirby grabbed my hand. "*We* will share it."

We gazed at each other for a long moment. As a silver-winged Valkyrie, I was prone to taking on the heaviest burdens. But Kirby and I had been working on helping me learn to share and lean on my sisters. We got together regularly as a group and on individual levels to build our bonds.

Mia took my other hand and smiled. It wobbled a bit. Mia struggled with a lot of insecurities, but she tried her hardest to overcome them and be there for us. She was here to offer that help—to share in the burden.

I smiled and squeezed both their hands. "Yeah, we'll share."

Diego returned with several sprigs of mistletoe. I thanked him and took the plant.

"The others are waiting in the main room as support," he said. "I'll wait out there with them, so I'm not in the way."

This left us with possibly the most difficult task any Valkyrie had to accomplish. And we had only one shot. *No pressure.*

I removed the vambrace and carefully attached it to Baldur's arm, ignoring the instinct to want to recoil at touching a body that should be dead, but wasn't quite.

Once secured, I repositioned his arm to cross over his chest. This would be the best way to ensure the soul didn't wander too far immediately.

I sucked in a steadying breath and held my hands over Baldur. My wings spread from my back. "Ready? You'll need to hold your breaths for this first part."

They repositioned so we were in a triangular formation, their wings also unfurling. Mia cut her arm with a knife Kirby gave her, smearing the blood over both her hands. They then held their hands to mine and each other but we didn't grasp. "Ready."

Focusing, I let instinct guide me.

Magic ignited in my veins. The sprigs of mistletoe smoked and were set ablaze by golden fire. I jerked my hands in opposite directions, spreading the burning plant over Baldur and the vambrace. Loki's magic fizzled.

In unison, Kirby, Mia, and I clasped hands, and I focused in, surging my attention down into the soul releasing from the armor. *"Baldur, if you can hear me, I beg your patience."*

A pulse of warmth answered me and my heart leapt into my throat. There wasn't time to dwell on it.

Kirby activated her shield first, then me. Mia followed up with hers and her fae magic coiled around it like a strand of sewing thread. It wove into the other shields, knitting tight until the three shields were nearly one. The power of them together was intense, and distracting. *Focus, Astrid. We're not done.*

Drawing up more energy, gold and black magic sprang from my hands. It wrapped around my sisters' arms and reached for Baldur. The tendrils snaked and coiled around him, until he was bathed in a roiling light that looked like dancing fire.

I summoned a dagger from my weapons arsenal and sliced my forearm. I winced. Blood splashed from the gash, the wound healing quickly. I then pointed the blade at Baldur and sliced his chest.

My blood dripped into his wound, the magical fire causing it to sizzle on impact. *"Come back to me, Baldur."*

A single tear rolled down my cheek, surprising me. It dripped off my chin and splashed onto the pool of blood.

Then the magic shattered.

I gasped for breath, weakness flooding over me. My hands remained in the air, shaking with the exhaustion threatening to consume me.

Fear crept up my spine. Had we failed? I hadn't felt his soul leave. But...

Baldur's chest inflated and he sucked in a deep breath.

My heart jumped into my throat, and I practically threw myself over him to stare down into his twitching face. "Baldur?"

His eyes fluttered open. Those achingly familiar icy-blue, foggy and confused eyes gazed up at me. "Sunshine?"

NINE

BALDUR

Heat swathed over my senses. Fire, blazing hot. I should be screaming in agony from the intensity. I should fear this fate I ran from for so long. But there was no pain with this fire. There was no fear of it. There was only recognition of its golden hue and warm caress.

"Baldur, come back to me."

I knew that voice. I needed to see the face that belonged to that voice.

Something cool and wet dripped into the flames, dousing their intensity. Tears. Why was she crying?

Air flooded into my chest and I gasped. My lungs both protested and relished the breath, as if I hadn't breathed in hundreds of years.

"Baldur?"

That voice. The sweet, low, and tempting voice I'd ached to hear for so long. *Could it truly be her?*

My eyes fluttered open, light blurring my sight. I blinked a few more times, clearing the haze. Hovering above me was a familiar freckled face framed by fiery hair. "Sunshine?"

My voice croaked out the name, my throat scratchy and dry. *Why does it feel this way? Why do I feel like utter shit?*

"Baldur!" Astrid shrieked, the pitch sending an uncomfortable sensation through me.

She swayed suddenly, and everything happened faster than I could properly process. Astrid collapsed. Something dark and blurry rushed into the space and caught her before the other two people in the room could react. Kirby? Who was the other woman? She was tall and she certainly ate well. A beautiful woman of wealth, no doubt.

Who was the man holding Astrid? He had horns, black and silver scales peppering his exotic complexion, and a tail. What was he? Besides handsome.

Two more people were in the room. The woman with pale hair, I recognized, even though her hair was knotted instead of braided now. *Freya.* The man, he loomed over Astrid and the man holding her. He seemed familiar, but I was struggling to place him… until he spoke. "Diego, is she okay?"

The man with horns nodded. "I think she just needs rest."

I squinted. What were these words they spoke that I somehow understood?

"She isn't the only one." Freya had gone to the tall woman's side to steady her. "That was a lot of magic used. Let's get them both outside for fresh air."

The room slowly emptied. My eyes tracked them all, and I noticed wings coming from Astrid and the new woman, both very different from Kirby's black ones. What was going on?

Tyr stayed, watching the others go for a moment before approaching me. I took him in, from his new hair to the strange clothes he wore. His hand was also back, which had to mean that really was Astrid.

"What are you wearing, and what did you do to your hair?" My words were also in this new language.

Tyr chuckled and patted me on the shoulder. "A lot has changed. Looks like the magic also gave you the ability to comprehend English, so that's one language barrier you won't have to worry about."

"English." I tried to process the word. "What magic? What's going on?"

"There's a lot that needs to be talked about, but we need you to orient yourself first."

Tyr encouraged me to sit up. My body protested in ways I wasn't familiar with. Standing wasn't much easier. Dizziness swam in my head as I stood, and my legs wobbled. Was this what it felt like to be drunk? Gods couldn't drink enough to be intoxicated, so I didn't know beyond what'd been explained to me or what I'd witnessed.

I stumbled through my house. How I got here, I didn't know. I wasn't anywhere near here when I'd been speaking with Loki. It was also in the same state I left it when Tyr and I went to investigate that lead, yet something didn't feel right about that. Or maybe there wasn't something right about me.

Light streamed through the open front door. I blinked when we stepped out. Familiar and unfamiliar scents wafted into my nose. The forest looked different for some reason. And the sounds… there were unfamiliar things in the air.

The man Tyr had called Diego sat on the ground in some soft moss, cradling Astrid's sleeping form against his chest. She looked so similar to how she used to in the past, from her short stature to the scar crossing her face. Were it not for some of her womanly features being more… pronounced, I may have struggled to believe she was in a new body.

I eyed the silver and gold feathered wings draping along the ground. *Is she now—*

A shimmer of color distracted me. The tall woman sat with Freya nearby, doing breathing exercises. Her odd wings, feathered but iridescent, flexed and shifted with her breathing. They were fascinating. What was she? A fae? There did seem to be a sharpening edge to her ears, but it was hard to tell from here.

Another woman with freckled skin and short black hair stood at the edge of the forest. Taller than the average woman and built like a bear, she gazed at me with wide blue eyes. "Baldur… you're… she… I can't believe it."

I squinted at her. She seemed familiar, especially in the way her presence wrapped around the area like a shield.

"It's me, Hlín."

Hlín? She looks so different. What's happened?

She walked up to me, slowly, as if she were afraid I'd jump away from her, and placed her hands comfortingly on my arms. "I never thought this was possible. It… doesn't seem possible, but yet here you are."

My brow furrowed. What was she going on about?

She nodded slowly. "You seem to need more time to adjust. I'll go back into town and tell everyone the good news. We'll make sure prayers flood in to help you recover quicker. When you've settled, come see me, and we can discuss handing everything back over to you, if that's what you want."

Hand what back over to me?

She patted my arms and turned away. As she left, she stopped in front of Diego and gazed down at Astrid. A small smile spread over her lips. "Back from the dead and performing miracles like no other before her. Make sure she stays safe. We can't afford to lose her again."

Diego gazed fondly at Astrid, and Hlín disappeared into the forest.

"Baldur!"

I jumped and jerked up. A black raven swooped down from the roof and flew around my head.

"Brother, you're back! You're back. She did it. She did it!"

"M—Muninn?" How was that possible? It couldn't be possible. My father's death would have ensured his ravens died, too. That's what he'd always told me since I was a boy.

It was the one devastating consequence I had chosen to bear by siding against him. I'd even tried to find Muninn and Huginn after the dust of the battle and Astrid's death settled, but they were nowhere to be found.

The raven circled me some more, briefly landing to tug on my hair like I always remembered him doing when he was excited.

"Muninn," Astrid mumbled sleepily. "Shut up. Sleepy…"

The others laughed. Muninn landed by her and grabbed one of her fingers. He tugged and she grumbled. "No muffins."

My brow arched. *What is a muffin?*

Muninn croaked and tugged on her finger again, seemingly trying to wake her. Diego also tried to get him to stop, but the raven was relentless. At first I thought he was being annoying, but then I realized his actions were out of worry. *What had she done to me to put her in this state?*

I wandered away, toward the outlook over Breidablik. The strange noises I continued to hear seemed to be coming from there. My feet halted at the edge, my eyes going wide. *What happened to my town?*

It was still there, but it'd grown and changed. The houses were bright and the ships strange. People moved about, as did other strangely shaped contraptions. This was not the town I last saw.

"It's a lot to take in."

I turned to find Kirby standing beside me. Her long blonde hair drifted in the salt-stained breeze. She looked similar to how I remembered her, though there was a guardedness about her now. This life she lived hadn't been kind to her. Or maybe it was the curse? How many lives had she lived since Odin killed her?

Kirby half-smiled at me. "Astrid worked hard to get this far. She didn't give up, and did what most thought impossible."

That sounded just like her. But what exactly had Astrid needed to do to me? "What happened? What am I missing?"

She turned to face me fully. "Loki killed you."

I stared down at her, unable to fully process what she'd just said. "He… what? No. Loki didn't…"

A gentle hand touched my back. I turned to look at Freya. While her smile was gentle, it made me uneasy. "Come sit down so we can talk. There's a lot to discuss."

I followed her, though my mind raced. Why did they think Loki killed me? Did something go wrong?

Freya had me sit near Diego. The woman with the unusual wings sat on his other side, with Muninn resting on her lap. He seemed to be enjoying the gentle petting she gave him. The woman introduced herself as Mia, and she was in fact a fae—an elf, to be more exact.

"And a Valkyrie," she said.

I blinked. "I'm sorry, what?"

She nodded. "Kirby turned me into one a few months ago."

I jerked my attention to Kirby. She could what? How was that possible? That was only possible through Odin, right?

Kirby settled down in this circle we were forming. "We can get into that, but it's best to start from the beginning."

I agreed. It would be difficult to understand the nuances of what's going on if I first didn't get my answers about myself. However, before anything could be said, Muninn perked up and croaked, and Astrid stirred.

Her eyes fluttered open and she sucked in a deep breath. She gasped and sat up quickly. Diego jerked back, narrowly missing her forehead slamming into his chin.

Eyes wide, Astrid stared right at me. I was already reaching for her. She shoved out of Diego's lap, and I grabbed her outstretched arms, pulling her hard into me.

Astrid buried her face into the crook of my neck. "You're back. You're really back. I'm… I'm so sorry."

Her shoulders shook, and her next words devolved into sobs.

I threaded my fingers into her silky hair and pulled her in tighter, inhaling her pleasant sweet and floral scent. "You stole my words, Sunshine."

After all this time, she was here. Truly here. Unless this was one elaborate dream brought on by another god, then I was holding my Sunshine again.

"Are you crying?" Freya murmured.

"No," Kirby said, though there was an unusual stiffness to her voice.

Mia, on the other hand, sniffled and dabbed at the corner of her eyes.

Astrid cried for a little longer before finally calming down. She sniffed and rubbed at her puffy eyes, murmuring to herself. "Thank you, magic makeup, for the little things. Like not making me look like a nineties-horror-flick ghost in a torn prom dress, come back to haunt my ex for causing my untimely death."

The corner of my lip quirked. I had no idea what that was supposed to mean, but the others found it funny.

She took a deep breath and then framed my face with her tiny hands. She stared up with those stunning green eyes framed by thick lashes that peered into the soul, past every wall and barrier to the vulnerability I tried so desperately to hide from others. "Welcome back, Baldur."

I cupped her face with one hand and caressed her cheek with my thumb, taking her in, from the same face-crossing scar to her freckles and her elegant, tapered jawline and high cheekbones, to the jewelry in her petite nose that accented her beauty in such a subtle way.

My fingers brushed the feathers of her wings, and I marveled at them. "I have so many questions. But, let's start with how you all think I died."

"Because you did," Tyr said. "Loki killed you."

I shook my head. "No. No, that didn't happen."

It didn't make sense. That's not—

"Baldur, he set a trap to split us up. I saw him over your prone, lifeless body," he insisted. "He walked around with your soul bound in—"

Sudden rage flared in my chest. "He didn't kill me!"

Tyr reeled back. I didn't lose my temper often, but I couldn't stand hearing his insistence. It wasn't right. That wasn't what happened.

"Hey, hey, shhh," Astrid hushed gently, taking my face in her hands again. "It's okay."

A sensation of peace washed over me, dousing the rage. I leaned into her touch. How much I missed that. I didn't know how she did it, but no one could pacify Tyr and me like she could—or rile us up, whatever she was in the mood for in that moment.

"Why don't you tell us your side?" Astrid suggested. "We only have a small piece of the puzzle, and it's clearly been put together wrong, with how much we've learned in the last few hours."

I didn't know why they didn't have the pieces. Loki could have just told them. Unless… something went wrong.

I took a slow breath. "Loki didn't set a trap. He followed me when I split from Tyr to check out a possible lead about Astrid. He had a theory on thwarting prophecies, and he seemed sure he knew how to stop the one who threatened me. I was skeptical, naturally, but he'd been so sure of himself, and since Loki and I never had issues with each other, I decided to try it. The worst we thought would happen was that it would fail to do anything to me and I'd continue on."

My brow furrowed as I thought about what happened after that. "The last thing I remember was him looming over me and things going dark. Occasionally I felt some things, like different emotions that weren't mine, and feeling like I was floating. Then I woke up to Astrid in Loki's place, and in my house."

"So, what, Tyr showing up messed up Loki's plan?" Diego said.

"Makes sense why he kept Baldur's soul and preserved his body," Kirby said. "If there was a long enough interruption, he may have lost his window to put the soul back in the body the way he wanted."

"Why keep it all this time, though?" Mia mused. "It's not like there is easy-to-access information about resurrection."

"It's Loki," Astrid said. "His ego wouldn't allow him to leave it be. So it makes sense he'd preserve Baldur's soul and body until he finally found his answer."

"And his answer was you." Freya slowly nodded "He was all too eager to give it to you, as if he knew you'd get to this point."

Astrid looked to Diego. "Do you think you could do a check sometime? It's not like stabby-evil-dickhead is going to give us answers."

Diego chuckled. "I'll check with Mom and see what I can find."

"But, why didn't Loki try to correct anyone when he was accused of killing Baldur?" Mia's nose scrunched. "With mistletoe of all things."

My brow rose. *Mistletoe? People thought Loki killed me with a plant?* I wasn't sure if I should be offended or impressed.

"He didn't confirm it," Astrid said. "Which means he was probably sarcastic when accused and people took it as admission. Even when Loki was being honest, people rarely believed him. So he probably figured there was no point in pleading his case. He doesn't care if people hate him or not anyway."

"How long have I been… dead?" I asked, struggling to process my reality.

Astrid pressed her lips together. "About six hundred years."

The earth beneath me shifted. *Six… hundred?* How was that possible?

Astrid placed her hands on my chest, as if to calm me. Even Muninn landed on my shoulder and cooed while pressing against my face. I touched him, relishing the familiarity that came with his presence. "How are you still here?"

"They're both my familiars." Astrid smiled wide like it was the proudest thing she could admit. "I took over their bond. Huginn is here in the trees somewhere, watching. He doesn't like me at all, still, but he was curious about my and Muninn's thoughts about bringing you back, so he came to investigate."

She pursed her lips. "He is happy you're back. But he's mad I'm here, so... yeah. He won't come down until I go away."

I squinted at her. "How? Odin died when you did. That shouldn't be possible."

A squirmy sensation wormed in my stomach when the others exchanged glances. "What?"

Astrid hesitated for a moment. "Your father... is alive."

What was left of my hold on reality shattered. *Alive? Odin is alive? How?* I leaned back on my hands to help stay balanced as I made myself breathe. "I need to be caught up, now."

Kirby, Freya, and Tyr took over from there.

Freya informed me she was going by the name Aya now for some reason. Kirby had lived a few lives before finally breaking her curse around a decade ago, prior to even remembering she was a Valkyrie. Once she relearned that, she also developed a way to turn others into one as well.

Apparently this wasn't an ability unique to my father, like he once claimed. That was part of why he'd ordered Astrid's death, because, even back then, she had a Valkyrie soul. Another Valkyrie made by another entity was hidden away until recently because of Odin's behavior. Kirby also revealed the Valkyries she was making, which included Mia and Astrid, were the only ones left. All of Odin's Valkyries were gone.

The knowledge unsettled me. Being Odin's son, I knew all the Valkyries by name. I was friends with so many, and knowing they were gone... *Where does a Valkyrie go when she dies?*

Astrid had also lived a few lives, where Garmr, the bastard, had been the one killing her as a child, to weaken Tyr for a prophecy, until Freya had finally gotten a leg up and kept her safe, though not until after a failed attempt on Astrid's current life as a child. Garmr had also been her first killer. Lucky for him, he was dead now, else I'd have skinned him alive myself for his treachery.

Tyr and Fenrir had patched things up, even around Tyr's blood oath. That was good news I could get behind. The idea that Fen had killed Astrid didn't make sense, and I was glad Tyr was proven wrong there.

Skuld, one of the dragon sisters, was dead, but apparently that began a path where more dragons were coming into their nature, like Diego, who was Urd's son. It took me a moment to process that revelation, along with learning dragons had been more abundant before, when Ragnarök apparently first happened and was pushed back, resulting in the near-extinction of the dragons and phoenixes.

My head swam with all this information already. So much had happened, and that didn't include even a fraction of what I wanted to know.

Astrid placed a gentle hand on my arm. "Do you want to take a break? It's a lot to process."

I shook my head. "I need to at least know how my father is still alive."

I had made my peace with siding against him, knowing it'd end in his death. I'd mourned the man he was from my childhood, not the crazed god he'd become. And to hear that he'd survived a ritual that would have killed others, that had killed many of his Valkyries who'd offered themselves up for the ritual… fury boiled just under the surface. *How dare he still draw breath. Only he could turn surviving into an act of arrogance.*

"We don't know how he survived the ritual," Kirby admitted. "He wasn't forthcoming with that information. But it left him weak most of this time. He wasn't even at his full strength when we battled him a couple months ago."

"And he's still out there?" My attention shifted to Astrid. "And yet you have the bond he once did with Huginn and Muninn?"

Astrid pressed her lips back together. "We used something to take away his power. Killing him wasn't going to work, so that was the best thing."

"Astrid also cursed him," Kirby said so casually it took me a minute to grasp the magnitude of what Astrid actually did.

I wasn't sure I was happy knowing Astrid could curse people, or that I should be pleased she'd cursed my father, of all beings, but given what he'd done to Astrid and Kirby, I wasn't going to see it as a bad thing. It was a punishment he rightfully deserved.

I scrubbed my face. "I think this is all I'm going to be able to process for now. Unless I need to know if Odin is going to be a problem anytime soon?"

"If he knows what's good for him, he'll take Astrid's curse as a way to grow and learn from his mistakes and finally become a good person," Diego said. "Though none of us are going to hold our breaths on that hope."

I grunted. I gave up that hope a long time ago.

Huginn flew out of the nearby trees and landed on my arm. He looked at Astrid, which felt like a glare, before looking at me. *"Go see Odin."*

I shook my head. "I have no desire to see him."

His chest puffed out and he made a displeased sound. *"Go see Father. He will be happy."*

I scowled. "I doubt it. Even if he would be, I don't care."

I no longer had love for the man. And knowing he'd ordered Astrid's death, there wasn't anything he could do to endear himself to me now.

Huginn growled and then screamed at me before pecking my hand. Blood dripped down my hand, and the most shocking word came from my mouth as the new, uncomfortable sensation burst through me.

"Ow!"

TEN

BALDUR

The ticking of a clock echoed through the quiet cabin. I sat on the back of the couch, taking in the small space I was calling mine for now, as if I hadn't been staying here for the last three days.

I couldn't help it. The cabin Astrid gave me was considered low-tech, to help me adjust, as we found out rather quickly that I was sensitive to the buzzing sounds the contraptions of modern-day technology gave off, and yet this place was so foreign-looking compared to my home.

The craftsmanship of all the wood furniture and counters was expertly done by Astrid's father, Darius, and Astrid herself for a few pieces. The thing they called a stove ran on wood, and apparently was considered decades old, compared to what other buildings on her property had.

The lights in here were magic lanterns provided by fae. The small table in front of the couch had a number of thick books Aya provided me to help start my reintegration into Midgard when no one was available to talk about events. I much preferred the books anyway. I was able to learn at my pace, which I definitely needed, given I was catching up on six centuries of time.

A part of me still couldn't believe I'd been in a semi-death state for that long. I was glad Astrid brought me back, though, even with the challenges I would face.

The clock, which ran on gears and pulleys from what I knew, chimed, its small hand ticking over to the nine on the face. I'd been in here long enough, and I wanted to find Astrid.

I stood and maneuvered through the room for the door, giving anything sharp a wide berth. I was not liking this whole feeling-pain stuff, and it was making me extra cautious right now. At least until we got answers.

Apparently Urd might have them, but she'd been busy since Astrid brought me back, so I was going to have to wait for answers until then—which was fine. I was merely thankful one of the oldest dragons would want to provide answers. And it wasn't like I was planning on testing how far pain went any time soon.

Opening the door, I stepped out onto the covered porch. Scattered clouds covered the sky, moisture thick in the air, threatening rain. A cool breeze rustled the trees. I shivered and grabbed the short, leather-like cloak with wool lining from a hook by the door. I looked at it, and then made a mental note to remember that Astrid had called it a jacket.

Technology wasn't the only thing that had changed in the last few centuries. There were new words and phrases for me to understand. New clothes to figure out how to fit into, because even now, my height required a specialized hand, and I just needed to understand how they worked. Shoes were especially difficult for the others to find me on such short notice.

Buttons were still used, but zippers were new, and I liked them. Quite convenient, especially for trousers… pants… I'd already heard both words used in the last three days between Tyr and Astrid, and wasn't sure which was the right term.

Pulling the jacket on, I left my cabin again, and this time, someone was waiting for me. Huginn sat on the porch railing. *Where had he come from?* I hadn't seen him since he'd pecked me in anger and flew away, and as far as I understood, while he'd accepted the familiar bond with Astrid, he hated her for some reason, so he was never seen around here.

And how had he gotten here if we were on another continent? Had Astrid allowed the ravens to keep their enchanted bangles? *I should ask her.*

"Good morning, Huginn," I greeted. "What brings you here?"

"Why are you here and not back home?"

That was a simple answer. "Because this is where Astrid lives, and she gave me an open invitation to live here."

Truthfully, I was the one who asked about current living situations, and I'd boldly asked if there was room for me. Astrid, bless her, had been insistent I not make any hasty decisions, and that it wouldn't be trouble if I chose to stay in the one place that was the most familiar for me.

But, besides my house, nothing was familiar. Walking through Breidablik was evidence of that. And I couldn't bear to be so far from Astrid. Not after how hard we'd searched for her. *Not after what I was willing to face to have her by my side.*

Huginn hissed. *"Why do you insist on following her around? You don't need someone like her."*

I frowned. "Why do you hate her? What did she do to earn your scorn?"

"She is a thief."

"And what did she steal?"

"You!"

I leaned back from the raven's intensity.

"And my brother. And Father's power. She stole it all."

My eyes narrowed. "Father lost his power due to his actions. Had he left well enough alone, Astrid would have never been a threat to him. She only ever wanted to live her life with us, like she deserved."

Huginn hissed again.

"She also didn't steal us. Just because I love this woman, doesn't mean I left you behind. The same goes for Muninn. We have room in our hearts for you, just as we always had."

"You don't love her. You can't. You don't know her."

I closed my eyes, her stunning face blooming in my mind's eye, and took a breath. "You're right, I don't know her now. The love I still feel is for a woman who died because of Father. But I'm not allowing those feelings to die just because she might be a little different now. I want to know this new her. I want to willingly fall into love's embrace all over again as we explore each other. If she wishes it."

"You are scared. Just like before."

I nodded. "Of course I am. I am not a god of courage because I lack all fear. I just know how to overcome it. And I would have that night, had she not died."

The raven snapped his beak. *"She makes you weak."*

I shook my head. "She is my weakness, yes, but she makes me stronger than I ever have been on my own."

Huginn puffed out his chest and made a low growl sound.

I smiled sadly at him. "One day, I hope you will allow her to show that love I would so willingly walk through fire for."

"You won't tell her."

"I will." I had to.

I'd waited so long to have her, when others would have lost interest and moved on. I'd waited with hope in my heart for the right sign from her that she wanted more between us. I'd spent countless nights imaging Astrid in my arms, enjoying each other's company, mind, and bodies.

How many nights did I service myself instead of seeking out a temporary lover? How many nights had I imagined she was who I was burring my cock into, instead of wrapping my own hand around myself? How many times since I'd been brought back had I shamelessly done the same?

If I didn't tell her after all that, then I didn't deserve my title as a god.

Muninn flew from the forest and landed next to his brother. *"Stop being mean. Astrid is great."*

Huginn screamed at his brother and flew away, disappearing. I sighed, my shoulders drooping. How was I to fix that? I wanted both ravens here.

I loved them dearly. I had so many fond memories growing up with them always around and willing to play and cause mischief with me. It hurt seeing them fight because of this one issue. It pained me to see Huginn hate Astrid so much, when all she would give him was love.

Muninn flew up to my shoulder and nudged my cheek. "Gwah."

My brow arched. He'd done that as a raven sound, not his telepathic speech. "Gwah?"

"Gwah." He made a few clicking noises. "Gwah."

I chucked. "Gwah."

"Gwah." Muninn bobbed his head. "Gwah."

I belted out a hearty laugh. I had no idea what he was doing, but it was silly.

"Astrid taught me that," he said. *"She's fun. She plays with me all the time."*

"Are you happy to be bonded with her?"

He bobbed his head. *"Yes! Odin became dark and gloomy, like a bad storm. Astrid is a ray of sunshine."*

I didn't stop the smile spreading my lips. "She absolutely is. Do you know where she is?"

"Of course. She's training. Follow."

He took off down the path, landing in the trees if he went too far. I didn't set a particularly fast pace. As eager as I was to see Astrid, if she was training, I didn't want to interrupt. It wasn't that I'd interject myself, she just had a habit of stopping what she was doing when I came around. Unless she was in those therapy sessions she did. Then, she was focused.

Her profession of healing others mentally to heal physically fascinated me. When I had more time around everything else I was learning, I wanted her to explain it more to me. And Diego.

I hadn't had a lot of time to get to know him, but I did like what I knew. Especially how well he treated Astrid. He had a clear grasp on how to romance her.

The forest path wound past other cabins. Some of their residents were home and milling about, others empty and quiet. I had noticed a large percentage of those living here in these small homes were fae. At least, the ones closest to me.

It'd been explained to me Midgard had become even more hostile to anything that wasn't an ordinary human. Aya had left me a small book that detailed the larger crusades the humans campaigned in an attempt to rid Midgard of us. I hadn't looked at it yet.

The fae royals had begun calling the fae to their realm to protect them from this continued hostility, but not all fae could enter the realm, and many others didn't want to leave. So, when they were displaced, they relied on sanctuaries like this one to thrive.

My surroundings opened to a clearing with a spectacular lake. I gazed around, still amazed how similar this place looked to back home, though different in its own way.

At the shore of the lake, Astrid stood with her father, Darius. Her dog, Angel, snoozed by Astrid's feet. They weren't training. Unless skipping rocks was training.

Muninn swooped down and landed on Astrid's shoulder. "Gwah."

She smiled and kissed his beak. "Gwah."

He repeated the word and then made an unusual clicking sound while nodding his head up and down until Astrid laughed. I smiled. I never recalled a time where Father had ever interacted with his ravens like this. Maybe in private he did, but never so openly.

The bond between Astrid and Muninn was always something special, ever since she healed him at Father's request. It was just one of Father's many schemes that backfired on him, as he underestimated Astrid in many ways and failed to account for how amazing she was.

Astrid skipped the rock in her hand, the flat projectile bouncing three times before sinking under the surface, then turned my way and waved, a brilliant warm smile on her lips. "Morning."

I approached. "Good morning. I hope I'm not interrupting anything."

She shook her head. "No, Angel and I needed a break, so Dad and I are trying to improve my rock-skipping skills."

Darius chuckled. "It's not going well."

She stuck her tongue out at him. I smirked. These two were fun to watch. Their father-daughter relationship was so much like the one she had with Bjǫrn way back when, but also very different. They were far closer than I was used to seeing fathers and daughters.

Maybe that was on account of me only ever hearing her mother mentioned with disdain, if she was ever mentioned at all. I'd yet to learn that dynamic, but I didn't doubt it'd come up soon enough.

A strange sound blared and I jerked, my pulse accelerating. Neither of them found the sound alarming, though Astrid's brow did crease with worry, for me. *Is this a normal sound?*

Darius reached into a pocket of his pants and pulled out a long, flat object. It had something moving on one of the flat surfaces. He pressed it and put the object up to his ear. "Darius."

I watched with fascination as he talked to this strange device as if he were speaking to another person. *What are these?* I'd seen the others use them, even Tyr had something that functions like them though looked different, but I hadn't gotten around to asking about them.

Darius said goodbye and put the device away. "That was James. He's got the licenses squared away."

Astrid squinted. "Isn't it the middle of the night over there? Why is he calling now?"

Her father smirked. "One of those 'oh shit' moments you remember just before you fall asleep."

She laughed and pecked him on the cheek. "Go get your gear squared away. Looking forward to seeing what you and Tyr bring back. I'll make sure the shed is prepped for your return tonight."

"Let's hope the game cooperates that well." He kissed her on the forehead and looked to me. "Keep her in line while we're gone."

I grinned, despite not knowing where he was heading off to. "No promises. I've been known to instigate."

Darius laughed and then scooped down to lift Angel into his arms. She groaned and rested her head and front paws on his shoulder, like some child.

"Is she okay?" I asked Astrid as he walked away.

She nodded. "We both worked hard today."

I scooped a few rocks from a pile at her feet and skipped one. It jumped six times. "What did you do for training?"

"I learned last week I could project my magic through her."

Project her magic? I'd never heard of a skill like that.

She skipped her rock four times. "I did it by accident then when I was stressed, but we're seeing how well I can master it. It's… difficult."

That was when I noticed the exhausted slump to her shoulders. "Tell me about this ability."

She explained roughly how she thought it worked, based on how it manifested. "I'm not as desperate when trying to do it this time, but that's really the only variable that feels different."

I turned the stone in my hand. "Maybe it's the most important component. You wanted to protect her and you succeeded. Maybe that's what you need to replicate it."

Astrid pursed her lips. "I could try more defensive spells. From what I'm told by those who were there with her, I'd used offensive spells, but maybe, because I was using them to protect her, it worked as a defensive, and she'd utilized them offensively."

She smiled. "Thank you. I've got something to try next session."

I returned the smile. "I'm glad I could help. Where are your father and Tyr going off to that needs... licenses?"

"Hunting down in Australia." I had no idea where that was, but nodded anyway. "We have regular get-togethers monthly, and since you're back, we thought we'd make the one this weekend into a big party in celebration. Means we have more mouths to feed."

A party in my honor? I could support that. "And why do you need these licenses?"

"Hunting is more regulated now compared to the past, to preserve populations without driving them to extinction. The licenses are pretty strict on how much a person can hunt in a season, so Dad is using his contacts to pull some strings to ensure we don't get into trouble in case they're noticed hunting more than mortal humans are allowed."

"Do you hunt?" I asked.

She nodded. "I go out with my dad whenever I can get away from my job, especially now that I have the ability to teleport us places. But I opted to stay here this time."

"Why?"

She glanced up at me and then skipped a rock, her cheeks turning a light shade of pink. "I have important things to take care of."

I smirked and reached out, tucking a wayward strand of her hair behind her ear. "Is one of those things me?"

"Of course it is," she murmured and skipped another rock. This one only went two jumps before sinking. She really was terrible at this. "How are you doing today so far? Did you sleep well? The new mattress should be done any day now."

Beds were still not large enough for someone like me by default. Astrid said she ordered a custom-made mattress, and she and her father would create a custom bed frame for me. In the meantime, we had to get two mattresses she called king-sized, and put them together on the floor, just so I could have something to sleep on.

"I slept well enough. I'm still getting used to the feel of these mattresses." Honestly, they were comfortable, even if the setup was unconventional, but maybe a little too comfortable if that made any sense at all.

She nodded. "Did you get the chance to answer any prayers?"

The thing about being dead and then revived, was that, while the universe still saw me as a god, I didn't have the following I used to. That put me in a precarious situation, given a god's power derived from worship. I would have assumed I wasn't a god at all at this point, given I could feel pain, but I did hear prayers. Most were nameless calls that I claimed ownership of, even if I couldn't answer it, but there were still a few scarce ones that came in my name. No doubt out of habit, but it was helpful.

"I heard three prayers sent out to anyone who would listen. I claimed all of them, and I was able to answer one." Nameless calls still gave us power if we claimed them, and even more if we answered, but nothing like if we answered the call of a follower.

Astrid grabbed my hand. "We'll get you more power, don't worry. We're working out a plan to safely share your return that will help you, and not cause an unwelcomed stir in the community."

I understood that perfectly well. As far as anyone knew, revival was not possible. Even the spell used on Astrid wasn't common knowledge, and everyone was keeping quiet on the exacts if anyone got too nosey when they found out she was reincarnated by force. "Contrary to what many may believe, I am a patient man."

That was an understatement. I'd waited an absurd amount of time for the right moment to tell Astrid how I really felt about her. And in the end, I lost that chance. *You have it now. Talk to her about it. Don't wait.*

"Aya is also working on feeling out where you can push your domain claim so you'll have a more stable source," Astrid continued, cutting into my mental urgings. "But I know that's also something you have to feel out, too, so hopefully we can get you caught up enough on the world for you to stake something soon."

From what Aya and Tyr explained to me, in the modernization of Midgard, and gods falling into obscurity with most humans, we had to keep our power alive differently. Gods had to adapt, and to do so, we needed to make claims on things in our domain that non-believers worshiped. This converted their worship into power for us, even if they had no idea. It was such an artificial concept to me, but if that was how we were to survive, then so be it.

Aya had control of something called cyberwarfare, as well as the battle within love, whereas Tyr had taken some various small claims in physical warfare and in the justice proceedings of violent crimes. My courage domain fit somewhere, I just had to figure out where, even if they were multiple small pockets.

I'd been warned that if I didn't, I could find myself mortal and fading away. Apparently, there were an unsettling number of gods this happened to when they couldn't adapt, or just decided it was time for them to move on. It made me thankful Creation hadn't stripped me of my godhood, and gave me the chance to adapt.

"Did you do anything else interesting this morning?"

I thought for a moment. "I have now experienced the unfortunate pain that is a paper cut."

Astrid winced. "Yeah, those are never fun. At least we have accelerated healing. I don't miss the days of those healing slowly."

Dealing with pain, I could handle. But if I'd woken up with no ability to heal quickly, I think I'd fight Creation.

A chiming sound came from Astrid and she pulled one of those devices out of her pocket. I crouched to look over her shoulder to get a better look as she started tapping the surface instead of putting it up to her ear.

"What are these things?" I asked.

"Cellphones, phones for short," she said. "They're a communication device that also seconds as an information center."

My brow furrowed. "You can talk to others with it?"

She nodded. "There are a few ways to do so, but you can communicate with just about anyone you want, no matter where they are."

Fascinating. "It's magic?"

"No, it's technology developed by humans." She pursed her lips, her brow furrowing. "Or, as far as I know it was. Who knows, the inventors could be immortals in disguise, mixing magic with technology without humans knowing. Or maybe they're using it as a way to make it easier for humans to accept us at a larger scale if the magical community is ever exposed…"

She trailed off, her eyes going distant. I watched her carefully, a bit concerned.

"*Sister,*" Muninn said.

She blinked, and her cheeks tinted pink. "Sorry. What were we talking about?"

I chuckled. "So, you can contact anyone you want?"

"If you have their contact information."

"How do you get it?"

"Well, there are a few ways, but the easiest is to get it from them directly if you know them." She cocked her head. "Are you thinking of anyone in particular?"

I did. "Do you… know how to contact Hodur and Váli?"

The smile she gave me was so sweet. "I do. Whenever you're ready for them to know you're back, I can help you arrange something."

I grinned. That sounded amazing. Of all my brothers, I actually got along with those two. Vidar could fuck himself, where ever the hel he was, and Thor… I couldn't say I hated him, but I didn't particularly like him, either.

"Can you show me how these phones work?"

She nodded. Phone calls, text messages, internet, social media and email. She went over all kinds of things on this phone. She called hers a smartphone, whereas Tyr's was just a regular phone.

"Why is his different?" I asked.

"Because Tyr is a dinosaur and is the most technologically challenged person I know."

I laughed. I may not know what a dinosaur was, but I got the feeling she was calling him ancient and unadaptable.

She grinned. "I actually am interested to see how well you take to technology once you can be around it more. I hope you adapt quickly, that way I can make fun of Tyr even more."

I chuckled. "I'll do my best not to disappoint."

A message popped onto her screen. She opened it, revealing a photograph of two small children, maybe a year old both. One of them had impressively red hair—a lot of it—and beautiful green eyes, and the other had darker hair with oddly perceptive-appearing green eyes. They were playing in some sort of box filled with sand.

"Who are they?"

"Magnus's twins. We call them Birdie and Bard."

My brow rose. I was assuming by her wording those weren't their actual names. "I'm guessing there's some context behind the names?"

"Well, Birdie is a phoenix."

I blinked. That explained the hair. "I wasn't aware there were any left."

She nodded. "Nico was the last until he and Magnus had Birdie. At least, as far as we know."

"And Bard didn't end up being a phoenix?"

She pursed her lips. "It's going to sound strange, and maybe unbelievable, because the statistical odds are so obscenely low, but Bard has a different father."

My brow rose high. "That's possible?"

She nodded. "It's called heteropaternal superfecundation."

She lost me. "Huh?"

Astrid laughed. "I wish I could say there was a simpler term, but there isn't. Because Magnus is technically a twin, her chances of having twins is much higher than most, so having two partners meant her chances of twins with different fathers also ended up being higher than most."

"What do you mean, technically a twin?" You either had a twin or didn't, right?

She blew out a breath. "From what she told me, her twin disappeared early in her mother's pregnancy."

My brow furrowed. "How does an unborn disappear?"

"Well, there is a phenomenon called vanishing twin syndrome, where for some reason a fetus is absorbed by its twin. We think that's what happened with Magnus. It explains how she's an amplifier and a conduit."

I needed a moment to process that. Amplifiers and conduits were rare, and were always twins—one person per power. "I didn't know that was possible."

She shrugged. "I don't think anyone did. But when you add chimerism into things, along with magic and all that shit, anything is really possible. And Magnus is living proof."

That was so fascinating. "So, who is Bard's father?"

"Bragi. Bard inherited his empath abilities."

"Bragi." I said slowly, trying to process. "The same asshole Bragi I would threaten to smash his lyre over his head all the time because he didn't know how to shut up?"

Astrid clutched her sides as she laughed. No doubt she remembered a few of those moments. "Yes, the very same."

"Huh…" I never pictured him wanting to be a father, or in a committed relationship at that, but here we were.

Another photo came in, this one of Birdie showing off the two teeth she had with her smile as she tossed sand. Astrid had the goofiest smile.

"You love them."

She turned that smile on me. "Don't let Dahlia fool you, I'm the best auntie. That makes you an uncle, by association, too."

Her joy was infectious. The very thought of being an uncle had never crossed my mind before. My brothers had been all fairly uninterested in having children. In six hundred years that could have changed, but as far as I'd known, I'd been the only one who wanted children. Of course, that option had been taken away from me.

Astrid did something with the photos on her screen. I didn't know what, as I wasn't paying much attention beyond her beautiful face. Each little freckle, the small way her lips moved with her unspoken thoughts, the curve of her nose, the way her scar looked so identical to her past life, and added a fierceness to her gentleness, she was all so captivating.

Those pains of disappointment prickled in my chest again. Even if I had come to terms with my misfortune, I couldn't help but sometimes wonder, *What if?*

She looked up at me when she was done doing whatever her task was. "How are you feeling being around this?"

I mentally shook off my mental state. She didn't need to see that. "Fine. I'm not feeling those weird sensations like with other things. The sounds the phone makes is the most startling part."

Astrid smiled. "That's good. I'd say, with slow, continual exposure, you'd be comfortable being around everything within a week or two maybe."

I liked the sound of that timeline.

She tucked her phone into her back pocket. "I've been asked to pick some strawberries and blueberries for a few desserts. Would you like to join me?"

I wouldn't say no to spending time with her. "Do those grow in the spring here?"

She shook her head. "We're going to the glade to do that."

My eyebrow cocked. I'd heard others mentioning this glade, but I'd never been. Astrid's eyes widened. "We never told you about the glade, did we?"

I shook my head. She smiled apologetically. "Sorry. It's a place on the north end of our property with one of the oldest trees in this forest. The fae have taken it over, and their magic does all kinds of amazing things to the flora vitality. As thanks for allowing them to live peacefully here, they grow all kinds of fruits and vegetables year-round for us to harvest."

That sounded especially useful in the winter months. But I also didn't know how food situations worked now for the average human, let alone one like Astrid, who had access to magic.

Astrid led the way to the glade. Muninn flew ahead, flitting about in the trees. The walk was peaceful and familiar. I could recall so many memories of the two of us doing just this in her past life. There were even deeper feelings of familiarity lurking amongst all that, like the memories went even farther back, as impossible as that could be.

"How are you feeling after Huginn yelled at you?" Astrid suddenly asked.

I blinked. "Uh, fine? I was surprised he was so mad, and I hope he comes around soon."

How much did she know? Did she hear my confession to the raven? "Did you hear all of it?"

She shook her head. "Just what he projected at me, which were all his feelings."

I frowned. "I'm sorry he hates you. I wish I could do more."

"It's up to him if he wants to accept me or not. No one can make him, and I wouldn't want to force something like that. I gave him an offer, and he's using it exactly how I expected."

She shrugged, as if it didn't bother her, but I could tell by her posture it did. Seeing how she interacted with Muninn, I was sure she wished she could have that with Huginn.

I touched her shoulder. "He'll come around. I'm sure of it."

She didn't look convinced, but I wouldn't allow for him to keep being mad at her for something she didn't do.

As we came up to the glade, the underbrush along the path thickened until it became a tended hedge and flowering arch at the glade edge. Astrid stored her phone in a basket outside, though not before she received another one of those text messages.

She tucked a few empty baskets under her arm before slipping into the glade. I followed, taking in the beauty of the glade. Fresh green grass and wildflowers spread like a carpet around the most magnificent tree I'd ever seen.

"Diego and I used to play here all the time when we were kids," Astrid shared. "Even back then, it felt so magical."

"How old is this tree?" I asked.

She shrugged. "I don't know. Urd says she's one of the oldest in existence. She is one of the last trees to ever see Midgard before the first Ragnarök."

Before I could respond, two faun children skipped up to us, their lower goat bodies not hidden behind a glamour.

"Astrid, are you picking anything today?" one asked, his eyes bright and shining.

The other one's ears twitched in his excitement. "Can we help?"

Astrid smiled and held out two baskets for them. "I am, and I'd love the help. Could you two get me strawberries and summer squash?"

The two fauns snatched the baskets and bounded away, promising to get her the best ones.

Astrid looked up at me with sparkling eyes. "We'll pick the blueberries."

I followed her to another side of the glade. "What are blueberries?"

"Only the best fruit ever." Her smile was contagious.

We came up to a row of bushes that stood about a head taller than her. Round blue-purple berries grew in large clusters all over the bushes. Muninn landed on the top of one and picked a few off to eat.

Astrid wrapped her hand around a large cluster and pulled them off in one go. She then plucked a large berry from the pile in her hand and popped it into her mouth. Her eyes squinted and she hummed. The expression was cute.

She offered the pile to me and I grabbed one to try. A splash of sweet with subtle tart flavor burst over my tongue. I nodded. This wasn't bad at all. Different, but not bad. The strangest part was the texture, but I could easily get over that.

Astrid's smile widened and she ate another, only for her face to contort. "Sour one."

Muninn cackled, which made me laugh. Astrid scowled and tossed a berry at us both. Muninn caught his, while the second projectile bounced off my chest and fell to the ground. A tiny hand that looked more like spindly twigs reached out from under the bush and snatched the berry, then retreated back to safety. I blinked. Seemed there were all kinds of fae hiding about.

We picked the blueberries with a goal of about half of the basket full for now. I was able to grab the higher up clusters with ease, while Astrid focused on the lower hanging fruit. We didn't talk. I wasn't sure what to bring up right now.

Being dead for so long put me at a disadvantage to know what to talk about with her. I didn't want our conversations to only be around me needing to be caught up. And while I could ask her about her hobbies and such, I doubted I'd understand a lot of it, forcing her to explain each thing to me. Maybe that wasn't a bad thing. If it was something she loved to do, she'd be passionate enough to want to explain all the details.

Despite my inner turmoil, this activity felt so natural to do with her.

My fingers brushed hers when we reached for the same cluster of berries. Astrid retracted her fingers, her cheeks turning a shade of pink. "Go ahead."

I plucked the berries and dropped them into the basket. She went for some more, but I didn't resume my picking. I watched her, feeling out the slight awkwardness that slid between us. Well, it had been there ever since I'd started staying here.

Huginn's accusations haunted my mind. He called me a coward. He said I couldn't admit to her how I felt. And as much as I'd said he was wrong, a part of me was nervous to do so. If this was the Astrid I knew in the past, there wouldn't be a single moment of hesitation. But this wasn't that Astrid. This was a new version of her, who I didn't yet know.

And yet, those same feelings persisted, pushing against my restraint to come out and confess. Why else would she bring me back to life, a memory of a man she once knew but had no attachments to in this life, if she didn't feel the same in some way? Kirby even told me she tried the hardest.

"Baldur, I want to… ask you something," Astrid said all of a sudden. She wasn't looking at me, but had paused with her hand latched around a cluster of berries.

That's when I felt it. The push and pull of fear and courage battling out inside her. I'd been so wrapped up in my own thoughts, I hadn't realized she was going through something as well.

"You can ask me anything, Sunshine."

The tide of chaos churned then the fear sank beneath. She released the berry cluster and turned to face me. Her lip trembled for a moment before she set it, and a spark of fire lit so intensely in her eyes my pulse skipped. I remembered that fire, but it was much more intense in her in this life, and I liked it.

"Are you happy I did this?"

My brow furrowed as I tried to understand her question. "Am I happy that you… brought me here to the glade with you?"

Her lower lip caught between her teeth and my eyes homed in, desire heating beneath my skin. "Brought you back, six hundred years later into an unfamiliar world, instead of just releasing your soul."

Her grip on the basket tightened. "I did it selfishly, and without thinking things through. I'm a Valkyrie; I could have figured out a way to communicate with your soul. I've done it once before. I could have asked you if this was what you wanted—"

I pressed my thumb to her lips to stop her babbling. She blinked up at me with those stunning eyes I could willingly get lost in. "I thought I had a fulfilling life. There was nothing I could have asked Creation for to make me happier. Until I met you. You were a ray of sunshine in a dark world my eyes had adjusted to."

My thumb slid from her lip down to her chin. "I wanted your light all to myself. But Tyr had already claimed you and had no desire to share. Out of respect for him, I settled for friendship, so I could still bask in your radiance when you came my way."

I tucked my finger under her chin. "When you became immortal, I wanted so desperately to show you the poetry I longed to share with you. I did everything to deepen our bond. But despite me even trying to explain to you that it was okay for you to have more than just Tyr, and you showing signs of feeling the same toward me, a disconnect or resistance in you remained."

Her mouth moved wordlessly for a few moments as we held eye contact. "I had always felt a pull to you, but because I swore eternity to Tyr, I tried to ignore it. Even though we had that conversation in the market, Tyr showed no signs of being okay with such a choice. So I didn't think it was okay to ask for eternity with someone else as well as long as I was with him. Tyr and I didn't quite have the best communication skills then."

I crouched to be on a better level with her, not breaking the touch I had on her. "I had made the decision to tell you my intentions after the battle. I never got that chance. When I saw your bloody, lifeless body, all the light in Midgard was snuffed out. Aya's promise was the only thing to keep me from falling into that darkness. I spent fifty years trying to find you."

I leaned in. "I was willing to do anything to have you back. I was willing to take risks with Loki so I wouldn't have a prophecy hanging over my head when we finally reunited."

Astrid leaned forward, her eyes hooding and mouth parting.

"I would have died and lived a thousand lives, if it meant I'd have my Sunshine again. Six hundred missing years is nothing compared to the joy I have experienced these last three days, basking in your radiance again. And now that I have you, nothing will snuff out your light ever again."

Her soft lips pressed against mine. My heart skipped a beat. Then it beat faster, and faster, igniting a fire deep inside me. Hundreds of years I'd waited and suddenly, here and now, I had the one thing I longed for.

I cupped her face and kissed her harder, desperation and need taking over. I needed her to feel what I felt. I needed her to share these same emotions.

I needed... her.

Astrid's fingers tangled in my hair and she tried to pull me closer, only succeeding in doing that for herself. I didn't know where the basket of fruit went, and at this moment, I didn't care. Hel, I didn't care who was watching us right now.

Her lips parted and my tongue slid in, tasting her, consuming her. She moaned, stoking the overwhelming inferno blazing through my veins. My hands slid over her soft, shapely curves, memorizing her by touch. She pushed into me more, her body molding against mine perfectly, like fitting a missing piece of a puzzle, as if Creation made her just for me.

My hands wrapped around her back and hips. I fell back on my ass, pulling her with me, lost in my desire—lost in her.

The kiss broke, but only for a heartbeat. She pulled me back in, our mouths melding into an all-consuming inferno that left us breathless.

When our lips parted again, I pressed my forehead against hers, breathing hard. Aching desire burned so deep in my body it reached the depth of my soul. I wanted so much more. But it wasn't the right moment. "I know you're a different person in this life, someone I have to learn about and explore all over again. Regardless, I wish to lay my heart as offering on the altar of your shrine, if you'll have me."

Her fingers trailed along my jaw. "I would like to explore what we are… what we could be. It's not a problem I'm with Tyr and Diego, right?"

"Of course not. I know in time I'll have others as well, but for now, I just want you." I kissed her again, long and slow, drinking her in. "I had always wondered what sunshine tasted like. You're even better than I imagined."

She chuckled and pulled away, her eyes dancing with alluring mischief. "And you've only had a sample of what I taste like."

A growl caught in my throat, desire shooting straight down to my cock. I'd taste every inch of her until she was seared into my mind.

Astrid played with my hair, taking the ends into her fingers. "I should call Carrie. You could use a trim to bring some life into your hair."

"Who is Carrie?" I asked.

"She's a former resident. She and her daughter lived here for a number of years until their rehabilitation completed last month. They decided to move into town. She's a hairdresser, and a damned good one. She does my hair."

"How much hair will I lose for a trim?" A lot of the men I'd met so far had their hair cut closer to their head. I wasn't sure if I was up for that much of my hair to be gone.

She smiled. "Just an inch or two. She can cut it short if you want, but only if you want."

"Is it most common for men to have short hair now?"

"Around here it typically is, but that doesn't mean you have to. Plenty of men still keep their hair long, and there are different ways to style long hair." She gave me an assessing look. "I think a half-up style would look good on you."

I had no idea what that meant, but I was willing to learn.

She turned her attention to behind me and I twisted to see who approached. Two tiny fae women cautiously walked up to us.

"Good morning, Bridget. Good morning, Dierdre. How can we help you?"

"We're sorry to interrupt," one of them squeaked out. "But, we were wondering, Astrid, if there's been any progress with the antidote. We know you're working hard, and it's only been three days since the breakthrough, and we don't mean to sound pushy, it's just… we heard Lugh offered his essence adding to what Tyr offered, and…"

She trailed off, what little courage she had petering out. I didn't take her for a confrontational type. But it seemed, whatever this antidote was, it was important enough for her to push that comfort for herself.

Astrid's warm smile eased the tension out of the two fae. "I understand where you're coming from. Our breakthrough was critical in moving forward. But I'm afraid I don't have the answers you seek. We're still waiting on responses from the light gods we reached out to. Lugh responded almost immediately, but the others have been more difficult to get answers from. And even with what he and Tyr gave us, it may take a while for an antidote to be made. This is the first time we're attempting to reverse the process."

Crestfallen sighs came from both fae. They then thanked Astrid for all her hard work and walked away. The smile on Astrid's face faded, weariness breaking through.

"Astrid, what's going on?" I asked.

"What isn't going on?" She blew out a breath. "Sorry, I don't mean to be flippant and sound like I'm not taking your question seriously. I just…"

She sighed, her shoulder drooping. Muninn jumped down from his perch on the blueberry bush and nuzzled her, crooning as if to try and cheer her up.

Astrid gave him an affectionate pat. "It's just been a lot to handle. I swear it's been non-stop since becoming a Valkyrie. It's hard to find a moment to breathe sometimes. And then I finally figured out how to bring you back, but I didn't want to overwhelm you—"

I pressed a finger to her lips to stop the rambling. "Tell me what I, a light god, can do to help."

I didn't care if I'd only been back a few days. I would help where I could.

Astrid nodded and then detailed everything about the situation with the corrupted goddess Malsumis, Astrid's deranged cultist mother, and the magic blockers they were using on the community after corrupting Mia's father's work that was only intended to protect her.

I listened to every word to come off Astrid's lips. I processed every emotion that threatened to break her. I felt the weight of expectation and responsibility she was shouldering—the mantle she, as a silver-wing Valkyrie, took upon herself.

When she finished, I sat there, not sure which emotion to feel more: outrage for the injustice this goddess has caused, or fury toward this Ingrid for everything she'd done to Astrid. If I ever met the woman, I'd break her neck.

"Whenever you need more essence, tell me," I said. "I'll give whatever I can."

She grabbed my hand. "I want to strengthen you first. That's our priority for you. Then we can discuss you giving some of that to help."

I squeezed her hand. I couldn't argue that reasoning. At my power level, I'd maybe be able to save an infected kitten.

We shifted our attention when someone ran into the glade. It was Sean. A quiet elf, I had only met him a few times, but he seemed nice, and it was clear he took his loyalty to Astrid seriously.

He was out of breath, as if he'd run across the whole property, and maybe he had, because when he spotted us, his face lit up. "Astrid, Urd arrived, and she's got news about Baldur's condition, and the antidote."

Nausea roiled in my stomach. Astrid gazed up at me with worried eyes, after she'd apologized profusely for no reason. It seemed teleporting on an empty stomach when I was still getting used to being alive was a terrible idea. She, of course, had no idea this would happen, so it wasn't her fault.

Diego opened the door to the deck and walked out. He offered me a glass of water. "This should help calm your stomach. My dad is almost done making some food."

I nodded my thanks and sipped the refreshing liquid. It took a few moments, but the water helped settle my stomach. Astrid fussed a little more before I convinced her I'd be fine. Xavier popping his head out the door to tell me my breakfast was ready didn't hurt, either.

Astrid took my hand and pulled me inside. Everyone was waiting in the gathering room. Tyr and Darius hadn't left for their trip, having been delayed with Urd's appearance. Urd herself sat on a couch, her posture regal. I'd only ever met her in passing once in my life, and even now, being in her presence in such a casual setting felt strangely wrong. How things had changed.

Next to her was a man I'd never met before. Mia was with him, and they shared enough similarities that I guessed him to be her father, Ronan. He had some sort of box at his feet.

In the kitchen, on the long thing they called an island, a plate with something yellow awaited me. Astrid left my side to open a tall box with a door that buzzed far too loudly for my tastes, yet she didn't seem to notice.

A cold breeze came from the box, and from the looks of the open door, there were food and other things inside. Curious, I stood behind her to peer inside. "What is this?"

"A fridge." She reached for a glass flagon filled with orange liquid. "It keeps food fresh longer so we don't have to preserve it."

My brows rose high on my forehead. "No salting or drying or relying on magic ever?"

"Not unless you want to. Freezer keeps some from going bad even longer, but the quality can degrade if they remain frozen too long."

How amazing this technology was.

Astrid pulled out two glass cups from some sort of suspended storage box on the wall and poured the orange liquid into both before storing the flagon away. She set one next to my plate of food.

"What is this?" I lifted the cup to inspect it, then gave the content a sniff. A fresh, zesty aroma shocked my nose.

"Orange juice," she said before taking a sip of hers. "Pairs great with that omelet."

I sipped the drink and my tongue was hit with a tangy, sweet taste. There was a texture to it as well that I didn't expect. I licked my lips and stared at the liquid in my glass, trying to process this new drink. "This is consumed regularly?"

"It's one of the most popular juices," she said. "What do you think?"

I drank some more, enjoying the freshness about it, reminding me of a nice summer's day. "I like it."

That left me to try the yellow thing she called an omelet. It looked similar to the egg thing I had yesterday they called scrambled eggs, just less messy. I poked it with a fork, finding it rather solid. When I tore some off with my fork, I found it filled with cheese, meat, and vegetables. One bite and a melody of flavors danced along my tongue. This was good. More than good.

I shoveled more into my mouth. Better than the scrambled eggs, but those were good, too. Everything I'd eaten since coming back was delicious. They had access to so much more in the way of spices and ingredients, it was hard to believe this was common for the average family now.

Astrid laughed when I almost choked on a bite. "Slow down. You don't have to rush."

I paused, realizing I'd almost eaten the whole omelet already. "I guess I was hungry."

She nudged me with her elbow, a teasing smirk on her lips. "Bottomless pit."

Xavier patted me on the back, a smile warming his face. "If you want more, I'll make more."

I nodded. I wouldn't say no to something like this. "Am I holding up this important conversation?"

Urd smiled. "I want to address your situation first, since I've made you wait. And I'd rather you satiate your hunger before any of that."

I didn't take that as permission to eat slower, like Astrid wanted. I wouldn't make a dragon wait, no matter how normal everyone else acted about her being here.

A few more swift bites and half of my orange juice later, I was ready to hear what she had to say.

Urd clasped her hands in her lap. "I have the answer you seek, but I want you to understand, it will likely not be what you want to hear."

"I'd rather the truth than a lie or false hope," I said. I could handle anything she said. Even if I didn't like it at first, I'd come to accept it in time.

Over these three days, I'd already prepared myself to learn I'd always feel pain going forward. It was my arrogance that landed me in this position, so I'd have to adapt.

"You will never be immune to pain again," she said bluntly. "Your previous immunity had nothing to do with your godhood, and everything to do with a spell Frigg placed on you."

My brow furrowed. "My mother cast a spell on me?"

She nodded. "When your parents heard the first prophecy Skuld had about you, they, like many others, assumed it meant your death, and they had very different reactions. Your father had the audacity to mock my sister. He refused to believe his perfect son could be killed, let alone by something like fire. Your mother, however, did believe my sister's vision and did everything she could to find a way to thwart it."

Mia tipped her head. "What do you mean by 'assumed death'?"

"Since visions are interpretations, it's possible the prophecy didn't even mean death, but most assumed it did," Diego said.

"But he did die," Kirby said.

Astrid shook her head. "Technically, he still had a pulse."

"And he didn't die by fire," Tyr said.

"What is the prophecy?" Mia asked.

I blew out a breath and spoke it.

The blessed son of the raven crown will be consumed by fire

She nodded slowly. "I could see where people thought consumed meant death. Hard to think of what that could mean otherwise."

Diego's brow furrowed. "Why does that prophecy not sound correct?"

I looked at him. What did he mean? That prophecy haunted me my entire life. I knew it perfectly.

Urd pursed her lips. "Because it's not. It wasn't a raven crown. It was a craven crown."

Several people shared looks that I didn't understand. "Is that an important distinction?"

"Not for your particular situation," Aya said. "But in general, yes. A raven crown and a craven crown are vastly different."

"We've seen this happen once before," Tyr said. "In the past, a völva recited a different prophecy for Odin and used the word craven. He was quick and adamant that she was wrong and it was supposed to be raven."

"*Odin lied,*" Muninn said.

Everyone looked at the bird perched on Astrid's shoulder. He hopped back and forth on his feet.

"Didn't want anyone to know. They couldn't know the truth."

My brow pinched together. "Know what truth?"

"The truth that Astrid accused Odin of," Kirby said. She looked to Astrid. "What was it you accused him of? Stealing a crown?"

A stolen crown? What did that mean?

Astrid nodded. "It's something I figured out. But it's not relevant to this situation. I'd like to understand more about this spell Frigg used."

I was torn. I wanted to know more about this stolen crown and this secret that Astrid seemed to have that no one else had yet to ask her further about. If my father had done something so terrible that a prophecy would call his crown craven and he tried to hide that, I wanted to know what it was. Yet, I also understood the spell was more pressing. Hopefully the appropriate time to broach the crown topic with Astrid would come after.

"I don't know how she found it, but Frigg discovered an ancient spell. My sisters and I hid these spells because they're dangerous." I noticed her eyes flick to Aya for some reason, then she continued as if she hadn't. "Before Ragnarök, there was more magic available, allowing for wider experimentation. Unfortunately, many of these spells had a heavy price."

"All magic has its price," Darius said.

She nodded. "Yes, this is true, however the magic we have access to now is nowhere near as powerful as back then. The most powerful spells required ritual, which helped mitigate the price as several casters were needed, and that price could be spread amongst them. For someone to cast one of these spells now…"

Ice chilled my blood. "It's what killed her."

The room grew unnaturally still. Urd nodded solemnly. "I was the one who warned her not to use the spell. I warned her that in order to protect someone so strongly, the spell required something just as strong in return, and that meant it would kill her. I knew she wouldn't be able to find enough magic-gifted individuals to share in the ritual burden, as it was still so soon after the divergence. She didn't listen. And because she didn't die right away, she assumed I was wrong."

I leaned my elbows on my knees, steepling my fingers in front of my face. "It killed her slowly, causing her mysterious affliction."

"It took a while for the protection spell to take full effect on you. And as you became stronger, the spell hastened her death."

Until it finally took her.

My fingers curled into fists. Her death was my fault. Had I not been destined to… what, die? Was I meant to die? Mia understood how the interpretation would be seen that way, but like Astrid said, I didn't die to fire or at Loki's hand. And now I didn't have that protection. Was her attempt to save me in vain? Did my arrogance in agreeing to Loki's plan waste my mother's sacrifice?

My pulse raced and my breathing picked up. *Am I still doomed to perish to fire?*

Astrid wrapped her hand around my bicep. I looked at her, snared by those stunning eyes of hers, like always. The building fear in me slid away. *Or have I already been consumed by fire?*

Astrid turned her attention to Urd. "Was it Loki or me who destroyed the spell?"

Urd pursed her lips. "That was difficult for me to figure out, as I had never seen that spell undone before. I believe it was a combination of you both. My best guess is Loki altered the magic protecting Baldur to preserve his soul and body separately. When you needed to put his soul back into his body, the only way to do that was to break the spell. Had Tyr not interrupted Loki, he would have foolishly attempted this himself."

"Are you saying Loki wouldn't have been able to bring Baldur back?" Mia asked.

"Of course not. Only the winged witch could have done that."

Eyes flicked between Urd and Astrid. I'd heard some of the fae call her that instead of a Valkyrie. It seemed to be an accepted term by Astrid, as she never corrected them.

"You knew? This whole time, you knew she'd bring him back?" Diego said.

Urd smiled. "The prophecy came to a gifted völva named Randi."

Astrid blinked. "My mother received it?"

Urd nodded.

Astrid's brow knitted together. "How did you know?"

"My sisters and I always made it a point to keep an eye on any magic-gifted mortal, especially those with seer abilities. Your mother in particular received unusual visions. She was an interesting one to keep an eye on."

"What was the prophecy?"

When the trickster steals courage
Tears of the winged witch will revitalize the fallen warrior

Kirby narrowed her eyes at Urd. "And all this time of us trying to work with you, you never thought to mention this to anyone?"

Urd leveled her with a calm yet cold stare. "And what do you suppose I should have said? I didn't know how Astrid would do it, as there was no ancient spell for her to find to revive a person as they are, nor has there been any current magic capable of performing such a feat. I also wasn't aware Baldur's soul was trapped in that piece of armor until Astrid brought it home. By that point it was clear she was on that path, making any mention of revival redundant."

I stopped caring about the two bickering women. None of that mattered to me. I couldn't take my eyes off Astrid. She had been prophesied to bring me back. *What kind of witch is she?*

Astrid, to her credit, didn't seem all that shocked by Urd's revelation. Contemplation masked her face. "So, there's no chance to get Baldur's pain immunity back?"

Urd shook her head. "None that I'm aware of that won't require that spell. And I'm not handing that over."

I wouldn't want her to. It'd been hard enough watching my mother's health mysteriously deteriorate. I would not allow anyone else to do that for me. "I'll adapt."

"Valkyrie shields might be a good substitute," Kirby said.

"I also have the shields Dad has been teaching me," Astrid said.

Darius nodded. "I'll bump more of that up on the priority list for your training."

With that out of the way, things turned to the developments of the magic blockers. A part of me hoped this would be quick. The buzzing in my ears was getting harder to ignore, but I also refused to interrupt. This was far more important than my comfort.

Everyone waited patiently to hear what Urd had to say. But it wasn't her news to break. Ronan grinned like a cat, and it both unsettled and thrilled me. That was a fae smile if I'd ever seen one.

He lifted the box at his feet onto the small table in front of them and lifted two latches. "We've done it."

Everyone seemed to stop breathing as he opened the box to reveal fourteen vials nestled in cloth.

Astrid slid off her stool to get closer. "Are they really…"

He nodded. "This is our first prototype that we're confident enough with to start trialing."

The room erupted in cheers.

When everyone quieted, he continued. "It's not a lot, I know. Unfortunately, we used almost all of the harvested essence on failed attempts."

Tyr ran his hand through his hair. "I think I speak accurately for everyone when I say we didn't think you'd be able to get a working prototype with the first harvest, so fourteen doses is fantastic."

Ronan shook his head. "Not fourteen—seven, max. At this stage, we're only able to get these effective enough to where in most instances, an affected individual will need two doses to reverse their affliction. For some beings, like fae, we believe a third or even fourth dose will be needed until we can create a more efficient antidote."

"On the positive side, we have determined the doses can be taken in rather quick succession," Urd said. "Instead of waiting weeks or months like traditional human vaccines, ten-minute intervals between administered doses should be safe. After each dose, the patient should be monitored closely to make sure there are no adverse effects and whether another dose is still needed or not."

"How confident are we about the safety of these?" Aya asked.

"We're quite confident even humans will be safe with this," Ronan said. "But that's also what the monitoring stage will help us with during the trials, on top of us being selective regarding who participates in the first few rounds."

"Since we only have enough for seven tests right now, how long until we have a larger batch?" Kirby asked.

"Lugh and I won't be able to provide more essence for another week at least," Tyr said.

"I would caution against doing more than two harvests per month for safety reasons," Urd said. "And two gods won't be enough for our needs, especially if we need to continue to improve the antidote."

"If we can cure even one person with this, that should give us the leverage we need to prove to any other light god on the fence that we're serious about this," Astrid said. "Then we can increase production and improve the effectiveness."

Discomfort pulsed in my head. All of this, plus the electronics, was getting to be too much. I excused myself outside. Muninn came with me.

"It will get easier," he said.

I stroked his chest with a finger. I knew that. It'd be nice to not have to isolate myself like this, but I had to give myself lenience and time.

We weren't alone for too long. Diego stepped outside, a glass of water in his hand. He offered it to me. "Feeling better?"

I nodded and took a sip of the refreshing drink. "Headache is subsiding."

He relaxed against the railing and tilted his head up to the sky, soaking in the sun. Having no concept of shame, I let my eyes travel down his profile and silhouette. He had a strong jawline with a light amount of facial hair accentuating its shape. His nose was straight and well-proportioned to his face. The breeze caught in his dark, tousled hair. The casual clothes he wore fit him just right emphasizing his broad shoulders and lean body which had a deceptive amount of muscle hidden beneath his bronze-brown skin. He wasn't a fighter, but he wasn't a pushover either.

Today he didn't have any of those dragon features visible, though the day was still young. There didn't seem to be any rhyme or reason when he looked human versus showing off dragon features. Either way, I could see why Astrid enjoyed him. I certainly liked the view.

"Not subtle, are you?" He cracked an eye open to look at me. "Not that I'm complaining that an attractive man is appreciating me."

I shrugged. "Never saw a need to be. If interest isn't reciprocated, I move on."

"Or hold out in the case of a favorite redhead?" he teased.

I chuckled. "That was different. There was reciprocation, but neither of us could act due to a number of factors. So, I was willing to wait until the opportune time."

Muninn cackled. I remembered vividly the number of times he teased and prodded me about my feelings for Astrid.

"What is it about Astrid that draws you to her?" I asked.

Diego hummed quietly, a smile tugging at his lips. "She's smart and funny. She's not afraid to get competitive even when she knows she won't win, all for the sake of fun. She doesn't do anything by halves. I love the way she dances and sings while cooking without a care who watches. Her smile. It's like the sun banishing the darkness of night. And her laugh. The carefree sound of her laugh lightens the burdens pulling on your shoulders." He grinned. "And can't forget her stubbornness."

My eyebrow arched. "You like that she's stubborn?"

He chuckled. "Yeah. It makes interactions with her more interesting. Plus, it's fun seeing who out-stubborns the other, her or Tyr."

I laughed. He had a fair point.

"What about you? What draws you to her, even now? What drives you to stay and try again?"

I smiled. "Her fiery spirit. She is radiance and intensity no sun could match. She's fierce and untamed, yet her warmth soothes like the first soft rays of sunlight of a new dawn after a long winter's night. She draws me in, like a moth helplessly drawn to a flame. I would burn for her a thousand times over, without regret."

Diego had a knowing smile. "Fire is all our undoing."

I winced when Muninn cried in my ear and flew off. I rubbed my ear. "Asshole."

Diego laughed.

We fell into light conversation about him and his hobbies. Most of the stuff, I didn't know what he was talking about, just like I'd feared would happen when talking to Astrid, but Diego was patient and even seemed to enjoy going into detail when I asked for it. There was so much to understand and learn. These things he called dirt bikes sounded interesting, and he was passionate about the topic too.

"Oh boy, he's got him all riled up on those bikes again," Kirby said.

We turned to see her, Mia, and Astrid exiting the house. Astrid carried another plate of that omelet stuff, though this one looked bigger.

"Not all of us can spend hours talking about guns," Diego shot back.

Kirby grunted. "That's Brit. Baldur, word of warning, don't get her on that topic unless you want to spend all week on it."

I chuckled. I didn't know who Brit was, or what a gun was for that matter, but I'd do my best to remember it.

"Just send Zeke in," Mia suggested. "The two can bicker about the best handgun model and you can slip away unnoticed."

The four of them burst into raucous laughter.

Astrid handed me the plate of food and my stomach rumbled in response. She picked on me again, Kirby and Diego joining in, and I dug into my meal.

Diego's phone pinged with one of those text messages. He typed back on the device. "Zeke wants to hang out for a few hours."

Astrid kissed him on the cheek. "Have fun. Don't get into too much trouble."

"That's my line to you three ladies. You're trouble with a capital T."

They grinned in a way that screamed trouble and he vanished. I shoved more food in my mouth.

Astrid turned to me. "When you're done, Eir messaged me, asking if you'd be interested in seeing her."

I paused my eating, something not feeling right. "Why is Eir in town? Is this a popular place for others to visit?"

Astrid frowned. "No, she lives here now."

"Why isn't she living in Fensalir?" My appetite was slowly waning as knots tightened in my stomach. "She swore to my mother on her death bed she'd always protect Fensalir in her stead."

Her eyes downcast, Astrid hesitated with her response, making my concern worse. "Fensalir is… gone."

My heart nearly stopped. *Gone?* That couldn't be. My mother's home and everything she protected couldn't be gone. "What happened?"

"Supernatural hunters," Kirby said. "They chased fae into Eir's protection, making them aware it existed. They amassed a force she couldn't protect against and destroyed it. We saved who we could."

Numbness crept along my body. Eir hadn't been a fighter. She healed the sick and injured. It was her passion to care and nurture. Even as a goddess, she couldn't fight back against much.

Astrid's lip twitched. "When we turned the town into a sanctuary, the townsfolk voted on a new name. It's mostly been called Valkyrie's Sanctuary, but we officially named it New Fensalir to honor those who were lost, and for the refugees we took in, which was nearly ninety percent of those who made it. The rest went to Runavík."

"Thank you for being honest with me." I lifted my gaze to meet hers. "And for taking them in. It pains me knowing my mother's home is gone, but it's a relief to know those who survived are in safe places. And I'm happy to hear Runavík is still around."

She smacked her forehead. "I just remembered I completely forgot to tell Bjarke you're back! That would help you out so much. I'm an idiot."

Kirby snickered and I shook my head. I wouldn't pick on her. She had a lot on her plate, she was bound to forget something. Hel, even if I didn't know Runavík was still around, I could have asked, or asked Tyr and Aya about reaching out to immortal followers discreetly to improve my odds of gaining power faster.

Astrid's expression went oddly blank for a moment and then she blinked. "I guess I have another reason to go into town. Nyx wants to see me."

Muninn must have communicated with her. That was my best guess, at least. My father had a similar look when he spoke long-distance with the ravens.

She looked to Kirby and Mia. "That's not going to be a problem, right?"

Kirby grinned. "You can't shake me that easily."

Mia nodded.

I watched them all grin at each other. It was good to see Astrid and Kirby had a bond again. And it looked as though it was even stronger than the one they had been forging before Kirby's first death.

I finished my meal and took Astrid's hand when I was ready to visit Eir.

TWELVE

ASTRID

The small clinic Eir ran was a converted Victorian-style house on the east side of town ten minutes from downtown. She'd been offered an open building downtown, to be more centralized, but the quiet neighborhood offered the atmosphere she wanted for her and her patients. It also doubled as her home, so it made her happy.

We walked up the wooden steps of the covered porch, past a fake Halloween pumpkin light display, and opened the front door, still decorated with a fake Christmas wreath, which held a few colorful plastic Easter eggs… for some reason.

The reception room was cozy and felt more like a lounge than a clinical welcome area with its palette of soft, neutral tones, plush carpeting, and suede upholstered furniture. Vibrant oversized throw pillows added a pop of color, which gave warning to Eir's… personality.

No one was in the room at the moment, though we could hear someone moving around behind a door.

A yellow bell with a sign reading *ring me* sat at the empty reception desk, which had a basic computer setup. I tapped the top of the bell and it chimed. At the same instant, the door with the muffled no behind it flew open and someone burst out in a frenzy.

She was a deeply tan and tall woman, with a wild, dark brown mane of curls decorated with an eclectic assortment of bobbles. A scarf on her head tied them away from her face. Enchanted glasses used to aid her healing efforts were perched on the tip of her nose, nearly obscuring her amber eyes. In her arms she carried a stack of overstuffed folders that looked two seconds from scattering all over the floor.

"Hey, Eir," I greeted. She didn't seem to hear me as she rushed behind the desk.

She moved around at a frazzled pace, as if she were perpetually dealing with an emergency. Given she acted like this all the time, one would guess life was one perpetual emergency to her.

"Eir," I prompted again.

"One moment, one moment," she mumbled in a thick accent.

She spun around, looking about wildly, as she was trying to find something, and then froze when she spotted Baldur. She gasped and then shrieked, "Baldur!"

The folder stack? It and its contents scattered everywhere as she practically threw herself at him. While Eir was tall, Baldur was still taller, and her arms were barely able to wrap around his chest. Baldur blinked in bewilderment as papers fluttered to the ground around us. I bit my knuckle, while Mia pressed her fingers against her mouth, and Kirby pressed her lips together, all of us doing our best to not laugh.

"Uh, hello, Eir," Baldur finally said.

"Oh, Creation!" She let him go and looked him over with wild eyes. "You're certainly in one piece. And breathing. This is the most blessed miracle. Come, come! I'll give you a check-over just in case and we'll catch up."

She grabbed his arm and dragged him away, not caring about the mess she'd made. Baldur shot me a pleading look and I just waved him goodbye with a big smile.

The door Eir dragged him through slammed shut. A beat of silence passed before the girls and I cracked, bursting with laughter.

When I got myself under control, I used my magic to clean up the mess. I didn't know how the papers should be organized, so I just stacked them neatly for Eir's benefit later.

"Is she always like that?" Mia asked as we left the clinic, her eyes a little wide.

"I don't think I've ever seen her in a state of calm," I said. Kirby nodded her agreement.

The three of us continued to chat while walking down the sidewalk toward Main Street, the maple trees lining the road shading us from the high morning sun. Occasionally my bond with Muninn poked at my mind. He'd found something unusual to him, but wasn't telling me what yet.

Huginn was also still hanging around. I got the vague notion he was back at Eir's. I did my best not to react to his presence, knowing it'd just get him riled up. If his only reason for staying was because of Baldur, then great. I was fine with that.

Pain pricked my chest, like someone twisting a knife in my heart. *Denial is a perfect coping mechanism, said no therapist ever.*

People, from humans to fae, to even demons—yeah, demons were real—and other creatures I didn't have names for, greeted us as we walked by. I still hadn't quite adjusted how diverse this place had become since last summer. Even the original townsfolk surprised me with how easily they'd adapted. We rarely had trouble from all the mixing, and if there was, it was worked out through mediation.

We came to a row of brick colonial buildings. Most were shops with small apartments on the upper floors. I stopped in front of an unmarked recessed door between two shops. This wooden door and its decorative frame were newer than the shops, and the bricks of the building had a fresh coat of black and white paint, making it stick out from the natural bricks of the surrounding shops. Potted plants in the recessed entryway gave the building a pop of color.

Mia wanted to grab something at the bakery down the street, so she and Kirby kept going.

Grabbing the door handle, I opened the door, calling out, "Nyx?"

The door swung open wide and as I stepped inside, a tingling sensation of magic ran down my spine, just like the first time I'd ever walked into her hotels, but didn't realize the sensation wasn't my nerves of living in a new city at the age of nineteen.

Instead of entering a cramped foyer or reception room that matched the age of the building, I stood in a modern and luxurious lounge with an elevator on the back wall. Plush furniture, potted plants, and artwork were meticulously placed around the room. A tall, willowy woman with dark, raven hair and pale skin stood from where she relaxed on one of the sofas.

She smiled, the gesture warm and almost motherly, and held out her arms. "Astrid, you're here."

We kissed each other on both cheeks and embraced in a quick hug. "It's good to see you, Nyx. This lobby is beautiful."

Her smile widened. "Your father thought it would be too much, but I knew you'd love it."

I winked. "Because unlike him, I have taste."

She laughed.

"Is everything set up?" I asked. "Or are you still working around the wards?"

Wards were crucial for a sanctuary. They kept those with ill intentions from finding it, and protected those inside from harm if it were to be found. My wards, reinforced by a number of others, also could eject someone should they not start as a threat but become one later. This had its downsides, however.

Certain types of magic were difficult to use inside the barrier, including teleportation and dimensional magic. I could easily do both, because they were my wards. However, Nyx had more difficulties.

Even though she wasn't a threat, the wards couldn't differentiate from her power and someone trying to invade the same way. So, when she agreed to install one of her apartments to help us with the influx of new residents, implementing them wasn't a quick snap of her fingers like it could be somewhere else.

Nyx dipped her hand into a pocket and pulled out a rectangular plastic card that looked a lot like a hotel key. "I only have one more task, and that's why I needed you to stop by."

A wide grin spread across my lips. I took the keycard and she ushered me over to the elevator. She pressed the call button and the doors slid open.

"Press the key to the reader and then push the ground floor button," Nyx instructed. "With the wards, I need a piece of your magic to trick the protections into thinking this dimensional travel belongs to you."

Made sense to me. I stepped into the elevator car and gazed at the button panel that was far too long for such a small building. Next to the panel was a bulky card reader I remembered from my college and intern days.

I touched the keycard to the reader and pressed the lowermost button on the selector panel detailed with a star. Magic rolled through me like a shiver, and then nothing.

Blinking, I cocked my head. "Did I… do it?"

Nyx grinned. "This lobby is now connected to my network."

I whooped. "Yes!"

Nyx laughed. We sat in the lounge, but the excitement coursing through me prevented me from relaxing.

"Thank you. I know I keep saying that, but I really do appreciate what you're doing for us, Nyx. I no longer have to worry if we'll have enough space for everyone we take in, and I can't describe the relief this gives me."

She took my hand into hers. "I'd have tried to do this even if you didn't ask me. I am not a fighter. I accept that. My strength lies in my sight of the Fate Weave and my apartments and hotels. I will use that to our advantage."

I hesitated a moment, not wanting my question to sound mean. "Nyx, why do you pretend to be neutral when you're not? Why aren't you neutral, where most of the other Fates are?"

She crossed a leg over the other and leaned back on the sofa. The way she looked at me sent a slight chill down my spine. It was so easy to forget that she was a being so old, she may rival even the dragons. But here, the way she sat, I could see the eons of experience and knowledge.

"We Fates never used to be neutral. Like the dragons, we enjoyed picking sides and tried to force a destiny path. But, in time, most of us found it foolish to do so, and instead decided to watch how the world played out."

She shook her head slowly. "I wasn't one of them. I always saw potential to steer destiny into a better path for everyone, even if others didn't agree with the one I chose. And I was almost always right."

The satisfied grin on her lips was comforting for some reason. Maybe because she was on our side.

"Then why the secrecy?" I asked.

"Protection," she said matter-of-factly. "Being seen as neutral meant I could get away with more. And once I began protecting others under the guise of profiting in an ever-changing world, my anonymity ensured my charges were safe."

My lips pressed together. "What made you show your hand now?"

Maybe her addition here would go unnoticed, but I highly doubted it. The world was vast, and rumors in the magical community spread quicker than old ladies gossiping in a bingo hall. It only took one person to notice or be careless. It took maybe three months for my reincarnation to be known. It was why I needed to be careful with Baldur's resurrection. I wanted him to get that needed power boost from worship, but I couldn't risk the wrong people finding out too soon or botch how we'd managed it.

"Because I can't continue the same path I was on," Nyx said. "The conflict brewing will only get worse. Everything the community has done to hide itself will come crumbling down. There's nothing we can do to stop it. We can only prepare with sanctuaries like this, and my network, until the dust settles and the world learns to live together like it once did, a long time ago."

My heart thrummed slowly in my veins, all my muscles tensing. "It's going to be bad, isn't it?"

She closed her eyes and nodded. "Great change is coming. With our efforts, we can twist destiny in our favor. But to get there—"

I sat ramrod straight. Chaos pinged in my mind at such a lightning pace I couldn't process it.

"What's wrong?" Nyx asked.

"I don't... know..." I slowly stood. "Something is happening... somewhere..."

"Astrid!" Muninn screamed in my head. *"Danger!"*

I was already sprinting for the door before the second word left him, his urgency flooding me with adrenaline. *"Where?"*

"The west wards. Refugees. Attackers." I felt him shiver. *"Dangerous magic."*

The hotel's door flew open and I veered west, nearly running right into Kirby and Mia.

"Whoa, where's the fire?" Kirby asked.

My wings spread from my back. "We're under attack."

Her expression darkened while Mia's eyes went wide. "Where?"

"West side is the best I know right now. Mia, go get the others, Kirby and I will handle the situation until we have backup."

Mia nodded. Her wings manifested and she took flight. Kirby slapped her hand on my shoulder and in a blink we were in the forest. I whipped around, searching for Muninn. I'd gotten us as close as possible without having an exact understanding where he was in the chaos of my mind. Huginn was also getting riled up, which didn't help matters.

Kirby's black wings unfurled from her back and her Valkyrie armor manifested. We both took to the skies, scanning for the trouble. Kirby pointed ahead of us just as the ward pings and Muninn's cries slammed harder into me. "There!"

In the distance the small black shape of Muninn darted around. He swooped into a dive bomb at something on the other side of the barrier, inside what only I could call chaos.

People ran around wildly, nature manipulated by magic lashed out, people screamed, some fell to the ground. My pulse beat deep in me. Black magic struck a woman and she collapsed. It disappeared, and she tried to crawl away, only for someone to rush her, a sword in hand. *No.*

My axe materialized in my hand and my armor suddenly covered my body. Magic coiled around my weapon and the head of the axe burst into golden flames. In a blink I was no longer next to Kirby, but behind the armed attacker. The person whipped around, sword arcing, but they were too slow. My axe drove into their back with a squelching crack, the blade of the axe head slamming into their spine. The smell of scorched flesh assaulted my nose.

The enemy collapsed and gasped for breath. I stepped on their back and turned my attention to the fear-stricken woman.

"Run!" I shouted, pointing toward the sanctuary. "The wards are just ahead."

She shook, her eyes wide. I gestured again. "Go. Now!"

The woman scrambled away, and luckily toward the sanctuary wards.

I whirled around, and my hand came up, magic springing from my fingers in time to create a temporary shield against a sword swinging at me. The weapon bounced off the shield, shattering the shield on impact and throwing my attacker back. I swung my flaming axe, plunging the blade into his chest. He gasped and collapsed.

Kirby swooped down and attacked another person, slicing their arms with her sword. I had hardly a second to question why she didn't aim for something more vital when two more enemies rushed me. These ones had armor, but not the modern, bulletproof stuff. They looked like they'd come right out of history. *Fae hunters.*

These types of supernatural hunters wore iron armor and wielded iron weapons, the one element fae were deeply affected by—the element that had permanently disfigured Ùna, after they'd attacked her village so long ago.

I slashed my hand, golden magic tendrils springing from my fingertips. They lashed out at the hunters, but just as they were about to strike them, the two hunters thrust some sort of artifact out and the magic nullified.

Fucking hypocrites! They'd attack any magical and non-human beings because they believed we shouldn't exist, but they'd use our damned magical artifacts to their heart's content to destroy us.

Kirby whirled around, drawing her hidden pistol, and fired twice. I jerked my attention away from the gore she created of their heads. *Leave it to Kirby to bring a gun to knife fight.*

A woman screamed. I turned in time to see her trip and fall. A fae hunter went after her, and she curled into herself protectively. In her arms, a small child clung to her. Thrusting my hand out, magic flared and flaming swords manifested around the hunter and skewered him.

The woman didn't hesitate to scramble away, running for the wards without my prompting, as if she felt the call of their safety.

I turned to face those threatening my home. I looked for those who would dare draw the blood of the innocent. My pulse beat slow and steady inside me, everything around me slowing to a crawl. The drums of war beat in time with my heart. It called to me as a Valkyrie. It sang its sweet siren song in a way my past understood better than my present could grasp.

Was it war itself that called me, or the need to protect? I wasn't a black-winged Valkyrie. I didn't feel compelled to fight wars like them. Sure, I had a temper that reared up every now and then. I needed to punch something every once in a while as catharsis. But I didn't like killing. I didn't want to hurt people if I could help it. And yet battles called to me for some reason.

Why? Why would a Valkyrie like me feel this compelled to fight? Because of injustice? Would that compel a Valkyrie, especially one like me who wasn't equipped to do that? I wasn't Kirby or Magnus, who were raised as soldiers. I was a therapist witch, who happened to be a Valkyrie.

I didn't know what it meant to be a Valkyrie. Yet I had to trust that side of my instincts to do what needed to be done. And that instinct said to fight. I had to tap into my past, to a person who had grown under those harsher world conditions, and knew what it meant to fight.

One day I might be able to handle it like she could, without relying on my rage or out-of-control emotions, but for now, I let her take control.

Dozens of weapons materialized around me and shot out, attacking our closest enemies. Kirby fired her gun until her magazine, plus the two extra she had hidden away, were empty, and then rushed in with her sword. Gold and black magic flew from my fingers, lashing and wrapping.

The fleeing refugees pivoted our way, and I tossed up temporary magical shields around them the best I could. Some felt bolstered enough to continue to fight back, but most were too fearful and sought safety.

There were so many hunters. And even more fae. Too many. Our sanctuary was too far out of the way for so many to be fleeing for our borders. It was like… they had been transported here somehow.

Kirby swore and I pivoted my attention. My blood cooled. Metamoura, lizard-like flying creatures, buzzed around her, swooping and biting. Magical spear tendrils sprang from my fingers and skewered several of the creatures. They burst into shadowy dust. Kirby pushed her Valkyrie shield around herself to protect her from the onslaught, and for good reason.

Metamoura were vampiric in nature, but instead of blood, they consumed an individual's life essence and assumed that person's form, while the individual they were became nothing.

A person could fall victim to these creatures at any time, but when they appeared in such great numbers like it, it meant Malsumis was involved. That meant only one thing.

Something like a distorted bull cry echoed through the battle. A hulking monstrosity of shadow and tendrils that vaguely looked like an upright bull charged right for me. I shifted my weight and shoved my palm forward. A wave of invisible force slammed into the bull, throwing it back. The beast crashed on the ground as if it were solid. The tendrils coming off its body lashed and writhed. The creature roared out its distorted cry again, a black ichor substance spitting from what should have been a mouth. Whatever this was, it reminded me of the possessed beings Ingrid commanded, but as if this one had shed its mortal skin or something.

The creature clamored to its feet, only to be barreled over by something just as large. I blinked. The newcomer looked like a wrestler on steroids with horns, tusks, and red skin. Reinforcements had finally arrived, and in the form of Kenta, an oni who had only been a resident for a few weeks.

He threw all of his impressive weight into beating the shit out of this shadow creature and then lighting it on fire.

Kenta wasn't the only one to come to our aid. I sensed it—a quick blip in my mind just before Diego appeared in the sky above us as a dragon. He descended, crushing three more creatures and whipping his tail into a group of fae hunters. Spear-shaped fire magic lanced out of his body, striking down some of the pesky lizard-things attacking Kirby.

Nature magic flew out of the forest at a greater intensity. Several fae and elves from the sanctuary had arrived, including Sean, and stood just inside the wards where they'd be safe from the iron weapons.

Blood magic rained down from above. Mia's brilliant wings shimmered like a beacon of defiance.

Gunfire rang through the forest. Tyr charged past the wards, Aya hot on his heels, firing his assault rifle and tossing one to Kirby without breaking stride. The added firepower was the last we needed.

"Fall back!" someone called.

The fae hunters turned tail, but before they could get very far, black tendrils of magic shot out of the ground and coiled around their bodies, binding and suspending them above the ground. *No…*

I'd really hoped I was wrong. I wanted it to be my imagination seeing that first bit of dark magic, and it was another cultist blending in with these hunters who was using the Malsumis minions.

A low *tsking* sound sent tension rolling down my spine. "Now, now, you can't leave yet. We've just gotten started."

A tall, middle-aged appearing woman with red hair walked into view. Her gray eyes, which seemed even darker than the last time we me, found me, and an unsettling smile spread her red lips. "There you are, my dear. You're looking well."

My grip on my weapons tightened. I took her presence in, unable to formulate any words. The last I'd seen her, Fen and Angel had bitten off her arms and strange black ichor had spewed out of her like blood. Now here she was, as if nothing had ever happened.

Well, not nothing. Her arms were back, but they weren't natural. They were impossibly black, like they'd been fashioned from the ichor of her magic.

"No warm welcome for your dear mother, Astrid?" She tsked. "Didn't I raise you better than that?"

My jaw clenched. My knuckles turned white from the grip on my weapons. "You have no right to say that after what you've done to me."

She shook her head. "You always were a stubborn child. I'm here to make amends."

Ingrid gestured to the captured fae hunters. "Look, I brought you new toys. I promise they'll be a lot of fun. That one there even knows a great deal of important information about other supernatural hunters. I know you'll have a lot of fun getting all that juicy information out of him."

She smiled wider, her eyes crazed. "And I brought you more friends. Only the best for my precious only daughter."

I shook my head slowly. "Do you really think I'm that stupid?"

She blinked too innocently and gasped, pressing her hand to her chest. "Astrid, why would you think such a thing? I know my actions in the past have put us at odds, but know I did what I thought was best at the time. And look at how much you've grown because of me. A protector of your own sanctuary!"

Muninn landed on my shoulder. He wasn't the only one. Huginn, who'd I'd been vaguely aware of in the chaos, uncharacteristically perched on my other shoulder. Their shared distaste for this woman wrapped around my senses through the bond.

Both hissed at my mother, which made her grin. "And look, you stole Odin's familiars from right under his nose. And you added a beautiful curse on top of that."

I shifted my weight, my unease growing stronger. *How does she know about the curse?*

She tapped her lips. "And you stripping him of his power? Oh, Astrid, I couldn't be more proud of you. I knew you'd see the importance of our work."

"I am not you," I said, my voice as cold and hard as I could muster while my heart beat erratically in my chest.

"No?" A wicked grin pulled her lips. "But, dear, what you did is no different than our own mission. You know this. You can't deny it."

I set my jaw. I wouldn't let her words get to me. I'd had my doubts and worries about that decision. It plagued me, knowing I had done something so similar to what my enemies were doing that it toed a dangerous line. But I couldn't allow her poisonous words to rile those doubts up.

I'm not her.

Ingrid clapped her hands together and let out a disgustingly sweet and fake gasp of excitement. "Oh! I have one more gift for you, dear. You're going to really love this one."

She flicked her hand and the magic holding the fae hunters solidified into dark crystals. At the same time, a black mass formed in front of her at her feet. It solidified from a shadowy mass and then dripped away like liquid, revealing a battered man.

My heart stilled, my blood running cold. Both of my ravens snapped their beaks in distaste.

Loki.

THIRTEEN

ASTRID

oki lay limply against Ingrid's legs, his hands bound and his mouth hanging open as he gasped for air. His eyes were nearly rolling into the back of his head. Blood dripped down his skin from open wounds that weren't healing. *What the hell did she do to him?*

Ingrid cackled. "See, Daughter? I know how much you want this one. I went out of my way to find him. I even rendered him powerless to make him a more compliant toy. Aren't you happy?"

I swallowed. *She… took his power away? No. The magic blockers only took magic. That's all they'd succeeded in doing for him. Our blocker for Odin was unique. She's bluffing.*

Loki's eyes slowly moved to focus on me. My pulse skittered. He couldn't speak, but his eyes did the talking for him for once, and for something I couldn't recall him doing in any life of mine—they pleaded for help.

Ingrid gestured to Loki like a prized animal. "Come, take a look. Tell me what you think, my daughter."

I took a cautious step forward, banishing my weapons. Tyr murmured my name in warning, but I ignored him. Months I'd spent hating this man. Months I wanted to see his blood spilled for what I thought he'd done. "You did this… for me?"

"Of course I did. I'd do anything to make up for all our misunderstandings. I just want my daughter to love me. I miss your vibrant smile. I want to hear you call me Mommy again, like you used to when we were all so happy."

My golden magic leaked from my fingers, in their usual tendrils. They crawled along Loki's body, feeling him out. Loki, barely conscious, stared up at me. None of that hate was there. None of that pull from the oath compelled me to revel in any of this.

Hidden within the magic tendrils, one golden strand tried to discreetly heal Loki. *No effect.* I pursed my lips as if I were thinking about this "gift."

"Well?" my mother said. "Do you like your gift, dear? Isn't it wonderful?"

I gently touched Loki's head. "I think…"

My fingers curled into a tight fist and my magic flared as I turned on her. "You're shit at manipulating a therapist, and all your love-bombing has made me therapissed!"

My tendril magic shot toward her as golden spears. She jumped back, her black magic springing from her body. Black and gold clashed.

Ingrid scowled, her fury sparking in her eyes. "Astrid! This is no way to behave toward your mother. I'm trying to—"

A fist flew out of nowhere, slamming her square in the jaw. She cried out and stumbled back, her magic stopping her from falling. I blinked at Baldur. He breathed hard, as if he'd run all the way here—which I didn't doubt he had—and he glared at Ingrid with more hatred than I could recall ever seeing from him.

Blood oozed from a cut in his knuckle, the wound already healing. I hoped he'd handled the pain okay. If he was lucky, his anger and adrenaline had numbed him to most of it.

"How dare you," Ingrid snarled, holding her face. "Who do you think you are?"

"I am Baldur Odinson, and I'm looking forward to wrapping my hands around your neck, witch, for daring to snuff out my sunshine."

I swallowed and shifted my weight. Loki chuckled and mumbled something about Baldur being a predictable puppy… or something like that. He was slurring.

Ingrid's furious expression shifted to surprise, then crazed joy. "It happened, just as she predicted."

Baldur repositioned himself more in front of me to act as a shield, when she held her hands out to me and took a step forward. "Don't come closer."

She grinned. "So obedient, just like the dragon and other god. You've done wonderfully, my daughter."

My stomach churned. I didn't like the way her gaze flicked from Baldur up to Diego, who loomed over us, and then back to Baldur. It was a lustful gaze, but in a greedy-power-type of way.

Ingrid stretched her arms out. "Look at the power you possess. To control a dragon and to bring back the dead—a god, no less—this is the power she expected of you."

My fingers curled. "I don't care what some corrupted shit goddess thinks of me."

"Oh, Astrid. These false gods have polluted your mind. Malsumis is wonderful!"

My lip curled. "You poison the magical community."

Ingrid shook her head. "No, dear. We're remaking it. Just like you can."

She gestured to Baldur. "Look at what you can do. Come with me, and we can reshape this world together in our image, as mother and daughter."

I clenched my jaw, emotions twisting in my chest. How long I had wished to hear such words from her when I was younger. How long I had wished my mother loved me. "You're not my mother."

She tsked and wagged her finger. "My dear, you can't change who you are or where you come from. I am your mother, and I am so proud of your power. She is, too. Malsumis will be so delighted to see you finally join us like you should have long ago. She wants us to be a family, like we were always meant to be."

I stiffened, and murmurs rolled through everyone behind me. "You're delusional."

An unsettling grin slipped up her lips and she held out her hand. My magic, the tendrils lazily swaying around me, twitched and I jerked when her power met mine. Unpleasant oppression ghosted over me like an invisible touch. It wound around my magic, and the black tendrils mixed into my gold weaved their way out and toward Ingrid.

She fondly caressed the magic, her unsettling smile widening. "I see your resistance to accept the truth, but I can help you, Astrid, I promise. We're so proud of you, your grandmother and me."

Ice chilled my veins. I'd questioned my dark magic ever since it manifested. I'd secretly feared it meant something more when I'd first witnessed hers. But this… this wasn't something I ever wanted to hear.

"You lie," Tyr snarled.

Ingrid chuckled and her magic came out of her body just like mine, in tendrils of black wisps. "I do not lie. Her beautiful magic is a gift from my mother, Malsumis, the supreme goddess. A blessed gift." Her eyes shifted to the golden parts of my magic. "One that needs a little purification to see its ultimate purpose, but that will be easy for us to do, my dear. Come with me, and I can show you so much. You'll see your true purpose."

My lip curled and I yanked my magic away from her. "My true purpose is here, protecting people from you and a deranged goddess."

She shook her head and sighed. "You're too worked up to talk to right now. I knew I should have waited until we were in a better setting to tell you all these truths. No matter. You'll come around soon enough. I'll be waiting for you, dear, with open arms when you're finally ready to allow me to help you. Enjoy your gifts."

Ingrid stepped away, the creatures she brought with her rushing toward her and her magic. The black tendrils swirled around them all until they were cloaked in blackness, and then they disappeared.

Silence followed.

I breathed as steadily as I could while my mind raced. *She's lying. I'm not related to Malsumis. My magic is this way because of something else.*

But even as I tried to convince myself of this, I knew the only one who was lying was me.

Shaking it off, I refocused my attention. All of that could wait.

My ravens took off, and I grabbed Loki by his tattered shirt collar. I exclaimed, to everyone but no one, "Take care of the refugees and deal with the hunters. I'll deal with Loki."

I didn't wait for anyone to confirm. I teleported us to the great room of the house.

Loki listed sideways. I tightened my grip on him, using what pathetic amount of strength I had, even with all the strength training I did, to keep him from crashing into the coffee table. "I need help!"

Xavier and Ùna ran in. Xavier helped me heave Loki's dead-weight ass onto the couch. I hovered my hands over his body, my golden magic springing forth and crawling over his wounds. I felt the healing attempts, and then it failed.

"I need the medical kit," I said.

Ùna rushed off. She returned a moment later, a large medical bag hauled over her shoulder. I tore into the bag, taking out the antiseptic and hemostatic dressings. Despite my love for my healing magic, in a moment like this I was happy I'd had first aid and trauma response training from all the search-and-rescue I'd done.

I instructed Xavier and Ùna where they could help staunch the bleeding. As we did, I collected a vial of his blood, knowing we'd need it for testing.

Loki's head rolled and I tapped his cheek. "Hey, stay with us, Loki."

His eyes fluttered and then he laughed in what I could only guess was delirium. "Therapissed. You really said that to that woman. Was that really the best you had in that moment?"

I gave his disheveled self a once-over before grabbing a needle and suture thread. "I don't think you're in any condition to be lecturing me about wordplay when you look like you're trying to slide into death's DMs."

He laughed some more, before devolving into a coughing fit.

I held up the needle so he could see it. "I don't have time for numbing agents. This is going to hurt."

Loki grinned lazily. "Don't pretend you don't know we both like a little pain."

I shook my head and focused on stitching a deep gash on his chest closed. Immortal skin was tougher than a human's; it made something like this a lot more difficult—not that I could recall a time a god needed healing to this degree. Magical weapons and certain types of magic could slow down the process, resulting in scarring if magical healing wasn't used to counter the slowdown, but self-healing never stopped completely.

He winced when the needle slid through his skin. "Why are you helping me?"

"Because, unlike you, I'm not an evil dickhead."

He grunted. "Says the woman who went berserk and tried to cleave my head from my shoulders. I know my handsome face would have made the perfect addition to your mantle, but I do prefer to keep it attached to my body."

I shook my head. "Blood oaths make us do rash things."

"Blood—" He rolled his eyes. "You were supposed to be the sensible one, not the meathead with impulse control issues when his redhead witch isn't around to keep him in line."

I shrugged. "Yeah, well, not all of us can be perfect and not vow an oath of revenge while in distress after finding out someone important to you is dead, after regaining your past-life memories all at once."

Loki blinked slowly and then closed his eyes. "Stop trying to confuse me. I've lost too much blood."

"Wow, did the mighty Loki admit I out-brained him?"

He rolled his eyes and I snickered.

Xavier turned away from his gauze patchwork. "You're back."

I looked to see Dad putting his hunting rifle on the counter. "Tyr disappeared on me all of a sudden, and I only just got a text response from Aya about what happened. What do you need now that the fight is over?"

I held up the vial of Loki's blood. "I need this tested."

Dad narrowed his eyes at Loki. "I should ask, but I think it's best I just let this go."

"I appreciate your discretion," Loki said. "I'd rather find out what that psycho witch did to me."

My father's brows knitted together. "So would I."

He took the vial and disappeared, Xavier going with him. Ùna wasn't sure how else to help, so she went to fetch some energy replenishers for Loki.

"Speaking of her, your mother is a piece of work," Loki said.

I grunted. "That's an understatement."

"What did she do to me?"

"Some sort of magic blocker is my best guess. But this is a first for it to be used on a god. What the hell did my egg donor do to you? How did she get you for that matter?"

He blew out a breath. "She ambushed me shortly after I left our little tea party in that warehouse."

I pursed my lips. *He'd been her prisoner for three days?* "Did she want anything in particular out of you?"

"Fuck if I know. After she injected me with something, her lines of questioning and choice of torture were as chaotic as Malsumis' magic flowing through her. The only thing I really learned was that she really enjoys waterboarding and—"

A muscle in my neck twitched when his lips quirked. "You say anything about a part of my magic being similar to hers and I'll slit your throat."

He seemed to ponder the threat a moment and then thought better of that line of thought.

The front door banged open and Baldur, Tyr, and Diego rushed in.

Loki's eyes jumped to each man before settling on Baldur. He smirked. "I'm quite pleased at how well you met my expectations."

"And why are you pleased by that?" I asked. "Why would you want me to bring Baldur back after what you did?"

He didn't respond, only grinned at me like a kid who wasn't sorry for being caught stealing from the cookie jar.

I wasn't biting. "You could tell me, or I, too, can become an evil dickhead and let you die. The Valkyrie side of me doesn't care either way, and the vengeance oath I made would rejoice to see more of your blood spilled."

He watched me in silence for a moment and then shrugged. "Fine, if you want the answers that badly. I had an idea on how to thwart

Baldur's prophecy. It was simple to try out, and wouldn't have taken long. If I was wrong, nothing would happen. If I was right, moving his soul in and out of his body would have been quick, and we'd have our answers about these senseless prophecies."

"Senseless, and yet you've spent your entire existence trying to thwart one about you," Tyr said.

I shot him a look to be quiet and listen. This was Loki's turn to share.

Loki ignored Tyr's quip. "Baldur agreed to my plan. And, as I predicted, it'd gone smoothly—until the boar of a god here interrupted and messed up my carefully laid plans."

His eyes briefly flicked to Tyr before returning to me. "I did make an attempt to place his soul back into his body after the others entombed him, but it was too late. The small window I had was gone. So, I kept his soul and body safe until the winged witch of the next prophecy arrived to fulfill it, if it was true. And here we are."

I pursed my lips. The moment Loki learned I was back from the dead and had ascended to a Valkyrie status, he would have known this path would happen. That's why he'd been so eager to give me the bracer. Maybe he'd rather have handed it over, but throwing it at me to pacify my rage worked for him too. "Baldur, are you avenged?"

"If he weren't already bleeding out on the floor, I'd say that needed to be arranged for his arrogance," Baldur said. "But, as it stands, yes, you being the one to bring me back more than satisfies my avengement."

A grip I hadn't realized was squeezing me released, and a sensation of peacefulness washed over me. That burning need to avenge Baldur, even after I brought him back, vanished. I could breathe again like I never remembered being able to.

I threaded my needle again. "Why don't you three go check on the progress on settling the new refugees or handling the fae hunters Ingrid dropped on our doorstep?"

Baldur opened his mouth to speak in protest, no doubt because they'd already done that, but Diego held up a hand. He understood the reason behind my request. As long as the others were around, I'd struggle to get anything else out of Loki. There was no guarantee he'd cooperate as it was, but this increased my chances.

Ùna returned with coconut water in a box with a straw, as well as a steaming bowl of bone broth, which she also provided a straw for. Loki's eyebrow arched when she held both out to him.

"You are to consume all of it before I go do other things," Ùna said. "Hurry up, I don't have all day."

I pressed my lips together and pretended to concentrate on my stitching as I tried not to laugh. Loki, though, did chuckle. "You've become bolder, I see, Ùna."

"I've done a lot of healing—something you could benefit from. Now drink up."

In the sassiest way anyone could manage, Loki sipped his water. He was far too amused with this situation.

True to her word, Ùna remained until he'd consumed both the drink and the broth. "I'm going to knit now, Astrid. If you need me, shout."

She then disappeared, using the magic around the house as a pseudo-fae doorway like Xavier did. Loki blinked bemusedly. "I can't say I understand what that was all about."

"The coconut water and bone broth will help with all this blood loss," I said.

"That's not what I meant." He then waved his hand. "Never mind. Care to share why you want me alone?"

I squinted at a particularly difficult point on his arm. "Why are you so suspicious?"

"Because it's you. I'll admit you're one of the most unpredictable women I've ever been acquainted with."

I grinned. "I'll take that as a compliment. And I'm sorry to burst your paranoid bubble, but I'm not turning this into some interrogation session. I sent the guys away because I didn't need them hovering over my shoulder while I stitched up a god worse than an overworked war medic."

He laughed. "Not much of a seamstress in this life, are you?"

I grunted. "Nor am I the best at cooking. Baking, yes. Woodworking, also yes. Needlework, not so much, which is why I'd rather be using my healing magic if I could."

Silence fell over us for a long moment while I worked on the gash in his arm. Loki broke it. "You really have nothing to ask me?"

I shrugged. "I've got plenty to ask, though I doubt you'll answer me."

"Humor me."

My eyes flicked up to him briefly, meeting his expectant stare. "What exactly did you tell people when you were accused of killing Baldur with mistletoe?"

He grunted. "Ah, yes, mistletoe. Of course, that's what I killed him with. I guess he wasn't as perfect as Odin claimed if he could be taken down by a measly plant."

The sarcasm leaked so heavily from him I had to stop my work as I rolled with laughter. It took me a moment to calm down, and Loki watched me with bemusement. "And you never once thought to try and correct them?"

"Oh, I thought about it, then didn't care enough to try. We both know with my reputation it'd be a waste of breath. Besides, I don't care what others think of me."

"No, of course you don't." I tried to match his sarcasm. "That's why you didn't listen to Fen and Baldur's heckling when you were challenged to fuck an unrestrained unicorn."

He chuckled. "Last I remember, you found that dare hilarious."

When Tyr had first told me the story before I had recovered my memories, I thought it a crazy tale. After I recovered my memories, I learned I'd been there, which was part of the reason why Tyr had been willing to share that real truth with me so soon.

I shook my head. "I thought you all idiotic and foolish."

"Oh, come now, little Valkyrie, you found it fun, don't you lie."

I chuckled. "All right, fine, it was a little fun. And the end result of you getting Sleipnir out of the deal was the best part. He was a cute kid. Fun adult as well."

Memories played through my mind. Fun and outrageous times those were. "Don't know how he turned out so well considering you're his parent."

Loki pressed his hand to his chest. "Me? A terrible parent? More like I have ungrateful kids."

I rolled my eyes. "Yeah, that's totally it."

"Don't try to therapize me, witch."

I dabbed a nasty-looking wound with antiseptic. "I wasn't planning on it. Just pointing out it's interesting that all of your kids, who are still alive, that is, don't have much association with you. How is Sleipnir?"

Loki was quiet for a long moment. "I don't know. I haven't spoken to him in centuries."

I could poke him more about it, but it wasn't hard for me to see the pain he tried to hide. Loki was fully aware of how much he'd fucked up. But he was too prideful to consider fixing anything.

Loki waved his hand dismissively. "If you're curious, you could always track him down. I'm sure he'd *love* to see you again."

I chuckled, knowing that interaction would be quite interesting, given how much of a charmer Sleipnir had become when he hit adulthood. "Maybe I will."

Dad walked into the room suddenly. I looked up and smiled. "Welcome back. What do you have?"

"It's definitely a magic blocker."

I pursed my lips. "That's it? My healing magic should work on him if it was just a magic blocker."

Dad nodded. "It might be a stronger dose than what's been used so far to our knowledge, but Loki has only been cut off from his magic, nothing else."

Loki leaned back on the couch. "So, the rumors are true that your little do-gooder group is making antidotes?"

Dad eyed Loki with outward suspicion. "Are you sure about this, Ace?"

I smiled at him and held out my hand. "Trust me."

He blew out a breath and placed three capped syringes in my hand. Something else touched my hand, but then vanished the moment it made contact with my skin. I didn't outwardly react. Dad then backed away. "Do you need me for anything else?"

I could sense his desire to stay and keep an eye on Loki, but I could handle him. "I've got it, Dad. I'll shout if there's trouble."

"Well, then he won't be gone long, since trouble is what I am," Loki said with a smirk.

Dad's lips twisted but he left me to handle the cocky god. And my first task was finding a good spot on his arm to do the injection. Finding and cleaning the spot, I expelled the air bubble from the first syringe and injected the first dose.

"We'll need to wait ten minutes before the next dose." I didn't doubt he'd need all three doses.

"Very well, then we can use that time to talk about why you don't plan to use those therapist skills on me."

My brow quirked. "Do I need to?"

"You have the infamous Loki—most would die to have me lounge in their client chair for them to *fix*. Yet you claim not to want that."

I nodded. "That's correct. I'm not them. I may have my thoughts, but they are just that. I have no need to dive deeper with you and help you save yourself, when you so clearly don't believe you need anything."

He leaned back. "Tell me, Therapist Valkyrie, what would you diagnose me with?"

"Most would diagnose you with narcissistic personality disorder and antisocial personality disorder. I would say you're an egocentric individual parading as a narcissist with ASPD to hide what you don't want others to know."

"And what is that?"

"You're afraid."

He grunted. "And, pray tell, what am I afraid of?"

My lip quirked. "That is the question, isn't it?"

Loki set his jaw for a moment then his flippant nature resumed. "And tell me, what's your non-professional opinion of me?"

"That you are the supreme dickbag of all dickheads who really needs to get laid and eat a Snickers."

"No head pats?"

I smirked. "Head pats are for good boys and girls only."

Loki grinned. "Just ask Davyn how good I am."

I shook my head. "I think he'd rather eat lava rocks than discuss his past with you."

The two hadn't been overly open about their relationship back then, but it wasn't much of a secret, either. And of course, with Loki after Azzie, it put Davyn in an even grumpier mood when Loki was mentioned in his presence.

I tested my healing magic on his arm when the ten minutes were up. Nothing worked. So I injected him with the second dose.

"Why are you doing this?" Loki asked. "Why would you help me? We're not friends. I've not been kind to those you call friends, which I won't apologize for."

"Some might say it's because I'm naïvely nice. Some might say it's because I'm a bleeding-heart." I grinned. "But really, it's mostly because it's a big giant fuck-you to Ingrid and Malsumis. Plus, my conscience is clear having you as our first guinea pig for these antidotes."

"I have the pleasure of being your first? I'm honored." Loki tried to hide behind the sarcasm, but I wasn't fooled. He wasn't quick enough to hide the alarm that flashed through his eyes.

I rolled my eyes and left to find a wash cloth. I did and ran it under the faucet. When I returned, I began wiping his arm with the warm cloth.

The blood washed away, and beneath where there had been a small wound not worthy of stitching up, there was now only pink skin. Seemed the serum was finally working. Not fast by the looks of his larger wounds, but my healing may just work on him now.

"You are both impulsive and collected." Loki said as he watched the golden light of my magic wrap around his bicep. "Dualities that make no sense, especially in the way you wield them. How does Tyr control a woman like you? It's clear the other men you've bewitched don't control you, but a god like Tyr…"

I shook my head and chuckled, making him frown. "He doesn't. He embraces the woman I am. And because of that, there's no need for a power struggle."

I glanced up at him, a smirk on my lips. "Sometimes, Loki, being on your knees is a lot of fun."

The air in the room changed as Loki scowled. It was inevitable. I hadn't thought of a better way to bring this up. Cajoling him like

I used to in my other life was my best option, but this was Loki. There wasn't a moment during all of this he let his guard down. He'd calculated various new outcomes every time we drew breath, assuming the worst from me. It was what he'd come to know. I pitied him for that.

"What is it you want, witch? I don't wish to waste time on games. Your feeble attempt at kindness did little to endear me to you."

I shook my head. "Small talk is hardly manipulation attempts, Loki. You of all gods will know this. But, since you are so eager to be done here, we'll discuss what you owe me."

His scowl remained, and he patiently waited. He'd anticipated there was a catch somewhere here, even if I'd tried to play off his earlier inquiry.

"Saving your life comes at the price of a life debt. I didn't have to save you from Ingrid. I could have allowed her to do whatever she pleased with you. So, under the rules of the old ways, I claim that debt as mine."

Loki's eyes narrowed, but he didn't argue. A trickster he may be, but not even he would contest this debt.

"The first two shots of magic blocker antidote are free. I'm not in the business of saving people only to allow them to bleed out on my floor. However, with the power of the serum used on you, you're fairly powerless still. You have a muted version of your accelerated healing, and I believe you've got a little bit of magic, though not much."

I held up the needle for the third dose. "This last shot, however, comes at a price."

He snorted. "And you plan to cash in your life debt for Azzie in exchange for that. Predictable and stupid—"

"You think you know everything Loki, when you don't."

Loki tipped his head, his lips slightly quirked, as if my words amused him. I knew the kind of power I now held over Loki with a life debt. As much as I wanted this bullshit to end between him and Azzie, with her not dying in the process, I couldn't use the life debt to do it.

"Your egocentric ways are showing. Of course you'd think I'd be foolish enough to waste a life debt in that way. But I'm not. That life debt remains mine. You can't get out of that one. This third dose comes in the form of a deal. And I know how much you love deals, Loki."

He regarded me a moment. "I'm listening."

"This antidote in exchange for leaving Azzie alone." I let silence hang in the air for a moment. "You will cease these attempts to kill her or have others kill her on your behalf. You will cease trying to destroy her in any way. Agree to these terms, and you'll be restored to your former self."

Loki chuckled. "Really? That's your play? Fine, fine. No more attempts on Azzie's life."

I shook my head. "No."

His brow furrowed. "No?"

"You will agree to my exact terms, or you don't get this."

He smirked. "And who says I won't be able to find an antidote somewhere else?"

I shrugged. "If you want to go through that hassle instead of agreeing to my terms, you're welcome to. But you will agree to the exact wording of my terms, or no antidote."

The two of us watched each other, not blinking. Then with lightning reflexes, he slapped my hand and snatched the syringe. "Sorry, witch, but I don't make those kinds of deals."

Loki stabbed the needle into his arm, injecting the serum inside. I sat there, watching him. He grinned as he flicked the empty syringe aside. "Next time, dear, you're going to have to be a better negotiator. Or, at the very least, not be so careless with your bargaining chip. You want to know my secret to making it out alive with that unicorn encounter? Never allow anyone to top you. The moment you do, it'll be your undoing."

He stood, straightening his ruined clothes. "Now, while our chat has been rather stimulating, I must be off."

Then he was gone.

I didn't move for a moment, and then let out a long breath and slouched against the couch. Weariness quickly set in. I glanced up when my guys entered. I figured Diego teleported them back in, out of sight in case I needed backup. I was also sure Dad was hanging around with them.

"Sorry it didn't work out, Sunshine," Baldur said. "It was a good attempt."

"Try not to beat yourself up," Tyr said. "We all know how difficult it can be to outsmart—"

He stopped when I burst out with raucous laughter.

"Valkyrie?" Tyr prompted when my laughter continued.

I calmed myself, though a few giggles continued to surface. "Why does everyone underestimate me? Is there something about me that screams *clueless woman who can't do anything right* or something?"

Tyr opened his mouth then shut it, looking to the others, who were just as perplexed.

I grinned and manifested a syringe filled with antidote. "I'm not a moron. I may not be as clever as Loki, but I understand how that man works."

Diego and Baldur laughed and Tyr crossed his arms. "What did you give him?"

"A placebo."

"Clever, Cielo, very clever," Diego praised. "I don't know how you two managed it with Loki right in front of you, but I shouldn't be surprised."

Dad and I had gone through enough together we could figure out what the other was thinking without speaking most of the time. Not only had he verbalized only three syringes when he'd handed me four, one had a different cap color. I knew then he'd already assumed I'd want to use this situation to my advantage, and since we could easily use magic to hide the real last dose from Loki with him unable to sense it in his state, it was the only chance we'd get to try to get a leg up on him.

"I knew weaseling out the deal I wanted was a long shot," I said. "But I had to try. Is it ideal that he's gone and we're no closer to keeping Azzie safe from him? No. But, at least we've bought some time while he's distracted figuring out what I pulled over on him and he tries a different way to get his magic back."

"And we always have that clever life debt if needed," Baldur grinned. "I'm glad you enacted that. Even if you don't use it, it'll piss him off that you've got one on him."

I smirked. That was the idea. It wasn't often a life debt could be fulfilled to its full extent. Most either wasted it on something small, or never used it. I'd rather it be the latter with the satisfaction of annoying the prick, than waste it.

I yawned, the last of the adrenaline pumping through me wearing off. Diego crouched in front of me, his fingers brushing my cheek. "What do you need?"

His smooth voice and soft words wrapped around me like a much-needed comforting hug. I hummed thoughtfully. "Hot chocolate, a fuzzy blanket, cuddles, and a movie. And to not yet talk about what Ingrid told me about Malsumis. I need more time to process that."

He grinned. "We can do that. Do you want me to tell Kirby and Mia raincheck for your plans today, or do you plan to invite them to the movie party? They're waiting in town."

I could sense his hope that I would choose the raincheck option, but I also had a feeling what he wanted to get out of this movie plan. "I have zero energy for sex, so if you're hoping that'll happen, you're going to be sorely disappointed."

He kissed my forehead. "I'll invite them, then."

FOURTEEN

TYR

The hammer gripped in my hand slammed down on the nail harder than necessary. The metal cracked and the head flew off, and the lumber split under the weight of my strike. I snarled and tossed the broken hammer aside. That was the third in the last hour. *Piece of shit.*

I shoved away from my work and paced the length of the living room. My feet pounded in rhythm with my racing heart. My fists clenched and unclenched as if I could release the pent-up energy building inside me.

It'd been like this all morning. I didn't know what was wrong, but my agitation had only gotten worse. I thought if I'd come to our Norway home and worked on something, I'd be able to work it out, but it'd only gotten worse.

The longer I paced, the more the room faded away until the tides of frustration pulled me under. I spiraled, my breathing staggering, almost choking out as if I were drowning.

A soft hand slid over my arm. Astrid's gentle voice sliced through the turmoil. "Tyr?"

Awareness melted the room back into existence. I was in the living room. Astrid stood in front of me, her hands wrapped around my arm. Concern creased the corners of her eyes.

"Tyr?" she said again. "What is it?"

"I…" I closed my eyes. *What am I supposed to say?*

She placed her hands on my chest and pushed against me. I didn't resist, stepping back until I bumped into the couch. She pushed more, this time harder than I expected, and I fell back onto the cushions.

Astrid climbed into my lap, straddling me, and framed my face with her delicate hands. "Talk to me, Tyr."

Calm seeped from her into me through our contact. It kept the chaos at bay, but not well, not like it usually could. "I… don't know what… to say."

"Aya said you snapped at her when she tried to ask you a question, then you stormed off. That was hours ago. I came to check on you when she mentioned it to me."

Besides the party, Astrid had been busy the last few days with all the new refugees, especially gaining the trust of a few after what Ingrid had pulled. It made it difficult for us to see each other. Not even Baldur was getting the time with her that he should, given he'd only been revived for a week.

Even when we found ourselves busy, we all tried to at least have dinner together, but Astrid was also missing meal times. She instead ate late and went to bed. Alone.

I must have been even worse off than I realized for her to take the time to deal with whatever was going on with me. I closed my eyes and tried to force these feelings away. "I'm fine. I'm just agitated. It'll pass. You can—"

Her grip on my face tightened. "Don't you dare dismiss me. Or yourself, for that matter. I'm here for you right now. Talk to me."

The way she gazed up at me, soft yet also desperate, it made my heart clench. I couldn't push her away. I needed her. "Okay, I'm not fine, but I don't know what's wrong. I'm agitated, like I said, but I can't figure out why and that's making it worse. Your magic touch usually helps it go away, but I can feel it trying to push back and explode out."

She caressed my cheeks with her thumbs. "Are you forgetting to do something important?"

"I don't think so."

"Are you neglecting one of your god duties?"

I worked my jaw, thinking. "No? Maybe? I don't think I am, but also I'm not sure. Nothing is coming to mind."

Astrid pursed her lips. "Have you answered prayers recently?"

I nodded. "Last night and this morning."

"Are you not doing something that you feel like you should be? Maybe, like, judging a crime or injustice?"

My eyes squinted as I thought. That didn't feel quite right.

"Have you not engaged in enough acts of war?"

I froze, something within me reacting. *Is that it?*

Astrid tipped her head. "Tyr, is that it?"

I shook my head. "No, it can't be. I've engaged in skirmishes several times this month. They were for a just cause and we won them all."

"But did those count as battles in the way a war god needs them to?"

My pulse slowed. My Valkyrie was too perceptive to let this go. She was right, they didn't count. Not any more than a brawl at the fight pits did. Those were more like little snacks instead of a meal. Just enough to stave off the hunger, but not filling for the body or soul.

The fight against Odin was the most recent battle that counted for my soul, and before that was our attempt to protect Fensalir. Before that had been the fight with Garmr, and Ingrid and before that... *I don't remember...*

Before I found Astrid, that was for sure. I'd engaged in plenty of battles up until that point, and frequently. But now...

"You haven't engaged in anything having to do with battle, have you?" Astrid said. "At least not to an extent you need to. Why?"

Because—My jaw set and the proper words tanged on my tongue. I couldn't say it. I didn't want her to feel responsible.

"Tyr." The hardness in her voice cracked me like a whip. She wasn't going to accept my silence. She was never happy when I stifled communication. It was a weakness of mine that I wasn't great at working on.

I sucked in a deep breath through my teeth. "I want to be the man you deserve."

Her brow furrowed. "What do you mean?"

I worked my jaw. "This isn't the Viking age anymore. Midgard is different. War isn't a way of life like it used to be. Your current life has experienced one of peace compared to the past."

Astrid's face hardened. "So what?"

I blinked slowly. "So, you deserve someone who isn't as hardened to violence."

"Says who? Who decides what is best for me besides me?" She cradled my face and made me look at her. Fierce determination seared my focus, challenging me—commanding me to not look away. "Tyr, I know what you are. You are a war god. You flourish in all the physical aspects of war. You breathe the brutality and thrive in the victory. War is a piece of you. It's a piece that I acknowledge and embrace. I accepted this back then, and I accept this now. I don't ask Aya to stop engaging in cyberwarfare even though she has a whole other angle to her godhood she could rely on. I would never dare ask you to give up your sword and live a life of peace the world only wishes could exist."

Her eyes softened. "I would never ask you to be anything but who you are: the man I fell in love with… more than once."

My heart thrummed in my chest. *This woman…* I didn't need to question any truths with her. I felt her conviction with each word. Even those last ones she hesitated on for only a moment. It sang to me like the second-most tempting siren—she being the first. This woman would be the death of me, and I'd welcome its cold embrace knowing I lived a blissful life with her by my side.

I brushed her cheek with the back of my fingers. "How did I manage to earn such devotion from the most perfect creature in existence?"

She pursed her lips and thought, the expression a bit sassy and I loved it. "Saving my life from an unjust trial helped."

I grinned and pressed my lips against her forehead. "I thank Creation every day I heard your prayer so loudly."

"I still don't know why you did, but…" she hummed quietly. "I'm glad you did."

She splayed her fingers over my chest. "Now, what do you need?"

I twirled a lock of her gorgeous hair. She and Diego said that to each other a lot. It was a form of communication I was learning better to have with her. She was giving me that chance to communicate my needs with her so she could help. "I need a battle. It doesn't have to be large, but it must have an injustice attached. I must tip the scales."

I felt uneven and out of balance. That was why my temper was out of control. Before Astrid, I did well regulating that of myself. But after her, I relied so heavily on her to carry that burden instead. And when I lost her, in my grief, I never learned to rebalance. I jumped into those chaotic tides, not caring if I'd ever come up for air again.

But now, I had her back, and she was here to help. However, I couldn't do what I'd done before. I couldn't push that burden squarely on her shoulders alone. She could help support me, but it was still up to me to shoulder the weight and hold myself accountable for my balance.

She leaned in and brushed her lips against mine. "Then find us a battle."

"You'll join me?" I couldn't hide my surprise.

"I am your Valkyrie, Tyr. Where you go, I go." She smiled. "I may not be the best fighter, but I am a good support. And I'm getting better at handling this bloodshed stuff, even if I rely too heavily on my past right now to get through it."

My brow arched. How did she do that? "You'll have to explain to me how that works."

"Later," she promised. "For now, we focus on you."

Closing my eyes, I pushed out my senses, doing my best to ignore intrusive thoughts about how much I enjoyed feeling Astrid's thighs pressed against mine. I could indulge in her later.

Battles large and small whispered along my senses. None of them struck me as one I needed right now. Then out of nowhere, it slammed into me.

Fear and hopelessness mixed with fury and determination. A battle of wills, both believing themselves vindicated, but only one spoke truths. The injustice was so palpable I could taste it on my tongue. My eyes flew open. "Found one. It's a decent size. We might need help."

Astrid was already whipping out her phone and tapping her fingers on the screen with more speed and dexterity than I had in my left pinky. At the same time her Valkyrie armor and wings manifested.

My fingers glided along her armored hips as she floated off my lap. Being a Valkyrie, she didn't need any of this against the average weapon, but the look inspired warriors and made her appear more formidable in battle. And I certainly enjoyed the view.

"Okay, Aya and Kirby are gathering others to be on standby."

I suspected I knew some of the people they'd gather—warriors we spent time with, like Starkad and Fen, as well as Bjarke and all of Runavík. Most of them were typically ready to spring in to help at a moment's notice. That was the nature of sanctuary communities, especially allied ones.

While most humans no longer knew of the existence of the magic-gifted and immortals walking among them, there were still plenty who did, and not all of them were pleased we insisted on living. They openly attacked our kind, forcing us to band together and create communities we now called sanctuaries. These sanctuaries seemed to grow in number as well as size every day, and that made them bigger targets, forcing further cooperation between us to ally and come to each other's aid when possible.

"I just need to relay the word and they'll—" she looked up from her phone and blinked. "What?"

I smirked. She was so completely unaware of how perfect she was. "Just enjoying the view."

She rolled her eyes, a smile tugging the corner of her lips. "Let's go. We've got lives to save."

I stood and she glided behind me. Her fingers slid into my hair and she pulled it back, braiding it as I'd been doing lately. Manifesting armor for intimidation purposes, and summoning my axe and shield, while ensuring several guns were in easy mental reach in case they were more useful against this unknown enemy, I enveloped her small hand with my larger one and focused on the aura of battle.

In a blink we went from the quiet cozy room to chaos in a glade. Magic and bullets flew. Steel clashed. People shouted and shifters snarled.

The drums of war thrummed in my veins. Astrid shot into the sky. Instinct pivoted my body, my axe swinging. It slammed into a body with a crunch and squelch. I didn't see my victim to verify they were an enemy, but I didn't need to. Bodies hummed with energy—those allied fell on one side of the scales, while our enemies weighed on the other.

It was a skill I'd developed long ago because you couldn't rely on your eyes to tell you such things, especially when your supposed enemies became allies, which was clearly happening here in this battle.

Pivoting, my axe cleaved through another person, their head severed from their shoulders. A wolf shifter snarled in irritation next to me. I swung my shield arm out, slamming it into someone and knocking them over, then shrugged at the shifter. He snorted and lunged for another enemy, sinking his teeth into their throat and tearing it out.

Magic, Astrid's black and gold power, flew above us. She speared enemies, shielded allies, and occasionally swooped down with her weapon wreathed in golden flames. She wasn't the only one. Kirby, Azzie, and some of the other Valkyries were here.

Witches and other magic-gifted lit up our enemies, but none so well as a woman with wild, dreadlocked red hair and light brown skin with a patchy-whiter skin tone around her hands. A small tattoo accented the underside of one of her amber eyes. It was Bjarke's wife, Alecia. Fire flew from her fingers, engulfing the invaders.

Fen's familiar war howl echoed through the trees. Then the over-sized wolf-god burst out, barreling over a cluster of hunters. Starkad, Arnlaug, Bjarke, and Davyn, transformed into their bestial berserker forms, and tore into the prone enemies.

A fist flew in my peripheral. I spun around to find Baldur pummeling someone.

"You shouldn't be here," I said.

He wasn't in any condition to be fighting like this yet. I'd sparred with him every day since Ingrid made her surprise visit—he wasn't nearly as strong as he once was, and he wasn't adapting to pain easily. This wasn't a place for him until he grew his power again.

Baldur chuckled. "And miss all the fun? I don't think so."

I engaged with a burly man who could compete with a berserker.

That was the only similarity, as he put up little fight against my own superior strength. "It's too risky."

His icy blue eyes met mine, calm and collected as always. "I'm not afraid."

My breathing leveled with the beat of the war drums in my veins. The chaos around us slowed, my senses synchronized.

A broad grin pulled Baldur's lips and he threw himself back into the battle. We moved around each other, each step practiced and deliberate. I drew a rifle, unloading the magazine. Baldur didn't flinch. He didn't recoil or make any deliberate movements to avoid me. The past and present mingled, our bodies harmonizing in the thrill of battle and our trust in each other.

And with each weapon swung, each trigger pulled, each life taken, the scales tipped.

Prayers flooded through my mind. I listened to them in a way only a war god could during the heat of battle, and answered many, their power bolstering me.

"Baldur, flank," Fen's words rolled through the battle and in my mind.

Baldur pivoted around me, and I realized Fen had joined us in the blood bath. Baldur's reposition formed a strong defense between the three of us.

Astrid wrapped her Valkyrie shield around Baldur and focused her magic around us. We'd drawn more attention, our enemies focusing in on the three gods they couldn't kill. Their mistake.

The battlefield blurred. I lost track of those I fought. I didn't think about which weapons I used. Instinct and the drums of war drove me. The only things I was constantly aware of were Astrid and my two friends by my side.

And then it was over.

My breath came in heavy bursts, and perspiration and blood dampened my skin. My body hummed with the power of victory, prayers, and justice. Baldur stretched next to me, an enormous smile on his face. He breathed as hard as me and his eyes glowed from the prayers that came his way, a relatively unique physical reaction he had to high volumes of prayers.

We'd wanted to go slowly with his reintroduction to the world. Partly for his safety, but also because as far as the world was concerned, there was no resurrection magic. The last thing we wanted was others trying to replicate our efforts without knowing all the facts on how it actually worked for our situation and causing issues. Hel, we had enough of those when others found out Astrid was reincarnated and tried to force us to explain so they could do the same.

But Baldur's decision to join appeared to be the best choice so far. As a god, he needed that power boost more than anything. Direct prayers were going to be his major source of power until he could make more domain claims for passive power boosts.

Aya and I were working on ways for him to claim empty domains. Baldur found a few unclaimed pockets here and there, most small, but it was a start, and better than none. And he had a feeling who had his former pocket, so we planned to have a discussion with that god to see if they'd be willing to relinquish the claim.

But all that still required more time. The more Baldur learned about the current world, and we figured out which gods still existed and which had faded away, leaving larger openings for claim, the better chance we'd have at finding him what he needed.

I lifted my gaze to the Valkyries hovering in the sky. They surveyed the battlefield littered with bodies. But it was Astrid who held my attention hostage.

The late evening sun shining over the trees caught in her feathers, bathing her in a stunning, blazing glow that matched the fire still burning on her weapon. I marveled at her, my magnificent Valkyrie, flame of my heart.

After another heartbeat of silence, all the Valkyries descended. They walked among the dead, bending down and touching certain bodies they deemed worthy. It didn't matter which side of the battle the fallen had been on—their Valkyrie nature didn't pick sides.

Each of the ladies reacted differently to taking a soul. Astrid's magic flared each time, and for a blip, a soul magically manifested, just like it had when she'd taken Officer Rory's son to Fólkvangr. And for every soul she took, the limper her wings became, as if the weight of the souls weighed her down. The same thing also happened to the other ladies, but it wasn't as noticeable. I suspected this was due to how many more Astrid was taking on. It was common for the silver-winged Valkyries to be the last to leave the battlefield, shouldering the burden of carrying the most souls.

"What are they doing?" someone asked.

I turned to a boy, no older than fifteen, wearing the colors of a fae hunter but the aura of an ally. *They really like to start them young.* "Doing what Valkyries do, taking souls to Valhalla and Fólkvangr."

"But there are no more Valkyries," he said.

"There are, they're just low in numbers." Best not to get into the specifics of how Kirby could make them. While it wasn't a closely guarded secret, this wasn't the setting to be spreading that information around. "Why did you turn on the fae hunters?"

He didn't answer right away, his eyes focused on the Valkyries. Eventually he sighed, his shoulders slumping. "I was raised with them telling us how bad non-humans were. They told me it was fae who killed my parents and that they'd raise me to avenge their deaths and protect others from suffering the same pain."

He'd be a superhero. What kid didn't want to be that? It was the same rhetoric TOM fed Kirby, Magnus, and Dahlia when they took them from their foster homes to be raised as soldiers.

"But after a while, I noticed things that didn't make sense. Every time I questioned it, I'd be reprimanded and expected to just do as I was told." He shook his head. "Then, when we started being trained on how to use counter-magic artifacts, things started falling apart for many of us. They told us humans who wield magic were also enemies, so of course using what they said was wrong didn't make sense to us."

Extremism did tend to breed hypocrisy, and it was well known that supernatural hunters used these artifacts. Who knew exactly how they were obtaining them. Naturally, raids and purges would be one source, but artifacts could be bought and sold if you knew where to get them. They weren't nearly as powerful as gifted ones, but that didn't mean they wouldn't be useful.

The boy shook his head. "Over the last few months it got worse, until last night they brought a fae to our camp. She was defenseless and frightened, nothing like we'd been told fae were. They wanted to use her as a live demonstration on how to kill fae. Adrian had enough and tried to stop it."

His face paled. "They shot him. Instead of trying to convince him he was being deceived or anything, they flat out called him a traitor and shot him in the chest."

The scales tipped as this boy told his horrific story. I watched the emotions play on his face as he lost himself to his memories. It was the same look all had when they witness horrible acts—the look of someone who needed the healing touch of a particular Valkyrie.

As if summoned, red hair glided past me, brilliant wings trailing behind her. Astrid placed a gentle, glowing hand on the teen's chest and gently hushed him in a soothing tone.

The tightness in his face smoothed, and his breathing evened out. "Chaos erupted in the camp after that and I don't remember much. I remembered some of us grabbed Adrian and the fae woman and we ran. She brought us here, and we tried to warn them of what was coming."

His lip quivered and he shook his head, unable to go on anymore.

Astrid smiled at him, wiping away a tear that broke loose. "You did a brave thing. It takes great strength to stand against everything you were told in order to do what is right."

"He was my friend," the boy whispered.

"And he still lives," a scratchy old voice said.

We turned to see an old woman hobbling our way by way of a large walking stick.

Hope filled the teen's eye. "Really?"

She nodded, her gray eyes solemn. "But he's not long for this world if we don't get a more experienced healer to tend to him. I hate to ask this of you, Valkyrie of Tyr, after everything you all have done to aid us, but—"

Astrid wrapped her hand around the woman's that grasped her walking stick. "Lead me to him. Kirby and the others can tend to the wounds of anyone else."

A quick glance told me they had already taken that initiative.

"You'd do that for us?" the boy said. "After everything…"

The woman tapped her staff. "Just as trees and flowers have no choice where they take up root, we do not choose who we are born to and raised by. You, however, were given a chance to break away from all that, and you made that choice. That accounts for more than you realize. But we can talk about that more once the injured are saved."

She pointed toward the town and gave Astrid directions. Astrid grabbed the teen boy and shocked the poor kid by flying off with him.

The woman watched them go before looking to me and Baldur. "Thank you, again. There is no amount of gratitude that can be given for what you've done. I don't know how much longer my magic would have held out had you not come to our aid. With age comes great power, but also a weaker body."

Baldur looked to me. "How did you know this assault was transpiring?"

"Astrid convinced me to search for a battle to cure my irritability."

The woman snickered. "Smart woman. I expect no less from the solar witch."

I tipped my head. "What did you call her?"

Her brow rose. "Solar witch, of course. Before she was called your wingless Valkyrie, which seems to no longer be the case, she was titled as the solar witch. Her story is one of legend and told in many covens. The rumors of her return were surprising to all of us."

Baldur and I shared a glance. I didn't know about that title. I'd have to talk to her about that. If that were true, that was an important bit of information to have known long ago.

"What else can we help with?" Baldur asked the witch.

She nodded absently as she thought. "I believe there are a few things we can help each other with. Come."

FIFTEEN

TYR

The evening passed quickly. We helped with refortifying the sanctuary, and we established an alliance.

Hearing of our fight against Malsumis and our attempts to thwart Ragnarök, as well as our recent success with the magic blocker antidote, made for a favorable chip on the table.

Our new allies brought magic, particularly in the form of imbued artifacts, as well as fighting numbers. Plenty of shifters, fae, and magic-gifted were eager to join the fight if it meant Midgard was safer for our kind.

The talks opened us up for other alliances, as well, through contacts individuals had. The more united we were as a community, the better.

As the talks wound down, the energy in the town ramped up. A celebration for the new alliance and to honor those who fought, and those who died honorably. I was all for a celebration, the thrill of victory and justice pulsing through every fiber of my being, but Astrid decided she wanted to bow out. The events of the day had taken their toll on her. So, I went with her. I didn't feel like straying far from her.

We now stood in the living room of the Norway home again.

Astrid yawned and rubbed tired eyes. Her wings hung limply in her exhaustion, yet she didn't pull them back. None of the Valkyries had through the evening.

I rested my hand on her upper back. "How are you doing?"

She chuckled. "That's what I'm supposed to be asking you. This was a hell of a lot more than I anticipated when I told you to find a war to fight in."

I tucked a finger under her chin and tipped her head up. "It was exactly what I needed. I haven't felt this at peace in some time. Thank you."

She smiled sweetly. "Good."

"Now, tell me how you're feeling."

She blew out a breath. "I'm exhausted. I used up almost all my magic. Plus talking to so many people. And then there was taking on those souls. That saps me more than my magic does, and there were a lot of souls in that battle."

I nodded. It was a heavy burden to bear.

My finger trailed the hard ridge of her wing. Astrid gasped, her back arching and eyes going wide. She jerked away and I retracted my hand.

My pulse rose into my throat. "Did I hurt you?"

She took a long breath and shook her head before glancing over her shoulder to her wing. "No. I was just surprised."

I realized her cheeks had turned a shade of pink. I grinned. "Sensitive, are they?"

Her color turned red. "I didn't realize that was a thing with wings. Maybe it's because I'm so exhausted. Or maybe they're always that way. I don't usually walk around with my wings out."

I tipped my head. "Why don't you?"

She blinked up at me, her eyes asking her silent, confused question.

"The Valkyries I knew in the past loved their wings. Most of them rarely folded them away. And, even though the new Valkyries now don't have them out as often, you seem to avoid using them as much as possible."

She caught her bottom lip with her teeth and her gaze fell away. "It's... complicated."

My jaw flexed. No. I was not going to allow that kind of answer. Not when she pushed us so hard to be open and communicate.

I knelt in front of her and tucked my finger under her chin so she'd look at me. "Talk to me, Valkyrie. You ask me to open up all the time. I'm asking you to do the same."

She softly smiled. "I'm being honest, Tyr. It really is complicated for me to express."

"Try? For me?" My thumb slid along her cheek. "I promise there is no judgment here, no matter what you say."

Astrid blew out a breath. "I… struggle a lot with feeling like I'm not a real Valkyrie. I know I am—I feel it deep inside. But I'm constantly struggling with this feeling of inadequacy… and maybe also with understanding who I really am."

I frowned. I'd never seen this struggle in her. She'd always seemed so secure in who she was. *Has she hidden it this well, or am I that unobservant?*

She pressed her lips together, her jaw working as she tried to piece her words together. "I can't say when I really noticed it, but I think that feeling has always been there in some way. I just have been noticing it more recently."

"What makes you notice these feelings?" I asked.

Her shoulders slumped. "It's stupid things…"

"It's not stupid if it bothers you. What are the things?"

"Everyone else seems to love their wings. I don't. I don't like how they feel as they drag on the ground, or how unwieldy they feel when I'm walking around, or how heavy they get when I carry souls. I love flying—it's so much fun. But I can't find myself loving my wings for some reason. It makes me question so much. Shouldn't a Valkyrie love her wings? And that makes me think it's tied to this problem with my identity."

I didn't have any advice yet to offer, so I waited. Even if words never came to me, I'd be here to listen so she could sort out her thoughts openly.

"I once knew who I was. I was just Astrid the therapist, with some normal human traumas. But now I'm Astrid the witch and Valkyrie with even more traumas, and titles, and insane responsibilities. And I've got these memories that are mine but also a past mine's. I have these thoughts and actions that are clearly influenced by my soul as a witch and a Valkyrie, as well as a past version of myself that I can weirdly tap into like some magic-influenced disassociation so I can get through uncomfortable situations the present version of me still can't handle."

That explained her comment earlier about relying on her past self.

"I've tried talking some things out with Kirby, but it's not exactly easy. We've both been reincarnated, but our experiences are different—along with how we were reincarnated—so what I struggle with isn't really the same as what she struggles with. This leaves me with no one else to help me sort through the mess in my brain."

Her wings slumped even more, and she continued before I could speak up. "And then there's this bullshit with Ingrid and what she said. I don't even know how to feel about all that. A part of me wants to scream and call her a liar. Another part of me says she was being truthful and I need to stop denying it. I just…"

She shook her head. "I just… I don't know anymore."

Framing her face with my hands, I pressed my forehead against hers. "When your wings are too heavy, lean on me. My strength will hold you aloft for however long you need."

She giggled quietly. "And you claim you can't create poetry."

"It would have been more poetic if Diego or Baldur said it."

Astrid rested her hands on mine. "It's your words I need right now."

I breathed deep. "I don't have a fountain of wisdom to pull from to offer. I won't say I understand what you're dealing with, because I've never questioned who I was."

She cocked her head. "Never?"

I shook my head. "I'm a god. What I am is set in stone."

She squinted. "Even hearing all these talks about sacrificed memories to stop Ragnarök, you haven't wondered if you're missing something?"

Missing something? Well, now that she's mentioning it, I have wondered a few things, but—I shook my head. "Don't turn this into being about me, Valkyrie. We're talking about you."

She blew a breath out through her lips. "Fine."

I chuckled and brushed her cheek. "Regardless, if I can offer you conversation or words to help you sort out your thoughts, I am here for you. If you just need to verbalize your thoughts without input, I can do that. If you need an opinion, I'll give it. If you need direction, I will help you find your way. Just don't shut me out, Astrid."

She leaned into my touch. "Thanks."

"And so you know, I support your questioning thoughts. Just because a path is set before you, doesn't mean it's the one you're meant to stay on forever." I tipped her face up. "Question everything about yourself. It's the only way you'll know how the pieces of who you are fit together into the true version of yourself. And I'll be right there to support you, no matter how long that takes."

I leaned in and kissed her, softly—passionately, pouring everything I felt for her into this one kiss. "I love you, Astrid."

She hummed and smiled, her eyes squinting in just the right way that was uniquely her, and her cheeks flushing a light shade of pink. "I love you too, Tyr."

Those words flowed over my being like the warmest caress and filled me with life I didn't know I still needed. How long I'd yearned to hear her say those words again.

Sliding my arms around her, I collected Astrid in my arms. She looped her arms around my neck and pressed her face against my skin, giggling quietly. "Where are we going?"

I maneuvered through the house. "You were amazing today. And you deserve to be rewarded."

She hummed and traced her fingers along the back of my neck. It sent a shiver of desire down my spine. "What kind of reward?"

The door leading out back opened, a flash of gossamer wings catching my eye. The corner of my mouth quirked. Una was always on top of things, even if I never had to ask or know she was around. "You deserve to be pampered."

Stepping outside under the deck awning, we were greeted by soft garden lights and the trickle of water running. Warm steam floated out of the large sunken bath that took up most of the covered space.

Astrid slumped against me and practically moaned. "Oh, a bath. I definitely need this."

She squeaked when our clothes disappeared, then grumbled out Ùna's name, making me laugh. She always hated it when Ùna did that. Not that she did often—it was usually after Astrid had used a lot of her magic, and she wanted to be helpful. Given it'd be difficult to get Astrid's clothes off around her wings, I was certainly grateful, even if it did mean I couldn't peel them off her body myself.

I sank into the water, the warmth seeping deep into my being. Astrid sighed contentedly. We sat there in silence for a while, soaking in the warm water and each other's presence. Eventually I took her arm and slowly massaged her. Astrid didn't fight me, her body languid and enjoying her much-needed pampering.

She did find the strength eventually to pull back her wings. I took advantage of the moment to slide my hands along her smooth back and gently massage her. Astrid moaned, and all the blood in my body drained down to my *very* prominent problem pressing into her back.

"Ignore that."

Her eyebrow arched. "Should I ignore it?"

"Yes. It's nothing to worry about right now."

Her eyes narrowed. "Who are you and what have you done with my Tyr?"

I laughed. "Is it so hard to accept I want to pamper you without it turning into sex?"

"Yes." Her tone was so matter-of-fact, I laughed harder.

She turned to face me better. "Besides, shouldn't I have a say in what pampering means?"

"Perhaps, but you also once asked if there was such a thing as too much sex in a relationship."

She grunted. "Yeah, and Aya looked so aghast, you'd have thought I asked her if she'd ever had sexual relations with her brother, and Kirby said I shouldn't look this big *fuck you Odin, you don't own us Valkyries* in the gifted face."

I chuckled and cupped her cheek. "Please, Valkyrie, let me do this the way I would like. Then we can consider sex after, if you're up for it."

She shrugged. "All right, if that's what you want. But I'm not going to monitor my moaning."

True to her word, she did moan—a lot. Most of it was exaggerated to mess with me, and it was working. It took every bit of control not to bend her over the edge of the bath and take her as my reward for a battle well fought. *Patience.* I didn't get my god reputation by being as impulsive as Fen.

Her teasing eventually stopped as relaxation set in and she was a limp, witch-Valkyrie puddle in my hand. That was when I knew she'd been sufficiently pampered. Astrid needed more opportunities to relax. She'd run herself ragged these last few days and it showed, beyond all the tightness in her body I'd worked out.

I gathered her in my arms and climbed out of the bath. She molded into me, wrapping herself in my embrace. I ignored the towels that had been left out for us and walked through the house. I'd clean up the tracked-through water later.

I carried her up to the loft, where our enormous bed waited. Muninn was perched on the sill of the dormer next to the bed, overlooking the lake. The bright moon reflected off its tranquil surface. Muninn perked up at our appearance but didn't move from his spot. I wasn't surprised to find him here. One of her familiars was always close by.

Laying Astrid on the bed, I climbed on with her. She snuggled into me. I ran my fingers through her hair, smiling at this perfect woman in my bed.

As she lay curled up against me, her fingers traced my tattoo of her. A few months ago, I had it redone. It now depicted her witch past and her witch-Valkyrie present, along with Angel.

"Muninn is still mad you haven't added him yet," she murmured.

I grunted and angled my head toward the open window, where the raven in question still sat on the sill, staring in like a creeper. "Well, you're going to have to wait. Tatiana is busy and her magic is limited."

Muninn snapped his beak and grumbled before hopping onto the bed and over to us. He jumped onto Astrid's back, touching her face affectionately with his beak, before finally perching on the nightstand. She smiled at her familiar and snuggled into me more.

"Angel will be showing up in a little bit. She's bugging Aya to let her through the Norway door."

I chuckled. "The bed is big enough."

She hummed, her eyes closing.

"Valkyrie," I said. I should let her sleep, but this one thing was bugging me.

She cracked her eyes open and tipped her head up to peer up at me. "Hmm?"

"Have you ever heard someone call you a solar witch? Before today, that is?" The witches at the sanctuary today used it frequently with her, as if it were the most important thing they could call her.

"No." Her brow furrowed. "Wait, actually…"

She grew quiet, and after a moment I prompted her. "Astrid?"

"I think I have heard it before, in my first life. I was little. A woman from a distant land passed through. She was a völva, though she didn't call herself that. She used the word witch, and thought our word völva was strange. She said…"

Astrid squinted as she tried to remember. "She called my mom a night witch. Mom liked it. Then she looked at me and smiled, telling me my embers were small, but soon they'd heat up, and I'd become a spectacular solar witch the world had never seen before. It made my mother really happy to hear."

She cocked her head. "When the stranger left, she told me… I needed to be careful. That if I burned too hot, those with jealous hearts would come and try to extinguish my fiery light."

Astrid's eyes fluttered and she looked at me again. "That's all I remember."

I stared down at her. That was a huge memory. It said so much with so little.

"What brought on the question?" she asked.

"Baldur and I were surprised by the title and it made me curious," I said.

"Because if we'd known, we'd have realized I was Baldur's undoing?" she mumbled.

I tucked a strand of hair behind her ear. I should have known she'd already figured out her part in Baldur's prophecy. All the pieces had been in front of us the whole time; we'd just never put them together properly. That one bit of information wasn't guaranteed to help us realize how the pieces fit, but it might have helped. "Not his undoing. His weakness, as you are mine."

She reached out and brushed my cheek with her fingers. "To this day, I'm still not sure if that's a good thing or not."

I placed my hand over hers, holding it captive against my face, and stared into her captivating eyes. "Everyone has a weakness. And I thank Creation every day that you're mine. I wouldn't ask for it any other way."

Astrid smiled and pushed up to lean over me. Her lips pressed against mine, soft and sweet and every bit luring. "And you're mine."

I tangled my fingers in her hair and slid my hand along the curve of her soft hips. I knew what she meant by that, but with the temptation of her right here, the primal side of my brain was seeing those words as something else. And as I kissed her, slow and deep, I knew she too felt the burning connection between us.

Astrid swung her leg over me and broke our kiss. Her thighs teasingly pressed against my hips, my hard cock curving along her perfect ass. Her hands slid down my chest, the trail burning and teasing. My erection strained harder as I gazed up at her, thoroughly enjoying this view while lying under her with her stunning body on display for me. *My confident, sexy Valkyrie.*

I tucked an arm under my head and slid my other hand up her belly, stopping at the tip of her sternum tattoo and tracing the outer lines. "Not tired anymore, Valkyrie?"

She made a fake thoughtful sound, her face twisting to look like she was thinking carefully. Her fingers tapped my chest, each impact jolting me with sparks of anticipation. "I think I need a little help sleeping."

Grinning, I wrapped my hand around the back of her neck. "I'm more than happy to help you with that. Come here."

I yanked her down and my mouth captured hers. She moaned and rubbed her breasts sensually into me, igniting the heat simmering under the surface. Her intoxicating presence wrapped around me, dragging me deeper into an embrace I refused to fight. I forced my tongue between her lips, devouring her until she was breathless.

Astrid ripped her mouth away, breathing hard. I tipped my head, kissing along her neck. My fingers curled around her thighs and I lifted her higher toward my chest.

She gasped when I kissed the hollow of her throat. "Tyr…"

"I'm going to worship and ravish your body until you're breathless and shaking," I murmured against her skin. "And each time you scream, the heavens will know the god who brought you there."

"Please," she begged.

My tongue dragged over her skin. My teeth nibbled and teased. I took my time, as difficult as it was with desire burning me from the inside out. I lavished her with my mouth, as I promised I would. Her gasps and moans were my reward, and soon her cries of ecstasy would be my blessing.

I slid my tongue teasingly along her breasts. Astrid gasped and arched, wordlessly begging her desired attention. I grinned and complied, licking, kissing, and lightly nipping her nipple.

"Yes," she moaned. "More of that."

I did, alternating between her breasts, using my hand to continue teasing the other where I left off, rolling and pinching her between my fingers. I slid one of them into my mouth and sucked on the erect bud.

Astrid moaned again. Her fingers sunk into my hair and she pressed into me, as if she could fuse us together. I slid a free hand along the curve of her wide hips and over her soft, perfect ass. My fingers dug into her skin, massaging and appreciating her particular asset that was certainly in the running as my favorite. When I'd thoroughly appreciated her, I slipped my hands around her ass and between her legs, sliding along her wet folds.

She moaned again and jerked into my fingers. I teased around her clit, never giving her quite enough. Astrid tried to squirm and pull me closer, but to her frustration, I wouldn't give her what she craved. Not yet.

Releasing her breasts, I kissed between them. Then a little lower.

And lower more. My mouth trailed along her tattoo and down the softness of her belly as I lifted her higher and higher on my chest.

Astrid wobbled and grabbed the headboard. "Tyr, what are you doing?"

"Worshiping," I murmured as I tasted the swells of her hips and lusciousness of her inner thighs. "Hold onto that headboard tight, Valkyrie. You're going to need it."

Her breath hitched. "Will I be praying?"

I slowly continued my teasing a path along her soft skin, my fingers circling her clit. "You'd better be screaming."

My finger slid over her needy clit. Astrid moaned and arched her back. I played with her until she was rocking into me and moaning. It wasn't enough for me. I lifted her up a little more until her pussy was aligned over my mouth, then slid my tongue between her silken folds.

Astrid gasped and groaned, grinding her pussy into my face. "Yes… Yes, Tyr."

I licked and sucked, greedily devouring her, searing her taste into every recess of my mind. My fingers slid inside her, drawing out a deep primal moan.

Rhythmically, I coaxed her closer and closer to the edge. She rocked her hips, her body tensing and shaking. She shuddered above me, then threw her head back and screamed as her orgasm tore through her.

I didn't let up, even as she came down. She panted and twitched and ground into me, needy for more. And more I gave, until she crested over the edge again. Ecstasy overtook her until she was a quivering mess.

She panted, her fingers gripping the headboard so hard her knuckles had turned white. I grinned, pleased to have succeeded, while also knowing I wasn't done with her yet.

Kissing her belly softly, I eased her down my chest before rolling her onto her back. I hovered over her, gazing deep into her beautiful face. "Ready for more, Valkyrie?"

She grinned and slowly spread her legs. "Always for you, my love."

Fuck. She had to call me that, the same way she used to in the past. Any control I still had snapped. Wrapping a hand around my cock, I gripped her hips and guided them into alignment. I grinned when

Astrid's fingers twisted in the pillows under her. Her eyes begged me to hurry.

I plunged into her tight, quivering pussy. I groaned as her tightness and warmth closed in around me. She was so perfect. So mine.

Astrid's mouth fell open as she accepted me, her back arching. I thrust into her without hesitation, harder and harder. Skin slapped skin as I fucked her. She moaned, the sound blazing the hot desire under my skin.

I braced myself on the head board, putting everything into my thrusts. Through hooded eyes and parted mouth, Astrid gaped for words that couldn't form.

Her fingers twisted into the fabric beneath her. Her walls clenched around me and her back arched as she screamed. Her ecstasy was intoxicating.

My pulse pounding in my ears, my body tightened, and then I crested over the edge, spilling inside her with reckless abandon.

Panting breathlessly, I stilled, relying on the support of the bed to hold me up. Or maybe that was the lack of blood in my limbs rooting me in place.

I sucked in a sharp breath when Astrid's hand glided up my chest. "Are you okay?"

"Yeah," I puffed out. With effort, I extracted myself from her and rolled onto my back. I grabbed her languid body and pulled her into me.

Astrid hummed quietly and snuggled in. I laid there, listening to her breathe and feeling her naked body against mine. Her breathing slowed.

As sleep took her, the house grew quiet. Muninn had left the room at some point, and I could vaguely hear the quiet patter of Angel's nails tapping along the floor downstairs.

No threats or god duties kept my mind occupied, yet it didn't follow Astrid's into a realm of comfort and dreams. It wandered until it latched onto the question she'd asked me earlier. I'd said I had never questioned who I was, but was that an accurate claim?

Something nudged the back of my mind, like a distant memory. Something painful to remember, so I had buried it deep. I closed my eyes and instead of running, brought it to the surface.

A day of confusion. The day I forgot Ragnarök ever happened—what I sacrificed to protect our lives.

Who was I? What was I? I knew those answers—Tyr, and a god. That was it, though. I had inklings of a past, knew faces and names around me, but there was something missing. I didn't know what, but it pained me that I couldn't remember. It bothered me to hear Odin claim himself king, though I didn't know why.

I wandered, trying to figure it out—trying to understand what was so important that I forgot.

But in my travels, I'd forgotten why I was searching and had stopped. I settled into my life and was adopted as a god of the people who became the Norsemen, alongside other gods I knew. I accepted my life, but a part of me could never forget that something was missing.

My gaze slid to Astrid's peaceful face. *Until I met her.*

I twirled my finger through her gorgeous hair. What had my Valkyrie figured out? What did she know when she accused Odin of stealing a throne? *What does she know that I've forgotten?*

And most importantly, how did she figure it out?

SIXTEEN

DIEGO

Chaos assaulted my mind: people shouting and crying; the clash of steel and magic; other sounds I couldn't put words to, but deep down I knew what they were.

Astrid leaned over me—or a woman who looked just like Astrid. She had the same red hair and piercing green eyes, the Valkyrie wings, and the armor, but there were other aspects of her that were different.

There was a fire-like quality to her golden feathers—and then there was her presence. There was something more ancient about her, rather than just being within the depths of her soul.

Blood coated her pale, freckled skin. The face scar I knew her to have was a fresh, deep cut here. Tears streaked her soot-stained cheeks. She spoke to me, but I struggled to hear the words. I could barely read her lips through progressively blurring focus.

The words she mouthed were something in a language I didn't know. Or maybe I did. I felt like I understood her, but I couldn't place anything. It wasn't English or Spanish; it vaguely reminded me of the language she sometimes used when she spoke to Aya and Tyr. There was always this sense of familiarity with that language, but I'd yet to learn it from them.

Whatever the other Astrid said, it felt like a promise. I felt it deep in me. I felt my dragon react in a way that made it desperate—desperate to protect her forever.

Hands not belonging to this Astrid touched my body. I jolted and vaguely heard, "Oof, why do you have to be so heavy?"

My vision snapped and the chaotic scene vanished. I was in the kitchen, on the floor. Astrid, the one I knew all too well, crouched beside me. One of her hands was planted on my chest, while the other touched my back. My arm was looped around her shoulders, as if she'd had to catch me.

Concern creased Astrid's pretty face. "Diego, are you back with me?"

I tried to speak, but the dryness in my throat caught my words. She handed me a glass of water. After a few gulps, I tried again. "Fuck, that sucked."

Her fingers glided along my cheek. "Are you okay?"

I blinked slowly and looked around the kitchen. "I think so. What were we doing just now?"

"You wanted to talk to me, and then you had a vision… I think. Then you fell over and I tried to catch you."

A vision. Was that a vision? Or was it a memory? *No, it can't be a memory.* There was no way that was a memory. Yet, it sure felt like one.

"Then you called me fat."

She laughed. "I did not. You've bulked up more."

I was glad she noticed. I'd been training with Zeke and Caleb. Dahlia was invited to our sessions, but she wasn't interested, saying she'd had her fill of watching boys beat each other up in school. I didn't blame her.

Caleb, being a seasoned brawler, didn't go easy on us. It didn't matter that Zeke and I didn't have the same strong fighting instinct or experience; he pushed us to be the strongest we could be in order to protect our partners. My dragon easily fed on this, driven to protect Astrid at all costs, even when I wanted to see the sparring as a competitive itch to scratch.

"Too much for the pint-sized Valkyrie?"

She swatted at me. "I'm a respectable size, thank you."

I laughed. It was too much fun poking her about that. Of course,

I loved her height, even if it posed a challenge for us when we found ourselves in a horizontal position—or made attempts to make it not-so-horizontal.

Astrid leaned into me. "What happened?"

I rubbed my temples; they pulsed with a growing headache. Not only that, the feelings from before were resurfacing, making me restless, as if the dragon inside me was crawling under my skin. Her touch on me didn't help, yet it also did.

I pulled Astrid into my arms and held her close, burying my face into her hair. I inhaled deeply, enveloping myself with her scent and presence. Astrid curled into me, giving me the closeness that I desperately needed.

She was safe. She wasn't dying or bleeding out. We weren't about to go into battle, and neither of us was going to die.

I inhaled her scent again. Lilac and vanilla, her favorite brand of perfume. It was mine, too. Pleasure whispered down my spine. My grip on her tightened. I needed her. I needed her closer, where she was always safe. I needed what was mine right now. I needed her to be *mine. Mate. Now.*

I released her and jerked back. The cold air filling the sudden space between us left a yearning ache, but I couldn't give into the sway. Those were dangerous thoughts.

"Diego?" Astrid murmured.

"I'm sorry." I blew out a breath and ran my fingers through my hair. "I'm just…"

Just what? So crazy about you that I want to claim you right here and now as my mate? I couldn't say that yet. It was too soon.

She took my hands and pulled us to our feet. "Let's go for a flight. The fresh air will clear your head."

My backside itched as if my wings and tail already wanted to come out. Flying with her sounded good—more than good. "That would be amazing."

We headed for the front door. I gave Tuggy and Angel each a quick head scratch as we passed them where they played, Tuggy laying on the counter and hanging her paws over the edge to bat at Angel. "Be good while we're out."

Buggy hopped up on the counter with her sister and watched us go. A sensation of "I'll watch them" fell over me.

The front door flew open before we reached it, and Aya strode in. "Ah, there you both are. Diego, yes or no?"

I blinked. "Huh?"

"You were going to think about whether you'd participate in the event."

Oh, right. The other day she'd asked if I wanted to be part of a pinup charity calendar. Aya had all sorts of themes she wanted to cover that would keep us set for years to come—her words. It was to help refugees of the magical community and anyone displaced by the increased attacks. The gods were loaded with their centuries of wealth accumulation, but not even they could fund everything. Plus, it added a bit of fun for everyone involved and felt less like pity handouts.

"Yeah, I'll do it." I didn't have any reason to say no. I'd asked for some time just to think it over and make sure Astrid wasn't uncomfortable with the idea. Not that I thought she would be.

"And you, Astrid?" Aya asked.

She nodded. "I'm willing to give it a shot."

Astrid had been asked to participate in the ladies' edition, though she'd been on the fence about saying yes. She was comfortable with the idea of the calendar, just not confident in herself. Tyr, Baldur, and I were quick to encourage her. The conversation might have also ended up with some promises for extra personal photos that wouldn't go public.

Aya's face lit up. "Great! Now I just have to find Tyr. Hopefully he won't bite my head off this time when I ask."

"He's with Baldur and Fen," Astrid said. "I think they're beating the shit out of each other."

Aya snickered. "I'll follow the sounds of a whimpering dog, then."

We all laughed. Astrid tugged me to follow her after Aya left. We found a good spot in the lawn for me to take my dragon form.

The transformation came on quickly. I rarely had issues going between forms, and had an easier time taking something in between. But today it came even easier. I clearly needed this.

Astrid's wings grew from her back and spread wide. The silver and gold feathers shimmered in the afternoon light, the fire quality from that vision noticeably absent. I didn't know why, but a sense of longing came with the realization, like I missed that version.

Her body lifted off the ground where she hovered. It was the strangest thing about being a winged creature like us—technically our flight ability was the result of magic, not our wings, yet we had them for some reason. They were useful for maneuvering, and there was an instinct to use them in flight, but it wasn't exactly necessary. No one I knew seemed to have an answer why that was, either, not even Mamá.

Mia joked it was superhero logic, and honestly, I wouldn't have been surprised to find out that was where the inspiration came from. For all we knew, superhero creators were also secretly part of the supernatural community.

Astrid smiled at me then took off into the air; I sprang after her. The wind whipped around me, my scales protecting me from the cold, and the land below grew smaller. When we were a few hundred feet above the tree line we leveled out.

We left the protection of the sanctuary wards and produced our own around ourselves. It wasn't fully needed, as we were so far up north, by the Canadian border in the middle of nowhere, we didn't get much in the way of mortal traffic, but it was best to be safe. Plus, it kept possible prying eyes away from us.

Astrid and I followed the curve of the mountain, our pace unhurried. The lush, vibrant green carpet of trees stretched for miles beneath us. Delicate blossoms from flowering trees broke up the emerald landscape with splashes of pink and white. Rivers and streams, still full from the winter's lingering runoff, wove through the landscape like shimmering ribbons.

The air glided over my scales, the fresh, crisp air filing my nose with the scent of flowers and earthly scents and invigorating my body. The remnants of the vision, while stubborn to leave as if it insisted on telling me something, no longer permeated a dark cloud over my mind. Astrid's flight patterns probably helped in that.

She circled me, first by rolling under me, then angling to roll above.

Her hair whipped around in the wind, as untamed as she was. The most brilliant smile brightened her face. The sight of her joy filled my chest until it ached. She needed this as much as me.

The mountain below us dipped into a deep ravine. Astrid rocked back and forth on the winds before diving. I tucked my wings in tight against my body and plunged after her.

The wind whipped past me, grasping and snagging as if trying to prevent my fall. I tucked myself in tighter, plummeting toward the ever-closer ground.

I flicked my gaze toward Astrid. She grinned and kept going. A chuckle rumbled through my chest. *A game of chicken it is.* She had an advantage here, being smaller, but I wasn't going to back down from her challenge.

The distance between us and the ground lessened by the second. My heart pounded in my chest as the adrenaline surged through my body. My survival instincts screamed at me to pull up, but I didn't listen. I'd hold out until the last minute.

Green flashed past as we re-entered the forest. The roaring of the ravine river enveloped my senses. My wings snapped out and my body jerked as they caught the wind and my fall halted.

Astrid continued several more feet before her wings snapped out. She hovered above the rushing water, no more than an arm's length above it.

I grunted when she whooped her victory. Next time I'd make sure to shift back so she didn't have such an advantage on me.

Astrid glided upriver, her pace now leisurely again. I tried to follow, finding my larger size too much for the narrow river, so I shifted. I dropped in altitude immediately. Focusing on keeping myself in the air, my magic flared and the wings on my back flapped wildly. Astrid paused to watch me with amusement.

"Yeah, yeah," I grumbled. I didn't usually fly this way; I found it more difficult than if I was a full dragon. But I wanted to change that. This half-dragon form had its advantages.

Astrid giggled and flew over to me. "Need help?"

I listed to one side, tried to fix it, and overcorrected, finding myself floating backward. "No, I've got it."

She laughed and watched me flounder for a few moments longer. Eventually I got myself stationary and upright... after I'd ended up upside-down.

I blew out a breath. "Finally. Why was that so hard? Dahlia and Caleb make it look so easy."

"Even if they're good at it, I don't think this is a natural flight form for a dragon," Astrid said. "It's not like me, where it's natural to open just my wings and fly away. I mean, Artura still gets grumpy when all of you take this form."

"Still shouldn't be this difficult," I grumbled.

She laughed and held out her hand. I gladly took it, linking my fingers with hers. We glided up stream. Astrid kept me steady when I needed it, and it wasn't long before I figured out my tail was useful for combating the imbalance.

Astrid eventually slipped her fingers from my grasp and flew ahead. She glanced back when I called out to her, but otherwise she ignored me. My tail lashed. The urge to chase after her built in my chest. So, I did.

Astrid smirked and took off into the forest. *Brat.* Flying after her, I wove through the trees, barely dodging some when she took tight turns. I managed to keep pace, but not gain ground. I had to get crafty.

Focusing in on her movement patterns, I repositioned myself to trick her into going the way I wanted.

It worked.

The distance between us lessened until I reached out and looped my arms around her middle. She squealed and struggled against my strong grip.

I pulled her hard against my chest and refused to let her go. Satisfaction pulsed through me. "Gotcha."

She went limp and sighed in defeat. "Not fair."

I laughed and pressed my face into her hair, inhaling her delectable scent. "Neither was challenging me to a game of chicken while I was a dragon."

She huffed air through her lips. "Truce?"

I pulled her closer, her presence doing me wonders, and nuzzled her neck. "*Yo gano.* I win."

Astrid giggled. "Feeling better, I see."

"Hmm…"

"Hey," she lightly reprimanded. "Grunting and one-word substitutions belong to Tyr and Tyr only."

"And what are you going to do about it, Cielo?"

She tipped her head up, gazing deep into my eyes. Her fingers glided up my cheek and into my hair. They brushed against my horns and a sharp *zing* of desire shot down my spine, making my tail lash. "If my dragon wants to come out and play…"

I leaned over her more, our lips brushing. She grinned and pulled away, right out of my grip. "Then he has to communicate how he's feeling after all this flying."

I blew out a breath. "Tease."

Her fingers trailed down my chest while she smirked, and then she floated down to a sturdy tree bough. I followed. I sat with my back against the tree's trunk and pulled her down onto my lap, wrapping her up in my embrace. I needed her right here.

Astrid pillowed her head on my shoulder and gazed up at me. "Do you want to talk about earlier?"

I pursed my lips. "I don't know how. It was so confusing."

She relaxed into me more, curling her body and adjusting her wings so she'd be more comfortable. She didn't have them out often; even between flying places she typically put them away. I liked that they were still out. "I can wait a few hours for you to figure it out."

"Not all day?"

"I've got a session at four."

I chuckled and tucked some of her hair behind her ear. "I can't tempt you to play hooky? I like having you to myself for once."

She merely smiled and I blew out a breath. "Fine."

"Tell me about the vision."

I worked my jaw. "It wasn't… a vision. I think it was a memory."

She tipped her head. "A memory of when you were younger? I wouldn't think that would be confusing. Or cause that type of reaction out of you."

"No… not that kind of memory." Damn, why was this so hard to say? Gods, magic, reincarnation, we'd seen it all, and yet I couldn't verbalize this weirdness I'd been experiencing?

Astrid shifted until she was kneeling in front of me. "What's going on, Diego?"

I sighed. "I didn't think it was a big deal at first, but it keeps happening, and it's hard to explain, but I'll do my best. I'm seeing… memories that aren't mine but feel like they are. I thought they might be visions, because I'm not touching an item with a memory attached, but the timeline didn't make sense. The first time, it happened when we were at the Norway house and I was waiting for you to regain awareness around you."

Astrid cocked her head, and she seemed even more interested. "What did you see?"

"You from the past. Like, Viking-age past. I was in this person's body and following you through a forest. I wanted to tell you something. You said my name. Well… his name."

"Ragnvald."

I stared at her. She said that name so quickly. So… surely.

Astrid chewed her lips and nodded, her eyes lowering. "I had some suspicions, but I wasn't sure."

I brushed my fingers along her cheek. Now I had my own questions. "What are you hiding?"

Her eyes widened. "I'm not hiding anything. I just… didn't want to say anything if I was wrong. I also didn't know if it mattered, even if I was right."

"Who is Ragnvald?"

"You know how I told you I was supposed to be married three times before I met Tyr?"

I nodded.

"Ragnvald was the third man, and…" She took a deep breath. "The only one of them I truly loved."

I gazed at her, suddenly seeing her in a new light. She never talked about those previous relationships in detail. She'd only glossed over the fact that they'd happened, so I had always assumed they were arranged marriages she didn't care had ended, besides the stigma it had gotten her in her community back then.

"He and I had known each other since we were little," she continued. "But his father was a traveling merchant, and once Ragnvald turned ten, he went with his father a lot, so I didn't see him much after that. It wasn't until I was fourteen, almost fifteen, did we reunite for a longer period of time. I'd had two failed marriages by that point. Both of them died soon after the engagement."

Her shoulders slumped. "The rumor mill was already working by that point, so when we started spending more time together, I tried not to think anything more than friendship with him. But…" A small smile spread over her lips. "He was persistent. And I found myself so head over heels for him. I thought I was going to be the happiest woman in Midgard."

A dark shadow fell over her face, heartbreak reflecting in her eyes. I hesitated to ask, but did anyway. "What happened?"

"A plague."

My gut twisted and something inside me roiled like it was in pain.

"I lost my sister to it. And Ragnvald… his entire family died." Her throat bobbed. "I was by his side the whole time. I refused to leave, even when everyone else told me the risk of catching the illness wasn't worth it. I… I couldn't leave him to die alone."

I reached up and brushed the tear that broke free down her cheek. *You never truly healed from that, did you, Astrid?* She'd buried those memories and grief and had tried to pretend it never happened. She'd lived in such a brutal world, weakness couldn't exist.

"What… does this have to do with me?" I asked after she took a few calming breaths.

The way she looked up at me made my breath hitch, and I knew what she'd say even before the words left her lips. "I think you're the reincarnation of him."

I blinked several times, trying to process that. "Well… shit. That makes a lot of sense."

She laughed, the gloom surrounding her breaking, just a little. "Of all the things you could have said. Though I guess I shouldn't be surprised you took that so well."

I rubbed the back of my neck. "Yeah, that does explain some of the subsequent memories I've seen. But why did it happen? Why did I find you again? It's not like your situation, where someone used magic to bring me back."

Astrid hummed quietly. "Souls can reincarnate on their own. And right before you died, you promised you'd find me again. So… maybe Creation took pity on us both, especially after all the bullshit my soul has gone through."

I tipped her chin up and kissed her gently. "Whatever the reason, I'm glad for it."

She smiled, and then it faded away. "Was it your death you saw earlier? Was that why you had such a reaction to it? The first one I brought you out of, you just looked really distant."

I worked my jaw. "Yes, and no?"

Her eyebrow quirked and she gave me her "go on" look.

I sucked in a deep breath. "This one was new, and it wasn't a Ragnvald memory. You were in it, though."

Her brow furrowed. "Then how do you know it wasn't a Ragnvald memory?"

I licked my lips, trying to piece together the chaos that was still fresh in my mind. "There was some sort of battle going on. You were there as a Valkyrie, but you were different. I was on the ground and you were covered in blood. You were saying something to me. I couldn't hear you but it felt like a promise."

I shook my head. "Then I came back."

Astrid blinked slowly. "And you're sure this wasn't a vision of the future?"

I trailed my finger along the crossing scar on her face. "This was a fresh cut."

She sat back and thought quietly. Her eyes spoke possible answers to what might be going on, but she didn't verbalize anything.

A strange feeling settled over me. "Astrid, do you know something?"

"Um…" She chewed her lip. "I might? But I don't know yet. It's something I've been trying to figure out for a few months now. And I think you just complicated things, but also enlightened them as well."

I leaned forward. "Are you going to tell me about this super-secret thing?"

She smiled sheepishly. "Would you accept, 'not until I figure it out more'?"

My eye twitched. "What if I told you no?"

Her lips pursed. "Could I bribe you?"

Laughter bubbled out of me. She wanted to bribe me? "Is it really that bad you can't share this information?"

"It's not that it's bad," she insisted. "It's just… that it's complicated. And I don't think I have enough information for myself to understand, let alone to explain it to anyone else."

A thought crossed my mind. "This has to do with that accusation you threw at Odin, doesn't it? This whole 'craven crown' stuff with those prophecies."

She nodded. "In a weird roundabout way, yeah, I think so."

Sucking in a hard breath through my nose, I curled my fingers around her hips and pulled her closer. "All right, then how do you plan to bribe me to let this go for now?"

She splayed her fingers across my chest and twisted her body in a coy way. "Hmm, I suppose that depends on what my dragon finds acceptable."

I hummed as I thought, tapping her hips. "Choices, choices."

Astrid pressed against me, her lips brushing mine. "Do I need to make suggestions?"

"Suggestions from the council will be heavily weighed for consideration."

She made a disappointed sound. "I'm only part of the council? And here I thought I would be at least a consort."

A growl threatened to rise up, my dragon instincts rising. *Mine.* "I didn't want to assign such a title without your consent."

Her tongue teased my lower lip. "How thoughtful of you, my dragon."

"Always. Now, why don't you tell me your thoughts?"

Her fingers slid behind my head and tangled in my hair. "I could slide down your hot body, appreciating every inch of you until I'm worshiping your cock. I could stand and give you the opportunity to do the same for me."

Her hips rocked against my too-hard dick, to emphasize her want. "Or I could slowly ease your cock into my needy pussy and ride you until the sun sets."

I groaned and dug my fingers into her ass. All of those sounded like fantastic options. "What else do you propose?"

A grin spread her lips. "I could make you chase me through the forest. Should you catch me, you could have your way with me over and over again, so much you'd make a sex god envious."

Desire crawled under my skin and heated my veins. I pulled her closer, curling my fingers around the back of her neck. "I already caught you, Cielo. So that means I can already do whatever I like… and all of your suggestions are so appealing."

Astrid kissed me, slowly, tantalizingly. My chest rumbled. I kissed her back, devouring her. My tongue swept into her mouth, dancing along hers. She moaned, setting my desire blazing through me.

"Tell me what you want," she murmured against my lips.

I wanted… I wanted… *To claim you.* I jerked back, gasping for air. *No. No, not yet.*

Astrid blinked in bewilderment. "Diego? What's wrong?"

Fuck. I did not want to have this conversation with her so soon. "It's… a dragon issue I'm having."

Her brow furrowed. "Is that a euphemism, or a legit dragon thing?"

I chuckled despite the turmoil inside me, with my dragon demanding I claim her. "It's a legit dragon thing."

"Is this something you've been dealing with for a while?"

I puffed out a breath and nodded. "It's… an instinct to… mate."

Her eyebrow cocked. "To mate."

I nodded again. "And I've been good at stuffing that away, but today I'm really struggling, probably on account of the memories."

Frustrated, I ran my fingers through my hair. "This wasn't something I was ready to talk to you about yet, especially as I don't quite know how it all works. Mom has avoided the topic—either she's too uncomfortable or she wants me to figure it out, I don't know. But I'm definitely not going to do something so permanent without talking it out with you thoroughly first."

Astrid gazed at me, her thoughts in her eyes. She then smirked and tugged at the button of my pants. "Well, if that's the case, why don't we work around that? You can't exactly mate my mouth, can you?"

I sucked in a tight breath through my nose. I couldn't believe I was about to do this. I wrapped my hand around hers to stop her. "That's not what I want."

Her eyebrow quirked. "Are you saying no to a blowjob?"

"No." I took another breath, this one to keep my hot blood from taking over all reasoning. "I'm saying, I want to get lost in you and find heights of pleasure together."

She walked her fingers up my chest, spreading heat through my veins. "Then we can try, and if you think things might go wrong, we'll stop. I highly doubt you can make a full mate bond without my consent."

A new wave of need surged in me. *Claim her. My mate.* She wasn't making this easy. "I'm worried something can change in the heat of the moment. You did make a blood oath on accident, after all."

Astrid blew out a breath and leaned back. "That's a good point."

I frowned, hating the gut-churning sensation now twisting my stomach. Frustration burned in my chest, and I wasn't sure if it was because I was denying what my dragon instincts wanted, or because I was disappointing Astrid. "You're upset I'm being cautious about this."

Her eyebrows rose high on her forehead. "Of course I'm not. There are many things I feel for you, and many others I wish to experience with you. But we're both on the same page for this. Neither of us is quite ready for the dragon equivalent of perma-marriage."

She brushed my cheek with her thumb. "And if you're not comfortable right now with any form of intimacy because of this heightened instinct, then I'm not going to push for anything, regardless if that causes the female equivalent of blue balls."

Yeah, that was a great assessment how my body was feeling, too. *Fuck.*

She pressed her lips against mine briefly for a teasing kiss, then pulled away, taking my hand with hers. "Let's go flying again. The cold air will help clear our heads."

My body stood with her encouraged tug, but my mind wasn't keeping up. My eyes roved over her curves, taking her in and assessing one thing: she was wearing too much.

Astrid turned, her wings spreading wide, and she lifted off the tree bough. I followed, but we didn't get far before my arms snaked around her and pulled her hard against me.

She squeaked. "Diego?"

I dragged my nose along her neck, inhaling her delicious scent. "I never said I wanted to clear my head."

Her breath audibly caught at the dip in my voice. She couldn't resist when I did this—when my dragon came to the surface to play just as much as the man.

"Diego, please don't tease me," she begged. "I can't handle that."

"I'm not. I just needed more time to think."

She turned in my arms and gazed up at me expectantly. My lungs struggled to breathe. I wanted her so badly. And I could have her right now, if I came up with a compromise my dragon could accept.

I tucked my finger under her chin. "*Te amo, mi cielo preciosa.*"

Her eyes squinted and a shade of pink spread over her cheeks as a brilliant heart-stopping smile appeared on her face. "I love you too, Diego, dragon of my heart."

My heart thumped hard in my chest. Warmth different from desire spread through me. My dragon, while not happy with the compromise, tolerated the step. *Pleased. She is mine. I have time.*

Astrid loved her friends and family with all her heart. She'd give her life to protect them if that's what was asked. She'd tell us she loved us, but the use was clear.

Whereas in the matters of romance, she didn't throw the L-word around. That was special to her. And I felt incredibly blessed to hear those words come from her lips—those tempting lips I was going to kiss.

I dipped my head and closed my mouth around hers. She sighed, her breath filling me with life I didn't know I needed. My fingers curled around the back of her neck and her hip. I pulled her into me, needing her closer. It wasn't enough.

Astrid's hands slid under my shirt. Sparks of desire heated my skin where she touched and explored. Breaking our kiss, I angled my mouth down her neck, lifting higher in my arms to provide me easier access. Astrid tugged my shirt up more, the cool air contrasting with the fire burning inside me.

I licked and nibbled her collarbone. She moaned quietly, the sound luring, like the sweetest memory just out of reach. Her fingers tangled in my hair and she tugged me down, encouraging more.

My fingers traced along her skin. My magic flared and her clothes disappeared in a theatric display of colored smoke. Astrid's fingers gripped my shirt and a moment later, it and the rest of my clothes were gone.

My erection pressed along the length of her thighs. She clenched them hard together, denying us both. But not for long. Lifting her higher, I kissed down along the curvature of her breasts. My hands glided along the swell of her wide hips.

Astrid moaned and arched her back, her fingers digging into my shoulders. "Diego."

I flicked my tongue over her erect nipple, the dusky rose buds begging to be tasted. Her gasp was music.

Flicking and circling, I teased and lavished, driving her wild. Her begs heated my burning desire into an inferno. My pulse pounded in my ears. Everything inside me screamed to claim her as mine.

I pulled her into my mouth, sucking and licking. My fingers slid along her inner thighs, teasing her. Astrid bit her lip and squirmed. I chuckled against her skin and increased my touch—coaxing and promising. Her body quivered her desire.

"Don't fight me, Cielo," I murmured. "Allow me to love you as you should be."

She snaked her arms around my neck, forcing me to let her breasts go with a satisfying *pop*. Her lips brushed mine. "Then love me, my dragon."

Her thighs relaxed, allowing my fingers to immediately slide between them. My fingers glided along her wet folds, teasing and spreading. When my fingers teased her clit, Astrid gasped and rolled her head back as she moaned. Her wings flapped as if my touch threatened to throw her off balance, even though it was me who supported us.

I stroked her, calling her closer to the paradise she deserved. My other hand slid up her back along her spine. My fingers brushed the base of her wings and her eyes popped wide, her breath catching. I grinned as I trailed a light touch along the ridge of her wing.

Astrid writhed, her thighs rubbing my cock just enough to be both relief and torture. Her fingers tightened in my hair and her other hand framed my face, guiding her mouth to mine. We devoured each other as if it were the first and last time.

My fingers slid deep inside her. Her slick pussy wrapped around me, begging me to give her more. She moaned deep, her chest vibrating against me, and rocked her hips into my touch. My fingers slid in and out of her rhythmically.

Desire coursed through me as each gasp and addictive moan from her perfect lips wrapped around my senses. "That's it, Cielo. Show me how much you like this."

Astrid tensed, her eyes hooding, and her grip on me tightening. Her head rolled back and her mouth fell open as my name screamed from her lips. The sound ignited a fresh wave of need in me.

She came down, her chest rising and falling with staggered breaths. I kissed her softly, withdrawing my fingers from inside her, and pulled away. She whimpered and grasped for me, as if she thought I was done. I was far from done indulging in her.

I glided around her until her back faced me, and pulled her into me by the hips. I bent over, kissing her along her neck and shoulder, following a trail of freckles, while crawling my fingers down her thighs. I smirked against her skin as my fingers pressed into her luscious flesh. My cock slid teasingly between her legs along the soft curve of her tempting body. Astrid sharply inhaled in anticipation.

Back and forth, I rocked my hips, teasing and slow. Astrid whimpered. She tipped her head back and reached up, threading her fingers into my hair. She tugged, lifting my head from her body enough for our lips to lock. Our tongues flirted and stoked the need burning hot in our veins until it fueled a frenzy.

Gripping her thighs tighter, I spread her legs and slowly, agonizingly, slid inside her tight, warm pussy. Astrid's eyes widened and her mouth parted as she accepted me. "Diego…"

I slid almost all the way out of her and then back in. Each thrust was just as slow and torturous as the last, but the unraveling mess she became was pure bliss.

"Diego…" she moaned again. "Diego, please."

"Good girl. You're holding up so well. I know you can keep going." I slid my hand along her soft skin, cupping her breast.

She bit her lip as I rolled her taut nipple between my fingers and shook her head. "My dragon, please…"

My restraint weakened with each plea. "Please what?"

"Please, love me more."

Those words were exactly what I needed to let go of all restraint. "Always."

Muscles bunching, I thrust harder into her. She gasped and then moaned as I found a more satisfying pace. Not frantic, but still steady and strong.

My pulse pounded in my ears. My body felt like a live wire as we fell into our desire together—our souls mingling, but not quite tangling up like my dragon soul desperately craved.

Astrid leaned forward and I caught her around the middle instinctively, fearing she was falling. She halted, but not from my support. She held her arms out in front of her with her hands curled around something invisible, as if she were suspending herself. At the same time, her feet hooked my hips.

I hissed as I slid impossibly deeper into her. Astrid let out the most primal groan I could remember hearing from her. This sound persisted as she used her invisible magic support as leverage to rock back into me, meeting my thrusts with vigor.

I let her take control of the pace, losing myself in the pleasure. My fingers slid along her luscious thighs and between her legs and I stroked her sensitive clit. Astrid responded with more pleasured gasps and moans and frantic movements. My body tightened and my breathing grew ragged.

Astrid tipped her head back, her eyes hazy with lust. "Diego—"

A shudder cut off her words. She clenched hard around my cock and then screamed in orgasmic release. The sound caressed my senses, pushing me over the edge. I grunted and spilled inside her in one strong erotic release.

I pushed past my limit, past being spent and the encroaching numbness in my limbs, desiring this euphoric sensation to remain just a little longer. Astrid's pussy pulsed around me, as if trying to encourage more even as her body tremored and she struggled for words through panting breaths.

"Shit…" I mumbled as I forced myself to still when I couldn't handle the stimulation anymore. I gripped her hips tighter to maintain grounding as numbness and euphoria pulsed through my body.

Astrid mumbled something incoherent in response.

When feeling returned to my body, I pulled her against me. I pressed my lips against the back of her neck and she shuddered. I smirked. Sometimes it felt like we were insatiable, and we couldn't stop. Other times, it didn't take much to find mutual bliss.

We drifted down to the ground. I gathered her in my arms and held her close as I sat at the base of a tree between its massive roots. She curled into me.

"*I love you,*" I murmured in Spanish. "*More than I know how to express.*"

She snuggled into my embrace. "*I love you too.*"

Hearing the Spanish roll off her lips made my heart melt for her more.

"And you express it without words every day," she said.

I smiled and tucked a lock of hair behind her ear, my fingers brushing her cheek and then her neck. "I'll continue to do so, for as long as I draw breath."

She hummed. "Well, then I guess I'll have to love you longer than that."

I chuckled. "Mine will be stronger."

Astrid turned in my arm and pressed a gentle kiss against my lips. "Not possible."

I grinned at her challenge. "We'll see about that."

My touch trailed down to her wings. She twitched and giggled as if it now tickled to be touched there. My fingers glided over her sleek feathers as I admired them. She rarely kept her wings out this long. I couldn't recall a moment I got to really take them in like this.

My path stopped when a silver feather snagged. My brow furrowed. I wasn't doing anything where that should have happened.

Hesitantly, I pinched the feather between my fingers. My intent was to fix it, as it was a bit askew, but it came free. "Uh…"

Astrid tilted her head. "Huh… That's a first."

"Did you feel me pull it out?"

She shook her head.

I twirled the feather between my fingers, then pressed the soft plumage to my lips. A familiar power sparked from it. I smiled. "There's a memory in it."

Astrid rested her head against my shoulder. "Of our impromptu date, or something else?"

I tucked the feather behind my ear. "I'll find out later. It's going in my hoard regardless."

"Woo, I finally have a memory object in your hoard."

I laughed and kissed her on the top of her head. "Don't worry, Cielo, I've got plenty of items with memories attached to you."

She hummed and mumbled a "good."

A nap sounded good, especially one with her in my arms. *She's probably going to be late for her client session.* I would have to make it up to the resident. I wasn't ready to let her go yet.

SEVENTEEN

ASTRID

The soft, rhythmic cadence of rain surrounded me. I leaned against a tree, breathing in the moist air and earthy aroma of the forest. My magic protected me from the falling water, allowing me to enjoy a moment of peace.

I shifted the basket in my arms, the weight reminding me I couldn't take long, but I didn't want to leave just yet. I'd barely had a moment to myself in the last twenty-four hours. Running a sanctuary had never been my goal, nor was I ready to do that. But here I was, and there was no turning back. Luckily, I had my guys to support me.

A smile tugged my lips, warmth filling my chest. While the balance of my duties and time with Diego, Tyr, and Baldur was shit, I had been thankful for the stolen moments.

Confessing things, getting them off my chest, had made me feel better and more connected with Tyr and Diego. It helped me cement myself when nothing seemed to make sense anymore. The only one I hadn't had enough time with was Baldur.

Guilt turned in my gut. It wasn't like I was intentionally ignoring him. Things were just happening everywhere and I wasn't keeping up well.

Muninn's presence entered my mind before he landed on my shoulder. Droplets of rain dripped off his feathers.

I made a face when I noticed the dead lizard in his beak. "Don't eat your lunch on me."

He chortled and swallowed his meal. *"What are you doing, Sister?"*

"Enjoying some time alone before I go find Baldur."

"Should I leave?"

I shook my head. "You're welcome to stay."

He looked down at the basket in my arms. *"What is this?"*

"I wanted to have lunch with him."

He crooned and his chest puffed out. *"Food for me?"*

I laughed. "You had your own food."

He snapped his beak unhappily and jumped on my basket. He tried to flip the lid open to peek inside, but I flicked his beak. He tugged on my arm sleeve a few times in his displeasure and flew up into the tree. I decided it was probably best to go find Baldur now.

I walked through the wet forest, Muninn flying above me. My magic was still protecting me, which did create some sensory confusion, but I was mostly used to it. The rain and soft ground beneath absorbed the sound of my footsteps. Rivulets of water trickled down the sloping landscape, washing over my shoes when I stepped on them.

My pace slowed when my vision blurred. I rubbed my eyes. Discomfort, like a growing headache, pulsed my temples. *Not now…*

My senses dulled. The patter of rain, the chilly spring breeze, and the dark cloudy sky, it all faded, replaced by warmth and laughter.

Mine. Theirs. I couldn't see them well, but I knew them. I was so happy. I never wanted anything more than this. Nothing could take this away from me. Nothing.

I gasped and blinked, my surroundings rushing back like a dam breaking. *It happened again…*

Muninn landed on my basket and tipped his head. *"Sister, what was that?"*

"Yes, tell us. "

I jerked my head up, my mind spinning a bit, to find Huginn perched on a branch above me, maybe an arm's reach away. I blinked slowly. Besides when Baldur first came back, this was the closest I ever remembered him getting to me. "You're here."

He snapped his beak. *"You project too much."*

Project? My eyes widened. "You both saw that?"

They bobbed their heads.

"It felt familiar," Muninn said.

My brow furrowed. "But that's the first time I've had that memory."

Muninn cocked his head the other way. *"Memory? Are you sure?"*

I chewed my lower lip and nodded. "I've experienced memory recovery enough to know that's what it was. But… they're not from the time I lived during the Viking age."

"They are older," Huginn said.

I nodded.

"We have those," Muninn said. *"Old and fragmented. From the time before."*

The time before? Did he mean before Ragnarök? I didn't know how old either of them was. I didn't think even Odin could put a number to their age. But from what I knew, Odin had his ravens before the first Ragnarök, so that meant the birds had fragmented memories, if any at all after the sacrifice.

"Are you old, Sister?" Muninn asked.

I grunted. "I'm forever twenty-nine, thank you."

He clicked a few times, then pressed the tip of his beak to my chest. *"No, old here. Older than anyone thinks?"*

I sucked in a quaky breath. "Maybe. I don't know. I'm still trying to piece some things together."

"Odin didn't trust you," Huginn said. *"Never trusted you."*

That was an obvious statement. He barely hid the fact he didn't trust me back then, even when I met him the first time. His first choice in interaction was to test me. And it was that mistrust that was his downfall.

"Lies and deceit, Brother," Muninn said. *"Not of her doing."*

My brows pinched together. What?

Huginn clacked his beak twice and puffed out his chest. *"You're going the wrong way."*

I watched him fly off in a different direction. "Wrong way for what?"

"Baldur is not this way anymore."

"His cabin is right up the path."

"Not here anymore."

Confused, I glanced down at Muninn. He watched his brother for a moment and then bobbed his head once before following. *Okay…* This day just got weirder and weirder.

I followed my ravens, away from the cabins without modern amenities, to a cluster of buildings made of rich honey-toned wood panels freshly treated and preserved with magic. These homes were provided with everything a resident could need. The birds flew past these and up a small path that veered away.

Residents who were home and noticed me pass through waved in greeting through their windows or from their covered porches. I greeted them back with all the warmth I could offer. As difficult as it was to run this place, it was rewarding, too. And I'd never allow anyone here to think they were a burden.

Heading down the offshoot path, I came upon a smaller cabin than the group ones, but of a similar style with large windows, shingled roof, and an inviting porch large enough for some patio furniture—furniture which was in the process of being moved around by Baldur.

I stopped and watched him, perplexed by this scene. Muninn and Huginn landed on the porch railing and crooned. Baldur paused his task of moving a patio couch and greeted the brothers. Then he noticed me. My heart did a little flutter when a grin slipped up the side of his face.

Baldur set the couch down and leaned against a sturdy support pillar. I stood there like an idiot, my brain short-circuiting. His pants slung low around his hips, showing off a delicious amount of his hip flexors, and he'd pulled his hair back in a half-up do like I'd taught him. He didn't have a shirt, showing off every cut of upper body muscle he had.

The way he leaned against the porch with his arm extended above his head, corded muscles stretched and pulled taut, gave me a perfect view of his delicious body marked with scars and protection-rune tattoos.

Baldur's eyes briefly flicked to the gray sky. "I was wondering when my sunshine would return."

My cheeks warmed, and I found it difficult to look at him all of a sudden.

"Astrid, that wasn't a reprimand."

I knew that. I knew his teasing tone all too well, but that didn't help me squash the shame spreading through me. "What are you doing over here?"

"Setting things up to my liking."

I blinked. "Did you move cabins?"

Baldur's brow pulled together. "No one told you?"

Great. I already felt shitty enough for not making time for him, and now here I was finding out he'd moved. "When did you move?"

"Yesterday."

Okay, that wasn't as bad as it could have been. But still.

Baldur pushed off the porch support beam and beckoned me with his fingers. I hesitated for a moment, then traipsed over. His fingers brushed my cheek. "What's wrong? And don't try to brush it off or deny it."

I pressed my lips together. I did not appreciate him calling me out like that.

He tucked his finger under my chin and lifted my gaze. "What's dimming your light, Sunshine?"

My lower lip caught between my teeth, and his icy blue eyes flicked down to my mouth. A mixed reaction of anticipation and guilt churned in my gut. "I'm sorry."

His brow creased. "For what?"

I shrugged noncommittally. "It's been, what, two weeks since I brought you back, and besides the first three days, I've hardly seen you."

"You've been busy." He said it with so much acceptance it hurt.

"That's not an excuse."

"It's not. It's a fact." Baldur tipped his head. "You're trying to run a sanctuary, be a therapist, exist as a Valkyrie and train your witch magic, and somehow fit in time to nurture connections you have with others, romantic or otherwise. That's more than anyone can do in a single day."

"But I—"

"Should be focusing on me? Why? You reviving me wasn't part of any plan. It's thrown off the delicate balance you already struggle to maintain."

"That doesn't mean I can accept neglecting you."

His eyebrows rose high on his head. "Who said you're neglecting me?" He chuckled. "I've got plenty of things to keep me occupied while I wait for you to be free."

I puffed out a breath. He was being too nice.

"It's been good for me, honestly," he said. "And probably what I needed most."

My brow knitted. "You think it's good I've ignored you?"

His head jerked back as he laughed. "You really want to look like the bad guy, don't you? If you want to play that game, then I ignored you, too."

I squinted. "Where is the logic in that?"

He shrugged. "I could have come seeking you out. I could have asked you to make some time for me. But I focused on other things."

I blew out another breath. He had a point.

Baldur poked the corner of my mouth, trying to lift it. "So, maybe instead of blaming yourself for no reason, we can catch up?"

I smiled despite the guilt, and lifted the basket in my arms. "I made us lunch."

He grinned. "Good, I'm starved."

I laughed. When was he not? I couldn't remember a time he and Fen didn't try to eat us out of house and home.

Baldur placed his hand on the small of my back, though his large hand curled up my spine, covering more of my back, and he guided me over to the patio couch. I dropped my magic the moment I was safely under the porch roof.

Baldur adjusted the couch's position to where he wanted, and then gestured for me to sit down while he brought the coffee table over. He plopped down next to me when everything was in place. "I see Huginn is tolerating you today."

My eyes flicked to the raven, where he sat on the porch railing, staring at me. "We shared a few words that weren't hostile."

Baldur's eyebrow arched, and he watched me as if he expected me to divulge more, but I didn't. That moment was between me and my ravens.

"Where's Angel?" he asked. "I saw her making the rounds this morning."

That was something she loved doing. She greeted all the residents on her rounds to make sure the property was secure and see if anything needed my attention.

I felt out my connection with her. A bubbling sensation in my mind that I recognized as Angel sparked in acknowledgement. "Looking for me, it seems. She was sleeping, after training this morning pooped her out."

"How is that going?"

I rocked my head back and forth. "Some progress, but it's still really difficult. We'll get there, though."

I folded back the lid of the basket. Muninn hopped onto the coffee table and tried to stick his head in. I tapped his beak. "Nosey, get out of there."

"I want to see."

I pinched the tip of his beak and pushed him out of the basket again. "You can wait for me to pull everything out."

He clicked at me, then hopped on top of the basket and tried sticking his head in that way. I laughed and grabbed him.

"Gwah."

"Gwah." I kissed him on the head and set him on the table. "Behave, or you won't get your meal."

He bobbed his head and crooned. Baldur smiled as he watched our interaction, and a slash of irritation from Huginn hit me. I didn't react negatively, and instead tried to push acceptance toward him, hoping it'd help him see I wasn't out to get him.

Dipping my hand into the basket, I pulled out a plate of caprese sandwiches. I set it on the table, giving Muninn a warning side-eye before retrieving a bowl of watermelon and feta salad, slices of fresh baked bread and a bowl of hummus, a plate of freshly baked chocolate brownies with frosting, and then a capped pitcher of freshly squeezed lemonade.

Baldur stared at the display while I grabbed the tableware. He licked his lips, his eyes gleaming. "You made all this?"

"I had a little help, but yes." Otherwise, I'd have come to see him sooner today. I wanted to really make up for all the missed time.

I set the picnic basket on the ground, and as I did, I pulled out one last thing—a plate of raw steak cut into digestible strips for the ravens, and finally, a chocolate chip muffin.

Muninn made a shrill popping call. *"Muffin!"*

Baldur and I laughed.

"So, this is the prized muffin I've heard about?" Baldur said.

Muninn tried to tear into it before I could cut it up for him and I laughed again. "This is his favorite thing in Midgard. It was alarming to learn at first, since a normal raven couldn't eat this without dying, but hey, who am I to question it?"

Muninn grabbed a slice and hopped closer to Baldur, offering it for him to try. Baldur took the confection, lightly pressed on it, as if testing its sponginess, smelled it, then popped it into his mouth.

He slowly chewed, his eyes lighting up. "I can see why. It's good. What's your favorite, Huginn?"

The raven puffed out, but he didn't growl like I thought he might. I sensed slight irritation from him, but also pleasure. Though, whenever Baldur talked to him, he was pleased, so I shouldn't have been surprised.

"Cheese puffs."

My eyes widened, giddiness bubbling up in my chest. I used my magic to pull a bag of cheese puffs from the pantry in the house to my hand. I smiled. "This one is my favorite brand."

I poured some on the plate with the meat and muffin, hopeful he might consider it. That hope died quickly. Huginn stared at me, his irritation slamming into me like a slap to the face. I frowned and tried not to deflate.

"Brother!" Muninn screamed at such a startling volume I jumped. *"Stop being this way. She's kind. She doesn't deserve your scorn."*

"Huginn, why do you hate her?" Baldur asked. "What did she do?"

The raven made a slow, almost growling sound. *"She sided against Odin."*

"I only did that when he killed Kirby," I defended. "I couldn't support a god who would do that to my friend who was nothing but loyal to Odin."

"She was not loyal," Huginn said. *"She loved another."*

"And Odin demanding that of the Valkyries was fucked up," Baldur said. "Everyone knew that. Especially since he also played favorites."

Muninn shuffled his feet. *"He hated our sister before that, though."*

I chewed my lip. "He was suspicious of me the very moment we met."

"You sided with Tyr," Huginn said. *"You couldn't be trusted."*

I threw up my hands. "I was mortal. What kind of threat was I to him?"

Huginn was quiet and for a moment I sensed his uncertainty. *"You sided with Tyr."*

I pursed my lips. He was being stubborn about that. But did he even know why? "Tyr saved me and I fell in love with him. That's not a crime. Yet Odin decided it was. I deserve to know why. So tell me, Huginn, what did I really do in Odin's eyes?"

Huginn puffed out his chest and then hissed. *"Betrayer."*

My brow furrowed. "What did I do to betray anyone?"

"Lies and deceit." Muninn cried back.

"Broken promises."

"Mask unveiled."

The two went back and forth, repeating the same phrases as if they were stuck in a loop. Each loop made my soul itch. Yeah, my soul. I looked to Baldur, desperately hoping he might know what was going on. His brow was furrowed in thought.

"I've seen them do this before," he said without my prompting. "My father said it was a problem with the magic in their bodies mixed with all the tasks he had them do, and that it caused them to speak nonsense. Though, I don't know how true that is anymore."

"Did you see how he stopped it?"

"He'd just concentrate and eventually they'd stop."

I bit my lip and tried. I didn't know what else to do. Concentrating hard on my familiar bond connection, I pushed calming energy into them. Muninn twitched and I felt his desperation. They were powerless to stop.

Leaping off the couch, I scooped both birds into my arms and held them close, hushing and cooing while desperate to sooth. *"Let go. I'm here. We can piece it all back together and together we can rebuild. Let the pain go."*

I didn't know why I thought those words, but the moment it appeared in my mind, something snapped tight, like a ribbon pulled taut. Huginn and Muninn's screaming halted.

Baldur and I blew out simultaneous breaths of relief. I set the ravens down on the coffee table and they sat still for a moment. *Are they rebooting after their 404 error?* Sure seemed like it.

They both puffed out at the same time and then shook themselves. Laughter bubbled up in my chest and I could only bite it back enough to stifle it into a giggle. I couldn't help it, it was too cute.

Muninn hopped onto my knee and rubbed his beak against my hand. *"Thank you."*

I stroked his head. "Of course, buddy."

I blinked when Huginn jumped onto my other knee. He shifted back and forth as if indecisive and then leaned over to lay his beak on my hand. I stared at him, unable to believe what I was seeing. I tentatively lifted my hand over his head and stroked his sleek feathers.

Huginn crooned so quietly I almost missed it. *"Lonely..."*

Gathering him in my arms, I held him close. "We're here."

"I wanted to be with him. But magic stops me."

I frowned, understanding what he meant. "I don't know how the curse works on Odin. I didn't know it prevented you from going near him."

"What was the wording?" Baldur asked.

"Summarized, I told him he'd have to wander alone for eternity unless Creation deemed he learned his lesson sooner."

He grunted. "That's a generous sentence, given what he's done." He then smiled. "But that just shows how much better of a person you are than him."

Huginn made a noise I didn't know how to interpret. *"I'm sorry."*

My brow raised high on my forehead. Even Baldur looked surprised.

"Odin said you were the enemy. I believed him. I thought this bond was a trap. It's not."

I stroked him. "I'm sorry you both were caught between it all. I don't want either of you to hate me, and I also don't ask you to hate Odin."

"Don't know how to feel anymore…"

"Take your time. There's no rush."

Muninn dipped his head. *"He played favorites, even with us."*

I frowned. "I'm sorry that happened. I try not to do that. And if you ever feel that I am, I want you to tell me so we can talk it over."

"Father didn't just mistrust you. He feared you," Huginn revealed.

My forehead scrunched. "Why?"

"Secrets," Muninn said. *"He thought you would reveal his lies and deceit. He thought you'd take us away from him and see all he has done. He did not know sharing those memories would be difficult even once the bond was passed."*

But what were the exact secrets he feared I'd find? The one I accused him of? Or were there even more dastardly things he'd done without anyone knowing? No doubt there were. But were they related to what I'd been trying to research, but failed to find time to continue as of late?

"You have seen it," Huginn said. *"The before times. Fragments, like us. You do know the truth deep down, just as he feared."*

Baldur stroked his jaw. "What's he talking about?"

I pressed my lips together. Could I tell him? I still didn't have enough to go on.

"I remember you now," Muninn said. *"Brought on by the memory you saw earlier. Different, but the same. Valkyrie, but not Odin's. Many who are not Odin's."*

Baldur leaned forward. "Memories? What is he talking about?"

My gaze never left Muninn. "Can you show me?"

"Yes," both of the ravens said.

Muninn half-jumped, half-flew onto my shoulder. *"Memories are my specialty. I remember everything. That is why you can see what I see."*

I looked down at Huginn. "And you?"

"I hear the best. I can't be confused by flowered words, disorienting speech, or magic. You will be able to hear the truths I do."

Memories and thoughts, just as their names meant. Muninn and I had struggled with the bond without his brother. They were both needed to make a complete connection. Together they made the perfect spies—spies who were my partners now.

"Yes," they both said.

Muninn pressed his head against the side of my face. *"See what fractured memory I have. See what I once saw before magic sealed it away."*

I sucked in a sharp breath. My vision cracked like broken glass. Large fractures flashed from the forest clearing to a sunny meadow carpeting the landscape with a sea of green, dotted with pink and blue flowers. A figure broke up the landscape, a woman with silver and gold wings—no, not quite gold… golden fire. Her wings were on fire! Yet she didn't appear to be in pain.

With her was a strange animal. It vaguely looked like a large, furry dog, but there were features about it that made it definitely not a dog… like the skull covering the top of its head. I couldn't tell if that was some sort of plating on top of the creature's actual head, or if the top half of its face was just a skull.

Power radiated off the creature, and its eyes… the eye sockets of the skull glowed with dark energy.

She turned to face this past memory of Muninn and my heart stopped. She was me. But she also wasn't. There were things about her that were slightly different, but her most prominent features were like staring in a mirror—minus the face scar.

The woman squinted as she smiled, and just as she opened her mouth, I felt Huginn rest his head against me. His connection added sound and physical sensation, livening this memory even more than it already was.

"How are my favorite boys today?" the woman said in a voice that sounded almost identical to mine.

My sight and senses snapped back to normal, the memory disappearing. I gasped in a lungful of air. Baldur's hand wrapped around my free shoulder, his grip grounding and comforting.

"That was…" I gulped. "Different."

I couldn't quite process. My mind pulsed. Something deep within me, the Valkyrie side of me, resonated with this memory more than any other memory I'd experienced. *Which was saying something, given how much I've had to remember.*

"Astrid, what is going on?" Baldur said.

I took another two good breaths to orient myself. "I'm… not sure how to explain. It's all been a bit chaotic, and what these two just showed me really cements that there's more going on than what I've uncovered."

Baldur grabbed a sandwich and bit into it; I picked up his quiet, pleased moan. His enjoyment of my food made my heart do a stupid flutter. "I'm a god who's lived for centuries and has been catching up on six hundred years of history after being pseudo-dead. I think out of anyone you know, I can do complicated."

When he puts it like that… I puffed out air through my lips and set Huginn into my lap. He nestled in and happily accepted a strip of steak when I offered it to him. "Well, I guess I'll start from the beginning. Everything started when I tried to learn more about what Valkyries are and where the dead actually go.

"We call it the afterlife, but none of us physically go there. I just have this instinct to send a soul someplace I'm calling Valhalla or Fólkvangr. And that ability to do so—while not unique, as reapers also touch the souls of the dying—is rather specific." Though, if I were honest, even with myself, I did recall a number of times it felt like the souls I touched didn't go to either of those places, yet I knew they were in the right place.

"There's also the fact that not just anyone can be a Valkyrie; they have to have the soul of one, which Kirby can somehow see, or feel it being different from another soul. Also, unlike reapers, we're specifically female, as far as anyone knows, which is strange in itself."

I grabbed a slice of bread. "What really got me thinking about this, though, was last fall, when Kirby and I connected with Elin and found out she'd not only awakened her Valkyrie abilities on her own, but was a Valkyrie long before Odin died, and wasn't one of his making. It created a lot of questions about the truths around Valkyries."

I spread some hummus on my bread. "Kirby also unlocked her own Valkyrie nature in this life, and she beat her curse by discovering what it meant to be a Valkyrie, which wasn't what Odin claimed a Valkyrie's purpose was."

"What does it mean to be a Valkyrie?" Baldur asked.

I shook my head. "I… don't know. I've been struggling with that identity for a while myself. Kirby has this vague idea that the answer is individual for each Valkyrie, but the thing we all have in common is we want to help people. I feel like there's more to it. Otherwise, the way she broke her curse would make more sense."

"What do you mean? How did she break it?"

I shrugged. "That's the thing, we don't know. When she hit a low point in her life at the place TOM called a school, and she tried to take her own life, the attempt failed. Something in her life by that point broke the curse, leaving her to rediscover the Valkyrie side of her, but Kirby has no idea what the trigger could have been. This leaves that question open, but whatever it is, it's not what Odin wanted us to believe."

Baldur drummed his fingers on his lap. "Keep going with your retelling of events. Maybe that'll help me piece something together than can help."

I nodded. "The logical conclusion we came to was that Odin lied about how he alone created Valkyries. This was compounded by the fact that each Valkyrie now connected to Kirby has unique abilities that aren't connected to her Valkyrie nature. Even Kirby's abilities aren't something she had in that first life of hers. At least, not that she remembers."

Baldur paused mid-bite of his sandwich. "What do you mean by unique abilities?"

"Well, Elin and Scarlett are both seers, but Scarlett's power goes further, allowing her to see special bonds linking people together. Tatiana and I have our witch magic, which manifests in its own unique ways. Magnus has rare channeling and amplifying abilities. The list goes on. But each one of us has something big and special about us that manifested separately from our Valkyrie awakening."

His brow furrowed as he thought. "I don't remember any Valkyries having abilities like that."

I nodded. "Kirby said the same thing when we were making these realizations, which added even more questions."

Baldur tried the hummus and then made a face. Looked like we found a food he didn't like. He held the bread up to feed it to me. I was all too happy to take a bite. I liked it when my partners fed me; I enjoyed that form of doting.

"So, all these revelations led you to research?" Baldur prompted.

I swallowed the food in my mouth. "I decided to make an effort to look into any remnants of the past, pre-Ragnarök, about Valkyries. Urd admitted she and her sister hid most of what remained, so I approached Urd about gaining access. Artura is the one who protects all the information, and I knew she'd deny me outright. Urd heard me out and how I felt it was important for us to look into this, and was willing to talk to her sister. Artura surprisingly agreed to allow me access, as long as I was supervised."

"Not all that trusting, is she?"

I shook my head. "She's protective, and I can't blame her. It's all that remains of the truth connecting us to the past."

I grabbed a sandwich to nibble on. "The archives are in languages no longer spoken. Some are similar to the language the gods know, but it's clear that what you spoke was a fragment of the real language. I've had to slowly work my way through this alone—translating what I can, and I'm no linguist, nor am I an archivist. It's taken me months to make any progress, and most of what I found isn't relevant to what I'm after."

My lower lip caught between my teeth. "This is where things might get confusing and weird. During my time researching, I had a strange dream. I was flying as a Valkyrie, but the world around me was different. Like it was ancient rather than me being in the future or something, and it strangely felt more real than the current world we live in. I assumed it was a dream brought on by all my research.

"Then… the day after the dream, Odin revealed he wasn't dead and was causing problems. Scarlett seemingly ended him again, but I wasn't convinced. Something deep within me told me that sword couldn't kill him any more than the ritual could. So, without anyone knowing, I started combing through the archive information to see if there was anything that could shed light on this feeling."

Baldur put his food down and turned his full intense attention on me. "Why couldn't you let it go?"

My brow furrowed. "I just told you—"

"You're not telling me all of it. We both benefit from you saying everything."

I chewed my lip. He was right. I just didn't want to sound crazy.

His gaze turned soft, and he tipped my chin up. "No matter what you say, I'll listen without judgment."

I blew out a breath. "During a college assignment, I ran into a theory that claimed Odin didn't always lead the Norse gods. At the time it resonated strangely with me, but I'd brushed it off, as it was all just myth to me. But after I had my memory restored and he'd returned, I started to wonder about that theory again. My dad always said myth was steeped in truths, so there had to be merit to that claim. The magic used during the first Ragnarök resulted in memory wipes and fragmentations. This could result in people making such theories from a truth, but with well-crafted lies by someone who didn't want the truth to be known, they could be dismissed as merely crazy theories."

Baldur thought for a moment. "So, you think my father used Ragnarök for his own gain and somehow bumped up his position of power?"

I nodded. "When we found Mia, Odin had returned again, just like I thought he would. I tried to do some more digging, but there wasn't a lot of time. It so happens, however, that I found a prophecy that mentioned him, and he was referenced as having a 'craven crown.' There was a scrawl of notes debating as to whether it was 'raven' or 'craven,' like it hadn't been written down improperly or something. That finding made me even more sure Odin had tried to manipulate what he could to keep his position."

I scrubbed my face with my hands. "When I accused him of stealing his crown and scheming to keep what wasn't his, I expected him to put up more of a fight to deny the accusations. But he didn't, and so I knew I'd been right."

Baldur smoothed his beard. "All of this in just a few short months."

"And I still haven't uncovered everything I need to," I admitted. "And the dreams... they didn't stop..."

Baldur regarded me a moment. "You know something. It's related to whatever Huginn and Muninn were talking about. And it's somehow all connected to everything you just told me, isn't it?"

I closed my eyes and tried to get my thoughts in order. "This is where I need to find more time to research. The ravens confirmed Odin was afraid I'd reveal his secrets. He never trusted me, even as a mortal. I had dreams of a time that I couldn't shake which were real, like memories."

Then I started having them while awake, only confirming they're memories. There was also the memory Diego told me about that matched what I'd been seeing, but I wasn't going to reveal that yet. That complicated things even more on a level I wasn't sure I was ready to tackle.

"And now... what Huginn and Muninn just shared with me all but confirms it."

Baldur leaned forward. "Confirms what?"

"That I lived as a Valkyrie once before."

EIGHTEEN

ASTRID

Baldur blinked. "You're going to have to elaborate on that one for me."

I pressed my lips together. "My dad raised me on the belief that there is no such thing as a coincidence. If it was happening but you didn't know why, it was because of some unseen event. Back during the Viking age, I had Valkyrie tendencies. They grew in intensity the longer I lived, even if I couldn't do everything a Valkyrie could. This all but confirmed I had a Valkyrie soul, and had I not died, I may have unlocked my potential all on my own. But why?"

I lifted my gaze to meet his. "With everything I've learned and seen, I can only come to the conclusion I was a Valkyrie once before. There were many sacrifices to push back Ragnarök. It could be that I was a Valkyrie who was part of that sacrifice. It makes sense that if I reincarnated for some reason, and Odin recognized me, he'd have worried that I'd remember the past, and he couldn't have that. This meant he did some dastardly shit to obtain his power and I was too much of a liability."

I blew out a breath. "I don't know how important any of this is. It could be meaningless in the end."

Baldur's fingers brushed my cheek before curling around the back of my neck. I looked up at him. "It's important. I can't say why it is, but the more you've talked about this, the more I knew this was important to know. Like you said, there are no such things as coincidence. You following this path to uncover the past has a point. Otherwise, you would have ignored it."

A small smile tugged my lips. He was right. I needed to trust my instincts and follow all this. *I need to confirm that what I read in college was correct. That the reason Odin hated Tyr so much, and feared I would expose him, was that he had stolen everything from my god of judgment.*

Baldur leaned over me. "I want to help in any way possible. It sounds fun to uncover all those mysteries lost to the past."

I smiled, the corner of my eyes creasing. "I'd love that."

His lips brushed against mine. My heart tumbled over itself. I leaned into him and kissed him slowly. There was no rush. We savored each other, enjoying this brief moment that felt familiar, in a strangely ancient way.

"Astrid," a quiet, sing-song voice called out.

I pulled away from Baldur and looked out beyond the porch. A child with dark hair and pale skin rushed down the path, Angel hot on her heels. A woman followed at a much more sedate pace. She had long dark hair and blue-ish pale skin. The water falling from the sky rippled her skin as if it were hitting a water surface.

The little girl ran up to the porch and latched onto one of the supports. Angel jumped onto the porch and shook. I squealed and complained, throwing up a magic shield to protect us from the water flying off her coat. Baldur threw his back and laughed. The little girl, who now hid shyly behind the pillar, giggled.

"Hi, Cora," I greeted.

"Hi." She practically whispered the greeting, a stark contrast to her exuberant call earlier. Her eyes flicked to Baldur.

Baldur smiled gently and waved at her. Cora waved her fingers.

"Why the sudden shyness, little water bug?" the approaching woman said in a thick Grecian accent.

Cora puffed out her cheeks, her skin turning a cute shade of pink. "Mamá…"

I pressed my lips together. She was too adorable.

Her mother chuckled. "Why don't you tell Astrid what you want from her? It looks like she's very busy."

Cora toed the ground. "Um… Astrid… can you… send a message to Babá for me?"

A sharp pain twisted in my chest. Cora and Naeda were two of the many survivors we'd helped after a raid. We'd caught wind of the attack late, and many lives were lost—including Cora's human father.

He'd fought bravely and I'd been the one to have the honor of guiding his soul to Fólkvangr.

"You want to send a message to your dad?" I asked, making sure I understood her correctly.

She nodded. "I want him to know how happy Mamá and I are."

Oh boy… I smiled. "Of course we can do that."

Liar, liar… But I wasn't a monster and I wouldn't tell her it wasn't possible. She'd lost enough. If she wanted to believe the Valkyries could pass messages to the dead, then so be it.

Huginn and Muninn looked at me and I felt their silent agreement to help. They hopped over to the edge of the coffee table.

"It's not actually me who sends the message." My brain worked overtime, trying to come up with something believable on the fly. "Huginn and Muninn do that. So, you'll have to tell them your message."

Cora smiled wide and came up onto the porch. She "whispered" her message to the ravens, telling her dad how good she was being, how happy she and her mom were, and how many new friends she was making in this new place. She didn't want him to worry about them.

I choked up the more she talked, and her mother wasn't able to stop a few tears from spilling.

When Cora was done, she smiled at me. "That's what I wanted to say."

I took a controlled breath, and slid off the couch. I offered my arm to Muninn and had Cora hold hers up for Huginn. The brothers hopped up and we walked out into the rain. They took off into the sky, climbing higher and higher until they disappeared, using their magical bracelets to teleport away.

My soul pulsed, as if her father had truly received the message. I smiled. I was willing to believe that was possible.

After a moment my ravens returned. They landed on Cora's and Naeda's shoulders and pressed their heads against the nymphs. Cora gasped and Naeda pressed her fingers to her lips, tears brimming her eyes. When the ravens were done with whatever they were doing, they flew to my shoulders, where they were content to perch.

Cora clamped her arms around my leg. "Thank you!"

Naeda, who couldn't stop her tears, grabbed my hand. "Bless you, Raven Valkyrie."

She ushered her daughter away, leaving me standing there in stunned silence.

"Raven Valkyrie," Baldur said. "You got yourself a new title."

"Yeah…" I murmured, barely hearing him as I got out of the rain. "What just happened?"

"We delivered the message like you asked," Muninn said.

"And he had a message in return," Huginn said.

I blinked slowly. "Wait, what? I was doing that to make her feel better. Are you saying, you can actually pass messages to the departed?"

The ravens bobbed their heads. Baldur made an impressed face.

I scrubbed my face. "I'm so confused. How long has this been a thing?"

"I don't know," Muninn said. *"I only realized I could do it when you asked."*

"Something unique because you're a Valkyrie?" Baldur wondered.

"But, Odin should have been able to do the same, then," I said. I paused. "Unless…"

"Valhalla was never originally his," Huginn said for me.

Baldur and I shared a look. That explained so much. Why Aya was able to give guardianship to Brit, and why Odin had gone through such lengths to try and reclaim it with magic instead of just use his power to.

Baldur smirked. "I think this is when you say, the plot thickens."

I laughed. I laughed so hard I almost fell over. Why that was so funny, I didn't know, but it apparently was to my overworked brain.

Baldur caught me around the middle and held me steady. "Why don't we get you sitting."

I nodded as I calmed. "And we can talk about you, because I've been doing a lot of talking about me."

Baldur sat back down and pulled me onto his lap. My ravens hopped onto the table and Angel jumped onto the couch with us. I gave her a good scratch before curling into Baldur.

"What do you want me to talk about?" he asked after grabbing another sandwich to eat.

"For starters, let's talk about you deciding to move out of the blue. The hell is that about?"

He took a bite of his food. "Well, while you've been busy with your own things, I've been working with Aya to better integrate myself around technology. The slow, casual approach wasn't working, so we've been steadily adding wireless items to my residence to increase stimuli to desensitize me."

I grabbed his hand and took a bite of his sandwich. The plan to get him used to the sound of electricity was simple on paper, but the desensitizing process was far from it. Plus, there was a chance, no matter how much Baldur tried, he may not be able to get used to the sound. There were plenty of people out there who couldn't, even when they'd grown up with it around them.

He continued. "I got to the point where I thought I was ready to fully integrate myself. Diego provided me this cabin, so I began moving what I had over."

I splayed my fingers over his warm chest and rested my head on his shoulder. The light scent of sandalwood and peppermint wafted into my nose. Someone had given him a new bottle of either beard oil or cologne, because I didn't remember him smelling this way before. I was guessing Aya's doing. She knew how much I loved sandalwood. "Is there anything you need?"

We kept the cabins rather empty to allow residents to furnish how they wanted. We found it helped them adjust better to their new situations. And with Baldur being brought back to life, he didn't have much besides what we'd been providing him slowly.

Baldur pressed his lips together, his brow furrowing. "I'm not sure. I'm still working out what I need to help myself integrate and what I'm curious about in my learning."

I hummed thoughtfully. "How about this then; how was your first night?"

He pulled a face that made me laugh. "The fridge is the most annoying part. I'm struggling with the buzzing sound it makes. It kept me up for a while."

"Well, I can't help with that, so why don't you give me a tour and tell me how you feel about things? Maybe that'll help me understand what you might need to succeed in this plan of yours."

He smiled and agreed. I slid off his lap, and he stood. His strong fingers snagged mine and he led me inside. I also somehow ended up with his sandwich, which I happily munched on.

We stepped into what should have been a living room but looked more like a warzone. Papers and books in various stages of being open and read were scattered everywhere. Not even the entertainment stand for the TV was spared. I was half surprised I didn't see any weapons sticking out of the wall or the furniture tipped on its side.

"Who knew Odin's perfect son was so messy," I muttered.

He laughed. "Tidiness isn't one of my stronger traits. It's why I rarely ever let anyone enter my house. I struggled with that need to keep up the façade."

That explained a lot. In the past, he'd insisted no unannounced visits, and really just seemed to rather have people not come over. I'd only ever been inside his house a handful of times. I never thought much of it at the time, especially since I'd been more than happy to host everyone if Aya didn't.

"So," I began, my eyes scanning the room. "Should we invest in a laptop for you?"

He pointed to the coffee table in front of the couch. "I have one."

I couldn't see it, but I guessed it was buried under everything else. "Are you feeling a lot of eye strain while using it?"

"Yes and no." He guided me over to where he had a printer set up. "I'm having a lot of fun with this printer thing. Aya did something with the laptop to allow me to print whatever I wanted as long as I had paper in it."

I gazed up at him as his voice took on a more excited tone. A broad grin spread over his face. "What do you like about it?"

"Everything! It takes all that I'm seeing on the laptop and puts it on a page. There's no need to transcribe with ink and quill, or now it's pencils or pens. And the way it does it, watching that… ink cartridge slide back and forth and magically know how to print the correct words or pictures, it's all so fascinating."

I bit back a laugh when he mentioned magic. I had a feeling that was going to be a common descriptor for a while as he learned.

He grabbed a book and held it up. It appeared to be some sort of spy thriller, from the cover. "That's how they make these books, right?"

I nodded. "The printing is done on a larger scale, allowing for more books to be made at once instead of one at a time, but the idea is the same."

His forehead crinkled. "Larger scale? But this book size is smaller than the paper I'm printing on."

I smiled and pushed him toward the couch. "Let's use the computer to show you a printing press and the bookmaking process in action."

Baldur didn't resist. No, I swear he would have sprinted had the couch not been only a few feet away. He gathered papers on the couch and dropped them in a messy pile under the coffee table so there was a clean spot for both of us. Without needing to search, Baldur slid his hands under a pile of papers and lifted the laptop lid, sending the papers scattering. *Good thing messes don't bother me.*

I watched him operate the laptop. While slow at it, he seemed to have a remarkable grasp on how the technology worked. I grinned. "You're going to be better at this than Tyr."

He chuckled. "Aya said the same thing. I think there's a betting pool on how long it'll take."

I belted out a hearty laugh. Of course there would be. I was going to have to get in on that.

Baldur searched printing presses and read the article out loud instead of in his mind. I let him, enjoying his enthusiasm. When he was done, I helped him bring up a video to show him the printing process. He was enraptured. Though, I wasn't sure if it was the video or printing technology he was more fascinated by. *Probably both.*

"Wow," Baldur said when the video ended. "Book making is both the same as it once was, but also not. It's amazing how this current process makes it easier for anyone to get their hands on books."

He picked up two books from the coffee table. One appeared to be a non-fiction book on war history—naturally. The other one was more of a surprise. I actually blinked to make sure I wasn't seeing this. He held one of Scarlett's books in his hands.

My eyes swept over the books I could see, and the range of topics both nonfiction and fiction amazed me. "Do you like to read? Or is it something you're doing because it's the easier way to obtain knowledge when you don't want to use the laptop?"

He grinned. "Both."

I propped my arm on the back of the couch. "Do you have a preference of what you're reading?"

He pulled out a few more non-fiction books from under the papers. "These help teach me what I missed. I'm also less worried the information in here is fake, so I don't have to rely on some program Aya put on my laptop that tells me if information is false."

My eyebrow quirked up. *She has a program like that and she isn't sharing it? That bitch. I'll have to have a talking with her about that.*

Baldur held up Scarlett's book and took the spy thriller from me. "These are like the tales we used to tell by mouth, but I can consume them at any time and more than once. It's fascinating seeing what another can make up in their mind and then share, knowing none of it is real."

"Do you have a favorite genre yet?" I asked.

He thought for a moment. "I don't know. I think I need to read more. But I'm also running out of room for the ones I have. I need another bookshelf."

Not that he's using the current one well. I grinned and pulled out my phone. "Or, you start going digital."

Baldur watched me intently as I opened my reading app and then showed him the covers in my library. His eyes went wide and he snatched my phone.

"These are all books?" he asked as he scrolled.

"Yup. It's the same thing as the physical, as long as you get the same edition, just digital. Your laptop can also use the app, but I find phones and tablets better. Or specialized reading devices. Some of these are even audiobooks."

"What's an audiobook?"

I smirked and pulled up one of my murder mysteries, pressing play. The narrator regaled the tale where I had left off, just as the killer was closing in on the heroine.

Baldur stared at my phone, awestruck. "It's like how we used to tell stories. How many of these books can your phone hold?"

"Thousands."

His eyes lit up, bringing a big smile to my face. I was so glad I could see this passion building. I wanted to see more of that.

"What else have you been experiencing ever since you were brought into the current century of technology?"

Baldur talked about the TV and more about the various internet things he was learning. I listened to him ramble on. I couldn't say I paid attention to everything, but I was enraptured. Mostly by the low timbre of his voice that maintained an expressive quality that was uniquely his. But also, by him in general. The shape of his face, and the dips of his muscular shoulders. The way his eyes lit up in his excitement. The curve of his mouth…

My eyes flicked to his mouth a lot. I really wanted to kiss him again. I wanted to do more than kiss him, but he hadn't really given me any signs he wanted more at this point. Maybe that was my fault. I had been fairly distant up until now. I'd probably all but killed what spark was there; what was left was barely hanging on by a thread.

Baldur abruptly stopped. "I'm boring you, aren't I?"

I smiled. "No, I love hearing your passion. It doesn't matter to me if I know all about it already or not. I want to see what now interests you, even if those interests change over time."

He slid his arm over the back of the couch, and leaned closer. "I'm at a disadvantage here. I still haven't learned all the things you're passionate about. I think that needs to change."

I made a thoughtful sound in my throat and leaned in, my fingers trailing along his chest. "Is that so?"

"Maybe you should share something now."

My mouth curled into a grin, and my voice dipped to something a little throatier. "Make me."

Baldur blinked slowly and then his brow knitted. "I… don't know if I can. Isn't that the point of you telling me things?"

I let out a slow breath. He couldn't be that clueless. "That means you need to discover it in the moment."

Unfortunately that didn't clue him in any better. *Okay…* I really wasn't sure what I should do. I wasn't even sure where this disconnect was coming from. I thought he was flirting with me with his posturing, but apparently not. *There's one last thing I can try.* It was bold, but Baldur liked boldness in the past. At this point, it couldn't hurt.

I scooted closer. "All right, fine, I'll concede. You get one thing from me."

Baldur watched me with growing interest and waited for me to say something, but it wasn't that simple. I climbed into his lap and curled into him. He froze, as if not understanding, then slowly wrapped his arms around me. His warmth seeped into my skin and presence closed in around me. It was comforting and familiar.

"This is something I like," I murmured.

Baldur pulled me in tighter and pressed his face to the top of my head. "I like this, too."

We remained like this for a long while. I listened to his strong heartbeat, the reminder of what an astronomical feat I'd managed. I lost myself in his presence. That was until he started laughing and squirming.

I sat up, my hand sliding against his torso. Baldur twitched again and grabbed my wrists. My eyebrow quirked. "You're ticklish."

"I am, and I don't appreciate you discovering this fact."

I grinned. Before he could clamp down harder to stop me, I broke free of his grasp and tickled his sides. He flailed and fought me off, both of us falling into a fit of laughter. This gave him the upper hand and I found myself pinned down on the couch.

I blinked up at him, a little confused how I'd gotten like this, though I also wasn't complaining.

"You need to behave," he said.

I smirked. "Make me."

Baldur stared down at me. Like last time, this seemed to confuse him. *I give up…* I clearly had done something wrong. We were once on the same page, but I didn't know about that anymore. It was best to stop pushing something that wasn't happening.

I huffed. "Fine. I'll behave."

Baldur hesitated, as if he wasn't sure if he could believe me, but after I put on my most sincere innocent face, he relented and I sat up. *Now what?*

After thinking a moment, I pivoted on the couch and laid my head on his lap. "Why don't you read me something?"

"Read to you?"

"I'm sure there's a book you really want to read right now. You can read it out loud and I can enjoy it with you." It'd keep me distracted—I hoped, at least. "And if that doesn't work, we can watch a TV show or something together."

"All right, we can try that."

Baldur grabbed Scarlett's book and opened it to the first page. I used my magic to clean up the coffee table and transport what remained of our lunch inside. Muninn complained, and I noticed why. My familiars had been helping themselves to some of the food. *Jerks.*

As Baldur read, a sense of familiarity washed over me. I looked up at him and my vision flashed. It was him, and we were in the same position, but the room was different. Well, frankly, so was he, but it was clearly him. He read from a different book, and the words that came out of his mouth were foreign yet familiar. Then all my senses snapped back.

"Baldur," I hedged.

He looked down at me. "Yes, Sunshine?"

I licked my lips. "You were born after Ragnarök, right?"

He nodded. "As far as I'm aware."

"He was," Huginn confirmed.

"Why do you ask?" Baldur asked.

I wasn't sure if I should tell him. Or even if I could. It was part of what I still wasn't clear on with this whole past-before-Ragnarök thing. "Let's just say, the plot thickens for now."

He chuckled, his eyes sparkling with amusement. "Okay, Sunshine. The plot thickens, then."

NINETEEN

BALDUR

Deep breath.

Deep breath.

Lifting my hand, I knocked on the wooden door. I stood there, shifting my weight and adjusting my grip on the bundle in my arms, waiting. After a few moments without an answer, I knocked again. Still no answer.

A muscle in the back of my neck tightened and I had to force myself to breathe. Astrid was there. Aya confirmed it on my way up. Astrid had also told me I had permission to enter at any time even if no one answered, but it felt rude to do so. And that wasn't an excuse in any way.

Yes it is.

My free hand clenched and unclenched and the strangest desire to flee tugged at every fiber of my being. Why did I feel this jittery? Why did I, a war god of courage, feel like I needed to run? That wasn't to say I didn't know fear. Courage wasn't the absence of fear after all. But I also knew this wasn't something I needed to be fearful of. I wanted to see her.

I closed my eyes and sucked in a deep breath. I'd never felt this way when thinking about her in the past. I wanted to always be near her. I wanted to bask in her radiance. But something had changed after I confessed that. It should have been easier to be around her, not harder. Yesterday couldn't have been more painfully obvious how messed up this was.

Fuck it. I grabbed the handle and twisted it. The door opened with ease, inviting me into the brand-new space. Before I could think of some excuse to come back another time, I stepped through the threshold.

The air shifted, as it sometimes did when you walked through magical portals. The sounds of the mountain house were replaced by gentle lapping waves and seabirds. Soft music played from somewhere deeper in the house. I called out for Astrid with no response.

Walking down a short hallway, I found myself in a spacious living room with a beachfront view. Pictures hung on the wall, with other décor like potted plants and items I didn't have names for, decorating the place. However, it was the entertainment center that was the obvious focus.

Angel, who lay sprawled on a large pillow like it was a bed of sorts for her, lifted her head on my entry. Tuggy and Buggy lounged with her like it was the most normal thing for them to hang around canines. It still shocked me to see them love her when they hissed every time they saw Fen.

Two raven heads poked up from behind Angel. Angel wagged her tail in greeting and the ravens crooned. Tuggy and Buggy acknowledged my presence but didn't offer any vocal greetings.

I smiled. Something about them all like this felt… familiar. I knew Angel and Muninn got along, but I'd not seen them like this before. And Huginn's quick turnaround after making that breakthrough yesterday was both surprising but also reassuring. Things were feeling right. At least where the familiars were concerned.

Suddenly my vision went askew and pain jolted in my head. My surroundings changed to something familiar yet foreign, like I'd been there a long time ago, but also imagined it, preventing me from describing what I could see. Angel went from a normal dog size to a monstrous black canine creature. Muninn and Huginn both seemed large for ravens. Even Tuggy and Buggy became a bit larger than their current fluffy oversized cat visages.

Then my vision returned to normal and the pain vanished. *That was weird…* I shook it off and focused on pressing matters. "Where is Astrid?"

"Down the hall," Muninn said.

I nodded and wandered down the hall. I stopped short in front of a door when Astrid appeared suddenly. Her cheeks were flushed with an alluring shade of pink, and her hair was tied messily over her shoulder, as if she'd hastily pulled it back.

"Baldur, hi." Her breath came quickly.

My eyes flicked from her to inside the bedroom where a large bed took up a sizable amount of space. Bright light shone in through the room's large windows, cascading over Diego. He lay across the bed, his arm draped over his face. His tousled curls framed his face, drawing the eyes to his cheekbones. A sheet barely covered his naked body around his hips. Based on his shallow breathing, he was asleep.

I grinned, taking a moment to appreciate the sight of him, and the fact that Astrid had tired a dragon out so much. "I'm not interrupting, am I?"

"No." She glanced back at Diego, a satisfied smirk on her lips. "We're definitely done right now."

"Well, good." I held out the bouquet of flowers I'd carried in. "I'd like my turn to spend time with you now."

Astrid's bright smile melted away some of my unease from earlier. She took the flowers and inhaled their sweet scent. "These are beautiful. Thank you. I should put these in a vase."

I nodded and my eyes flicked to Diego again briefly. He was a bit more distracting than I would have liked right now.

Astrid chuckled and her hip bumped me as she pushed past. "I licked him first."

I grinned. "That's impressive tongue work."

She glanced back at me, her eyes sparkling and the curling of her lips alluring. "He thinks so, too."

I swallowed, an image of her kneeling in front of me, eager and wanting, flashed through my mind. Shaking that tempting image from my head, I followed her back down the hall. My eyes roamed her, from the sway of her hips to the way her tank top and cotton shorts clung tight to her curves. I very much appreciated the fashion in this age.

Astrid headed for the kitchen but then stopped when she saw the cuddling pile of familiars. "Buggy, Tuggy, when did you both get in here?"

I blinked and glanced at the felines. Their eyes were squinted and they both trilled at Astrid. I hadn't thought anything of their presence, given Astrid was home. I had just assumed she'd let Aya's cats in.

"Angel let them in," Muninn said.

Astrid nodded and resumed her searching as if it weren't strange her dog was opening doors. I could only guess she was used to it. She opened a cupboard door and tried to reach for a large rectangular container made of glass that was well out of her reach.

"Need help?" I asked.

"Nope," she puffed out.

I chuckled. "It's no trouble."

Astrid stopped reaching and I thought she might have reconsidered. Nope. I blinked as I watched this tiny woman climb onto the counter and grab the vase instead of using her magic. I said nothing as she jumped down and went about filling the glassware with water. What else was I supposed to do? That might have been the oddest thing I'd seen her do. Okay, maybe not, but it was high on the list.

"How did you sleep last night?" she asked while setting the partially filled vase on the counter and poured some sort of powder from a pouch that'd come with the flowers.

"Okay." My eyes cut to her fridge. "One of these days I have to get used to the buzzing, right?"

Astrid grabbed some scissors and began trimming the flowers. "I hope you do."

That lacked the confidence I was used to. "Do you not think I will? You seemed confident yesterday when we were talking."

She glanced back at me. "I'm confident you'll work hard. However, I'm also realistic. Some people never get used to the sound of electricity.

If you end up being one of those people, we'll work on ways to make things easier for you."

I smiled. I appreciated her being honest and not hiding a possible reality.

"There," she announced. The flowers were now neatly arranged in the vase. "Now where to put it?"

I watched her walk around and try a few places until she settled for the kitchen table. Her beaming smile was everything I'd hoped to see. I didn't care that it was over just flowers.

She spun on her heels to face me, clasping her hands behind her back. "So, what do you want to do?"

I opened my mouth, but the moment our eyes met, all thoughts vanished. "Uh…"

She grinned and closed the small gap between us. She bent forward a little, tipping her head all the way back on her shoulders to look up at me, while cocking her head just enough. It was cute and alluring at the same time. "What's wrong, Baldur? Valkyrie caught your tongue?"

Yes. I didn't know why, but just like before, when she was like this, I forgot what to do or say.

A crease formed on her forehead as her brow pinched together. "Baldur?"

"Um…" I rubbed the back of my neck. "I came here with an idea."

She tipped her head a little more and blinked slowly. Heat rose along my cheeks into my ears. *What was I going to say?*

Astrid chuckled, her lips tugging into a type of smile that made my pulse leap. She lifted a finger and beckoned me closer. I crouched to be better on her level, though I still towered over her. I bent over as she continued to command me closer. I couldn't deny her.

Her fingers slid through my beard along my jaw. Closer she drew me, her presence the most bewitching of poetry. Our breath mingled for a moment before her soft lips pressed against mine. My heart lurched.

My eyes hooded and my nose flared, breathing her in. Just as I began leaning into this kiss, Astrid pulled away. Both disappointment and relief clashed within me.

She hummed thoughtfully. "I'm more curious than ever why you're so tongue-tied."

I pressed my lips together. That was a damned good question.

Astrid took my hand in hers and tugged me to follow her. I didn't hesitate to comply. We sat on the sectional sofa. She tucked her legs up, her knees touching my thighs, and propped her arm on the back of the sofa. She rested her cheek on her palm.

Her piercing eyes stared up at me—through me, like she could see past any type of armor I erected to hide the darkest secrets that branded my soul. "I think we should talk, over anything else."

I swallowed. "Why does that sound so ominous?"

She laughed, the whimsical sound making my stomach swoop. I always loved her laugh. "I tried to make that line sound less terrifying, but I guess no matter how you word it, it's not an easy one."

I didn't have a response for that. Hel, I was still failing to think properly with her looking at me.

"I guess I'll start with the obvious question," she started. Her words made me twitch on the inside. "You still want to see where this goes with us, right?"

My eyes widened. *Shit.* I should have known she'd start questioning this. "Of course I do. I just…"

I puffed out a breath as the right words failed me. I had never failed to articulate myself. Why was this so difficult?

Astrid slid her hand into mine. Her warmth and gentleness seeped into me. Something inside me relaxed. "Take your time. I'll hear everything on your mind if you want to dump it in one go. I can help you sort it out after."

My eyebrow quirked. "So, you're my therapist now?"

She laughed. "No. I can utilize my therapist skills in some way, but this is just me trying to communicate with you. I'm here for you, no matter what that thing is. That's how healthy relationships work."

My fingers closed around hers. I wanted that with her. "I don't know what's going on with me. I've never had this issue before. When I want to show interest, I do. I don't hesitate and I always have the right words to say."

I hesitated and then pushed on. "But when I'm with you, that confidence is gone. I forget everything I wanted to say or do. Today, as I walked over here, I knew what I wanted to tell you and what I wanted to propose for plans. Then I get here and you look at me…"

She smiled in a way that made my heart thump in my chest. "I make you nervous."

Was that what I was experiencing? "I suppose you do in a way. You're a startling woman, in a good way. But that's not the issue, I don't think. Or the main one at least."

"Maybe you're struggling to jump from friends to lovers with me? Given how long we felt we had to avoid our true feelings."

Something clicked in my mind, like we'd just found the correct linking puzzle piece. "I spent centuries being your friend hoping one day that'd change, but never pushed. I knew how to talk to you as a friend. I thought I knew how I'd approach you to change that status. And now here I am, centuries later, and I don't know how to properly court you in this day and age."

I squeezed her hand. "It's confusing how I have maintained these strong feelings toward you when I'm still trying to learn who you are. How can I court you if I don't know this?"

"That's the point of courtship." Astrid's sweet smile remained in place. "Yes, there's getting to know how compatible you are with someone on a romantic and sexual level, but there's also an element of learning who that person is. There's a level of getting to know them deeper than any other person alive could. It doesn't happen in a course of a day or three, but over a long period of time, until you come to a point you can't imagine a time never not knowing that person so intimately. And then, even when you hit that point, you still learn more. It's not something that really ever stops."

Her fingers trailed up my arm, sending a jolt through me. "Yesterday was a great example of how I got to know you more. You've been in a death-like state for over six hundred years. By all accounts, you theoretically shouldn't have changed at all. And yet, I learned something about you."

She laughed. "Sure, yesterday had plenty of awkward moments, but I can tell you I've had even more awkward dates in my life."

My brow pinched together. "Yesterday wasn't a date."

"Wasn't it?"

I didn't understand. Nothing about yesterday remotely came close to what I'd been reading on dates in modern courtship.

"A date is a moment of time where you and your partner spend quality time together," she said. "They don't have to be as extravagant as dinners and costly live entertainment. They could be simple, like taking a walk together, or playing some video games while stuffing your faces with pizza. They don't even have to end with you tangled up doing the horizontal tango."

Her hand rested on my chest, right over my heart where I could feel it beating as her words sank in. "They're stolen moments together in a busy life that seems to always want to keep you apart."

I curled my fingers over her hand, pinning it to my chest. Warmth spread through my body. We had stolen a moment together, hadn't we? We were both so busy with our own things, we'd had to force time to just stop and be together. That's why she'd been so hard on herself even though I hadn't faulted her for being busy.

I sucked in a deep breath and shifted to give her my full and intense focus—maybe a little too intense, because she shifted back a bit and her eyes widened a little. "I want to take you on a classic date, with dinner and entertainment."

Astrid blinked and then smiled, her shoulders relaxing. "I'd love that. But before we do, I think we should talk about the pacing of all this. I'm not the most skilled flirt out there, much to Aya's chagrin, with all her failed attempts to help me get better, but you freeze up every time I do. So I don't know if I'm pushing too much for your comfort level, and if we're going on a date, I need to know where the line is."

That was a fair and sensible request. There was only one problem. "I don't know…?"

She laughed when I added a questioned inflection at the end.

"Being completely honest, you're the first person I can recall pursuing for any form of long-term relationship."

Astrid blinked, her surprise plain as day. "Really?"

I nodded. "That might be what's compounding my issues, now

that I think about it. My intent with others was always physical and temporary. But with you… I want to do this right, whatever that means for this modern age."

She smiled gently. "The correct way isn't defined. Some people might claim otherwise, but really, it's what those in the relationship want. Some people fuck on the first date, while others wait until they're married. Some people aggressively date with defined goals they want to meet by certain times, while others are more casual."

"What pacing are you expecting?" I asked.

My eyes flicked down to her mouth when she chewed her lower lip. "How to put this so it doesn't sound like a deflection… Um, whatever pace makes you comfortable."

That intrigued me. "How did things go for you and Tyr and Diego?"

She awkwardly half-laughed. "That's why I'm saying it's probably going to come down to your comfort level. My relationship with those two started off unconventionally. Diego and I have been friends since we were kids, and danced around each other until last year. He decided to kiss me after a conversation to finally tell me his feelings, and then we danced around each other for a while longer until we fucked and then decided we were just dating. Going on classic dates didn't happen until a while later."

Well, that wasn't what I expected to hear. "And Tyr?"

"Even less conventional. He showed up and tried to get me to remember him. Eventually I did, but not our previous relationship, so Aya had us pose as a couple during a reenactment event in hopes to help. It did."

"Let me guess, so you two fucked and didn't do dates until later."

Her eyes squinted. "Um, well, dates aren't a big thing for Tyr. Unlike Diego, who is a big romantic and into grand gestures, Tyr is more… physical. Sex removed from the equation, his idea of taking care of me is doing manual labor and ensuring I'm comfortable.

"We'll spend casual time together and maybe go on walks or do some carpentry projects as a date, but grand gestures in the form of date activities would most likely come from Diego's brain rather than his. Tyr tries to make up for it by spoiling me with all the money he has, when I don't frustrate him by insisting he doesn't need to pay for everything in my life."

I chuckled. Those two explanations didn't even remotely fit what I'd been learning. "I see your point. I guess to your question, I'd like to take things slow to get a feel for where we stand, but be open if something changes."

She smiled and leaned up to kiss my cheek. "I can agree to that."

"Do I hear healthy communication?" Diego's voice drifted down the hall. A moment later he walked into the room, awake and dressed. Angel padded along with him. *When had she left the room?*

Astrid laughed. "Duh. It's me."

His brow lifted. "Then explain Tyr."

She stuck her tongue out. "It's Tyr, not me."

Diego chuckled and turned his attention to me. "Keep her out of trouble."

I grinned and leaned back on the sofa. "I was always the one helping her get into trouble, not out."

He rolled his eyes. "Don't expect bail money then."

I didn't quite know what that meant yet, but Astrid thought it was funny. The two of them shared a few more words, and a kiss, before he went off for a therapy session. Angel left with him.

Astrid stood in front of me with her hands on her hips. "You wanted to do dinner and entertainment. Did you have anything in mind, or do we want to brainstorm?"

"I know what I'd like to do." While I was still learning about this modern Midgard, I had put effort into learning a few things in regard to this. Aya helped a lot, but some of it was from my own research.

Her lips curved into a tempting, sultry smile. "Are you going to tell me?"

"What if I told you it was a surprise?"

She thought for a moment, tossing her head to the side and pressing a finger to her lips as she did. She was cute with these over-emphasized reactions. "Well, how am I supposed to dress appropriately if I don't know whether this is a casual or formal date?"

That made me pause. "I didn't think about codes of dress."

She looked me up and down. I hadn't thrown on anything special in particular, just a shirt and jeans. "Maybe I should assume casual. Unless you had everything planned and you just don't know if there's a dress code."

I blew out a breath. "I'll tell you the plan, then."

She poked the corner of my mouth where it'd turned down. "Don't be upset. It's okay that I know. Once you're more comfortable with your knowledge, we can talk about more surprise-style dates."

She was right. This didn't ruin anything.

Her sultry smile returned. "Plus, I think I can make up for it."

Now I was intrigued. "How?"

"First, tell me the plan."

"I thought watching immortals pummel each other within an inch of their life, including Fen and Tyr, would be fun entertainment. Then we could go to dinner at a local place."

She chuckled. I frowned. "You don't like the idea?"

Astrid shook her head. "It's not that. I had a feeling that's what you'd say is all."

"Is that Tyr's idea of a date when he's not helped?"

She gave a half-hearted shrug. "Pretty much. That's not a bad thing, of course."

I wasn't convinced, if it was that predictable of a choice.

Astrid took my hands in hers. "Really, Baldur, it's not a bad thing. I like going to the fights. They're fun. My concern is whether you're ready for people to find out you're back."

I gripped her hands tighter. This was one thing I was absolutely sure about. "That's why I joined the fight to save that sanctuary. I'm not interested in hiding. I want others to know it was you who brought me back. I want them to know the power my Sunshine has, so they think twice before crossing her."

"Or they'll try to take me for their evil bidding." She delivered that with a smirk.

I leaned closer to her and kissed her gently on the lips. "They'll have to get through me first."

She grinned and tugged me to my feet. "Come. You can help me pick out my outfit."

I complied, following her into a different bedroom than the one I'd found her and Diego in earlier. This room, too, had a large bed, though it had a canopy as decoration. The large windows allowed for a great deal of sun to stream in, and it was decorated in a way that felt like her.

"Do all of you have separate rooms?" I asked.

"Yeah." She walked over to a tall standing mirror. "Having our own space is important, so we agreed to separate rooms, but with big enough beds for when we didn't want to sleep alone at night."

Made sense. I didn't know how conventional that was this day and age, but I doubted that mattered much.

Astrid gestured for me to sit on the bed. I sank onto the comfortable mattress and waited, expecting her to disappear into a closet to bring out some clothes, but she remained in front of the mirror.

"Dress, skirt, or pants?" she asked.

I squinted. "How can I choose that if I don't know what they look like?"

"I'll pick the style depending on what you think I should wear."

I shook my head. "I don't know. Is one more appropriate for our outing?"

She pursed her lips. "No, it's more what you'd like to see me in."

Nothing at all. Of course that would mean our date plans would change and I needed to behave. Slowly, I told her, "Any?"

"All right, a long game of dress-up it is." She snapped her fingers and before my eyes her clothes changed to a green dress with floral patterns. There were no sleeves or collar to the dress. It somehow stayed on over her breasts without supports at all.

Her dress skirt swished around her knees as she rotated her hips back and forth. "Yes or no?"

My eyes trailed down her body, taking in all of her exposed skin. "It looks good on you. But not the outfit."

Astrid snapped her fingers and the dress transformed into a black one. This one had sleeves that covered the length of her arms, cut low around her chest, and clung to every curve of her body.

My pulse jumped. This was certainly a nice dress. It tempted me to run my hands along her, feeling the realness of her curves myself. My voice was a little strained when I spoke up. "Not that one."

Astrid hummed thoughtfully, tapping her finger against her lips. When her clothes changed again, it wasn't into a dress. This time, her skirt was much shorter, up around mid-thigh, and she had a white shirt that had a high collar and no sleeves.

I sat forward more and motioned for her to turn around. Astrid happily obliged, swaying her hips as she did. "The skirt, yes, that shirt, no."

She turned away to face the mirror and her shirt changed to something incredibly appealing. Gone was most of the back of the shirt, exposing almost all of her skin. The mirror reflected the low-cut nature around her breasts, putting them beautifully on display. The shirt stayed on somehow by the use of something, but I wasn't paying attention to what it was.

I stood. My body heated with more hunger the longer I looked at her. "This one."

Astrid grinned in the mirror at me. "You look very pleased."

I approached, forcing my eyes to stop trailing up and down her body. "I am."

She fussed with her hair next, though she didn't ask my opinion as she used her magic to try out different ways to style it. I may not have been of much use even if she had. I couldn't stop myself from standing a little too close to her.

And when she stopped at a hairstyle that pulled her gorgeous hair into a high ponytail and her locks had been curled, I lost control on my reasoning to take this slow. My fingers trailed along her shoulder, toward her spine.

She shivered under my touch. "You really like this halter, don't you?"

I didn't say anything, too intent on my current objective. Astrid shivered again and bit her lip as my fingers glided down her spine.

"What are you doing?"

My fingers stopped when they reached very particular spots around her shoulder blades. Gently, I rubbed them, the motion instinctive and practiced. Astrid gasped and grabbed her mirror for balance. I leaned over her, intently watching her wide eyes and gaping mouth as I worked her with a sensation she'd never experienced before.

Astrid's eyes hooded and her mouth moved as she struggled to sound out my name. I couldn't help but smile. Seeing her like this brought me great satisfaction… and a throbbing hard cock.

Before she could manage more than stuttering out the first letter, she gasped. Her wings popped out and she shuddered beneath me. My motions stopped, yet I didn't retract my touch from her back. My eyes roamed her languid features and limp wings.

I grinned. "You're welcome, Sunshine."

Astrid panted out a quiet breath as she used the mirror to keep herself balanced. "What… did you do to me?"

I took a step back so I wouldn't be crowding her anymore. "Just a little something I learned. It's not just a Valkyrie's wings that are extra sensitive to touch."

She spun around. Her cheeks were flushed and her brilliant green eyes had darkened in her lust. "And tell me, perfect son of Odin, how would you know that the wings of the forbidden-to-touch Valkyries were erogenous zones?"

I grinned and took two steps back. "Now, if I told you that, then my perfection title would come into question."

Astrid matched my retreating steps, her movements graceful and deliberate, like a huntress on the prowl. Heat sparked in my veins. My cock strained in my now-too-tight pants. *I should stop this. I'd wanted to go slow.* But if I'd actually wanted that, I wouldn't have gone so far already.

My legs bumped into her bed. She kept advancing until she was on my toes. She placed her hands against my chest and shoved me. I fell back, my arms catching me from lying flat. The view of her at this angle was stunning.

She summoned a gold ribbon into her hands. "Tell me, Baldur, how many Valkyries were you secretly sharing a bed with behind your father's back?"

My pulse jumped at the sight of her with Gleipnir. I always liked it when she brought that out. In the past, I may have gotten Fen and me into extra trouble just so she'd threaten it. "I never brought a Valkyrie back to my bed."

It wasn't a lie, technically.

"But you did enjoy their company intimately."

"Define intimate." Because what I did was not anywhere close to the current thoughts I had running through my mind about her.

Something silky slithered along my arms. Before I realized what she'd done, Astrid twisted her finger and my arms pulled tight together. I lost what little balance I had and fell back. Or I expected to fall back. Instead, I was suspended.

Astrid twirled the tiny bit of ribbon in her hands around her finger. A grin spread wickedly across those lips of hers. I played my part and struggled against Gleipnir's hold, though I had no intentions of truly trying to break free—not yet, at least.

I stifled a sharp inhale when Astrid slid onto my lap. Her heat seeped through my clothes, teasing—begging me to touch her.

"Did you give them orgasms?"

Did I catch a note of jealousy in her tone? I grinned. "Not in any way that would have gotten them into trouble." At least, not at first.

Her fingers walked up my chest, ribbons appeared in their wake, twisting and coiling in various patterns. They looped into the ribbons binding my arms, confining me tighter, in a pleasant manner I had yet to experience in my life.

"Why don't you tell me the story of how that worked out?"

I clacked my tongue, my eyes lazily roaming her. "And if I decide not to?"

The ribbon tightened, sending a rush of pleasure mixed with pain through me, and compounded with a jolt of desire when she shifted her hips. "I don't think you can handle the punishment for your silence."

I gazed at this bewitching winged witch, the sun catching in her orange locks and golden feathers, setting them ablaze and intensifying everything she was. My body pulsed with intense need which only increased the longer she bound me. "Being bound beneath your radiance is hardly a punishment, Sunshine."

She grinned, her fingers playing with a bunched section of my shirt and a knotted section of ribbon. "This isn't the punishment. This is merely decorative fun, with maybe a little lesson for you to enjoy a little pain with your pleasure."

She rocked her hips again, grinding into me just right. "But I wonder how long you can hold out before you break."

I clenched my teeth. The friction spiked my growing frustration. "Are you sure you're not breaking rules?"

Was I grasping? Yes. But it kept my head clear for a moment longer.

Astrid made a thoughtful sound, and then bit her lip right before she used her magic to remove my shirt. "I don't think you're in a position to be lecturing me about rule-breaking, when you told me not ten minutes ago that you wanted to go slow, only to give me an orgasm by manipulating my wings."

I exhaled slowly when her fingers trailed along my chest, sparking desire everywhere she touched. "Did I break any rules?"

She leaned closer, her breasts brushing my chest. Her hot breath puffed against my neck, chilling my skin where beads of sweat had begun to form. "If you didn't, neither am I. So, tell me, my god of courage, which rules are you following? The old ways, or the new ways?"

The way my god title rolled off her tongue, it did something to me. I needed to touch her—needed her to touch me. Far more than she already was.

I struggled against Gleipnir's hold, but it held as strong as always. Her teeth grazed the skin of my collarbone. "Old ways…"

She made a thoughtful sound in her throat. "Then tell me, am I breaking any rules?"

I swallowed, distracted by the way her fingers teased my skin just below my navel. "No… but I want you to."

The grin she gave me was dangerous. The way she rocked her hips was maddening. The way her fingers touched me made me want to beg for more.

"Tell me how you learned this Valkyrie pleasuring trick." She pressed her lips against my neck. "And maybe I'd consider breaking a few rules for you."

I released a strained breath. "I wasn't always a man you would have liked. I'm sure—I know—you would have hated me. My status as my father's favorite and perfect son made me into an asshole beyond what any language could articulate."

Astrid stopped tormenting me with her hips so she could properly listen, but her hands were a complete other story. She would not stop touching me, and it was making it difficult to focus. "When did that change?"

"When I found a Valkyrie crying alone." My libido cooled at the visceral memory of that day. "She was one of my father's favorites. Or, she had been until that moment. On a whim, he decided to replace her with another Valkyrie."

Astrid made a face. "Scumbag."

"Despite my behavior, I never had any bad interactions with the Valkyries, but I also had never felt the need to get close to them. They belonged to my father and I accepted it. In that moment I realized how blind I had been to their mistreatment, and just how much my father played favorites with them. I made a decision that was the first of many to tarnish my title as the perfect son."

I closed my eyes, trying to keep those memories from overtaking me. "I'd only tried to comfort them at first. I was there for them to vent to, and I didn't tell a soul what was told to me in confidence. I learned a lot from those conversations, and it inspired me to use my terrible public view to my advantage."

Astrid tipped her head, her attention intensifying. It kept my veins simmering. Her undivided attention was something I had always craved.

"The Valkyries my father rejected would spend notable time with me. We never did anything inappropriate, so none of the gods made any comments. I led them to assume I was just surrounding myself with beautiful women. Well, a few had figured it out. Aya, Tyr, and Fen were among them."

"Gods who took issue with Odin?"

I nodded. "Typically. Which is why they didn't say anything. And that choice would open options to truly befriend them later on."

Astrid smiled sweetly and brushed her thumb along my cheek.

"My father eventually started to question my attention toward *his* Valkyries. He was paranoid even back then about anyone giving Valkyries too much attention, even his own sons. But, I was able to convince him I wasn't doing anything wrong, and"—I made a face—"and I made up a convincing lie that I was getting to know them better so I could help them become better Valkyries for him. Clearly they'd been lacking, which was why they didn't have his favor anymore, so I was taking it upon myself to make them perfect."

Astrid made a disgusted face. "Did the Valkyries hear you say that?"

"Yes, but I'd befriended them for so long at that point, they knew I was just trying to keep them safe."

"When did things change after you told your father your fake plans?"

I thought for a moment. "I don't know exactly when, but it was after I'd started to get to know Tyr and Fen better, and by extension Aya and a few others. That first Valkyrie I mentioned? Her name was Elsa, and she was having a particularly bad day. She'd lost my father's approval again and she was just feeling lonely. She wanted companion-ship, but feared permanently losing my father's favor, so she couldn't bring herself to take a lover. I was trying to comfort her the best I could, but I didn't know what I could do without telling her to stop trying to gain my father's approval."

I blew out a breath. "Things just kind of happened. In my attempts to show her comfort, I found myself doing what I did to you. I didn't think about doing it, I just felt compelled to."

Astrid's brow furrowed. "You never saw anyone else doing that? Not even your father by some chance?"

"To this day, I'm the only one who knows that trick." I still didn't know how I knew to do it. I just did.

"Then what happened?" she asked.

"At first, just that. Word got around, so on occasion when things got bad enough, the Valkyries would come to me for that kind of attention. We weren't technically breaking rules, so the ones who were still determined to get my father's favor again decided it was okay to come to me without feeling guilty."

Astrid tilted her head to the side, her expression relaxed yet fully focused. Her inquisitive look that lacked any judgment was so alluring on any day. And right now, being vulnerable with her about my fall from grace, that look was what I needed most.

"You got nothing out of this arrangement?"

"Not at first, but after a while the Valkyries who came to see me the most—the ones who were losing their love for my father—they insisted they give me something in return as thanks." I grinned. "Still, I didn't want them to get into trouble if I could help it, so we worked around the rules that applied—until it got to a point where we all stopped caring if my father learned the truth."

I expected a change in her expression. Or maybe I hoped for it. There was a little bit of excitement in the idea of her being a little jealous. But she didn't show that.

"Did your father ever find out?"

I smirked. "Not until it was too late for him to do anything about it. I'd created a better reputation for myself, and given he'd pushed the perfect son title, it meant he couldn't call me out without tarnishing his image. So, it forced him to make up a lie that, as his perfect son, he trusted me with full access to his Valkyries, freeing them from his awful treatment."

Astrid's expression softened to something gentle. There was still that underlying allure to her, which added to her expression. Her fingers brushed my cheek and then she slid her arms around my neck. Her breast pressed into my chest, the exposed skin teasing my heated flesh, and her body molded into mine.

Her soft lips pressed against mine, gentle and luring. "Thank you for taking care of my sisters. You're a good man."

Warmth spread through me. I eagerly kissed her back, groaning deep in my chest, desperate for more of her. She listened, didn't judge, and still saw me as a good man. How could I not want this perfect woman?

Our lips parted and our tongues danced, tasting each other, memorizing each other. Her body rocked against me, reigniting my desire for her, the heat blistering me from the inside out. She was everything I wanted—everything I needed.

Our lips parted again; this time we breathed each other in. "You really are my weakness."

"I'm sorry." Her expression said otherwise.

"I'm not." I kissed her again, straining against my bindings. She chuckled, which only made me struggle more.

I needed to touch her—to enjoy her—to break every rule for her.

Her hands trailed down my chest, fanning my desire until I thought I might combust. Her fingers reached the hem of my pants and the button popped loose. I breathed hard out of my nose as she slid the zipper down, both in anticipation and relief.

With agonizing slowness, Astrid worked my boxers until my hard cock sprang out into her waiting hands. I groaned when she wrapped her hands around me. "Impressive enough for you?"

A smirk slowly curled up her beautiful face. "You certainly pass the first impressions. But further inspection is required."

"Inspect me all you want, Sunshine. You will not find me lacking, I can assure you." Or, I hoped. There was one issue I'd found these last few weeks that I prayed to Creation would not rear up now. It was too embarrassing to think about, let alone talk to her about earlier.

With slow, gliding strokes, Astrid coaxed my foreskin down, exposing the head of my cock. Her thumb brushed the sensitive flesh, jolting me with pleasure and coating my head and her hand in my essence dripping out of me. The sensation of her touch was maddening and pleasing me all at once.

I breathed hard through my nose and continued to pull against the restraints. All that did was cause the ribbon to bite into my skin more, the pain sending surprising sparks through me. Her will remained stronger. I needed to touch her like I was allowing her to touch me.

She slid off my legs and knelt between my knees. My pulse pounded in my ears. Seeing her like this with her wings trailing on the floor behind her… the way she gazed up at me… it was too much. *No!*

I squeezed my eyes shut and white exploded behind my lids. "Fuck!"

Astrid gasped, not expecting me to suddenly come any more than I'd wanted to yet. My breath puffed in ragged bursts and I hung my head. Heat seared my cheeks and I refused to open my eyes.

"Baldur?" she said quietly.

My lids cracked open, but the shame wrapped too tightly for me to meet her gaze. "I'm sorry."

She pressed her hand against my cheek. "Baldur, look at me."

My eyes flicked to her, and then away. I couldn't.

"Look at me." Her voice was hard and no longer asking.

I looked at her, expecting judgment or teasing amusement, but there was none of that in her eyes. I only saw gentleness and affection.

"You have nothing to be ashamed about."

"Yes, I do."

"Why?"

I glanced down at the sticky mess I'd made all over her hand and my pants. "I think that's obvious."

"You're sorry you were enjoying my touch so much you couldn't hold back?"

"That's not—" I closed my eyes and concentrated on the shame that was twisting into frustration. I didn't need that being projected onto her. "I've been dealing with this since you brought me back."

"Considering your body has been involuntarily celibate for six hundred years, I'm not all that surprised."

I stared at her, confused how she could be so accepting of this. "I'm a god, Astrid."

She nodded. "And you also seem to still be hung up on needing to maintain some bullshit perfection title." Her attention flicked down to my cock in her hand. "And considering you're still hard after that, you're already a leg up on a ton of other gods out there."

"It was rumored my mother had a sex-demon parent. She had such a strong sexual appetite my father couldn't keep up."

Astrid's brow ticked up. "And he was able to still entertain Valkyries?"

I chuckled, the humor helping shake the shame clinging to me. "No. Many said he was terrible in bed. Which likely didn't help him keep them loyal."

Astrid laughed, the sound making my heart tumble over itself.

"You really aren't upset at me." I didn't mean for that to come out of my mouth, but it happened.

She gazed at me with soft eyes. "Baldur, just because you're a god doesn't mean you can't have performance issues. Tyr also experienced this in the past. It happens."

My brow spiked. "Tyr, really?"

She nodded. "His was brought on by stress. We worked through it each time."

Their marriage wasn't perfect, no union was, but no one could say the two didn't have a strong one. I had envied that.

I groaned; my mental tracks halted when her hot, wet tongue slid over the sensitive head of my cock. "Sunshine…"

She grinned as she licked me off her lips. "Don't tell me you want to be done."

I swallowed. "No. Not even close."

"Good," she purred out. "Because I still need to properly thank you."

Her tongue slid around and under the head of my cock. She licked runes down my shaft. Heat thrummed under my skin, my heart pounding hard in my chest with each added rune. She sealed them with her mouth like a kiss, as if laying claim. She could claim me all she wanted. Creation knew I wanted to do the same to her.

She made her way back up my hard shaft. Her soft lips pressed against the head of my cock. She flicked her eyes up to meet me. Those piercing eyes snared me. My breath hitched, the anticipation agonizing.

Astrid smirked and eased me slowly into her mouth. I groaned and rolled my head back. "Yes, Sunshine, do that."

Desire blazed under my skin, stoking hotter and hotter each time she slid me in and out of her mouth until I thought I'd combusted in more ways than one.

I tried one more time to break from my restraints. She refused to release me. "Please, Sunshine, I need to touch you."

She chuckled. The vibrations hummed through my body. My mind fuzzed and my breath labored as the threads of my control frayed. Astrid's worship hastened, her hands joining in. My body tightened and after another ragged intake of breath, I crested over the edge, convulsing and spilling my hot seed into the back of her throat.

Astrid greedily swallowed it all until I had little left to give. She leaned back, wiping me off her lips, her eyes flicking from my face down to my still-erect cock. "I've got so many questions about how long you can go."

I focused on controlling my breathing. Pleasure coursed through me in ways I couldn't get from amusing myself or ever remembered from anyone else. This was everything I'd hoped for with Astrid, and there was so much we'd yet to explore with each other. "A while."

The grin she flashed me sent my pulse skittering and my blood heating. Creation did I want her.

Astrid rose and her wings folded away. She leaned in and gave me a chaste kiss on the lips. "Impressed by my tongue work?"

I chuckled. "Absolutely."

"Good." She spun her finger and Gleipnir vanished.

I relished my freedom while looking over my arms at the red marks on my skin that were healing quickly.

"You seemed to enjoy that. I wasn't sure you would." She trailed a finger along a large red mark that took longer to heal. "I was worried not turning Gleipnir into proper rope would be damaging, even for a god."

"I liked the way you did it. I'm discovering new things about myself as well. It seems I'm finding ways to enjoy pain." I brushed her cheek with my thumb. "I only hated that I couldn't touch you."

She smirked and pulled away. "I didn't want to risk us getting so caught up in things that we'd break actual rules we established."

Astrid turned and used her magic to fix herself up, as well as me. "I shouldn't delay us anymore. I'm sure the others are—"

I curled my fingers around her perfect hips and pulled her into me, making her gasp. I kissed her shoulder. "They can wait longer."

"Baldur…" My name came out as a heady whisper. "You asked for this to go slow. Doing anything more would remove us from the gray line of slow and not-slow that we're already teetering on."

I pulled her in tighter and kissed up her neck to the shell of her ear. "I've changed my mind. I want to bring you to the heights of pleasure no skáld has ever dared write about."

TWENTY

ASTRID

Baldur's hot breath sent a shiver down my spine. His words ghosted along my skin, caressing me with temptation. His erection pressed hard against me between my thighs, teasing me through my flimsy panties. My lungs struggled to take in air.

I swallowed. "Are you sure you've changed your mind? These choices should be made with a clear head, and not in the heat of the moment."

His fingers trailed up my arm. "I've never been more sure in my life."

I sucked in a tight breath through my nose. "There's no turning back once we cross that line."

"Good." Baldur tugged the strings of my halter top. They didn't resist and my top slid down, freeing my breasts. His finger trailed along my collarbone. The callouses of his fingers bit into my skin, yet he was tender with such a fragile part of my body.

His lips pressed against the soft spot behind my ear. Then he kissed me a little lower, and then a little lower. "I've had a taste of the sun, and I want nothing more than to bask in her radiance a little longer."

I sighed and leaned into him, releasing any resistance I had. If he truly wanted this, I would indulge as long as he allowed. "And what do you plan to do with the sun, now that you have her?"

His fingers trailed along my skin, down to my breasts. He touched and explored my body like it was the finest wonder in all existence. "I will worship and indulge until we're drowning in each other for all eternity."

"Hmm, tempting, tempting. Unfortunately, I don't think we have that kind of uninterrupted time."

I sucked in a tight breath as he slid his touch over my hard nipples, sending a hot spike of desire through me. He kissed my shoulder. "Then maybe I need to bewitch you with poetry."

I grinned. "You can certainly try."

> In the soft embrace of twilight's glow
> A love story begins, destined to grow.
> She, my sunshine, in every dawn's kiss
> The radiance of her love, pure bliss.
>
> In her eyes, constellations gently swirl
> A cosmic dance, a celestial twirl.
> Her laughter, a melody, sweet and light
> Echoes through the quiet of the night.
>
> Her touch, a gentle, warm caress
> Ignites a fire, a tender finesse.
> In the quiet whispers of the breeze
> Her love, a symphony that never shall cease.
>
> She's the sun of my world, a beacon bright
> Guiding me through the starry night.
> Her presence, a tapestry of hues
> Paints my life in love's vibrant views.
>
> In the quiet moments, just us two
> Love blooms like roses kissed with dew.

Her essence, an intoxicating spell
In the dance of hearts, we both excel.

So, here's my ode to the woman divine
Whose love makes every moment shine.
In the soft glow of passion's flame
She's my forever, my heart's true claim.

His words whispered over my skin, wrapping and tangling around me, until I was trapped in a binding I didn't want to break free from.

I hummed appreciatively and tipped my face toward him. Reaching up, I tangled my fingers in his hair. Baldur dipped his head when I gave a light tug. "I do believe my heart's been ensnared by a god."

Our lips met and a hunger took over. Our mouths and tongues locked in a battle of sensual need. His hand continued to tease and explore my breast while his other slid along my bare thigh, sliding up my skirt as he explored. My heart beat in my ears, harder and harder as my desire for this man ramped up anew.

How long had I ached for him and kept it hidden. How long had I craved his touch and never had it. How close in another life had we come to having something so potent and consuming, only to be ripped apart. *Again.*

My heart hammered against my ribs. Was I right in those thoughts? Was it more than just me who lived and lost that long ago? *Will we have that happiness we deserve, or are we destined to repeat a twisted, endless cycle?*

I gasped in a relishing fresh breath and blinked up at Baldur. I had somehow ended up on my back, my hair splayed out around me on the bed, and my shirt was in his hand. When had that happened?

He tossed my shirt aside and tugged on my skirt. It offered little resistance. My panties were last, and unlike Tyr, he took care not to shred them off me.

Baldur's appreciative gaze raked over my naked body like a physical touch that set me on fire. Lifting a hand, I reached out. I needed him, more than I needed to breathe.

He grasped my fingers and pushed my hand down, pinning it beside my head while leaning over the bed and kissing me. My lips, my neck, between my breasts along my sternum tattoo, no part of me was safe as he explored me, claiming each piece until almost all of me was his in this moment.

"If this is how you treat all Valkyries, it's no wonder they came back," I said, my voice breathy.

"Only you, Sunshine," he murmured against my skin. "Only you get this treatment."

I chuckled. How absurd. "Please, don't lie to me. Aya and I were your wingwomen a number of times. I knew how women acted after a night with you."

His teeth grazed the underside of my breast. "It isn't hard to please an unloved woman. But you…"

I gasped when his tongue slid over my nipple.

"You are worth far too much to give such basic attention."

Was that a compliment? I assumed it was. My brain wasn't doing well processing anymore as his fingers teased my thighs in time with his mouth. "Then make me feel like I'm the only woman who matters in existence."

He grinned against my skin. "Sunshine, I'll worship you until our souls are bound beyond eternity."

Creation, did I want that. More than anything right now.

My back arched into him when his mouth closed around my aching nipple. He sucked and licked and played it with his tongue. His fingers teased and played with my other breast until I lost myself in the sensations of pleasure.

His hand slid between my thighs to the quivering, needy wetness between them. I gasped as his thumb slid between my dripping folds and rubbed rhythmically against my clit. I tipped my hips into his touch, needing more.

Baldur obliged, sliding his fingers inside me. I moaned out his name.

My pulse pounded in my ears. Desire burned in my veins until I thought I'd combust. My body coiled and tightened with pleasure until I came undone.

My head tipped back against the bed and I screamed, my orgasm taking over and flooding every sense I had.

When I came down, gasping and feeling lighter than ever, Baldur made a pleased sound against my skin. His mouth released my sensitive breast but instead of pulling away, he kissed down my body. "Not enough."

"What?" I mumbled out, my brain still fuzzed.

"Your soul didn't reach Fólkvangr yet. That will be fixed."

His mouth pressed against the bare, sensitive flesh of my pussy. His tongue slid between my lips. My eyes rolled back and I moaned.

His tongue stroked my clit with so much pleasure I almost forgot to breathe. His fingers slid in and out of my pussy, igniting the burning fire within me. I tangled my fingers into his hair and ground into his face, desperate for more.

"Baldur," I moaned when he began sucking my clit. "Yes... oh yes..."

He sucked more. The threads of my control frayed and I wanted it to sever. His tongue flicked my sensitive button and that was the end to those last threads.

My eyes rolled back. Baldur's name came out just as I screamed and my hips bucked as ecstasy took over. Baldur didn't ease his attention until I came down, prolonging the high just enough.

I lay there languid and panting. "Fuck..."

Baldur leaned over me. "Good?"

I smiled. "Most definitely. And you get to now say you've truly tasted the sun."

He stood and shoved his pants off his hips. "And I'm not done indulging in her radiance."

I tucked my arm under my head and took my time appreciating him while I got my breathing under control. Hard planes of cut muscle moved under his skin with each shift of movement. Scars crossed his body in ways I wanted to trace and follow and discover their individual stories.

I'd seen him naked before, but not like this. This was different. And I was enjoying every moment of it. *It's been worth the wait.*

His eyes felt like a physical touch as they roamed over me. "Do you understand how stunning you are?"

I made a thoughtful sound as if I were thinking. "I believe I've been told that before."

His knee pressed into the bed and he leaned over me, bracing his hands on either side of my head. "Yes, but do you understand what that means? Do you realize what you do to a man like me?"

His hot breath ghosted along my neck, his mouth hovering and sending heady anticipation skittering down my spine. "I am a god who holds so much power, mortals bow and revel at the sight of me. And yet I am powerless against you. I crave your worship as much as I desire to offer everything I am at your feet. I would wrangle the sun for daring to attempt to burn brighter than you."

His cock slid between my legs, rubbing against me, teasing me. "You leave me breathless while breathing life into me. I crave you like nothing else in existence. And if something were ever to happen to you again, I would burn Midgard to the ground until Creation gave you back."

My heart about stopped beating. I framed his face with my hands and pulled his lips to mine. I kissed him with so much desperation, it startled even me. All the longing and loss that I'd shoved down couldn't be held back anymore. "Don't ever leave me again."

Baldur chuckled against my lips. "That's what I'm supposed to say to you."

He kissed me a moment longer, then pulled away. His hands gripped my hips and then he slowly eased inside me. My back arched and my mouth fell open with my silent gasp. Baldur's hold on my hips tightened as I accepted him until he was fully buried. His breath was as strained as mine.

Slowly he pulled almost all the way out then thrust into me again, a little faster the second time. Then a third. Thrust after thrust, breath upon gasping breath, we lost ourselves in each other.

Need burned inside me, like an inferno that soon could never be extinguished. I wanted more from him—needed more. I needed everything he was now and everything he would become. A permanent forever I couldn't request of him. Not yet.

Baldur's movements slowed as he gazed down at me. "What is it, Sunshine?"

My thoughts were projected to my face too much. I needed to focus on the us in the now. I grinned, knowing exactly how to ensure that. In one quick movement while he was buried in me, I twisted over onto my knees.

"Fuck!" Heat filled my pussy. His hands slammed into the bed, his shaking arm bracing him over me as he gasped for breath.

I bit my lower lip and glanced over my shoulder. "Oops."

He chuckled and grazed his teeth along my shoulder. "Don't lie. You're not sorry at all."

I bit back a moan. "To be fair, I didn't think that would push you over the edge."

"I don't believe you."

I wiggled my hips, making him suck in a sharp breath through his teeth. "I swear I'm not that mean."

He thrust into me, drawing out a deep moan from my chest. "No?"

I rocked back into him. "Never."

Two of his fingers trailed down my spine, sending a shiver crawling through me. "Well, that makes one of us."

I bit back a startling gasp when his fingers found that perfect sensitive spot he'd worked earlier. His hips continued to rock, the sensation of him sliding in and out of me adding to the overwhelming pleasure his fingers provided.

My breath quickened and desire took over. I rocked into him, heightening the pleasure coursing through me. I needed this, and yet it still wasn't enough. I wanted everything from him.

My breath caught when his other hand trailed lower along my backside. I glanced over my shoulder and locked eyes with him.

"Can you take more?" he asked.

I swallowed hard. "Lube is in the nightstand."

He broke our visual contact for a moment to glance over. "Too far."

I rolled my eyes which earned me a harder thrust and deeper twist by my shoulders. I groaned. I then used my magic to move the bottle of lube from the drawer to hovering where Baldur could easily reach.

He liberally coated his fingers. The cool sensation of the lube slid over my skin. It took a much greater dosage of control that I could barely muster to stay relaxed in all my craving anticipation.

Baldur's thick fingers worked inside my tight hole. I gasped, then moaned. The sensations he poured into me flooded my mind until I thought I'd be overwhelmed. I thought I'd come undone at the seams, and yet, as I teetered on the edge of pleasure, I didn't crest over. Not yet. But I wanted to. I wanted him to undo me.

My eyes snapped open when a pair of hands slid into my hair. Not Baldur's hands. They still worked me in ways that would threaten to make me blush to attempt to share details with even Aya.

No, my gaze met Tyr's as he knelt on the bed and towered over me, his huge cock eagerly on display. *When did he show up?*

"Look at you, Valkyrie," he rumbled. "Little whore you are, you couldn't wait to be dicked down by another god."

My lips parted, tongue poised to lick the pre-cum dripping from his cock. "Why don't I show you how much of a whore I am?"

My tongue darted out, teasing his head and taking in the burst of his taste. Tyr's grip tightened and he pressed his cock against my lips. I eagerly opened for him, easing my lips around his thick member.

His head tipped back and he groaned, pushing deeper. I relaxed my throat to accept his size the best I could. Not to be ignored, Baldur picked up the pace of his thrusting, skin slapping skin, and his fingers worked me more in ways I'd never imagined.

Tyr slid in and out of my mouth, choosing the pace. He grinned down at me. "That's it, Valkyrie. Be good for us as we use your pretty holes."

I moaned in response. I wanted this. I wanted my two gods to want me—to use me in all ways that were pleasurable. I'd waited so long—too long.

I lost myself in the sensations. I let the tides of passion take over until I nearly couldn't take it anymore.

"Pleasure yourself, Valkyrie," Tyr rumbled.

I did. My fingers slid between my legs and played with my over-worked clit. My eyes rolled back, the sensation pushing me over that edge I so craved. Tyr's cock muffled my scream of shattered release. My body writhed and my wings sprang out.

My gods didn't ease up, even as I finally came down from my orgasm. I was a twitching, oversensitive mess, and completely at their mercy as they fucked me.

Tyr's cock swelled in my mouth and Baldur's thrusts became more punctured. Barely breathing and nearly unable to see straight, I gazed up at Tyr, and that was all it took for him to lose all control. He convulsed and exploded, spilling his hot cum down my throat.

Baldur's breathing labored and then roared out his release. They slowly stilled and then pulled out of me, leaving us all panting messes.

Tyr's fingers stroked my hair, then dipped down to capture my chin and tip my head up. "Ready for more?"

My eyes flicked down at his still-erect member. I didn't remember battling with him, but I wasn't going to complain.

Baldur pulled me to the edge of the bed and held me against his hard body. "One more."

I swallowed. How did this day take this turn? Did it matter? I wanted this. "Please."

Tyr grinned. "Good girl."

He climbed off my bed and walked around it. Baldur drew me to my feet and held me in place against him, his hands around my middle. My gaze followed Tyr. All hard planes and dangerous cuts of muscles rippled with each prowling step. His intense gaze on me sent my heart skittering and breath rushing through my nose. Or maybe that was Baldur's touch as he traced runes along my skin.

Both, it was definitely both of them doing this to me.

Tyr wrapped his large hand around my neck and forced my gaze up. My teeth caught on my lower lip. They both towered over me—powerful war gods I held power over, and yet they held the same of me.

Tyr bent over, his mouth crashing into mine. I let out a startled gasp that he devoured. Baldur's hands slid up my body and cupped my breasts, his fingers rolling and pinching my nipples. His hot breath ghosted over my sensitive wings, sending an unusual, pleasant sensation down my spine.

To be pressed against them like this was fantasy come to life. And as Tyr wrapped his hands around my thighs and lifted me, and their cocks nudged both my entrances before sliding into me slowly, it became the most intoxicating, orgasmic riding dream I never wanted to wake up from.

I didn't resist the sensations they fed me. I fell into the pleasure, moaning with each thrust, each sensation of them both impossibly filling me. Pain and pleasure mixed, and I was so greedy, I wanted more.

"Good girl," Tyr praised. "You're taking our cocks like the perfect Valkyrie you are."

"More," I begged, my fingers digging into the skin of their necks. "Please give me more. I've been good."

"You have."

Their thrusting increased, harder and harder they fucked me. Feeling them like this in me, it was everything I'd ever wanted, and still not enough, even as I lost myself to the burning desire in my veins.

Baldur's hand slid down my belly and between my legs. He scrawled runes along and inside my folds. It drove my overworked senses wild. When his fingers pressed against my clit, I was done. Everything shattered in one powerful, dizzying explosion of erotic release.

I screamed, my body convulsing and clenching around their hard, pulsing cocks, milking them harder. My senses were so overwhelmed, I barely heard them both groan out their release.

We all stilled, our heavy breathing filling the room. My body shook with the aftershocks of my orgasms, completely overspent. Tyr and Baldur, being gods, fared a little better, but I felt the slight quivering of their muscles.

They carefully extracted themselves from me, and Tyr lay me down on the bed. I pulled my wings back to make myself more comfortable as I gladly lay there in a cloud of bliss.

Baldur curled against me, his hand gently pressing against my stomach. "You were incredible."

I grinned. "That assessment belongs to you. I might already be addicted."

Tyr reappeared by the bed, a towel in his hand. *When had he left?* He took the time to carefully clean me up. Even though I had magic, I let him tend to me. I always did before doing the thorough job myself. The aftercare treatment was just as important to me as the sex. And I liked when he was tender with me, as much as I enjoyed his roughness.

"Are you always that vulgar and rough with her?" Baldur asked Tyr.

"Depends on the day." Tyr tossed the towel somewhere when he finished his task and lay on my other side. He also slid his hand over my middle. Such a subtle claim that didn't impede Baldur's.

Baldur shifted his attention to me. "And you enjoy it?"

I grinned. "I'm a woman of many desires."

He brushed a damp lock of hair away from my face. "I look forward to discovering them all."

I smiled and then turned my attention to Tyr. Gentle affection cracked his stoic face as he gazed at me. "So, were we taking too long?"

He chuckled. "Baldur told me fifteen minutes. I gave you double. And since Baldur wasn't telling me to get lost when I walked in, I didn't see any harm joining."

I slid my hand up his chest. "I'm glad you did. That was fun."

I tipped my head back to look up at Baldur. "You were okay with that, yes?"

"As Tyr said, I would have told him to leave if I wanted to keep you for myself longer."

"No, instead I'm sure you're going to keep that wing trick of yours a secret still," Tyr grumbled.

My brow rose. "You knew about it?"

"I'd heard Valkyries gossiping about it once. Didn't think much of it until I witnessed it just now."

Baldur leaned over and kissed my forehead. I let out a content sigh. "It's my special secret for now."

Tyr grunted but didn't argue.

"I guess this means we need to get ready for real?" I said.

"Fen is waiting for us," Tyr said.

Baldur pulled me against him tighter. "He can wait a little bit longer."

I giggled. I was okay with a little more cuddle time. Fen wouldn't stay mad if we took another five minutes.

TWENTY-ONE

ASTRID

We stood outside a one-story, nondescript building. Nothing about it screamed important, and if I were an unwanted guest, the magical charm humming along my skin that protected this place would ensure I forgot about it the moment I turned away. But as it were, Frey loved me too much to banish me from this place.

I opened the door and magic danced along my skin as I stepped into the club. While the club wasn't technically open right now, it was all set up for when patrons would begin filing in.

Neon lights created an ambiance that was both alluring and mysterious, perfect for bathing the centrally located stage in the neon glow. Sturdy and well-crafted wood tables were strategically arranged around the stage. The warm tones added a touch of sophistication. Plush and comfortable seating accompanied the tables, upholstered in deep blacks and purples, encouraging the relaxed atmosphere.

Private booths with soft, indirect lighting and cozy seating created an intimate retreat to the rest of the vibrant atmosphere and offered more secluded viewings of the stage.

"What is this place?" Baldur murmured, his eyes on a half-clothed woman practicing her routine for the show later tonight. Dimmed, spotlight-like neon lights emphasized her movement, adding to her alluring dance.

"A burlesque club," I said as I scanned the room. I was still slightly disappointed Frey wasn't interested in my suggestion to add pole dancing to their show lineup.

"A what?"

Ah. For some reason I assumed Aya would have given him information to read about types of sex clubs—especially given Frey ran one with special rules, particularly after show hours. "Too much to explain right here. Remind me later to give you the full rundown."

I finally spotted Fen over by the bar, brooding with a drink in his hand.

"Only the Berserkers are allowed to look that grumpy, Fluffy," I teased as we approached.

"Grumpy Fluffy, Grumpy Fluffy." Muninn taunted from my shoulder. Huginn cackled from his perch on Baldur's shoulder.

Fen looked up and he narrowed his eyes. "About damned time you showed up. What, did you get detoured to Istanbul?"

"I had needs that required attention that couldn't wait. If you were that bored, you could have asked Frey or Dahlia to entertain you."

"They're out on a date, because it was assumed I'd have been gone, *an hour ago.*"

I shrugged. "Cry more."

He placed his drink down on the bar. "Besides, you're supposed to wait to fuck until after the fights, once the blood gets pumping."

"Who says I can't have both?" I winked and stole a sip of his drink. The smoky, malty flavor with a hint of vanilla burned all the way down. "But, hey, if you want to keep being mad, I can book you a cozy ticket on the next Greyhound bus out of here and you can meet us there, instead of utilizing the amazing witch-Valkyrie taxi service right in front of you."

He grunted and held out an arm for a hug invitation. Instead of reciprocating, I calmly placed the drink down on the bar and Muninn hopped off my shoulder, sensing my thoughts. I slipped behind Fen, using the bar to help as I jumped onto his back and wrapped my arms around his neck.

Fen grunted again and supported me with his arms. "Brat."

I kissed him on the cheek. "Love you too."

The corner of his lip twitched up. Tyr and Baldur snickered. Muninn hopped back onto my shoulder and we left the club so I could teleport us. A moment later we were in a dingy alley. Graffiti covered the worn bricks around us and the air reeked of decay and smog.

Everyone looked around.

"Is this the location?" Baldur asked.

I slid off Fen's back. "It's a little down the street, but yeah."

He stepped around a pile of broken garbage bags and tires. "I was expecting a nicer location."

"There's a lot of movement in and out of the locations where the entrance moves to," Tyr said. "So, to keep people from paying too much attention and putting extra pressure on the magic to keep things hidden, run-down areas of larger cities are chosen."

"What city are we in?"

I peered casually out of the alley. "Detroit."

The street, once smooth and pristine pavement, was now neglected and riddled with cracks, potholes, and faded road markings. Buildings lined the street, some with boarded or barred windows, others with broken or worn signs and faded painted bricks and graffiti. Some abandoned shops were blocked off by "temporary" chain link fencing that looked as though it hadn't been maintained in a decade.

A car drove by, ignoring the stop sign at an intersection, as if they feared something would happen to them if they stopped. Or they didn't care about traffic laws. Several people walked down the street, their paces quick and heads down. None of them would notice our odd group with two ravens.

With the coast clear, we walked two blocks to a corner building with a worn sign and recessed doorway. There were no windows to this place, and even the door looked uninviting. That also wasn't including the magic charm on the place that made even me feel unwelcomed. *Neat trick.*

Fen and Tyr went first, since they were fighting. The door opened on its own before they could do it themselves, the opening beyond dark. These fights didn't actually happen here in the city. They were in the fae realm, which was handy to keep the wrong people out. And it was how the entrance moved around all the time.

"Don't disappoint me," I said.

They both grinned and stepped inside, the darkness swallowing them. The door didn't close, as if it could sense Baldur and me. Baldur entwined our fingers. I felt the nervous, excited energy from him. I squeezed his hand and led the way into the darkness beyond.

The door slammed shut, trapping us in. Baldur's grip tightened, as tingles of magic washed over us. The magic neutralized my own—not enough to disrupt my familiar bond, but enough to ensure I wouldn't be a danger to anyone.

Magic, amongst a few other things, wasn't allowed in these fights. It was why I never participated. I wasn't terrible at hand-to-hand combat thanks to my own training, but I couldn't take on Berserkers, shifters, and the like who were made for such fighting.

The darkness faded, revealing a dimly lit hallway. Shouts and jeers and the palpable taste of battle lust slammed into my senses. I sucked in a tight breath, trying to not be overwhelmed by it. Being a Valkyrie, I was sensitive to the tides of war and battle. It helped me find it when I needed, though I usually relied on Tyr for that, as his sense was far more accurate. But as I watched Baldur inhale deep and his eyes dilate, it was clear whatever I felt was nothing to that of a war god.

"This place…" he said slowly, his voice strained. "It's amazing."

I smiled and tugged him to follow me down the hall. Tyr and Fen were nowhere in sight, but that was to be expected.

At the end of the hall, a centauride stood as a sentinel, her scars proudly on display. "Battle maiden."

Her lip twitched ever so slightly, clearly appreciating I acknowledged her experience. "Valkyrie. Fighting or watching?"

I wasn't surprised she knew what I was, even without my wings out. The magic here seemed to make any sentry aware of what we were at all times. "Watching."

Her gaze shifted to Baldur and she paused for a moment. Her eyes gave away her masked surprise. "Welcome back, god of battle courage. Fighting or watching?"

"Watching."

His response made her pause again and then she nodded to a staircase to her right, our left. "Go ahead."

We ascended the stairs until we broke through to the arena with grand tiered seating. Rows upon rows were packed with spectators of all walks of life, from fae to shifters and berserkers to gods and even humans. At the heart of all the excitement lay the recessed fight pit. A cage covered the top, acting as a protective barrier between participants and spectators, as well as adding a primal touch to the already brutal sport. There were already two people in the pit, blood dripping from slow-to-heal cuts and splattering the permanently stained arena floor.

Surrounded by chaos and bloodlust, it was easy even for me to get consumed by the energy in here. I squeezed Baldur's hand. "How are you feeling?"

"Alive," he said, his voice heavy. "It's like bathing in all the sensations of battle without needing to get your hands dirty."

I smiled. "If at any point you want to get your hands dirty, you can go downstairs and become a fighter."

His gaze stopped roaming our surroundings and pinned on me. "Now, why would I choose that, when I can relish in this feeling with you?"

Heat touched my cheeks and my heart did that pitter-patter thing. A war god choosing you over a good fight was an incredibly high honor.

We found a place to sit, not easy when one of us was seven feet tall and the other was barely over five. While the crowd was mostly engrossed in the current fight, I didn't miss the whispers around us in regards to Baldur's presence.

None of them were brave enough to come verify it was really him, and Baldur was far too engrossed in the fight to notice the attention. I did my best to follow his example.

This was what he wanted. And I knew it was best for him. He needed the world to know he was back so he could regain the power he'd lost, especially now that he could feel pain. But I couldn't help but feel protective. I couldn't lose him.

Baldur's hand wrapped around mine. My eyes flicked down to our hands then up to meet his gaze.

He smiled. "You're overthinking about something."

I ducked my head, heat singeing my ears and cheeks. "I'm distracted, yeah. That obvious?"

"You didn't react to the knockout."

My attention flicked to the arena where one of the fighters was being carried out. *Oops.*

Baldur lifted my hand to his lips and kissed the back of my hand, then he turned back to the fighting when an announcer boomed through the arena announcing the next fight.

Pushing my worry out of my mind, I fell into the intense atmosphere. When Tyr's first fight finally came up, I was maybe a little too pumped up and shouted maybe a little too excitedly, because he knew exactly where I was in the stands. I may have also told Tyr to beat his opponent to a pulp, which got Baldur to laugh. *Oh well.*

I couldn't hear what taunt Tyr threw at his opponent, a panther shifter from what the announcer said, but I read enough from his lips that he was apologizing but he couldn't disappoint his Valkyrie. I didn't stop the pleased smile spreading on my lips.

The match started and Tyr didn't hold back the brutality. Even if the shifter could take on his bestial form, which he couldn't in the pit, Tyr wouldn't have given him much of a chance to attempt to. My heart skittered in its cage, my breath coming quick. There was some primal reaction in me anytime I saw this side of him that got me a little hot under the collar. Okay, a lot.

As a therapist, I shouldn't condone such behavior. But as a Valkyrie? Hell yes.

Tyr's opponent yielded and I cheered. Was the fight a fair match-up? Probably not, but that was part of the risk reward this place set up.

Two fights later, Fen finally got his shot; his opponent was a Berserker. I only half paid attention to the start of this fight, as the bond made me aware of Huginn's and Muninn's attentions sharpened to someone approaching.

"Loki," I greeted without looking at him.

He sat down next to me. "Astrid."

"What brings you here?" I asked. "Not for the entertainment, as I'm sure it's still below your preferred levels of intellectual engagement."

Loki chuckled as I cheered Fen on. "Maybe I'm here to see what I've been missing all these years."

I raised an eyebrow in his direction. Like I'd believe that. "You can try harder than that."

He didn't say anything as I cheered for Fen's victory. The Berserker didn't want to go down, forcing a tough knockout on Fen's part.

I leaned back in my seat and let myself calm down before paying attention to Loki again. As expected, he wasn't watching the fight. "You're not getting that last antidote until you agree to my terms."

He exhaled a harsh breath through his nose. "Do you have any idea how frustrating it is to have your magic messed with?"

I grunted. "Try having it forcibly suppressed to nothing for the first twenty-nine years of your life."

"Not the same."

I shrugged. "Maybe you should be glad you can at least still teleport. Otherwise, Bragi and you could swap riveting tales about dealing with the TSA."

He half laughed. "Pass."

When I still refused to budge, he blew out a breath. "I can appreciate the trick you pulled. I'm quite proud of you, really. But I do need my magic, and I'll be happy to negotiate a deal with you to get it back. Just not the one you proposed."

"No deal."

"We were friends once," he tried.

Not that you'd ever admit to having friends. I gave him a pointed look. "You don't know the meaning."

"Oh, I know the meaning."

I rolled my eyes. "You don't believe in the meaning, how's that?"

He chuckled. "Fine, I'll give you that. We were at least on friendly terms in the past."

I had many good memories with Loki, and defended him on numerous occasions from unjust accusations. But that didn't mean anything in this moment. "In the past, yes. That doesn't mean I'm just going to give you the antidote."

He scowled. "She can't mean that much to you. She's just another Valkyrie."

"I don't expect a god who eschews the concept of loyalty to another to be capable of grasping the strength of loyalty I have with my Valkyrie sisters, or anyone else in my life for that matter."

His frustration radiating off of him was so palpable he might as well be shouting it at me. "You can't begin to comprehend the havoc an unchecked prophecy can wreak."

I leaned closer, getting in his face without a care. "No, Loki, it's you who doesn't get it. You have not once thwarted these supposed outcomes. In your fear, you have met every single one of them to the near-exact interpretation. Maybe, if you actually used your brain for once, you'd see these attempts at Azzie are doing nothing more but ensuring you see this predicted outcome. If you left her the fuck alone, she'd have no reason to be anywhere near you and cause this supposed damning downfall that you see this prophecy as."

I turned back to the fights. The buzz I felt from the battle aura here had ebbed in my irritation. I didn't know why his continued fear of this prophecy agitated me so much. Sure, it put Azzie at risk, but there was something else about it that bothered me.

"Is that your professional advice as a therapist?" Loki sneered.

I gave him a side glance. "That's my advice as a Valkyrie who has seen and experienced far more than you'll ever know. Including prophecies."

The truth of that statement pulsed through my body from my soul. There was ancient knowledge somewhere deep inside me, something that understood this far better than I presently did.

"Beasts, monsters, and immortals," the announcer began for the next match. "The most anticipated fight of the night is about to begin. Returning to the cage, Fenrir."

Cheers erupted as Fen walked back out into the pit.

"As well as his opponent, Tyr."

I threw a fist up as I shouted along with the rest of the crowd who supported Tyr. This is what I'd hoped to see. Fen and Tyr sparred all the time, but they rarely got to go all out like they could in a place like this.

"Care for a wager?" Loki said. "My son against your god?"

I glanced his way. He held his hand out, palm up. "How much?"

"One hundred."

"Thousand?"

He smirked. "You don't have that kind of money."

Technically no, my bank account wasn't that big. But Tyr insisted I spend the stupid amount of money he'd collected over the centuries, so I had unfettered access to his accounts. "Don't assume what I do and don't have, trickster god."

Loki chuckled. "Then, deal."

I slapped my hand down onto his waiting palm.

"Wager! Wager!" Huginn and Muninn screamed out.

"We've got a wager!" the announcer declared. "Throw in your bets."

The crowd cheered with even greater intensity when a magic board appeared and showed Loki's and my bet. People partnered up, declaring their own bets and clasping hands, or their species equivalent. That was the rule here. You needed someone to wager against to play.

Fen stared at me with his arms held out, pretending to be offended I'd wager against him. I blew him a mock kiss.

Tyr, on the other hand, glanced at my wager amount and shot me a "Really, that's what you finally spend my money on?" look. At least, that's how I interpreted it as I grinned at him.

Baldur laughed. "Well played, Sunshine."

Loki's brow arched. "It's not really your money you're wagering, is it?"

"Of course it is," I said with far too much sweetness in my voice. "You can't wager money that isn't yours. The magic doesn't allow it. It doesn't, however, prevent you from wagering money your partner gave you unlimited access to."

Loki's head tipped back as he laughed, and for a moment, it was like the time we used to have a long ago.

The fight began and I focused fully on the match. The intensity between the gods embodied what these fights were all about. The brutality. The control. The thrill. Everything those built for conflict and war needed, in a world that didn't support them anymore.

Alarm shot through me, cutting through my focus. I stilled, pushing out my Valkyrie senses. What was wrong?

"*Sister,*" Muninn warned to my mind alone.

"*We feel it too,*" Huginn said. "*Something is coming.*"

Baldur noticed my stillness. "Sunshine, what is it?"

Loki focused on me as well.

My body tensed and coiled, reacting to something I couldn't understand. I was readying for a fight, but why?

My attention jerked to the stairs. Standing at the top, and out of breath as if he'd run a marathon to get here, was Diego. With him were several fae sentinels, all with very alarmed looks on their faces.

I shot to my feet, my wings manifesting on their own. I felt his panic from here. I felt the need to fight an unseen battle. "Diego, what's wrong?"

The crowd died down as they noticed, confused murmuring rippling through them. Even Tyr and Fen halted their fight, their heightened senses tuned to the growing tension, and no doubt the same energy my Valkyrie soul was feeling.

"Everyone has to get out now!" Diego shouted.

Baldur stood. "What's going on?"

"They're coming. Everyone needs to get out."

"Who is coming?" someone shouted.

Fear reflected back at me in his eyes. "Malsumis—"

The roof of the fae realm pocket exploded.

TWENTY-TWO

TYR

Chaos erupted above us. Fen and I watched as the impossible happened before our eyes. *What the hel is going on?*

The magic binding us for the fight snapped, and power rushed into me in a dizzying wave. Fen immediately shifted into his wolf, his large head swiveling as he tried to sort out the chaos. A door materialized behind us—a way out—but that wasn't what we needed. I gazed at the cage above us. That needed to go. It was the only way we could get out of here and help.

Fen and I instinctively crouched when a bear berserker was thrown against the cage. The metal creaked and bent under his weight. Without any magic to shield it, it was nothing more than metal.

Fen snarled and lunged at the cage, slamming his head into the metal with a resounding *bang!* The pre-weakened metal bent a bit more, but it didn't break.

Magic flashed, and the familiar gold tendrils of Astrid's magic slashed the cage, cutting the metal. The metal sang with each strike. Fen bashed against the cage again, and this time, the metal shattered. I ducked behind Fen as metal crashed to the ground around us.

"Grab on," Fen ordered.

He barely gave me enough time to snag a fistful of fur before launching us into the now-demolished arena.

The chaos swarmed us, along with the potent sensation of battle—not that we couldn't see it ourselves, but this wasn't like any battle I'd been part of. Malsumis minions swarmed. Fight spectators and arena combatants scattered—some trying to flee, while others fought back. The battle spilled out into the streets of Detroit, buildings around the arena's fight entrance suffering damage.

How the hel had they done this? How were they keeping this realm pocket open and exposed to the public? None of this should be possible.

My attention snapped to the sky. Astrid soared high, with shadowed lizard-like creatures chasing her. Her magic lashed out, exploding the creatures on impact.

I summoned my axe and shield. I couldn't help her from here, but I sure as hel could deal with the annoyances on the ground. I slammed my axe into a mutated person, black tendrils lashing out of their body, trying to latch on to anyone it could. Fen bowled over an infected wolf berserker, tearing his head clean off.

The drums of war thrummed in my veins, pushing me harder and harder. I'd destroy every last Malsumis vermin. I'd make them rue the day they crossed us.

Midgard ceased to exist as my focus tunneled. The only thing I knew was my rough awareness of allies around me. Magic caressed my skin. Astrid's magic. She was here—somewhere. Fen and Baldur battled nearby, sometimes alongside me. I always knew with them. Centuries may have separated us, but that didn't break the bond we once shared.

Baldur shouldn't have been fighting in his condition, and yet he was. I felt his courage flowing through me. I recognized his wild movements and the spark it ignited in others. If anyone doubted his return, they wouldn't anymore.

A flash of warning pierced the haze of battle. Something was wrong. But what?

Then, the battle ceased.

Our enemies vanished into puddles of oozing ichor, like Ingrid always did. I whipped my head around. Was she here? Had I missed her presence in all the chaos?

My breath rushed in and out of my lungs. The intoxicating sensations of war thrummed in my veins, invigorating me even more than the fights had. Yet I couldn't shake the concern rising up in me. What was still wrong?

My eyes darted about. Besides all the destruction, the city street had been turned into an urban warzone I'd seen far too often with human wars. Mortals gathered with phones and cameras. Even though this had been a rundown area, that didn't mean it was completely abandoned. *Shit.*

Immortals and others who had been part of the battle helped each other. Many were wounded. I couldn't see if there were deaths.

I whirled when frantic movement caught my attention. Diego wove through the cluster of warriors, his head bobbing and whipping around as he frantically searched.

"Astrid?" he called out. "Astrid!"

Muscles in my neck tightened, and that sense of unease grew in me. Baldur, Fen, and I glanced at each other and then rushed over to Diego.

He turned to us, the worry lines on his brow accentuating his wide, distressed expression. My blood ran cold.

That was only a look the younger dragons had when their Valkyrie partners were in trouble. It was that unusual, special connection none of us understood. And the next words from his mouth shattered any hope I was possibly misreading him.

"They took Astrid."

TWENTY-THREE

ASTRID

"Astrid," a gentle alto voice said. "Astrid."

Awareness bubbled at the edge of my mind, but I didn't want it. Warmth cocooned me, a comforting weight that banished all the bad in my life.

"Astrid," the voice said again.

Who was calling me?

"Time to wake up…"

Wake up? I wasn't asleep.

Consciousness flitted through my mind, and with it the shocking and visceral memories and sensation of battle. Magic, war cries, blood. My heart raced, pounding in my ears and my ribcage. My eyes snapped open, panic seizing my senses. I gasped for air, each inhalation a struggle. My body jerked and I frantically clawed at the tangle of sheets trapping me.

The voice from before, now clearer and right beside me, made hushing sounds, and warm hands touched my shoulders. "Easy, Astrid, it's okay."

I gasped and jerked away. My eyes leveled with dark gray eyes that I never wanted to see again.

Ingrid smiled, the expression gentle and kind and all kinds of revolting. "Good morning, sleepy head."

I clutched the sheet to my chest, my eyes darting around the room. Pink blankets with Hello Kitty print covered the bed I sat in. A white cat-head rug covered the pink shag carpet. All the walls were pink. The dresser in the corner was white… and pink. Fake curtains over false windows were also… yeah, pink. *What the hell?*

I felt out my magic and found it surprisingly all there. But as I thought about teleporting away, my understanding of how to do so vanished from my mind, like I never knew how to do it. The moment I stopped thinking about it, the knowledge returned to the back of my mind, but that's where it was only allowed to stay. *What the fuck?*

"Where am I?" I didn't trust her kindness, but she wasn't being hostile. Until I knew what was going on, it was best to play along for my safety.

"Your room, silly. I've decorated it just how you like it."

How I liked it? Yeah, when I was five. Okay, maybe when I was ten, too. Fine, fifteen-year-old me would have liked it. All right, maybe forever twenty-nine me also didn't hate the theme. It could just use a little less pink. Moderation, please.

"Where are my familiars?" I looked around. When I tried to pull up my familiar connections, only Muninn's felt clear. Huginn's and Angel's connections felt like static on a bad TV or radio channel.

Ingrid smiled and pointed behind me. "One of them is right there."

I whipped around to find Muninn nestled on a pillow with his beak under his wing. He seemed okay, just asleep.

"Don't worry, he's fine," Ingrid assured. "He's a very well-trained familiar. He thought we were going to hurt you, and tried to protect you when you were unconscious, so I had to sedate him. I didn't want him hurt. I knew you'd be quite upset if that happened."

"Thank you," I said in my most neutral tone. I couldn't see why she'd care if I was upset about something she did, but I wouldn't count my blessings that Muninn was okay. "What about my other raven?"

Ingrid dramatically sighed. "I tried to find him, dear, I really did, but I think all the fighting scared him away."

I nodded. "He doesn't like fighting. He'll find me when he's calmed down."

"I've got sentries looking for him."

I blinked and played dumb. "That's not necessary, Mom. He can teleport to me."

Her eyes fluttered when I called her "Mom" and then she gave me an apologetic smile. "I'm afraid, for everyone's protection here, we don't allow teleportation in the area. I'm sure you understand that all too well, with your sanctuary, dear."

I didn't, because we allowed such travel in and out of the sanctuary. The wards were only set up to tell if someone was a threat. That was why it took time to make open-ended portal connections like the hotel or the southern home. *These people are even more paranoid than I thought.*

"But don't worry," Ingrid continued. "I have sentries posted with instructions to not cause him harm once he shows up. Now, let's get this one woken up and then we can go have dinner."

"Dinner?"

She patted my leg over the blankets. "I know I said good morning, but it's actually dinner time. You've been asleep for a while. I would have let you sleep longer, but I need to make sure you have a balanced diet, and I won't allow you to skip a meal unless it's absolutely necessary."

Yeah, sure…

Ingrid flourished her fingers and Muninn's eyes snapped open. His head shot up and he screamed and hopped to me immediately, somehow not tripping up in the mound of pillows. I gathered him in my arms and held him close.

He crooned. *"You're awake."*

"I am buddy," I replied back in my mind. I'd never had to do so when he was right next to me, but it was definitely necessary now. *"I'm so glad you're safe too."*

"Can't leave. Hard to communicate with Brother."

I kissed him on the head, taking the time to make a show of the affection in front of Ingrid. *"We'll have to bide our time. I'm sure Huginn is aware of where we are and will tell the others."*

"He knows."

That was good. Hopefully I'd figure out a way for us to escape before anyone else needed to be involved.

Ingrid patted my leg. "Come now. Dinner will get cold."

Muninn perched on my shoulder and I climbed out of bed. I still wore my date clothes. I was thankful Ingrid or any of her goons hadn't taken the liberties of changing me. Though from the assessing look she gave, she wasn't pleased with my attire.

"What?" I said, pushing out defensiveness.

"We'll need to have a talk about dressing appropriately," she said. "You need to have more self-respect."

Self-respect, right. "I was on a date."

"With the whole world? Honestly, Astrid. It looks like you're trying to whore yourself out."

"Baldur liked it," I muttered. I wasn't stupid enough to tell her he was the one to pick it out.

She sighed and shook her head. "Then you need to train him better. He's a fresh slate. You can mold him into a respectable man."

I tried not to make a face at her suggestion. This was way too uncomfortable.

Ingrid led me out of my pink room, down a small hallway with wooden floors and white walls, to a small bathroom with all the necessary amenities. I washed my hands and used my magic to freshen up my appearance. She continued on when I finished.

We passed another bedroom, this one less weirdly decorated. Well, it wasn't decorated at all. There was just a bed with a gray and white bedspread, and an old alarm clock that looked like it'd come right out of the '80's with its long rectangular body, wood paneling, and red lit digital face.

We came to a living room. It had a TV, more fake windows, and a nice couch. There were some picture frames, but they were all weirdly empty. *What is this, one of those doomsday condos?*

She continued on with this strange conversation. "You should start by teaching him not to take you to some barbaric place as that fight pit."

I frowned. "I like going to the fights. They're fun."

She dramatically sighed. "I told your father you weren't a boy. He shouldn't have raised you as one. Look at how you turned out."

It took everything in me not to lash out at her. "Dad raised me to like what I wanted. I like the fights because I chose that. I also like makeup and other girly shit."

She flicked a stern glance back at me. "Watch your tongue, young lady. It's not becoming to swear."

I rolled my eyes. Creation, was she making me feel like a teenager again. Defiance and immaturity were so easy to call up in order to deal with her, it was sad. But if this didn't backfire, then so be it.

I knew what she wanted. She wanted to worm her way in and pretend she deserved the "best mom of the year" award so she could control me, all the while doing so by demeaning and degrading me until my self-esteem took too many hits. It was such textbook manipulation. I would put up a fight, but in a way I didn't like having to do.

To beat a manipulator, you had to manipulate right back.

We walked into another room with a small table and kitchenette. The table was set for two and had what looked like more food than the kitchen setup could have handled.

"Come, sit." She was too excited for this.

I took my seat, my eyes roaming the food. It did look good at least. "What's for dinner?"

"We have Greek salad, fried green tomatoes, ground lamb balls, braised lamb with turnip, Three Sisters soup, and I have a dessert in the fridge if you're still hungry after that."

My stomach rumbled. I was certainly ready to eat. Immortality came with a high metabolism, and I'd worked up an appetite all afternoon. "That's a lot of food."

She smiled brightly. "Only the best for my daughter. And I know how much you love lamb, so I made sure it was cooked to perfection for you."

Lamb was one of my favorite meats. How did she know that?

"Oh, and tomorrow we'll have bison. There are a few recipes I want to try, and I know how much you love bison."

I did. *How does she know that, too?*

Ingrid excitedly gestured to the food. "Go on, try it."

I looked it over, warring with myself whether I should. She'd kept me alive this long, so it wouldn't make sense for this to be poisoned.

"I'll try first," Muninn said. *"I don't trust."*

He loved eating my food, but he was usually acting all goofy when he did. This was the most serious I'd seen him be.

I cut into a lamb ball and held it up to my mouth as if I was going to eat it. Muninn reached over and plucked the meat from my fork. I chuckled, acting up my amusement. "Like it, buddy?"

He bobbed his head and spoke to me only again. *"Real food. Safe to eat."*

That was reassuring, though it hadn't occurred to me the food was fake. I didn't want to know what he considered the meat actually was, or how he'd know it wasn't real lamb.

I took a bite myself. A melody of spices danced along my tongue. It was actually really good. I noticed Ingrid watching me without touching her food. "Something wrong?"

"Oh, no, I was just thinking about your familiar." She finally took a bite of food. She barely chewed it. *Strange.* "Do you always allow him to eat from your plate?"

"Usually they get their own, but I don't mind sharing this way, either. Are you uncomfortable with that? I don't want to be rude. I could go look for another plate."

She laughed and waved me off. "Oh, don't be silly, Astrid. Your familiars are welcome here, just like you are. They're an extension of you, so they can eat at the table, too. Do you like it?"

I nodded. "I'm impressed. I'm not this great of a cook. Diego is the master in the kitchen, so I let him take over that duty."

"As you should. You shouldn't have to lift a hand with… three men, is it?" She grinned. "You get that from me. Before your father, I had a number of boyfriends eating out of the palm of my hand. But your father wanted to be the only one, so I agreed. It's good you asserted yourself and made them be okay with you having them all."

The way she said that made my skin crawl. But I knew correcting her about how my relationship worked wasn't smart. "I'm blessed to have snagged them. I want for nothing."

"That's what I want to hear. I need to be sure my daughter is taken care of." She took another bite of her food, and again basically just swallowed it.

"I don't like the way she eats, Sister. It's not right for a human."

"Mom, why am I here?" A bold question, but I also couldn't see it hurting.

Ingrid blinked. "To spend time with me, of course. It's all I wanted."

"So you… abducted me?"

She sighed dramatically. "I had no choice, Astrid. That magic they had on you wouldn't allow me to get through to you. I need to get you away from it so that I could have a proper conversation with you. We deserve to catch up and see what we missed."

Yeah, I'd rather eat hákarl for the rest of my life.

"So, let's catch up."

And we did. I had the strangest, most normal conversation with Ingrid. I didn't tell her anything that would be compromising, but telling her parts of my life wouldn't hurt. At the very least, it kept her from getting angry.

She would get frustrated when I wouldn't allow her to disparage Dad, but then would easily redirect to something different so she could try to paint herself as the good guy in the scenario.

All throughout this, she hardly ate. It didn't feel right.

I stopped eating when I lost my appetite. I wasn't sure if I was full or just unhappy with my situation now. I couldn't help but notice a part of me liked this situation. In the past, I'd wanted nothing more than to have a sane mother who loved me. And this situation really fed that side of me.

"All done? Do you want dessert?" She looked hopeful, too much so.

I shook my head. "I need to digest a bit."

She clapped. "That's fine. What would you like to do? We have all kinds of movies and board games to choose from."

"Um, can I have a tour?" I needed to see more of this place.

Ingrid blinked. "A tour? You've seen everything."

This was a risk, but I had to take it. "Please, Mom, don't treat me like I'm dumb. I know we're underground. Those windows have photo prints of scenery, and none of them look real or match. There's no way one apartment is underground."

I played with my fingers, leaning on what I'd seen Magnus and Dahlia do from their interrogation training, hoping I could pull it off even a fraction as well as they could. "You also told me last time there was a lot more you wanted to show and teach me. I thought that's what you wanted now, that's why I was here."

Ingrid smiled, that crazed look I'd seen last time sparking. "You're just as smart as I knew you were. You get that from me. I'm happy to show you around."

We left the table without cleaning up, most of her food untouched, and she led me down a hall that went to an elevator. I noted the number of floors on the elevator was only eleven and we were at the bottom.

"Mom, is this a small facility?" I asked.

She blinked. "No, of course not."

"Oh, okay. Eleven levels is just smaller than I expected."

"The top three levels are the largest. They hold most of our operational needs here."

"Is this layout common between other locations?"

Ingrid's eyes narrowed. "What makes you think there is more than this location?"

I shrugged. "There's so much widespread reach, it makes sense to me there are multiple bases. Kinda like how the military works."

She burst into laughter. "Your father has you watching those military movies of his, doesn't he? Oh, the things you think up, Astrid."

She patted me on the head in the most condescending way I could have ever experienced. "We're nothing like that. We have this place, and that's it. It's all we need. Malsumis provides everything else."

Yeah, right. I hadn't gained her trust yet for that information was what she was saying. And I doubted I would, not unless I became a permanent prisoner, and there was no way my family would allow that. They'd burn the world down for me. *Hmm, maybe that's what Ingrid is hoping for.*

We arrived at the floor Ingrid wanted to show off. Some sort of recreation room. There were people in here, relaxing and doing activities.

Not just humans, either. Fae, demons, and all other creatures I may or may not know the names for. I didn't expect such a diverse group. *Why would so many of these creatures side with Malsumis? What do they get out of working with her?*

Most of them were pleasant with their greetings, but something felt… off. The way they spoke and interacted felt too stilted, as if they were forced to say certain things. And I swore, when I stopped looking their way, I caught them in the corner of my eye going unnaturally still and quiet.

"Muninn?" I prompted.

"Something isn't right," he agreed. *"They don't replay back in my memories correctly. We need brother."*

Even without Huginn, that was enough for me to be extra cautious.

Ingrid led me away to another floor. I wanted to call it a training facility, but it was the most normal-looking gym I'd ever seen. It was too normal. All of this was too normal. The only thing that wasn't normal were the people. Again, on this floor, the interactions were just like the lower floor.

"Something the matter, dear?" Ingrid asked when she ushered me into the elevator again.

I nodded slowly. "Yeah, it's just… this isn't anything like I imagined."

She wrapped her arm around my shoulder. "I told you I wasn't the bad guy. Those… false gods have painted such a horrid picture of us, when it is them who invaded our lands and enslaved our people."

Our? That was such a strange thing for her to say. From Malsumis, yes I understood that completely. But aside from Malsumis's essence in her—I wasn't even sure whether it was DNA or not, given the specific circumstances under which the chaos goddess had been able to impregnate women while sealed away is quite unclear—Ingrid looked Western European, like me. And if Azzie's upbringing was anything to base things on, I had my doubts Ingrid was raised hating her European ancestry.

"They're not false gods, Mom. They're real gods."

"Not here they're not. They should return to where they belong."

"Malsumis was affecting their lands, too. She didn't stay here." I put a little extra indignation into my words.

She scoffed. "More lies, Astrid. Everything they told you was a lie. Why can't you see that?"

I crossed my arms and looked away from her. "They're my friends."

"You're their pawn." Her hands on my shoulders were gentle and warm. "I understand you don't want to believe this, but I'm trying to tell you the truth. Just see what happened with Odin. He is one of them, and you had to put him down. They'll all turn out to be like him one day. They're cut from the same cloth."

I threw my hands out and faced her. "They're not like that! They wouldn't use me and then throw me away. They care about me. If you just met them, then you'd see it, too."

Ingrid shook her head. "I can't reason with you when you're like this. Once we purify you of their influence, then we can have a better discussion. And a nap. You clearly could use one."

I snorted and crossed my arms. "Of course. I should have known this wasn't a real tour."

Gods did I hate having to act like this. I felt like a spoiled, snotty teen.

"Astrid," Ingrid warned. "There's no need to act like this."

I leaned against the elevator wall and refused to look at her. Mustering up hatred was easy. I couldn't stand the way she saw those I loved. *How can she not see how amazing my people are?* She wasn't even trying to see it from my perspective.

Muninn pressed against me, pushing calming vibes through our bond. Apparently it was a little too easy to fall into these feelings.

"Well?" I prompted when Ingrid didn't select a button. "Are we going back down to my gilded cage or not?"

"Astrid…" Her eyes were soft, almost sad. They had the audacity to tug at my heart. "You're not a prisoner. I love you."

"You have a fantastic way of showing it." I snapped. "All you've done is criticize everything about my life. My hobbies, my fashion, my friends, even my magic. I've never once been good enough for you."

My voice may have broken a little at the end. The emotions were too real—too close to what I actually felt about her never being there for me like a mom should be.

Ingrid sighed and her finger hovered over the bottom floor. I expected as much. I couldn't be too eager to side with her, otherwise she'd be suspicious. I had to push back a little, else I'd never get out of here. It was a delicate balance, and not one I felt totally equipped to maintaining.

"I do love you, Astrid," she said. "I want what's best for you. You have so much potential that you just can't see."

To my surprise, she pressed the level three button.

"Where are we going?" I muttered out, keeping up the annoyed act.

"You wanted to see the truth. I will show it to you. Then you will understand what I'm trying to tell you."

The ride up was quiet. I kept up my act of being mad at her but vaguely curious. It seemed to help me with the way her attention focused on me. While I didn't have to watch her, Muninn could, and he relayed the various emotions that seemed to play over the woman's face.

The most infuriating problem was that each emotion seemed real. She seemed to really want me to understand her and what she was trying to accomplish. I couldn't fall for her manipulation, but I was also struggling with how to deal with this. Could I save her? Was there an innocent person somewhere within her I could save from Malsumis?

The elevator door slid open and Ingrid led me down a gray hall with concrete floors. Pipes ran the ceiling and bright LED tube lights illuminated the passage. People and other supernatural beings moved about, these ones less relaxed, having an air of business and work about them. And unlike those I met at the lower levels, these beings didn't act strangely when I didn't have my full focus on them.

Cult members noticed me, but they didn't stop for greetings. No, there was an air of suspicion about them. But one look from Ingrid sent most of them scurrying. She clearly held power here, and wasn't afraid to use it.

The hall opened to a large circular space. An opening in the ceiling revealed glimpses of levels one and two, which allowed for surveillance and communication between the floors. My eyes darted around, searching for a way out.

"*I don't see it,*" Muninn said.

"*It has to be just out of sight on the first floor.*"

"*Do you want me to check?*"

"Not yet. It might make her suspicious. We'll wait for an opening."

Muninn had other ideas. He snagged a lock of my hair with his beak and tugged on it while making cooing sounds. Ingrid noticed. "Is he all right, dear?"

I pulled my hair from him but he grabbed it back. "He's bored and restless. He doesn't like sitting on my shoulder for long periods of time."

I glanced around, as if taking in the size of the room. "Um… would it be a problem if he flew around this room a few times? It's just so he can stretch his wings."

Ingrid smiled. "Of course that's okay, dear. It's important to take proper care of your familiars. So as long as he doesn't cause anyone trouble. Ravens are cheeky."

I chuckled. "Don't worry, he'll be good. Won't you, Muninn?"

He bobbed his head while pushing cheeky, mischievous feelings through the bond, and darted off my shoulder. My raven winged his way around the room, avoiding the center circle at first. To my surprise, I felt him taking in everything he saw, committing it to his memory to be stored forever.

This was the first I'd ever felt that sensation. It was this pressure on my senses, like, if a bubble in my head popped, I'd see what he saw without issues.

A man, human by the look of it, came up to Ingrid. His gaze was downcast, but he didn't hesitate to approach her. "Priestess, a word if you would permit?"

The friendly aura she was trying to maintain for me was turned toward this man and it clearly made him uncomfortable. It was a stark contrast to how those below reacted. She clearly wasn't like this with these cultists normally. "Always. Astrid, I'll be right back."

I said nothing, watching them walk off to speak privately. Unfortunately, between their distance and the loud sounds around me, I couldn't hear what they were talking about. This forced me to focus more on Muninn.

Taking advantage of Ingrid's distracted state, he angled toward the center circle and then banked up. I sighed when he flew into the second level. Looked like I was going to have to be more involved here.

I approached the inner circle and placed my hands on my hips while looking up. "Muninn, this isn't what we agreed. Come back down."

He croaked in response and continued flying around.

I blew out a breath. "Muninn."

Muninn called back, then made another sweep around that level before diving down at me. He swooped up just above my head and circled around the third level again then flew up to the first. I crossed my arms and shook my head. He was good at this, and I'd play along as long as I could.

He returned to me and landed on my shoulder after a few more laps. *"I can't find a door."*

A muscle twitched in my neck. That wasn't a good sign. *"Why would they hide an exit door?"*

"Maybe there is no door."

Discomfort rolled through me. I didn't like that idea.

"They spotted Brother."

I blinked looked at him. *"Huginn is here?"*

He bobbed. *"He and Loki were scouting. They only spotted Brother, though. He knew, so they retreated."*

My brow furrowed. *"Loki? Why would he be here?"*

Muninn shook his body and puffed out. *"Not sure. I'm struggling to connect with Brother. I can only send small moments of memories, and he is struggling to send me what he sees and hears."*

I didn't like that. It made this place that much more oppressive. Without any doors, and a magic disrupting communication and teleportation, how were we going to get out? Even if they informed the others where Muninn and I were, escape wasn't going to be simple.

Muninn pressed against me and cooed. *"We will escape. Have faith."*

I wouldn't need faith if I weren't so useless.

"Not useless…"

I was. I had all this magic, and here I was, a damsel in distress.

Muninn pecked my head and I winced. *"Not useless! Gathering intel. Seeing how far crazy priestess will go. Seeing what they hide here. All important."*

"Astrid," Ingrid said.

I jumped and spun around. She stood behind me. The guy from before was nowhere to be seen. "Yes?"

"Did your familiar just hurt you?"

I shook my head. "He does that when he's upset with me, but it doesn't hurt. I was about to remind him that wasn't appropriate behavior."

"Good. Otherwise, we'd have to have a talk about his improper training. A familiar should never, under any circumstances, harm his witch."

Unless they really needed it. I knew all the complex rules between witches and familiars. But some could be broken or bent if a situation truly called for it. And I wasn't very strict on the rules, either. That's why the ravens could come and go as they pleased and I never ordered them to do anything unless absolutely necessary. They weren't my slaves. They were my partners.

"Are we going to see what you wanted to show me?" I asked.

"Of course. I need you to see this."

Ingrid ushered me toward a hall on the other side of the room. It went on for what felt like forever, and we passed closed doors with no windows to glean anything from inside. None of them opened with people coming or going, and no sound could be heard. Yet, despite not knowing what lay beyond them, I couldn't shake the feeling something wasn't right behind those doors.

The longer we walked, the more suspicious I became. Had Muninn and I tipped our hand too quickly? I wouldn't be surprised. It wasn't like I was raised as some soldier or spy.

"Mom, what are you trying to show me that needs us to keep going this far?" I asked.

"The truth."

I pursed my lips. That answer made me even more suspicious.

She suddenly stopped in front of an unmarked door. She touched the handle but didn't open it right away. "Before I show you this, Astrid, I need you to open your mind and shed all misconceptions you've ever had. I need you to see with unclouded eyes, as much as you can."

I nodded, not trusting myself to say the right thing. After everything she'd done, it would take a lot for me to see that as a misunderstanding.

Ingrid twisted the handle and pushed open the door. A relatively large room lay beyond, with walls painted in soothing neutral tones. Fluorescent lights illuminated the space, gleaming off stainless steel countertops lined with neatly arranged instruments and tools. Medical stations were dotted around the room, broken up by treatment areas outfitted with examination tables, monitoring equipment, and beds. Most of the beds were occupied, while a few areas had their privacy curtains pulled. *An infirmary?*

At first, I expected the patients to be cultists, those who returned back after whatever dangerous job they'd been sent out on to cause chaos. But on closer inspection, these looked like ordinary people and supernatural creatures. Creatures I would have taken in to the sanctuary.

Some looked like they were fine and in good health, while others were severely harmed and had several nurses in scrubs tending to them. None of them were chained up or being tormented. They were all seemingly here on their own accord and receiving medical attention. *Why would the cult do this? What benefit did they get from helping the people whose lives they also destroyed? Why aren't these people distressed?*

A nurse noticed us and a look of surprise crossed her face. "Priestess! What a surprise."

More eyes turned to us. Some, reverent, as if Ingrid's presence was some sign from the gods, while others surprised yet pleased. No one, not even the patients, looked as though a bad omen shadowed their doorstep.

Ingrid smiled with warmth and tenderness. Too much so? "Sisters, I would like to introduce my daughter, Astrid. She's been kept away from us and our Mistresses' truths for longer than I have wished. But she is here to learn and understand. She shares the gift my mother bestowed upon me and utilizes it in a way that will ensure our Mistresses' embrace reaches more lost children."

A shiver ran down my spine. I did not like this one bit.

"It has not been purified, but nonetheless her gift will help our injured siblings so they can enter their purification cleaner."

Reverent eyes shifted to me. I swallowed. *What the hell has she just signed me up for?*

TWENTY-FOUR

DIEGO

Tension coiled every muscle in my body. Fury roiled in my veins.

Go now.

I couldn't. I didn't have a direction.

Find her.

Where? I didn't know where she'd been taken.

Make them pay for taking my mate.

Someone said my name. I barely heard them.

Pace, back and forth. Back and forth.

Where was she? Why couldn't I have gotten to her sooner?

My tail lashed. When had I grown that? Didn't matter. Astrid was missing.

Someone tried to touch me. I pushed them away. How dare they try to stop me?

Stop me from what? I was here, at the house, not where Astrid was. I wasn't out there searching.

I shouldn't have to search. I should have been there sooner. I reacted the moment I felt something was wrong. I knew that pull. All of us dragons with Valkyrie mates had this bond.

Astrid wasn't my mate yet.

Yes she is. Go, protect her. I can't fail her like I have in the past.

Images flashed in my head: that same memory of her hurt and looking down at me during some battle; another memory, of her hurt because Leif and I weren't careful; the cut on her face, identical to all the versions of Astrid I knew, freshly bleeding.

I needed to calm down. I couldn't think logically when I was like this.

Something, some sort of feeling, pressed against my mind. I shoved it out. It wasn't Astrid. That was all that mattered.

The others failed to protect her. They were right there with her. How could they have failed her?

"I choose you, empathy baby," a muddled voice whispered.

No, I couldn't blame them. I should have been better at protecting her. I'd seen her. I could have let my dragon out. The chaos was already open to the public; they'd seen the battle. A dragon wouldn't have caused any more damage. It would have stopped those filth from taking *my* Astrid.

My feet halted and I blinked. Warmth and calm seeped in from… my legs?

I looked down to find little toddler Bard at my feet. His tiny hands gripped my pants, holding him up on his wobbly, still-learning-to-walk legs. He stared up at me with intense, far-too-aware eyes for someone so young.

"He's super effective," Dahlia cheered in a hushed voice.

I blinked and looked up. Everyone in the room was staring at me. *Shit.*

"Are you calm now, Treasure?" I looked up to Mamá. She stood behind me, her hands poised to touch me, but hesitant.

I was. Stooping, I lifted Bard into my arms. "Thanks to this little one, I am."

I kissed him on the head. Bard giggled. "Habby."

I felt it. This tiny little empath radiated happy feelings into me. I still worried for Astrid and needed to find her, but at least my head was calm.

I was more aware of what everyone was up to. We were all clustered in the great room and kitchen. Everyone who was close to Astrid was here—even if they may not have had the ability to help, they'd gathered.

Tyr looked pensive, a reflection of the feelings I had about this situation, but he was somehow managing to stay controlled better than I had, which was an impressive feat for him. Baldur sat on a chair, leaning his forearms on his legs. While he appeared mostly calm, his frustration reflected in his eyes.

I needed to keep my head on straight. We couldn't save Astrid if we were flying off the handle. "What are we supposed to do?"

Aya looked up from a laptop. "We're not having luck with Dahlia's program, and none of us who can sense immortal signatures can find her."

A muscle twitched in the back of my neck. Frustration flared, and then fizzled when Bard patted my cheek with his tiny hand. "How is it she can be that hidden?"

"There are plenty of ways to hide something or someone," Mamá said. "Abilities to find people aren't perfect. They can be thwarted in many ways."

"Ingrid isn't going to want us to find Astrid," Darius said. Every feature in his face was tight and radiated danger. I'd only ever seen him like this once, when Garmr and Ingrid attacked the town last year. "We're going to have to be more strategic in the way we search. She's too smart for the usual tactics."

"So, what, we keep trying to find their bases and hope one of them has Astrid?" Azzie said. "That's going to take too long. Who knows what'll happen to Astrid in that timeframe."

"Astrid is strong," Bjarke said. "We have to have faith she can hold on while we figure this out."

"But if Ingrid messes with her magic in any way…"

I blinked slowly. Astrid's magic. *Her familiars.*

Whirling around, I looked for them. In my panic, I hadn't checked whether the ravens came back with us. And Angel hadn't been near me, trying to work her therapy-dog attempts to calm me.

No ravens were in sight. Angel, however, sat in front of a large window, staring out at the sky. I handed Bard off to Bragi and sat down next to Angel. She turned her attention to me, those expressive eyes of hers watching with eerie intelligence. *The familiar bond is still active.*

No one could communicate with her in the same way Astrid could. I doubted even empaths could figure her out. But if she was gaining the intelligence I thought she was from the interactions I gleaned between her and Astrid, this should work.

I held up my hands. "Angel, I'm going to do *yes* and *no* questions. This is yes, and this is no." I moved each hand to indicate which. "Do you understand?"

Her ears perked and she barked, slapping her paw down on my "yes" hand.

I felt everyone's attention on us. People scarcely dared to breathe.

"Do you know where Astrid is?"

No.

"Can you feel her through the familiar bond?"

Yes.

"Is Astrid unharmed?"

Angel took a moment. *Yes.*

I blew out a breath. That was reassuring. I wanted to know about her safety status, but I wasn't sure of a yes-and-no question that would work. "Are the Ravens with her?"

She cocked her head and lifted her paw, but hit the air between my hands. My brow furrowed.

"Is that a maybe?" Magnus asked. "Or did she get confused?"

"No, I don't think that's it… Angel, is Muninn with her?"

Yes.

"Is Huginn with her?"

No.

My heart beat faster. Why wasn't he with her? "Is he injured?"

No.

That didn't make any sense. He and Astrid had patched things up. If he wasn't injured, why wouldn't he be with her if Muninn was?

I turned to Aya and Dahlia. "Can you search for him? Does it work on familiars?"

The two looked at each other, and Dahlia spoke with uncertainty. "We can try."

Before they could make the attempt, Angel leapt to her feet and rushed toward the kitchen. I whirled around. Leaning against the island, with Huginn calmly perched on his arm, was a well-dressed man I'd only seen twice: when Ingrid dropped him off in a bloody heap at Astrid's feet, and next to Astrid at the fight pit.

Angel stood in front of him, not aggressive, but attentive, as if waiting for something.

"What the hel are you doing here, Loki?" Davyn snarled. Hair of his bear form was already growing as he barely kept his Berserker side contained.

"Davyn," Darius said in a deceivingly calm tone. A shiver ran down my spine. I knew that tone all too well, growing up here. It was one step down from his dad voice. "You will abide by the rules."

The Berserker snarled and narrowed his eyes at Darius. "I will not tolerate anyone conspiring with the likes of him."

Loki sighed. "Or maybe, Davyn, you could use that tiny Berserker brain of yours for once and consider he already knows I have the information you seek and he's not moronic enough to send me away."

"And you're going to just hand this information over because you're a good person?" Dahlia said, the sarcasm extra thick with her.

Loki rolled his eyes. He opened his mouth to speak, but stopped when Sean placed a plate of fruit and nuts and a small bowl of water down on the island next to him. Loki's brow rose.

"Huginn needs his strength back," Sean simply said.

With all the immediate tension, I hadn't taken the time to make sure Huginn was okay when I should have. My eyes roamed the raven as he ate and drank Sean's offering, but I couldn't see anything wrong with him. Maybe it was something specific to Sean's abilities.

Loki refocused on us. "I don't do charity. I do, however, settle my debts."

Confusion passed through those not in the know. This made so much more sense to me. Saving Astrid likely counted as a life debt repayment.

"You say you know where Astrid is," Tyr said, calm like me, as if it were normal for Loki to be here. "How did you figure it out?"

Loki gestured to Huginn. "Isn't it obvious? Those idiots were so focused on capturing your precious Valkyrie, they didn't pay attention to the fact they'd missed one of her most important familiars."

Tyr's eyes narrowed. "You saw them take her and you didn't stop them?"

"I don't think you're the right god to be lecturing me about protecting a Valkyrie."

Fen growled, yeah, actually growled, and Loki ignored him. "Now, do you want to hear me out, or am I leaving? The clock is ticking for Astrid. I doubt she'll last long. She is quite soft."

My eyes narrowed. "Don't underestimate her."

That was always the downfall of those around her. It was something even I did far too often. Her sweet and gentle nature made her seem like she was something she wasn't. There was a warrior and deadly witch inside her, and neither were to be trifled with.

"I will show the memory dragon what my brother sees," Huginn said.

My brow furrowed. It wasn't hard to figure out he meant me. "I'm not bonded with you."

"I can only do this with you. Your gift… resonates with ours."

My ability to see memories was an actual useful skill? Sign me up.

I sat at the island, remembering how disorienting Astrid said this ability with her ravens was, and Huginn hopped up onto my shoulder. He sidled closer and pressed his head against the side of my face.

My vision blurred and then, I was no longer in the house. I was in some building. Or a box? It was hard to tell, as the colors in the room weren't what I was used to. The best I could tell, maybe the vision was in some sort of elevator?

Astrid's familiar red hair came into view and I realized I was seeing through Muninn's eyes. He perched on her shoulder, watching everything. His emotions bled through this strange share, or maybe they were Astrid's? Fear mixed with frustration and pain. A spark of hope mingled in there somewhere.

From the looks of it, Astrid was conversing with Ingrid. I couldn't hear, but the feeling I got was that it wasn't a pleasant conversation. Not that they were fighting. No… it felt like Astrid was having to use uncomfortable methods to converse. Was she trying to manipulate her mother? Or maybe counter-manipulate. Ingrid did try to gaslight her when she'd showed up here. I wouldn't put it past her to try again with Astrid alone.

The vision got staticky. Yeah, static, like a bad TV channel signal, and then suddenly they were in what looked like a hospital wing. It was hard to tell what exactly was going on, but I saw people on hospital beds, and felt Astrid's worry through the connection.

The vision faded from my eyes and I blinked back to the house. *Shit.* "They have hostages, on top of holding Astrid."

Curses rumbled through the house. This added a layer of complication.

"Tell us what you saw," Darius said.

And I did, every detail I could remember.

"Given the familiar bond is still active, we can assume Ingrid hasn't used a magic blocker on Astrid yet," Aya mumbled. "Why she hasn't, I don't know, but that indicates they're blocking her ability to teleport out, and our way in. I'm guessing that's why you didn't just go in and grab her and get out."

She'd directed that last part to Loki. He had a smarmy smile on his face. "Very good, Aya. Gold star for you."

She flipped him off.

"I think Ingrid is trying to manipulate Astrid," I said, making sure this didn't derail. "The two of them were talking, and I sensed how uncomfortable things were from Astrid's side. If Ingrid had taken Astrid's magic away, that wouldn't help her angle."

Darius nodded in agreement. "That would be an angle Ingrid would take. Too bad for her, Astrid is well equipped to handle that, even if it makes her uncomfortable."

Azzie opened her mouth to question, and then mouthed "oh," when she realized what Darius meant. Never make an enemy of a therapist.

"Where is Astrid being held?" Kirby asked.

"A hidden bunker facility two hundred kilometers south of here," Loki shared.

That close?

"Then let's go," Davyn said.

"With what plan?" Kirby asked. "It's not abandoned."

"There are human and tech-based sentries that will alert the compound the moment you're spotted," Loki said. "No one can just walk in."

"We have to worry about getting out, too," Magnus added. "That's always the hardest part, and if we have an angry cult on our ass, we're not leaving without a fight. We know nothing about their numbers, abilities, anything."

"Is other magic disrupted beyond teleportation?" Darius asked Loki.

"I don't know," he admitted. The others seemed suspicious of this answer, and I remembered, no one else knew about Loki's condition.

"Astrid can use her magic," Huginn confirmed. *"She can only not teleport. Loki and I also needed to leave the area before we could as well."*

"That's an oddly specific target. Were you able to get close enough to the facility to get an idea of what might be blocking teleportation?" Darius asked.

"Malsumis' energy is all over that place," Loki said. "I wouldn't be surprised if it's just that causing the interference."

Magnus tapped her lips. "Could it be overpowered?"

Aya shook her head. "Not easily. Remember, it took almost a dozen gods to seal Malsumis originally. With her seal broken, her power isn't something to be easily overpowered."

"No, but you probably didn't have both a conduit and an amplifier."

Kirby's back straightened. "Or a witch who gets a power boost with her emotions."

Darius smoothed his beard. "That might just work. Maybe not permanently, but long enough for the rest of us to arrive."

"Or leave," Kirby said. "If Magnus can get in and overpower the magic, they can leave right under Ingrid's nose."

Bjarke shook his head. "Astrid won't leave the other hostages, so unless you've got a way to gather them all up and overpower the magic quickly, that plan won't work."

Kirby swore.

"I don't think I can do this alone anyway," Magnus said. "I'm good at amplifying, but even if I'm touching Astrid as my source, it won't be an instant thing."

Baldur lifted his head. "I can get Magnus in and we can act as a distraction long enough for all of you to enact a second entry plan."

Everyone turned to him. He had one hell of a serious look to him. "Ingrid called me obedient. She thinks Tyr, Diego, and I will do anything for Astrid, no matter what Astrid asks, even side with Malsumis. If we can make her think we're only loyal to Astrid, it might keep her distracted long enough. But all three of us going would seem suspicious, especially if she's not expecting us to find this place."

"How does that get Magnus in?" Bjarke asked.

"I could play off as the weakest-willed of the Valkyries," Magnus said. "Someone who's easily swayed by Astrid. I've had to pretend a lot worse."

"You're not wrong." Loki crossed his arms, his eyes critical. "How are you going to explain finding the bunker?"

To my surprise, Baldur pointed at Angel. The shepherd's ears perked up and she bolted to the god. She sat in front of him, eager and alert, barking once in agreement of his choice.

"The dog?" Loki didn't hide his disbelief.

"Huginn is too obvious a choice," Baldur said. "Ingrid knows Astrid has both ravens as familiars. Bringing Huginn could play into a trap. However, she can't gain much from Angel. And it's still logical that Angel could track Astrid down."

"Huginn can also act as a relay for us," Fen said. "If he and Diego work together, we can keep tabs on Astrid's situation and pivot accordingly."

Huginn puffed his feathers and bobbed his head. Seemed my job was chosen for me. My dragon twisted and moved so close I could feel the shift just under my skin. It moved in sync with the irritation and conflict within me. I should be there to save Astrid, but I would likely only get in the way, putting her in even more danger.

"I don't like the idea of you going in there," Nico mumbled to Magnus.

"I'll be fine," she reassured. "I've had worse jobs with even lower odds of success."

"I'll go with you, for a team of three," Azzie volunteered. "Being Malsumis' daughter might be useful in this situation."

Davyn snapped his attention to her. "You won't."

Zeke shook his head. "I don't like that idea, either. So many people will start looking like a rescue party. And without us knowing if Magnus can get anyone out, we don't know if you'll be trapped there. You being trapped in a Malsumis cult building is the last thing we need."

"It'll look like a rescue party no matter if it's one person going, or five," Darius said. "Ingrid will be expecting one. So it wouldn't hurt to play to her ego a bit. However, we need to ensure the right people go in for the first team. And while I appreciate your willingness to volunteer so quickly, Azzie, I need your skills with us on the second team."

Azzie smiled at him. There seemed to be a spark of pride in her eyes that Darius had expressed himself in that way to her.

"I'll be the third person going," Loki said.

Davyn snarled. "Like hel—"

Darius held up a hand, silencing him. His hard stare on Loki was unwavering. "You think you can convince her?"

Loki smirked. "I can be very persuasive. And charming when I need to be."

Davyn grunted. Darius ignored the Berserker and nodded. "Then we're sending in two gods, a Valkyrie, and a familiar. The rest of us will hash out a plan and pivot as you learn more from the inside."

Kirby was the first to nod in agreement to the plan. I was surprised she wasn't calling the shots more here. But maybe it was because she understood and respected Darius' experience.

Birdy waved at the infiltration team when they grouped up. "Ba-ba."

Then they were gone, leaving us to continue planning.

TWENTY-FIVE

ASTRID

Ingrid held her hand out to me, to emphasize the awesomeness that was me. I didn't know what I was supposed to do. Heal these people? That contradicted what I'd seen when we saved people after the cult infected them with the magic blockers.

And what was she meaning by my magic needed to be purified? She'd said that before to me.

The nurses stepped aside, their eyes never leaving me, and revealed a path to a particularly injured woman who appeared to have some fae features. Ingrid ushered me toward her.

"Astrid, dear, this poor fae was attacked by hunters," Ingrid explained. "We don't have the means to heal her. But your blessed power might."

Might was a strong word. My healing could do a lot, but it still had limitations. Fae wounds inflicted by iron were still incredibly difficult for me, especially the older the injury was. That didn't mean I wouldn't try. No matter how fucked-up this situation was, I wasn't going to leave someone to suffer to their wounds just to spite Ingrid.

I tried to speak with the woman, to reassure her I would do my best, but she didn't say anything back. She just blinked up at me with weirdly dull eyes. Even Muninn was uncomfortable with the behavior.

Forced to take her silence and calm nature as compliance when I really didn't want to, I summoned my magic. The room filled with gasps when black tendrils of magic sprang from my fingers and wrapped around the fae.

What the hell? Where was my golden magic?

The magic snagged on her wounds and seeped in, knitting her flesh back together. My brow furrowed as I worked. Most watching might assume my expression was focus, but it was far from that. She was healing too easily. My magic slithered along her in a way that it didn't normally. There was almost no resistance, and that wasn't right.

I let my magic die and the woman was completely healed. Everyone in the room murmured and marveled.

Ingrid held up her hands. "Behold. Even unpurified, Malsumis' power flows through my daughter in miraculous ways."

A nurse fell to her knees and tipped her head back. She murmured things in a language I didn't understand. Others looked as though they'd been overcome by witnessing my almighty power of… whatever healing I was doing.

Ingrid wrapped her hands around my shoulders and ushered me toward another patient. "Daughter, please, show them again."

Unsure how to process this, I complied. This person was more talkative than the first, but they babbled about truths and becoming beyond their current self. They also healed just as abnormally fast as the first patient.

"A true Valkyrie!" Ingrid proclaimed, making another theatrical motion about this. "Not some poor imitation made by a false god. My daughter, my beautiful, perfect daughter, not even purified, and showing us a fraction of what our Mistress is willing to give us all, should we give ourselves to her."

Her words made my skin crawl. She made me sound like a prophet come to life, and I didn't like it.

Muninn pressed against my neck, cooing softly. He helped me stay calm and centered as the people around us fell into reverence.

My brow pinched when wooziness fell over me all of a sudden. I blinked rapidly when the room began to spin. Muninn squawked in alarm.

Ingrid grabbed me by the shoulders. "Oh dear. It seems you overdid it, my daughter. Let's get you resting. Then you can help the rest of our brothers and sisters with their injuries, so they'll be ready for their purification."

"Their purification?" I mumbled out.

She didn't answer and ushered me out of the room, promising the others we'd be back once I rested.

"Mom… what's going on with me?" Were my words slurring? My body felt so wrong. "This has never happened before when I healed. It's never… looked like that, either."

"It's your lack of purification, dear." Her voice sounded far gentler and reassuring than it had all day. "Here you're able to channel Malsumis' power as you were always intended. Her power protects you more from the outside influences that have tainted your magic and essence."

That… made sense. My eyes fluttered. No it didn't. Why was I thinking it had? "There's nothing wrong with me."

"Of course there isn't," she said. "You are my perfect daughter. But those heathens have tainted you."

I shook my head. This didn't make sense. It was this cult that was the problem. Yet, why did it also make sense?

"*Sister!*" Muninn's alarmed voice pierced my mind. "*The food. The food was poisoned!*"

Poisoned? No, I ate it too long ago for it to be poisoned. And it was so good. Mom had made it just for me.

"*Listen to me.*"

"*I'm always listening.*"

He tugged on my hair. My precious familiar was always worried about me. He'd never lead me astray.

"*Never, Sister. I love you.*"

The haziness in my mind lifted a little. Just enough to know that, no matter what, I could trust Muninn. Everything he'd show me was truth.

I smiled and rested my hand on him, pulling him closer so I could nuzzle him with my face. "*I love you too, buddy.*"

I looked up when someone came running down the hall. It was the man that wanted to talk to Mom—Ingrid—before. At the same time, Muninn's mind stirred against mine. He noticed something that I couldn't see.

"Priestess, I need another word," he said.

Ingrid glanced at me as I leaned against her for balance. "You can speak freely in front of us."

He hesitated for a moment, the man's eyes flicking to me, then he held up a tablet-like device. "We found intruders. One of them is the same one we spotted earlier. The two others, we do not know. They also have a dog. How do you wish us to proceed?"

A dog? The haze in my brain lifted more. I was able to process the image on the device better. *I know those people.*

I reached for the tablet device. The man had the audacity to try and pull it away. I scowled and my magic flared. A knife manifested by his face, the sharp blade pushing just enough into his skin to be a threat, but not yet make him bleed. "Give it to me."

His jaw muscles flexed and he flicked his eyes to Ingrid. She smiled. "Listen to my daughter."

He nodded once and extended the device to me, careful not to move his head and cut himself on the blade. I snatched it from him and looked hard at the image displayed on the screen.

"Do you know them, dear?" Ingrid asked. "Well, I know the answer is at least one. That appears to be one of your god-pets."

I nodded and smiled up at her. "Baldur. He'd burn the world for me."

The way Ingrid smiled, it sent warning shivers down my spine.

"And you know Loki—my newest pet, thanks to you, Mom."

She seemed pleased with my praise of her supposed influence. "He seems to be well trained already if he's returned in search of you. I do wonder where your raven went, though, if he was tasked with caring for it in your absence."

"I'm not sure. I'll have to have a good talk with him."

She nodded. "As you should. And who is the woman with them?"

I smiled. "Magnus. She's my best friend. I'm not surprised she's here. She'd be one of the first to come searching for me. I'm sure she was in a panic as much as the others."

"I wonder where the others are..." Ingrid murmured.

I made a face. "Knowing Tyr, he thought he knew where you had whisked me away to and wouldn't listen to anyone. And I'm sure he's now gotten himself lost. He's terrible with direction."

Ingrid threw her head back in her laughter. "Most men are, dear, you'll learn that. What's with the dog? That is the most surprising part about this photo."

I blinked up at her. "That's Angel, my familiar."

Ingrid laughed as if I'd told a good joke. "Funny, dear. Now really, tell me."

I cocked my head. "I'm telling the truth, Mom. Angel was my first familiar."

"Dear, you're afraid of dogs."

I shook my head. "Not anymore. Angel helped me through that. And..." I looked away shyly. "You did as well, by bringing Garmr to me."

Ingrid hummed, sounding pleased. "Yes, I did do that."

"All of them can come here, right?" I asked her. "I'm sure they're worried about me. They've come this far to find me."

Ingrid looked down at the device and thought over my request.

I latched onto her arm and gave her my best pleading eyes. "I promise they won't be any trouble. If they are, I'll take full responsibility."

"You trust them fully?" she asked. "These ones won't cause us problems? After I've shown you truths firsthand, I don't want to worry about them trying to corrupt you again."

I shook my head. "No, I promise. Out of everyone I know, they'll understand."

"Very well." She smiled gently at me and then shifted her attention to the man I still threatened with a knife. "Bring them in. See to it no harm comes to them."

The man swallowed. "Priestess, I don't mean to argue—"

"Then don't," I said. My knife pressed into his skin, breaking it just enough to make him wince. Dark blood dribbled down his cheek. *Is that... black?*

His jaw set. "I was addressing our priestess, not—"

Ingrid stepped forward and he took a stumbling step back. "You will not speak to my daughter that way. You will speak to her with the same manner of respect you give me."

"With all due respects, Priestess, I do not trust her yet. And I question how these heathens have found us here."

Ingrid dismissively sniffed. "My daughter already answered that question. Her familiar, you dunce. They are an extension of her. They would find their way to her, no matter how far or secretly she went."

"Hidden words," Muninn warned me.

"I know." It was something I was hoping would go unnoticed by her, but that seemed to be a stretch. She wanted all of my familiars here. Then no one could find me if she moved me.

"Now, go." Ingrid dismissed the man with a wave of her hand.

"And don't harm them," I warned. "Or you'll regret it."

His lips pressed into a thin line and then he nodded his acceptance of Ingrid's order.

"Now," Ingrid said after the man left. "Tell me about Angel."

She placed her hands on me in a gentle, guiding way, and I allowed it. My mind was clearer than before the man arrived, but I felt it best for her to think I was still suffering under the effects of whatever put me in that state.

"She's the best dog ever," I said. "She's my protector, my safety, and my friend."

"What is your bond with her like?"

I blinked. "What do you mean?"

"Is it the same as your ravens or different?"

I shook my head. "Oh, no, nothing like with Huginn and Muninn. It's a bit more basic. While I can have conversations with my ravens, Angel can only communicate feelings to me that I have to interpret."

At least, that was how it'd been in the beginning. Now, it was something more. I wasn't having verbal conversations with her yet, but I just knew, on some instinctive level, exactly what she wanted, as if she'd verbally communicated with me.

"Can your ravens communicate with her? Or anyone else?"

I shook my head again. "Only I can."

"She seems pleased by this answer," Muninn said.

Yes, Ingrid was smiling oddly. I hoped I'd fed her the information she was after. If she wanted me trapped here, then she'd see Angel as the weak link from being my most basic familiar. She wasn't a threat. And that was exactly what I needed her to believe.

"How do all your familiars get along?" Ingrid asked. "I can't imagine it's easy having so many with individual personalities."

She patted my head—it felt almost motherly—maybe it would have if she had been a real mom to me. "I am proud of you, if I haven't told you that. A witch usually is only able to handle one familiar. Any more would take too much strain on her magic. But here you are, with three."

A part of me basked in the praise, but it was so fucked up. As much as I knew this was some bizarre trip and manipulation scheme, she fed into that side of me that wanted my mother to actually love me, like Dad did.

The central room came into view and awareness bloomed in my mind. *Angel.* My connection with her was still struggling, but not as much. She was furious and anxious, but didn't feel to be injured. She was almost here for me to see for myself, though.

Ingrid and I made it to the central room first. The activity here was the same as before. *Actually...* "Muninn?"

"Yes, Sister, there is something strange about their actions. They're... too much the same as before."

Were these people just working on the same shit still, resulting in repetitive movements, or was something else going on?

I didn't get much time to ponder when the man sent out to fetch the others returned. He came from a hallway I hadn't noticed before that appeared to house stairs. I wasn't sure if it was to the level up or somewhere else.

"That was not there before," Muninn confirmed.

Behind the man were their new hostages, who were flanked by more cultists. Baldur, Magnus, and Loki were blindfolded and had their hands bound. Lucky for the cultists, unfortunate for me, Angel was not restrained. I would have enjoyed making a few of them bleed.

Angel stuck close to Baldur in the perfect heel position. Her head swiveled and she searched. She spotted me and barked once before bolting to my side.

I crouched and she crashed into my open arms, nearly knocking me over. She let out her shepherd whine while she tried to lick my face and her whole body wagged in her excitement. I kissed her head as I held her, murmuring how she was so amazing to have found me.

Muninn bobbed up and down as if feeding on all this happiness. Angel finally calmed down, and then gazed up at both of us with those exceptionally intelligent eyes.

Muninn cackled in my head. *"Stupid cultists. Angel knows the way out. Hidden by magic. Magic you and our other sister can dispel together."*

I snuggled Angel more. *"You're amazing, girl."*

I didn't know what kind of plan we could make to get us out, but we could work on something as long as we could find time alone without ears to hear us. If that was even possible in this place.

"Don't move," someone ordered. "I said don't move."

I jerked my head up. Baldur and Loki had ripped off their blindfolds and Baldur appeared to be mid-motion of doing something with his wrists. He shot the cultists an uncaring look, not bothered by the gun being pointed at him, and then yanked his wrists. The cuffs binding him offered no resistance. The shattered pieces clattered on the concrete floor.

Loki wiggled his fingers like he was doing a magic trick and then somehow just slid his hands through his restraints, as if he didn't have any bones.

Magnus lifted the bottom of her blindfold to peek if it was okay to follow their lead. She looked so cute and innocent, just like I figured she would.

The cultist threatening Baldur shifted his weight and poised the gun in a way I was not going to allow. My magic flared up, and a black tendril shot out, wrapping around his wrist and yanking him down on the floor.

"Harm them, and I will make you wish you hadn't." My threat rumbled low but strong through the room. Several people even stopped their work to mind the commotion.

"You would do well to listen to her," Ingrid warned. "Afterall, these are our guests, and we are gracious hosts."

The cultists lowered their weapons and backed away.

"I sense Brother." Muninn launched from my shoulder and flew up to a higher level.

Thankfully, Ingrid appeared nonplussed by his behavior, and kept her attention on the others. She opened her arms dramatically. "Welcome. Astrid was just telling me all the wonderful things about you three. It's a pleasure to have all of you here."

Magnus shoved her blindfold up onto her forehead. "Are you okay, Astrid?"

I smiled and jogged over to them. "Of course I am."

Before I got to her, Baldur swept me up into his arms and held me close. "Don't scare me like that."

I nuzzled his neck. "You didn't have to worry. I was never in any danger."

Magnus popped up next to him and held up her wrists. "A little help?"

Baldur chuckled and put me down. He broke her restraints.

"Or you can do that," Ingrid muttered. She'd apparently followed and had a key in her hand.

"Sorry, Mom," I said with fake sheepishness. "We're still working on civilizing him."

Baldur nudged me. "You like it when I'm uncivilized."

Loki rolled his eyes and scoffed. I pointed a warning finger at them both.

Magnus stepped closer to me, her arm brushing mine, and glanced between Ingrid and me. "You two seem to be getting along."

I smiled and grabbed her, feeling the small bits of power she was already trying to push into me. They had a plan, and I just hoped I could help even if I couldn't communicate with them with Muninn gone.

"We've had some good long chats and come to an understanding," I said. "Right, Mom?"

Ingrid smiled. "Yes. We've had a lot to talk about. Like you, beautiful Magnus. Astrid tells me the two of you are close."

Magnus leaned into me and smiled. "We're like—"

"Sisters," I said at the same time as her, to help sell it.

Ingrid clapped. "You two even finish each other's sentences. How wonderful. I always wanted another daughter, and now I will. Welcome to the family, Magnus."

"Thank you…" She hesitated for a moment. "Mom?"

Ingrid's smile beamed. It was almost like she was truly happy to hear that. She then turned her focus to Baldur. She assessed him with her eyes in a way I didn't quite like. "Yes, dear, you sure know how to pick them. You are a fine man indeed, Baldur. And your devotion knows no bounds."

Baldur smirked and placed his hands on my shoulders, playing along as the obedient, dutiful partner.

Loki slipped around behind me as well. He'd been quiet, and his presence really did confuse me. He had no reason to come after me. *Unless…*

"Are you absolutely sure we can trust her?" Loki asked in a lower tone that made it seem like he was trying to be more subtle with his question, but failing to do so.

I nodded. "Kirby and the others got it all wrong."

Magnus snorted. "Kirby getting something wrong? Color me surprised."

I forced a laugh to make it seem like something we discussed all the time.

Ingrid took great interest in this topic. "I assume you two don't get along with her?"

Magnus made a face. "She struts around like some queen peacock, bossing us around and all that. Both her and Azzie get so insufferable."

Gods, Kirby and Azzie would kill us if they overheard us talking like this.

"Azzie…" Ingrid nodded. "Yes, Malsumis was quite disappointed in her. So much potential wasted. Unlike you two ladies." Her eyes flicked to Loki. "You, however—"

"Loki, where is Huginn?" I needed to keep her distracted by being slightly annoying. Magnus' power was pushing against me again. She was trying to do something with my magic, but secretly. Unfortunately, with Ingrid being magic-sensitive, if she was given the chance to pay attention, she'd feel such a shift. "I'd tasked you with keeping an eye on him."

Loki rolled his eyes. "Yes, well, he's still an unruly bird. He decided to fly off the moment we arrived. We were ambushed soon after, so I didn't have a chance to go after him."

Ingrid's eyes focused intently on the trickster god. "So, all of Astrid's familiars are here?"

"Somewhere, yes. We're all loyal to our contracts."

Ingrid's eyes narrowed with suspicion.

I grunted. "You make it sound like you're a familiar."

Loki laughed and then ran his fingers through my hair as if he were an affectionate lover. "For you, my dear, I can be anything. But no god can be turned into a familiar."

Ingrid's suspicions didn't abate. "You are the most surprising of all to see here, Loki. I wonder what your intentions are."

"I owe Astrid my life," he said, smiling pleasantly. "And through that act, we've come to an accord that is most agreeable to the two of us. Mainly, I serve her faithfully and she helps me work to better improve myself until she deems me worthy of being called *fixed*. It was long overdue; I realize that now. And Astrid has the…" He smirked. "Magic touch. We see it all the time with meathead Tyr, and how she keeps him under control when he goes off the rails."

He was laying it on a little thick in my opinion, but it seemed to be working with Ingrid, so I wasn't going to contradict anything if I could help it. "Speaking of Tyr, where is he?"

"Gone off the rails," Magnus said, struggling to bite back laughter.

I rolled my eyes. "Of course."

"He insisted on going in a different direction, even though both Angel and Huginn were telling us where to find you," Loki said with a shrug. "He doesn't listen when you're gone."

Magnus bumped my hip with hers. "Don't worry, Diego followed him to make sure he didn't get into any trouble."

"It shouldn't be too hard to find them, right, Mom?"

Ingrid blinked and then her happy mask slipped on again. "Of course, dear. Whoever you trust here is welcome. Our Mistress loves all. Now, we should get you all settled in. I'll have to work out accommodations for you two men."

I cocked my head. "They can sleep in my room. It's big enough."

Ingrid shook her head. "Absolutely not. Not until you're married."

She gasped, her face lighting up. "We'll have to start planning your wedding."

I choked. "I'm sorry, what?"

Magnus snickered. A real one.

"Well, you're not getting any younger, Astrid, really. And I want grandchildren before it's too late."

Loki laughed—actually laughed. *Asshole.*

"Too late? Mom, I'm immortal. I've got time." And really, I did not need her dogging me about this, too. Why did I care? She wasn't actually serious about this. She wasn't serious about anything when it came to me and her. She didn't care about me. *But what if she actually does?*

Ingrid waved her hand dismissively. "That doesn't mean you don't still have a prime window." Her glance shot to Loki. "You're not a prime candidate, though."

Loki held up a hand. "I would say Astrid agrees, given her opinion of my parenting skills with my other children."

I snorted.

Ingrid glanced at Baldur, her eyes appreciating him again in a way that made my hackles rise. "You, though…"

Baldur cleared his throat in a way that told me he was very uncomfortable with this topic. "I'm afraid I cannot sire children."

Ingrid waved her hand dismissively. "All things are possible with Malsumis. She will approve of you, god of courage. You weren't part of the problem, and the stories of you in battle… let's say she would appreciate your methods."

So, Ingrid believed Baldur was reckless and chaotic. That was good to keep her thinking we were on her side.

She turned toward the hall for the elevator. "Come, we can…"

I pressed my lips together and my brow furrowed when she trailed off, her attention drifting. "Mom?"

"I sense an unusual power."

Magnus glanced nervously at me. Had she pushed her power too much? "Maybe that's me? My power sometimes leaks out. It's been a major contention point between Kirby and me. She thinks I'm not trying hard enough to control it."

Ingrid waved her hand. "No, dear, don't worry. I felt that too. This is something different."

Muninn returned to my shoulder and pressed against my cheek, cooing like he was purring. *"They're here."*

I nuzzled him. *"Is this part of the plan?"*

"It's the part if Magnus' plan failed."

That didn't sound good. *"Did I mess something up?"*

"No. She was to boost your magic to overpower the chaos preventing us from leaving. She's having trouble connecting to your magic. I let Brother know, so the others moved in using Angel's memory of the path."

Magnus was having trouble? Why? She'd never struggled with that before. I assumed she was just being careful, not blocked.

"Ingrid knows they're here, then."

"I don't know if that is what she senses or not. They're disguised."

Ingrid held her hand out to me. "Let's get you downstairs to rest, Astrid. You still need to recover."

Baldur's grip on my shoulder tightened just a little. "Recover? What happened? You said you were fine?"

I blew out a breath. "I am fine. I used my magic earlier and it drained me more than normal."

"Do you want me to try to rethread it?" Magnus asked.

"What do you mean by rethread?" Ingrid asked, her attention intense, but it was unclear to me whether she was interested in Magnus' fake power, or suspicious.

"Oh, I can see magical energies," Magnus lied. "When someone uses too much, their magic scatters around them. When they rest, it comes back to them. I can rethread it, allowing them to recover their magic faster. That's why it leaks out of me. The more magic around, the more it happens."

"Fascinating." Ingrid's eyes gleamed. "You will show us this. Downstairs."

"Is there a reason she can't do it here?" Baldur asked. "If Astrid isn't feeling well…"

Ingrid held up a hand. "I need to investigate something, and I don't want anyone in the way of processes up here. The apartment is comfortable, which should be beneficial for Astrid."

"We can go to the apartment, it's fine," I said. I didn't want to if the others were here to rescue me, but the last thing I needed was to anger Ingrid. She needed to think we were on her side for as long as possible. "It's just an elevator ride down."

Baldur bent down and hooked his arm behind my knee while bracing my back with his other. Muninn hopped onto his shoulder just as Baldur lifted me and held me close to his chest. "I'll carry you, then."

I noticed Ingrid's jaw clench slightly. "That's not necessary. She can walk."

That didn't make any sense. Earlier, this protective, doting behavior would have been praised by her.

"Come here, Astrid," she said in a calm voice.

I glanced between her and Baldur. "It's okay, Mom. He can—"

"Come here." Her voice wasn't as gentle as before.

My bonds with Angel and Muninn stirred. They didn't like something about this situation. Neither did I.

Ingrid huffed. "I didn't want to do this, but you've left me no choice, Astrid."

Faster than I could blink, her dark magic shot out of her. It slammed into my companions, while black tendrils wrapped around me. I gasped and was yanked from Baldur's hold. Angel snarled and yipped. Muninn squawked. *No!*

Ingrid's arms clamped around me. I struggled against her hold, desperately trying to call up my magic. I didn't manifest. It was there. I felt it. But I couldn't call it. *No!*

"You all thought you were so clever." The manic edge to her voice had returned. "You thought you could take my baby girl from me. But you're wrong. Your plan was so predictable it was painful. Like I'd believe my daughter was so easily swayed by my words. Like I'd believe you'd all follow her without question. It would take more than that."

She backed away, pulling me with her—and Muninn and Angel. She had them grappled in her magic, hovering in the air.

Baldur jumped to his feet. His hands curled into fists and he pulled himself into a fighting stance. "Ingrid, give her back."

"She is ours." Her voice sounded bitonal, like I was hearing it in layers. "She has always been ours. I am taking her back. The purification process has already begun. Soon, she will be one with our beloved goddess, just as we all are."

I swallowed and my pulse accelerated. *More than just poison, then. What had she given me to eat?*

"You will give her back," Baldur snarled. "Or I'll wrap my hands around your throat."

She tsked. "Temper, temper. You, Baldur, are welcome to join us. She approves of you. But the others, I'm afraid… She does not deem them worthy of our dear Astrid."

I struggled against her grip, but her hold only tightened more and she scolded me for being so unruly. *What the hell?* Why couldn't I break free? Were these fake arms of hers that magical?

Baldur took a step toward us. The energy radiating off him screamed danger. There was no fear in him. "Release. My. Sunshine."

My pulse fluttered in a way that wasn't so appropriate in this situation.

Thoughts flashed in my mind. Not my thoughts, but chaotic ones through my familiar bond. Then a flash of black, and chaos erupted around me. I struggled to keep up.

Huginn attacked Ingrid, breaking her concentration enough to release her hold on my familiars. People in what were the cultist uniforms turned on others, some transforming into bipedal bears and wolves. Gunfire erupted and magic flew.

The sound of tearing and Ingrid's furious screaming filled my ears. Hands wrapped around my wrists and yanked me out of Ingrid's iron grip.

I stumbled and found myself surrounded by wings. Kirby, Magnus, and Azzie were in full Valkyrie mode, protectively standing in front of me, blocking me from the disturbing sight that was now Ingrid. *What the hell?*

Black veins crawled up Ingrid's pale skin, and her eyes had become consumed by darkness. Wing-like appendages grew from her back, but instead of fully formed feathers or leather, it was a webbing of dripping black ichor.

Ingrid's unnaturally black arms had split. Four arms now grew from her body, each of them dripping with that same black ichor.

Tyr, Fen, Angel, and Baldur all made attempts to engage with Ingrid, but her black magic twisted and lashed out from all sides of her. Ingrid herself wasn't even paying them any mind. She engaged physically with Aya, decked out in her warrior armor. In each of Ingrid's hands, she held shadowy weapons, like the ones I could create if I didn't put in enough magic to make them appear more real.

With precision and strength no human should be capable of possession, she met each of Aya's strikes, a crazed look in her eyes.

"Freya, how nice of you to join us." Ingrid's sarcasm was saccharin sweet. "And here I thought after all this time, you'd be too weak to fight. My mistake."

My eyes darted to Aya, whose face twisted with rage.

Ingrid gasped in fake surprise and pushed Aya back. "Oh, Freya, you're keeping secrets from our darling Astrid."

"Shut your shriveled mouth," Aya snarled, repositioning herself for another strike.

Ingrid wagged a finger and tsked. "Oh, dear, they deserve to know. Especially my daughter. She should know the longer she lives, the closer you come to death."

"Aya," I murmured. "What is she talking about?"

"Why, the spell to bring you back to life, of course, my daughter." The most sickening grin spread over Ingrid's face. "Didn't you know, all magic has its price? Especially one such as that."

Aya's jaw tightened. "I paid the price when I cast that spell. Nothing more."

Ingrid cackled. "Goddess, are you that arrogant, or are you truly more naïve than a goddess of your age should be? Even my mistress knows you are doomed to die so long as Astrid lives. A life for a life, that is what you agreed to."

My blood ran cold. That couldn't be true. None of this was true. Aya wasn't dying because of me.

But as I looked at Aya and saw the grim resolve, I knew I couldn't deny my mother's words. *Aya, what did you do?*

"It just so happens, the power of undying makes it more difficult for the spell to take you quickly." Ingrid's eyes glowed with utter reverence, as if this chaos fed her. "This does mean you can be saved, of course. Step aside, Freya, and give me my daughter. Once my mother remakes my daughter, you'll be free of that curse."

Azzie stiffened. "Mother?"

Ingrid smiled wider. "Oh, Astrid, you didn't tell her? The secrets that you, too, have kept, darling. Hello, Sister."

My hand curled into a tight fist. I hated hearing that word from her mouth. It wasn't right.

"You're no sister of mine," Azzie managed through clenched teeth.

"No?" Ingrid's eyes went wide and then her expression smoothed to one of indifference. "Well, you are one of her rejected children. You had so much potential and chose to squander it."

"Considering what she's made you into, I'll take the reject title."

Ingrid shook her head. "Astrid, darling, don't you see how much they're holding you back? Come with me, and you will be more magnificent than you could ever dream. And together, we'll remake this world into a paradise of our own image."

My stomach churned and every muscle in my body coiled. I couldn't stand hearing these twisted promises anymore.

I wrapped my hand around Azzie's wrist. "I'd rather be a disappointment."

Deep within me, in a place I hid away, something snapped. That small side of me I never wanted to admit existed—the one that still wished for my mother's love and approval. No more.

As she stared at me, lips tight and eyes pinched, her disappointment radiating off her in waves, I felt nothing. I didn't care how she saw me. I didn't revel in her dissatisfaction, but I didn't feel any desire to fix it, either.

Her opinion of me, in this moment, truly didn't matter.

Ingrid's face twisted as her fury rose to the surface. "You impudent child!

I will teach you a lesson you will not forget. And then I will force you to watch as I replace you with someone more worthy before I destroy you."

Her magic explodzed, sending all four gods and Angel flying. My Valkyrie sisters threw up shields, protecting us. I ducked behind them, unable to find the ability still to use my magic or call upon my Valkyrie nature.

Ingrid didn't hesitate to spring, but Aya was just as fast. She combined her physical battle prowess and her magic in a beautiful, cohesive style I'd yet to see anyone else pull off.

Out of nowhere, Dad appeared, his magic colliding with Ingrid, and complimenting Aya. Ingrid blew him a mocking kiss. Kirby and Azzie launched toward the corrupted witch while Magnus latched onto me.

"I'm going to try again," she said.

My breath came out rushed as I tried to take in the overwhelming battle. "Can you? I can't reach my magic. I can't reach my Valkyrie. I'm cut off." *I'm useless...*

"We have to try."

Sucking in a deep breath, I tried to calm my thoughts and let her power flow over me. It took all my focus not to pay attention to battles going on around me. Even when Ingrid got too close; even when Bjarke, Davyn, and Starkad joined in to protect Magnus and me; even when Ingrid screamed in agony when the Berserkers ripped off one of her fake arms, and she regrew it almost immediately, I somehow focused inward, searching for that part of me that was lost.

Magnus's energy wrapped around me, trying to seep inside and fill my magic—fill the emptiness that was me—a void of uselessness.

Black magic slashed at Magnus. A dagger caught it. Loki now stood between her and Ingrid, who'd broken away from everyone somehow.

"Results, please," he said. "We don't have all day."

"I'm trying," Magnus muttered. "Something is wrong."

Ingrid cackled. The jet-black eyes and sclera accentuated her twisted glee. "Give up, Astrid. You are ours. You are nothing without us."

No, that wasn't true. *Yes it is.* No it wasn't. I was something. I always was something. *But what? What am I? Who am I beyond a name and a few silly titles?*

Pain lanced my mind. My vision cracked and for a moment I saw something other than a bunker and battle. I saw a meadow with beautiful flowers carpeting the ground. I saw the charred earth and fallen bodies of Valkyries. I smelled the stench of blood and war. Exhaustion and pain, fear and determination, hopelessness and resolve. Emotions flooded through me. Hands touched me, reassuring and supportive.

Ingrid's voice whispered across my senses. "You're useless without us."

She was wrong. She was wrong.

"I'm not useless!" I screamed.

Something in me cracked. Magnus' power flooded in, filling me, building in me. Magic swelled. Emotions overpowered.

My magic exploded. Metal whined and cracked, boxes crashed, concrete shattered. The ground trembled beneath my feet.

Black magic slashed and twisted, destroying everything in my path. Ingrid shrieked.

Then, nothing.

My magic dissipated. The sounds of battle were gone.

Weakness flooded over me and I stumbled, then fell to my knees, panting hard. Ingrid and the rest of the cult were gone. The bunker was gone. We were still in it, but the pristine, well-maintained version I'd seen wasn't here. This one was some old, abandoned bunker from who knows how long ago.

A lie... Everything, from the apartments, to the elevator, to the infirmary, had all been one elaborate lie to deceive me. I hadn't done jack shit on my own. I hadn't done anything but play into her hand the whole time. *Useless...*

My head swam and I lost my equilibrium, even on my knees.

Arms wrapped around me, but they didn't belong to any of my guys.

"I got you, Ace. I got you," Dad said.

He did. He always did.

I pressed my face into his chest, tears welling in my eyes. He was always there when I needed him. No matter how tough it got, I could always rely on the unwavering love of my daddy.

And, right now, that's what I needed most.

TWENTY-SIX

ASTRID

My fingers flexed. *Nothing.* Nothing at all. No magic, no Valkyrie power. Whatever I broke into with Magnus' help was now gone. I didn't even feel my magic like I could before. It was just… empty.

Huginn and Muninn perched on my shoulders, preening my hair as they tried to comfort me, while Angel sat at my feet, her head in my lap where I sat on the couch in the great room of the retreat home. Diego sat on one side of me, while Baldur sat on the other, their hands resting on my thighs.

I sat in Tyr's lap, where he'd insisted I sit. His fingers pressed against my back, stroking me with wordless reassurance. The three of them knew speaking wouldn't help, but they didn't want me to give into any despair. Dad was testing my blood, but I wasn't sure it'd give us any clue what was going on.

I still had my familiar bonds. My immortal healing was still active—I checked. I'd used my magic with Magnus' help—a twisted version of it, from what everyone had told me. There was no way I had magic blocker in me. There was no way. *But if I don't, what's wrong with me?*

Shame hung over me. I was so pathetic and weak. I hadn't done one damned useful thing while I'd been captured. Even that last blast of magic that sent Ingrid running like the Wicked Witch of the West was because Magnus amplified my magic.

The TV played the news, which was covering the incident in Detroit. My stomach churned seeing all the destruction from this angle. Occasionally the news replayed captured footage of the fighting and made speculations as to if this was actually real, or if it was some stunt gone wrong.

"It's just like when Vidar pulled his stunt," Magnus murmured.

Baldur looked at her, his brow furrowed. "What did my brother do?"

She blinked at him. Dahlia's attention snapped to them. "Did you say... brother?"

My brow lifted when Fen pushed off the wall. "Fuck, forgot about that."

Dahlia held up her hand. "Did you say brother?"

I pursed my lips as I studied the way the corner of her eyes pinched, and the tightness in her jaw. *She's upset.* It wasn't completely common knowledge that Vidar was Baldur's brother; he didn't talk about it, but it wasn't a total secret.

"Thor and I are the only ones who have the same mother," Baldur said. "Vidar was one of Odin's least favorite sons, to the point that our father would sometimes deny Vidar was even his son, even though he was most like him."

Fen grunted his agreement.

Baldur scrutinized the two women. "You both seem... are you two all right?"

The two of them passed a glance. Magnus then spoke. "Were you told about TOM and what they did to us?"

A displeased scowl pulled Baldur's mouth. "Enough that I don't like where this is going."

"He was one of the gods who ran the facility, and one of our instructors who took the most enjoyment in our suffering," she said.

His scowl turned downright furious. "Where is he?"

"Dead."

"Good."

I blinked slowly. I'd never seen someone in one conversation call someone family and be happy said family was dead with such conviction. There was also the matter of Dahlia. She wasn't looking at Baldur, and seemed more interested in her painted fingernails.

"Dahlia," I hedged.

She pressed her dark lips together. Frey placed a comforting hand on her knee and opened his mouth to speak, but she beat him to it. "I'll tell them. Just… I need a sec."

I didn't care about my issue right now. This was far more important, and she could have as much time as she needed. Kirby had never quite gone into detail about what happened to them at that place, but they didn't need to.

I saw it in the way the three of them held themselves. I saw it in their mannerisms. Hell, I saw it in how they saw day-to-day life. The trauma was right there, so plain, my Valkyrie soul didn't need to alert me to it.

I'd offered them my skills to help them heal. None of them had wanted it, desiring to go their own path, as some people did. I didn't begrudge them, and my door remained open if they ever changed their mind.

That door was open.

"The students they had were all orphans, or so we were led to believe. Plucked from foster care and orphanages, we were told we were no one, but that with their training, we could be special—the kind of heroes who saved the world." Dahlia took a slow breath. "More than a few of us were actually Vidar's offspring. He kept us close, to see which of us would manifest power, so he could use us as needed."

Every muscle in my body tightened. I felt Baldur shift beside me. I didn't need to see the growing realization in him. I had the same realization dawning on me just as she spoke the words.

"I was one of those children."

Silence.

No one scarcely breathed as her words sank in. Baldur had grown unnaturally still.

Then, he stood and walked over to her. Frey rose from his position on the couch, as if expecting Baldur to sit next to Dahlia, but instead he knelt in front of her. He reached out and framed her face with his massive hands.

Baldur pressed his forehead against hers. "I am sorry I wasn't there to spare you that fate. You deserved far better—you deserved so much more. And he was a fool for not seeing it. He should have been honored to call you his daughter. I would have."

He pulled her into a tight hug. Dahlia didn't reciprocate for a moment, her face merely pressed into his shoulder. Then she reached out and gripped the back of his battle-torn shirt. Baldur pulled her in tighter, practically burying her with his large stature.

My chest swelled. Something deep inside of me stirred, like the Valkyrie in me was approving of this. Tears pricked the corners of my eyes, but I didn't let them fall.

"It will never happen again," Baldur promised.

"It definitely will not," Fen snarled out.

I choked on a laugh. Overprotective of her to a fault.

Dahlia sucked in a breath, as if she were trying to hold back her "weaker" emotions, and pulled away. She had a painted-on smile, one that was clearly trying to hide those emotions she didn't want us to see. "He doesn't deserve the air it wastes to say his name."

Baldur placed his hand on her head, something gentle and affectionate, and returned to my side.

I should have kept my mouth shut, but the smart-ass side of me decided it wanted to come out and play with all the tension in the air. "I guess you're more than an uncle by proxy now."

He gave a short, disbelieving laugh that then tumbled into a real one. The room soon filled with laughter.

"What was it that you meant by the Detroit events resembled something Vidar did?" Diego asked.

Magnus blew out a breath. "He had some deranged plan to bring on Ragnarök. It caused all sorts of strange magical happenings that hit the news."

"What do you mean?" I asked.

She seemed surprised I asked. "You didn't see the newscasts last year? Every channel was covering them for days."

"I made sure she wasn't exposed to it," Aya said. She'd remained quiet until now, not looking at anyone. "I didn't want her to find out the truth that way, so I created an extended power outage."

I blinked. "You bitch."

My tone was light enough to make her smile and finally meet my gaze. I wasn't angry with her about what Ingrid revealed. I just wanted an explanation when she was ready to give it.

"We won't be able to sweep it under the rug like last time, however," Kirby said. "I don't care what Urd said about trying to get the right coverup going. A few random happenings are easy for us to keep everything hidden, even if caught on camera. Another larger-scale situation a year and a half later, with even more witnesses…"

I felt the fear coming from her and many of the others. The supernatural world couldn't stay hidden forever. We all knew this. But no one was ready for the struggles of integrating back into the world. The world wasn't even ready for that. And yet, I knew this was only going to get worse.

"Ingrid said something about having plans," I admitted. "They were big ones, and it would be chaotic. I don't think the attack in Detroit will be the last scene they cause."

Azzie narrowed her eyes. "You think they're going to openly attack people and expose the world to the truth that way?"

I shrugged. "That, or they're going to be more open about who they are. They might use magic openly, or not wear glamours. There aren't just humans who are part of that cult. I saw a number of different creatures."

"They all had their own reasons for being there," Muninn said. *"I heard some of them. The cult makes it easy for them to further their goals."*

"So, some of those people were real?" I asked him.

He bobbed his head. *"I couldn't tell the difference at the time, but some do replay in my mind clearly, in contrast to the illusions."*

Azzie scrubbed her face. "This cult makes less and less sense the more we learn about it."

Wasn't that the truth.

I looked up when Dad returned. "Hey. What'd you find out?"

The scowl on his lips told me everything I already suspected, but I needed to hear it. "There isn't an ounce of magic blocker in you."

It took everything in me to keep my breathing measured.

"Then what's going on with her?" Azzie asked. "None of this makes sense."

Dad shook his head. "I'm not sure. We're still running tests. Hopefully, the reason she can't feel her magic is because she used it all up, and it'll return with rest."

"And if it doesn't?" My voice was quieter than I would have liked.

He rested his hand on my head. "We'll figure it out, Ace. I promise."

I nodded, hoping the hopelessness weighing on me wasn't obvious on my face. What if Ingrid was right, and my magic really did only exist because of Malsumis? What if my full rejection of her took that away?

I needed a distraction. Something more important. "I believe it might be time for some answers from you, Aya."

Aya blew out a breath and nodded. "I'm sorry."

"I only want you to be sorry if you knew," I said.

She shook her head. "I knew the spell asked a high price. It was laid out clearly that in order to bring you back, not as you once were, but still you, I had to offer something of equal value. So, I used my power. I felt the spell siphon my power each time I cast that spell. I knew the consequences and accepted them without hesitation. But I swear I didn't know my power wouldn't be considered equal value and I'd offered my life instead."

"Thank you, for being honest." My smile wobbled. "I just can't help but wish we'd known, so you wouldn't have done the ritual."

Aya held my gaze, her expression serious. "I don't regret doing it. And I'd perform that spell again if I had to, even knowing the true price. I can accept this fate."

I shook my head. "No. No one is going to die for me."

I wasn't worth that sacrifice.

Baldur roughly ran his hands through his hair. "This is like Mother all over again. What are we going to do?"

"What can be done?" Azzie asked. "We're talking ancient spells that no one really understands anymore. Except maybe the dragons, and a lot of help they'll be."

"My mom will help," Diego said, his posture defensive. He didn't like it when the others made snide remarks about the older dragons, especially his mom. Urd was trying to change, but that didn't erase the bad taste she'd left in the others. "There's just no guarantee there's a counter. Maybe people in the past had a way to reduce this risk, but that's not to say they didn't accept the results if they couldn't circumvent the requirement."

"I might know of a few places to start for research," Dad said. He turned his gaze to Aya. "But, in the meantime, I have an idea that might work to slow the progression until we find a permanent solution. We can talk about it privately."

Aya nodded. I pursed my lips. Why couldn't he just talk about it here? Was it that complicated? Or maybe it was some sort of secret spell that he also shouldn't be using? I hoped it wasn't that. Dad wasn't stupid, and he was always careful and respectful of magic, but I couldn't help but worry.

I needed to redirect my thoughts. I tapped Azzie's leg. "We need to talk. But I also need some fresh air."

Not a complete lie. There were too many people in here. Air would be great. This conversation also deserved a little more privacy.

She nodded and followed me outside. To my surprise, Loki leaned against the deck railing, his arms crossed. He looked annoyed, like I'd been rude and made him wait or something.

"You're still here?" I casually plunked down on the deck swing. Azzie insisted on standing, her posture tense and her eyes flicking between Loki and me. I grabbed her hand and tugged her down next to me. There wasn't a need for her to be ready for a fight. "I expected you to bail a while ago. Hell, I'm surprised you helped as much as you did."

Loki didn't unfold his arms. "I settle my debts."

I nodded. I had my suspicions why he'd shown up. "So you do. Is that why you've hung around, then? To ensure I understood I used it up?"

"No." His eyes flicked to Azzie for a moment. "I wanted to talk to you in private about what we were discussing earlier, before we were rudely interrupted."

I shook my head. "I'm not in the mood for that, Loki. My answer remains no."

He scowled. "Why must you be so stubborn?"

I smirked. "Because you'd be more concerned if I wasn't."

He grunted in concession.

"Goodbye, Loki."

His brow arched and then he disappeared.

Azzie chuckled. "That was amusing. I didn't know you could banish people."

I shrugged. "Only inside my wards. I have no idea where it sends them when it happens."

"Hopefully to Antarctica," Dahlia quipped.

Apparently some of the others decided to follow us outside. *So much for a private talk.*

"Is no one going to say it?" Davyn grumbled. He seemed tense. Well, tenser than usual.

I arched an eyebrow. "Say what?"

When no one else spoke up, he snarled. Yeah, he bear-snarled. "How the hel did you have a debt from Loki and never say anything? Why the hel are you talking to him anyway, like you two are on friendly terms, as if his entire goal isn't to kill Azzie?"

"Why don't you try that again without growling at me, and add an apology for doing so?" My words came out flat and tired.

His eyes narrowed. "Are you serious right now?"

"I don't have the patience for your grumpy-ass bullshit," I snapped. "I just spent hours trying to out-manipulate a manipulative, unstable bitch who I have the unfortunate displeasure of calling my egg donor. I don't have to put up with you and your single brain cell, too! So yeah, I'm fucking serious."

Maybe that was too harsh, but I was too emotionally frayed at this point to care.

Davyn scowled. True to how he was, he didn't say a word. I could count on one hand where I'd heard this man apologize, and really, most of them couldn't even be counted as true apologies.

Azzie nudged me. "Ignore him. He might spontaneously combust if he says 'sorry.'"

He glowered and crossed his arms.

I blew out a breath and leaned back, telling them how I'd obtained the life debt.

"You saved him?" Magnus sounded scandalized. "You should have left him for dead."

"It's because she's a damned sentimental bleeding-heart," Davyn muttered.

"I'd rather care too much than not care at all." I refused to be shamed for being a good person.

"And that bleeding-heart of your means Loki now walks around free to be a problem."

I rolled my eyes. "Yeah, because I'm such a stupid, naïve fool."

I motioned to Dad, who flourished his hand, procuring Loki's last dose from the safe place I'd asked him to store it. The air around me shifted as everyone focused in.

"Is that the antidote?" Kirby asked.

I nodded. "One of the three doses."

Dahlia squinted. "Why three?"

"Because it's that brand new. Urd had just given us the news that morning about having a tiny batch of antidotes ready for testing. None of this had been trialed before Loki ended in my lap. As much of a *bleeding-heart* that I am, I'm also practical. Instead of us going through the process of vetting volunteers, I chose to use Loki as our first guinea pig. This was the third dose intended for him."

"Why didn't he get a third dose?" Dahlia asked.

"He clearly didn't need it," Davyn grumbled.

I ignored him. The two of us got along fine when he and I weren't both in bad moods. "Because he didn't want to agree to my terms."

I shifted my gaze to Azzie. "I tried, and unfortunately failed, to negotiate his agreement to leave you alone."

Her lips parted and eyes widened in surprise. "You did?"

I nodded. "He doesn't have all of his magic back. He either needs this last dose, or to go through the trouble of figuring things out himself. Loki thinks he can convince me to renegotiate the terms. That's what he wanted to talk about before I sent him away. But I'm not budging. He knows my stubbornness can rival a Berserker's at times."

Tyr let out an amused snort. Even Davyn's grumpy scowl broke a little.

"I'm sorry I wasn't able to convince him," I said to Azzie. "I'm going to—"

She rested her hand on mine and smiled. "Even though you knew it was a long shot, you tried. That's what matters to me. It's not like we lost any ground."

I nodded. "You're right. And I do plan to keep trying."

"How?" Zeke asked.

"I'm in a unique position compared to everyone else. I never experienced firsthand the horrible shit Loki did to people. I can accept the things he's done in recent times have been terrible, the same way I can accept that barely a single one of us here doesn't have some dark smear on their past, myself included."

Not a single immortal, maybe besides Azzie and Zeke, could voice a counter to that. We all had done things we were not proud of now.

"I'm not under some delusion I can *fix* Loki." My wording got a grunt from Davyn. "But I'd also say there's nothing of Loki that needs to be fixed. Because he's not broken. My professional diagnosis of him is vastly different than any other would give him, and I really do believe that makes the difference for our situation."

I ran my fingers through my hair. "I'm not saying I'll succeed in any of the interactions I might have with him in the future, but that doesn't mean I won't try. Even if I have to use the most underhanded psychological tricks that make him remain a selfish dickhead and think every change in him is his choice rather than mine, then so be it."

Azzie laughed. "That's actually terrifying to think you can do that."

I honestly didn't believe I could. Loki was significantly smarter than me. He'd know how to win the perfect game of chess before I even considered which piece to move. But that didn't mean I wouldn't try.

And so long as I had his antidote, and Loki believed I'd be the only person in existence who would even consider giving it to him, I held the right cards for a possible win.

This only left one last thing hanging in the air. I rested my head on Azzie's shoulder. "I'm sorry I didn't tell you sooner. About being related."

"Let me guess, it happened at the same time as the hostage-Loki situation?"

I nodded. "Ingrid lobbed that at me like a hot grenade. And I knew I should have told you, but I… I didn't want to think about being related to Malsumis. It ended up with me going down the rabbit hole of questioning my magic, and that's not something I'm ready for."

If I could forget all about this and pretend parts of my magic were just like my past mother Randi's and not my current, I'd be so much happier. *Why are they so similar?*

Azzie chuckled. "Yeah, I get that. And while I could poke fun at you for avoiding something this important when you're a therapist, I really can't blame you. I could hardly believe Ingrid called me her sister. And it means you're not some perfect, programmed robot."

I laughed. "I'm just as imperfect as everyone else."

Her nose scrunched. "I don't have to call you my niece, do I? That… feels weird."

I grabbed her hand and squeezed. "I'd rather call you my sister."

She blinked slowly. A beaming smile lit up her face and she threw her arms around me. I wrapped my arms around her. My chest swelled with warmth. That felt good to say. Azzie and I weren't as close as Kirby and me, but that didn't mean that couldn't change.

When we released each other, Dad reached over and placed his hand on Azzie's head. He didn't say anything, but there was fatherly affection to the gesture that made Azzie smile more, her cheeks turning a shade of pink. Dad had taken in all the Valkyries as his daughters, if they wanted that, but this felt like a little more, given the circumstances.

"So, the sister Valkyries are dating the cousin dragons," Dahlia started, ticking off on her fingers. "And one of their cousin dragons, who is the niece of the god dating one of the sister Valkyries, is dating said sister Valkyrie's wolf-god brother. We really like to keep it in the family."

Everyone burst into laughter, easing the tension that had become a little too suffocating. That also let in the exhaustion and the intrusive thoughts lingering under the surface. I yawned so wide my jaw popped.

With me now safe, everyone agreed to disperse, allowing me time to rest. Tyr didn't let me walk, instead lifting me easily in his arms and holding me close. His embrace was strong and protective, something I needed as the feelings of uselessness from earlier pushed in.

"Not going to protest?" he said, amused.

"Too tired," I mumbled into his neck, yawning again.

Huginn and Muninn landed on Tyr's shoulders. *"Tired. Tired."*

"Jerks," I grumbled.

They cackled.

When we arrived in our island home, Tyr picked the sofa as our destination. Diego grabbed a controller and popped up a streaming app as he sat down next to me. I was encouraged to lie down, using Tyr's lap as a pillow and Diego as a leg rest. Baldur sat on the floor in front of me. Diego threw my favorite fuzzy throw blanket over me.

Huginn and Muninn tried to settle on my chest, but Angel wasn't having it. She *insisted* on climbing up on top of me and being my heavy second blanket. The ravens then settled in between her and the back of the sofa, up by my face, where they preened my hair again.

None of this was comfortable, but I didn't dare say anything. It didn't take mind-reading powers to understand what was going on.

I let out a slow breath. "I'm sorry I worried you all." *If I was a better witch and Valkyrie, none of this would have happened.*

Diego rubbed my leg. "Don't place blame on yourself, please. You did nothing wrong."

"And you were amazing in there," Baldur said.

Yeah, amazingly pathetic.

Tyr brushed his fingers through my hair. "What's wrong, Valkyrie?"

I shook my head. "I'm just exhausted. Today was rough…"

"You can always talk about it with us," Diego said. His warm hand on my leg was as reassuring as his voice.

"I know." But not right now. I couldn't. I couldn't admit these feelings of uselessness to them. I was a sorry excuse of a Valkyrie and an even poorer excuse of a witch. What made me think I could also help Azzie with Loki?

The negative thoughts cycled in my head as the movie on the screen played. I didn't pay attention to it, too stuck in my head. And when my exhaustion finally took me, they followed me into a restless sleep.

TWENTY-SEVEN

ASTRID

Waves gently lapped against the shore, the rhythm soothing. Palm fronds rustled in the light breeze, swaying branches occasionally creaking. Seabirds called overhead, while Muninn mimicked a tiny dove brave enough to perch on the house near my raven familiars. Angel raced up and down the island shoreline, chasing tiny sandpipers or harassing the occasional crab, all the while carrying a piece of driftwood in her mouth like a prized possession.

I lounged on the patio furniture under the shade of the pergola above. Books and papers were scattered around me, in various states of use. The cool metal of my amulet weighed on my palm. My fingers traced the etchings making up the tree. I should have been working on translation work, disguised as psychology study should someone appear who shouldn't get a glimpse of my works. But I couldn't concentrate.

My skin crawled with magic below the surface, but it wasn't right. It'd taken three days for my magic to return, and it wasn't as it once was. It looked just like Ingrid's, and felt all kinds of wrong.

On top of that, my Valkyrie was still missing. None of my Valkyrie sisters could help me find that side of me. It was like… she'd never existed.

Nothing made sense, and I was so lost. *Who am I, really?*

The patio door slid open. I looked up, expecting one of my guys to be checking up on me. I hadn't exactly been overly sociable these last few days.

I didn't expect to see Urd gracing the doorway. "Oh, hi, Urd."

She smiled and stepped out. "Hello to you, too. Not who you were expecting, I'm guessing."

"I would be lying if I said yes." That got her to chuckle. *Win?* "Are you looking for Diego? I think he's still in the garage, trying to get Baldur hooked on dirt bikes."

"I'm actually here to speak to you." She gestured to the open cushion beside me. "May I sit?"

"Uh, yeah, sure." What could she possibly want with me? I couldn't recall the last time she went out of her way to spend any sort of time with me.

Urd was doing her best to be less aloof, but that didn't mean she socialized with us regularly. She spent most of her time with Xavier and Diego, otherwise she was typically off doing… something. We were fairly in the dark about her activities. Well, maybe except Xavier. He always seemed to know what she was up to.

Urd sat, her posture rigid and regal as always. "How are you?"

I rested my arm on the back of the couch. It was a normal, small-talk question, but this was Urd. She didn't do small talk. She wanted truths, and wouldn't appreciate it if I dodged her question. "Frustrated, and feeling like I'm drowning. Every time I think I've finally got a handle on things, everything seems to crumble around me and I'm left feeling more lost than when I started."

She nodded slowly. "You've had a lot thrown at you in your short life. All of your lives, really. Your tenacity to keep moving forward despite the setbacks you experience is commendable."

Tenacity? I chuckled. "I certainly don't feel tenacious right now. More like a miserable wet cat who's found herself on top of a flag pole with no way down."

Urd made a thoughtful sound in the throat. "That is an oddly specific image that feels… rather accurate."

"What type of flagpole are you stuck on?" I asked. The dragons had withdrawn for so long, doing everything themselves in secret, anything could be bothering her. But what could she see in me that she felt would help her with her problem?

Urd sighed. Her shoulder sagged, destroying the typical regal visage she had. Right here and now, she just looked tired and overwhelmed, like me. "I feel as though I am standing on two poles, motherhood and guardianship. Each pole swaying in the tides of fate in different directions, making it difficult to find balance for them both."

I tucked my feet up. "If you're seeking advice, I can try to offer it. I don't know if someone with as little life experience as me can provide the insight you might be needing, but I can do my best."

She smiled. "It's your youth that has me reaching out. Even though you are older than some of the other Valkyries, due to your unique situation, you are still but a child compared to the length of time I have existed. You see Midgard much differently than I do, and I'd be a fool not to see that as an opportunity to help me understand what I struggle to on my own."

"All right then. How do you want me to handle this? Do you want my opinions, or would you rather I prompt you with self-exploring questions?"

She thought for a moment. "Both. I value your opinion, Astrid. You have impressed me over this short time of knowing you. I know you will provide your insight with rational thinking, and not as a child lashing out. I also know I can trust you will guide me to self-explore without your opinions when it's appropriate."

I regarded her for a moment. She'd really thought this through before coming to me. "I can certainly help you with the motherhood aspect to the best of my ability, even though I don't have personal experience there. This guardianship you mentioned, I would need to be told more to be certain I can offer my help."

She nodded slowly. "I know. I spent much time wrestling with this before coming to you."

"I'd be more surprised if you hadn't," I admitted. "You aren't secretive to be malicious. You hold the cards close, because you wish to protect us. That's admirable. And also foolish, to try and do alone."

She smiled, despite the uncertain emotions playing on her face. "As Xavier has made me realize. But before we go into that, I'd like to discuss the other topic first."

I nodded. "Please tell me what's on your mind."

Urd's lips pressed into a tight line. "Do you think I am a good mother?"

Took a moment to properly word myself. "I think only a mother who loves her child and mate more than anything would give up everything she ever dreamed of with them to ensure they were safe, knowing she would have to live for all eternity with that decision."

"But does that make me a good mother?" Her fingers curled into a fist on her lap. "Do I have a right to call myself a mother after I abandoned him, when in the end that choice had done nothing but cause him pain? When the event I so desperately sought to escape happened anyway? I lost so much time... and for what?"

I watched her, taking in all her tight features and searching for the cracks in the mask she wore to hide the emotions she didn't want others to see. "Urd, you may be an ancient dragon with the ability to see the future, but you are not infallible. Nor can you control what you see. No seer can. We both know this. You only see a snippet and have to make a judgment call from something like that. And sometimes—a lot of times—that interpretation is wrong."

I reached out and laid my hand over hers. "Diego loves you. He talks all about the time he spends with you. There is so much joy that comes off him every time he does. He gets so angry when anyone tries to disparage you."

She lifted her gaze to me, unshed tears brimming in her eyes. "He does?"

I nodded. "He doesn't hold it against you, Urd. He understands why you made that choice. Yes, it might bother him a little that you weren't there for all the important parts of his life, but neither was my mother. At least the reason you weren't present was out of love."

Urd sucked in a deep breath through her nose to calm herself.

"What brought this on?" I asked. "Is this something that's been bothering you for some time, or was there a recent event that brought these questioning thoughts to the surface?"

She worked her jaw. "Xavier… he…" She blew out a breath. "He wants us to expand our family."

My eyebrows rose high. Joy and excitement rose from deep in my chest, but I didn't let it out. She was too conflicted for me to express any of those emotions right now. "But you don't want to?"

"It's not that I don't want to… it's… I don't know if we should." She sighed. "I'm worried Diego might resent me, because this child would get what he had been deprived of."

I was already shaking my head before she finished. "No, Urd. Diego would never resent you or any future sibling he may have. He'd be so excited. Truly."

Urd smiled. "Thank you. You know my son best, besides Xavier, and as much as I'd like to confide in my mate about my doubts and worries, I know I can trust you more to provide me the full truth."

I shook my head. "Lying wouldn't be productive. And even if you were a terrible mother, that doesn't mean we couldn't fix that, as long as you tried. But you are trying. Even when you and Diego struggle to see eye-to-eye, you're both trying."

Urd closed her eyes and blew out a breath. "It is difficult. My son is a grown man, not a child. He has his ways of doing things that are set in stone, just as I do." She opened her eyes and smiled. "But there are other times we learn to change and grow from each other."

I smiled. It was good she saw that in such a healthy way.

She reached out and pinched the pendant I held in my other hand with her fingers. I let her take it and watched as she gave it a good long look over. There was tender affection in her gaze. "I can't think of a better partner for him to have given this to."

My heart fluttered, and I couldn't stop the embarrassed smile from forming on my lips. "He told me it was a family heirloom that he was supposed to give to someone special."

Urd nodded. "Yes, that is what I told him. But it wasn't the whole truth."

I tipped my head to the side. "What do you mean?"

She swallowed, as if pushing back emotions. "One of my sons had this pendant made for his mate. Their bond was… something special. When they died during Ragnarök, I kept this. I've kept mementos of all my children. I thought it was my way to keep his memory alive. But when I had Diego… I don't know how to say it without making me sound like a terrible mother."

I placed my hand over the pendant. It was oddly warm in her hand. "I can assure you, I won't think poorly of you, no matter what you say."

She sucked in a slow breath through her nose. "I remember the feeling of laying my eyes on each of my children the first time. I *saw* them do great things the day they were born. That sensation I had when I first held Eero was the same when I had Diego. I'd never experienced such a strong resemblance before with any of my children. And the vision I had… it was so similar to his brother."

My throat tightened, as did my grip. "I'm guessing there were other reasons you were convinced there was more to you keeping this pendant, given you gave it to Diego."

"Yes. Even though there were those similarities, I had plans to hold onto this. There was no reason for me to think it was more than that, a similarity. Then, somehow Diego found it. I'd hidden it well, and yet he came to me with it in his hands, asking about it. I knew then that I had kept it so that he could have it… again."

There wasn't enough air in my lungs. What I had been speculating about Diego… and maybe even about me… she'd just confirmed. "Reincarnation is a mystery to us."

Urd lifted her gaze to meet mine. "Not when magic is involved, right, Valkyrie?"

I nodded slowly, the words to respond hard to find. It was the way she looked at me, those wise, ancient eyes that knew so much, yet seemed to maybe not know as much as they should.

"How long have you also known?" she asked.

"I've had my speculations for a little while." There was no need to deny this topic with her. Not when she'd been so open with me—not when she could hold answers I sought. "I've slowly found evidence to support some theories, though I've been missing vital information to confirm."

"I'm assuming this has been related to your Valkyrie research, yes?"

I nodded. That was something else I'd wanted to ask her about, but this didn't feel like it was the time. Not yet, at least. "I've been finding more than I expected, with what little progress I've made. And… I've been seeing things… in my memories that I don't think magic intended for me to see."

Urd closed her eyes and breathed slowly. "You're a lot like her. Different, too. Just like Diego."

Reincarnation didn't create carbon copies of ourselves when we were reborn. We weren't guaranteed to be similar to a past life unless magic was involved, and even then, there were always differences. "What's one big thing that makes Diego and Eero the same that makes you so sure?"

She took a moment to respond. "Our children have almost always found their affinity in the domains of their parents. The past for me, the present for Artura, and the future for Skuld. There are exceptions, of course, like Callie and Caleb. Separate, one is the future and the other is the past. Together, only as twins, do they make the present. And even then, our visions can sometimes show us something that is outside our affinity if Creation believes we must see an event."

I thought about the current dragons, and saw how that was still true. Though one thing confused me. "If you are the past, why does Artura protect the archive library?"

"Because I asked her to." The answer was simple, but made sense. "I am the one who put most of the information there as I've found it. I'm the one who still seeks out small remnants of evidence that may still linger out there beyond our current sight. Artura protects it for me, keeping the present stable from past fragments that could destabilize the tentative balance."

That made even more sense. I encouraged her to keep talking, apologizing for derailing for a moment.

"Even if all my children found their gifts in the past, there was only ever overlap. Diego and Eero were the only ones to both be true memory dragons. It was too much of a…"

I grinned. "Coincidence?"

Urd chuckled. She didn't believe in those any more than Dad and me.

"You seem unsurprised by the reincarnation," I observed, based on how calm she was with me also being in the know. "Is it because you've come to terms with it, or something else?"

Urd bit her lip, which surprised me. This dragon was always so regal. I'd never seen her so nervous and hesitant. "As we know, I didn't realize Diego was a dragon when I made my choice to leave. While I saw the similarities, I couldn't be one hundred percent sure I was right that he was the son I lost. And even if he was, I assumed he was merely human this time around. But there's been some changes that have been weighing on me, that have also allowed me to accept some of these truths, while also struggling with them as well."

"This has to do with your guardian duties?" *This must be the other thing she wanted to talk about.*

She nodded. "I already know what you're going to ask. What do those duties entail?"

It wasn't a hard guess. She'd only once mentioned her guardian status, and that was just to explain to us how Ragnarök already happened once.

Urd pressed my hands into my necklace pendant, forcing my fingers to curl around the hard surface. "What I'm about to tell you, I ask you to be discreet about. It is a sensitive topic that we're trying to keep quiet about. Not out of maliciousness, but to protect."

I nodded. "Everything you tell me is in confidence, Urd. I won't tell a soul unless you want me to."

"Midgard is vast, in more ways than one. Energies that many do not understand tie it together. They are volatile, but necessary. They congregate into specific areas of Midgard. We call these 'vaults.' And we guardians protect them."

I pursed my lips. "Where exactly were they located?"

"In the roots of the world tree."

I looked at the tree on my pendant. "Like in the myths?"

She nodded. "Yggdrasil, the tree of life, Pandora's box, Adam and Eve, the list goes on. All stories and ideas formed from fragments of the truth, fractured by magic."

I glanced around at the open blue sky. "Was Yggdrasil an actual place then?"

"She was the most magnificent tree." Longing reflected in her eyes. She'd seen beauty like none other could ever experience. "Her roots were vast and crawled all over Midgard. She offered herself as sacrifice when the time came, leaving her children to oversee the world, not knowing they would struggle to communicate with those left behind."

Her children, like the tree on my family's property. The fae loved that tree. *Maybe they're the only ones left who can speak with them.*

"Where are the vaults now, if not in the roots of the tree?"

"Hidden, where only guardians and their mates can find them."

I chewed my lip. *That was good, right?*

Urd continued. "When Ragnarök first appeared, the vaults became unstable. This is why we made the sacrifice. The lives of those who offered themselves up, were converted into the power needed to seal the vaults. It stabilized Midgard, though did take away the ability to connect to it like we used to."

That was the loss of magic she told us about once.

Urd hesitated. "The vaults are growing unstable again."

My hand clenched my pendant so hard my fingers ached. "What do you mean?"

"I told you once that my sisters and I noticed a change in magic. That was our first clue. Then, it got worse early last year. And then…" She sucked in a deep breath. "Over the winter, mine destabilized."

My brow furrowed. "Your vault?"

She nodded. "Mine was the only one that did not need to be sealed. It had stayed stable through Ragnarök. Until recently."

I thought on this. "That was the event you saw Xavier dying in, then?"

She nodded. "That's how I interpreted it, at least. That wasn't what came to pass and that was how he unlocked latent power within him."

That made so much sense. And it explained why Xavier had been so vague when I asked for clarification. "What does this have to do with reincarnation and Diego?"

Urd sucked in a steadying breath. "The guardians are returning."

My eyes widened. "What do you mean?"

"When the guardians gave their lives, they vowed to return. And they are. I believe Diego was my early warning sign, which I didn't understand at the time. One of the new guardians has already been found, and I'm fairly certain I've located another. For one of them, I recognize her energy in the same way I had with Diego."

"This should sound relieving, but why does it sound like terrible news?"

Urd's lip trembled. "Because as I just told you, the vaults are destabilizing. Xavier and I managed to stabilize my vault without a sacrifice of death, but… I don't know if we can do the same again for the other vaults."

Her head bowed, a heavy weight pulling on her shoulders. "I can't… find these former friends and children, only to sacrifice them again. I can't ask that of them. I can't… go through that again. But if we don't… Ragnarök…"

Her words died, and the weight of her responsibilities dragged her deeper into these emotions she wrestled with alone. What was it like to hold the responsibilities of the world on your shoulder to bear alone? Yes, she now had Xavier, but one person couldn't support her.

I grasped her hand with mine. "You said you stabilized yours without death. Then, I believe that it's possible to do the same with the others."

Urd lifted her head. "How?"

I shrugged. "I'm not sure. I'm still at a disadvantage here with my understanding, but maybe if we hash some things out, we can figure out a path."

It would be good for me. I could keep myself busy, and maybe finally prove my worth. Maybe it didn't prove my worth as a Valkyrie, but it was something, right?

"You said the vaults were part of the world tree—located at the heart of Midgard. There are stories that seem to correlate with that. The one I know the best is the nine realms of Norse myth."

Urd nodded. "Yes, the Norse people gave names to the vaults and associated it with the gods who took up residence in their area."

"So there are nine vaults?"

"No—including my vault, there are seven." Urd's brow furrowed.

"Eight? No, definitely seven. Midgard doesn't have a vault." She paused again. "Or… did it?"

I pressed my lips together. It was disconcerting that she was questioning this. "Urd, are you sure you and your sisters weren't affected by the magic?"

Her brow furrowed. "Of course I'm sure. We, the eldest of the fae, and the fates were careful with the spell. We knew what we asked others to offer up, and the curse we laid upon ourselves by keeping all our memories intact."

I couldn't shake the feeling that, while she believed this, it wasn't the truth. "What vaults did your sisters oversee?"

She blinked. "They… they didn't. Only I took a vault. Our children and some of the phoenixes oversaw the others."

"Why is that? Why wouldn't all of the oldest dragons protect vaults? Wouldn't it make sense if they did?"

She shook her head. "They didn't want to. They didn't want that responsibility when there were other ways to oversee Midgard's protection."

But while she said the words, the doubt reflected in her eyes. I rested my hand on hers. "It's okay to question this, Urd. Take it from someone younger, it's okay to feel so certain about something and find out you were wrong."

She nodded slowly. "You are right. I can't run from this out of fear."

"Think hard about what's happened as of late. You and your sisters have watched for any anomalies that would indicate Ragnarök was returning, even if in the end, your goals for this monitoring weren't the same. This past century has had the most significant changes, correct?"

She nodded. "Yes. Though it was the last two years that's been the most concerning."

I tipped my head. "Why is that? What's happened?"

She shook her head back and forth. "I'm not sure. There was a lot of activity that Dahlia and Magnus involved themselves in. Dahlia had even gone to Artura for something. She needed a trinket…"

She trailed off, and stared at nothing.

"Urd?" I prompted when she remained quiet.

"The vaults have keys—artifacts. Physical items used in the rituals to seal them. Skuld had gifted Artura an artifact. It was the last gift my sister ever gave before pursuing their own goals. We thought it nothing, but…"

She pressed her lips together. "I had always wondered what Skuld's true motives were for creating FU, beyond to make a mockery of my name. We came to the conclusion, they were trying to ensure all prophecies came true, given they were the dragon of the future. But… what if my sister knew something that I had forgotten? Me, the dragon of the past."

"Magnus said that Vidar was trying to bring on Ragnarök last year," I shared. "Dahlia is his and Skuld's daughter. If they had a plan together, it could be that Vidar knew more about the vaults than anyone else, because of Skuld. And if he was willing to continue Skuld's work… if he was willing to break the world for Skuld… then…"

Urd pressed her lips together. "My sisters were guardians to a single vault, and Vidar, Skuld's mate who could be the only one to find the vault in Skuld's absence, broke the seal." She swallowed, her eyes tight. "If we forgot that, what else have we forgotten?"

I patted her hand comfortingly. "I'm still trying to understand what Valkyries are. You've never once offered information, just allowed me to search for myself."

"I… that is true. I didn't question why you wanted to know your origins, yet I should have. We were the first. I would know all there was to Valkyries and gods. Yet, now that I try to remember, it's fuzzy. I know the knowledge is there, but I can't reach it."

"It's possible the answers we both seek are related. Maybe the library archive has a book that tells us whether there are eight or nine vaults."

Urd shook her head, struggling with this. "I knew all of their names. Every child we lost, guardian or not. I still remember them. I refuse to believe I forgot one."

"But it wasn't just your children who were guardians," I said. "You also said there were some phoenixes."

She nodded. "Yes, two. I knew them well. And I know they're coming back. I can't explain how I know this, but they will return, as all phoenixes do."

I pressed my lips together. Something was nagging me about this last vault. Something about recent events. "Maybe Nico or Alecia could help? Maybe they've got memories of these phoenixes and don't realize it."

Urd's brow furrowed. "I beg your pardon?"

"Well, they're also phoenixes. I can't be certain they're old enough to have been born before Ragnarök, but maybe… Alecia might have been, considering her unique circumstance."

"Who is Alecia?" Urd asked.

I blinked slowly. "Oh, right. You weren't able to make it to the party. Alecia is Bjarke's wife. She thought she was just a solar witch with magic that only manifested as fire. Come to find out, Nico recognized her. She's a phoenix who lost her memories. Apparently she came back a few years ago, and never recovered her past, so she never learned the truth of her identity until now."

Urd was quiet for a moment, contemplating my reveal. "Bjarke wanted her as a mate…"

My brow furrowed and I opened my mouth to question what she meant, but then she stood. "I will speak with her. And my sister. You may be right, in that the answers we seek are right under our noses, and we were too afraid to face that truth."

She smiled. "Thank you, Astrid. I now have a clearer path to take, with more hope than I've had in a long time. I'll let you know when I have Arura's blessing to further investigate these theories in the archive. We may just find a way to stop Ragnarök for good this time."

I shook my head. "I will fully admit, I don't believe that's possible."

Urd's brow furrowed. "Is that not what you've been trying to achieve all this time?"

I sucked in a breath through my nose. "One of my Valkyrie sisters once put it poetically: Ragnarök is a cycle of rebirth and change. I believe there is merit to that. Ragnarök wasn't stopped. It changed the world. Our actions to stop it dictated how that change would take place. And now that it has returned, it will be our actions now that will decide how that change will once again take hold."

Urd tipped her head. "Then why look into the past?"

I gave a weak smile. "I wish to understand who I really am. And if those answers lead me to a path that will help us with handling Ragnarök, all the better."

The ancient dragon before me gazed thoughtfully, and then smiled. "I think I better understand why my son chose you. I approve of you more and more, Lost Valkyrie. I'll be in touch."

Then she was gone.

I blinked slowly. She may better understand, but I certainly didn't. Did she know something about me that I didn't?

I jumped when Angel barked. She stood in the shallows of the ocean, watching me and wagging her tail. She hadn't felt the need to come over and comfort Urd. That was unusual for her. Angel pushed against the bond. I was being too serious for her liking.

Taking a deep breath, I clasped my necklace back around my neck. It settled comfortably on my chest, where it weighed a little heavier than before. I then stood. I needed to walk and get out of my head, as difficult as that was when I was alone.

Angel barked again and took off down the beach. Muninn and Huginn flew off after her, leaving me to follow and take in my private island. Maybe I'd figure out what else I wanted to do with the available land. I could only hope that distracted me from all the shit that was still wrong with me, at least for a little bit.

TWENTY-EIGHT

BALDUR

oft soil shifted under my pounding feet; the yard flashed past. My breath puffed out in strong bursts, my heart pounding in my ears. Diego's pumping arms brushed mine. He and I glanced at each other, and I grinned, pushing more into my run.

Diego swore when I broke out ahead. I chuckled and kept pushing, the front porch of the house coming into view. He caught up a bit, pushing himself as hard as he could.

My hands touched the porch first.

I leaned against the support pillar, breathing hard. Diego let out a frustrated groan and used the other pillar as support.

I grinned at him. "Told you… I was faster."

"Not by… much," he puffed out. He lifted a shaky finger. "I'll beat you next time."

I shook my head and took another calming breath. "Not if the bet is the same. I'm winning that one every time."

He punched me in the shoulder, the sensation not as jarring as it had been in the last few weeks, and entered the house. I followed.

A delicious scent wafted into my nose. The savory aroma brought on excessive salivation and my stomach rumbled. Diego snickered and I smacked his arm.

Xavier walked out of the kitchen. "Ah, mijo, you're back. *Sígueme.*"

We followed him into the kitchen where a plate of pastries they called empanadas sat on the counter. *Those are the source of the deliciousness I smelled.*

"Take those to Astrid, please," Xavier said. "No one has seen her all day. They should cheer her up."

Diego and I passed each other a silent look. That wasn't a good sign. She'd promised she wouldn't keep to herself today. *The bet can wait.*

Diego grabbed the plate of food. "We'll figure out what's up."

I followed him upstairs. When we walked through the door to the separate house, silence greeted us. My lips pressed thin. That wasn't a comforting sign.

Entering the living room, we looked around for any sign of her. She wasn't in the house. Nor were her familiars.

I wandered toward the patio doors and peered out. I spotted several books, paper, and writing utensils spread out on the furniture. "Diego."

I slid open the door and stepped out into the warm air. I took in the sounds of the ocean and environment. Even that interesting bird they called a dove. It was one that Astrid seemed rather fond of, because it insisted on living on top of the house, and it showed no fear of the ravens.

"Well, she was here." Diego looked around. "But where is she now?"

I glanced up when I heard wing flaps. Muninn and Huginn swooped down. Muninn landed on my shoulder, while Huginn claimed Diego's. Diego gave the raven an affectionate beak rub. It made me smile. The two of them had bonded better after the events a few days ago. It was good to see Huginn integrate more into Astrid's flock.

"Where is Astrid?" I asked them.

"*Walking,*" Muninn said. "*Her mind is unkind.*"

I blew out a breath. I was afraid of that.

"*Ancient dragon came and distracted her, but being alone brought it back,*" Huginn said.

Diego's brow furrowed. "Ancient dragon? My mom was here?"

Huginn bobbed his head. *"Yes. They spoke, in confidence."*

Diego made a surprised sound that I didn't know how to interpret. "Is that a good or bad thing?"

Diego shrugged one shoulder. "Hard to say. That term means my mom came to her to talk about something that was weighing on her."

"Why not go to you? You have the same skills as Astrid, and you're her son."

He shrugged again. "She could have also gone to an immortal therapist with far more experience than us. With everything she's seen, it's not likely she'd trust just anyone to hear what's bothering her, and I guess she figured Astrid could help her best. I don't hold that against her. I'm just glad she's willing to talk to someone."

"Astrid did help," Muninn said. *"More than either expected."*

Diego smiled. "She's good at that. That Valkyrie side of her really knows how to dig into deep-rooted issues."

"Can you two tell us what Astrid's been dealing with for herself?" I asked.

She'd been out of sorts for the last few days. She wasn't interested in spending time with people if she didn't have to. It's why Diego and I tried to get her to promise not to sequester herself again today. She said she wouldn't, as long as we didn't hover like worried hens, or something like that.

Huginn puffed up, and let out a sound that seemed like a displeased grumble. *"Useless Valkyrie. Pointless. Weak."*

Muninn bobbed up and down. *"Not weak. Hurting. Lost. Confused. Struggling."*

I frowned. We'd suspected all of this was messing with her self-esteem, but to hear her familiars repeat words she actually thought of herself… I didn't like it.

"Narcs," a light alto voice said.

I jumped and whirled around. Astrid blinked bemusedly while Diego snickered. Angel was with her; she had an absurdly large piece of driftwood in her mouth. It was so large that it dragged on the ground. I saw said drag marks in the sand, showing the path they'd come.

I blew out a breath and pressed my hand to my chest, my heart beating a little too fast. "Don't do that."

She smiled, though it seemed a bit forced. "Did you two have fun today?"

That was a strange thing for her to ask after overhearing her familiars tell us what was going on in her head. "Yeah. I've been introduced to the amazing world of motocross."

She laughed, an actual one. Her face lit up just enough to bring out the light in her. "I was wondering if he'd get you hooked."

"He might be ready to do tricks," Diego said. "He's got the balls to start trying, at least."

I grinned. I'd had a lot of fun watching Diego show off some of those tricks.

Astrid rolled her eyes. "No self-preservation, either of you."

I didn't quite understand her lack of enthusiasm. "We're immortal."

She pointed at Diego. "He was doing that when he wasn't."

I was impressed, and didn't hide that from my face as I looked at Diego. It did explain how he did those flips with practiced ease, but I wouldn't have assumed a mortal would try something like that. Then again, mortals had always fascinated me with their courage, even outside of battle. *Though, some, like Astrid, might call it stupidity.* I had a feeling, from her reaction, that's what she called the motocross tricks as well.

Diego held up the plate of food. "Empanadas for you. Papá made them."

Astrid's expression flashed from suspicious to pleasantly pleased. I could only assume she would have thought the food was a bribe if it came from us.

She took the plate and set it down on a small table before cleaning up her scattered work to make room of us. Her ravens perched on the roof and Angel managed to hop up on one of the pieces of furniture with her enormous stick, though some furniture did get knocked around in the process. It was quite amusing how stubborn she was about it. *She gets it from Astrid.*

I plopped down next to Astrid, and Diego on the other side. My arm slid behind her on the top of the patio sofa. Diego's did as well. His hands brushed along my arm, sending a *zing* through me. I did my best to ignore it.

Spending time with Diego these last few days had been fun. I was enjoying his presence and getting to know him better. The longer I spent with him though, the harder it was to ignore my attraction to him.

Normally I wouldn't. Any other time, I'd lean right into it unless he told me to back down. But given I was so newly revived, and I wanted to give Astrid as much of my time as possible to develop our relationship, I didn't want anything distracting me from that.

My eyes traveled down his profile as he looked at Astrid. And he was definitely distracting. Diego's gaze flicked up to me for a brief moment, and I swore I caught a faint smirk before he focused on her again.

Astrid looked between us. She had an empanada held in her mouth mid-bite. "Is there something going on that I should know about?"

She didn't appear mad, just like the last time she caught me appreciating him, more curious. I glanced at Diego, who shrugged and answered her. "Nothing is going on."

"Uh-huh." She took another bite of her food. "Well, if you two wanna fuck, you can. I'm not stopping you like some possessive girlfriend."

Diego chuckled and tucked a lock of her hair behind her ear. "Thanks for the non-jealous permission. I'll remember that if it comes up. But right now, there's nothing going on, like I said."

"Hmm…" She bit into another empanada. Did she sound a bit disappointed?

"Sunshine," I said.

She glanced up at me, her brow arched. "Yeah?"

"Do you want to talk about how you've been feeling?" We were all awkwardly avoiding this after she startled me, and I didn't want that. She always talked about healthy communication, so here it was, no matter how difficult it might be to ask such questions.

She let out a heavy sigh. "No, but I should. Though, what Muninn and Huginn said about sums up what I've been wrestling with."

She slumped against the back of the sofa unhappily. "I can't shake this feeling of uselessness. I don't know what it means to be a Valkyrie.

Which means I don't know how to be a proper Valkyrie, yet I feel like I've failed in every aspect. I'm a mediocre witch with no true mastery of my magic. I can't fight my way out of a cardboard box, and the other day was proof of that. I'm pathetic."

She threw up her hands with a surge of emotions that came with the last part of her outburst.

I took her hand in mine. "You're not pathetic or mediocre, especially in your magic. You can do so much with it, where others cannot."

"I couldn't hold my own for one lousy altercation and got my pathetic ass captured and my magic suppressed. I needed to act like the pathetic damsel I was while I waited for other competent people to come rescue me."

I shook my head. "You held your own as best as me and Tyr. We're gods. I feel pain now. It was so damned difficult to fight. Tyr has had all these centuries to keep his skills and power, and yet, between us and Fen, we still managed to fail you. Even Diego, who has this fascinating connection with you that tells him when you're in trouble, he couldn't stop you from being taken."

Diego slid his fingers through her hair, speaking up before she could protest. "He's right. You're far from pathetic or weak. You are so amazing, Cielo. You were taken captive and held your own when others would have broken under the pressure of Ingrid's manipulation. You kept her distracted while the rest of us infiltrated the facility. Just because you weren't able to out-manipulate her, or do some mystifying feat to get yourself out, doesn't mean you're a failure."

Her shoulders slumped. "But I almost broke. If it weren't for Muninn, I would have fallen prey to the poison worse than I already had."

He shook his head. "No. Muninn may have helped, but it was your will that prevented that poison from taking over your mind. You broke through it."

She looked down at her hands. Well, the one I wasn't engulfing with mine. "I feel so useless. This magic that's come back is... so wrong. The way it works, the way it moves under my skin, all of it is just... wrong. And my Valkyrie powers..."

"You're still a Valkyrie," I said, already seeing where her mind was going. "Kirby already confirmed your soul is still a Valkyrie soul."

"Then where is my power?" Her head snapped up to look at me. Tears brimmed her eyes and it sent a jolt of pain in my chest. "Why can't I find it? Why am I so damned useless? All of my Valkyrie sisters are more useful than me."

My grip on her tightened. "Don't. Don't you dare say that. You know that isn't true."

She swallowed and her lip trembled. "I suck at fighting."

"So? Many Valkyries did. You know as well as I do most Valkyries didn't fight."

"I need to fight!" Her burst of anger stunned me. "I don't have the luxury of sitting on my ass and waiting for someone to need mental or physical healing. There are people dying and suffering, and I'm so damned pathetic I can't help them."

I set my jaw. "That's not true. You help people every day. There are hundreds, if not thousands who owe their lives to you. You protect them. You heal them. You do everything in your power to make a better life for them."

She opened her mouth, but I wasn't finished. "You may not be a master of a million skills, Astrid, but that's because you don't need to be. You fit every role that has ever been asked of you. Maybe not perfectly, but it's been more than good enough. You're the putty that holds everything together."

"Glue," Diego corrected with a cough. That got Astrid to laugh a little.

"I see you with the other Valkyries. You connect with each one of them on some level. You bind them together." I brushed her cheek, smearing the wet trail where a tear had broken free. "Even if you can be aggressive, which hel, it's attractive when you are, that doesn't mean you have to be a physical fighter. Because you fight a different battle than anyone else. You bring out the best of everyone around you, making them stronger."

Her lip trembled.

Diego smiled and ran his fingers through her hair some more. "Besides, it's not like all your Valkyrie sisters are fighters. And some are deceptive fighters. Look at Azzie. She may fight, and she's good at it since she's more than capable of taking on a bear Berserker, but she'd rather be a protector. We see it in how she'll hesitate to join a fight for the sake of fighting, but won't think twice to protect. It's why her wings are gold. She excels in her shielding. She even picked up a few tricks from your dad that she somehow was able to use with her Valkyrie powers."

I tipped her chin up so she'd look at me now. "You're a perfect Valkyrie. Every time I look at you, you're exactly what I think a Valkyrie should be. Sometimes, it feels even more real and perfect than the Valkyries I knew in the past, like they were mere imitations."

She closed her eyes and took in a deep, calming breath. "Thank you. Both of you. I still feel like shit, but I do feel better. I just need to be patient and not put some much pressure on myself."

I bent over and kissed her forehead. "We'll help you find your Valkyrie powers and figure out your magic. Malsumis can't take those from you. She'd have to kill everything you are to do that, and you're far too strong for her to handle."

Diego leaned in and nuzzled her neck. "She'll have to pry you from our cold, dead hands before she can take you from us."

"Careful, she's already tried it," Astrid said through bouts of giggling.

Diego mumbled something in Spanish, his hands finding her sides as he kissed her neck. Astrid squirmed and laughed, trying to push away from his tickling fingers. She pressed into me, and my hands wrapped around her arms, holding her in place.

She glanced up at me through her lashes. "Don't be mean, Baldur."

My eyes traveled down her body. The thin layers of fabric she wore hid none of her curves. "Oh, I won't be mean, Sunshine. I promise you that."

Astrid squealed when Diego wrapped his arms around her waist and tried to pull her away from me. I refused to let go. "I won."

Astrid's brow listed. "Won what?"

Diego scowled and then muttered something else in Spanish. Astrid gasped. "Diego!"

Danger mixed with desire in his eyes. Clearly the dragon had some choice feelings about my claim. A grin flashed on his lips. "And what are you going to do about it, Cielo?"

She grabbed his shirt and yanked him forward. I suddenly had two people half on my lap, not that I was complaining. "I'll make you behave."

My pulse thrummed under my skin. That was a threat I wanted directed at me.

Diego's nose flared and he flicked his gaze up to me. "I think someone else would enjoy that a little bit more."

Astrid made a thoughtful sound in her throat, her attention flicking between us. "No one is going to enjoy anything until you tell me about this bet."

I slid my fingers into her hair and tugged, making her gasp. The sound sent a pulse of desire straight down to my cock. I could see why Tyr liked doing that. "It's nothing nefarious. We had a footrace. Winner got to claim solo time with you next. I won."

Astrid pursed her lips. "So, you're sending Diego away?"

I leaned over her. "He can stay if he likes. I believe you deserve a little extra after being so open with us."

My mouth closed around hers and she sighed, leaning into me. I slowly kissed her, enjoying the softness of her lips on mine. The heat of her skin burned hotter than the sun, teasing me with her presence.

Diego's presence grew and she gasped. Our lips parted and she tipped her head to give him better access. He kissed a leisurely path up her neck and along her jaw.

I kissed Astrid's forehead, then the tip of her nose. She rolled her head back, her lips brushing mine. I kissed her again, quick and teasing. My hands roamed down her arms. They brushed Diego's hands as he pushed up her shirt. The contact was electrifying. Even Astrid let out a small gasp against my mouth.

Our lips parted and I gazed down at her. Her eyes were half-lidded from our combined touch on her. I wanted to kiss her again. Diego tried the same. We halted before we collided. Our breath mingled as the three of us shared the same space. His mouth was so close.

"Well?" Astrid said, her voice heady with desire. "Are you two going to or not?"

I chuckled and Diego grinned. Then his mouth was on mine. I inhaled deep through my nose, my hand flying up to grip his face. His stubble brushed my callouses. Astrid made a pleased sound.

Our tongues flitted, energy coursing through our connection—strength and passion that swirled in an intoxicating battle needing to burst to the surface. Where Astrid was a consuming fire, Diego was powerful passion. He was as incredible as I hoped.

The kiss ended with us panting and staring into the other's eyes. There was something there, a connection deep and wanting. In unison we turned to look at Astrid.

She sat with her hands shoved between her crossed legs, framing her amazing breasts threatening to spill out of her disheveled shirt. Her bottom lip was caught in her teeth and her eyes glinted with her lust.

I grinned. "Enjoying the show, Sunshine?"

"Maybe," she said coyly.

I chuckled and grabbed her, pulling her onto my lap and kissing her with all the passion I had for her. She moaned against my mouth and snaked her arms around my neck. My hands roamed her body, yanking at her clothes when they were in the way—until they weren't.

I wasn't sure where they went, but they vanished. Mine had, too. I didn't care. Feeling her bare skin against mine drove out all thoughts. My hard cocked strained, desperate to have her. But I wanted something else first.

My mouth trailed down her neck, over her collarbone and along her heaving breasts. She moaned as I licked a path along her sensitive skin, then whined when I didn't linger. Diego could have that fun. I'd allow it.

I trailed between her breasts, appreciating her tattoo for a moment, before kissing lower. I eased Astrid back as I went and tucked her legs loosely around my hips. They wouldn't stay there, but this would be more comfortable for her as I laid her along my legs.

"Baldur?" My name was so breathy off her lips, it was maddening. "What are you doing?"

I chuckled and kept going, enjoying the taste of her skin and the sounds of her quiet gasps before Diego cupped her face and cut her sounds off with a deep kiss.

Hooking Astrid's legs over my shoulders, I leaned back against the armrest of the sofa, pulling her by her hips with me. Astrid squirmed as I kissed along her inner thigh. My fingers dug into her luscious skin as I spread her legs until her glistening pussy was on display for me.

I slid my tongue teasingly along her wet folds. Astrid gasped and her hips bucked. The motion sent a surging wave of desire through me. Without hesitation, I dove in, greedily licking and sucking, devouring her. Astrid writhed and moaned. I was sure she would be begging, if Diego hadn't claimed her mouth.

She reached for me, but Diego intercepted her reach and pinned her hands to the sofa cushions. He tsked. "I don't think so, Cielo. You're at our mercy, not the other way around."

"You call this at your mercy?" she said through panting breaths. She bit her lip and stifled a moan when I sucked her clit extra hard. "I'm sure I'd have you both at my mercy before you manage it of me."

The challenge riled up the heat burning in my veins. Diego grinned. "Challenge accepted, Cielo."

He descended on her, kissing and licking trails along her skin to her breasts. He lavished her with attention. My tongue and mouth worked her needy clit, changing up my rhythm just as she grew too comfortable. It drove her mad.

Astrid fought back, trying to resist the pleasure we provided. It only made me want to try harder.

I slid my fingers inside her, gliding in and out in a competing rhythm.

Diego released her nipple with an audible *pop*. "You're losing, Cielo. Just give up now."

"Never," she half-moaned out just as I changed it up with a new pattern with my tongue.

Diego chuckled. "Have it your way."

He tipped her head back and eased his hard cock into her mouth. Her throat bobbed and she moaned as she took him. I might have as well. At this angle, seeing him slowly slide in and out of her, it turned me on even more.

"That's it, Cielo. Keep sucking this cock. Take even more. I know you can." Diego leaned forward, pushing deeper into her and she moaned. He played with her breast, his fingers pinching and rolling her taut nipple while he moved her hand he still held captive. I closed my eyes and groaned when he wrapped her hand around my hard shaft. "I think he deserves a reward for treating you so well, don't you think, Cielo?"

Astrid didn't hesitate to stroke, renewing the burning heat in my veins. It stoked hotter with each pump, their combined grip tight and amazing.

I licked her favorite runes while sucking on her clit in hungry response. Blood pounded in my ears. Closer and closer I came to the edge, but she needed to give in first. I grinned when she bucked against my mouth and gave her one good, long, consuming lick and then sucked, hard.

Astrid screamed, the sound muffled by Diego's cock. Her orgasm had her bucking and writhing. Her grip on my cock tightened and white flashed through my vision. I came quickly and hard.

I released her, gasping for air. As was she. She lay languidly on her back, panting, with Diego and me looming over her, quite satisfied.

"We win," Diego said.

"Barely," she puffed out. "I almost got you both. I felt it."

He grinned. "Almost isn't a win."

I slid my hands up her body, taking controlled breaths. "And that means you're ours. I hope you didn't have any plans."

I pulled her up and pressed her soft curves against me. I kissed her deeply and she groaned before pulling away just enough to speak. "Only with you two."

Diego pulled her from my arms and lavished her with attention. I watched, enjoying her expressions to each of his gentle, loving caresses. And the way her eyes hooded and her mouth parted as he slid inside her, it made me hungry for her.

I wrapped my hand around the back of her neck and crashed my mouth to hers. I devoured her moans and relished her fingers sliding along my shoulders.

Astrid broke the kiss before I was ready, and she grinned when I let out a frustrated huff. "Lean back, please."

Her hand trailed down my chest to emphasize her request.

"Only because you asked nicely."

She closed her eyes and moaned when Diego slammed into her harder, reminding her he was still there. "I'll be extra nice, I promise."

The throatiness to her words sent a pleasant *zing* of anticipation. I relaxed against the sofa arm and Astrid bent forward. I closed my eyes and sucked in a sharp breath through my nose when her warm tongue slid over the head of my cock.

My eyes cracked open as she traced her tongue down and then up the underside of my hard shaft. Her lustful gaze met mine and she slid me into her mouth. I groaned and grabbed the back of her neck.

Astrid found a quick and maddening pace, sucking me off as Diego pounded into her. His pleased expressions were just as amazing to watch as Astrid's.

The desire building in me stoked hotter and hotter. My breathing labored, my pulse pounding in my ears like drums of war. I thrust my hips forward, pushing myself deeper into her throat. Astrid let out a startled sound, but she couldn't pull away. My hand gripped her hard as I fucked her mouth in time with my battling pulse.

Diego reached around her between her thighs and stroked her clit. Her moans of pleasure vibrating through me became my undoing. My body tightened and with another ragged intake of breath, I toppled over the edge, convulsing and spilling in her mouth. Diego threw his head back and also came, filling her pussy until he was fully spent.

Astrid took another moment of coaxing, but she, too, fell into the tides of orgasm, my still-hard cock in her mouth, barely muffling her scream.

Diego and I fell back. Astrid leaned against the sofa, running her hand messily through her hair. Our heavy breathing filled the air.

When I'd gotten myself under control, I reached for Astrid. She smiled and climbed into my lap. Her mouth found mine and I kissed her softly—leisurely, enjoying the feel of her against me, and her presence wrapping around me.

The embers of desire stoked again. Astrid giggled against my lips, probably on account of my cock pressing against her. "Are you ever not raring to go?"

I pretended to think. "I think I'd lose my perfect-son title if I wasn't."

She rolled her eyes. Diego puffed out a breath. "Why are you gods so lucky?"

Astrid rolled her eyes again. "Don't complain. You only have to wait five minutes now."

He leaned over and pressed a kiss to the back of her neck. "Or you could speed up the process."

My brow rose. *She could?*

Astrid shook her head. "You know I can't right now."

His dragon horns grew from his head, and silver and black scales appeared in patches along his skin. He pressed his lips to her ear. "Try for me, and I'll come out and play."

His voice dipped to something gravelly and very appealing. Astrid definitely thought so, too, with the way she sharply inhaled and her eyes fluttered.

"I can't... my dragon," she whispered. "It's not my magic..."

"It is," he said. "You just have to take it back. Take it back, Astrid."

She closed her eyes and shook her head. She wasn't ready. And while Diego was clearly disappointed, he wasn't going to do anything she didn't want.

I pressed my lips to her. "Then I can have fun while he has to wait."

Gripping her hips, I slid inside her, her slickness and warmth welcoming me. Her lips parted with her breathy gasp and her eyes hooded as she enjoyed the feel of my cock inside her—filling her.

I thrust hard, the motions easy with her filled with Diego's cum. Her perfect breasts bounced in time with my thrusts, their motions hypnotic. She moaned. The unmuffled sound was so perfect. Desire and need built quickly, and I came soon and hard, filling her more with my hot seed.

Astrid pouted when she tried to rock her hips and I held her still so I wouldn't pull out too soon as the remainder of my orgasm pulsed into her. "Not fair..."

I smirked. "We won. We get to use you as we see fit, Sunshine. And if we want to fill you until you're dripping with cum, then that's what we'll do."

She sharply inhaled, her pupils dilating. "Promise?"

Diego bent over and chuckled in her ear. "Do you have a kink to confess to?"

Astrid swallowed. "Destiny is a bitch, and I'm not going to tempt it by admitting to anything right now."

I didn't understand the term they were using, but the way Diego's hand slid along her lower belly, I got an idea of the hidden implications. My pulse jumped.

Diego's teeth grazed her shoulder. "One day, though, yes?"

She shivered. "One day, yes, my dragon, but not now."

My hands slid along her thighs. What would it be like to have that with her? Even just once.

"Baldur," Astrid said.

I looked up. They both watched me, worry creasing both their brows. "I'm fine."

"Are you—"

I bent forward and kissed her, cutting off her words. "I said I'm fine."

And truly, I was. I could wonder what it'd be like while also accepting my reality.

Astrid slid her fingers along my cheek and sunk her fingers in my hair. Her mouth met mine again. Slowly and lovingly, she kissed me. The connection knitting us together wasn't frantic or filled with lust. It built a slow, warm heat that wrapped me in desire and left me craving more.

My fingers pressed into her luscious hips, and I pulled her closer, pushing myself deeper inside her. She moaned against my mouth. The sounds she made for me undid me.

Her hips rocked, slow and steady, a rhythm that spread the simmering heat in my veins until I was on fire. I slid my hand up along the smooth valleys of her back, enjoying the feel of her soft skin. My fingers pressed into that special place on her back and she moaned a little louder.

Diego slid her hair away from her neck and kissed her. Astrid leaned her head to the side, offering herself. He took full advantage, claiming all of her exposed skin. His hands roamed her, his touch brushing my hands in his path.

Astrid's rocking increased. I met her motions with my own thrusts, spiking our pleasure. Her eyes hooded and her breaths turned into delicious pants and moans.

Diego's hand grazed the base of my shaft, startling me and throwing off my rhythm. Or not his hand?

Astrid gasped and stilled. "Diego?"

He pressed his lips to her ear. "You can handle Tyr. I think you can handle the two of us just fine."

The head of his cock pressed against her entrance and my buried shaft. Astrid swallowed. "I know he's huge, but I think you've under-estimated both of your sizes."

She and I both sucked in a sharp breath as he slid the head of his cock inside her tight pussy with me. "I know you can handle it, mi amor."

"She can handle it." I could feel it in the way he stretched her—in the way her walls wrapped tightly around us both.

Astrid nodded and swallowed again. "I can. I want it. I want you both inside me."

Diego kissed her gently and eased himself in, slowly. Her nails dug into my skin, the pain a delicious mix with the pleasure I felt, and no doubt a mirror of what she experienced from the expressions that played on her face.

Astrid groaned something deep and primal as she accepted him in with me. The sound did something to me. As Diego eased himself in, I withdrew. Astrid's eyes popped wide, her mouth gaping wordlessly.

"Are you okay?" I murmured.

She nodded. "More of that."

Diego and I grinned, and when I was nearly all the way out of her, I thrust back in, Diego pulling out. She was so slick and tight.

Astrid's eyes practically rolled back in her head as we found rhythm in this pattern. "Yes… fuck yes, keep doing this."

Gladly. Our rhythm continued, even when she begged for more or tried to make our pace more frantic, which Diego easily kept controlled with his hands on her hips. I enjoyed this slower build, feeling her and him. The molten heat in me burned hot. My pulse thrummed hard in my veins. I fell into the sensations and sounds and savored the view of her enjoying everything we gave her, feeling the connection building between us.

My fingers resumed their work on her back, and Diego slid his hand between her, rubbing her needy clit, his other hands reaching around to play with her supple breast. Astrid spasmed and then tipped her head back as she came apart and screamed her orgasm. Her walls tightened, squeezing us and milking our simultaneous releases.

I squeezed my eyes shut and saw white, coming harder than I could recall ever doing before. I felt Diego's pulsing cock and hot seed as much as my own and it only intensified the euphoric sensations crashing down on me.

I cracked my eyes open, breathing hard, when I came down. Astrid lay limply in my arms, her beautiful wings sprawled out behind her. Diego barely held himself up over her with his quivering arm on the back of the sofa as his support.

His fingers flitted over her feathers, earning a quiet gasp from Astrid. "Look who came out to finally play."

"You two are just too amazing for me to stay away." She hummed and snuggled into my chest. "Thank you."

I ran my fingers through her hair. If this was how we could help her find her confidence in herself to where she could find herself again, then so be it. I only wanted to help her become the best version of herself, whatever that immortal looked like.

When pain pulsed in my back, I repositioned us so I was a bit more comfortable—as comfortable as I could be, given the furniture was still too small for me.

It was also apparently too tiny for Diego, as he grumbled while trying to get comfortable with us. "We're buying new furniture."

Astrid giggled, a sleepy weight heavy in her voice. "I'll ask Mr. Money Bags for my allowance to buy a bigger set."

Diego and I chuckled. I stroked her back to coax her into relaxation. She'd need it. We weren't done enjoying her yet.

TWENTY-NINE

BALDUR

Magic was a fascinating thing, even to a god like me. When I opened the portal door to Astrid's home, I did not expect to be met with loud sounds, laughter, and talking. It made me pause in the threshold as I tried to place much of it.

Many of the loud noises were coming from a TV. The laughter and talking were all women. Did Astrid have friends over? I may have come at a bad time. *Well, if she doesn't want me around, she'll say so.*

I walked into the living room. Astrid did have company over, in the form of Dahlia, Magnus, Kirby, and Brit. Aya was also amongst the group. They all sat on the sectional sofa, holding those things Astrid called video game controllers. Well, except Brit. She focused on a book.

The other thing to catch my eye was the presence of extra TVs now in the room. They all played similar moving pictures on them, though were different enough to add to my confusion of what was going on.

Astrid glanced my way briefly before refocusing on the TV. "Hey."

"Hey to you, too." The movement on the screens distracted me. The environment for the picture was dingy, and those things I was introduced to called guns fired at oddly humanoid-looking creatures that had a strange resemblance to draugar. "I'm not interrupting, am I? If this is a girl's day, I can come back later."

I definitely didn't want to intrude on that. It showed her mental state was improving.

"I don't mind if you stay," Astrid said. She squealed and mashed her finger on her controller. The main TV turned red and displayed some sort of death message. Astrid hung her head.

Brit snickered and looked up from her phone. "That's what you get for having such an impractical build."

Astrid stuck her tongue out. "It's perfectly fine, thank you. I just ran into a horde while trying to escape another one."

"Yeah, sure," Brit said before shifting her focus to me. "As long as you don't whip your dick out, you can be an honorary member of team estrogen today."

I blinked as the ladies laughed. *Why would I whip that out?*

Dahlia held up a finger. "And I get to paint one of your nails purple."

"Uh, sure." These were such strange requirements, but I wasn't going to point that out.

I waited for them to finish their game. It'd be rude to get in the way of their view of the TVs. One by one they all died, until Kirby was the last one still playing. The ladies' excitement grew the longer Kirby survived in this game. From what I gathered, the objective was to kill these draugar-like creatures before they swarmed you. I guessed there was some increased difficulty in some way, by how excited they were Kirby could survive this long alone.

However, in the end, these enemies killed her, too. A chorus of disappointment rumbled through the women, then they congratulated each other. It was interesting to watch the comradery over something like this.

Astrid stood and waved me over. "Come sit, instead of hovering like some outsider."

"I didn't want to be the cause of any deaths."

I walked around the sofa and Astrid had me sit in her spot. Before she could possibly consider finding another place to sit, I pulled her down on my lap. She didn't complain or try to insist on sitting elsewhere, which was good, because I'd have fought her on that. Having her in my arms, even in such a casual setting, was everything to me.

Dahlia grabbed a glass vial from the coffee table and demanded my hand. I held it out for her. She uncapped the vial, revealing a shimmery purple goopy substance dripping off a tiny brush attached to the cap.

She applied it in two swift strokes, then waved her hand over my finger and announced, "Gorgeous."

That was a lot faster than I expected the task to take. And now one of my fingernails was a shimmery purple. It was a nice color.

"Magic is great," Astrid said as she tapped on her controller button. Something was changing on her TV screen as she did. "I don't miss the days of waiting for that to dry naturally."

"Or thinking it was dry and then smudging it," Dahlia said.

The ladies grumbled. I guessed that to be an issue with this nail polish stuff.

"So, what exactly are you all doing?" I asked.

"Shooting Nazi zombies in the face." Dahlia vocalized that so casually, like it was the most normal thing for them to be doing.

"What is a Nazi zombie?"

"Have you read up on World War II yet?" Astrid asked.

I shook my head. "No idea what that is."

"Then, the first part won't make much sense. But basically, they were a political party that followed an ideology that ended up promoting the genocide of millions of people that they deemed unfit to live in society."

"On paper it appears only humans were the target, but it was another attempt to rid Midgard of non-humans as well," Aya added.

I scowled. Despite being a war god, I did not condone the blood of innocents to be the price of it. "These... Nazis... are no more?"

"Some of their ideas have unfortunately stuck around in small groups, but the party itself is gone, and has been reviled in history since," Magnus said. "Hence using them as bad guys."

"And what is a zombie?"

"It's the human's current understanding of draugar," Aya said.

I didn't understand. "Do humans not know what draugar are anymore?"

She shook her head. "The more we hide our existence, the more the generations forget the truth and try to make sense of stories passed down, or even explain accidental sightings. Zombies are one of those interpretations."

I'd have to add zombies to my research topics. "How does this game work?"

Kirby jumped into an explanation about rounds and zombie hordes they had to survive. As I thought, the zombies become more difficult each round. They had different abilities that became stronger, so certain guns and upgrades helped fight off the different types.

Brit made a quip about unrealism and Kirby rolled her eyes. "Ignore her. She's only here to heckle our skills and grumble about inaccurate firearm representation in modern media."

Brit's eyes glanced up from her book. "I don't know how none of you have a problem with it, so someone has to do it."

Astrid held her controller up for me. "Do you want to try?"

"I'd like to watch first to get a better understanding."

They started up another game. My attention flicked from the TVs to the women as they bantered, laughed, and, well, shrieked as they tried not to die. It was all entertaining, even though I struggled to grasp this whole video game concept. I also didn't understand the TV setup, even after Magnus tried to explain what a LAN was, so I just accepted that multiple TVs were needed for them all to play.

Astrid had me try to learn how the controller worked by me holding her hands in mine and feeling her movements. I was, however, more focused on her face. All the little expressive changes were interesting to watch. And seeing her not once look down at her controller to press buttons while she played was fascinating.

Even though this activity was still overall foreign to me, I was having fun watching them.

Astrid held up her controller to me. "Your turn."

I hesitated. "I don't know—"

She pushed the device closer to my face. "One round, just for fun."

"I'm going to get you killed."

She shrugged. "Oh well."

I took the controller and tipped it in multiple angles to get a good look at it. "How does it all work? I didn't learn much from your movements, except that each button has a complicated purpose."

She gave me a quick rundown of how to use the controllers. She admitted she was only telling me the basics so as not to overwhelm me and that should do me just fine, but I wasn't convinced.

Kirby started the next round before I thought I was ready, thrusting me into the chaos. Astrid tried to help me, shouting out what to do. Though it turned into her doing a lot of squealing and laughing as I flailed around with the controls.

The red death screen appeared when I was overwhelmed.

Aya slapped my shoulder and continued playing. Her eyes didn't leave her TV screen. "Not bad for a noob."

"Did I do well?" I had no reference beyond how great these women were at the game.

Astrid patted my hand. "You did great for your first time ever touching a game. Tyr was *way* worse."

"Didn't he have his character run in a circle?" Dahlia said.

Astrid laughed. "Worse, he only spun his camera in a circle."

The women laughed with her. I grinned. Tyr wasn't a great technology bar to measure against for success, but I'd take any win over him.

Several more rounds were played before Aya was the last to be taken down. Astrid held out her hand to play the next game. I kept the controller.

"I'd like to try again, if that's okay."

The brilliant, excited smile on her face was everything I'd hoped for in a response. Even if I didn't manage to grasp this, I was seeing another aspect of her life. I was sharing in something she enjoyed and I wanted more of that.

Grasping it became less of an issue as I played. Each time, I got a little better. And, even if I wasn't improving, the fun I had increased. It wasn't as serious as I thought, making each death less annoying.

When I'd made it five rounds without dying, beating Dahlia when she miscalculated and died in round four, I felt pretty good about my improving skills. Then I blew up.

I sat there blinking like an idiot while Astrid and Brit laughed. How had I done that? The zombies with that power were the slowest and easiest to avoid.

Astrid pressed her hand against my cheek. I looked down at her, drowning in those eyes of hers. I leaned over and she met me halfway, kissing me quickly. "It's okay. We all make those mistakes."

"Yeah, just look at Dahlia," Magnus said.

Dahlia scoffed and smacked her in the arm. I chuckled. It was fair, but no less annoying.

Astrid jumped when a bird suddenly landed in her lap. We all laughed as she pressed a palm to her chest and panted for air. Muninn gazed up at her with a cocked head.

"Don't scare me like that," she complained.

Huginn landed on my shoulder. *"Don't be so jumpy."*

Astrid pointed at him with narrowed eyes and he cackled.

Muninn grabbed one of Astrid's fingers and pulled. *"Time to go."*

Her brow furrowed. "Go? Go where?"

"With me."

We looked up to find Urd standing in the room.

"Oh, hi, Urd," Astrid greeted. "Does that mean we've got permission?"

"Permission for what?" Kirby asked. Her expression had closed off to one of suspicion.

Astrid's eyes flicked from Kirby to Urd, as if she wasn't sure she could say. *Interesting. What were these two up to in private?* Diego had assumed the two talking the other day was therapy-related. But maybe there was more to it.

Urd nodded once. "No more secrets, right?"

Astrid smiled and then filled in everyone about the research she had started about Valkyries and their origin. She didn't reveal to them her revelations about a previous life before Ragnarök, but she did divulge a discussion she had with Urd. They had somehow figured out that even the dragons had lost memories when they didn't think they had.

The two of them planned to do more research to see if there was any connection, as Urd didn't even remember the true origins of Valkyries. Urd admitted that she had received similar confirmation from Artura about this missing information.

"Searching a hidden library for ancient clues about the past sounds like fun, actually," Brit said. "Do you need any help?"

Astrid looked to Urd. The older dragon thought for a moment then nodded. "We can trust everyone in this room with the knowledge we learn."

Dahlia raised her hand. "Sifting through old books that haven't been digitized isn't my preference, so I'm going to pass."

Magnus agreed. Aya and Kirby were happy to help with the search, and I didn't say no. I'd promised Astrid I'd help with this research whenever I could. It also intrigued me what we'd find.

"Oh, before we go, I should inform you that Callie will be present," Urd said.

"Really?" Astrid said. She sounded hopeful. A few of the other women seemed happy to hear this as well. I was curious who this person was. I'd never heard of anyone by that name mentioned before.

Something seemed to dawn on Astrid. "Oh. How does she seem to be doing?"

"Well enough, though I do believe you know some of the boundaries she'll still need," Urd said.

Boundaries? Now I was concerned. Was this woman dangerous?

Astrid looked at her familiars. "Please behave."

"We will," Muninn said. *"Promise."*

Huginn tapped his brother and they seemed to share a private word, then bobbed their heads. We watched them half-fly, half-jump their way over to a wooden perch with pouches and toys attached. They rummaged around in the pouches before taking something each and flying back to Astrid. Both ravens had something small in their mouths.

Astrid smiled. "I think that's a nice thing to do."

My brow spiked. *Why the sudden private discussion?* "So, who is Callie?"

The air in the room shifted. It felt... tense but also somber.

"Callie is Caleb's twin sister," Astrid said. "They were separated at birth, and… she unfortunately didn't have the best life." She chewed her lower lip. "Odin made things worse for her, when he found her just as her dragon nature made itself known."

My hand slowly curled into a fist. "What did he do?"

I didn't mean for that to sound threatening, but the tension came out anyway.

"He held her prisoner," Magnus said.

"And used the whole *pain makes you stronger* abusive bullshit," Dahlia muttered darkly.

I exhaled a hard breath. *If I ever see him again…*

Astrid placed a gentle hand on my leg. "We're helping her heal. Slowly, and as much as she allows. She just has some triggers we do our best to work around."

"Like the ravens?"

She nodded. "I won't hide them from her, as that won't help, but we will compromise on the types of interactions she'll have with them."

That seemed fair to me. I trusted she knew what she was doing. Healing people's trauma was her specialty.

"Say hi for us?" Magnus said.

Astrid happily agreed.

After some goodbyes with Dahlia and Magnus, Urd used her magic to teleport us. The thick scent of aged parchment was the first to greet my senses. I looked around, taking in the most magnificent library I'd ever seen.

Towering pillars, carved with intricate artistry, supported vaulted ceilings that seemed impossibly high. A labyrinth of enormous bookshelves surrounded us, their shelves filled with countless scrolls, artifacts, and tomes with all manner of bindings. There were even piles on the floor, as if there wasn't enough room for all the knowledge contained in this place.

No doors leading to the outside existed from what I could see. Elaborate stained glass windows, depicting scenes that were vaguely familiar, scattered prismatic light across the polished floor.

A pale, dark-haired woman in stylish dark clothes carrying an armload of books stared at us with wide mismatched eyes, the left one blue, the right one brown. With her was a muscular dark-haired man with bronze skin. He carried a single book in his hand at his side. His dark eyes squinted at us suspiciously.

"Uh, who the fuck are you?" the woman asked.

Urd stepped out from behind me. "They're with me."

The woman relaxed. "Oh, okay. Artura said you were getting someone; I didn't expect so many."

"It wasn't part of the plan, but I think it's best for the task we have."

She nodded and held out her hand to Astrid, who was closest to her. "I'm Raven. Apprentice archivist and maybe guardian? Still unsure about that part."

Guardian? What was that? Astrid didn't seem confused, more interested when the woman said the title, but didn't speak of it.

"Astrid. Valkyrie, witch, and therapist."

Everyone else introduced themselves. Raven's companion was Axel, a crow shifter, and her personal bodyguard. *She must be someone of great importance to have a bodyguard.*

Huginn and Muninn loudly proclaimed they didn't like him because of his shifter type and Astrid scolded them.

Raven shifted the books in her arms. "I never expected to meet so many new supernaturals, let alone two gods. This is exciting."

She seemed more overwhelmed than excited. I wondered how recently she'd been introduced to our world.

"Why don't I show you where the others are set up," Raven offered. "I need to drop off these books anyway."

She walked down the long hall, Axel right on her heels. He walked unusually close to her, as if he expected someone to jump out from the bookshelves and attack at any minute.

We followed her into a spacious new room with a center table. Books and scrolls covered most of the table's surface. Two people, a man of average height and wiry yet muscled build, and a petite woman with a slight frame, hunched over some scattered papers. Both had such pale hair it looked almost white.

No, hers is white. I realized the woman was Verdandi—Artura. It'd been a long time since I'd last seen her, and she hadn't aged a day. The man took a moment longer to recognize, as I'd only met him once. Mia's partner Caleb, and Artura's son.

Both looked up upon our entry. Artura's eyes narrowed. "There's a lot more of them than we agreed, Urd."

"They'll be useful and careful," her sister replied.

Artura made a displeased sound in her throat.

"You're as warm and welcoming as always, Artura." It took me a moment to realize I had been the one to rudely say that.

Kirby and Brit choked on laughter while Aya, Astrid, and Urd stared at me. Huginn and Muninn cackled.

Artura looked me up and down indignantly with her intense violet eyes. "And you speak well for a walking corpse."

Raven's mouth fell open. "Corpse?"

"The myth where he died is said to be a twist of the true story," Axel told her.

"It was," I confirmed. "And the Valkyries brought me back."

Raven swiveled her attention to Astrid and Kirby, her eyes intent. "Is that something you can do?"

Astrid shook her head. "It's a bit more complicated than that. There is no magic that can bring the dead back to life the way they were before they died."

Raven's shoulders drooped. "Oh…"

Axel touched her shoulders in support and then encouraged her to put her books down so they could find more. Seemed that topic wasn't the best for her.

Astrid glanced around. "Where's Callie?"

"Right here," a quiet voice said.

We turned to another doorway leading into another grand book room where a person with soft, androgynous features, short pale hair, and loose-fitting clothing stood. She carried a few books in her arms.

Astrid smiled. "Hey."

"Hey." Callie seemed a little hesitant to enter, but then did, setting books down next to her brother.

Muninn cooed softly and hopped onto the table. Huginn followed his brother. The two slowly walked toward Callie, who stiffened. Caleb placed a reassuring hand on her shoulder.

The ravens set their shiny gifts on the table—a pretty ring and an interesting multicolored stone. Muninn cooed again and nudged his ring gift with his beak, then they both flew back to Astrid.

Callie hesitated, then picked up the gifts. A small smile appeared on her lips. "Thank you. These are… pretty."

The ravens puffed out and cooed again. Astrid petted them. "Huginn wants you to know he's sorry for being angry with you. He says he was wrong to be."

I could only assume Huginn had treated Callie similarly to the way he'd treated Astrid.

Callie's lip trembled and then she nodded. "Thank you."

Astrid turned her attention to Artura and jumped right into discussing business, taking the focus away from Callie, which the timid woman seemed to appreciate. *Astrid really has no fear of these dragons.* Surprisingly, Artura seemed to respect this quality in Astrid. Or she'd been working with the dragon long enough that the animosity had been quelled.

Artura had never been an outright antagonistic dragon, but she'd also never been known for her warmth, either.

Caleb showed Astrid some papers with scrawled notes. "These are some rudimentary translation notes Callie and I have been able to come up with for the most common languages she and Raven found in their searches. Your preliminary notes were helpful even with the errors, so thank you for trudging through that. One of them still isn't finished, as we've been struggling with a few aspects of it."

Astrid sifted through a number of the loose pages. "There's so much here. It's impressive what you've been able to do in such a short amount of time."

The praise brought brightness to Callie's whole person. She seemed to relax a little more, too, though there was still a guardedness to her that reminded me of a cornered animal. It was so easy to see the damage my father had caused her, and it infuriated me.

"I'm glad to have been given the opportunity to do it," Callie said, a giddiness to her voice. "It's been a lot of fun. And the more I find, the more questions I have. This is a really interesting situation you've uncovered, Astrid."

"How many have you found?" Kirby asked as she approached the table.

"Nine distinct languages, with even more dialects," Callie said. "There could be more that we haven't found yet, though."

I noticed Astrid and Urd share a look when she mentioned nine languages. That was somehow relevant.

"Has there been anything that's stood out with any of these language finds?" Urd asked.

"Two things, actually." Caleb gestured to a leather-bound book inlaid with silver plant designs. "That is written in a fae language that reads more like a dialect than a completely separate language."

Brit lifted the book in her hand and carefully admired the design work. "So, unlike the rest of us, they kept their language intact. I wonder why?"

"It's actually not that uncommon," Callie said "Greek is a great example of a language where the ancient and modern use is nearly the same. Whereas Old Norse's closest modern counterpart is actually Icelandic, rather than any of the hundreds of Norwegian dialects that exist. It has to do with how well a language is preserved and controlled when exposed to outside languages."

I was impressed already by this woman. She clearly was a scholarly type.

"We think the fae may have writing enough of their language down to retain it after the memory loss and then protected it from non-fae influence," Caleb said. "Take a look at this."

He pushed a translation sheet toward me and Aya. "Does this look vaguely familiar to you two?"

We both peered at the paper. An odd sense of familiarity washed over me. No, more than just familiarity, I was certain I understood a portion of these words, even if their translation was just out of reach in my mind. "Yes."

Aya nodded. Astrid and Kirby took a look as well.

"This reminds me of the language the gods speak. At least the Norse gods," Kirby said.

"That's what I think this is. I think this language was one the gods used to speak," Caleb said.

"But why did theirs change so much, whereas the fae didn't?" Brit wondered aloud.

"We didn't have it written down," Aya said. "It was something we all spoke, and Odin claimed it wasn't needed for us to waste time writing down. At the time, we didn't have any reason to disagree with him, so we didn't."

"It's a fairly common control tactic," Callie said. "We see it a lot in history, and even today, where literacy is heavily monitored in order for those in power to remain there."

"That might be why the fae are so protective of their ways," Kirby said. "Similar reason to what Odin wanted, but a different method. I wonder if their anti-human consorting rules might be a product of that. I can't recall a time they didn't push that hard."

Astrid's eyes swept over the books. "It's possible that answer lies in these books. Or it's hidden in the fae realm. It's something we can look out for, but I'm not sure if it's fully relevant to what we're after."

She looked over the translation notes and paused on one. Well, pause wasn't the correct way to put it. She nearly ate the sheet of paper trying to hold it up to her face so quickly.

"What is it?" Aya asked.

"I… can read this," she said.

All eyes fell on her.

"Like, it's difficult, but I'm understanding it in a way I'm having a hard time articulating."

Kirby looked over her shoulder to read it. "Strangely, so can I."

Aya and I shared a look. It was like when we read the other translation sheet.

"That's the one we couldn't figure out," Caleb said. "It only had one book so far that Raven found."

"Damn, did someone crack the code already?"

We turned to see Raven strolling into the room with another armful of books. She had a bright smile on her face. Clearly this stuff was a passion of hers like Callie.

"We can read it," Kirby confirmed. "Not clearly, but enough to struggle through it without a translation guide."

Raven blinked, surprised. "So, it's some form of Valkyrie language?"

"Yes, but look at this." Aya was comparing the text of the god language and this presumed Valkyrie language. "There are no similarities between these two languages. They're distinct, as if—"

"As if Valkyries weren't created by the gods after all," Kirby finished for her. She looked at Astrid. "You said you had a theory, right? One that started because of Elin?"

Astrid nodded. "This only confirms what I'd been looking into. Odin couldn't have created Valkyries, because they existed independently of the gods."

That took a moment to sink in for the others. Luckily my discussion with Astrid the other day helped prepare me, but at the same time, I was still surprised to see how separated the Valkyries might have been from us.

"So, then what are Valkyries?" Brit asked.

"That's the million-dollar question, isn't it?" Kirby muttered.

Raven set her books down and scanned the rest of the piled books on the table. Like magic, she precured a sizable tome with gold detailing, as if she knew where every single book she'd placed down was.

She offered it to Astrid. "This was the book I found. If you're somehow able to read this language, maybe it's got what you need about Valkyries."

"I still don't get why you two can read it," Brit said. "I get Aya and Baldur reading that god language; they still speak the current dialect. But neither of you have ever known a Valkyrie specific language, right?"

"Maybe this book can help us understand," Kirby said. "Similar to the fact that all these individuals with interesting abilities also have Valkyrie souls this time around, our understanding of this language may be another lost aspect of being a Valkyrie."

"It's also not like we've found literature to read in the language before," Astrid said.

Kirby shook her head. "No, but I don't remember speaking a language like this, and you'd think, if I was a Valkyrie already after Ragnarök, then I would have had to live through it. So why didn't I speak this language post Ragnarök?"

That was a great question. There were so many questions around all the forgotten languages that made me wonder, what happened to them? Why did we forget?

My eyes slid over the translation papers, to the books. *Or did someone capitalize on the memory loss and try to erase certain languages from history?* "Maybe Valkyries didn't speak it, because they forgot, which aided Odin in his lies about how he made Valkyries."

Quiet glances passed around the room.

"Let's read this," Kirby said to Astrid.

"What should we be helping with?" Brit asked.

"Search for any reference to gods and Valkyries, maybe?" Astrid said. "As well as guardians and vaults."

Her brow furrowed. "Guardians and vaults? How are those words relevant?"

I was curious about that as well. This wasn't the first time the word *guardian* came up in conversation. But from the looks of it, neither Astrid, Raven, nor any of the dragons were intending to explain yet.

"Not sure yet," Astrid said. "But trust me when I say we should look for those."

While Astrid and Kirby focused on the Valkyrie book, the rest of us each took a language translation and got to work. Callie ended up excusing herself. While disappointed, Astrid seemed to understand Callie's need for some space.

Minutes turned into hours. The book Astrid and Kirby scanned through didn't have exactly what they were after, but it did have some interesting insight on what Valkyries could do and how they lived. There were some references in the tome that they struggled to understand, so that didn't help them.

The two of them then decided to scour the library to specifically find any Valkyrie-written books. With their wings, they were able to grab the higher books on the absurdly tall bookshelves with ease.

My search was coming up about as empty as the others for any of the keywords we sought. The only thing that kept me going was Astrid's determination, and the occasional moments I got to steal with her. When she wasn't rushing around, she sat in my lap doing her own reading. I especially enjoyed those moments.

Huginn and Muninn heckling Axel, and him dishing it back, came in a close second. That was entertaining as hel.

Then, all of a sudden, Brit exclaimed. "I found something!"

Kirby and Astrid flew back into the room. Raven and Axel weren't far behind. Even Callie poked her head in the room.

Brit pointed at a line in the small book she'd chosen.

> *We met the illusive winged women others spoke of. They rarely left their realm and many stories were told of how they seduced or stole the men of others.*

Raven's face contorted with thought. "That's eerily similar to the story of Amazons."

"What if that's where those stories came from?" Aya pondered. "Valkyries have always been female, as far as we knew. What if that's one truth that remained?"

"That implies we're a species," Kirby mused. "Which… I guess that makes sense. That passage referenced a realm. What would that mean?"

"Their home, maybe?" Brit said. "I'm only roughly translating, so I could have gotten the word wrong."

I noticed the dragon sisters, Raven and her guard, and Astrid all exchanged a look. What weren't they revealing yet? I didn't want to call them out, in case it caused an issue, but I hoped they would be forthcoming soon. *I can always ask Astrid later if it doesn't come up organically.*

"So, if we're a species, one that is only female, we'd need to be able to breed more Valkyries to keep us from going extinct," Astrid said. "Which would explain the rest of that passage, and how fractured memories would create stories about warrior women who kept men as slaves and all that."

"How did Odin make us infertile, then, if that's the case?" Kirby murmured. "Something isn't adding up. Is there more on it?"

Brit scanned the text and scribbled her translations. "Uh, there isn't much, but it seems that whoever wrote this made contact with the winged women. I'm struggling with the rest. I don't think this is actually all in the same language."

Aya went over and peered over her shoulder. "Strange. There's god writing in this."

I smoothed my beard. "So the person who wrote this not only had access to both languages, they were so comfortable with them, they wrote in both."

"Maybe a child of both?" Caleb said. "It's the most logical conclusion I can think of."

"Does this mean gods are a species, too?" Raven asked.

Everyone paused. That was a damned good question.

Aya steepled her fingers. "I'm wondering if we all were distinct species that somehow were able to breed, creating the vast possibilities we have today."

"Gods aren't guaranteed to have god or even immortal children," Kirby said. "And yet seemingly ordinary people with no god parents can have the potential to be gods. If it's a genetic chance, that could explain that a bit."

No one had any more theories to throw around, so we went back to searching. A few of us finally found references to guardians, and a singular vault reference. The dragons took those books to set aside for later. I found a lot of references to realms, which Raven took interest in the more I found them. She took those books from me after a while to look into herself. Seemed that was a word that really stuck with her.

Caleb picked up what looked like a worn journal. It didn't have anything fancy written on it, but Astrid looked at it oddly. Her entire focus zoned in on that book.

"What do you have there, Caleb?" I asked him, prompting the others to look, too.

Before he could do anything with it, Astrid snatched it. She touched the cover with a gentle caress, then she cracked it open. "It's a Valkyrie's journal."

A loose piece of paper fluttered out and hit the ground. I bent over and retrieved it, then I unfolded the paper and scanned it. This was the first time I'd looked at the Valkyrie language—but what struck me was, like the god language, I knew this.

"What does it say?" Caleb asked.

I made sure I was correct in my translating before reading it out.

If you are reading this, then I have failed. Not just in my mission, but my sisters and all the realms. I only pray Creation takes pity and those who remain can remember enough to build a beautiful new world that can learn from our mistakes.

I am sorry.

I looked up from the paper and stared at the stunning red-haired woman gazing at me in a completely new dawning light.

Fire Soul Valkyrie Astrid.

All eyes all fell on me. My lungs struggled to take in air. The moment I'd laid eyes on the journal in my hands, I'd felt inexplicably drawn to it, like I'd recognized it on some level.

Raven broke the silence. "Why is everyone staring at her? Astrid is a fairly common name, and an old one."

I chewed my lip. How was I to explain this? I wasn't ready. My mind was still so jumbled, and now this?

Muninn nudged my hand and spoke only to me. *This is the truth we sought. Don't shy away. Everyone will help put the pieces together. That's why they're here.*

He was right. "Because I did write that note."

As the words tumbled from my mouth, I knew without a doubt I spoke the truth. For months, I'd been seeking information about Valkyries and diving into the truth of the past. For almost as long as that, I'd suspected I had played a deeper role. When Huginn and Muninn confirmed what I was seeing in memories, breaking through what I now knew was a powerful magic mind shield, I never expected to find such clear confirmation as this. But now, I had it in my fingers.

Brit's brow rose. "Come again? What do you mean you wrote that?"

I took a deep breath and explained to them what I'd discovered over the last months, leaving out the specifics around Tyr. I wasn't ready to tackle that yet, nor did I think it was a good idea, unless I had evidence in front of me, to let others know before I got the chance to speak to Tyr about it.

Kirby ran her fingers through her hair when I finished what I understood so far. "Well, damn. That's a lot to handle on your own."

"Why did you shoulder that alone?" Aya asked. "This is something we could have helped with."

"I didn't mean to keep it a secret. I thought I was just doing some light, fun research that would explain what a Valkyrie actually was. Then I went down this rabbit hole, and…" I puffed out a breath. "I was so deep in I didn't know how to bring anyone in to help. I'm still surprised Baldur was able to follow along last week when I finally decided to give it a shot."

Baldur shrugged. "I didn't find it that difficult to follow your lines of thought."

Kirby shook her head. "Speak for yourself. This… wow. I thought learning Valkyries were a species was going to be the biggest mind blow today."

Brit winked. "I could grab a gun."

Kirby rolled her eyes.

"So," Raven hedged. "You're an ancient Valkyrie? Like as old as Artura and Urd?"

I pressed my lips together. "My soul is almost that ancient, yes, but not my body. None of my reincarnated bodies lived even a faction of the length of that life pre-Ragnarök. Until I started my casual research for Valkyrie information, I only had memories as far back as the Viking Age. I thought that was my first life all this time."

Caleb turned to his mother. "Can magic be so powerful that it can block memories even after death?"

Artura nodded. "Do not underestimate magic, especially ancient magic. It is powerful enough to transcend a body and attach eternally to a soul. Were I not seeing it myself with Astrid, I'd have told you it was impossible for anyone to break through such a powerful barrier. But even ancient magic has its limits, it seems."

"Does this mean others living among us could have these locked-up ancient memories?" Brit asked.

"Are you implying that more people in the world are reincarnations?" Raven said. "That sounds a bit far-fetched."

"Except you might be one of those people, too," Axel murmured. "It explains a bit more about what you're experiencing."

"But why?" she asked. "Why now? Astrid lived hundreds of years ago. I'm living now and as far as I can tell, there are no hidden memories in my brain."

Kirby shrugged. "You may have had more lives before this and no one knew. We don't know how often souls reincarnate. Hel, we don't even know why, unless they're forced into that cycle through magic, like all of Astrid's reincarnations. There are so many working parts to the world that it's impossible to understand it all. Happenings we can't explain, we chalk it up to destiny or Creation's will. Some of these things could be a result of the Ragnarök prevention magic, or it could be something else."

Caleb took the letter from Baldur and scanned it. "The note connects Astrid to Ragnarök, but also tells us she knew what was going on. Maybe this journal can shed some light for us."

I agreed.

I leafed through the old journal pages, skimming the text that was becoming almost as familiar to me as English. This was a personal journal. It had all kinds of topics from what I'd eaten on a given day, to magic I'd tried to perform. Hell, there was even a whole page dedicated to a sketch of someone's dick.

Aya leaned over the table to get a good look. Kirby and I cocked our heads as I twisted the book to understand this entry more.

"Your drawing skills weren't half bad," she complimented. "Though, why?"

I squinted at the page. "Uh, I think it's about a one-night stand I had."

Raven's brow furrowed. "Really?"

I nodded. "Something about being a great lay, but lacked any capacity for stimulating conversation."

She, Aya, Kirby, and Brit all laughed. I was pretty sure I heard Callie cackle in the other room.

I continued thumbing through. *I wouldn't have put that note in this journal if there wasn't important information in here to explain why.*

My flipping stopped suddenly, and I gazed at a rough sketch of a raven head. My eyes skimmed the page until I found something.

There is jealousy in the raven god's heart, sisters.

Everyone stopped their idle tasks to listen. Baldur stood behind me, gazing over my shoulder.

He covets a crown that is not his. He does not say it, but his actions speak it. He does not deserve the crown my beloved carries. His heart is too selfish… too unjust.

My lungs seized. This was the confirmation I sought. There was no mistaking that passage was about Odin and Tyr. All this time, the answers were here in this journal.

Baldur's fingers curled over my shoulder. "What does this mean?"

"It means Odin is a lying bastard," Kirby snarled. "Just like we thought he was."

I continued reading.

It displeases him that I love his favored ravens. He broods that they will not spy on me and my beloved as he has demanded. He seems to fear I will take them from him. They have told me all of this. How I wish I could steal their bonds. But they love him as much as they love me, and I will not make them choose.

Huginn and Muninn puffed up and crooned.

Baldur rubbed the back of his neck. "This is oddly too reminiscent of what has happened already between you two."

"History repeats itself," Raven said. "At least that's the common claim. Given the nature of Ragnarök, and the magic used to try and stop it, it's not much of a surprise that history was destined to repeat, even if slightly differently. Keep reading, Astrid."

I nodded and skimmed more.

> *It happened today. The jealousy in the raven god's heart was shown. He tried to scheme and plot, but all was for naught. None, not even his own favored son of courage, would look upon him with love. He stood by my side and the side of my other beloved, the rightful king. The raven god left with rage in his heart, sisters, and I can't help but worry for what lies ahead.*

"Son of courage," Baldur murmured. "He had no other son that claimed the courage domain besides me. You asked me if I was born after Ragnarök. Why?"

I chewed my lip. "I had a memory. Just a brief flash… of being with someone who reminded me a lot of you. And given everything I'd been learning up to that point, I thought maybe—"

"I'd also lived back then." He finished for me. He drummed his fingers on my chair. "But Huginn and Muninn confirmed that my memories of being born after Ragnarök weren't wrong."

"We are not wrong," Huginn said. *"This text is not wrong, either."*

"How likely is someone to be reincarnated into the same family line?" Brit asked. "Seems crazy Baldur would be reborn as Odin's son again."

"Given how I was born into my brother's line over and over, I wouldn't discount anything from the realm of possibility," I said.

"I've also always had the same face and name," Kirby added.

"And there was magic involved in both cases," Aya said. "Whenever you involve powerful magic, it's likely to have a heavy effect."

"This would mean I died, just like you," Baldur said. "If this is a correct assumption to make. And if I died, did Odin know I was reborn as his son again?"

Kirby glowered. "I wouldn't put it past him. He seemed to know things others really shouldn't have."

"He encouraged you to choose the path of courage," Muninn said. *"Don't you remember?"*

Baldur smoothed his beard. "Yes, that's true. When I realized I was a god who could claim a domain, I had gravitated to war first. My father had advised not to, and to go with courage and wisdom. I felt a pull toward courage over wisdom, so I combined it with war, and that worked even better. Let's see if Astrid's past-self has any more insight."

I had to flip a few more pages, as the next passages weren't about Odin or anything else useful. There were a few instances where I'd noted strange things happening. Urd and Artura confirmed those were the early signs of Ragnarök.

My fingers stopped flipping, and my eyes pinned to a passage that sent a jolt of pain through my chest.

> *The raven god has betrayed us, sisters. He has broken the sacred truce between our kind and theirs. He uses a despicable magic to enslave us, taking our power and our ability to bring life, stripping us of everything we are and making us a mockery of who we are meant to be.*
>
> *Fury rages in my heart. How dare this god touch us? How dare he think us beneath him, with a purpose only to serve his depraved whims?*
>
> *My loves try to sooth me. They try to talk me out of taking revenge and saving my kind. They fear for my life and my freedom. But my heart's burning desire for vengeance cannot be quelled. Not when he has enslaved my blood sister.*

My hands shook. My breath came in harsh pants through my teeth. All the rage and pain—from a past I could barely recall—now consumed me like I'd experienced it yesterday. Baldur tried to sooth me, but like in the past, this rage... this pain I once felt... could not be stopped.

Aya pressed her fingers to her lips. "We knew he was capable of despicable things, but this?"

Kirby slammed a fist on the table. "That fucker! This was why he always kept us on such tight leashes. If we strayed too far, he knew we'd discover the lies he'd created."

"Does the journal say who your sister was, Astrid?" Brit asked.

I hardly heard her. My vision flashed with memories and sensation. They rushed in like a flood, and I gasped for breath and grounding. So many things I didn't understand, but also did.

And then it was done. Baldur gripped my arms to hold me upright, and Kirby and Aya had closed in.

"Astrid?" Kirby hedged.

I lifted my gaze to her, tears pricking my eyes. "It was you. He stole you from me."

Kirby stared at me, the reality of my words slowly sinking in. Then her gaze shifted to the journal. "We didn't get the chance to know each other for long, and yet I felt drawn to you. You were the type of person I'd want to be my blood sister if I had one. Odin… didn't like that I was friends with you. He didn't outright tell me to stop, but he implied I shouldn't associate with you. I'd assumed that it was because you associated with Tyr, and those two always struggled to get along."

"His punishment had also been far too severe, compared to what you'd done," Aya said. "I don't know anyone who thought otherwise. Taking lovers against his wishes happened a lot with Valkyries, given he played favorites. Kirby preventing Starkad's soul from leaving his body, effectively bringing him back to life as an immortal, was a crazy happening, but not something that should have been punishable by death. Odin could have easily used that to his advantage. But he chose to kill you…"

"Because he feared I'd learn the truth," Kirby said. "If my original Valkyrie powers were starting to manifest, then it meant the magic he used was failing. That would threaten the web of lies he'd crafted, and he couldn't have that."

I took a controlled breath and grabbed Kirby's hand. "That's why he killed me, too. He knew who I was the moment he spotted me. He feared I'd unlock the past if given too much time. He couldn't allow either of us to live if he was to protect the throne of lines he sat upon."

Muninn lowered his head. *"Valkyries died by his hand."*

My brow furrowed. "What do you mean?"

Aya gasped, tears pricking her eyes at the realization of what lengths Odin really had gone to in order to keep his lies hidden. "Valkyries would be found dead. They'd go missing for a while, or were just found the next day after they had been alive and well. Odin pretended to be furious and would make a spectacle of trying to find their killers, but nothing ever came of it."

My eyes widened. "Those Valkyries were also remembering."

Baldur's hand curled into a fist. "All the Valkyries who were sacrificed in that final ritual of his when we tried to kill him, how many of them weren't actually willing, and were his attempt to be rid of more Valkyries who were breaking out of his magic snare? He knew he'd survive that ritual."

"And the moment everyone thought he was dead, the Valkyries moved on rather quickly, going about finding their own purpose," Aya confirmed. "Not that there were many of them left after that ritual. He'd sacrificed a lot of them, and that should have been a warning indicator to us all."

"Damn," Brit mumbled. "The asshole really was unhinged."

"We're sorry. We were sworn to secrecy," Huginn said. He sounded just as regretful as his brother. *"But that magic doesn't bind us anymore."*

I stroked both their heads to reassure them. I didn't blame them at all. They didn't have a reason to share that information until now, so it wouldn't have crossed their minds to say anything.

"The question remains, how did he do it?" Caleb said.

I leafed through the journal. I could try to sort out some memories, as I could feel the answer somewhere in my overworked brain, but this would be quicker at this rate. *Found it.*

> *This may be my last entry, sisters. The guardians are*
> *attempting to save us from a doomed fate, but I fear it will*
> *not be enough. The raven god has sided with chaos. He seeks*
> *what he should not have. The magic he has obtained… it*
> *is dark and wrong. The ravens say their god did terrible*

things to obtain this power. He has sacrificed his sight for this knowledge. They say he will have marks around his neck to perform a spell that will devastate the crumbling balance. I must stop him. My gods and dragon, and my unbound sisters are with me. I do not know if we will survive this. But we cannot stand idle and wait for the darkness to spread. If my fire is to be snuffed out, let it be on my terms, fighting back the darkness for the hope of a burning and bright future.

I do not wish to die, but I also do not wish our realms to perish. And I refuse to allow a usurper to sit upon a throne he is not meant to have. I will stop him from using his magic. I will free my sisters and our realms. Or I will give my final breath trying.

There was no more. Blank pages were all that was left in the worn journal, never to be used again.

The room remained quiet, everyone taking in this last entry.

"So," Raven said tentatively. "Does that mean Odin caused Ragnarök, or…"

"It means the raven god took advantage of the chaos for his own gain," Artura practically snarled. The sound was very dragonish, and also rather intimidating. "While the rest of us were making sacrifices to preserve what we could, he was taking what didn't belong to him."

"He used the memory wiping to his advantage," Baldur said. "That's how he was able to convince everyone of the power he'd taken from this other god. But how did he manage that? How did he keep his memories, or at least enough of them, that he could manipulate everyone?"

"It must have been that last spell," Aya said. "Whatever he did, it gave him what he needed."

"Myth is steeped in truth," I mumbled as I blinked slowly, processing what I could. "The sacrificing of his eye… the hanging on Yggdrasil… That all happened, but not in the way he spread the story—not in the way the fragmented minds could remember, and thus were so easily manipulated." I scrubbed my face. "My brain hurts…"

"Why don't you call it a day for now?" Raven suggested. "You seemed to have found out more than you bargained for."

I shook my head. "This is only a piece of what I was after."

She smiled kindly. "We've learned that Valkyries and gods are each distinct species. We learned there's more to your kind, which was something you were seeking. You've gotten extra answers on top of that, that unexpectedly connect to more than one question you came here with."

She and Axel looked at each other and seemed to communicate somehow without words. "We came here to help Urd and Artura with vault research. Your journal provided some insight for me to search for in these tomes. I can keep an eye out for more information on your Valkyrie questions and pass it along to you. How does that sound?"

I bit my lip. It didn't feel right to abandon this.

Baldur rubbed my back. "We need time to process all of this. I know I do before I ask more questions."

If even Baldur wanted to take a break from this, instead of diving deeper, then maybe I was being too stubborn. I reluctantly nodded. "All right, we can do that then."

Callie entered the room, her steps timid and her mouth working as she hesitated to say something. "Um, Astrid. Can I… can I pet one of the ravens?"

I blinked and then smiled, warmth blooming in my chest. That request wasn't one I thought I'd hear for a long time. I honestly didn't think she'd react so well to my raven's gifts.

Muninn hopped down onto the table and bobbed, making a happy throat noise that sounded like "La-la-la."

I was worried that him verbalizing anything, even if not actual words in the mind, would act as a trigger for Callie, but to my surprise she smiled and giggled a little. She approached with tentative steps, and reached out to touch Muninn's beak.

She sucked in a sharp breath on the contact, then relaxed as he remained perfectly still for her. Her fingers stroked his beak. Muninn, the cheeky bird he was, managed to show some affection by rubbing his beak back against her finger. That about put her to her limit for the moment, and she retracted her touch.

"Thank you," she said before fleeing from the room.

"Gwah," he quickly called back from his bird vocals before hopping back onto my shoulder.

I patted and praised him. I was also very proud of Callie. Her kind of trauma wasn't one that would go away in a few months. She had a long road ahead of her, but we'd support her in any way we could.

Kirby nudged me. "Now I can go back to kicking your ass at video games until we're ready to address the jötunn in the room."

I grinned. "You are mistaken as to who was kicking whose ass, and I'll be happy to remind you."

"I think you're both mistaken," Aya said. "It's definitely Baldur who will win."

Brit snickered. Knowing her, she was already thinking about how she'd heckle us the whole time.

I closed the journal and stood, but found it difficult to lift my fingers from the worn leather. This was a link to a past I was only just scratching. It held the key to understanding the jumbled mess in my mind.

"Take it," Artura said.

I blinked, stunned to hear those words from her mouth. She didn't like giving permission to take books. Whenever she did, it practically required a full Master's dissertation on why I needed to. "Are you sure?"

Her ancient eyes watched me. "It's not mine to keep, Fire Soul."

My heart thumped against my ribcage. Of all the titles I'd managed to accumulate over the last year, that one resonated the best.

I hugged the journal against my chest. "Thank you."

THIRTY-ONE

TYR

The cacophony of battle assaulted my ears. The wind carried the metallic bite of blood. Weapons clashed. Magic, thick and tingling in the air, exploded and warped both land and warriors. Combatants cried out, either in victory or death.

None of that mattered. I held her body carefully in my arms. One of her silver and fire wings was bent askew, the other completely gone, ripped off at the base. A gouge cut diagonally across her face, and a life-threatening one ran up her arm. Her hair, the color of blood, splayed around her like the pooling life liquid dripping from her wounds.

She gasped for breath, her stunning, soul-piercing eyes dulled with each gurgling inhale. "Tyr…"

"You can't leave me, Valkyrie." My voice quaked. I'd never feared for something more than this moment. I'd never felt pain as strong as this. "You can't die. You're undying."

But she was. The magic he used was killing her.

She reached for me with a shaky hand coated in blood. "I'm… sorry. I tried…"

I held her hand against my cheek, my mind frantically thinking of ways to save her. "We'll find you a healer."

Her lips trembled. "It's too late…"

I refused to believe that. "He can have the crown. I don't care. As long as I have you."

She smiled, tears leaking from the corners of her eyes, and what was left of my heart shattered. "I love you. I… always will. Until eternity ends."

I shook my head, my control and sanity fracturing. "I'll die with you."

"No… live for me. Until we find each other again."

Her hand slipped and the light in her eyes dimmed. I was losing her. Losing my light in the darkness—my calm warmth when the cold injustice threatened to encase my heart—the fire to my soul and my blade.

I pressed her hand to my chest, her blood smearing with mine. "I swear, on the undying life you gifted me, I will find you again."

She smiled, that sweet, loving smile I didn't deserve. "I swear… my love will be eternal… and I… will… find…"

Her words faded, as did the final light of life. Her body went limp. *No…*

Power surged in my chest and around me. My vision flashed white. "No!"

I jolted upright, my cry still projecting. Something metal clattered. My pulse thundered in my ears. My breath came out in short bursts. I flicked my gaze around, searching the living room. *Where is she?*

I was on my feet and moving before I could think. I needed to find her. Where was my Valkyrie? *Where is she?*

I shoved through a door, my vision tunneled. *I swear, I'll destroy Creation if anything's happened to her.*

Someone said my name, but I didn't process who. They didn't matter. I needed to find Astrid.

I reached the stairs and didn't recall taking them down, just reaching the bottom landing. I pivoted away from the front door and came up short. *Valkyrie.* She sat at the island casually chatting with someone, unharmed and okay.

Astrid paused mid-conversation and turned my way, her brow creasing with worry. "Tyr? What's wrong?"

Wrong? Nothing was wrong. She was here. She was safe.

I scrubbed my face. "Nothing."

Because it was nothing. This was stupid. I panicked over nothing. Astrid was in the same condition as when I'd seen her earlier today. It'd been a bad dream that I'd reacted to instead of thinking logically. *Why had it felt so real?*

"Nothing. I… just forget about it." I turned away, but halted when her warm hand grabbed mine. I looked down. She was so tiny compared to me, yet she had the strength to stop me in my tracks.

"Tyr, what is it?" she said.

I hesitated. How could I explain to her that I had panicked for no reason? *Was it for no reason?*

She was here, safe and alive in front of me. But she had died in my arms. *More than once…*

I fell to my knees and pulled her into me. Her soft and soothing scent permeated my senses, enveloping me until I could only feel her. She wrapped her arms around my shoulders the best she could and let me seek comfort in her. She didn't know what plagued my mind, yet she was still here, offering the comfort that only she could.

"Let's go upstairs to talk in private," she murmured.

I nodded and released her, even though I didn't want to. If I did, she might disappear, and I'd be alone again.

She took my hand in hers and led me back upstairs. I followed, more focused on the connection between us than where we were going. She was here. Our hands were linked and she was warm and very much alive. *It was just a bad dream.* One that was brought on by the stress of everything going on with the attempts on her life ever since I found her last year. I was just afraid of losing her again.

Because I knew this time, if she died, she wasn't coming back. After finding out what Aya was going through because of that spell, there was no way Astrid would allow anyone to use it again for her sake. *I can't lose her. I won't lose her again.*

Astrid pushed on my chest and I found myself sitting on the sectional sofa. She glanced around, where I'd left a mess of weapons in various states of upkeep and repair. Some were even on the floor. I suspected that was the source of the crashing sound when I woke up and rushed out.

She's trying not to scowl. I knew that neutral look. She hated it when I left weapons out in common areas. It was fine for my room to be however messy I wanted it, but she had stern feelings about anywhere else.

I was better these days about at least cleaning up, rather than leaving them out until she exploded in anger like her first life with me. *Second… No.* I needed to banish that idiotic nightmare from my mind.

Apparently choosing to ignore my mess for now, Astrid slid onto my lap, her legs straddling me and her hands pressed against my chest where she could no doubt feel my accelerating pulse. How could it not, when she pressed against me like this and gazed at me with those eyes that saw through all the armor I could ever use to hide behind?

"I'm going to ask you again, and this time, I'd like it if you didn't avoid answering," she said. "What's got you all freaked out?"

I shook my head. "It's nothing. Just a bad dream I reacted to, instead of allowing myself to wake up and realize it hadn't been real."

"A bad dream wouldn't have caused the utter terror I saw in your eyes."

"That's what it was," I insisted, more to myself than her.

Her fingers glided along my cheek. "Tell me about the dream."

I hesitated and then told her every detail I remembered, which was eerily close to everything. Like I was regaling a recent memory.

"See, it was just a bad dream," I insisted. "Brought on from all the stress lately and fear of losing you. I can't lose you. Not again."

Not when she wouldn't come back. "I couldn't bear it. I can't keep living in this world if you're not in it."

She framed my face with both of her hands and pressed her lips gently against mine for a soft, tender kiss. "I'm not going to die. And I'm not going to leave you. I promise you, I'm not going anywhere."

I pressed my hand against one of hers and leaned into her touch, my eyes hooding. I wanted to believe that promise. But so long as there were threats out there that wanted to take her from me, I couldn't believe the past wouldn't repeat. *Creation won't give us a fourth chance.*

I tried to banish this strange thought, but it wouldn't leave. And the more I fought it, the more a pressure in my head built.

"Don't fight it, Tyr," Astrid murmured. "Let the memories return."

"What…" A spike of pain lanced my mind, flashes of images and sound coming with it. "What's going on?"

"Memories. The ones you lost because of Ragnarök," she said. Her voice was so soothing and understanding, as if she knew what was going on.

A crack. Something deep in my mind fractured more. She did know what was going on. She was so certain about what I was experiencing. "How—"

Pain slammed my mind so hard that my vision blacked out. It came back, but not where I had just been. I was in a room I recognized, but didn't have words for. Astrid was with me, but she was different. She had no scars. She wore clothes that were foreign, yet familiar. She sat on my lap in the same way as before this mind change.

"Don't fight it." Her words came from this Astrid's mouth. "Accept the memories Ragnarök stole from you. Remember who you are, my god of judgment."

Her words flowed over me like the warmest caress, wrapping me up until I was shielded from all pain and suffering. It allowed me to let go.

The crack splintered and then shattered. Images, sounds, names, taste and touch—all of my locked-away memories—flooded into my senses. I couldn't keep up, overwhelmed. The only thing that kept me from tumbling into insanity was Astrid. She was here, being my steady rock when I couldn't be.

When the onslaught finally subsided, I was left gasping for air, completely overwhelmed yet feeling more whole than I had in a long time.

Astrid framed my face with her hands again, her touch gentle and grounding. Her visage was back to how I knew it in this life, but as I gazed at her, I saw her differently—more clearly, like I'd been seeing her filtered through a half-awake state.

"Valkyrie…" My Valkyrie. She had always been my Valkyrie, since the day we first met, when our people made our first contact with hers, and I laid eyes on the most magnificent woman I'd ever had the pleasure of viewing.

I pulled Astrid into me, holding her close, and feeling more than I could really process. "I'm so sorry."

"Why?" Her voice was so soft and caressing. "You promised to love me for eternity, and find me again. You've done that more than once now."

"I should have listened to you." I tried to think as everything over the centuries pieced together. "You told me your concerns about Odin. I brushed you off because I trusted him. He betrayed us—betrayed me. He stole…"

"Your crown and named himself king after the dust settled," she finished for me. "I know. There's nothing to apologize for. You already did when we discovered his treachery and tried to stop him. I don't need you beating yourself up over it again."

I released my tight hold and held her in front of me, gazing into her eyes. "I do need to apologize. I trusted him as my advisor. It was my failures that caused so much pain to you and your sisters. If I'd been more willing to see, he wouldn't have imprisoned them. Hel, he wouldn't have been able to work with the others like him to trick your kind into binding yourselves with ours."

I lifted my shirt and felt a scar that ran along my ribs where a sword had plunged in and pierced my heart. I once wondered why I felt shame with this one. Now I knew. "I deserved this wound you inflicted on me for my failings and breaking your trust. I should have learned then to trust your word. I should have learned not to be so blind. I always lose you when I am."

Astrid pressed her hands against the scar, her expression bittersweet. "I could have also exercised more restraint. You weren't the one who betrayed me."

"You had every right to believe I had." I closed my eyes, my mind pulsing from too much remembering. "Before we continue to act like remembering this far back is normal for us rather than new, I need to understand how you knew this was happening. Don't leave anything out. Please."

She smiled and revealed everything, from how her causal Valkyrie origin inquiry ran her down a bigger rabbit hole of information pre-Ragnarök. She also confessed how, years ago, she'd heard a theory from historians about me being the leader of the Norse pantheon, and that it was that theory that pushed her to keep searching once she started learning more.

I was a little hurt to hear Baldur had been the first person she opened up to when she felt ready to reveal something after lone-wolfing it for months. But I also understood. Even with these unlocked memories, I was struggling to keep up with her thought processes and how it led her to discover more. Baldur would have followed much more easily.

"So, when did you unlock your memories of back then?" I asked. She'd mentioned dreams and all that in her explanation of what kept spurring her on, and Huginn and Muninn confirming them as memories, but that wouldn't have given her the knowledge on how to talk to me after I'd gotten mine back.

"Two days ago, when a few of us went to the ancient library to continue my research," she admitted. "I've needed some time to process everything I unlocked before talking to you and Diego."

Diego. He was somehow involved with the past, but I couldn't place how I knew that.

Astrid kissed me. "Give your brain a rest, my king."

A king. Not of all gods, like Odin had tried to be and failed, but of our region. I shook my head. "I don't have a crown anymore. Nor do I want it."

"No, I didn't think you would. Things have changed too much for crowns to be needed. Even if everyone miraculously remembered their pasts one day, those days are over." She pressed her forehead to mine. "And you don't need a crown to hold my fealty."

I inhaled slowly, enjoying our closeness. She was the only constant that made sense. She was the light of a new dawn, when the darkness of night became too long. She was the only thing I wanted—forever. "Marry me."

I knew I shouldn't ask. Not yet. We talked about this. She wanted at least a year of dating before I started entertaining these thoughts. And it wasn't an unfair request.

"Marry me, right now."

Astrid chuckled and slid her hand down my chest. The motion shouldn't have been as arousing as it was, but given my state, I wasn't surprised. "Just the two of us here?"

"And Eternity as our witness."

She leaned in, our noses touching. "On one condition."

My heart lurched. "Anything." Anything as long as she didn't say no.

Her breath puffed against my mouth. "I want a real wedding when this is all over."

I slid my fingers along her cheek. "Absolutely."

My mouth claimed hers in a hot, mind-searing kiss. Astrid moaned and pressed her body into me, her fingers sliding into my hair. I wrapped my arms around her, pinning her to me, and stood. She instinctively wrapped her legs around my waist, but I supported her with ease as I carried her to my room.

Our kiss didn't break until I gently set her down on the bed and turned to find the item that would bind us. Tucked away in my closet was the box I'd hidden, made of rich, dark wood and detailed with masterful carvings.

I pulled it out and sat on the edge of the bed. Astrid scooted closer to peer at it. "I had this made as a betrothal gift for when it was time for me to ask you."

She glanced up at me, her eyebrow arching. I chuckled. "No, I wasn't planning on going back on what we agreed on. I just wanted to have it ready for when the moment came. Here it is."

Astrid traced the intricate details of knotwork along the edge of the box and then flipped the latch. Inside, nestled in satin, were two knives. They looked more ornamental than practical, with their silver rune-engraved onyx blades and bone hands embellished with delicate metalwork and gemstones, but that was intended. If she only wanted to display them, they'd be a stunning piece. If she wanted to use them, they'd be deceptively deadly, enhanced by an enchantment.

"These are beautiful." Her words were breathy, matching the awed sparkle in her eyes. She took one out of the box to better inspect it.

I took out the other and set the box down on the floor. I casually tested the sharpness of the blade, to make sure this wouldn't hurt her too much.

My actions caught Astrid's attention. She lifted her gaze to mine. A zap of nervous energy flowed through me from her, but I didn't see any fear or second thoughts in her eyes.

"You can say no, Astrid," I said. "If this is too fast, we can stop. There is no pressure to do this."

"I know." She swallowed. "I have come up with every excuse I can think of to justify why I needed to take all my relationships slowly, even if… even if a part of me didn't want to. I've warred with myself on what is appropriate and too fast or too slow."

Astrid took my shirt collar between her fingers and pressed the knife to the fabric. The blade sliced through with ease, as if I were wearing paper. "But the reality is, those goal posts are arbitrary when you live for eternity. Waiting won't make our bond stronger; it's already unbreakable. We've found each other over and over, no matter how hard others tried to tear us apart."

She pressed the blade to my chest. "This is what I want, my god of war and judgment. I vow to you on my soul as a Valkyrie and a witch, to eternally be your heart's shield."

The blade sliced my skin with unnatural ease, blood flowing freely.

I pinched her shirt with my fingers and easily tore the flimsy fabric without a blade. Astrid grinned. Was I lucky this wasn't a favorite shirt of hers? Maybe, but she'd ripped my shirt, so this time it was only fair.

I pressed the knife to her chest. "I vow to you on my soul as a god, to eternally be the strength of your sword and your convictions."

The knife sliced a shallow cut. Blood dripped from the wound. I slid my fingers across her skin and coated them in her blood. Astrid did the same.

My heart pounded in my chest. This was nothing like our wedding in the Viking age. But it did mirror our bond before that.

We pressed our hands together, our blood mixing, and we spoke in unison. "Our blood as our bond, and Yggdrasil as our witness, our vow of love and loyalty be eternal."

Energy pulsed from my chest and expanded. I sucked in a deep breath as it filled me. Astrid let out a quiet gasp and her eyes dilated. The energy thrummed in my veins, growing stronger and potent where we touched. My senses had never felt more alive than in this moment.

The knife slipped from Astrid's hand and she surged toward me. I dropped my knife and wrapped my arms around her. Astrid's hands framed my face, and our mouths locked.

My pulse pounded in my ears and my desire flared hot.

My witch.

My Valkyrie.

My wife.

Rolling her onto the bed, I sunk my fingers into her hair and held her down with my body, kissing her until we were breathless. "You're not going anywhere tonight."

"What if I'm needed?" she said breathlessly. "This was a bit impromptu."

"They can figure it out." I kissed along her neck, and brushed my lips against her ear. "As long as you're in my bed, you're mine tonight. Only mine."

Her breathing hitched. "And if I try to get away?"

"I'd rather you behave for me." My teeth grazed her skin. "I don't want to punish my wife on our wedding night. So be a good girl for me."

She tried to stifle a pleased whimper.

I hovered over her, my knees between her legs. I trailed my fingers down her neck toward the tear in her shirt. "What was that, beautiful? Speak up."

Her throat bobbed. "Only if you make it worthwhile to be good."

I grinned and leaned down, kissing her nice and slow until she whimpered for more. "Don't you worry, Valkyrie, I'm going to love you nice and good. Your prayers are going to be delicious."

My hands trailed along her body while I kissed her some more. Her soft skin was hot under my touch, matching the burning desire inside me. My fingers gripped the torn fabric of her shirt, and it ripped further. Astrid gasped as air hit her exposed skin. I kissed her deeper, plunging my tongue into her mouth, devouring her.

She moaned and arched into me, her own fingers finding the tear she created in my shirt. She tugged several times, the fabric giving away little by little. My veins sizzled hotter. She didn't destroy my clothes often, and I was starting to hope she'd do it more in the future. That primal need to be closer to her without barriers no matter the cost was an intoxicating sensation.

Her bra released with ease. I knew better than to ruin that. I removed it and her ruined shirt, along with shrugging off the scraps that used to be my shirt, leaving us half-naked and frantic with desire. But not for long. Her jeans ripped with only slightly more resistance than her shirt. Astrid gasped but didn't fight me stripping her naked.

I stared down at her, drinking her in. "Perfection."

Her mouth twitched, as if she found something funny. "Take a picture, it'll last longer."

I chuckled and dipped my head, my lips brushing her ear. "I told you to behave."

Astrid's hands slid up my chest. "You know I'm not good at that."

"You behave for Diego." My hand wrapped around her throat. "So, you can behave for me, wife."

She tipped her head back and squirmed under me, each moment of contact teasing. "He gives me reasons to behave. You give me reasons to misbehave."

We loved her differently and she liked that. But tonight, I wanted to love her in a way I didn't normally. My mouth brushed hers. "I don't want to pull out the restraints. I don't want to be rough right now."

Her eyes softened and she tapped my hand with her finger. "Then you need to be gentle."

My grip loosened and then I slid my hand up to cup her cheek. Her eyes fluttered in the way I saw when Diego had his time with her. I was sure she did this too with me, but it felt different this time.

I kissed her, gently and slowly, savoring her. Astrid moaned quietly. Her hand slid along my bare chest, down to the waistband of my trousers. She popped the button, my zipper next. Her motions weren't frantic or desperate, but it made my pulse quicken that way.

Then, my trousers were gone, her magic sending them somewhere, and my cock fell into her waiting hands. I groaned when she wrapped her hands around me and stroked. Slow and steady, the same pace I took with her.

My mouth trailed down her neck, my contact featherlight and teasing. Her breath hitched and she arched into me. Everywhere her body touched me, it sparked a burning sensation that made me feel like a live wire.

My hands traveled along her body, feeling her every curve like I'd never felt her before. I tasted her skin like I'd never had the pleasure of feasting on her. I listened to her sighs and moans and quiet begs for more in a way I'd never heard her so clearly. It was like I'd lived life with her half awake. And now that my eyes were opened, I wanted nothing more than for our souls to fuse for all eternity.

I slid my fingers between her thighs, trailing them along her soft flesh and feeling how wet she was for me already.

Astrid arched into my touch. "Please, Tyr."

She whimpered when I continued to tease her. "Please, my husband."

I groaned. Creation, had I longed to hear her call me that. "You're so beautiful when you beg."

She sucked in a breath through her nose and swallowed. "Please. I'm being good."

Her begs whispered over me as prayer. I felt it tangle into my essence. "You are. You're so good for me."

I slid my finger between her wet folds, quickly finding her clit. She gasped and arched. I stroked and played, watching the pleasured expressions she gave as she enjoyed my touch.

Dipping down, I kissed her, and she met me with a hunger I wasn't expecting. Her arms wrapped around my neck and she tangled her fingers in my hair. Her tongue grappled with mine and we devoured each other until we were gasping for breath and the desire in our veins threatened to catch us on fire.

Astrid moaned and tipped her head back when I slid my fingers inside her begging pussy. "Yes, please give me more."

"How could I not, when that pretty mouth of yours begs like that for me?"

Withdrawing my fingers, I slid inside her with barely a missed stroke of sensation for her. Astrid's mouth fell open and her eyes hooded as I filled and stretched her. Unable to hold back anymore, I braced myself over her and thrust, hard.

Astrid moaned. It rumbled deep from her chest, vibrating into me. Her pleasure called me. Each moan, each beg for more, it drew me deeper and deeper into my desires. Rhythmically I thrust, feeling her clench tighter and tighter around my cock, milking me closer to the edge.

Balancing with my arm, I reached between us and found her clit. Astrid gasped and jerked into my touch, thrusting me deeper into her, making her moan. Her legs wrapped higher around me, and she rocked her hips. The added sensation undid us both.

Astrid arched into me. Her nails dug into my back, the pain delicious. A scream tore through her and her body convulsed. Her pussy clenched hard around my cock. My pulse roared in my ears, deafening me to my own sounds as I crested over the edge, and spilled inside her.

We stilled, gasping for breath. Euphoria pulsed through my body, as did a deep craving for more. Astrid hummed appreciatively, her fingers sliding along my back. I swore I felt that connection buzz between us.

I dipped my head and nibbled her ear and neck. She giggled. "Is my war god finally ready to play?"

"Hmm…" I sunk my fingers into her hair. Her breath hitched. "Is my Valkyrie ready for me to play?"

I'd had my moment of gentleness with her. Now, after the prayer she gave, I was ready to claim her with stronger love.

"Please." Her voice was breathy with a hint of desperation.

I grinned against her neck, then pulled away. Gripping her hips, I flipped her over with ease. Astrid inhaled sharply and her fingers gripped the sheets. Sliding my hands over her ass, I enjoyed the view she presented me.

Astrid glanced over her shoulder and wiggled her ass, earning her a nice smack. Her gasp was delicious. I wanted more.

Tangling my fingers in her hair, I pulled. She gasped again, her mouth parting as I made her look up at me. I grinned and then surged deep inside her. Astrid moaned, her fingers gripping the sheets tighter, and her eyes closed.

I thrust into her hard again. "Look at me."

Her eyes fluttered but she didn't comply.

I wrapped my free hand around her throat, yanking her hair harder and slammed into her. "Look. At. Me."

Her eyes snapped open, and our gaze met.

"I love you."

Her mouth twitched with amusement. "I love you, too."

"Good. Remember I do, because I'm about to fuck you like I don't."

Her breathing hitched and her eyes went wide. That was the last I saw before I shoved her face into the bed. Pinning her head and gripping her hips, I slammed into her.

Astrid let out a strangled cry, her fingers scrabbling at the sheets. I pulled out almost all the way, and thrust back in, hard. Over and over, I fucked her strong and hard. She gasped and moaned. She jerked against my hold, sometimes writhing in pleasure and other times fighting me.

When her hands flailed around helplessly for a little too long, I snagged them with my massive hand and pinned them together behind her back, giving me total control over her.

"Tyr," she moaned. "Tyr."

"That's it," I panted out. "Keep taking my cock like the whore Valkyrie you are."

I fucked her until my senses were frayed and she was a begging mess. My orgasm suddenly exploded through me. I came hard, filling her greedy pussy with hot cum. After several more punctured thrusts, I stilled, breathing hard, and released my tight grip on her.

Astrid let out a slow breath and half turned to look up at me, her eyes pleading. I grinned and gave her what she wanted, sliding my finger between her dripping folds and playing with her clit. Her orgasm rolled over her quickly. I held her down as she thrashed and screamed, and didn't let go until she came down and was a panting, twitching mess.

After taking a few controlled breaths, she rolled onto her back and smiled at me. It was such a relaxed, languid smile that didn't match her words. "More?"

"More?" I chuckled and leaned over her. "Greedy today, aren't you?"

She slid her fingers into my beard and tugged me down lower to kiss me. I didn't resist, enjoying the gentle feel of her on my mouth after I'd been so rough. "You told me I was stuck in bed with you for the rest of the day. And I'm quite certain you weren't insinuating sleep or playing board games."

"That is true." I kissed down her neck. I couldn't go another round for a few more minutes, but that didn't mean she couldn't. "Be prepared for me to break our previous record."

She sighed and arched into my touch. "With how much daylight we still have, I hope seven isn't my peak."

I was up for that challenge. I wouldn't stop until our bodies demanded rest. And I held myself to that.

Hours passed before we hit that point.

I gazed down at her blissful sleeping form curled into me, my fingers trailing through her damp hair. Satisfaction hummed through my body, both from the sex and this new connection. I felt her in my senses. It'd been overpowered in the heat of passion, but now that I was calmer, I could feel whatever it was knitting us together.

We'd done this before, in her true first life, but I couldn't recall what it did exactly. The answer was somewhere in my head, but the memories were all jumbled up. It was those memories that kept me from falling into sleep alongside Astrid before we made love some more.

In the silence that settled in, my memories started piecing together. It was all still confusing, but I wasn't rushing to figure it all out. I'd learned from watching Astrid piece her memories together that rushing the process made things worse.

The pieces coming together now were of a time where the Valkyries and we gods were making an alliance of sorts. We both were to benefit from it.

My hand touched the large scar on my ribs. I knew somehow that hadn't gone as planned at some point, but the memories of what exactly happened weren't piecing together quite perfectly. I just knew Astrid's fury had been justified. *Was her name Astrid back then?* I didn't have anything yet to tell me. I called her Valkyrie all the time, just like now.

Another memory clicked into place. I had gained something big in the alliance exchange. How my power worked had changed from this. How all gods got their power had changed. We became more powerful from our worship, but we also were more reliant on it.

And I'd gained something physical. A piece of their land—realm… where were we from, exactly? That information had yet to sort itself out, but Midgard—this realm—was not it. That much I felt for sure, for some reason. *I need to talk to Aya.*

Glancing down at Astrid to be sure she was asleep, I carefully slipped out of bed. Hopefully she wouldn't wake before I returned, or I'd be in a shit load of trouble.

Throwing on some clothes, I searched for the goddess, finding her in her room with Baldur. By room, I meant her actual house in Norway. Like our door, Aya's also now acted as a portal.

They were in her living room, with several old books between them.

Aya gasped and then glowered. "You asshole. You could have waited."

Baldur's brow lifted. "Waited for what? You told him he could come in when he knocked."

I chuckled and made myself comfortable on a couch. "Don't get angry. I promised her a full ceremony."

It took another moment for Baldur to clue in. "Oh! Wow, I thought she was going to make you wait longer. Congratulations."

He truly was happy for us. I saw it in his smile. There was maybe a little jealousy, but he and Astrid were still fresh in their relationship. It may take longer for them to reach that step. Or maybe not. It depended on whether my bond to her now changed things.

"She did ask for a year before you proposed," Aya said. She was watching me with unmasked suspicion. "What changed? And why not have an engagement for a while?"

"I remembered."

I let the words sink into them both.

Aya's eyes widened, all her irritation vanishing. "You remember pre-Ragnarök?"

I nodded. "My memories are still piecing together, but I'm certain it's all there."

She sat forward. "How? How did you do it? I haven't had a single inkling, and Baldur hasn't worked out anything, either." She paused. "You do know how Baldur fits into all this, right?"

I nodded. "Astrid told me everything she'd learned, after I'd had a memory leak and then everything came flooding back to me. It's been an unusual day."

"But you don't know what triggered it?" she asked.

I shook my head. "Beyond me questioning what I've forgotten every now and then, I didn't really pursue those missing memories. It just came to me."

"Maybe Astrid was some sort of trigger," Baldur mused. "She began leaking memories when she was digging in more. It wasn't until we found a journal of hers that she unlocked everything. Maybe that has some sort of effect on those around her with blocked memories."

The theory had merit, especially with the type of Valkyrie Astrid was. But my remembrance felt so sudden. Could she really have that kind of power, even if she didn't know herself?

Aya huffed in frustration and leaned back. "If she's a trigger, why are we not getting any inklings, either? We were there when she got her memories back. And the two of us are actively trying to remember based on these books Artura loaned us. But Tyr got his back on a whim."

"Maybe it's so I could talk to you about something specific," I said. I'd come here with a goal. "Something that can help us win this brewing war. And maybe this knowledge will help you remember what you forgot."

Aya squinted at me. "I'm listening."

THIRTY-TWO

ASTRID

My fingers glided over the worn journal page. Two stunning cats had been sketched out, from a few angles. Flipping the page, I found a diagram comparing their size to a few things. They were huge. From what I could compare, possibly the size of ponies.

Kirby looked up from the book she had nosily peered over. "You really liked to draw."

I nodded and flipped another page. There was more handwriting here but still, a sketch of these cats dominated the page. My journals were filled with pages like this, and my memories would flash to the front of my mind, remembering when I would sit down and passionately sketch or paint. "It's interesting seeing how similar I am to this past version of me, but still so different."

My sketches weren't anywhere near as nice in this life. I didn't quite have a passion for the medium. But, I could make something pretty cool from wood, so that creative passion managed to stay alive in some way.

I glanced over at the book in Kirby's lap. "Have you found anything interesting?"

She shrugged. "Maybe? This appears to be some sort of transcript of important meetings that were held. Most of what was discussed in these meetings doesn't make sense without more context around events going on during those moments, but the word 'ascended' comes up a lot. It appears to be used as some sort of title."

My eyes squinched as I tried to dig up the memories related to that. I winced when pain lanced my brain. "Guess that's a *not today* memory."

Kirby snickered. "Maybe soon."

Even though I'd broken through the magic and recovered my memories, there were still times I was finding the magic held strong and fought my attempts to piece together the fragments. It was why we were still going through any library finds we could. Plus, even if I could remember everything, I was only one person. There was no way I'd have all the answers from the past.

Kirby nodded to my book. "What does this journal talk about?"

Raven had miraculously found two more journals that belonged to me. She hadn't realized they were mine, just that they were in the Valkyrie language, but after getting my hands on them, I knew they couldn't have belonged to anyone else.

"It's my thoughts about my first meeting with Aya and getting to know her." I flipped the page. Yet another drawing, but this time of Aya petting one of her massive cats. "Bygul and Trjegul too."

Kirby's brow arched. "There's no way that's them. Those cats are way too big."

I shrugged. "From all these notes, their personalities match. Besides, there are too many stories of her cats pulling a chariot; there has to be some hidden truth there. And what Norwegian Forest cat can pull a chariot?"

Kirby laughed. "Okay, fine, I can follow the logic. But why are they so small now?"

I shrugged. "Magic?"

She rolled her eyes at my cop-out response. She then set her book on the coffee table and picked up the other journal. "Have you gone through this one yet?"

I shook my head. "No, but why don't you? Maybe it'll help you unlock your memories."

Tyr and Diego were still the only ones who had unlocked their past memories alongside me. Aya and Baldur were trying, but they weren't making progress. Kirby really suffered on the remembering side, too. She was sometimes experiencing physical pain when she tried. I worried it was a side effect of the magic Odin had used to bind her. *I really hope her diving into these books will help.*

Kirby's lips twisted. "You sure you want to risk that? I might see sketches of your guys' dicks in here."

We laughed. Past Valkyrie-me definitely had no shame. I'd found three more dick drawings in my first journal after I'd gone back to the skipped-over pages. All of them were of men I'd been with as one-night-stands, or for a short relationship.

"Don't act like you haven't seen Baldur's or Tyr's dicks in the past. And I caught Starkad with his pants down many times."

She shook her head. "They have no shame."

That was an understatement.

The door opened, and a lively burst of chatty voices echoed down the hall. A moment later, our Valkyrie sisters, along with Dahlia, Brit, and Lucia walked into my home. Lucia appeared to be animatedly telling some story to them.

I looked at my phone and saw the text I'd missed from Mia, telling me they were here and on their way up.

Lucia's story cut short when they entered the living room. Those who hadn't been here yet gazed around. I was happy to see they'd all shown up, especially the stunning woman with pale skin and jet-black hair in chic business attire, Brigid. The high-profile executive queen she was, she ran a hugely successful humanitarian aid organization. As a result, we rarely got to spend time with her. *But I was told this super-special event couldn't be missed, so I'm glad she managed to sneak in the time.*

"Nice place," Brigid said. "You know how to live in style, Astrid."

That wasn't a jab. Even though she helped people in need, Brigid never begrudged people for living comfortably. She also knew how hard I worked my angle to help people, even if it'd turned more toward the supernatural community lately, where hers was people as a whole.

Dahlia jumped onto the sectional sofa next to me and wrapped her arm around my shoulder. "Rumor has it you'll have to start thinking about expanding."

I shushed her and practically launched off the sofa to make sure they'd closed the door. They hadn't. "Don't let the dads hear you say stuff like that. I swear to Creation it gets worse every day."

The women laughed. *Everyone* knew of our dads' obsession with being grandparents. They loved Birdy and Bard to pieces, but it wasn't enough. They wanted a gaggle of grandchildren running around.

Magnus made herself comfortable on the sectional. "Well, my nuggets need cousins to grow up with, and no one else in a permanent relationship right now but you wants to admit they eventually want kids too. So hurry up."

I rolled my eyes. "It'll happen. Just not right this instant. I'd like to get through the whole 'my mother is a cult priestess and causing problems' issue first. Then I can see about my upgraded timeline of life events, including family planning."

I nudged Dahlia. "Besides, we need wolf-dragon babies to complete the wacky family tree we've got going on."

"Yeah, you both have to make up for what I can't do," Azzie razzed.

"Hey!" Dahlia smacked my arm and pointed a warning finger at Azzie. "Don't you be dragging me into this, bitches."

The room filled with more laughter.

"How many would you want, *hermana*, when the time comes?" Lucia asked me.

"I'm thinking three or four," I admitted. "But who knows what Creation might have in store."

Kirby snickered. "You mean what Tyr has in store for you. Because let's be honest, he's going to want three or four... or seven, himself."

I fell back into the sofa as I laughed. She wasn't wrong.

"I still need to understand how bad the grandbaby obsession is for your dad," Brigid said. "Since I only hear about it in the group chats."

I blew out a breath. "Let's put it this way, when Aya spilled the beans about Tyr and me having our impromptu elopement ceremony before I could say something myself... I swear, stabbing my dad in the heart with a god-killing knife would have been a kindness. Whereas, if I didn't have any partners and got knocked up by a one-night stand, he'd be putting on a party all of Midgard could attend. Why his priorities are this way, I cannot fathom, but that is my dad in a nutshell."

More laughter filled the room.

Tatiana, a tall and slender, statuesque woman with rich black skin, lifted an old book off the coffee table. "Have y'all learned anythin' new from all this reading?"

"Not much," I admitted. "But we've only just gotten started today."

Scarlett, a curvy bombshell blonde, leaned on the back of the sectional sofa. "I'm still trying to wrap my head around what you've already shared."

After some discussion with Kirby, we decided it was a good idea to bring the others in on the secret. Artura had also relaxed some of her grip on her book-loaning rules for the Valkyrie-related books, on account of them technically belonging to us, especially now that I'd gotten most of my memories back.

"Are you sure that was the TL;DR version?" Dahlia asked.

I rolled my eyes. "Trust me, from what I've got ping-ponging in my brain, yeah, it's the TL;DR version. If Huginn and I could figure out how to project these memories to others, we definitely would."

Elin, a pale woman with wavy copper hair, looked around. "Where are your familiars? I always thought at least one of them was glued to your hip."

I chuckled. "No, luckily I do get to reclaim my personal space from time to time. Angel went off with Diego and Caleb to visit Callie."

"Why did they bring Angel?" Azzie asked. "I know she's a therapy dog and all, amongst other jobs, but can she actually help Callie in these visits?"

Mia tipped her head toward Azzie. "You've never actually experienced Angel's help first-hand, have you?"

"Nope."

I smiled. Mia, on more than one occasion, had utilized Angel to help her through an emotional difficulty. "Angel is very good at her job, especially so now that she's an ultra-intelligent familiar."

"She has this way of just making you feel so much better, like she's taking away all the chaos of negative feelings storming inside you," Mia gushed. She paused and blinked. "Actually, it reminds me a lot of you, Astrid."

"Most familiars are an extension of their bonded partner," Tatiana said. "The magic used reshapes them, penetratin' their essence. Astrid's magic and personality influence what Angel is potentially capable of. It's why every familiar is different, and why they're so prized amongst witches, beyond the rarity that something is capable of handling the bondin' magic to be our familiars. I'd about die if I found the perfect partner to make my familiar."

"You said most are an extension, not all, what do you mean by that?" Elin asked.

"Non-beast ain't the same."

Azzie squinted. "Non-beast familiars? What are those?"

"You know, like fae, shifters, demons, all them."

I blinked. "I didn't know that was possible."

To be fair, most witch knowledge was obtained by passing it down through a coven or something similarly named. If a coven were to die off, their cumulative knowledge would disappear if they hadn't passed it to someone else.

Völva didn't operate in covens, though. We passed our knowledge within the family, but it wasn't common for more than two or three völvur to be alive at any given time in a family, immortal family members aside. And völvur didn't engage in the practice of familiars, so it wasn't a knowledge that was passed down. I only got on this path of having them because Aya had shown me how.

Tatiana nodded. "It's not a common practice, as it's more complicated and there are even more rules around it, but it does happen. There's a coven in Nevada who is known for the practice. Last I heard, the current matron has an incubus partner and her daughter has a vampire."

Elin nearly choked. "I'm sorry, did you say vampire? Those are real?"

"Called it!" Lucia said, a little too excitedly.

Tatiana blinked. "Y'all didn't know?"

"To be fair, they're rare," I said.

Brigid shuddered. "And nothing like the stories."

Eyes shifted between the three of us. There had been a reason Louisiana had a lot of vampire superstitions, giving Tatiana and her family ample knowledge, and Brigid, while not a fae to our knowledge, was connected to her Celtic roots. I knew due to my unique living situation, being part of a sanctuary.

"Vampirism is a fae infection that only befalls humans," Brigid shared. "No one knows how the first human contracted it, or how it continues to crop up when all vampires are thought to be eradicated. We only know that it spreads through bites when someone survives an attack. It turns the person into a feral, blood-hungry beast. It's a horrible affliction."

Mia, eyes wide, swallowed nervously. "Um… so, what's the cure?"

We didn't answer right away, but it was Tatiana who spoke the grim word. "Death."

Silence. No one scarcely breathed.

"That can't be the answer," Elin finally said. "There has to be a real cure other than them dying."

Tatiana shook her head. "'Fraid not. Once the infection takes over, the feral nature will drive the vampire to attack anything until someone comes along and puts them out of their misery. A familiar bond can stop the infection spread, which is why those rare ones that are still sane are always familiars, but the moment that bond is severed, the infection spreads again."

Melancholy fell over the room. It was a bleak situation for those poor people. But there weren't always magical solutions to save people from something so unfair.

Dahlia clapped her hands together, her energy surging. "Astrid, tell us what you use the ravens for."

I wasn't sure if she was actually interested in the answer, but it was certainly a good distraction. "Well, they're not therapy birds, that's for sure. Those two would rather be annoying instigators than help."

Laughter rumbled through the room. No one had been spared from these birds' antics.

"They still prefer to do what they did for Odin, and spy on people."

Brit's brow rose—not with skepticism, but of piqued curiosity. "You're spying on people?"

I held up a finger. "With great power comes great responsibility that I don't wield properly."

My sisters laughed. I grinned. "I love the soap opera drama they bring me. It's entertaining. And the ravens love it, too, because according to them, Odin was way too serious about the spying and wouldn't let them have this kind of fun."

"Well, don't be stingy, ¡*suelta la sopa, hermana*!" Lucia's eyes practically glowed with excitement. She loved good gossip. "What's your favorite segment? Are they gathering the gossip right now?"

I hummed and felt out the connection. "Yep, they're still in Italy, collecting on one of our favorites. There's actually two I love a lot."

Using my magic, I conjured an iffy image of three older women. I still wasn't great at projections. "We have the three nonnas, who are Neighborhood Watch badasses that we're convinced are secret super-heroes. We're eager to catch them in the act of crime fighting. On their 'off-time,' they're on the cases of their very handsome grandsons about not getting married. Their attempts to set them up are hilarious."

I altered the image to show a large man with tattoos. "Then we have Priest Theo, also known as Archangel by his biker gang. When he's not hitting the road on his prized motorcycle, he loves to garden and play with his teacup yorkie rescue. He also helps with the homeless and battered women's shelters. Oh, and he delivers justice and punishment to abusers and rapists when the system fails their victims."

"That method doesn't sound very priestly to me," Elin mumbled.

I winked. "I never said what kind of priest he is."

"He could be my priest any day." Brigid fanned herself. "I vote him for my favorite and offer my temple as tribute."

The others laughed and whooped.

"I think, for a fair vote, we need to see these three grandsons from Italy," Tatiana said.

Lucia held up a finger. "And, if they have a sister who's single."

I laughed. "Actually, one of them does, and she's more stubborn than all three of them."

She rubbed her hands together. "Excellent."

Brit nodded her agreement.

Before I could show off the nonnas' grandchildren, a fluffy cat trotted around the sofa. Tuggy hopped up on the coffee table and sat in front of me.

"Hey, girl," I greeted, scratching her under the chin.

Her eyes closed and she purred. When she'd had enough, she pulled away, yet stayed sitting, staring with those eerily intelligent eyes.

I bent forward to get a better look at her. "Tuggy, I was doing some reading in this journal, and it has some interesting information. So, I have a very important question for you. Are you really a skogkatt? Are they more than just a story, and now you're forced by magic to be this tiny version of your true magnificence?"

She blinked those intelligent eyes slowly. Then she trilled and booped me on the nose with her paw before jumping down and trotting off for the door. I sputtered on a laugh with the rest of the girls. *That felt like a confirmation to me.*

"I guess we're being summoned," Scarlett said. She was looking down the hall. "She's staring back at me from the door."

"Finally," Dahlia said dramatically. "Now we can find out what's up with all the secrecy."

I couldn't blame her. I'd asked Aya several times what she was up to when she told me this morning to prepare for a fantastic surprise.

I tidied up the books on the coffee table and we all filed out into the retreat home. When we made it to the kitchen, Tuggy was up on the island counter with her sister. I gave them each a good scratch on their heads. They enjoyed it, but when I finished, they didn't move. *Odd.*

I figured we'd be led somewhere else by one of these two. Nothing was special about the great room, and both cats enjoyed leading others around. It was quite comical, really, especially when they decided you just needed a good walk.

The door to Dad's room opened, and both he and Aya walked out. I pursed my lips. They'd been spending a lot of time together privately ever since he promised to help her find a temporary solution to her impending death until we could find a permanent one.

I shook my head. I didn't want to know.

Aya snickered. "What's wrong, Astrid?"

"Nothing."

"You sure?" She slung her arm over my shoulder. "I think there's something on your mind."

"Nope. I don't want to know."

Aya hip-checked me. "I know you're dying to know. Just ask."

"Nope. Nope. Nope. I don't want to know."

Dad's massive hand came down on top of Aya's head and he shoved her down as he passed. "Leave her be, Freya."

My brow quirked up. *When did he start calling her that? And why?* I couldn't imagine it was part of keeping her alive. Otherwise, we'd all be doing that.

Aya grinned at his back. "Why don't you make me?"

Dad shook his head and headed down to the basement level, calling back as he went. "Hurry up. We're going to be late."

"Oh, but I love taking my time," she said in a throaty voice.

I gagged. "Stop it! I don't want any gross images in my head."

Aya grinned at me. "I can promise you, they're anything but gross."

"LA-LA-LAH!" I stuck my fingers in my ears.

"Don't be that way, Astrid," Aya shouted. "I've got plenty of fun stories to tell you."

I threw my hand out and clamped it around her mouth. She licked me. I made a grossed-out face and rubbed her saliva on her face. "Bitch."

She batted her eyes. "Love you, too."

The girls around me cackled at my expense.

Aya then hooked her arm around mine and dragged me toward the basement. "Now, we really will be late if we keep goofing off."

"Are you going to tell us what's going on yet?" I asked.

"Nope. That'll ruin the surprise."

I huffed and didn't fight her. We moved through the recreation area downstairs and out the door. I noted how empty the place was. There should have been plenty of residents utilizing this space. But it looked more like when we only had four residents, including Tyr, last summer—completely empty.

And when we stepped outside, there was no activity. Not even the children. This was not right.

"Does anyone else feel like we stepped into The Twilight Zone?" Magnus asked.

Dahlia and Tatiana both hummed the theme song, making us laugh.

"Don't question it, just follow," Aya said.

I huffed. Normally I didn't mind surprises, but this… this bugged me for some reason. Maybe it was because *everyone* was acting weird. Even Tyr and Baldur were clearly in on this, because they were doing the same stuff. Diego was the exception. He'd been just as out of the loop, and almost considered not going with Caleb to see Callie because of everyone being weird.

Buggy and Tuggy bolted past us at top speed. They didn't run in a straight line either, stopping suddenly and changing directions at times. *Someone has the zoomies.*

After a while of walking through the woods, I realized the direction we headed. *Why are we going to the glade?* The questions continued to pile up.

Dahlia looped her arm around my free one. "So, I've been dying to ask something. Well, a few things."

My eyebrow arched. "Have you? You look fine to me."

She rolled her eyes while the others laughed. "This… eternal bond thing you did with Tyr, it can't be accidentally done, right?"

Interesting question. "Uh, not that I'm aware of. It's basically a blood vow, but we both had to actively participate."

I looked to Aya for confirmation to be sure I was right. I might have a lot more memories in my head, but a lot of things were still instinct-driven.

She nodded. "*Enthusiastic* consent is needed."

"So, no finding yourself accidentally married after a wild night in Vegas, good to know," Brigid said.

"No, that's an accidental immortal pregnancy because Creation thinks it's funny," Magnus said.

We laughed.

"Next question," Dhalia said. "Are you just eloping or do we get to attend a real wedding?"

"Definitely a real wedding," I said. "It was part of my condition."

"Good, because I had ideas."

I smiled. "I absolutely want help in my planning. It'd be fun."

An excited clamor rose in the group.

"Related question, are you planning this with Baldur and Diego? Maybe it's too soon for Baldur, but I figure I need to ask because you never know. And is it going to be multiple weddings or one big wedding?" Dahlia lobbed at me at a dizzying pace.

"Um…" *How to put this.* "Baldur and I haven't had any discussions yet. Diego and I had a conversation a few weeks ago about a dragon mating ritual, but we agreed at that time it wasn't the right time, and haven't yet revisited the conversation."

I planned to; I wasn't avoiding it. Tyr and I had only been bonded for a few days.

Dahlia tripped on nothing. "I'm sorry, did you say *dragon mating ritual?*"

Mia and Azzie closed in, their attention intense.

Hmmm, yeah that was about the reaction I expected. "Yes."

She stared at me, goggle-eyed. "Well? Are you going to say any more?"

"Um… I don't really know much. Diego wasn't totally clear on it, which was part of the reason we put it on hold, but it's some sort of intense feeling dragons and phoenixes get, and then when it happens…"

Magnus grabbed my arm. "Phoenixes, too?"

I nodded. "I guess it's some special thing they can do. Dahlia has probably felt the one Xavier and Urd have. Diego said it's something only you guys can feel."

"Wait, that's what *that* feeling is?" Dahlia said. "It's like feeling a flashing neon sign. You know how weird it is to *feel* a neon sign?"

I laughed. It sounded weird, that's for sure.

"Is this bond something I can see?" Scarlett asked.

I thought that over. She'd called me the day after Tyr and I bonded, asking if something had happened. Her abilities had shown that my connection with him had changed. She couldn't tell how, due to the distance, but it was different and not something she'd seen before. She was curious rather than worried. "Your gift is rather unique, so it's possible you can."

Azzie poked my back. "So, what is this bonding, exactly? Is what I feel with Zeke, and Mia has with Caleb, the start?"

Dahlia gasped. "It better not be. I'm not mating with Magnus."

Magnus made a face. "Because Dahlia hogs the bed."

Aya cackled. She was finding this unfortunate situation I'd found myself in far too amusing.

"I don't think Dahlia and Magnus have anything to worry about," I said. "I'm confident the bond between you two is unique."

Dahlia pursed her lips. "So… I still have to worry about this with someone else?"

I shrugged. "I don't know. I don't know what triggers the need. I only understand that the longer we're together, Diego feels this increasing need to create a mate bond with me."

The entrance to the glade came into view. Diego and Caleb were standing outside chatting with Dad. Angel sat at Dad's feet, enjoying a scratch behind the ears. She was the first to notice me and barked. She then rushed over and greeted me as happily as any dog, but the feelings she pushed into me were even stronger. Diego smiled that sultry, panty-melting smile of his when I was able to focus on him again. I slipped away from the girls to give him a hug. He kissed me on the head.

"How was the visit?" I asked as I pulled out my phone and stored it in one of the available baskets.

"It went well." His tone was warm and affectionate. "She's showing the same progress you saw the other day. It was great seeing her smile and be happy."

"She really loves Angel," Caleb said as he pulled Mia to him. "Bringing her was a good call."

"Maybe we can look into getting her a dog if she likes the idea," Mia suggested. "A companion and protector might be good for her."

This conversation filled me with more satisfaction than I could tell them. I wanted nothing more than for people to heal, and as long as they didn't close those doors of opportunity when they presented themselves, anyone could.

Aya convinced everyone to store their electronics and move along into the glade. When we filed into the glade, I halted. There was a crowd of people. Most were residents or those living in town, but some were others we knew outside, like friends in Runavík. Tyr and Baldur were among them. Even Ronan and Thac were here.

That wasn't the only thing to catch my attention. The glade had been decorated. Everything was organic and alive. *Clearly fae-made, but why?* Was there a party about to happen?

"Why does it feel like we've just ushered you to your wedding?" Dahlia murmured as eyes turned to us.

I shot her an alarmed look. "No."

Aya rolled her eyes and scoffed. "Please, I wouldn't do that to her. She'd at least get *some* say in that."

"Gee, thanks, Aya." Sarcasm laced my words.

She grabbed my arm and dragged me forward. "C'mon, you're going to love this. Trust me."

The crowd parted, revealing a lineup of nine wooden posts about the height of a table, with cloth covering something slightly bumpy on them. Ùna, Sean, and a few fae stood behind the posts, smiling at us. Tyr moved to stand with them but more off to the side, as if he were clearly involved, but the fae were the center of this whole surprise.

Aya had me stand in front of the post before Ùna, then she pulled each of my Valkyrie sisters to very specific posts of their own. All the other ladies who accompanied us were ushered into the waiting crowd, as were Dad, Diego, and Caleb, and then Aya stood by Tyr. *Okay…*

I blinked when Huginn and Muninn suddenly landed on my shoulders. "Good timing?"

"We promised not to be late," Huginn said. *"We were not."*

"Promised who?"

"Me," Ùna said. "Are you ready?"

"I guess? I'd love to know what I'm ready for, though."

She laughed, as did many others. "This is something special we put together. It started out as just us fae, as a way to thank you for the kindness and hospitality you've given to us. For not seeing anything wrong with our flaws or choices. For loving us in ways that our other closed-minded cousins could possibly not."

She smiled. "Then, we thought it best to extend this to all you Valkyries, for everything you've done for not just us, but everyone you've helped."

Ùna gave a side-eye to Tyr. "Then the gods had a plan that worked perfectly with ours, so we combined them."

She and the other fae grabbed the cloth coverings. "Please accept these humble gifts as a show of our thanks."

They yanked the covers off the posts, revealing round shields. I blinked slowly and then grasped the shield in front of me. The moment I lifted it off the post, the wooden structure pulled down into the ground, like some video game. All that was missing was the theme music telling me I'd secured a special treasure.

The shield, while made of white- and gold-painted wood with what looked to be a solid silver backing, was surprisingly light. In the center was a domed silver boss designed to look like a sun. The rays branched and formed into a wolf, dragon, and a pair of ravens. The tip of the north sun ray split down, creating Tyr's rune. A colorful array of gemstones decorated the silver and a silver rim finished the shield, engraved with Norse and fae runes.

Magic pulsed from the shield. Protection... something else... something... deeply familiar. My soul began resonating the longer I held the shield.

A brief glance around revealed to me that all of my Valkyrie sisters had a shield. Theirs each depicted something unique to them. *Every shield is personalized.* The fae had gone out of their way to learn about each of us so they could show such strong appreciation.

My fingers glided over the surface of my shield. Love and hard work seeped everywhere, so palpable that my soul felt it. Emotions twisted in my chest, choking my throat and threatening stinging tears in the corner of my eyes. "I don't... know what to say..."

The other Valkyries didn't, either. They each appreciated the gift as much as me. And we'd have been foolish not to.

Any object augmented with magic became stronger when gifted. As corny as it was, love was an easy and strong emotion for magic to bind to, amplifying it every time love was involved. An item passed down many times through love was a rare but powerful artifact.

But this was especially so with fae magic. Emotion had a strong impact on fae magic, and when they worked that emotion into an item and then offered it with emotion, the magic intensified. Silver and other pure elements also acted as excellent conduits, which only fae could work with.

"Thank you…" I said.

The gathered fae smiled, shimmered, murmured, and reacted happily in their own way to our gratitude.

My fingers continued to trail along the silver details as if I felt compelled to do something, yet I didn't know exactly what. The sensation on first contact had grown, but I didn't know what it was. No one was explaining what magic lay in these shields, as if they expected us to figure it out.

I wasn't the only one still exploring a shield. Every one of my Valkyrie sisters seemed just as compelled as me.

My eyes half closed and I twirled my finger around the boss. My Valkyrie power pulsed and then bloomed out, my magic flaring. I gasped and took a step back when the magic formed in front of me and then solidified into a woman.

She was my height, with matching red hair and green eyes. Dark makeup dusted her face, making her both alluring and dangerous. Her dress and jewelry were just as old as the memories I had of her.

The shield slipped from my hand and crashed to the ground. "Mom?"

THIRTY-THREE

ASTRID

My mouth fell open. It couldn't be her… It couldn't be my mother Randi. And yet, it was.

Her lips pulled into the warm smile I could never forget. "Astrid."

Her voice. I always feared I'd forget it, as time continued without her.

"Look at you, Sunshine." She lifted her hands and framed my face. My heart skipped. Her touch was warm, as if she were really here. "You're as beautiful as ever."

Tears stung my eyes. "Mom!"

I threw myself at her, colliding with a solid body. She wrapped her arms around me and I cried like a damned baby, my hands clutching her dress desperately. I'd lost her too early, and it'd been all my fault.

It was my fault there'd been a battle. It was my magic failing that kept me from saving her. It was because of me that she left my life when I needed her the most.

Mom hushed and cooed, rubbing my back in the soothing way she always had when my emotions got the better of me. "It's all right. I'm here."

She was. She was really here. For me. It was the one thing in my life I'd always craved. And I now had it.

Eventually I got myself calmed and under control. I wiped my tears away, still sniffling a bit. "Thank you Creation for magic makeup, so I don't have to look like the mess I feel right now."

Laughter rippled through the glade.

"I'm happy to see you," I said. "But also really confused. What's going on?"

She wiped a smudged tear from my cheek. "I'll let the gods speak on that. It's quite the situation they created."

I turned to look at Tyr and Aya. This had something to do with them. It made the most sense.

Aya crossed her arms. "You make it sound sinister. We're doing a fascinating thing here." She smirked. "Besides, it was due to Astrid's meddling that we were able to make this possible."

Kirby nudged me with her elbow. "Who would have thought that quirk would come in handy."

I laughed. "So, what did you do?"

"You reminded us how we were connected to the afterlife," Tyr said. "Or, you reminded me that I still was and needed to reclaim what Odin stole."

I blinked slowly. "You said you didn't want your title back."

He nodded. "I don't. There's no need for it. However, I made an oath when I was given what we now call Valhalla, to always protect those in my care, and in return I could call upon them, with a Valkyrie's blessing."

I glanced at all the spirits who stood before us. Some didn't go to Valhalla though, like Mom.

Aya smiled. "I remembered that promise as well."

"It's like the myth," Mia mumbled. "When Ragnarök came, Odin would call upon the warriors of Valhalla to fight."

Aya nodded. "Yes, and it's that story that had us thinking how true that could be."

She approached and touched Elin's shield. It briefly pulsed with magic. "When we learned the fae wanted to provide you a gift, we devised a plan to combine our magic that would resonate with a Valkyrie's power so that we could uphold our promise. It required us to connect each shield to one soul who was willing to act as an adviser of sorts. Because I was already trying to communicate with Randi about questions having to do with your magic situation, Astrid, I was able to find a few souls willing to take that mantle."

"Once I remembered what I needed to, and took back my mantle from Brit's guardianship, I was able to help," Tyr said. "Though I will admit, reconnecting after Odin severed my connection wasn't easy."

I wouldn't assume it was. I couldn't imagine what they had to do in order to make that stick. Odin made his attempt, but his was unnatural, since he wasn't the rightful guardian of Valhalla.

"So, every soul here volunteered to help one of us?" Scarlett said.

"We wouldn't be here if we hadn't, *cherie*," the tall black man with Tatiana said. He had his hand affectionately wrapped around her shoulder, as if the two knew each other.

The woman standing in front of Scarlett smiled. "This connection is paramount. None of us can say why, as the magic of Ragnarök makes it difficult for us to communicate, even with this special magic making this possible. But I promise you, this is a good thing."

A stunning fae woman, who had the most elegant flowers growing in her hair, stopped inspecting Mia's amazing wings—*Did she ask Mia to do that?*—and spoke up, her voice gentle, like raindrops. "Not all of us are from those places your gods are connected to. That's how important this is."

I looked to Mom, who smiled. "You are following the correct path, dear. You've always been good at that."

I swallowed the lump forming in my throat. I knew my random choice to dig into the past had become something more important than I could have imagined, but being told it was the right path that we needed to take meant more than she knew.

"So, what does this mean?" Azzie asked. Her arms were crossed in front of her chest, and there was a bitter edge to her tone. *That's strange, does she have a problem with this?*

"It means you can call upon us whenever you need our guidance," the man in front of her said. "And, should you require the aid of war-riors, you only need to summon us."

My heart skipped and I looked at Mom hopefully. She smiled as she nodded. "They're all eager to heed your call."

I wouldn't cry. I wouldn't cry. I'd done that enough. But the very thought of seeing my father, brother, and all those I loved in the past once again, threatened the waterworks. I scooped up my dropped shield and held it close. It was now possibly the most precious thing in my possession.

"So, does this mean Brit no longer has anything to do with however you connected her to Valhalla?" Kirby asked Aya.

It was Tyr who spoke up. "Not exactly. We worked something out where she'd still be connected as a way to help both Aya and myself. It wouldn't be right to outright take that from her after the lengths she's gone to protect it all this time. Especially since it should have been me doing so."

I smirked. "She's an honorary Valkyrie, then."

My sisters cheered at that suggestion. Brit rolled her eyes, though I was pretty sure she was trying to hide her embarrassment. *She is one of undying, and a pure soul. This trust is right.*

My eyes fluttered. That was a weird train of thought. But, it felt right, too.

"So both of you gods can speak with the dead?" Brigid said. "Is that a unique thing for you?"

Aya blew out a slow breath. "That's complicated. None of us have ever had to communicate with those who've died. When Diego gave me the idea weeks ago, I just knew I could do it. As it turns out, the magic used during Ragnarök puts limitations on us. I can't speak to just any departed soul. They must be attached to Folkvangr, and I must ask the right questions."

Tatiana tapped her lips. "So even if the dead are in another place, we can still talk to them? You're saying the dead don't have the same restrictions talkin' with each other? Cool."

"The path you currently walk will lead to more answers," her advi-sor said. It was cryptic, but we'd been warned the advice might be.

"So, what makes things so special for us Valkyries?" Azzie asked. "Why do we need to be involved? What does it mean that a Valkyrie's blessing is needed for this to happen?"

When no spirit answered, she blew out an annoyed breath. However, I chewed my lip. Something nagged me, like I knew the answer.

Mom placed her hands on my shoulder. "You do know. You just need to piece the memories together."

I focused in and tried to find those still-shattered pieces, only for pain to lance my brain. I winced. "Not today, I guess."

She shook her head. "Don't give up so easily. I know you have it in you."

That made one of us. I didn't have much confidence in myself these days.

She frowned. "I hate seeing you like this, Sunshine. I see the doubt. You've always doubted yourself when you shouldn't. You are an exceptional witch, and an even more spectacular Valkyrie."

Was I? I definitely didn't feel that way. Not with me still so messed up. "What is wrong with my magic?"

The way she gazed at me, she was bothered by the way I worded myself. "Nothing, Astrid. There is nothing wrong with you."

I let it leak out—the dark, icky tendrils. "Yes there is."

She shook her head and her own magic came out, in the same way mine did, and the same color. "No, dear, there isn't. Because this is the source of our most powerful magic."

The floor dropped from beneath me. "What?"

She exhaled slowly. "As you know, our family had access to magic for generations before you or me. That is true of our family line even before Ragnarök. But... our magic wasn't always offensive. Most of our women were seers, healers, or defensive witches, like your current father."

I glanced behind me, finding Dad had moved closer, as did my cousin Randi, to take in this important piece of family history.

"It wasn't until one of our ancestors traveled to a distant land and brought back a wife with exotic features and unusual magic, did things change."

I swallowed. "She was a native of this land, wasn't she?"

Mom nodded.

I chewed my lip. "Was that common?"

She shook her head. "No. Not many traveled this far, at least not for a long time."

Not for a long time. She meant long after my mortal life would have ended back in the Viking age. Not until our people started setting out for places like Iceland and beyond, searching for new, better land and riches.

"So, she was a follower of Malsumis, then?"

Mom nodded. "Yes. She converted to our ways, but kept her connection to Malsumis as she claimed it was her source of power."

That might explain how Malsumis' influence managed to get to Europe, even in small amounts. Not even Odin's influence was able to spread like that, despite his hard attempts.

"So, her magic influenced the family's magic?" I asked.

"Yes. The magic-gifted daughters she bore were able to use the same magic she possessed, even though they were not raised to have that same connection with their mother's goddess." She let out a slow breath. "And they were not subjected to the insanity that befell their mother."

My heart lurched. Was that the fate for all who used Malsumis' magic? "But why weren't they also affected?"

Mom took in a deep breath and then took my hands in hers. "For the very same reason you couldn't be corrupted. Your Valkyrie soul."

I blinked rapidly. "I beg your pardon?"

She laughed. "Our family is blessed to be descended of Valkyries."

I opened my mouth but nothing came out. Valkyries… beings who could create shields and had healing capabilities. Some even had seer abilities.

"Witch got your tongue?" Kirby teased.

I smacked her, making the others laugh.

"I can't say whose line we come from, as much as I wish I could," Mom admitted. "But know this, you were born to this line for a reason after your sacrifice."

My brow furrowed and I looked at Kirby, who also looked perplexed.

"Did we have kids?" Kirby asked. She almost sounded concerned, not that I blamed her.

"I don't think so." I thought really hard. "I don't have any memories popping up that shows we did."

"Did you maybe have another sister?" Mia asked.

Kirby and I stared at each other, concerned by the prospect. Did we? I thought even harder, only for pain to lance my brain. "Guess I can't know yet…"

Fuck, this block was frustrating. All the information was right here in my head and I still couldn't reach it.

I sucked in a tight breath through my nose. "Before I get mad for no reason, Mom, please explain to me what's going on with my magic. It was gold in my life with you, and when I discovered my witch powers in this life, it was gold here, too. There was one black tendril, and now that Malsumis got her claws in me for a moment, that's all I've got. There is something wrong."

"There is nothing wrong with your magic," she insisted. "At least, not in the way you think."

My brow furrowed. That didn't make any sense.

"Your magic isn't corrupted, Astrid. It's just out of balance, like the rest of you."

I pursed my lips. "What do you mean?"

"Tell me, who are you?"

My brow furrowed. "I'm Astrid."

"Yes, but *who* is Astrid?"

Who… who indeed. I had been questioning that very thing these last few days. *Who am I, and what is a Valkyrie, really?*

She smiled gently and tapped my chest with her finger. "The answer lies within you, Sunshine. It always has. You must break through that wall you've imposed on yourself."

Imposed on myself? No, my issue was a magic block. *Stop lying to yourself.*

The words rattled around in my skull.

I was lying to myself. I made up excuse after excuse instead of actually facing my issues. I blamed everything on my weakness and failures, when… the only thing I was failing was myself.

Closing my eyes, I took a long, slow breath. *Who am I?*

Astrid.

Witch.

Valkyrie.

But what did that mean? What did those words truly mean?

My heart slowed and the world around me faded, but not everything. The connections I'd built flowed around me, all having purpose and strength, like a thread in a web.

I felt my Valkyrie sisters. And I felt my family. I felt my three lovers, and all those I would die to protect. Again.

I had gone after Odin for his crimes against those I loved. I found out what else he was trying to do, and put my life on the line to save everyone else from the atrocity he was about to commit. I failed.

No.

Delayed. I was merely delayed.

Because even though he tried to kill me, many times, I was one of undying. That was the gift we Valkyries had before we bestowed it to others. And only we Valkyries knew what that truly meant.

What does it mean?

It meant a responsibility—a curse to those who were not ready—a madness for those who were weak—a power for those who were meant to be.

A burden—an acceptance, to never rest and see the fields of Elysium as those we protected could.

I sucked in a deep breath. Power pulsed deep inside me, growing stronger and stronger. *I am… Astrid.* I was always Astrid. Every life, no one could take that from me. And that made me…

A kind and gentle healer.

A fierce protector.

A gifted witch.

An unbreakable Valkyrie.

I am Ascended.

The power exploded. Warm and radiant, overwhelming and soothing. Familiarity and longing.

I reconnected with myself. My true self. Who I am, not who others thought I should be. Not who I made myself believe I needed to be.

What did it mean to be Astrid? What did it mean to be a witch? What did it mean to be a Valkyrie?

Myself, in all its imperfect perfections.

My eyes snapped open and my wings flared behind me. My feet were no longer touching the ground as I hovered. Magic coalesced around my hands—one side gold, the other black. My wings flapped, golden fire now consuming the once plain gold feathers.

Gasps echoed through the glade. My Valkyrie sister stared at me with surprise and wonder, and probably the same disbelief that I had.

Mom gazed up at me with the proudest smile, her arms spreading in a sweeping gesture. "Behold, the once lost Ascended Fire Soul Valkyrie, now found and freed."

My heart pounded strong in my chest. *Ascended. Fire Soul.* Those titles, of all the titles I'd ever been given, felt the most right.

Huginn and Muninn flew around me and Angel barked like mad, making an excited racket. As I looked at them, I saw them differently. All three of them. Two ravens, larger once, when the magic was more plentiful. And one dog, massive, with the top half of her head a skull, a gift from my dragon once before, faithful and powerful until her last breath… until she found me again.

My magic wrapped around them, gold and black trailing off them like wisps, showing me these versions, seeping into them as my familiars, and empowering them as I now was.

I landed, tucking my wings close to my back but not putting them away. They didn't feel so heavy anymore.

"What. The. Hel," Kirby said.

I laughed. Genuinely, I couldn't help myself. "Surprise?"

She laughed with me. It was so stupid. This wasn't a time to be laughing, yet here we were, nearly about to fall over.

When I finally got myself under control, I looked at Mom, who smiled at me. "Why is my magic still different? It should be all gold, shouldn't it?"

"Should it?"

I blinked slowly.

"Malsumis may be one originator of our power, but that power isn't hers. It is ours to mold. Your magic is different in this life because you are not the same Astrid you once were. You are so much more, my daughter. Embrace it. Embrace every side of you and be the unstoppable force you are meant to be."

Emotions swelled in my chest. She was right. That was all part of me accepting who I was. This new look to my magic was its true self. The self it wanted to be months ago, but I couldn't see it yet.

"So, uh, what exactly is an Ascended?" Mia asked.

I smiled, the memories flowing far more freely now. "It's a state that all Valkyries dream of achieving. We become one when we understand ourselves to the fullest and accept it."

"What it means to be a Valkyrie…" Kirby mumbled.

I smiled. "You were right all along. That meaning is unique to each of us."

"So, we all can become this?" Scarlett asked. "And do we take on this same look?"

I squinted as I pieced the memories together. "Yes, and no."

They laughed.

Tatiana looked to Mom. "You knew, didn't you? How? How do you know what an Ascended Valkyrie is? How did you know all this stuff about Astrid when she only just recently found out she's a reborn Valkyrie? How would you know all this when you died ages ago?"

Mom smiled at her knowingly. Being dead had its perks, it seemed. We just didn't know what they all were.

And that was okay. Those answers would come in time. We just had to be patient.

All of the spirits' forms flickered.

I frowned. "Time limit?"

She gave me a bittersweet smile. "This will not be the last time we see each other. I am always here to help you. You only need to call."

She placed a gentle hand on my chest over my heart. "And remember, souls don't break, they bend."

I nodded. "I'll remember, Mom."

She and the souls faded, and with it the magic in the shields went inert. My own power faded, and my magic around me and my familiars dissipated.

My heart lurched, the pain of losing her rearing up. I took a steady breath and grasped the vertical handle of the shield. She wasn't gone. She never had been.

As a Valkyrie, we were always connected to the afterlife. Even if we could no longer reach that place physically, this was proof it was still there. *I will find our realm again.*

I closed my eyes for a moment, letting that thought sink in. I would help the guardians find those, if they ever called on us. Change was coming, it couldn't be stopped. We just had to make sure we were ready.

THIRTY-FOUR

ASTRID

The rock I poorly skipped sunk into the dark lake water with a *plunk*, my magic lights barely enough to keep it visible for a moment before the darkness took it. Discomfort churned in my chest as I watched it disappear.

Unsettling thoughts plagued me, mixing with conflicting, unrelated ones that left me confused and uncertain. Unable to sleep because of them, I'd hoped coming out here and skipping rocks would help sooth me. It usually did. But I wasn't so lucky this time.

This shouldn't be so difficult to come to terms with. After everything I'd gone through and accepted, and everything I understood, these decisions shouldn't have weighed on me so much. But they did. Like a rock sinking to the bottom of a lake.

I grabbed a flat stone from a pile collected by some of the fae children to make rock skipping easy for people, and skipped the rock. It jumped the usual three times and then sank into the dark abyss.

I tipped my head up, gazing at the dark, new moon sky. Stars twinkled, and the luminous band of the Milky Way arced across the sky, its ethereal glow painting the night with an otherworldly luster.

The movement of a shooting star streaking the sky in a brilliant arch of light caught my eye. When I was a child, I would have wished so many wishes on that falling meteor, believing it could perform magical miracles. Now, I only wished I could believe in that kind of magic.

I could laugh. I was surrounded by magic and wonders beyond my imagination just a year ago, and here I was, wishing for those simpler times back.

A twig snapped.

I turned away from the lake, my senses calm. Nothing could pose a threat to me here, not even the wild animals that could roam, unobstructed by the barrier magic.

In the dark of the night and forest, a soft, flickering light danced and swayed. As it emerged from the forest, it grew in brightness, illuminating the outline of a man—a man with glowing blue eyes.

My magic lights hovering around me slowly floated toward the approaching person until they lit up Baldur's face. He paused to gaze at the light before continuing his approach.

I tracked him, unable to look away from his eyes. He must have been answering prayers before coming out here. I hadn't seen his eyes glow like that in so long. The corner of my lip twitched. That was a sign I liked to see.

His lips quirked into a smirk. "Enjoying the view, Sunshine?"

The question broke the spell on me, and my gaze trailed down his impressive physique. He'd forgone a shirt again even though the night was on the chilly side, and gray sweatpants slung low on his hips. From the outline barely visible in the dark, I was pretty sure he'd gone commando tonight. *Does he do that often, or had he thrown some pants on before coming out here?*

"Always," I said. "What are you doing out here?"

"Looking for you," he said. "Huginn appeared in my cabin, complaining you were still thinking too loud on your late-night walk and I needed to help. Then he left to try and get some sleep."

I rolled my eyes, making him laugh. The familiar bond made it very difficult to hide my thoughts. I honestly wasn't even sure if I could. I wanted to, because my familiars deserved rest and didn't need to be dealing with the chaos of my mind.

Baldur stood next to me, watching me stoop to grab another rock to skip. He was quiet until after I tossed the rock, this one managing to skip four times. His fingers trailed the ridge of my wings. I shuddered, desire sparking. "Did you go flying?"

I shook my head. "Even with the lights I can make, flying at night is too sketchy for me. I just... have them out."

He smiled. "Not so heavy anymore?"

"I guess so." I hadn't really thought about it, but now that I was, having them out did feel more natural than before I ascended yesterday. Before, it felt more like a farce to have them, whereas now, the very idea of not liking them seemed so absurd.

Baldur brushed my cheek with the back of his finger. "What's wrong? What's got you up this late skipping rocks in the dark?"

I blew out a heavy breath, my shoulders slumping. "A lot of things. The big decisions are weighing me down, and I don't know how to handle them all."

"Tell me, then, no matter how chaotic," he said. "I'm sure I can help."

I was sure he could, too. I just didn't know if I was ready to talk about it. "There's a lot in my head. I'm still struggling to focus on one topic."

Baldur held out his hand. "Then maybe walk with me while you do that?"

I smiled and entwined my fingers with his. He guided us away from the tranquil lake, into the forest. A mournful hoot of an owl echoed in the distance. Unseen nocturnal animals and fae skulked around in the shadows, barely detectable except for the occasional crunch and rustle of leaves or snap of a twig. Not even my lights and Baldur's lantern caught glimpses of them.

Baldur and I didn't speak as we walked, just enjoyed each other's company. His presence soothed me, the chaos in my mind quieting. I leaned into him, wrapping my arm around his, embracing the comfort that came with the calm. The things bothering me ordered into a line of importance and possible actionability.

The heaviest subject remained a giant weight, and I still didn't know how to handle it.

We passed some cabins and turned down a path. I blinked slowly when we came to Baldur's place. A warm, inviting glow emanated from the lights inside.

I nudged him. "This was your plan all along, wasn't it? Lure the unsuspecting Valkyrie with the promise of comfort and safety, and then trap her."

He chuckled. "You weren't supposed to figure it out so soon. Now I really can't let you go."

I gasped when he suddenly lifted me into his arms and hauled at top speed for the door. I laughed and struggled against his grip, knowing he was too strong for me to break away from without magic. The door slammed shut behind us, and the living room flashed past. His feet thumped on the hardwood floor, carrying me to the back of the cabin.

I squeaked when he unceremoniously dropped me onto the mattress of his unkempt bed. I pushed my hair out of my face and propped myself up by an elbow. "Jerk."

Baldur snickered and loomed over me, his hands on his hips, thumbs tucked into the waistband of his sweats. He seemed to be thinking about shoving them off, but wasn't for some reason. I folded my wings away and made myself comfortable on his bed, waiting to see what he'd do.

When he continued to watch me, I spiked an eyebrow. "Are you going to drop those pants and get comfortable and join me, or keep standing there like you're lost?"

"How do you know I don't sleep like this?"

I snorted. "Yeah, and my hair is blue. You threw those on when an annoyed bird pestered you at"—I checked my phone—"three A.M. Now get your ass in bed."

He grinned and his pants dropped. *Yup, went commando.* I took great pleasure in checking out every visible inch of him as he climbed onto the bed that he made look small instead of the sea of mattress it was.

Baldur laid comfortably on his back and then pulled me halfway onto his chest. "Now I've trapped my Fire Soul Valkyrie."

I grinned and laid my head on him. "You say that like this wasn't my plan all along to get my god of courage naked and in bed."

He lightly tugged on my flimsy tank top and yoga pants. "But, you're still clothed."

I walked my fingers up his chest. "If I give you everything, instead of slowly feeding you what you want, it's harder to keep you compliant."

He captured my hand and pressed it against his lips, his eyes never leaving mine. "For a taste of your radiance, I'll be as compliant as you wish."

My heart fluttered. I smiled and trailed my fingers down his face, along the vertical tattoo so few would ever be bold enough to carry. "I missed that look."

"What look?"

"The one where I'm the only thing in existence that matters even after you've answered hundreds of prayers." I lightly rubbed his cheek with my thumb. "Especially when your eyes glow after answering all those prayers. I really missed that."

He was the only god I'd met to have such a strong reaction to prayers where it had a visual effect on him. It happened to him in our first life, too. Tyr sometimes would have a temporary glow when he received a prayer, but that was usually only when I gave him a special prayer during sex.

Baldur's was only cosmetic, it didn't actually give him any advantages like seeing beyond his normal sight, or seeing in the dark, but that never seemed to bother him. *We never did figure out why it happened.*

Baldur grinned and cupped my cheek. "Because you are the most important person in my life, Sunshine. When you were mortal, I'd have laid my immortality at your feet given the chance. I'd walk through the hottest flames, just to hold you. I'd reject recovering any past memories if it meant I never had to leave you again."

Warmth spread through my face and my heart beat a little faster. My eyes hooded and I leaned into his touch. "I want you to remember. Everything between us makes so much more sense now that I remember it all."

"I wouldn't mind having them, but I don't need those memories to understand why we make sense. And I can just keep making new ones with you."

I smiled and laid there with him, a comfortable silence falling over us. His gaze would unfocus and then return, the glow around his eyes intensifying little by little.

My clothes went missing at some point while we laid here. Baldur's hand had slowly worked my shirt off me. I hadn't fought him, and enjoyed the warmth of his skin on mine. So much that I slipped the rest of my clothes off. There was something comforting and extra relaxing about cuddling naked in a non-sexual way with your partner.

My thoughts sorted out the longer we lay here. I was able to brush off things that seemed like big issues but really weren't. I also figured out how I'd handle other problems, down to a good plan to tackle them. That only left two things in my mind, and they were a bit more complicated.

"Thank you." I resisted a pleasant *zing* when Baldur's fingers casually slid down my back. "Even though you aren't doing much, you just being here has been really helpful. Huginn was right to bother you about this. I don't know why you make these things easier; you just do."

Baldur ran his fingers through my hair. "I'm always here for you. I'll listen to every problem you have, even if I have no idea how to help."

I propped myself up better to look at him. "There is one big thing weighing on me that I do believe you can help with because of experience. It may be a difficult topic even for you, just so you know."

He tucked a few strands of hair behind my ear. "Tell me everything on your mind. I'm listening."

"How…" I blew out a slow breath. "How did you come to terms with siding against your father, knowing the intent was to kill him?"

He sucked in a sharp breath through his nose and sat up, bringing me with him. "That… wasn't easy, but also in a way it was. I think my relationship with my father is about as complicated as yours is with Ingrid."

I chewed my lip. "I don't have any memories of her being a good mom. Dad said she was the perfect mom for the first couple of years, but I don't remember that far back. It's not like anything traumatic happened to me, unlike my previous lives, when I died at those young ages."

I traced a tiny circle on his chest with my finger. "She's a horrible person. Everything she's done…" I sighed. "There are just some people who can't be helped with therapy. And she's one of those people. I could never break her away from Malsumis, because she'd never want to. She revels in the power she has and what Malsumis asks her to do."

My actions ceased. "I may call her my egg donor and wish she'd just disappear or die on her own, but going out of my way to try and make sure she stops breathing… I… I don't know if I can do it. Therapist training aside, where I'd be horrified by half the things I've had to do since becoming immortal… including contemplating if murder is okay, Ingrid is my mother. I just…"

My words failed me. I didn't know how to describe this conflict within me. I didn't care anymore that I didn't have her approval. I didn't care that she saw me as some failure. None of that mattered to me anymore. That part of me that cared stopped the day I chose those I loved over her in that bunker. I knew she was an evil bitch who needed to be stopped. *So why can't I come to terms with needing to take the ultimate action against her?*

Baldur slid his hand over my hair. "Odin was a good father when I was a child. He was attentive and loving, to all of his kids, truly, and honestly, even looking back now, besides how he treated the Valkyries, he made for a good leader. He actually tried to fill the role that he'd stolen."

Baldur frowned and my heart sank at the sight of the lingering heartbreak that was in him. "That all changed when my mother died. It was like she was the only thing keeping him from succumbing to insanity."

"Maybe she was," I mumbled. "Maybe that was part of the price Odin had to pay for his treachery and she kept it at bay."

With a small nod, Baldur continued. "The problems I had with my father started slowly, and only appeared in private, never public where it'd tarnish his reputation. At first he'd become more nit-picky about how I, as his perfect son, should present myself. Then things gradually got worse until my father, in a fit of rage, called me a worthless, imperfect son, unworthy of his affections and my mother's last ounce of love in her dying breaths. It… it devastated me to hear that from his mouth."

I frowned, my hand sliding along his cheek. "I'm sorry you had to hear that."

"His treatment of me in private grew worse until he went from loving father to a strange, unhinged man who wore my father's face." Baldur closed his eyes for a moment. "That's when I made my decision to side against him. I thought he'd killed my love for him, which made that choice easier, but as the fateful day loomed closer, I knew it wasn't a lack of love that drove me. It was because I still loved him, in a sad, twisted way, that I had to do it. I had to save him from himself, even if that meant he had to die in order to be saved."

I nodded slowly. He really had been in a similar position as me. His thoughts even reflected my own in many ways.

"I do admit, it's hard knowing Odin lived through that when he shouldn't have, and, not only returned, but caused so much trouble in the process. And it bothers me a little you had to resort to cursing him because there was just no way to kill him. I'm not sure if I'm hopeful he'll finally learn his lesson, or pity him for the isolation he caused himself."

"I'm sure it's both, which isn't wrong to feel," I said. "As much as he's caused me problems, I would like to see him become a better person. I could learn to move on from the past and his transgressions if he truly strove to better himself and genuinely apologized to us. I'm just more cynical and not so optimistic that'll happen."

Baldur slid his fingers through my hair. "Did this help?"

I shrug. "Maybe? It's nice knowing you went through similar struggles, and that you seem to still feel the emotional gambit of that choice all this time after, but I don't know yet how I'm going to come to terms with the decision."

"Why don't you pray? You can pray to me to help."

I grimaced. "You know I don't do that. It's always felt weird to pray to gods when I know them. I only do prayers and blood sacrifices to help with power boosts, but they're always done as rituals, not personal calls."

I also couldn't admit to him that I never felt worthy of asking for favors from them. I had struggled with that this life and my Norse life prior to meeting the gods. I always believed those prayers belonged to someone better. That feeling only grew worse after knowing the gods. It was like knowing them made me less worthy to make such requests.

"Try."

Blowing out a breath, I thought about it a moment and then figured it couldn't hurt. It wasn't like I could embarrass myself.

I closed my eyes and took a deep breath before praying. *Baldur, please hear my prayer. I ask for the strength and courage to make the right decision that will have irreversible results. I ask for the courage to snuff out the life of someone I'm supposed to love and be loved by, but do not and am not. I ask for strength to protect those she would otherwise harm should she continue to be left to her own devices.*

Something warm and wet trailed down my cheeks. I didn't have a right to ask this of him. I needed to find my own strength somewhere and buck up. This was what needed to be done. There was no other way.

I'd failed to get through to her when she abducted me. I wasn't good enough, or she was in too deep. Both, really. It wasn't like I'd been at this therapy stuff very long outside of school. And my schooling couldn't help me now. This issue was beyond that. *And I'm too weak to make the choice that's needed.*

Baldur's thumb brushed over my cheek, swiping the stream of tears trickling down my face. As he touched me, the turmoil inside me began to quiet. That creeping fear of making the wrong choice slipped away. In its place, a strong warmth grew. I felt stronger. Not invincible, but like I could make an appropriate decision.

My eyes snapped open and I gazed up at Baldur. "What did you do?"

He smiled. "I can't answer your prayer; that would be too self-indulgent since I told you to pray to me. But I don't need to answer your prayer to help you. My power doesn't come in the form of giving others courage. It comes as a suppressant or enhancer of fear."

I blinked slowly. I never asked him how his powers worked. I didn't know why. Maybe I'd just assumed courage was courage, no matter where it came from. But I was glad to know now. And I didn't hate how he did it.

The warmth in my chest solidified into steely determination. He wasn't giving me false hope or strength. He was just muting my irrational fears, allowing my true feelings to surface like they needed to. *This is what I have to do to save her.* It wasn't the ideal solution, but we had no others. And sometimes… the person we wanted to save, couldn't be.

I framed Baldur's face with my hands and kissed him. "Thank you."

He tucked his finger under my chin. "I will give you whatever courage you need to stand up to the evil that threatens this realm and the next. You need only ask."

His lips pressed against mine again and I kissed him back. My hands slid up his chest, my pulse picking up. I felt so much better than I had in a while. The weight of the unfortunate task still loomed over me, but the conflict of choice wasn't suffocating me anymore.

"What was the other thing bothering you?" he murmured against my lips.

"You."

He jerked back, his brow furrowed, and I laughed.

"Not in a bad way," I insisted. "I've been thinking a lot about your pain situation and how we can better help you, since temporary shields are only going so far."

"Oh." He leaned forward. "Tell me, Sunshine, what nefarious plots have you been making on my behalf?"

I laughed more. "Don't be so dramatic. I'm not thinking up anything drastic." I paused. "Okay, it might be drastic, but it's not nefarious. I might have figured out something. Might. I can't guarantee it."

I really wasn't sure if it'd work, which was half of the conflict I'd been dealing with. The other half of the conflict… well…

I chewed my lower lip. "There's a catch. Something permanent needs to happen, and I need your enthusiastic—"

"Yes."

I choked on a laugh. "You don't even know what you're agreeing to."

He cupped my cheek with his massive hand. "I will marry you through an unbreaking vow."

My heart thumped hard in my chest and my mouth dried. It took me a moment to find my words. "Just like that? You want to bind yourself to me on the slim chance this crazy idea of mine might work?"

I couldn't be sure my theory was correct. I just was going on gut instinct. When I bonded with Tyr, I felt something inside me change. Like a piece of me filling and changing as a result, as if I was truly becoming whole. I felt him in me, like a presence. It wasn't overwhelming, but it was comforting.

"I don't give a damn about this idea of using it to block pain." The strength and conviction behind his words startled me. "I had you for I don't know how long before I lost you because of my father's transgressions. I almost had you again when we reunited. I waited far too many centuries to tell you my true feelings. You were the woman I wanted to come home to after war and fall to my knees and worship like a goddess.

"I waited for you, when I would have never waited for anyone else. I was so desperate to find you when I lost you a second time, when I wasn't even there to protect you like I should have been."

The intensity in his gaze sent my heart racing. "I haven't been more sure about a decision in my life than now. My love for you has never faltered, and it never will. I promise I'll never leave again, and stay by your side for eternity—if you'll have me."

Emotions tightened my throat. I swallowed them down and nodded. "That's what I want."

He smiled and brushed his thumb along my cheek. "To think, it was you I feared all this time."

"Are you still afraid?"

There was no hesitation in his reply. "I willingly offer myself to your flame."

He kissed me, soft and slow and sweet. My heart swelled. Just a few weeks ago, I'd have thought this decision crazy. The very idea of binding myself to someone I'd only just started dating *was* crazy.

But Baldur was right. Our situation was different. And if I had gotten over my mortal concepts of relationships and how fast or slow they should go, I didn't doubt I'd have done this sooner with Tyr, and Diego too, rather than make a year become some random goal post.

"Does this mean I don't have to live alone anymore?" he asked when our mouths finally parted.

I smiled. "You never had to. All you had to do was ask, and I would have moved you closer."

He dragged his thumb along my jaw. "No, I mean with you. Do I get to live with you and the others?"

Ah. Yes, that was a bit more complicated. "We'll have to build you a room, but I think we can accommodate you until that happens."

"Good, because I'm not keen on living so far from my wife."

My heart fluttered. Sucking in a steadying breath, I summoned the daggers Tyr had given me, and offered one to Baldur. He took it, but then set it down beside him before climbing out of bed. I was tempted to ask him what he was up to, but he moved with purpose to his dresser. He rummaged around until he found a small box. He opened it and pulled something out, then put the box away.

I tipped my head when he sat back down on the bed. He grabbed my hand and placed something in my palm. It was an amulet of a sun, with runic lettering engraved into the rays.

"This was my mother's," he said. "I had it made for her, in hopes it would help cure her of the mysterious ailment afflicting her. It didn't work, but even still, she never took it off, except on her deathbed, asking I take good care of it. I'd wished at the time she'd kept it on her until the very end, but now I'm glad I get the chance to pass it on to you. I know you'll cherish it like she had.

My throat closed up and my lip trembled. Was I crying? *Dammit.*

I unclasped my necklace and slid the amulet onto the chain. It settled in next to the pendent Diego gave me. The moment the amulet touched my skin, a wave of strength and rejuvenation rippled through me. The enchantment on it was as strong as ever. *Now it's stronger, with how many times it's been gifted.* "Thank you. I promise I'll cherish it forever. For both of us."

Baldur smiled brighter than I'd ever seen him before as he wiped my tears away. I had vague memories of Frigg pre-Ragnarök, but nothing after, and I wished that weren't the case. I'm sure we would have gotten along so well, and she would have been so proud of the man her son had become.

Baldur picked up the dagger again. "Ready?"

I held mine so I could draw his blood and nodded. "I vow to you on my soul as a Valkyrie and witch, to be the eternal flame of your soul and ever-burning light in the dark."

The blade sliced his skin with ease.

Baldur pressed his knife to my chest. "I vow to you on my soul as a god, to eternally be your strength when your heart feels too heavy to carry, and banish all your fears and worries."

I flinched when the blade cut and blood dripped. He coated his hand in my blood and I did the same. My pulse thrummed in my ears, the anticipation almost too much to bear. Memories of our past together swam in my head, including us performing this very ritual in a beautiful private location.

We pressed our hands together, mixing our blood, and spoke in unison. "Our blood as our bond, and Yggdrasil as our witness, our vow of love and loyalty be eternal."

Energy pulsed in my chest, and Baldur audibly inhaled. That sensation I had with Tyr happened again. I felt him—his essence in me, like an awareness in my mind. Something else slid into place—a sense of near fullness settled into my very being.

My magic suddenly leaked out of my hands, one side black, the other gold. I stared at my hands and the power built, but never overpowered.

"Wow," Baldur said.

I jerked my gaze up at him and he blinked, then smiled. "Yeah, that's neat."

"What's neat?"

"Your eyes. They're filled with magic. It's in the same way as Randi's, but half and half for you."

I summoned a mirror, and sure enough, black veins crawled up one side of my neck, while golden ones did the same to the other side.

My eyes glowed with their respective side's color of magic. And yet, I didn't see or feel any different in my face. "Wow…"

Baldur tipped my chin up to look at him. "You're stunning."

His mouth claimed mine and my heart leapt. I wrapped my arms around his neck and eagerly kissed him back. My god of courage. I had him again. After all this time, chasing each other through different lives and never quite finding what we had.

And now we had.

I couldn't ask for anything more.

Baldur pressed me down on the mattress, his body covering me. Our kiss broke, our breaths panting and mingling. "Just like last time."

I blinked up at him. "You… remember?"

"A small little leak." He grinned. "I'm sure more will come as we continue to stay together."

I tangled my fingers in his hair. "You're not going anywhere on me."

Our mouths collided, desperation and lust taking hold. Our hands roamed each other, feeling and enjoying, memorizing and remembering, craving more as our everything enveloped each other until we were consumed. Each dip, peak, and valley of hard muscles and scars, I felt them all on him. I couldn't get enough.

Baldur's mouth devoured me. Our tongues wrestled until he kissed and licked down my neck, leaving me panting for air. My veins simmered and my body craved with need.

His calloused hands slid up my sides and cupped my heavy breasts. They teased and played, his kisses angling lower and lower. I moaned and arched my back, my mind fuzzing with desire.

Baldur tasted every part of me he desired, my collarbone, along a path of freckles, between my breasts, under them. He tasted a little higher on them, then a little higher. Right under my nipple. Not quite the sweet spot I craved, but that agonizingly teasing place.

"Baldur…" I moaned.

He answered with his hot, wet tongue flicking my hard, aching nipple. I sharply inhaled. And then he did it again. And again. All teasing flicks, both breasts, but never the satisfying attention I craved for them.

The teasing continued, until I was writhing under him for more. I desperately needed more. My hands pawed him. I let out a whimper when he pinned me to the bed. His mouth never stopped teasing, and no matter how much I arched and writhed, he didn't give me the one thing I craved.

He rocked his hips into me, his hard cock rubbing my thighs. I tried to spread them, tried to entice him to give me more, but he had me pinned. My whole body was on fire and I was powerless to take more.

I whimpered. "Baldur, please."

He chuckled. "That's it, Sunshine. Beg for me to pleasure you."

I squirmed, my bratty side desperate not to give in, but I was too worked up. I begged. "Please, Baldur. I need more. I need all the pleasure you can give me. I need you inside me, filling me with your cock and pumping me full of your cum."

A pleased rumble reverberated from his chest into me. "Good girl."

I moaned. I'd do anything to keep hearing him call me his good girl.

Baldur's lips wrapped around my aching nipples and sucked. Gentle at first, then suddenly hard in between. My head rolled back and my back arched. A pleasured moan rumbled through me.

He switched between breasts, each hard suck and teasing lick fuzzing my mind and driving me crazy for more. His hands forced mine together above my head, allowing him to freely roam my body with his unoccupied hand.

I was on fire, burning from inside out, and yet it wasn't enough. I craved a raging inferno.

I gasped in a sharp breath when his fingers slid along my inner thigh. The sparks of sensation were delicious and agonizing. My hips wriggled under him, my silent please for more.

Baldur took his time, his unhurried pace maddening and desirable. How could this man drive me to the edges of sanity and yet make me crave even more?

He slid his fingers along my soft flesh, slowly working his way between my folds. His chest rumbled and he released my nipple with a hard *pop*. "Perfectly wet, just for me."

I moaned when he rubbed my clit. The pleasure I so desperately craved rushed through me, igniting the flames of my desire into a wildfire. My hips rocked, intensifying everything. My breathing hitched and tension coiled deep within me.

My toes curled, just as Baldur said, "That's it, Sunshine. Shine brighter for me."

His fingers slid inside me and I gasped. With it came a snap of the building tension inside me, my orgasm coming on so suddenly that my head flew back, his name screaming off my lips. My hips bucked wildly, his body the only thing keeping me tamed.

I gasped for air as I came down, and moaned when Baldur resumed kissing my skin along my collarbone and up my neck to the shell of my ear, his hands doing wicked things to the sensitive skin between my thighs.

"I'm never going to grow tired of that," Baldur murmured against my ear.

I bit back another moan. "Tired of what?"

"Your sounds of pleasure and the amazing faces you make."

I slid my hands up his abs, and purred out my next words. "And I still have so much more to offer."

His fingers slid out of me and gripped my thighs, spreading them apart. His cock teasingly slid along my quivering folds. "I hope so."

A deep, gasping breath rushed out of me, my back arching as he slowly slid inside me. Inch by inch, he stretched me. My body accepted him, greedy to take all of him.

"I'll never grow tired of this feeling, either," he rasped out.

I grinned and slid my legs up around his hips, driving him in deeper. "And how about that feeling?"

He groaned and braced himself with his arms on either side of my head. "Even better. You're perfect, Sunshine."

I bucked my hips into him, driving him harder into me. We both sharply inhaled and I smirked. "We're perfect together, love."

Baldur's chest rumbled and his thrusting increased. "I could get used to that name from your lips."

Good, he'd better, because I was going to keep saying it.

Baldur thrust harder and faster. Pleasure coursed through me in an intense inferno that threatened to burn us both. I craved it—him and everything he offered.

My nails dragged along his back and he groaned. I wasn't sure if my theory had stuck, but in the moment I didn't care. He found pleasure in this, and I would provide.

My pleasure coiled deep in my core as the building orgasm sparked to its peak. It overtook me. I screamed, clamping down hard on him.

Baldur groaned and his thrusts became punctured until he succumbed to the tides of his own orgasm. We collapsed in a tangled, sensitive heap. My body quivered and shook, yet still craved more from my god. It did not help I still felt his readiness buried inside me.

We lay there a moment longer, collecting our breath before I nudged him lightly against the hip. He took the hint to roll over. He didn't release me, bringing me with him. I sat comfortably on top of him, his cock still fully buried in me, much to my delighted pleasure.

I didn't hesitate to rock my hips, my sensitive body igniting with so much pleasure it fuzzed my mind almost immediately. I bit my lower lip and my eyes hooded, hot desire blazing through me. I wasn't done with him. I wouldn't be done with him for a while. And from the way he held my hips, Baldur had no intentions of stopping, either.

Not until we were completely exhausted and falling asleep curled up together, blanketed in utter bliss.

Until the light of morning came too fast, and the birds outside didn't understand that some of us needed a little more time to catch up on sleep after our long night of lovemaking.

I yawned until my jaw popped and I looked up at Baldur. He'd held me against him the whole time we slept, and from the looks of it, not even the birds were going to wake him. I smirked. *But I can.*

Should I let him sleep? Sure. But that didn't mean I was going to.

Careful not to wake him too soon, I slipped out of his grip and crawled a little lower on the bed. His morning erection was already presenting and I licked my lips. *My other guys really enjoy a pleasurable wakeup, let's hope Baldur is no different.*

I carefully laid myself on Baldur's legs and lightly dragged my tongue along his semi-hard shaft. He stirred for a moment, but not by much. I continued to casually lick him, using my hands to ease his foreskin back gently until the head of his cocked was fully exposed.

Baldur mumbled something, slowly coming out of his deep sleep.

I slid his cock into my mouth and casually licked and sucked him. Nothing hurried or frantic. I enjoyed the slow, sensual glide of him in and out of my mouth; of my tongue licking and swirling around his sensitive head; of his bursts of taste luring me to do more to him.

Baldur's hand gripped my hair, and he mumbled my name. *Well, at least he knows who is giving him a morning blowjob.*

I continued, my pace as unhurried as ever, even when he fully woke and gazed down at me, his breathing labored. I stayed my casual course until his body tightened and he grunted, hot seed spilling into the back of my throat.

I hummed as I cleaned him off my lips. "Morning, love."

He chuckled. "Morning to you too, Sunshine."

Baldur grabbed me by the arms and pulled me higher onto him until I was seated perfectly for him to thrust his hard cock into me. I gasped and braced my hands on his chest. Pleasure sparked and burned into an inferno as I rocked my hips to meet his thrusts.

"We never checked to see if my theory was correct." Was I really starting up casual conversation while my god gave me a fantastic morning fuck? Yes, yes I apparently was, and it seemed he had no issue with it, from the smirk on his face.

"I already know," he said.

"That you can or can't feel pain?"

He grinned more and thrust into me a little harder, making me gasp. "That only you now can mix pain in with my pleasure."

I licked my lips, my pulse accelerating, and dug my nails into his chest until he hissed. "Perfect."

"That's what I'm supposed to say about you." He pulled out of me and hauled me higher by the hips, until I was hovering over his face. "And since you got your fill, it's my turn to satiate my ravenous hunger this morning. So, thank you, for presenting me with a hearty meal, wife."

He pulled me down by the hips and devoured my pussy. I moaned, bracing myself with one hand on the headboard, my other hand sinking into his hair, and falling into the pleasure I was never going to grow tired of.

THIRTY-FIVE

DIEGO

The basket's lid clacked on the island counter from the movement I caused while I secured the plates to it. Baldur slid a bottle of wine into the basket for me, next to the food I'd piled in. When the plates were secure in their holder, I double-checked I had enough silverware packed and then made sure I wasn't missing anything. I may be able to pop back and grab anything I'd forgotten, but that'd ruin the mood.

I froze when an uncomfortable sensation flowed through me. *Not now…* My eyes snapped shut and images flashed in my mind. Chaotic and difficult to process. Gunfire and flames. Roaring. Someone crying. A hand pulling a trigger. A woman screaming. A flash of wings.

The vision vanished. I gasped for air and braced myself on the counter as my senses flooded back in. Baldur's hand gripped my shoulder.

"Are you okay?" he asked after a moment.

I nodded. "It's just… a lot. You'd think I'd get used to these."

"What's it like?" he asked. "Is it always the same, or…"

I shook my head. "Some are easier to handle than others. It depends on how clear or chaotic the vision is. The choppy and chaotic ones are the worst, because I'm supposed to figure out what is different in my vision."

"Different?"

I nodded, and breathed deeply when my head pulsed. "I mostly receive visions someone else already had, but I see it differently, like from an alternative angle. And before you ask, it's an instinct that I know someone already saw what I did."

Baldur made a thoughtful sound. "That sounds annoying. Do you understand what this vision was trying to tell you?"

"Something about a father... a mother's blood... and..." I tried to push through the chaotic slush in my head. "Freedom? That's all I've got right now."

He rubbed my shoulder. "Don't hurt yourself trying to figure it out. It'll come to you when it needs to."

Maybe. These visions sometimes felt so random. Like why did we even get them? I understood the plight of the older dragons the more I dealt with these visions.

The front door opened and boisterous laughter filtered in. I looked up. Angel trotted into the house and went straight for her water bowl. Darius entered behind her, carrying Astrid on his back. It looked like she was about to fall off of him with the way she hung on him; it was clearly throwing Darius off balance, by the way he stumbled. If immortals could get drunk, I'd assume the two of them were.

Tyr walked in after them, his hands full, carrying gun cases.

"Right on time," Baldur mumbled.

I wasn't surprised. Darius was a punctual man. If you gave him a time, he rarely missed it. Centuries of training did that to a person.

"Are we enjoying a successful hunt or bringing up the endorphins to make ourselves feel better?" I asked while trying to be casual about closing the lid of the picnic basket.

"I got two boars!" Astrid cheered.

"Nice sized ones, too," Darius complimented.

"Tyr also got one," Astrid said. "We would have gotten more, but Muninn and Huginn decided to harass the herd and then Angel joined in, running them off."

I chuckled. Angel usually behaved during hunting, but the ravens were showing to be quite the instigators. The ravens in question weren't around, so I was guessing they were off doing their own thing right now. "Dad will be happy to work with what you brought home, I'm sure."

Astrid hopped off of Darius and skipped over. "What's with the basket?"

I used my magic to send it to where it needed to go. "It's a surprise."

She squinted and then her eyes flicked between me and Baldur. "Are you two going on a date?"

Baldur and I glanced at each other. He smirked. "Tempting, but no."

It was tempting. When Astrid set out to revive Baldur, I never expected I'd find myself attracted to him. I also thought Astrid would be the sole focus of my attention for some time. Yet, the bit of time I'd gotten to hang out with him, and that hot-as-hell kiss last week, I found myself in quite the position.

Neither of us had talked about this clear mutual attraction. Maybe because we were both still trying to focus on Astrid for now. He had a steeper hill to climb with that. Plus, there was a discussion that would need to be had with Astrid about other relationships beyond her.

Baldur slapped my shoulder and left the kitchen. Astrid blinked as Tyr and her dad followed him out.

"Um…" she mumbled.

I grinned and swooped around the island, pulling her into my arms. "They were just a distraction."

Her eyebrow rose. "A distraction?"

"I needed to get everything ready. So, your dad agreed to bring you on a quick hunting trip under the disguise of showing there was no hard feelings about your eloping twice. Baldur had planned to go, but then he decided to stay behind and help me."

Aya spilled the beans both times about the elopements, before Astrid was ready. She was excited. At least, that's the reason we used to excuse her. We also knew the friendship she had with Astrid meant she was a shit sometimes.

I paused. "Uh… that sounds more nefarious than I intended."

Darius had been, understandably, the most shocked of all of us about the news the first time it was announced. Up until recently, Astrid had been quite clear she wasn't ready for marriage, so he hadn't prepared for that life change with his daughter yet. Hell, he was still getting used to her living semi-separately with us.

Astrid had assured us her bonding with Tyr wasn't a planned thing, for her to go get hitched behind everyone's back. Her bonding with Baldur was less of a surprise, and her explaining that part of it was her attempt to help Baldur with his pain issue did help with the reveal, though because she'd only waited a few days, it was a lot for everyone to take in so quickly.

"Your dad is supportive of everything, don't think he's not. This just gave him a chance to get used to everything and…" I trailed off, realizing my rambling was making it worse. Normally I was a much smoother talker than this. I blamed it on the jitters. Luckily Astrid was too busy laughing at me to be offended.

"I know he's supportive," she said when she calmed down. "We talked a lot today about everything. I also respect that he's a little upset things happened so suddenly. Tyr assured him nothing else was changing immediately."

My mouth lifted into a smirk. "No secret baby?"

She laughed. "Still much to both our dads' displeasure."

I laughed with her. That was what made things so funny about this. Darius would have handled a baby announcement a hell of a lot better.

She slid her hand up my chest, sending a prickle of warmth through me. "Are you sure you're still okay with things? We talked about waiting so recently, I want to be sure—"

I pressed my fingers to her lips and hushed her. "We'll talk about that later. I have a date to take you on."

Astrid pursed her lips. "A date, where?"

"It's a surprise," I said. Her eyes narrowed, making me chuckle. "Why are you so suspicious?"

"Because you don't want to talk about this, and would rather focus on a surprise date."

I spun her around, hoping to distract her. She was paying too much attention to things. "Mi cielo, you need to trust me."

She swayed her hips, rubbing against me. "Do I?"

I spun her back around and kissed her quickly on the lips. The house disappeared and the sounds and smells of an evergreen forest enveloped us. "Yes, you should, mi amor."

Astrid looked around. Hemlocks towered over us, creating a dense foliage canopy. Dapples of light broke through in golden patches, highlighting lingering snow and the carpet of mosses, ferns, and lichen. "Where are we?"

I rested my hand on the small of her back and encouraged her to walk. "Somewhere not near the house."

She rolled her eyes. "You're going to be a pain in the ass the whole time, aren't you?"

I grinned. "Only if you don't stop trying to ruin the surprise."

She flipped her ponytail over her shoulder haughtily. "Me, ruin something? As if."

I snorted and she shoved me. I stumbled two steps before catching my footing. She skipped off, with her nose in the air. I watched her walk off. The desire to chase her tugged deep in me, stirring the dragon. *Not yet.* I set a slow pace following her.

Astrid glanced back every now and then. Each time, her suspicion grew. Finally, she called me out. "Are you going to tell me if I'm going the wrong way?"

"You're not."

She walked a bit longer before finally huffing and coming to a halt. I snickered and came up to her, sliding my hand over her hip and pulling her close. "Done being a brat?"

"Yeah…"

I kissed her on the head. "Enjoy the walk with me. It's been a while since we did something like this."

"Can you tell me at least where we are? Besides, clearly the northern hemisphere and somewhere high in altitude."

"Washington."

Her brow rose. "You brought me to Washington? Why?"

I smirked. "You'll see."

She rolled her eyes, pretending to be annoyed, but I saw the tiny smile pulling the corners of her mouth. Her arm snaked around my waist, and we walked together with no trail to guide us and just the symphony of nature as our companion. We used to do this more often, but with how crazy life had gotten, we hadn't been out for a hike of any kind in a while.

It helped my plan that the weather had cooperated with us today so we could do this. It was on the chilly side, but nothing a light jacket and our immortal Valkyrie and dragon cold resistance couldn't handle.

At this time of year, one would have expected to be trekking through deep snow, but much like in New York, this area, too, was experiencing warmer than usual weather.

It was all the news wanted to buzz about. Worldwide weather patterns were off-kilter. We suspected it had something to do with the chaos brewing the last year or two.

The trees around us thinned until we walked in a stunning meadow of vibrant hues of wildflowers. Their sweet fragrance perfumed the air, overpowering the rich, earthy scent of the forest. Majestic mountain peaks dominated the horizon, their caps covered in snow. The crystalline waters of the glacial lake below sparkled with the mid-afternoon sun overhead.

Astrid's surprised gasp was everything I'd hoped for. She spun in a slow circle, taking in the spectacular view. When she turned back at me, her eyes sparkled. "We're at North Cascades National Park, aren't we?"

I smiled and took her hand in mine, lifting it so I could plant a gentle kiss to her skin. "You told me you always wanted to visit. And with the bizarre seasonal issues going on around the world, I thought we could take advantage of it for once."

She also had Glacier National Park and few other North American national forests on a bucket list we seriously needed to check off.

Astrid squinted. "This meadow is full of flowers. No seasonal weirdness would ensure that happened."

Dammit. "Okay, maybe I enlisted Dad, Ùna, and Sean to help make this extra special."

Her lips curved up into a pleased smile. She curled her fingers over my shoulders and pushed up on her toes. I bent to meet her half way, and she kissed me softly. "Thank you. This is a wonderful surprise."

I grinned against her mouth. "Then you're going to love the rest."

Slipping my arms under her, I lifted her in a bridal carry and walked over to the plaid blanket and basket she'd missed in her gazing.

Astrid's eyes lit up when I sat down at the prepared space, her in my lap. "A scenic picnic? You do love me."

I kissed her on the forehead and she sighed. "Of course I do, mi amor. You are the most important person to me."

She sat forward and grabbed the picnic basket. "Well, until Baldur steals you from me."

My head tipped forward as I gave her a stern look. "Astrid. There is no stealing."

She stuck her tongue out. "Just don't forget I exist."

I rolled my eyes. "Never."

"Good. What's for lunch? It smells heavenly."

I shook my head. *This woman.* "Only your favorites."

She pulled the food out of the basket, from caprese sandwiches to empanadas and lemon blueberry cake. I'd even packed a cluster of grapes.

Astrid leaned back into me when everything was spread out around us. "Yep, you love me."

I gently took her chin in my fingers and tipped her head back so I could gaze into her stunning eyes. "Never question that I do."

Pink tinted her cheeks and she smiled. "Never."

I grabbed a sandwich triangle and offered it to her. Instead of taking it from me, she bit off a corner. She hummed contentedly. I took a bite from the triangle as well. It was a good sandwich. Papá had made sure I had the best ingredients. Only the best would suffice today.

Popping the cork on the wine, we ate and casually chatted in this idyllic moment on the mountain. Wildlife appeared every now and then. Even a marmot made an appearance, and serenaded us with the chirps of his people.

Connection flowed through us, that sensation I always felt with her, and grew stronger the longer we enjoyed this moment together. All I wanted to do was foster it until I could physically grab it so it'd never leave. The dragon in me stirred, primal wants and desires creeping up. I knew exactly what he wanted. He wasn't alone.

Astrid swirled her glass of wine. "So, what's the occasion for this date?"

I paused mid-bite into an empanada. Her tone was casual, but there was a subtle shift about her presence. She was suspicious again. "Am I not allowed to plan a surprise date just because I want to?"

She pursed her lips. "You are, but that doesn't usually require you to enlist a host of others to help you set this up in some way. Plus, you're still avoiding the conversation I wanted to have earlier."

My dragon awoke more. Desire stronger than I'd ever experienced before surged through me. *Mate.* I couldn't deny this anymore, not after everything that had happened.

"I'm not avoiding anything." I set my food down and took her wine away. "I wanted a perfect moment with the most incredible woman in my life, without interruption, because the world is burning down around us."

Astrid turned in my lap so she was facing me with her legs crossed over mine. She gazed at me as if seeing more than the surface of who I was.

I brushed her cheek with the back of my finger. "No matter what life throws at us, I want so many more of these moments with you for the rest of our, hopefully, long lives."

She smiled. "It will be long. I won't let the past keep repeating."

I slipped my finger under her chin and pressed my forehead to hers. "I won't either. I waited too long to allow anyone to take you from me again."

"That's my line," she mumbled. "You died first each time."

"The second time was bullshit."

She laughed, the sound luring as any siren song.

"What isn't bullshit is how much I need you. You, Astrid. With all your loveable quirks, sharp and soft edges, and amazing and strange hobbies."

"And broken pieces," she added. "Can't forget those."

I chuckled. "Especially those pieces you've been fusing back together with gold. I need everything that makes up the amazing woman right here with me."

My thumb slid along her cheek. "I need you… as my light in the dark. As my life partner. As—"

"Yes," she breathed out. She then half-laughed at the same time as me and averted her gaze. "Sorry. I jumped the gun. Say it."

I tipped her chin up. "Be my mate, Astrid."

She slid her fingers into my hair and tugged me closer, our lips barely a breath apart. "I said yes to you, Eero. I said yes to you, Ragnvald. I again say yes to you, Diego. My heart is and will forever be eternally yours."

My heart thumped hard in my chest for each name she called me. I claimed her mouth with mine and wrapped my arms around her, pulling her flush against me. Her warmth, her presence—I needed it. I needed to brand every aspect of her essence onto my soul, where she'd never leave.

I rolled us onto the blanket, my mouth still melded to hers. My tongue swiped inside her mouth, desperate to claim her. Her fingers in my hair tightened, as if she were trying to fuse us together. I wanted nothing more.

Astrid finally broke our mouths apart, allowing us to come up for air, but only for a moment. Our lips claimed each other's again. My heart beat strong in my chest. She was mine. *No one is taking my heart flame again.*

Memories flowed through my mind. Memories from times before with her—of us together. Every single one. It wasn't painful or jarring. They washed over me like a warm caress, filling me with life I didn't know I needed, but desperately craved.

Astrid's fingers slid over my horns that were now growing from my head. The pleasant sensation her touch brought shot down my spine. My fingers flexed and my claws grazed the soft skin of her cheek and neck. My tail slid side to side, knocking the picnic basket before loosely wrapping around her leg.

Slanting my mouth, my kisses migrated down her neck, following the path of my fingers. "My powerful witch I will always stand behind."

I kissed her neck. "My stunning Valkyrie I will kneel for."

My lips pressed against her chest, right where her heart thundered below the surface. "My perfect mate I will cherish and love for all eternity."

Astrid hardly breathed each time I kissed her with a vow. When she finally spoke, it was breathy. "My eternal memory dragon I will always shine as a beacon for, so you'll never be lost again."

Power pulsed deep in my chest, and Astrid inhaled through her nose at the same time as me. Something shimmered along her skin, and awareness flooded my mind. Awareness of her. Awareness of how much she needed me, as much as I needed her. Right now.

My hands grabbed the hem of her shirt and pushed the flimsy fabric up. The warmth of her soft skin teased and lured me in. I pulled her shirt off and tossed it somewhere. Her bra was next, the front clasp no match for my need for her.

Astrid pulled at my shirt until it was over my head. We used magic so often on our clothes, not using it now felt so much more exciting and fun.

My mouth descended on her again, kissing and licking all her exposed hot skin. My hands roamed her, eager to claim every inch I could.

Astrid moaned and arched into my touch. "Diego…"

I loved the sound of my name off her pleading tongue. "Patience."

The words rumbled out as my dragon and I finally synced. Everything we were, fusing into one existence. "I will enjoy you until our souls mix and can never be torn apart again."

I tasted her, leisure in my exploring. My tongue slid along her breast, intermingling with quick kisses and light nips with my teeth. Astrid whimpered and squirmed underneath me, her legs rubbing my hips, making me even harder for her.

My tongue danced around her taut nipple, teasing until she was begging. The sound set my veins on fire with desire. My mouth closed around her sensitive peak. Astrid moaned as I sucked and licked and teased, arching into me and tightening her grip in my hair.

My hands roamed her, my claws teasing her skin. I rolled my thumb over her other breast, playing with her free nipple. The hard bud slid under the pad of my thumb, stiff and unyielding. I rolled it between my thumb and index fingers, gentle and coaxing. Astrid moaned and writhed underneath me, enjoying every moment of torturous bliss I gave her.

I released her nipple with a *pop* and gave the other the same attention with my mouth. My fingers played with her newly released one. Sensitive and wet, my warm fingers played and contrasted against the cooler air caressing her.

"Diego, please, more," she begged. "Please."

I released her, enjoying the sound of her gasp as the cool air rushed over her damp, sensitive skin. I kissed between her breasts, tracing parts of her tattoo with my tongue. My hands glided down her sides and over her jean-clad hips. My fingers slid along the hem of her pants, my claws skimming her skin in the most teasing way. Astrid squirmed under my touch, her hands grabbing for me, in hopes I'd hurry. But I wouldn't. I was enjoying this too much. I was going to savor this moment and draw out our ultimate pleasure.

I undid the button of her jeans and slowly slid down her zipper. My mouth kissed along her soft belly, migrating down. I tucked my fingers beneath the hem of her pants and the band of her panties, careful not to cut her perfect skin, and tugged. Her pants resisted for only a moment and then her clothes slid off her hips and gathered at her knees.

I kissed her lower and lower, over the swell of her wide hips and down her luscious thighs. I tugged her clothes more, but they caught on her shoes. Without my mouth breaking contact with her body, I made quick work of her shoes and her other clothes. I lifted my head to gaze down at her naked visage.

I marveled at her. "Stunning."

Astrid smirked and spread her legs. Her fingers glided down her stomach and spread her pussy lips, putting herself on full display. "And now?"

A swallow caught in my throat, my blood burning even hotter. "Perfection."

She grinned and hooked her foot around the back of my head. "Then why don't you come and appreciate this perfection?"

I turned my face into her leg and kissed her. Then again a little higher. And a little higher. Slowly, I migrated up her leg, my kisses quick and teasing. Astrid's fingers slid into my hair again as I came back into her reach.

Her nails slid along my scalp, sending prickles through me. The sensation intensified along my spine as her fingers slid up my horns. This only happened when she touched me there. Or maybe it'd happen if I were intimate with someone else, but so far, that privilege was hers alone.

Gods, did I love it. And she knew it. She stroked my horn in the most provocative way possible, torturing me as much as I was her. Or maybe more, because as she drew me in with her promises of pleasure, my body remained untouched by her. It hummed with desire, craving the primal satiation I was about to promise her.

My mouth pressed against her inner thigh. The musk of her arousal invaded my heightened senses, luring me in. I fell into her spell.

Astrid gasped. My tongue slid along her dripping folds, her taste searing into every facet of my mind. I greedily licked her outer folds, then slid my tongue between them, along her begging clit.

Astrid moaned. Her hips pushed up and her grip in my hair tightened, forcing my face down into her. I eagerly obliged her demand, devouring her with hungry fervor.

Licking then sucking, sucking and licking in tandem, I brought her higher and higher into the throes of pleasure. She writhed and moaned. She ground her pussy into my face and begged for more. I wasn't ready to provide.

I savored her, feasted on her. And only when my craving was sufficiently sated of her taste did I slide my fingers inside her begging pussy and send her the heights of paradise.

A deep, rolling moan turned into a shrieking scream as the tides of Astrid's orgasm tore through her. Her hips bucked and she arched her back. I didn't let up until she fell back onto the blanket, panting and languid.

I grinned as I wiped her off my lips and then licked my thumb and fingers to savor her remaining taste. Astrid's eyes tracked my motions, her eyes intense with lust and satisfaction.

"Come here, my dragon," she said, her alto voice even lower with heady desire.

I leaned over her, lazily taking in her stunning beauty. "Yes, my Valkyrie?"

Her lips spread into a deep grin and she practically purred. Her hands slid up my chest, the contact creating sparks of desire, heating the flames that had yet to die within me. She wrapped her arms around my neck and her legs slid up my hips.

Astrid's lips brushed my ear. "Come love me some more."

Her magic flared and the remainder of my clothes vanished.

Astrid hooked her legs around my hips, and lifted herself into me. She kissed along my neck and nibbled my collarbone as she rocked her hips, teasing her pussy against my hard cock. I tried to resist, just for a moment. I wanted to draw this out a little longer, until I was so sure this bond between us was more than complete.

"Diego, come love me." Her words caressed me like nothing else in existence. "Please."

My moment of resistance snapped. How could I deny her anything? "As you wish, mi amor."

Urging her to let go and lie back on the blanket, I gripped her hips and eased myself inside her. Deliciously slow and blissful, I watched in slow motion as she forgot to breathe, and how her lips parted and her eyes closed with her silent moan. I took in every movement of her expression and every small twitch of her body as she accepted me.

When I was fully buried, I didn't wait or hesitate. I pulled out of her just as slowly and then eased myself back in. Slow and rhythmic, I made love to her, her breathy sighs and moans delicious and luring. "That's it, Cielo. Enjoy my cock. You take it so well."

Astrid's hand slid up my chest, and she gazed up at me with silent pleading eyes. I dipped down and kissed her, softly and gently as I thrusted. She slid her arms around my neck and laced her fingers in my hair.

She tried to kiss me more urgently and grumbled in frustration when I didn't give in. She tried to thrust into me, to hurry my motions, but I held her hips down.

I needed to keep feeling this slowly building connection between us. It hummed along my senses, wrapping me in everything she was.

"Diego, please," she begged against my lips.

"Patience," I murmured. "Just a moment longer. I know you can do it."

She whined and kissed me with more frantic force while her hips jerked against my hold, her desperation breaking through. "Now. Now, my dragon. I need all of you, now."

Fuck. I liked to pretend I had some sort of control in our love making, but I knew I didn't. She had total power over me, and there was only so long I could resist.

Her insistent kissing was finally met with my own. My pulse kicked up, thrumming under my skin and in my ears. My tongue swiped the inside of her mouth, greedily wrestling with hers for dominance.

The rhythm of my thrusting increased, slowly at first, then harder and more frantic. Astrid moaned and her body bucked in time with my movements. The increased pleasure coursed through me, overwhelming what control I had.

I fell into the tides of passion, her moans and pleas for more pulling me deeper and past a point of no return I had no intention of running from.

My breathing grew short, every muscle in my tightening. I braced myself and slid my fingers down her body, my claws drawing out quick extra moans from her.

Astrid arched into me more when I slid a claw-tip over her needy clit, driving me into her deeper. She panted and started mumbling my name before her scream cut it off. She came with soul-shattering intensity, bucking and writhing. Her walls clamped around my cock, milking me.

I lost control, groaning and convulsing. White seared the back of my eyelids. Abandoning myself to pleasure, I spent myself inside her until there was nothing left.

I stilled when I could no longer continue, my body trembling with the effort to hold myself over her. More than just euphoria coursed through me. Our panting breath mingled, our bodies breathing each other in until we felt each other in our souls.

Never had I felt this whole before in recent memory. Only once in the past, when we'd bonded ourselves together. Feeling her in my senses, I could no longer imagine a life not ever knowing this. The very thought was too painful and empty.

I lowered myself next to her and pulled her into me. "Te amo. I love you, more than life itself."

Astrid hummed. "I love you, too. I feel so… complete."

She then reached up and touched a patch of scales on my face. "Your scales changed. There's amber here now."

Somehow I already knew that before she said anything. "You're a part of me. We're bonded for eternity and I'll wear that publicly for all of Creation to see."

She snuggled into me, rubbing her face into my neck as if embarrassed. I chuckled and ran my fingers along her arm and she giggled and twitched. I loved teasing her when she was this sensitive.

My teasing stopped when energy sparked from contact with her shoulder. Even Astrid noticed it. She pulled back, and I saw what I'd missed a moment ago. Faint, intricate patterns of magic crawled up her arms and along her chest.

I couldn't make sense of any imagery, but it felt ancient. And even when I tried to peer into my memories, my life as Eero didn't even know their true meaning.

"What is this?" Astrid said, both sounding alarmed and awed.

I shifted and looked at myself, finding its twin on me. I smiled and dipped down to kiss a part of the mark on Astrid that curled around her heart. "Our mark. A physical reminder for us."

Astrid traced a part of the mark on her arm, and then the same section on mine. "I feel it."

I felt it, too. More than just physically, though. I had this sense in my mind, and this presence that made me aware of just… her. *This is why it's so special.*

"I guess we're going to have to explain this when we get back." There was amusement in her tone.

I shook my head and kissed her. "They can't see it."

She blinked up at me. "What do you mean?"

"I mean exactly that." It was why I could feel Mamá and Papá's but not see anything beyond it. It was why Mamá mistakenly thought I had mated with Astrid previously. "It's only for us to see. And only dragons and phoenixes can feel it."

Astrid closed her eyes and then nodded. "I remember that now. Though, I think Scarlett will be able to see a change in our connection with her unusual ability. Not that it's a big deal either way."

I kissed her happy little smile. She sighed contentedly and slid her hands along my chest.

She let out an excited groan and pressed into me when my tail wrapped around her leg. "My dragon still wants to play as much as me?"

I slid my fingers along her cheek and tangled them into her hair. "Always."

Astrid pushed harder into me and I rolled back, pulling her with me. She braced her hands on my chest, her arms framing her perfect breasts.

"It's more fun to play with them than to just look," she said.

My hands ran up her thighs, over the perfect curve of her hips and waist. "I enjoy appreciating you in all ways, Cielo."

She pushed my hands up quicker until I was cupping her soft, perfectly sized, breasts. "Tyr appreciates my ass enough. The rest of my assets deserve attention."

I grinned and gladly fondled her, feeling her supple fullness and enjoying her pleasured sighs when I played with her sensitive nipples. I loved all of her, but if I had to claim a favorite part, these would absolutely be it. But—my tail snaked up her back and around her waist—that didn't mean I'd ignore the rest of her.

Astrid's eyes hooded as I slid my tail between her legs and teased her. She appreciatively ran her hands along my tail. There was no apprehension or disgust. She enjoyed all of me, no matter how human, or lack thereof.

I pulled her back with my tail until she was hovering over my newly hardened cock. Astrid licked her lips in anticipation and then lowered herself. I groaned as I slid inside her.

Astrid moaned, her hands bracing on my chest. Our desire for each other flowed through us in a palpable, heady aura, overwhelming my senses. We enjoyed each other until the sun slid low in the mountain sky and not even our immortal nature could stave off the cold. But I wasn't giving her up to anyone tonight.

I got her back in my bed where I held her close. Everything felt so right now. No one would ever take this from us ever again. I'd make sure of it.

THIRTY-SIX

ASTRID

A mini pretzel stick bounced off my cheek, making me blink rapidly. I turned my attention away from the window just in time to be pelted with another pretzel right in the face. "Bjarke…"

He chuckled and ate one of the pretzel sticks in his hand. "Stop spacing out and make your move."

I glanced down as the Risk board laid out on the breakfast nook table. Colored soldiers and infantry units were scattered around the map of the world. Bjarke and Dad had a large portion of the territory, while Azzie and I were struggling to stay on the board. Kirby and Brit, though, were sitting pretty with the most tiles, thanks to them getting their hands on Australia and teaming up from there. Yeah, we weren't technically playing a team's version of this, but it had turned into that. And good thing, too, because I couldn't focus.

I wasn't the only one. Azzie and Kirby also couldn't shake a weird feeling, which was partially why they were over. The other part was just so we could hang out before D&D later. Dad figured a nice family game of Risk would be a great idea to calm us down. Bjarke just so happened to want to stop by and hang out, so he joined in, taking Diego's spot.

While a competitive strategy game was something Diego could enjoy, it was surprisingly not his favorite type of game. However, he did enjoy watching us. Tyr and Baldur also watched on, their war-god brains working hard to come up with strategies as they learned the game on the fly from watching. Seeing them play when they were ready was going to be interesting.

Azzie and I conferred on strategy and made our move. It earned us a territory steal from Bjarke and Dad, though it was short-lived when Kirby and Brit's turn came up and they swooped in and took out our units in the fresh territory. Brit had other units destroy us on another side, taking that territory from us, too. I stuck my tongue out at them and they smugly smiled back.

My attention wandered again, this time because Aya came trotting down the stairs from the loft. "Hey, anything yet?"

She shook her head as she entered the kitchen. "Nothing."

I frowned. She, Magnus, and Dahlia had been hard at work trying to track down Ingrid, and either cult or Malsumis activity. But they'd remained MIA since our last encounter almost two and a half weeks ago.

While the lack of activity wasn't unusual, given the cult's elusive nature, I knew they were up to something big. Most of what I saw in that bunker might have been fake, but not everything. My ravens and I had worked on replaying the memories over and over again, to spot what was real and what hadn't been.

The cultists who had been real were doing work that couldn't be stopped for the charade Ingrid had put on for me. They'd just taken it all with them when they escaped. What Muninn had seen, though, in his flights around the main chamber didn't have anything cohesive enough to piece together even an inkling of a plan. Well, except something chaotic. But that was a given.

"If you need any extra resources, just let me know," Dad said as he made a move on the board. "I'm sure I can find something to help."

Aya winked at him. "I'll be sure to let you know."

I gagged, making everyone else laugh.

Everyone froze when an alarm blared from upstairs. Aya abandoned her glass of water and rushed for the stairs. The rest of us stampeded after her.

My heart raced as I ascended the stairs. I'd never heard this sound before, but my Valkyries senses flared. Something was wrong.

I came to a halt in the war room. Computer screens everywhere were filled with all manner of hacked-into surveillance cameras. Aya typed furiously on her keyboard and she spoke to what sounded like Dahlia through a headset.

My blood ran cold when some of the feeds changed to cities where chaos had erupted. Magic and gunfire, beasts and men. The camera feeds couldn't keep up with it all. "Aya…"

Azzie swore. "Those are Malsumis minions, look."

Sure enough, those lizard-like flying creatures flew by one of the camera feeds. "Where is this?"

"London," Aya said, her voice grave. "Moscow. Harbin. Cairo. Los Angeles. Sidney. Buenos Aires. Baghdad."

My breath rushed out of my lungs. This was it. This was the chaotic plan they were working on. Attack eight major cities around the globe to spread panic and chaos. Expose everything the supernatural community tried to hide. "What do we do?"

Kirby placed a hand on my shoulder. "First we breathe. Then we come up with a quick plan."

I sucked in a shaky, calming breath and nodded. She was right. We couldn't save these people if we weren't acting rationally.

"First, why eight locations?" Bjarke said.

"Beyond the fact that this spreads out the chaos, making it harder to cover up," Dad said. "Ingrid knows we have some sort of force to compete with her. This forces us to split our numbers."

"Eight locations. That's one for almost each Valkyrie," Diego observed.

"No doubt they figured out how many of us there are," Azzie said. *No such thing as a coincidence.* "But why eight and not nine?"

"To make me pick." The very thought made my stomach knot. "She may not know everyone's powers, but she knows I can heal and possess powerful magic. Whoever gets me to aid them will benefit greatly. And… it fucks with me. She'll think she's teaching me some twisted lesson for crossing her."

Azzie grimaced. "That bitch. How can we make that kind of choice?"

Two ravens cried and suddenly both Huginn and Muninn appeared in the room. They landed on my shoulder, each carrying something.

"Sister!" Muninn said. *"Hurry! This will help. Hurry."*

My brow furrowed and I took the envelope from his beak. The envelope had nothing written on it. I flipped open the flap to find a piece of paper inside. I slid it out. *Coordinates?*

I handed it off to Aya. "Enter these into your computer."

She shot me a quizzical look, but did as I asked. A few keystrokes, and a map pulled up what looked to be an aerial view of something grassy and urban.

"What is that?" Bjarke said.

"A golf course and what appeared to be an industrial lot right next door," Aya said. She zoomed in on the properties. Nothing seemed special about the images that appeared. "Astrid, what is this?"

I didn't know. But I knew it was important. My ravens were sure. Just before I was about to ask them about it, I felt something inside the envelope. Popping it open further, I found something green inside. I pulled it out.

In my hand was a woody stem with smooth-edged oval leaves and a cluster of white berries. *Mistletoe…*

"Astrid," Azzie said cautiously.

I chuckled. "That dickhead. He figured out where she was."

Everyone exchanged glances. Azzie spoke up again. "I'm sorry, what? Loki sent this?"

I nodded. "Yeah. And I'm certain it's legit."

Both ravens bobbed their heads. Muninn spoke up. *"Crazy witch made the wrong god angry. Trickster won't dirty his hands, but he gives freebie help."*

Dad gave an amused snort. "It was clever, too."

"How so?" Tyr said.

"She hated golf. No one would think to look for her there."

"It's that or a ski lodge," I said.

Baldur's eyebrow spiked. "What else didn't she like?"

Dad and I shared a glance. "Fried chicken."

The room was silent, then Bjarke spoke up. "Did we ever mention your—"

"Egg donor was psycho? Yeah." *Now I want fried chicken.*

"So, what do we do?" Brit said. "Ingrid will be too busy causing mayhem to suspect she'd be attacked at this facility. This is also too good of an opportunity to pass up. But it also spreads us thinner or we have to abandon a city."

I thought a moment, grim resolve settling in. "I'll go after her."

"Ace..." Dad warned.

Kirby spoke over him. "Are you ready for that? That's a huge burden to take on."

I nodded, resolve hardening in my chest. "I've been working up to this moment. I'm not backing down now."

"We should go with you, for backup," Azzie said. "You shouldn't do this alone. We can send other powerful allies to handle the cities."

I shook my head and summoned my shield. "Ingrid doesn't know about the undead army we have at our disposal. It will be our biggest advantage. We Valkyries are the only ones who can summon and command the dead to fight for us. We are needed at each location to tip the scales of battle."

Diego suddenly went still and then spoke as he interpreted the vision presented to him.

From grief, courage will breathe again
And the witch with silver wings shall command
Sworn warriors to heed her call
The false Valkyrie will fall

He blinked, his gaze clearing. "I think that settles that choice."

Kirby and Azzie shared a look and then nodded, Kirby speaking up. "Then we'll organize with the others to bring an end to their attack, while you focus on ending her." She placed her hand on my shoulder. "Be careful."

"Yeah, you're not allowed to die again in battle," Azzie added. "It's really a bad habit."

I laughed, despite the gravity of the situation.

Diego offered to teleport them anywhere they needed to go before joining in our planning. Bjarke went with him, promising to be back with an army of Berserkers to help me. I knew that'd be his choice. Runavík was loyal to me, and I to them. I could count on them to have my back whenever I needed it.

Huginn tapped me, the package he carried still in his mouth. It was a tiny paperboard pouch, with twine wrapped around it in a bow. I took it from him and opened the pouch. Inside was a folded note and a bullet. I looked at the bullet for a moment and then read the paper.

"What does it say?" Baldur asked.

"Use it well," I mumbled. I stared at the bullet. This round fit Dad's long-range rifle.

"That's an immortal-killer," Aya said, her voice strained.

I blew out a slow breath. These were rare. I'd never come into contact with them, but Kirby and the others talked about them from time to time. One of these nearly killed Fen.

It might be overkill, but we didn't know what Ingrid was. We couldn't be sure she was even human anymore after whatever she turned into at that bunker.

I hesitated and then offered it to Dad. I didn't want to place this burden on him. He'd loved her once. Involving him in any way when it came to my mother just reopened old wounds. I knew he'd never been the same after her. He never sought out companionship that I had ever seen. I didn't want to risk this choice being what killed his heart completely. But at the same time, I had to give him that choice.

And he took it.

I watched him roll the bullet between his fingers and then curled them around it. Resolve hardened his face, and for the first time, I saw not my dad, but a warrior witch who'd lived centuries fighting hidden battles no one would know the stories to.

In a strange way, it helped me align myself. I hated fighting. I hated the thought of taking another's life. But we didn't have the luxury to walk away. We were at war, and war had its price, just like magic.

As Dad spoke strategy, the war gods in the room helping, I focused in on myself, aligning my past with my present. Each part of me was unique, with different experiences that shaped me individually. And now, it all shaped who I was about to become.

"Muninn, Huginn, you're to do surveillance," I instructed.

Both birds perked up.

"We need actual eyes on the ground to know the current movement of the cult. They're probably using both the golf course and the industrial lot." I rubbed their heads. "I want you both to be extra careful. Don't do anything that puts you both at risk. They're going to be suspicious of any ravens in the area."

Both of them touched their beaks to my cheeks. *"We will be careful. And get you all the knowledge you could ever desire."*

Aya outfitted them with their body cams, then they were gone. My heart thumped hard in my chest. I worried for them, but had to trust them, too. They hadn't lived this long by being careless.

Dad nodded his approval to me, which helped with my decision. Next was Angel. She stood in the doorway, staring at me. Her intelligence had grown even more. I recognized her thoughts, similar to when I had her in the past. Soon, she would be no ordinary dog. She may look like it, but that would be all that would remain from her life that started as the puppy Diego gave me as a gift years ago.

She wanted to be included. I didn't want her hurt, either, but I wasn't going to deny her wishes. "You'll protect Dad. He's going to need someone watching his back."

She barked once, the feelings of agreement pushing through the bond. She would protect him, at all costs.

Dad and the others continued to strategize. I would do what they asked. This wasn't my area of expertise, so all I could do was listen and relay whatever my spies provided me through the link or camera feeds.

My ravens proved as useful as I expected. There was a barrier around both the industrial lot and golf course. The ravens could get inside, though were cautious about doing so in case the familiar bond magic triggered something. I did suspect the barrier would pose a problem for us if we tried to teleport in.

What we thought was an industrial lot wasn't actually one. The barrier made it seem like it, and maybe it was one before the cult took it over. But Muninn relayed the truth that he could see the military compound it now was.

Cultists moved around in the compound the most, but there was some activity on the golf course. Or, more accurately, under the golf course.

My birds couldn't see that activity, but they spotted the odd movement. We all agreed it had to be where the bunker had been built. I would have loved to have access to the layout, but I wasn't risking either raven for that. I had to assume it was similar to what I'd seen when Ingrid abducted me.

Even with Malsumis powering her magic, it would have been difficult for Ingrid to just make up an illusion that powerful on the fly. She would have needed a reference to lean on.

Dad used what I could remember from all that to make some temporary maps. It wasn't perfect without Muninn's help, but I needed him to stay focused on his task, and this would be good enough. While we wanted to draw out the cult, we'd need to sweep the entire area to ensure this sect of the cult was wiped out.

I wouldn't be so foolish to believe Ingrid was Malsumis' only priestess—or whatever she was. It would make sense to have multiple branches to ensure that if one group failed, or needed to be removed like a diseased limb, Malsumis wouldn't lose all of her following in one go. However, this would be a good blow to the goddess, making her that much easier to deal with.

Diego returned with Bjarke and the other warriors. There were so many of them we had to move our discussion downstairs. Siobhán was also with them. Her druid abilities would come in handy. Her formidable battle attire wasn't for show. There was a reason she'd captured Hilda's beastly heart.

We shared the plan with the rest and broke everyone up into smaller infiltration units.

"I'm going with you," Diego said.

I shook my head. "You're not a fighter."

"I am when I need to be. And I know how to crunch a few bodies as a dragon. And if there's some sort of barrier, I can disable it. I've been practicing with Dahlia."

I blew out a breath. I didn't like it. I knew he wanted to protect me like Tyr and Baldur, but that didn't mean he should. But I couldn't stop him. "If that's what you want."

"How are we going to flush out Ingrid?" Bjarke asked. "Make enough of a mess she's forced to show up?"

"Yes and no," I said. "I'll be the bait."

"No," Dad and my guys said.

I rolled my eyes. "I'm the perfect bait. She won't be able to resist coming out to either pretend to be happy I learned my lesson and I came crawling back, or she'll want to mock me. Either way works."

"I'm going with you," Baldur and Tyr said at the same time.

I nodded. "That's fine."

They blinked, as if they'd expected me to argue or something. It made sense. And I didn't have an issue with Ingrid knowing I wasn't showing up for tea and cookies. She'd fall for the bait either way. She thought herself too invincible. Her pride would be her downfall.

When we'd finalized weapons, potions, and magical artifacts, everyone split into their squads and we handed out communication devices. They would be largely useless for the Berserkers once they shifted and fell into their fighting instinct, but the non-bestial transforming warriors were more than capable and were split into the Berserker groups accordingly.

Diego, Dad, and Aya would move the squads into position far outside the perimeter of the compound and the warriors would sneak in from there. This way there was lower risk of them being detected.

When everyone was there, Tyr and Baldur took my hands and I teleported us. I attempted to do so smack into the middle of the compound, but just as we expected, the barrier pushed me to the outskirts. Warning alarms sounded, making this place feel like an invaded military base, even though, besides the unusually sturdy walls, it didn't look like it from this side of the barrier.

The barrier protected this wall, but not for long. The invisible magic became visible when it rippled, and then dispersed when Diego disabled it from where he was sneaking in. I summoned my magic and made quick work of the wall.

Cultists on the other side weren't panicked. On the contrary, they were already aiming to fight. Yet they were no match for us, as we dispatched them quickly. It hurt my heart to have to draw their blood, but as they died, and the uncomfortable black tentacle shit started coming out of their corpses, forcing us to kill them a second time, I quickly became comfortable freeing these people from this torment.

We marched toward the center of the compound. While I manifested my Valkyrie armor for this, I kept my wings hidden for now. It was all part of my plan to prove to Ingrid who she'd messed with.

My hand gripped my shield tightly, the magic in it resonating with my soul. The warriors were gathered. I heard Mom's voice leak through the connection, even though I wasn't tapping into the shield just yet. I felt her praise and encouragement. I could do this. Once we engaged with Ingrid, I would summon warriors all around the compound and they'd join the spread-out numbers. *Her goddess is going down, and Ingrid will feel the fall with her.*

Cultists swarmed in, their numbers noticeably small. *They're just fodder.* Ingrid was waiting. She just wanted to slow me down and waste my energy a bit. *Good, it's working.*

Aya and Bjarke's squads reported in. They, too, were engaging, but didn't need the backup yet. Siobhán's unit was still well hidden and working their way to the bunker, Huginn being their scout.

Diego waited with Dad. He hadn't wanted to hang back; his intent was to fight with me to keep me safe, but Dad convinced him at the last minute to help him find a secured hiding place. It also seconded as a surprise ambush when Diego was ready to swoop in.

Don't show the enemy all your cards. Dad drilled that into my head all the time, ever since I was a kid. It was just fun competitive play to me then, but I was thankful he'd had the foresight to teach me, just in case.

Tyr and Baldur, shielded by basic, non-draining magic from me, cleared a path for us. We needed to ensure I had the magic needed to fight Ingrid. I wouldn't fight her alone—Mom's presence hummed at the edge of my mind—but that didn't mean she'd be easy to take down. If Malsumis was desperate to ensure Ingrid prevailed, or died taking us all out, she'd pump Ingrid full of her corrupted magic.

The compound's layout that Muninn had projected to me was easy to follow. He had spotted Ingrid briefly before having to duck somewhere safe. And sure enough, she came into view. Cultists stood on guard nearby, but even when they spotted us, they didn't attack—yet.

Ingrid, in her twisted dark Valkyrie-like form, stood in the center of the compound, all four of her hands resting on her hips. Her eyes and sclera were now solid black, and black veins crawled along her pale skin.

Now that I was getting a better look at her, I couldn't quite believe how monstrous she'd become. I couldn't understand the level of insanity she had to reach to allow Malsumis to turn her into this. *Are you even in there still, Mother?*

I pushed out the thoughts. I couldn't go down that road of doubt and indecision now. I'd chosen my path. Ingrid would die today, and if there was still a small piece of the real her in there, I'd be setting her free from this torment.

"Astrid," Ingrid cooed in a sickeningly sweet voice. "You came."

Breathe. I took one step forward and straightened my back. "You can't play your games with me, Ingrid."

She tsked. "You're such a bad girl, Astrid. Leaving all those people to suffer. I thought you wanted to help them?"

I grunted. "You assume my Valkyrie sisters can't handle those attacks. You miscalculated."

Ingrid laughed. "What possibly could eight Valkyries do against our armies? You may think you're powerful, dear, but you don't know what power is." She held out her arms and her corrupted wings flared. "Look at what Malsumis has given me. Look at what you rejected."

I grunted. "I'm supposed to be impressed by a pathetic imitation?"

Tyr and Baldur snickered. Ingrid scowled. "You impudent child. You could not possibly understand—"

My Ascended wings flared and my feet lifted off the ground until

I hovered a foot above. My sword, the one Tyr gave me long ago on our wedding day—the one I'd given him as a gift originally in our first life together, ignited in gold and black flames. My magic flared in my chest and I knew, from the way the cultists took startled steps back and Ingrid's eyes widened, they saw the splendor that was me, an Ascended Fire Soul Valkyrie.

"No, Ingrid, it is you who does not understand. Your goddess could never create anything close to what we Valkyries are. Her lust for more than she deserved drove her to the madness of her mind. She was weak and could not handle the gift we Valkyries bestowed her."

My lip curled. "I am an Ascended, while you are nothing but a poor imitation who will never live up to the glory of a single one of my feathers. And you've underestimated me for the last time."

The magic in my shield initiated. Magical lights appeared around the center compound, in the open, and in nearby alleys. The lights coalesced into the people—warriors from different times and lives. Not all who were sent specifically to the mysterious places that were Valhalla or Fólkvangr, but could reach it if they so chose to fight. And choose to fight they did.

The magic pinged in my mind as warriors manifested with other squads and fanned-out positions. Hundreds of fighters, witches, creatures I had no names for, showed Ingrid just how much she'd underestimated me.

My mother Randi stepped up beside me. To my other side, a gentleman with blond and gray hair and beard flanked me. My father, Bjǫrn. Gone was his gentleness and kind demeanor I saw most in him, and replaced was the fierce determination of a warrior and a protective father.

Behind me, a man around my age with braided blond hair added to my protective circle. His blue eyes sparked with fierce protection, as if it weren't my job as his older sister to protect him. Leif's gaze darted to me, and he grinned. My heart swelled. My family was here for me, fighting with me. With them, my current dad protecting me from afar, my partners, familiars, my closest friends, and other warriors of my past by my side, I couldn't lose.

Ingrid whipped her head back and forth. "What is this?"

I chuckled. "You were right to fear me, Ingrid. That's why you used me as a test subject. Your goddess knew the risk I'd pose if I was left unchecked. She recognized who I was and what a problem I'd become for her, and look at what wrath it has brought her."

Her lip curled in disgust. "Pathetic illusion magic. You're just like your father, so weak you must create illusions of greatness to seem better than the pathetic, worthless person you are."

"Illusions, are we?" Randi's dark magic flared to life, taking over her eyes and veining up her neck. Black tendrils, not corrupted black ichor, but dangerous sparkling magic like mine, leaked from her body. "Don't worry, Ingrid, I can assure you, our love for our daughter is far more real that you could have ever possessed."

Ingrid's face twisted. "If you want that reject of a girl, have her. You will all perish under the power of Malsumis. This world will be hers!"

Chaos erupted. Magic flew from Ingrid; her cultists attacked. My warriors engaged. Randi and I went for Ingrid and she met us with the same intensity, magic versus magic. Bjǫrn and Leif worked with Tyr and Baldur, keeping the cultists off of us.

Magic lanced my shoulder, the corrupted feel of Ingrid's magic more uncomfortable than the pain. Randi and I lashed Ingrid with gold and black tentacles, and I took a moment to summon weapons and spear a cluster of cultists trying to overwhelm my two gods. I shielded them and fought Ingrid in the air.

Her power was intense, but I had my true mom with me, aiding me. We worked in synchronization—me from the sky, her from the land. A cultist thought he would be brave and take on the terrifying vǫlva, but her undead body showed just how ill-equipped these cultists were. Randi barely cast him a look before spearing him dead with her magic.

Ingrid screeched like banshee, magic in strong force exploding out of her. I shielded my gods and myself, protecting us from most of the harm, but the blast sent me crashing into a building. Pain seared my senses and disorientation fell over me.

Tyr hollered my name, but it was drowned out when another

concussive blast hit where I'd landed. I cried out in agony, my body feeling like it'd been lit on fire.

The intense pain subsided, though my body ached like no one's business. My wrist popped painfully back into place due to my self-healing.

"Get up, Sister," a voice said. I couldn't tell if it was in my head or right next to me. I didn't recognize it, and yet a part of me did. "Get up. Show this pawn of the betrayer our wrath."

My body ached and protested. Sharp metal and concrete stabbed me and I blasted it away with my magic. The building Ingrid had thrown me into was mostly rubble now.

Outside, Ingrid and Randi dueled. Their dark magics clashed, their differences now so clear to me. To think I worried once that the dark magic I harnessed was like Ingrid's. It wasn't.

"Your line will perish," Ingrid screamed. "I will see to it personally that it will perish. Your line will pay for corrupting my mistress' gift!"

My mother, unfrazzled and confident as always, grinned. "You could never understand the blessing it is to be of a Valkyrie's line."

Magic clashed and exploded. Ingrid was forced back, but not down. She breathed harder from all her exertion, but wasn't anywhere close to being taken down.

"You picked the wrong side," Ingrid sneered. "My mistress will destroy you all. You and that pathetic girl I once called my daughter."

The insults should have hurt me. It should have pained me to hear a woman who was supposed to be my mom spit such vitriol. But I felt nothing. Because the look of utter disgust on my mother Randi's face was everything I needed.

"You cannot fathom the gift it is to have a Valkyrie daughter," Randi said. "You'll never understand the pride it means to have Astrid as my daughter. You could never comprehend the blessing and gift she is."

A cultist raised her weapon at me. I threw up a shield, but Baldur got to her first, pummeling her into the ground with flaming fists until she was a limp, flaming corpse. *Was I doing that?* I couldn't tell. My magic was everywhere.

A dragon roared overhead, and Diego swooped down in all his

magnificence. He rained magical fire down on buildings and people, careful of Tyr, Baldur, and me.

Ingrid whipped around back and forth as two ravens swooped in and attacked her. My heart lurched. They weren't supposed to be here. They were supposed to be safely hidden.

Their bodies collided with her, magic flaring through the bond and out of them. It was a startling feeling. Never had my magic so easily crossed the familiar bond before, especially not with them. I had only been practicing with Angel.

A dog snarled and my magic flared again. I whipped around in time to see Angel, encased in magic, tackle a cultist and rip into his throat. *What is she doing here?* She was supposed to be protecting Dad.

My heart lurched when she looked up at me. The magic made her look so much larger, fluffier, with a skull-like outline for her upper head. Her eyes glowed with the dark side of my magic. *Meja…*

"Ace." Dad's voice crackling through my earpiece made me jump. "It's time."

My pulse slowed, as did everything around me.

"Listen to me carefully. You must restrain her. We can't risk her moving. Can you do that for me?"

Could I? I steeled myself. A long ribbon coiled around my fingers. *I have to.* "Yes."

Pushing my focus onto Ingrid, she chaotically moved, trying to dodge my ravens and attack them, Randi, and all of the other warriors. She breathed hard and yet had too much power still. My restraints were strong, but I couldn't guarantee she would remain still long enough in them.

I flew in, my sword reappearing in my hand. I wasn't a strong melee combatant, but it put me at a better advantage against another witch.

Ingrid saw me and tried to blast me out of the air, only to be countered not by Randi, but Aya. My heart leapt as not only her squad, but Bjarke's, rushed into the chaos.

Bear and wolf Berserkers and shifters alike tore into the bodies of living cultists and clashed with those of the corrupted. For a brief second, I recognized Jarl Rune's massive form, fighting alongside his son, as well as two of Bjarke's sons who died long ago.

I gasped when another enormous amount of magic exploded out of Ingrid. I threw up as many shields as I could, but it protected us only so much. Concrete split, metal creaked. Pain ricocheted through my body when I slammed into the ground. Something broke. More than just one something, I was sure. It wasn't enough to keep me down. Between my healing and the pendant Baldur gave me, my wounds sealed and bones mended.

I breathed hard as I flung magic and weapons. Fire and shields. I used everything I had against Ingrid and her forces—the force that was dwindling by the second.

Hope soared that we'd actually win—until Ingrid belted out an ear-splitting screech, her insanity taking over. The ground around us erupted, massive black tendrils breaking through, grabbing and spearing undead and alive warriors. *What is this, a battle with Cthulhu?*

One grabbed me and slammed me on the ground, again and again. Pain overwhelmed me, my vision blurring. Diego roared and I felt his presence as he grappled with the magic tentacle. Strong arms gripped me and ripped me out of the tentacle's hold. *Tyr.*

Baldur's blurry form, heightened by the magical flames around his fists, beat the magic back into submission.

"Hold on, Valkyrie." Tyr tried to steady me. "We're going to win this."

"My vision…" I was pretty sure I'd hit my head.

"What do you need?" he asked.

Those four words rolled over me, powerful and strong and supportive. My guys were always there when I needed them. I just needed to ask.

"I need to pin Ingrid down. But I can't see her right now." I winced as my Valkyrie healing tried its best to fix me up as quickly as it could.

"I'll shield her," Diego's dragon words sounded in my head and outside it at the same time, like how it worked for Fen and my ravens.

"We will be your eyes, Sister," Muninn and Huginn said in unison. *"We are always your eyes where you can't see."*

My vision shifted and I saw through them. Not as separate flying birds, but one combined look at the battlefield. I leaned on Diego for balance as he wrapped around me, his dragon scales protecting us from most attacks, his magic from the rest.

Tyr and Baldur rushed for Ingrid. She tried to fly out of their reach, taunting them. That was her mistake. Tyr summoned an axe and threw it at her. I focused on the flying projectile and wrapped my magic around it. A gold ribbon coiled around the haft. The weapon missed her, but it didn't need to meet her as the mark.

Like a poised snake, my ribbon struck, snagging her around the wrist. Ingrid jerked back, trying to escape my spell, but this was Gleipnir, and I hadn't been rendered useless.

The axe landed on the ground, acting as a tethering weight, reinforced by my ribbon wrapping around the broken ground. Ingrid screeched and thrashed against the restraint like a wild animal. Randi, quick as ever, used her magic to grapple Ingrid's other arm and yank her down. Gleipnir tightened, fighting against Ingrid's beating wings and desperation to fly away.

Tyr threw another axe, this time intentionally past her, another ribbon lashing out and grabbing her. Baldur fearlessly charged in, grabbing one of my ribbons and yanking Ingrid harder toward the ground. He yanked again when she tried to fight, and I used him as another anchor, wrapping my ribbons around him and shooting out to grapple Ingrid.

She thrashed against her bindings, her wings now useless and magic unable to cut through my hold. Not that I believed she could cast magic anymore. Terror mixed with crazed glee as she screamed and battled incoherently. The woman who was Ingrid was no more, sacrificed to Malsumis' desires.

Once I worried I was making a terrible mistake. Now, my heart beat as steady as my resolve.

Ingrid was grounded, still a moving target, but grounded. My ravens noted ways to restrain her more tightly, and so I did. It wasn't pretty, but it was what we needed.

I cut my contact with my birds when I felt the fatigue setting in. I needed all the strength I could muster to keep Gleipnir's hold.

Ingrid continued to scream, but no one came to her aid. I wasn't sure there was anyone left to help her. The sounds of battle were dying down.

Something told me this was the time. I didn't know what. Maybe my

Valkyrie instinct, or maybe training with Dad. But I felt the tug—the tug that caused everything to slow.

Diego shifted, apparently on my request, though I was a bit numb to my own mouth moving, and I pulled us, as well as Tyr and Baldur, aside with my magic.

A gunshot rang through my ears.

Ingrid jerked.

Her screaming stopped.

And then she collapsed.

THIRTY-SEVEN

ASTRID

Silence blanketed the battlefield.

No more fighting.

No more magic.

No more screaming.

My lungs gasped for air, my body aching from exertion. My vision, while better, still wasn't great. *Can immortals get concussions?*

I took one unsteady step toward Ingrid's prone form. Diego caught me when I wobbled, but didn't stop me. He walked with me to what was once my mother. I had to. The compulsion was too strong to ignore.

I stopped when I stood over her. My gut twisted. The bullet had gone right through her head. Her eyes were still open, the crazed look no longer there. Nothing was there anymore in those dead eyes.

She bled black and her skin had grayed. *No, not gray….*

The black veins in her skin pulsed and spread, turning her skin the same color. My heart raced. This wasn't right. *I can't let Malsumis take her.*

I dropped to my knees. I had no idea what I was doing or thinking. I was just following my instincts as a Valkyrie.

I pressed my hand to Ingrid's chest and gasped when black ichor exploded out of her and grabbed me. My guys shouted my name, but I didn't jump back in fear. No, I shoved my hand further into the ickiness that was Malsumis' energy. It was wrong, so wrong.

"Give her back, you corrupted bitch!" I screamed.

My Valkyrie power pulsed and I swear I heard Malsumis scream in my head. Then, my hand clasped around something. It was small and faint, like a weak heartbeat.

My heart leapt into my throat. I knew this feeling. I knew what I had.

I yanked my hand back, holding on for dear life. The ichor couldn't hold me, and broke apart.

I held my hand close to my chest, clutching Ingrid's soul for dear life. Tears streamed down my cheeks. Malsumis didn't get to claim her after all. No one could take her. *I did it.*

I held on extra long to her soul. I knew I needed to let it go and send her off, but I couldn't. I couldn't let her disappear. Not when she was this weak.

"It's okay, Sister." That voice from before had returned. Her words whispered across my ears as if she were here with me. "You can let go. We have her. She will be safe with us."

Then I heard my mother's voice—weak, but there. "Listen to them, dear; it will be okay. I'm sorry my poor choices forced you down this path. I'm so proud of you. Truly. Now, go be the chaos you want to see in the world."

I let go. The weight of holding on just snapped, and a lightness came to my chest. Tears fell and my shoulders shook as I sobbed. I did what I had to, and in the end, I'd saved her. Maybe not her body, but her soul.

When the father spills the blood of the mother
Broken wings will rise

Diego mumbled the prophecy. It was as ominous as it was eerily relieving.

I cried, and cried. The weight of everything had dropped. Ingrid was stopped. Malsumis was waylaid. There was one less part of her cult to harm Midgard.

My guys comforted me. Randi comforted me. Hell, even Leif comforted me. I was a downright mess.

I finally calmed down. Wiping my tears away, I took in the devastation. I was pretty sure all of Bjarke's and Aya's teams were okay, minus some wounds that would heal on their own.

Siobhán's team were rushing over, the summoned warriors with them.

My eyes bugged out when I saw Hilda. She was in her bear form, but she was carrying one of her arms. "What the hell, Hilda?"

She shrugged and everyone laughed. I rolled my eyes and motioned for her to come over to me so I could reattach it. Luckily I had enough magic for that.

When I was done, I looked around again. Something wasn't right. "Where's my dad?"

Everyone looked around. He should have been here by now. I tried to reach him on the communicating device, but got no answer.

"Where's Angel?" Diego asked. He was looking every which way. "She was just here."

My pulse kicked up a notch. My instincts screamed at me; something wasn't right. I needed to find Dad.

A gun fired.

I jumped, but no one here fell victim to it.

Muninn screamed and flew into sight. *"Sister!"*

My fear skyrocketed and without me requesting it, my ravens projected their sight into me. Angel was rushing for a man looming over a prone body. A gun poised to shoot again. *Dad!*

Everything happened at once.

My vision snapped back. My sword manifested in my hand. My magic flared and I was no longer in the open compound but inside, descending on the unsuspecting man of the vision, my arms above my head.

The man choked and gasped as my sword plunged into him. Angel snarled and lunged, grabbing the man around the throat, tearing it out. His red blood splattered everywhere on the stairwell.

I spun around. "Dad!"

He laid prone on the stairs, blinking at me. In his hand he had a pistol. "Well, you can do that too, Ace."

I stood there, my heart hammering in my chest. He was okay? "But… the gun…"

Dad chuckled and pulled back his vest, revealing a Kevlar shirt reinforced with magic shielding. A bullet was stuck in it. "I'm immortal, not stupid."

I huffed out a disbelieving breath and then threw myself at him. Apparently I still had more tears to shed.

Dad held me and patted my back, murmuring reassuring words. I wasn't losing him. I wasn't going to lose him like I'd lost Randi.

When I managed to finally pull myself together, we collected his things. The man who had attacked him was the same one I'd met when I'd been abducted, the one who spoke with Ingrid and was outspoken of his distrust in me.

Muninn confirmed he wasn't a corrupted cultist. He'd caught the man talking to others about some of his desires from working with the cult, none of them good. *Good riddance.*

I gave Angel extra love for her help. Even though I had wanted her to stay with Dad, apparently he thought I needed her more, so she'd left when Diego had. He admitted that as useful as she was on the ground, he probably should have kept her with him like I wanted.

I also made sure to give my ravens the love they deserved, too. They'd been instrumental in all of this.

When we returned to the others, there was a bit of a commotion. Some new people had shown up—people in an eclectic mash of outfits, from business-suit types to hemp hippies and bingo-hall old ladies. They weren't seemingly hostile, but the others clearly didn't trust them. Well, the living didn't. The spiritual warriors looked rather unbothered.

One of the newcomers, a business-suit type, noticed me and nodded. "Valkyrie."

I paused as I took them in. Somehow I knew who, or rather, what they were. "Reaper."

"Forgive us for intruding on what is normally your agreed-upon domain if you or your chosen gods are involved with the battles," he said. "But given the circumstances, we thought we'd lend you a hand with soul collection. I assure you they'll all go where they belong."

I nodded. "I'm a little too tired to be doing any of that, so have at it."

The strange people went about doing what Valkyries did, unaccosted. Everyone knew at least vaguely what a reaper was, so they didn't argue with my choice. I was just surprised they showed themselves. I always had this feeling they showed up to the aftermath of battles after the Valkyries vacated the battlefield in order to collect what we left behind, but I never expected to have that speculation confirmed. *Everything is changing.*

I blew out an exhausted breath. "Do we know how everyone fared?"

Aya nodded. "I recently got done contacting them. Kirby and Azzie are still dealing with some cleanup at their locations, but overall, everything went smoothly. Ingrid was not expecting the force we brought them."

That was good. That was really good.

The warriors flickered, the magic in my shield almost used up. Most took that as their cue to say farewell and leave with little fanfare. Most of them were people I didn't know personally, so that made sense. I thanked them for their help.

Mom came up to me and pulled me into a warm hug. "I'm so proud of you."

I choked up, and it took me a moment to not burst into tears again. I was tired of crying, dammit. "Thank you. For helping."

"Sunshine, you don't have to thank us for that." She cupped my face. "We're always here for you. Whenever you need us."

I smiled and gave her another hug. "I love you."

"I love you, too. You try to behave for a while."

I chuckled. "No promises."

Leif was next. I punched him in the arm.

He pretended it hurt. "Rude."

"I'm your sister, I'm allowed to be."

He smirked and then embraced me in a hug. "Missed you, Astrid."

"Missed you too, Leif."

Bjǫrn-dad was last. He'd just gotten done shaking hands with

Darius-dad. It was this moment I was so glad he was sticking to that name rather than going back to his birth name. This was confusing as it was.

Bjǫrn pulled me in for the warmest of hugs. "I'm so proud of you. Don't you ever forget that."

I choked up. "I won't. I promise."

Randi gave Dad a hug and made sure he understood she was proud of him, too, and made him promise to keep me safe. Jarl Rune had some passing words of advice for me, which I was more than happy to take. I spoke a moment longer with other people I knew, and then they, too, had to return to the other realm.

Seeing them go hurt, but I knew it wouldn't be the last I'd see of them.

I breathed out a steadying breath, and a wave of weakness fell over me. "Um… I need someone to catch me."

I wasn't sure if I got all those words out before my vision went dark.

It returned a moment later, bringing a pounding headache with it, and I found myself not in a blown-up military compound, but the retreat home, lying on the couch. I also was staring into Dahlia's far-too-close face.

We both shrieked and jerked back. Laughter filled the room.

"I told you not to get too close," Kirby teased.

"I was just checking on her," Dahlia muttered. "Her breathing changed."

I winced when some more pain lanced my brain. "How long was I out?"

"About an hour," Aya said. She offered me some water. I sat up and eagerly drank it. Maybe a little too much, because I choked on it.

"Your lungs don't need water," Magnus said.

I rolled my eyes as I coughed. After a moment the fit subsided and I glanced around. Not too many were here in the great room, just the typical family members. "Everyone else home safe and sound?"

Kirby nodded. "Yeah, you were the only one to come out so rough, and it sounded like what we dealt with was a piece of cake in comparison."

I was given a rundown of what they had to go through, and the type of cleanup they'd attempted. The situations didn't escape the news, so that was going to be a thing. We all agreed it was likely things were going to get worse, and we'd need to be extra diligent.

Fen, Tyr, and Baldur entered the home and I was about crushed by all three of them. Apparently they'd been sent out to walk because their nervous energy was too much. Considering they'd lost me to battle before, I didn't feel it appropriate to reprimand them, and reassured them I was indeed alive, as long as they didn't crush me to death.

Once everyone calmed down, Xavier and Diego brought out food. Diego and Aya did some delivery runs to everyone else, ensuring they were well rewarded for the weight they'd pulled today.

I blinked when Dad dropped a gaming controller in my hand. The TV had become several, along with a few gaming systems. I blinked. *When had he done that?*

He grinned at me. "I thought everyone might be too exhausted for today's planned D&D session. So, mindless violence against zombies seemed a more appropriate speed."

I laughed. It was such a ridiculous proposal that sounded amazing right now. And it was. The hours ticked by full of laughter and fun. More of our friends and family showed up when they learned about the fun we were having. The house got a little cramped, but I wouldn't have it any other way.

This time last year, I could count the number of friends and family I had on one hand. Now, my home and heart was full of so much love. The path here may have been a little messy and painful, and we hadn't reached the end of it either, but that was okay, because we had each other and would always be there when anyone needed it.

We enjoyed our time as a family for hours, until people were quite literally falling asleep at the controller. We got everyone home, or tucked away in a guest cabin. I wouldn't have minded the idea of some doing the whole slumber party thing at the island home, but I'd been catching my guys' eyes all night and they clearly wanted tonight alone with me.

I got a chance to speak with Dad privately. He insisted he was okay after what he had to do. Similar to what happened to me while I was fighting Ingrid, seeing what she'd become made it easier for Dad to pull that trigger than he anticipated. I did notice some relief in him when I told him about saving Ingrid's soul from Malsumis.

We wished each other goodnight, promising each other if anything from this came up that bothered us, we'd talk about it. No secrets. No hiding. Which did mean I unfortunately learned what the temporary measures to keeping Aya alive were. Dad didn't outright say it, but just told me *I didn't want to know.*

I knew sex was involved somehow. It was Aya; that was part of her domain. And really, they could do what they wanted. I just didn't want to know any details. *And if it keeps Aya alive until we find a real solution, so be it.* I also made a mental note to perform some blood rituals tomorrow for the gods. They could benefit from it.

When I headed for the island home door, Tyr caught me and hauled me into his arms.

"Tyr, I can walk," I said.

"I know."

I huffed playfully and let him do his thing. His way of doting was nice.

Baldur and Diego were already inside. Tyr didn't set me down in the living room. He carried me instead to my room, which had been temporarily turned into my and Baldur's room until his room was finished.

Tyr laid me down on the massive bed that I swear could fit all three of us comfortably. *I think I need to upgrade all of our beds to this size now.* Tyr braced himself over me.

I grinned and looped my arms around his neck. "I think my gods and dragon need to be rewarded for their hard work today."

Tyr's chest rumbled and he dipped his head for a breath-stealing kiss. "So does our Ascended."

My heart thumped hard in my chest. Creation, I couldn't even vocalize how much I missed hearing him say that.

Tyr kissed me again, my mind fuzzing from the devouring intensity. I tangled my fingers in his hair, pulling him desperately closer.

My clothes tore. I didn't care. The faster we were naked, the better. I'd have removed theirs with my magic, but I didn't have anything left in me for the day.

I gasped and moaned. Each kiss, each soft and firm erotic caress, I fell deeper into the sensations of pleasure they gave me. Baldur's mouth enjoyed my breasts. Diego's fingers pleasured my clit and competed with Tyr's mouth as he tried to devour me. No part of me was safe from their love.

My hands fisted the sheets. The orgasm that burst through me came on quick and hard. None of them eased up after it subsided.

"Again," Tyr murmured against my thigh.

"Definitely again," Diego said before dipping his head to lavish my breasts with Baldur, who was enjoying his job far too much to say anything.

My core tightened and my breath panted out. Each flick of a tongue or finger, each slide of a hand along my sensitive body, built an overwhelming fire in me until I couldn't take it.

I screamed and arched my back, my soul practically leaving my body as the tides of orgasm swept over me. I came back down in a gasping, sensitive heap.

"Fuck me," I murmured. It was supposed to be an expression in my overwhelmed, pleasured state, but from the way all three of them chuckled, and then I found myself suddenly straddling Baldur, they were taking that as a command.

I gasped and my mouth fell open as Baldur slid inside me. He gripped my hips, rocking me into him. I struggled for air as I enjoyed his thrusting slowly into me.

Diego came up behind me and kissed along the shell of my ear, down my neck. His hands roamed my sides and his hard cock pressed against my back. "Ready for me?"

"Yes," I breathed. "Please."

I didn't care where he put it, he just needed to be inside me, now.

Baldur paused his movements and Diego's cock pressed into my very full pussy. My lungs ceased to function. *This feeling again.* I wanted it.

Diego slowly slid into me with Baldur, filling me impossibly. My eyes rolled back and I moaned deep in my chest and my nails dug into Baldur's chest. Both men groaned.

"This is becoming my favorite way to take you," Diego managed to say.

Baldur lifted my chin so I'd look at him, as difficult as it was with the way the two of them found that same mind-fucking rhythm the last time they did this to me on the beach. "She's loving it, too. Look at her."

I was a right mess with these two, and I wanted it. I wanted more of them.

My hips rocked. Only a little. It was difficult to push for more with them like this. But it was just enough. Pain mixed with intense pleasure. I moaned as they pushed deeper into me.

Tyr wrapped his thick finger around my chin and pulled my attention to him. The moment I saw his waiting cock, my lips parted to open wider. I wanted him, too. I wanted all three of these men to wreck me for anyone else.

His cock slid into my mouth, his size filling me. His rocking rhythm and taste mixed with Baldur's and Diego's thrusting, drowning me in desire. It crawled under my skin and found its way into my veins. It ignited a craving I needed to satiate. I needed it now.

Wrapping my hand around Tyr's thick shaft, I sucked his cock with vigor, my hips rocking just enough to bring my pleasure to a new high. All three men groaned, their eyes gleaming with their lust for me.

"That's it, Valkyrie." Tyr slid his hand into my hair. "Take us nice and good."

I moaned, which did something wicked to these men. Their paces intensified, their words of praise and desire flowed over me as the most erotic touch.

And then I was falling apart at the seams. The blinding rush of ecstasy took over. I convulsed and screamed around them, milking them to the edge until they crested that peak, groaning long and low and spilling inside me.

We stilled and collapsed in one giant heap, our hard breaths filling the night air. Bliss pulsed throughout my entire body. I couldn't think how I could be any happier than in this moment with them.

Tyr pulled me into his hard body, kissing my shoulder, then the crook where my shoulder and neck met.

I hummed. "Not done?"

"Never done with you, Valkyrie," he mumbled. "Not after a century. Not after three millennia. Never."

I sighed at the sensation of his touch along my hips. I knew the feeling. I'd never grow tired of them, either.

As his fingers pressed into my skin a little harder, I realized his touch was more intense with this hand than usual. "Tyr, did you regain feeling in that hand?"

He kissed the side of my head. "A little bit. You've been freed, but my choices had a permanent consequence, and I accept this. I accept this is how I am forever. It will remind me to never fail you again."

I turned my head just enough to kiss the corner of his mouth. "I know you—"

My gasp cut me off. His fingers slid between my slick folds, offering me more pleasure.

"No more talking, Valkyrie," Tyr rumbled. "Only feeling the pleasure I'm providing you."

Diego, who was on Baldur's other side, leaned on Baldur and grumped. "He's stealing her for himself."

Baldur turned to look at him. "Well, then I guess we'll have to have our own fun while we wait our turn."

I might have squeaked when the two of them kissed. Just a little. And they definitely heard me and found it amusing. *It was hot, okay, sue me.*

So was watching them feel each other up while Tyr pleasured me, and then fucked me nice and good while Diego sucked Baldur's cock. *It was extra hot, okay?* And I made it known. And it seemed to make those two enjoy it more.

I lost track who was enjoying who as I was passed around between them, or Diego and Baldur explored each other. I lost track of all time. It was late before we all succumbed to bliss and exhaustion.

My guys slept soundly—well, they did after we managed to get Tyr to stop snoring. I laid awake longer, staring into the darkness.

"Thank you," I thought to Creation.

It didn't matter what was in store for us in the future. I had my memories and my men back. Creation allowed us this chance to have it again, not once but twice. It believed in our love as much as we did. And I'd be forever grateful.

EPILOGUE

ASTRID
ONE MONTHS LATER

A gentle summer breeze swept through the glade, rustling tree leaves and bringing with it the sweet scent of wildflowers. Songbirds sang overhead, perched in the old tree's branches. I sat next to Baldur while he read, laying my head against him, the massive oak tree shading us from the midday sun. Her leaves danced in the breeze, casting shimmering dapples of light on the ground that Muninn hopped around chasing for fun. Angel snoozed by my side and Huginn nestled contently in my lap, his eyes closed as he enjoyed my fingers gently stroking him.

I gazed at the journal page where I'd written some thoughts. Or, they were supposed to be thoughts. I wanted to make sure that, no matter what happened with Ragnarök nearly upon us, if the past repeated, then we'd have more information than the last time. But my words… they'd turned into more of a rough story of sorts. Nothing amazing like Bragi could have created, but it wasn't terrible.

My finger grazed a loose scrap of folded paper. Muninn had delivered it to me earlier. It'd come from Raven. I hadn't looked to see what was written yet, though.

Baldur looked up from his reading after turning a page. "How are you feeling?"

I smiled. "Much better."

He ran his fingers through my hair. "Good."

Ever since I woke up, I'd felt… off. I wasn't sure how to describe the feeling, as it wasn't something I was familiar with, though a bout of fatigue accompanied it for a short time. And it wasn't like I could get sick like mortals could. Being immortal had many perks.

Even if I could, the healing charm I wore every day should have helped me. But it didn't.

Luckily today was a day off, allowing me to recover, though not because I didn't have anything to do. Everyone was enforcing healthy habits with me, including setting boundaries with my workaholic nature. I had been doing better last summer with it, but after the sanctuary opened and my life was subsequently turned upside down even more, that had gone out the window.

A dark shadow flashed over the glade. I looked up, spying Diego in his dragon shape descending. His amber and silver scales shimmered in the sun, creating a stunning image against his black scales. He landed and shifted. I waved at him as he approached.

Diego smiled and bent over, pecking me on the lips. "How are you?"

"Doing better."

"Good."

"Did you have fun?" I asked after he'd settled down next to me.

Angel rolled over into him for belly rubs. Diego happily obliged. "Of course. And the guys say hi."

I smiled. In all the craziness of life's changes, it was easy for things to fall between the cracks. When you went from thinking you were human only to find out you're an immoral Valkyrie or dragon, then you started making non-human friends and learning what immortality entailed, it was easy for past non-immortal friends to be left behind.

Not with Diego, though. He still had his dirt biking human friends and was trying to ensure they all got together and out on the trails once a month. Soon enough, Baldur would probably join him on those adventures, when he got the hang of the sport enough to go as wild as Diego and the rest. *Bunch of crazies.*

"I still think you need to come out with us," Diego said.

I rolled my eyes. He brought this up all the time. "No thanks. I'm never going to be like you crazies. Rope Zeke into that."

Diego smirked. "Already did. He's more interested in Baldur's current speed."

Which made it closer to my speed if I got on a bike. "Because he's smart."

Baldur chuckled and flipped another page of his book. He'd heard this conversation a few times now and found it amusing each time.

"We can go your speed," Diego insisted. "I don't even have to go out with the others. It can be the four of us, taking it slower with no insane tricks."

I exhaled slowly. I was hearing the silent request. He desperately wanted to include me in a hobby of his. "I will think about it."

It wasn't like I hated the sport. I would say I was neutral about it. But maybe that was because Diego went so hard at it compared to me. *I swear, he should have done it competitively instead of going into therapy like me.*

Diego leaned over and kissed my head. He paused mid-action and inhaled my scent. Then again.

My brow rose. "What?"

"You… smell a little different."

I pursed my lips. "Like, in a bad way?"

"No…" He sniffed my head again. "No, it's pleasant, but I don't know how to describe it."

That was weird. I hadn't changed what I used for soaps or perfumes any time recently.

Diego wrapped his arms around my waist and pulled me into him, his nose still firmly pressed into my hair. Huginn squawked and jumped off my lap. He pecked Diego's shoe, but Diego paid him no mind.

"Diego," I mumbled, my face smooshed into his chest. "What are you doing?"

He didn't answer, instead nuzzling the top of my head and hugging me tighter. I flicked my gaze to Baldur, who was watching with a perplexed and slightly amused look.

"Diego, what are you doing to her?" That sounded like Dahlia.

I tried to turn my head to see the new arrival. Diego didn't make it easy, but I could kind of see Dahlia, Azzie, Kirby, Fen, and Tyr approaching.

I flailed my arms. "Don't mind us. My dragon has just been possessed."

Baldur barked out a laugh. Kirby crossed her arms and shook her head.

"How are you guys?" I asked, trying to pretend this wasn't weird at all. "I didn't expect you and Azzie for another few hours."

Azzie blew out an annoyed breath. "Davyn is being extra grumpy today, and Zeke wanted to work on a project in his forge, so I thought it couldn't hurt to come by early."

"I wasn't doing anything," Kirby said.

"Fen and Dahlia just got here when I got her phone call since you didn't have yours on you," Tyr said.

Dahlia's hand shot up. "And since I was asked to play dragon taxi, I'm self-inviting to this party."

I laughed. That was fair. "You're always welcome to hang out with us. And I wouldn't mind more input on the wedding plans."

"Just no black," Azzie said.

"Always needs more black," Dahlia countered.

"I'd love to join you in the black-versus-no-black debate, but I'd need this dragon to stop being weird and let me go before I can do so properly." I tapped Diego on the arm. "Love, please?"

He jerked away from me when a shrill shriek pierced the air. Everyone whirled around to the entrance of the glade. Aya stood under the elegant arch, her eyes wide. She'd dropped a binder, which had landed open, revealing what looked to be full of photos of women. The were probably from the recent photoshoot for the charity calendar we were hoping to have ready in the fall. Of course, that wasn't the focus anymore.

Aya's shock was morphing into something else. Joy?

She shrieked again and dashed towards us—toward me. I jerked back when she slammed down on her knees in front of me. Her hands hovered in front me, shaking in her excitement.

"Aya?" I managed, concerned and confused by her state.

She squealed and threw her arms around me. I grunted from the life-crushing squeeze. Aya let me go and gazed at me with those wide, excited eyes.

Dahlia gasped around the same time realization dawned on me. "No…"

Aya squealed, again. "You're pregnant!"

The only sound to penetrate my mind was Baldur's book snapping shut. *Pregnant?* "I can't be…"

I was. Aya, of all people, would know. A pregnancy test could fail. A passion and sex domain deity could not.

My hands slid along my flat stomach. "I'm… how?"

"I'd joke it was magic, but we have Magnus' twins," Kirby said.

"I was careful," I insisted. "I wanted to wait a little longer, so I made sure I was… careful…"

I'd been careful with Diego and Tyr. I turned to look at Baldur. "Except with you."

Because he couldn't have children. He'd helped me come to terms with my infertility in my second life, because he'd gone through the same. He'd been open about it when the topic came up a few times since his revival.

Baldur stared at me with wide, disbelieving eyes. "I can't… I couldn't have… There's no way."

Unless Creation was pulling a huge move over us like it'd done to Magnus, then it wasn't possible to be Tyr's or Diego's child.

Diego went rigid next to me. I whipped around to look at him. His eyes were unfocused and he stared at nothing. A stupid, goofy grin spread over his lips.

Then after a moment, he came back to us, still smiling. "Well, it's nice having a clear vision, especially one that no one else has had before."

Because of the nature of his gift, he somehow knew when he was seeing visions someone else had already seen. "What did you see?"

He brushed a strand of hair behind my ear and leaned over to kiss my forehead. "Our happy future. The baby is Baldur's."

Baldur and I gazed at each other. And then it clicked. "The spell. The spell required a life sacrifice. It took it from Frigg, but it also took it from you…"

"In the form of creating life," Baldur finished, his words barely above a whisper.

He hesitated for a moment, then reached out and rested his hand over mine on my belly. The way his face relaxed and a mix of indecipherable expressions formed one after another, emotions swelled in my chest and choked up my throat. *I'm pregnant.*

"We're having a baby…" Baldur murmured.

I squealed when he grabbed me and launched to his feet. He spun us around and unrestrained joy broke through the ebbing shock that was numbing me to the reality thrust on me. Angel barked excitedly with all the joy pouring out of us.

Baldur halted and we stared at each other, big smiles on our face. I kissed him. "We're having a baby."

Dahlia squealed and did a happy dance, making us laugh. She was clearly holding that in a little too long.

Baldur set me down and Diego scooped me into his arms. He was all smiles as he held me close and kissed me. "We're having a baby."

My heart swelled. Baldur may be the biological father, but this child would have more than one loving father.

Diego released me when Tyr approached. He'd been quiet, and for a moment, doubt crept into my happy little bubble. I didn't think about how he might feel, after everything we went through in the past and never having this moment, and then seeing someone else getting that chance first.

Tyr dropped to his knees and pulled me into him. His body engulfed me and his face pressed against my neck. He didn't say anything. But he didn't have to.

I felt it in the way he held me, in the way his muscles bunched and slightly tremored; I felt it in my soul, that deep connection I had with my men.

I wrapped my arms around him and held him as close as he held me. We were all embarking on the next stage of our lives together. Maybe a little earlier than planned—I couldn't help but look up at the sky and be slightly amused at Creation getting the last laugh—but I wasn't angry.

Even with Malsumis and Loki still being an issue, along with Ragnarök and everything, I was gladly stepping onto this path that had presented itself.

Neither Aya nor Dahlia could keep behaving any longer and they yanked me out of Tyr's grasp, both of them squealing. Azzie and Kirby were both laughing, as was I. The joy inside me couldn't be contained.

They finally released me, and totally not because Kirby and Azzie had to come to my rescue.

Fen came up and pulled me into a light headlock. "Congrats. I'm so looking forward to being their uncle."

I pointed at him. "You need to behave with them. No being a bad influence."

He snickered; the look he gave was downright wolfish. "Oh, I'll behave, don't worry."

Dahlia clapped as she gasped. "Astrid, I got the cutest photo earlier with him and the twins."

"Dahlia," Fen warned, the words more a growl.

"Oh?" I said. "Do tell."

"Don't tell," he warned.

She stuck her tongue out at him. "Grumpy wolf totally *hates* it when the adorable ankle biters climb all over him when he's shifted and treat him like a horsie."

I laughed when Fen released me and lunged for her. She danced out of the way, taunting him with flirty smirks.

I retrieved my dropped journal. The thing had landed face down on the pages. I brushed some loose dirt out of it and glanced at the little story I'd started. I placed my hand on my belly, unable to stop smiling. Maybe I had the perfect way to tell this story after all.

Something crunched underneath my foot. The paper from Raven had fallen out. Before I could bend down to retrieve it, Muninn did that for me. He flew up onto my shoulder. Huginn flew down from the tree where he'd retreated to in all the excitement, and perched on my other shoulder. They both crooned, their happiness bubbling through the familiar bond. Angel nudged my hand, she, too, happy with all the news.

"I also expect you three to be good influences on the baby," I said.

The raven cackled, mischievous ideas already passing through the bond to each other and to me. At least I knew Angel would be a good influence. And an amazing protector.

I flicked open the note when Muninn handed it over. Raven's impeccable penmanship didn't say much, but it said everything.

Helheim

I'll let you know when he returns.

I tucked that in my journal to be addressed another day, then faced the others. "Who wants to plan the big surprise reveal for the grandpas?"

ABOUT THE AUTHOR

Shannon Pemrick is a full-time USA Today bestselling author of slow-burn romantic fantasy, fuller-time geek, and dragon obsessed. She also has too many novelty mugs, not enough chocolate, and a forbidden love-affair with all things shiny. When she's not burning her fingers across a keyboard handing out adventures and HEAs, she's rolling dice and getting lost in RPGs or searching for brides for her dragon overlords.

You can learn more about Shannon by visiting her website at:
shannonpemrick.com

www.ingramcontent.com/pod-product-compliance
Lightning Source LLC
Chambersburg PA
CBHW051423190726

48289CB00001B/21